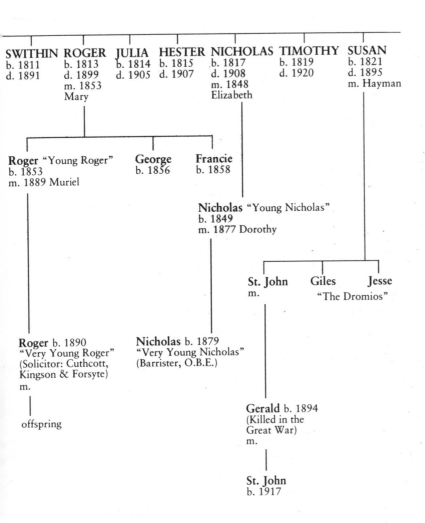

SWITHIN	ROGER	JULIA	HESTER	NICHOLAS	TIMOTHY	SUSAN
b. 1811	b. 1813	b. 1814	b. 1815	b. 1817	b. 1819	b. 1821
d. 1891	d. 1899	d. 1905	d. 1907	d. 1908	d. 1920	d. 1895
	m. 1853			m. 1848		m. Hayman
	Mary			Elizabeth		

Roger "Young Roger"
b. 1853
m. 1889 Muriel

George
b. 1856

Francie
b. 1858

Nicholas "Young Nicholas"
b. 1849
m. 1877 Dorothy

St. John
m.

Giles

Jesse

"The Dromios"

Roger b. 1890
"Very Young Roger"
(Solicitor: Cuthcott,
Kingson & Forsyte)
m.

offspring

Nicholas b. 1879
"Very Young Nicholas"
(Barrister, O.B.E.)

Gerald b. 1894
(Killed in the
Great War)
m.

St. John
b. 1917

D1298715

The Forsytes

The
FORSYTES
Suleika Dawson

SINCLAIR-STEVENSON

The author and publishers are grateful for permission to reproduce words from
songs as follows:

"SOUTH AMERICAN JOE" (Cliff Frend/Irving Caesar)
© Warner Chappell Music Ltd., London WIY 3FA.
Reproduced by kind permission of
International Music Publications Ltd.

"GUILTY"
Music by Richard Whiting & Harry Akst, and words by Gus Kahn.
© 1931, EMI Catalogue Partnership/EMI Feist Catalogue Inc, USA.
Reproduced by kind permission of EMI Music Publishing Ltd./EMI United
Partnership Ltd., London WC2H 0EA.

First published in Great Britain in 1994
by Sinclair-Stevenson
an imprint of Reed Consumer Books Ltd
Michelin House, 81 Fulham Road, London SW3 6RB
and Auckland, Melbourne, Singapore and Toronto

A CIP catalogue record for this book
is available at the British Library.
ISBN 1 85619 255 5

Typeset by Falcon Graphic Art Ltd
Printed and bound in Great Britain
by Mackays of Chatham plc, Chatham, Kent

For Graham Goodwin, *sine quo* . . .

Acknowledgements

My first thanks fall due to George Greenfield. George was the first to back this project (then only a thin and hopeful outline), and generously launched it on its way by introducing me to Ed Victor. My second thanks are due to Ed, for seeing me, and encouraging me, and for leading me to his colleague, Graham Greene. My third thanks go to Graham, for taking me on. His constant kindness, good humour and subtlety over the last three years have nursed this book – and often its author – to completion.

Further thanks go to Peter Delaunay, Elizabeth McKane and Barbara Rudolph, for their friendship, support and wise counsel; also to Sioban Phelan, for excellent word processing and research.

And I should like to thank my publisher, Christopher Sinclair-Stevenson, who was the first to offer me the immense privilege of seeing my own name in print.

Suleika Dawson,
London, April 1994

*"What is to come? Will contentment yet be caught?
How will it all settle down? Will things ever again settle down
– who knows? Are there to come fresh wars, and fresh
inventions hot-foot on those not yet mastered and digested?"*

John Galsworthy: *Preface to 'A Modern Comedy'.*

*"Yes, my young lover of justice, everything happens
all over again. That is how it is."*

August Strindberg: *Easter.*

Contents

Book Two
Dark Clouds

PART ONE

PART TWO

Book Three
One More Affair

By Way of an Introduction

In seeking to pinpoint – with the acuity conferred only by hind-sight – the exact origin of the second great and bloody war of this century, and thereby to understand at least in part the rise of aggressive nationhood which was at its root, historians often cite 'the Schleswig-Holstein question'. Only three people in the world, it was claimed, ever fully understood the convolutions of this. Of those three, the first was said to be mad, the second dead, and the third – no less a personage than Lord Palmerston – when asked to explain the intricacies of the issue confessed blatantly to having forgotten them. Subsequent commentators would have done well to note that, this being the case, 'Old Pam', whatever else he may have been, was certainly no Forsyte. In matters of property and possession (for when was the war that was not thus principally concerned?) a Forsyte, like the elephant, is disinclined to forget, especially when the conflict lies in the bosom of his own family.

The war among the Forsytes – declared over the building of a certain house in 1887 – had enlisted four generations of family members so far, volunteer and conscript alike, and was at this very moment preparing, with its rallying bugles and clarion call to arms, to stir the blood of the fifth. As in any military engagement the advantage was with him who held the high ground, and the high ground in Forsyte campaign chronicles historically lay within three miles of Richmond, and was known as Robin Hill.

Whether this patch of earth, after this fifty-years' war, was of size enough to bury its dead was, in the best tradition of military history, a moot point. Indeed it already contained the mortal remains of two long-serving combatants: Old Jolyon, the first good general of the conflict buried like a knight of old with the faithful dog Balthasar at his feet, and his son Young Jolyon, in keeping with the metaphor his lieutenant and squire, interred beside him.

Old Jolyon's estranged brother James, and his son Soames – the matchless fallen of the other side – were entombed elsewhere. Yet, in the case of Soames at least, the proprietorial shade may have wandered there still, through the beech wood and larch coppice, seeking – revenge? – or absolution?

And the damsel of the piece – for one of the many things which every schoolboy is obliged to know is that there must be a woman in all such weighty disputes – the stolen Helen whose distracting beauty was at the very heart of this long conflict, who was she?

Irene. Her name meant peace, but no Forsyte who ever looked at her knew what that precious commodity was, once he looked away. For her sake, brother had spurned brother, and cousin had fought cousin in the divided Forsyte ranks. And for her sake still, the civil war between the two encampments of this great English family was now, in the summmer of 1939, entrenched in its sixth decade.

Book One

1939

The Echo of a Song

---

*"Of love that never found his earthly close,
What sequel?"*

Lord Tennyson

Part One

Chapter One

Fine Fleur Mont

For most of the thirteen years which had passed since she last encountered her first – and only – true love, her cousin Jon Forsyte, and certainly for all of the twelve and a half since she had become aware that her husband Michael knew of the unhappy affair, Fleur Mont had succeeded in becoming the womanly woman.

Realising that a man finds scant comfort in a critic on the hearth, she had championed her husband tirelessly through several small but significant successes in his parliamentary career and, more importantly, supported him after one or two better remembered defeats. Her name – as his, since the death of Sir Lawrence, now embellished with a title – was to be found among the patrons of a number of *mondaine* charities, at whose meetings she showed an active understanding not only of their proclaimed intentions for the year ahead, but also of their finances from the previous quarter. And she was a mother – of Christopher, abbreviated even before his birth to Kit, now nearly sixteen and the future eleventh baronet – and of his sister, Catherine, almost six years younger and inevitably dubbed Kat.

By such weights and balances was Fleur's life regulated, and guided along that always tricky central path. But to suggest that, as lives go, hers was complete or – an even more hazardous notion – fulfilled, would be to fly in the face of the hereditary principle, and to discount utterly the fact that its owner was a Forsyte.

Forsytes – whatever their names are in the world, Lambe, Hayman, Spender, Mayhew, since Forsyte is more by way of being a biological or social classification than a name – Forsytes are by nature never happy unless they can possess the objects of their desire. For most of

5

their breed this is simply the relatively easy matter of wealth, property and the social position which either of the preceding usually secures. But should a Forsyte's desire exist in the realm of the senses, where the possessive instinct is admitted only on the most extreme sufferance, to wander as a beggar, then he – or she – is likely to remain dispossessed of that desire for life. Peripherally aware of much of this, Fleur found herself increasingly given, in solitary moments, to assessing the extent of her commitment to this present middle way.

So it was that Fleur's as yet unlined forehead wrinkled momentarily with a passing displeasure which had insisted its way into her otherwise private thoughts as she sat on the knole sofa in her sun-filled, *art deco* drawing-room in South Square, Westminster, one bright afternoon in June, 1939.

Her son stood before her, his hands deep in his trouser pockets, one foot sullenly tapping the asymmetrical metallic screen which masked an unlaid fire-basket in the hearth, and looking up with a steely absence of appreciation at the masterpiece from the jazz-age that was hung over the mantel.

His sixteenth birthday approaching, the man that Kit Mont would soon become was beginning to show himself in all manner of subtle ways – in the quick, certain light in his cool grey-blue eyes, at present hidden by sleepy boyish lids and lashes; in the imperious height of his forehead, camouflaged by the school cut given to his tawny hair; and most significantly in the set of still youthfully full lips over his white, perfect teeth, where the incipient look of a well-kept cat was beginning to play.

"It isn't on and you know it," Fleur said. "If Finty wants you to go with them, then that's all there is to be said."

"But it'll make my hay fever play up," Kit protested, hearing in his own changed voice how the excuse had acquired a lame foot since the previous summer.

Fleur shrugged her shoulders, beautifully fitted in their suit of amber silk.

"It's rather a selective problem, don't you think? It doesn't seem to *play up* at Lord's."

She didn't need to look at her son to know this was a direct hit, since he had begun to pull at a loose strand of wool on his cricket jumper as she spoke.

6

She added simply,
"I'm sorry."

Kit left the room, less in temper than in the plain understanding
that further debate with his mother was futile. With the click of the
doors behind him he took the stairs up to the top floor at a disdainful
trot. His preoccupation since returning home that morning for his
last week-end out before the long vacation was the counterpart to
his mother's, had he but known, for how best to be the manly man
was now his chief concern. Caught at that bicuspid age when neither
voice nor bearing can quite be trusted to play the part, Kit was
on guard constantly against downfall and embarrassment, and as
a consequence perceived both lying in wait everywhere. Finty had
once been the dearest person in his world, and the memory of that
not-so long lost emotion pricked his cheeks with unmanly points of
red. But she was Kat's nurse now, and the thought of having to walk
with them both in the Park on his first half-day back was just *too
much*; hence the appeal to his mother, now overturned.

However, Kit was beginning to be a pragmatist, the first to
show itself in adult form of many traits he had inherited from
Fleur, and by the time he reached the top landing he had squared
himself to the sentence she had upheld. On the way to retrieve his
school blazer from his own room, Kit paused in the doorway of
the nursery. The redoubtable Finty – Miss MacFintlock she had
once been, before she made her life over to the top floor at South
Square – was applying a final, impatient brush to his sister's unruly
length of dark auburn hair. This deep-glinting, coppery mass with its
row upon row of tightly packed waves had defied the plain-handed
force of Finty's brushing twice since lunch, as its very nature defied
rational explanation, at least in the nurse's strict, chapel-taught
universe. That such a slight, pale wisp of a girl – why, you could
all but see through her – that she should have such hair! It was as
if all the life in her was contained in these shining, cascading locks.
And mindful of her Old Testament exemplars, Finty thought this a
dreadful and probably Pictish aberrance. The girl herself submitted
silently to the harsh plaitings of the nurse's fingers, casting a glance
which didn't quite dare to seem hopeful towards her brother as he
poked his head through the space in the half-open doorway.

"Come on. It'll take all day at this rate," Kit said, sounding less charitable than he actually felt, and wishing he could bring himself to follow such a masterful exhortation with a wink, as his father might. "Mother says I'm to take the dog."

Left alone once more in her drawing-room after her son's departure, Fleur returned to those thoughts which recently had been gnawing at her equilibrium like mice at wainscoting. Denied no whim since her birth which money, social position and a doting father could satisfy, she had found it no simple task to reconcile herself to the hard truth that the only thing she desired in the world was not to be hers. Perhaps she had never truly found the reconciliation she sought but, for many years now, she and this stony fact had at least found a way to rub along together without too much detrition on one side or the other. And indeed, if there was any weathering caused by this uneasy juxtaposition it was not visible, for it lay in Fleur's own soul.

On the day of her wedding, almost twenty years ago, to Michael – it should have been Jon! – she had experienced a bad moment when going up to change after the reception. June Forsyte, Jon's much older half-sister and her own second cousin, had been with her and did her best to help, to try and soothe the aching wretchedness of all she felt, and all she could not stand to feel any longer in that minute of crisis. In theory, there should have been no one better qualified than June for the task – she too knew that serpent's tooth of true love lost in youth, and her story was not by any reckoning unconnected with Fleur's. But the little woman's philosophy of rugged determination struck a sour note with Fleur. After all, she had been determined to have Jon, and now — now she was Michael's wife.

'*I shall forget him, I suppose,*' she said then '*—if I fly fast and far enough.*'

At the time June took this as a sign of recovering composure and left Fleur with her blessing, the second she had received that day. '*From this day forth*' — thou shalt live without Jon! As if recovery from that were possible — never to have — never to hold! In that second she would have given a world of composure twice over to recover her loss.

For one whose genetic inheritance was derived from a French

8

mother and a Forsyte father, defeat was galvanising, and Fleur held resolutely to her plan, if at times it was as one drowning at sea will cling to driftwood. Thence she had arrived at the seeming perfection of her present life. But perfection without the beloved, if not a sword through the heart, is still likely to bring a dull ache to the stomach from time to time – and so it proved with Fleur. For all her striving, and her achieving, the wisdom of the ancient poet[1], that they only change their skies, not their souls, who run across the sea, had been her single unequivocal reward. Her loss, recovery and, thirteen years ago, her final surrendering of Jon – to that American girl, his wife – were indeed indelible marks upon her soul. Now, in the hot summer of this restless present year, Fleur's clear-eyed and unsentimental appraisal was that she had made a poor fist of forgetting, only succeeding in the costly charade of self-deception. For quite a while, she knew, something within her had been wearing thin, but she did not know what it was.

The telephone rang, and Fleur answered it listlessly.

"Fleur, dear?" The voice, still vigorous as its owner in her eighty-first year, belonged to Winifred Dartie, *née* Forsyte, Fleur's aunt.

Fleur held the mouthpiece slightly away so that her mood, which she felt disinclined to relinquish, might not be detected.

"Hello, Winifred."

With the exception of her mother, Fleur had long since dispensed with all prefixes among both her own relations and Michael's. Her aunt was now just Winifred, as Michael's family were all only their first names to her. Even her mother-in-law was simply Em, to which foreshortening the Dowager Lady Mont did not demur. Winifred Dartie, who in her youth had taken up the same fashion – then quite daring – and called her own mother Emily for several seasons, welcomed the loss of an appendage she considered ageing.

"Fleur? You sound very distant, dear. Are you well, or is it just a bad connection?"

Fleur rallied her voice: "Is that better?"

"Ah, yes. Now I was wondering, do you think you could ask

---

[1] **Horace:** *Epistles – 'Caelum non animum mutant qui trans mare currunt.'*

9

Michael to ring me up when he returns from the House this evening? If he has a moment, of course."

Fleur was puzzled.

"Yes – but you haven't forgotten about supper tonight, have you?"

"No, dear, I haven't."

Winifred's tone acquired a sharp edge. After a bout of rheumatism during the winter and a couple of minor falls in the spring, she had lately become rather over-aware of her age, and was alert for allusion to it.

"It's just that I'd appreciate Michael's opinion on something, that's all. It happens not to be a subject I'd want to raise in front of a stranger."

"I see. Well, I'll tell him, of course – I'm sure he'll make time to ring you."

Winifred softened her edge. She was in danger of becoming the very thing she abhorred most — a crone! Old age was the pest!

"How is your visitor, by the way?" she asked, more cordially.

"I haven't the faintest notion."

"Oh – is he very abstruse?"

Fleur smiled despite her mood.

"I haven't met him yet. He was supposed to call for tea yesterday, but he sent his man instead, carrying a huge bouquet and begging that I excuse his master on urgent business."

"Well! That's *some* style. They always seem to have a flair for the grand gesture, these Spaniards – look at the tango."

Fleur was grateful for this unintentional humour, and let herself go along with the distraction it offered.

"He's not Spanish, Winifred, he's Argentinian. And so's the dance!"

"Oh," said Winifred, mostly to herself. Her single association with this noble South American country was that her late husband Montague had gone to Buenos Aires in the autumn of 1899, taking with him all his own belongings that he could carry, and Winifred's pearls. This last was the straw which broke Winifred's long-suffering back in regard to her husband, not so much for the fact that Monty had himself given the pearls to her, but because her father James had been required to pay for them. That he also took with him an exotic dancer – whose liberal embraces, pursuant to the transfer of the necklace, he hoped to enjoy – seemed Dartie's lesser offence. His greater was to part a Forsyte from some of her most valuable possessions – a piece of jewellery and a spouse. Certainly, when she opened the case and found her pearls were gone, it was perhaps the worst shock Winifred had ever received. Indeed it was not until the errant Dartie's return from the Argentine in the following spring (*via* steerage, another body blow since no person associated with the Forsytes had ever travelled in this manner, not even a servant) that Winifred could have said with any certainty of which piece of property she felt the more deprived. A pearl, after all, keeps its value – a Dartie, in an unpressed suit and with one boot split across the toe, does not.

"Mother thinks him charming," Fleur said, "so perhaps he will be."

"I'm sure. Annette always did have excellent taste. Besides, in my case it will be jolly interesting to meet someone new for a change. I'm far too much among Forsytes these days!"

Both aunt and niece concluded their conversation measurably cheered, particularly Winifred, who never made a call these days without a stiffening of her nerves against the trials of the new 'automatic' exchange. To know that Michael would be telephoning later was a great comfort, and quite overwrote the small guilt she felt at not telling Fleur the exact truth of her situation. It wasn't advice she wanted from Michael at all, but a favour; fortunately her nephew was such an obliging fellow she felt certain that to ask him for something was only a precursor to his giving it. And as for being too much among Forsytes, it was her intention to surround herself with them. In short, Winifred had decided to visit the past, her past, and she needed Michael to help her do it.

When Montague Dartie lost his balance, and consequently his life, down a flight of stairs in Paris in 1913 – the Spanish dancer then merely a hazy memory – most of her family considered Winifred to have been granted a merciful release. (It was like Forsytes to consider the benefit that way around, for none of them set much of a premium on the probability of an after-life.) But Winifred's affection for her husband lingered, and even grew a little, after his demise. In his youth, which of course was also her own, Monty had been so –

dashing was the adjective she wanted to use. How dated the word seemed now! From the start it was *the* word for Monty – along with a lot of others whose suitability was to surface later. *Spendthrift* and *wastrel* had been her father's personal favourites, commonly found embedded in his habitual expression *'There! The fellow's a—! I knew how it would be!'* Other words – rogue, drunkard, womaniser and worse – followed as their applicability came to light. Winifred's own final definition was *'the absolute limit'*, though she had used the phrase only once.

Nonetheless, Winifred had been fond of her husband and his passing left a modest gap in her life. She had never depended on him for advice or financial support and hardly, towards the end, for companionship, but there was a capacity which neither her son Val, nor her father James, nor even her brother Soames, but only Montague Dartie had been able to fill. He was not a *Forsyte*, and was unique in her life by this fact alone.

For Winifred's present purpose he was sorely missed. So Michael would have to fill in.

Chapter Two

Meeting in the Park

In Kensington Gardens, only the very last of the latest-blooming trees kept their blossoms, mostly Spanish chestnuts, red hawthorn, and sweet white lime, while all the others – copper beech, sumach, Oriental cherry, European plane and English oak, a veritable arboreous League of Nations – were once more light enough to nod and sway in the breeze for a few weeks before their various fruits and berries would weigh them down again by summer's end. A crisp easterly wind, which had set the day fair from first light, still in mid-afternoon prevented many of the strollers from lingering as they might have over the flower-beds, and kept the pace of pedestrian traffic up and down the sweep of the Broad Walk unseasonably brisk. But the Gardens seemed nonetheless tranquil, unruffled save by the breeze and strains of *'Barbara Allen'* coming from the bandstand, and discreetly segregated by the Serpentine lake from the more communal goings-on in the park proper. What a pity the digging of trenches last year had not been confined to there!

As the small groups and configurations of people, drawn from as near to a cross-section of humanity as any city could decently provide, took their slightly wind-chastened turns along the paths, it would have been a safe guess that uppermost in each mind was a single shared thought: *What is it these others do for their living, that they can spend time so wastefully here, and not risk dereliction of duty?* The corollary to this very reasonable question was the understanding that it did not, of course, apply to oneself. So in the course of their perambulations did these unwitting representatives of social theory prove that mutual disdain can be a force for national unity quite the equal of more charitable impulses.

The little group, which might well have caught any passing painter's eye – brother, sister, and nurse with dog – having set out from South Square a quarter of an hour since, was deposited by the driver, Riggs, in the sepulchral shadow of the Albert Memorial, and proceeded from there due north through the Gardens along Lancaster Walk. Kat held Finty's hand, as always in public places and often in private ones, while Kit walked a few paces ahead and a little to the side, firmly holding one end of a saddle-stitched lead pulled tight by the eager straining of the dog.

When he had been picked from his siblings five years earlier, to replace the suddenly departed Dandy Dinmont (Dandy Goodfellow of High Dean, as he is remembered in Kennel Club records – reduced by Fleur without ceremony to Dan), this spotted bundle of a dog was chosen specifically because he was quite the smallest of a litter of six pups. Fleur had insisted all along, after the Dandy's injudicious altercation with the coal merchant's dray, that to get another dog straight away was a bad idea, since it was likely to be over-indulged in the wake of the other. She also told Michael that the particular breed being so persistently requested by their ten year-old son was too large to be kept even part of the time in London. But between acquiescence bordering on complicity at Lippinghall, the Mont country seat, where opinion held that one more dog among them of any sort would scarcely be noticed, and the solemn protestations of a young boy to his less than hard-hearted father, Fleur had been out-voted. Thus the present dalmatian had been acquired.

But being the runt, as any dog fancier or sociologist will confirm, is a position of only relative status, and the piebald hound had set about catching up on opportunities for physical and emotional growth the minute Michael brought him home, to whoops of unabashed joy from both children. He had become a vigorous, happy, long-legged beast who, so far now from being a runt, had for some years harboured the suspicion that he was being senselessly overlooked for promotion to leader of the pack. To the extent that his narrow, ink-blotted head could contain such an item, the dalmatian was certain he knew his own mind on this issue, and so was determined to be first on the path into the heady world of sounds and smells which was the park that afternoon.

As the little procession moved along, with the dog's jet black nose on chalk white muzzle pointing the way forward and the girl's diffident heels sometimes obliged to break into a shuffling sprint to keep up the rear, it met with no major obstacles until, after completing two sides of a rectangular route, it turned again at the Italian Garden and headed south. Finty held to the doubtful saw that seeming is next to being and so, in order that her charges might approach rectitude in their spirits, encouraged straight lines and right angles wherever possible in their actions.

This was where the animal broke with the consensus. For the first time on this walk he could not only smell water but actually *see* it, and the reckless need for a plunge overcame him. It was true that the fountains and ornamental ponds were enticing, and this appeal had been the very reason why Finty insisted they pass quickly by. Quite a number of people occupied the seats around the geometrical pools, or helped their children to set down little boats of various riggings on the rippled water. There were even one or two dogs – mincing things, to judge by the dalmatian's pied expression – content to sit in the shade beneath their owners' benches. But people, it was universally accepted, meant germs and contagion, and Finty, who always suspected Master Kit's hay fever of being the herald of a summer cold until half-way into the season, intended to take no chances.

Up to this point in the walk, Kit had encountered no particular test of his burgeoning adult credentials, aside from the fact that he was there at all and in the company of his sister and his – *her* nurse. Mercifully, he hadn't been called upon to make conversation, Kat and Finty seeming content to walk mostly in silence, only occasionally pointing out leaves or feathers or flowers to each other. And after all, he had his dog as mascot, a badge of rank, as if to say to anyone who doubted his status – *I'm here to exercise my animal, in case you care to know, and these two chose to accompany me.* Kit found great comfort in this notional distinction, so when the beast began pulling madly at its lead, gasping and straining to get to the tantalising pools, the boy automatically checked the animal by speaking its name sternly, in the deepest and loudest register he could summon. Alas, such is the tyranny of nursery fairness that, since Kit had been allowed to choose the pup, Kat, then very young indeed, had been awarded the prestigious task of naming him. Heedless of

15

the contradiction inherent between stripes and spots, Fleur's little girl had not hesitated to name the dalmatian after her best and most favourite character, from her best and most favourite book. Consequently, it was this name Kit now had to shout.

"*Tigger!*"

That idiotic name! It seemed to Kit for one awful moment that his voice echoed across the Park. He was certain a small child in the company of its parents and previously engrossed in a game of 'peek-a-boo' stopped to laugh outright. Kit cursed the day his sister had been allowed to give the beast such a stupid, childish name. How could they have let her? The whole assembly of passers-by would be laughing, even if only inwardly, at that ridiculous nursery name. Kit was unaware, though he was in no state to derive solace from the fact, that the Park was that day littered with any number of wagging, scratching Tiggers, Ratties, Badgers and Pooh-Bears, all similarly christened in times blessed by ignorance of such a thing as social embarrassment. No matter. We are seldom comforted by the knowledge that others have yet to suffer as we do. At the sound of that ludicrous name cast aloft by his own voice Kit felt as if his entire past had been stripped bare, the fragile fabric of his manhood reduced to shreds. To add insult to this vividly imagined injury, moreover, the dog took not the least morsel of notice of his young master, but dug in his heels and would not be distracted from the shortest path to the water.

"This way, please, Master Kit!" urged Finty, now walking ahead with her younger charge, while the older grappled with his disobedient pet.

At this unnecessary instruction from his old nurse, Kit was all the more determined to be masterful. Feeling all eyes still on him, he took the dog by its collar, unclipped the stout lead, and then, in a gesture unmistakable down the ages and inextricably associated – from Kit's reading at least – with decisive manliness, he raised the strip of leather above his head and prepared to strike. The dog cringed, and then both dog and boy started at a sudden plaintive cry.

"Oh, don't! Kit, *don't!*"

Kat stood with one thin hand clutching her nurse's arm and the other stretched out towards her brother. Over her pale ice-green eyes came a wild look; what little colour had been raised to her cheeks by the exercise drained completely. Finty turned at the girl's shriek and the tug on her arm. When the nurse saw what had alarmed Kat, her brows and mouth contracted towards each other and her features fell crossly in at the centre around her small pointed nose, like a doughy pudding taken sad out of the oven.

Kit would not have been deterred by his sister's distress alone, since she was '*only a kid*' and couldn't know the value of demonstrating manly intent by manly actions, but he dropped the lead soon enough when he saw the old nurse's expression. This second's pause was all Tigger needed to bolt, and bolt he did, not towards the water which seemed to have lost its appeal suddenly, but straight down the path ahead, past his two other humans, and into the Park at large. Within seconds he was out of sight.

"*Hell!*" Kit employed the mildest of a growing battery of adult words at his disposal to curse under his breath and, leaving another redundant command from Finty trailing in the wind, set off to recover the dog.

He ran, or more accurately jogged – that same dismissive trot as before which was his unconscious response to having to kow-tow to forces he had outgrown but not yet learned to outmanœuvre – for some hundred paces before he saw the wayward beast. With one front paw raised in supplication, it was sitting at the feet of a young girl who was standing on the bank of the Long Water. She was holding a brown paper bag from which she tossed pieces of bread to the swiftly gathering wildfowl. Approaching, Kit saw her turn to the dog and look at it with an expression of such sweet-faced pity that the boy was afflicted by a twinge of guilt he might otherwise not have experienced. She dipped her hand into the paper bag and brought out a crust. She offered it to Tigger, who took it as if it were communion bread. Judging by her height, Kit guessed the honey-haired girl to be a good three or four years older than his sister though she still had her hair plaited, a long single plait which hung right down her back until it ended in a wide blue bow at her waist. It swung as she threw small pieces of bread across the water. Yes, definitely a good bit older than Kat. (Kit was in the habit of assessing all members of the opposite sex by the degree of their resemblance to his female relations, none of

17

whom he liked too well at this stage of his development.) Nothing about her was like his sister – she seemed quite jolly in fact, with a sort of sun-coloured look that went with her hair. Thankful he didn't have to haul his dog from the water or, worse still, from the remains of someone's picnic, but had only to confront this open-faced girl, Kit slowed to a confident stroll as he drew close. Then he heard an unfamiliar sound. The animal was making the strangest little noise, a sort of soft, high-pitched keening, while its eager ebony eyes clung devoutly to the girl's face.

Just as Kit came up level with her, he heard the girl say cooingly, as if naturally replying:

"I'm sorry, poppet, but that was the last scrap. If you'd arrived earlier I could have given you more – I'm sure the birds wouldn't grudge it you."

Tigger tilted his head first to one side and then to the other as she spoke. He understood perfectly, his attitude seemed to say, and he would be a gentleman about it – but mayn't he stay there at her feet the merest moment longer, just to be sure? Just then he recognised his master's footfall at his back and, with a confirming glance over his shoulder, slipped between the girl and the water's edge and crouched there in her shadow.

Kit spoke assertively:

"I say, grab him, will you? He slipped his lead, and he's not supposed to beg."

The girl looked up and smiled.

"It was only a very little bit of bread," she said to Kit, and then looked down at Tigger who rolled his eyes up to meet hers. "Look, he's sorry for it already."

Kit, who knew that the hound had greater indiscretions to be sorry about, thought he saw his chance and made a sudden lunge. But Tigger once more took his cue and bounded off, this time through a half-shut gate which let into the small enclosed garden around the statue of Peter Pan. The area was empty and Kit followed quickly. He wanted to catch the dog and bring the ridiculous episode to a close. He also wanted to escape the girl's certain derision at his ineptitude with this animal he was supposed to own. But instead of laughter he heard the light tap of her shoes running after him. She was coming to help!

It was little more than a mad minute's dash, during which time Kit managed to get more than a few streaks of green on his flannels as Tigger led him through a series of very sharp exercises in the grassy enclosure. The last of these led to his total disgrace, as he skidded on a particularly tight turn and hit the ground with distinct impact to the seat of his trousers. Unmanned! Rear down on the grass and this girl with a ringside view of his humiliation – and that wretched animal was sitting once more at her feet! Kit scowled in anticipation of her first giggle. But again the girl's reaction was not what he expected. Casting the same look of sweet and unfettered sympathy quickly in Kit's direction, she bent over the dog and held him sensibly by the collar.

"You nearly had him that last time."

Kit realised she was speaking to himself and not to Tigger.

"He's a wretch," he replied, still scowling and taking a few seconds to pass some dirt from the heel of his hand to the front of his sweater before getting up.

"Do you have his lead? We could clip it on before he realises he's had."

"No – I – it's back there, with my—" Kit didn't finish his shambling explanation but watched entranced as this unknown girl, in whose company he had passed three of the most taxing minutes of his life, did the simplest and yet the most astonishing thing. She flicked her head so that her long golden plait fell over her shoulder, and, with right hand under Tigger's collar, she pulled at an end of the bow with her left and deftly removed the ribbon in one fluent movement. The next moment she had furnished the dog with a brand-new lead of blue satin – secured in a pretty good slip knot too, Kit noticed. Without a trace of triumph she offered the free end of the ribbon to him as he stood up.

"He's not such a bad dog, really. He's just got himself in the wrong story, that's all."

Her soft dark eyes smiled back at Kit as he looked at her uncomprehendingly. The girl nodded to the statue of the boy Peter blowing his pipe as all the animals and fairies gathered round. Throwing her unravelling hair back over her shoulder she gave the dog a fond pat on his narrow head.

"You want to be Nana, don't you? But you're quite the wrong

sort of dog, I'm afraid." She felt for his tag. "Goodness! You *are* in the wrong story. Poor old Tigger!"

Tigger gave her his best two-way tilt again – this new person with the tid-bits had his name!

At this juncture Kit sneezed.

Amid all his other besetting preoccupations on this walk Kit had forgotten to give this handy ailment – now fading with his growing maturity, he suspected – his best attention. Unaccustomed to such neglect, the condition chose its moment and retaliated by forcing a great sneeze upon him, which for decency's sake Kit only just managed to stifle on the sleeve of his blazer. As he looked up through bleary eyes, he thought he heard the girl say "Ascot!" as she held the satin lead out for him to take. Before he could ask her to repeat herself, he sneezed a second time.

"Goodwood!" the girl said, and this time gave the smallest giggle. Kit peered at her again, needing to establish whether this was finally the treachery of mirth he had expected all along. When his sight cleared she had retracted the makeshift lead and was holding out a small square of patterned lawn instead. It was her handkerchief! Kit took it, knowing that the gesture with his sleeve had betrayed the fact that he was without one of his own on his person at that moment. Besides, he could feel a third mighty explosion coming upon him, and sheepishly he turned away from her to deal with it. When he turned back he saw the girl was leading Tigger out of the Peter Pan garden. The dog went with her like a lamb. Kit followed.

"That was a dash, wasn't it?" she said.

Kit jammed the now very damp square of coloured lawn into the deepest recess of his trouser pocket before he spoke, so there should be no chance he would risk the final embarrassment of having to return it in that condition. He took the ribbon's end from her.

"Thanks," he said gruffly, then cleared his throat and repeated himself, this time sounding less surly.

He was about to ask her what she had said previously when she offered:

"Hay fever's miserable. My brother has it, too. Our uncle says it always starts with Ascot and finishes at Goodwood."

As Kit had an elderly cousin, whom he only saw about once

20

every summer but who each time said the same thing to him, he was able to sniff sagely at this evidently well-known maxim. Just then the girl looked past him and stood on her toes to see over his shoulder. He heard a rather shrill voice calling, "Ann, dear! We're going!"

Kit turned to see a diminutive and, as he thought, rather batty-looking old lady appear round the turn of the path. To Kit she looked about a hundred in the shade, maybe even as old as his Great Aunt Winifred and he had always imagined her age unassailable. But this one seemed sprightly enough, with her great hat above an arrangement of orangey-white hair shifting unsteadily like a badly perched bird's nest as she walked. And what a chin – you could hang a lantern on it! By her side was a boy of exactly the same height and colouring as the girl, though he looked a lot younger. Feeling the confidence of rank returning, Kit instantly thought him a sap. He must be this girl's younger brother then, and the old lady surely their grandmother? Crikey! Not all the awful people in the world were his own relations!

The girl stopped to give the dog's ear a last scratch, said a swift "Good-bye!", and ran off to join her family. Tigger started after her, but was checked by the gentle lead. Kit called the newly compliant dog to heel and looked up again just as the girl and her two companions were turning back around the bend in the path. The last he saw of her was a bright face turned over her shoulder as she threw him a happy farewell wave.

Chapter Three

Meeting by the River

As he walked along Victoria Embankment in the fair light of early evening, Michael Mont – the prominent Member for Mid-Bucks and now, incongruously for one of such an egalitarian disposition, the tenth baronet – wondered whether it was actually possible to leave his workplace with a heavier heart each day, for that was how it felt. The inevitability, as he saw it, of unspeakable consequences if the Government held to its present course weighed upon him like a stone under his ribs. Uncertainty about his own direction doubled the weight. How to avoid the worst excesses of appeasement towards German demands and yet not take steps which might commit his own country to another war in Europe – it seemed incalculable as the value of π.

He stopped and leaned his elbows on the embankment wall and drew a hand over the brief, rather grizzled fair moustache he had acquired on his upper lip. In a face naturally quizzical – comical, some said, with its pointed ears and earnest eyes – this and the look of sorry appreciation which had lately grown above it seemed ageing, despite a cap of boyishly fair hair. Soon he would turn and walk home to South Square, but it had become his little habit when time allowed to walk in the evening along the river to Cleopatra's Needle or thereabouts and, with the Palace of Westminster blessedly at his back, to stare across or sometimes simply into the waters of the Thames. He found something unaccountably therapeutic in this small deviation from the exigencies of duty. His essentially genial nature had been severely taxed in recent months and these few empty moments were disproportionately precious to him after the regular clamour of the Lower Chamber. In these present days even

Michael's liberal scepticism had taken a beating – that tendency to take the humane view in matters where one was not considered possible, which his opponents called 'Montism'. Previously this had been the great standby of his career, but now even it wavered; hence the need for these few snatched moments of quiet by the river. Strange to think this great, grey slick was the same twisting band of water which ran past Lippinghall.

> 'Through wood and dale the sacred river ran,
> Then reached the caverns measureless to man,
> And sank in tumult to a lifeless ocean:
> And 'mid this tumult Kubla heard from far
> Ancestral voices prophesying war!'

It seemed to Michael that he heard these now, as he stared out, while under its filmy surface the river churned ceaselessly. Paraphrasing Doctor Johnson, Michael thought Old Father Thames looked at that moment tired of London and Life together; even the gentle evening light could barely raise a shimmer on his weary back. Staring without focus into the opaque current, Michael reflected on the insidious regularity of events. The century had virtually begun with the Boer War, and within twenty years they had celebrated the Armistice of the Great War, in which he himself had fought. Now, another twenty years on, the war to end all wars was promising a sequel and, unlike Mafeking, there appeared no relief in sight. Wasn't it the same good Doctor who called a second marriage the triumph of hope over experience? What then a second war? The confounding of collective experience in mass folly? Evidently the war to end all wars has still to be declared, he thought, the one where we manage to blow ourselves to smithereens so that the whole process can start again from atoms! At this Michael smiled wryly to himself – it required more effort than ever to believe it was all comedy! And skipping authors once more, without as much as a nod in the famous lexicographer's direction, he decided that it must be a comedy of errors if it was anything at all.

He became vaguely aware that someone was approaching him along the line of the wall. Anyone but a fellow Member, he prayed, and was relieved on turning his head to see his prayer answered in the form of a tramp, diffidently holding out a calloused hand in the age-old gesture for alms. All his life Michael had been what, in vagrant circles, is referred to as a soft touch, and no sooner had he seen the man's hand and the threadbare cuff of the undersized jacket from which it poked than he had put his own hand into his trouser pocket and found a half-crown.

Michael turned to offer the coin but to his surprise the tramp started to back away, now shaking his hand in an equally unmistakable gesture of embarrassed refusal. Keeping his head down as he turned, he mumbled a few words.

"I couldn't, sir . . . I never realised . . ."

But Michael insisted and narrowed the gap between them, holding out the money.

"Here! Really, it won't break me, I promise you—"

He tapped the man's shoulder with a forefinger to press the coin on him and when the fellow turned to plead his final refusal, saw his face full on for the first time. Even before memory could supply a name, Michael felt in his stomach the clutch of an old, neglected loyalty. Small wonder the man did not wish him to see his face!

Knowing he was recognised the man straightened his shoulders, but would not meet Michael's eye.

"Didn't know it was you, Captain Mont, sir. Very sorry to 'ave disturbed you."

Michael looked at him with rising pity, at the weather-grimed face with its hunted brown eyes – like a rabbit's, he thought, through a shot-gun sight – at the worn suit and the shirt with no collar, and knew that what he was seeing were the remains of a man he had once known better than he might have known a brother. Michael simply spoke his name.

"Lewis—"

Lance Corporal Lewis the man had been, when he was Michael's batman during the War.

He was saying "Sorry I troubled you, sir—" again as he tried to edge away.

Michael caught him by the sleeve and held the thin material as firmly as he dared.

"Well, I'm not. Take this for a start, or I'll pitch it in the river."

He dropped the piece of silver into Lewis's jacket pocket, and hoped there was no hole in the lining.

"Thankin' you, sir." The eyes looked more hunted than ever. "Glad to see you lookin' so well."

"I only wish I could say the same of you — hadn't you better tell me about it?"

Michael steered the man to a nearby bench facing the river and sat down. Lewis remained standing, in a position suspiciously like attention.

"Oh, Lord!" cried Michael, suddenly laughing. "Those days are long gone for both of us! As a matter of fact, I'm by way of being your lackey now — so take a pew, please."

Michael's heart was no lighter when he inserted his latch-key at his front door an hour or so later. Now it bore the extra burden of a portion of guilt which he knew to be ridiculous, but which with unparliamentary soundness he felt unable to duck. Guilt for having a door to turn his key into; guilt for having a house in the city, an estate in the country and a wife with capital. In a phrase, guilt for 'having it made'. Socialist principles and a rich wife maketh not good bedfellows. He went straight up and found Fleur almost dressed.

He watched the delicate line of her back as she leaned over her dressing-table to correct the angle of an ear-ring. Her sheath of emerald green *moire* rustled faintly with the movement, its primary colour drawing an unwonted red from her dark chestnut hair. Michael knew that here above all was where his guilt lay; in this fine, bright, quick, perfect creature, whose adoring husband he had been these almost twenty years, but only *faute de mieux*. She saw him in her mirror and he returned her smile, though not its speed. Her ear-rings, also emeralds — what their daughter had called green diamonds when she was little — sparkled at him.

"There you are!" she said. "You'll have to bathe in ten minutes flat."

Michael clapped a hand to his forehead.

"Oh, Michael, you hadn't forgotten? Can you stay?"

"Only just. There's a vote at midnight — I'll have to be back for that."

Fleur neither frowned nor said anything but by the familiar little flat look which came into her eyes as she continued her

25

toilette, changing the emeralds for garnets set in pearls, Michael could tell she was coming to resent the demands of his work, and was growing tired of its incessant incursions into their life. He went over to her and kissed her shoulder. The touch of creamy skin to his lips made him wish to offer more than a single kiss, but he contented himself with a lingering glance at the perfection facing him in her glass. Whatever the disparity between his own desires and those of his wife, this was self-evidently not the moment to attempt to bridge them. Nor had it been, Michael reflected, for some time.

"Sorry, darling, I was waylaid. War paint?"

"White waistcoat, please."

As he moved to his dressing-room she added:

"Kit's back, and dying to see you. And Winifred wants you to telephone her before she leaves Green Street."

Michael had to keep the irony out of his voice.

"Right-o! I'll make the duty calls first, and be down in two shakes."

Chapter Four

Supper at South Square

About a month before the evening of Fleur's supper party, her mother telephoned from France to say that she had made the acquaintance of a very interesting and cultured person whom she wished Fleur to meet on his next visit to England. Fleur assumed that all her mother's acquaintances possessed free amounts of these two qualities and paid little attention. Annette had returned semi-permanently to Paris several years before her husband Soames Forsyte died in '26, and since then seldom visited England herself. But she and Fleur spoke regularly on the telephone so Annette knew by now all the nuances of tone in her daughter's voice. This current one denoted ennui and Annette's own voice took on an ironic purr.

"He is from the Ar-rgentine – but he speaks the most delightful English. I do not think he will bor-re you, Fleur."

"Then by all means send him here. What should I know about him?"

"Oh, there is no need: *il est très mondain*. But he is a financier of some sort, I think. He will tell you, if you care to ask."

Fleur had given really very little consideration to his visit, which was arranged entirely over the telephone by her mother, with the complication of two or three telegrams from the Argentinian to herself containing successive changes of dates. When he excused himself from taking tea with her the day before, Fleur had decided that in this instance her mother's judgement was substantially awry and that he would indeed bore her. The last thing she needed to do in this period of diminishing dividends in her life was to put herself out for someone who was too busy to be entertained. So with all her guests assembled that evening bar one, Fleur expected either a final telegram or another apologetic garland to arrive at any instant. Above the chatter of the drawing-room her ears caught the sound of hooves and wheels pulling up outside in the square. Her cynicism was confirmed. No doubt this was the florist's boy with a special delivery.

What she did not expect, as she kept one ear tuned to the door while monitoring two separate conversations in the room, was to hear a man's footsteps in the hall, and the murmur of a resonant bass voice intermingled with the comparative squeaks of the maid. They had been without their 'man' since he joined up in the spring, provoked by the invasion of Czecho-Slovakia. Timms, their maid, diminutive as she was, seemed never quite to rise to these occasions – but even she would not have let the delivery boy in! The footsteps continued, and approached the drawing-room. Surely this could not be her last guest just arrived? Heavens – no one kept a carriage these days!

Fleur turned to see a tall figure in the doorway. Timms had barely caught up with his stride: she already held his hat and cane, and he was removing his great cape with a practised sweep of his arm as she did her best to announce him.

"Mr Allyhan—Hallyan—Mr—"

"Alexander Barrantes," said he, bowing his head.

For one second only there was perfect silence in the room, but in that moment Fleur's agile mind understood completely what it was her mother had done in ordering this introduction. The second passed and he moved towards her almost before she could disengage herself from her other guests. He took the hand she offered, and again inclined his head; his hand was warm and dry, and felt smooth around her own.

"Your servant, Lady Mont. I hope you can forgive my impossible lateness."

Fleur looked into large, calm eyes of unfathomable brown and instantly her own of dark hazel became brighter than ever. Quite suddenly and instinctively she felt the need to deflect any attempt to gain access to her thoughts.

"Not at all, Señor Barrantes. As guest of honour it's your pre-rogative to be the last to arrive. Now, my mother said you wanted to meet our family, so – here we all are."

Apart from Michael, the assembly more accurately comprised Winifred Dartie's family – her son and daughter, and their respective spouses. But since Fleur was an only child these were all her own immediate English relatives too; except for those she owned through marriage and her mother had made a point of saying that the Argentinian particularly wanted to meet 'the Forsytes'.

Fleur covered the ground briskly:

"This is my husband, Michael; my cousins – Mr and Mrs Val Dartie, Mr and Mrs Jack Cardigan; and, of course, Mrs Winifred Dartie, my aunt. I'm sorry there are so many names between us but we were mostly Forsytes originally."

"We're quite a specific breed, you know," said Winifred, whose hand he still held. "I wonder you wanted so especially to meet us."

"It is quite simple, Mrs Dartie. I myself am half English but have never known my English relations. When Lady Mont's mother told me of her family here, it seemed to me that I might see how my own family would have been, if I could have known them. I trust you will forgive my candour, but I already feel as if I have somehow come home."

Winifred, who hadn't Fleur's trick of deflection, found herself fixed by his great, dark eyes, like an elderly deer caught in headlamps. He released her hand and the spell was broken. Jack Cardigan was heard to say:

"There's a thing, now – never thought of the Forsytes as a paradigm!"

Imogen Cardigan, for whom Jack's sense of humour had lost much of its currency over their thirty-three years of marriage, responded lightly:

"You mustn't pay the slightest attention to what my husband says, Señor Barrantes. None of the rest of us does."

Amid companionable laughter at Jack's expense, Fleur slipped her hand through her guest's precisely tailored arm and led the party in to dinner.

In Fleur's Spanish dining-room, unchanged since the newly-wedded Monts had first taken possession of the house in South Square, Alexander Barrantes' dark, slim and elegantly poised figure seemed

29

the perfect and only possible addition. Seeing him amid its brightly-coloured porcelain fruits, its Moorish panelling above a tiled floor, its copper articles, tooled leather, and the copy of Soames Forsyte's Goya – a woman of a certain age and usage, wearing a cascade of black lace, and whom the Argentinian instantly identified – the outside observer (that mythical beast) might have suspected him of being hired for the evening, for that very purpose. In a room devised to offer sultry charm, here suddenly was more.

And how he charmed them! Fleur watched as one by one her guests fell like flies under the spell of this elegant foreigner. She had placed him at the top of the unclothed refectory table, with herself and Winifred on his either side. Next to her sat Val, opposite Jack – poor Val, but someone had to! – then Michael at the other end, flanked by the two remaining women. From his position, Barrantes seemed able to hold all her guests in thrall, with no more effort visible than a conjurer at a children's party. Even Michael's ears were pointing up, Fleur noticed; she did like him in white waistcoats. Only Holly Dartie remained somewhat aloof, but as Fleur knew to her own past cost Holly was always watchful. Val and Imogen were quickly won over, as if they had recovered a long-lost friend from their childhood. Odd, she noted, how Val had aged so exactly as his wife, not as his sable-eyed sister whom in feature he more closely resembled. He and Holly had just the same degree of grey in their hair and, short of counting, identical numbers of lines over their eyes with matching wrinkles below. It was said to arise out of contentment, growing alike with age. Well, those two were as like as a pair of Staffordshire china dogs on either side of a hearth! And had – Fleur made no attempt to stop her inevitable next thought – had Jon grown more to resemble Holly, his quiet sister, or did he look like his wife now? Had Jon really found his life's mate in that American girl? Was contentment theirs on the Downs at Green Hill? From what she had heard, and that mostly from Winifred in unguarded moments, it seemed it might be so.

Fleur picked up the tail end of a question which passed in front of her. Val was quizzing Barrantes across the corner of the table – the question was about horses. No surprises there, Val had a stud farm on the Sussex Downs. Ah — so the Argentinian had a ranch? That would mean an invitation to Wansdon for him before the evening was over. Wansdon! — even the name of the place was unpalatable to Fleur. The fellow was welcome to go there. Wild horses would be insufficient to drive her back — back to the place where she and Jon had found themselves staying together, quite by accident, she visiting her cousin Val, and Jon his half-sister Holly, all those years ago. It had been only their second meeting, after that first fateful encounter in June Forsyte's gallery off Cork Street. At Wansdon they had become young lovers – young fools, she had thought countless times since, for they had loved only in words and looks, not in deed. A single deed then, and history would have changed its course. But history had been the one enemy she could never better. Now Jon lived on those same Downs, just a few miles away from Wansdon, with his wife and their two children . . .

Fleur was brought back to full attention when Jack brayed at a witticism, too close for her ear though he sat as far away from her as it had been possible to arrange. He seemed set to split his tails over the Argentinian's last remark, which she had missed. Barrantes paused graciously to make room for Jack's response, and then continued without missing a beat. He *did* have charm, this dark stranger – seemingly endless reserves of it – and yet he appeared to be doing so little to achieve the effect. Yes, that was his trick! And with another momentary lapse of concentration, Fleur realised that she had identified the trick so quickly because it was her own.

Jack whinnied again:

"Oh, I say! — I shall have to remember that one!"

He was no conquest, a ready ass for any distraction, but still he too was won. Fleur turned her observation to her aunt, and found the chain of enchantment to be complete – she might have been a young girl at a dance to judge by the glow on her cheeks!

At the next convenient break, of which Fleur somehow felt the Argentinian to be the engineer, Winifred undertook an explanation of the intricacies of family connection around the table; how Fleur was her late brother's daughter and so a Forsyte by birth, but that Holly was also a born Forsyte, a daughter of her late cousin; so Val and Imogen were first cousins to Fleur, while she and they were all second cousins to Holly. By his expression Barrantes was absorbed in the genealogy.

"Then you are all very fortunate indeed, Mrs Dartie," he said.

"How so?"

"Because you are all so close. In a family, and such a large one too, that quality is rarely achieved."

To this last proposal Winifred was bound to agree. Returning her smile, Barrantes' face was a paragon of sincerity.

Against her conscious will to the contrary, Fleur found her own eyes drawn to that face, at carefully chosen moments when it was not turned towards herself. His skin, she noticed, was finely textured and flawless, his clean-shaven face rather tanned than dusky, with a look as though a fine resin had been rubbed into it; a pronounced brow and rather long, straight nose gave him the profile of a Greek poet; a full yet precise mouth offered the sincerity of a chorister, and length of limb allowed a dancer's poise. His dark eyes, heavy-lidded yet strangely absorbent and open, held an undisclosed intelligence behind them. And like his eyes, his hair was a brown that was all but black, with the slightest wave to catch the light and shine. Top to toe, every part of his appearance owned a deep patina of unfaultable elegance. Was ever darkness more fair! And there was a scent about him, a slight and subtle mixture – what was it? – amber? – and sandalwood? – which Fleur knew from the first was the kind which could undermine her capacity for objectivity in a matter of moments, were she ever to let it.

There was one point later on – after Imogen remarked that her father had once gone to Buenos Aires on business – when Fleur caught Winifred and Val in an exchange of private glances which she could not interpret, but that was the single detraction from near perfect harmony around her Spanish table. By the savoury, Barrantes' conversation had been so diverse and so much to the delight of all her party, that Fleur even allowed politics to enter the dining-room. Previously this topic was known to be beyond the pale of her supper table, and now she kept a careful watch on its advance. The Argentinian drew his host on to the subject of the Peace Ballot. Michael – who still owned beleaguered pacific tendencies, who had dutifully sent in his post-card to the Peace Pledge Union, and who had passed on membership of the Left Book Club only because of a troublesome inability to overlook the Moscow Trials – was easily drawn. It had, he believed, shown up a sad failure of nerve on the part of Democracy to act by its own basic principles.

"They called it the largest plebiscite in history: over eleven million votes, and massively on the side of peace. But seen by the Government as little more than the co-ordinated beating of breasts."

"Are you then a peace-at-any-price man, Sir Michael?"

"A peace-at-*almost*-any-price man – like Lord Avebury – certainly."

"— Like the chap who's *almost* stopped beating his wife, what?" was Jack's observation.

"That better than nothing, surely?"

Jack was temporarily chastened.

"I imagine that around this table many of us have already paid the high price of war. The question therefore asks itself – could the price of peace be so much higher?"

Fleur relaxed her watch. Barrantes' easy urbanity, it seemed, could be trusted with any subject.

"Isn't it that no one wants war, but if it has to happen then everyone wants to do his bit?" Holly suggested. "I know that's how Val and I felt going out to the Transvaal."

"But that's just it," said Michael, not wishing to take on a guest, and least of all Holly, but feeling the need to add something for the record. "If only more of us would do our bit in peace-time. I ran into an old acquaintance today who certainly must have had a basin-full of doing his."

Fleur asked: "Who was that?"

"A friend from the War: fellow by the name of Lewis."

Winifred's ears pricked up.

"One of the Shropshire Louises?"

"No, Aunt – Mile End, I rather think. He was my batman." Rather than make a fist in his frustration Michael ran his hand through his hair. "Poor devil! He told me his story and I felt ashamed to be coming home to my supper. The man went through four years of trench warfare in France, and twenty years on he has to beg for coppers on the street just to keep body and soul together."

"Wouldn't he have been in the regular army if he was your batman?" Barrantes asked placidly, as if reluctant to offer a point of information to his host.

"Yes, he was a regular. But after the War his King and country

33

didn't need him any longer – or thousands like him. So he tried his hand at running his own business for a bit, just small trading, and had the spots knocked off him in the Depression. He couldn't find his feet again after that so he took it as a sign to return to soldiering and volunteered for the International Brigade. Now he's back from Spain and absolutely down-and-out."

"Can't he go back to Mile End?"

Imogen's question was more careless than callous: beneath the recesses of her ample bosom there beat a heart which was by no means unkind, only one which had not been allowed any significant contact with classes other than its own. And further in her defence, Imogen was probably not alone in this sentiment in Fleur's Spanish room that evening, nor would she have been in many another gathering of Forsytes.

"No such luck. Apparently he's no family, and what few contemporaries survived the Somme and Passchendaele have disowned him for being a Communist sympathiser."

"Is he, Michael?" asked Winifred earnestly. "He might be dangerous, you know."

"Not unless you consider Kipling the voice of radical dissent. His only considerations when I knew him were King and country – His Majesty's most loyal servant."

"But *Spain*?"

Winifred's tone elicited an amused flicker from the Argentinian's eye which caught no one's attention. Michael shook his head adamantly.

"The outlet of a generation, Aunt. Almost three thousand of them went out from here, volunteers one and all – over five hundred never to return."

"Poets and intellectuals mostly, romanticising it all—" Val put in.

"Not so. Oh, it's true, Auden and Spender and their lot went out, but the greater part was made of working-class blighters like my batman, his age and younger. And believe me, there's not much of the bard in old Lewis."

"Nor of the patriot, I should say," Winifred said, and squared her still fashionably fitted shoulders. "It's a very peculiar thing, wanting to fight other people's wars for them."

"All he wanted was to be of use somewhere," Michael answered

34

patiently. "England was no go, and Spain offered the chance of commitment – 'the war in which the rights and wrongs seemed so beautifully simple', as Orwell puts it. Lewis just wanted to help keep the Fascists out and a half-way decent, legally elected government in, that's all."

"But he was fighting on the side of Bolshevism," Val said. "That's not to be condoned, is it?"

"Not condoned, no," Michael admitted. "But I doubt the Communists have the monopoly on atrocity. And as for Lewis – well, if he does believe in the Manifesto, can you blame him? Look at the good the present system's done him, poor snipe! – left him no job, no home, and no prospect of either."

"Where *does* he live, Michael?" Holly asked.

"Around. He hangs about the Eton Mission some of the time, or so he told me. At night I suspect it's generally on the Embankment under a copy of the Manchester *Guardian*."

"But that's dreadful." Holly's sympathetic features knotted into a frown of concern. "Can you do anything for him?"

"I can try, but he's not in my bailiwick. I said I'd speak to his local man, but frankly I don't see what else I can do except offer him a handout." Michael's hand sought his hair again. "The more I stick at this business, the more convinced I become that the only constitutional powers of a sitting Member are to slander with impunity, and be sure of getting one's letter published in *The Times*. In this instance I feel driven to do both. Not a lot for the cost of universal suffrage though, is it?"

Fleur had listened intently to her husband for the last two minutes. Michael cynical? Had the mood which prevailed with her finally reached him?

"Michael suffers from a safe seat," she said to the table in general. "The less he has to do to be re-elected, the harder he tries."

There followed murmurs of assent from Winifred and Imogen, but no noise sufficient to shift the conversation to different ground.

"Is he desperate?" Barrantes asked unexpectedly in the lull.

"Lewis? Not yet; there's a certain torpor that seems to come with hitting rock-bottom, and that's certainly where he is now. But who knows? How can one know what life must be like for him?"

"It is ironic, is it not—" and here Barrantes pursed his full lips in reflection, "that, despite this man's fighting so long in its cause, it should be Democracy which has deserted him. When in theory, of course, it should be his to command."

"Yes – that is the theory," Michael responded sadly. "And indeed it does serve *us*, because we're the Establishment, and supporting us keeps things going. Lewis and his sort, they need something else. They'll never matter to entrenched power, except as statistics, so understandably they cast their allegiances elsewhere."

"*El tenir y el no tenir.*"

Barrantes made no attempt to explain his expression. He was perhaps unaware that he had used it.

"So," he continued, in the same rhetorical way, "the privileged and the people form two nations still?"

Michael could only answer him with a bleak, choric "Alas, yes."

Jack, who had kept abreast with most of the key words of this exchange, bleated: "Well, we're all privileged around this table – no earthly use pretending we're not."

His immediate female relatives both turned to Jack, wearing between them a joint expression of despair that he might one day say something which would advance a conversation, however modestly. It was Barrantes who actually made use of the comment.

"Quite so, Mr Cardigan. But not all of us have always been."

Here fell the second total silence of the evening. Forsytes can talk about poverty and deprivation with the next man – so long as the next man is not deprived or poor. Barrantes appeared not to notice their sudden unease. Winifred was slower than the others to draw the inference. Her *a priori* assumptions about Fleur's guest were a little confused. Hadn't he said earlier that half his relations were like themselves? How then could he have been unprivileged? – except that he did not know these people, which no doubt was a loss. She felt the need for clarity.

"Didn't you say your mother's family were English, Señor Barrantes?"

"Forgive me, Mrs Dartie, but I did not. My mother was from Seville. The English part of my heritage I derive from my father. It is his family I have not known, since he did not marry my mother. I take the name Barrantes as a courtesy from my adoptive step-father."

"Oh," said Winifred, enlightened. "I see."

Fleur suggested the women withdraw.

"Well, Fleur, I think your guest is perfectly delightful," Winifred said, advancing her original and more acceptable theory about the Argentinian in order to stymie the implications of his last statement, over which she still puzzled. She seated herself on the knole sofa and declined a glass of liqueur, as did Holly when Timms moved on to where she stood by the unlaid hearth. The maid, then finding no takers at all among the ladies, squeaked a "— M'm!" to Fleur and left the room.

"He's certainly immensely articulate, and I'm sure Val was very impressed with his knowledge of horses."

In Holly's gentle voice this assessment carried no edge, though Fleur listened hard for one. Perhaps her fairmindedness might be something to mark for once.

Imogen sat down next to her mother, and looked herself every bit as comfortable as the cushions around her. Although what was once lusciousness in her figure had become a fullness overblown in the rounding-off of middle age, in her dark sloe eyes, and in her hair carefully maintained in a matching shade, she still kept from girlhood that air of having a rich secret about her. She hadn't, of course, or if she ever had then half a lifetime with Jack Cardigan had worn it away utterly – but the illusion was a pleasing one. She announced:

"Do you know, I believe he reminds me of someone."

"Really?" Across Winifred's face passed a queer frown, of which she may not have been conscious, as if the same thought had first approached her and had not been entertained. "Of whom?"

"I don't know," Imogen replied, with that blank simplicity which came to her like an obedient spaniel whenever it was summoned.

"How very irritating, dear," said her mother.

Fleur had joined Holly by the hearth. Holly was looking at the painting over the mantel.

"Is that a Mondrian?"

"Yes. We wanted something geometric in here, and De Stijl seemed to catch the mood."

"'The renunciation of form' – that was a tenet of belief with them, wasn't it?"

"That's the blurb. They gave up the shape of things to see the substance more clearly—" Fleur gave a short sudden laugh at a bitter thought which passed through her mind. She knew Holly would understand the family shorthand when she concluded: "I expect I'm the only Forsyte to own one! What do you think of it?"

Holly paused before replying.

"It's very clever, and stylish – but a little modern for me."

Once again there seemed no edge in Holly's voice, even though this might have been an exact expression of what this soft-eyed cousin thought of her hostess. Fleur's cynicism, having prowled about all evening, went still unhoused – a wolf at the door – and from that slinking beast within her crept her next question.

"How is Jon these days?"

Fleur had not seen Holly for over a year – nor Jon for thirteen! – so the enquiry possessed a cover of plausible innocence, even when she added:

"— Still the happy farmer?"

Both were facing the picture, and Fleur knew without looking across that her cousin's quiet discretion was too complete to allow her to be caught off-guard. Holly smiled at the Mondrian and tilted her head fractionally, as with growing appreciation.

"Yes. Very much so – he and Anne both. And the children are dears."

"Mm."

Whether deliberately or not – and Fleur was not inclined to be charitable this evening, for everything had gone too well – Holly had just sealed up the last thirteen years of her life, those long years endured completely without Jon once she finally surrendered him to that American girl, Anne; sealed them up and cast them adrift like a hopeless message in a bottle, and in only as many words. Provoked, the Argus-eyed beast stalked on:

"And his mother?"

"Still in Paris. In fact, we—"

An interjection from behind them required Holly's attention.

"— what's that, Aunt?"

38

Because of the interweaving of family connections, Holly always used this form of address for her mother-in-law, who replied:

"I said, you'll be able to visit her in Paris, won't you?"

Holly hesitated.

"Yes—"

"Are you going there?" Fleur asked quickly. She and Holly separated and sat in opposing walnut bergères at either side of the hearth.

"Yes – we leave tomorrow. The Courvette stables have an Arab strain that Val wants badly. We thought we'd take a look."

"Quite," said Winifred. "So it would be just the easiest thing for you to visit Annette while you're there. How nice!"

"Oh," said Holly, sparing Fleur the need to say it herself.

Chapter Five

A Letter to *The Times*

By the inadequate yellow light from a small reading-lamp in his caricature-lined study, the conscientious Member for Mid-Bucks again ran a hand through his hair as he set about exercising the second of his two constitutional powers on the matter of his batman. He was writing to the newspaper and finding that inspiration was an insipid creature at one-thirty in the morning. He had returned from the House a little before one o'clock, and in the ensuing half-hour, with the ironic gaze of the White Monkey bent upon him from its frame on the wall above his desk, had scribbled several indifferent versions. Now, as Big Ben once again chimed its phrase from Handel, Michael picked up the sheet of his latest draft and gave it a hard look. It badly needed something to lift what he considered the proficient but lack-lustre quality of his prose. He rocked back in his chair and stared up at the ceiling. He should quote someone – but whom?

The answer, given the hour, was surprisingly forthcoming. Michael crossed the little room and took down a slim volume entitled *Counterfeits*. Whom better to quote than Wilfrid?

The book was heavy with many times its own weight of bitterness and gall. Glancing through the poems Michael wondered how he had managed to escape these sentiments burrowing their way into his own character. After all, he had fought in pretty much the same places on the line as Wilfrid, though Wilfrid had been a flyer some of the time. We suffered from equivalent shelling, he thought, and ended up in the same hospital. What's more, we were disabused of the same ideals, and clung to the same false promises in their place, yet I saw nothing but hope after the War, while Wilfrid saw none at all.

'*We're a generation who lost the ballot without ever being old enough to vote,*' Wilfrid once said of themselves. That would account for a good deal of asperity, Michael supposed. But there had been another ballot, or rather a draw, into which both their names were entered. As Michael's lucky star would have it, Fleur had pulled his name out of the hat and not Wilfrid's.

Michael remembered the rocky shallows of that stretch at the end of the second year of their marriage when Wilfrid Desert – his best man no less! – had declared himself in love with Fleur. For several bad weeks he had stood to lose both his wife and his best friend at a stroke. He was certain that Fleur didn't return Wilfrid's love, but therein lay the danger, for neither did she return his own. Michael did not then have the details of her first, her one great love, but he knew that his own suit had succeeded only because the straight favourite in the race for her affections had fallen inexplicably at the last fence. Instead of '*also ran, Michael Mont*', he had romped home in a clear field to take the trophy. So, if the plain truth was that Fleur didn't love either of them, why not go with Wilfrid? At least she would have the change.

Yes: it had been a wearing time. Then quite suddenly Fleur had elected to stay with him, and Wilfrid had gone East. Michael had never completely understood either decision. Heigh-ho!

His eye fell on a line of relentless, pacing iambics which seemed just the thing he wanted. He turned one page back to read the poem from its start. It was a lament for the forgotten victims of the Great War – those men who had survived. With his wormwood irony, Wilfrid had called it *Encomium.*

As he finished transcribing the couplets Michael felt a light touch on his shoulder. He looked up and saw Fleur standing over him, her hair gently ruffled from her pillow. Her wrap, a silk kimono of some sort, was warm at his back.

"Sorry if I woke you, darling."

"I saw the light; I couldn't have been asleep very long."

She covered a little yawn with the back of her hand, and Michael thought for the unnumbered time how prettily she looked when she was sleepy.

"Is that your letter?"

41

"It's trying hard to be. 'Frustrated' of Westminster — what do you think?"

Fleur picked up the sheet of paper and studied it. When she came to the lines from Wilfrid's poem she recited them softly:

> *'No worse to lie forgotten in the field*
> *Where poppies thrive, Elysium's only yield,*
> *Than, here return'd, forgotten to survive,*
> *Rememb'ring Death, in nought but name alive.'*

She put the paper back on Michael's desk.

"Hmm. It's bitter, but I suppose it's right. You'll get no thanks for this."

"I don't expect any. As a public servant I'm told it's my greatest strength."

He smiled but she had already turned away.

"You're too devoted, Michael. Come to bed."

Chapter Six

Mornings

In the world of the family as in the world of science there is a primary law which is irrefutable and applies to all things. This law holds that matter cannot be destroyed. While it may be dispersed as energy, or separated into its elements, it will nevertheless be found in all cases that the total of parts, if measured, remains constant. So it was on Forsyte 'Change, that crucible of family occurrences formerly located at Timothy's on the Bayswater Road and now, after a lapse of several decades, effectively reconvened in Winifred's elegant Empire-style[1] drawing-room in Green Street. It was late in the morning after the supper, and the matter of Fleur's visitor had already generated a good deal of energy as it was atomised by those present. They had analysed him up, and analysed him down, but whichever way they approached it, the answer they came to was constant – the Argentinian was an enigma.

From first light Winifred had possessed her soul on this subject, while she saw Val and Holly, who had spent the night at Green Street, off to the boat-train for Paris (even though they had said expressly there was no need). It was possible that Val would have encouraged her in this urge to talk about the Argentinian had they been alone, he had seemed quite taken with the fellow last night, but there was Holly too. Much as she could not have been fonder of her daughter-in-law, Winifred always felt that Holly was a little reserved in her

---

[1] *To which Winifred had returned, chastened and full of self-reproof, after a brief and largely unrewarding flirtation with Expressionism in the twenties. The room was presently a shrine to ormolu.*

opinions, and that around her she ought to follow suit. So by the time her present company arrived in the middle of the morning she was, in the vernacular of the smoker, 'positively gasping'.

Imogen had brought her two daughters-in-law and, despite her protestations that they couldn't stay long and definitely not for lunch as they were meeting their men at Jack's club, it soon became clear that she shared her mother's priority, and had even been whipping up enthusiasm for it *en route*.

In short order the events of the previous evening were detailed in their every minute particular. The foreigner's entrance – from a *carriage*, my dears – his height and composure, and the power of his dark good looks. And his conversation – *so* urbane, and so *knowledgeable*! By the conviction of their testimony Winifred and Imogen held their listeners enthralled, now venturing into observations and inferences which the constraints of social propriety barred from the drawing-room at South Square the night before. It should be said that their audience were willing captives to gossip, but what they heard would have brought the most pious ear to attention. Even as the hour for a pre-lunch cocktail approached – always a great attraction for the Cardigan wives – there were still more wonders to hear.

"And then Mama asked him about his mother's family's being English – and what do you think he said?"

Not a murmur of a suggestion was offered. Two breaths were held in tightly while Imogen paused, and then continued:

"He said it was his *father's* family who were English, and that his father *hadn't married* his mother!"

There was a satisfactory gasp as two breaths were let out.

"Then who *is* he?"

This came from Celia Cardigan, the twenty-one year old wife of Imogen's elder son John. She was sitting on a giltwood piano stool – usually the preserve of St. John Hayman, when he called – her ankles crossed prettily to show her favourite new pair of shoes to their best advantage. Behind her the little rosewood upright, a relic from Timothy's[2], might have struck a suspenseful chord if it could.

---

[2] *Bought back by Soames, surreptitiously, from its buyer at the sale there after Timothy died, thus saving it initially from a sitting-room in Fulham, and ultimately for the greater glory of the First Empire.*

Instead of this accompaniment, her question was seconded by the other daughter-in-law, Cecily, barely twenty and still the bride of the younger son, James. She leaned forward eagerly on a firestool by her grandmother's chair.

"Yes – and how does Fleur's mother know him?"

"My dears, if only one knew," said Winifred. "He spoke of his step-father, and of his farm – ranches they call them – in the Argentine. I believe he breeds polo ponies, which is nice for dear Val. They'd quite become chums by the end of the evening. But it's most mysterious about his background. Certainly, he's every inch a gentleman now—" In this last she was adamant, for with Winifred some of the old standards – behaviour and appearance chiefly among them – were imperishable, and grew by steady degrees as her own years advanced.

Celia smiled sweetly enough, but the light in her dainty eye was coy. She flexed her pretty ankles and said:

"He can't be, though, can he? A gentleman, I mean. Not if he's a bas—"

"Celia!" Winifred's rationale was hoist roundly by its own petard.

"Well, I think he sounds dreamy. Lucky old Fleur!" Celia concluded, undaunted.

"I wish we'd seen him – how romantic – and mysterious!" said Cecily.

Imogen smiled tolerantly as she raised her comfortable person to leave. These two young women were very much the daughters that she never had, and she embraced them uncritically to her substantial bosom as companions thereof. Her sons had turned out as surprisingly sober young men – *fit* and sober, naturally, being sons of Jack – and so she felt entitled to the whimsicality of Celia and Cecily as fair compensation. Winifred's affections, as ever, followed those of her children and she even looked forward happily to the arrival of any future 'very little Cardigans', as she was already calling them – though they would make her a great-grandmother! That the girls were each the other's best friend before their marriages was simply a delightful bonus. They were so infrequently seen apart that their cousin-by-marriage St. John Hayman, who was much their age and fancied (not always mistakenly) that the family quota of wit had passed diagonally down to him from his Great 'Uncle' George, always referred to them as *Gwendolen* and Cecily.

On the mantel, Winifred's great ormolu clock, with some grinding of parts, began its own internal rise to the mid-day hour. Beneath the bell-jar, its filigree hands were closing chastely upon the time when cocktails were expected, if not overdue.

"Is he staying with them?" This was Celia again, as she took her cue from her mother-in-law and the clock, and got up to go. It might as well have been Cecily, following her friend, who spoke, for they sounded as they looked, these dun-haired, sweet-faced and sometimes naughty-eyed girls, so much alike and were always in such fluent succession that it could have been one voice all along.

"No," Winifred replied. "At the Dorchester."

Here came two exclamations of candid disappointment.

"He said he had taken his usual suite there," Winifred added, not knowing quite what she made of this fact except that it suggested habituation with London and a longish stay.

"Oh," said Cecily again. "Then we shan't see him unless we're invited to Fleur's."

She knew this was barely a possibility. Fleur to the Cardigan daughters-in-law was a near-ethereal being who had attained a state of perfection depressingly remote to lesser mortals such as themselves. If the Argentinian had been staying at South Square they might have called during the day – 'on spec', as they said. As it was, both despaired of a formal invitation.

"Unless you should see him here, of course."

Winifred's eye twinkled as she saw the effect of her words. It stopped the girls on their way to the drawing-room door and brought them back to her chair with a snap worthy of corsetry elastic.

"Oh, Grandmama – you've invited him here! When? When are you expecting him? Will he come do you think?"

This was both in tandem, united in an undisguised enthusiasm which shaved a good five years off their respective ages. Winifred had to hold up her hand to make a space in which to answer.

"I have no idea when he'll come, but I see no reason why he shouldn't. I said he would be welcome to call any day, and he seemed quite jolly about it. So perhaps you will both get your wishes after all."

There may well have been times when Winifred felt like a fairy godmother to these young things, whose experiences and sensibilities were so very junior to her own, but with a wand in her hand she could not have conjured the next moment, nor would she have improved upon it if she had.

Trained *in situ* at Green Street by the long-since retired Smither and therefore more confident with unfamiliar names than poor little Timms at South Square, Winifred's maid Miller opened the drawing-room door and announced:

"Mr Barrantes, ma'am."

As the old clock began its set of chimes, the tall and just sufficiently languid figure of a man, not looking at all as if his ears burned him, appeared in the doorway. While the pleasant C major of noon continued to sound from the mantel, Barrantes took in the female assembly with a calm sweep of his dark, prominent eyes, ending in a single, slow blink of dusty lashes. He shot his cuffs discreetly, a little gesture of implicit deference, and hung poised on the threshold of the room.

"I hope I don't intrude myself upon you, Mrs Dartie," he said gently, glancing at the clock as its last note decayed into the corners of the room. "Perhaps it is a little late to be making a morning call."

"No, no, no! I should have been quite alone if you hadn't – my daughter and grand-daughters are just going on their way. You must take a glass of sherry and stay for lunch, Señor Barrantes – your timing is excellent!"

That theirs was not was precisely why the two young Cardigan wives so flatly despaired of ever coming within a mile of either Fleur's social perfection or her formal guest-list. They tried to glint intriguingly as they were introduced in turn by Winifred, but honestly they felt that their cause was one St. Jude himself could not have salvaged. What eyes he had though; and that scent which just reached them with his hand – subtle and alluring – if only they could be!

Fleur spent the morning after her supper party in a silent rage at her mother. She had only to pick up the telephone and put through a call to Paris to say exactly what she thought of this *chicanerie* of hers. It would be a simple transaction; Fleur knew exactly what she

47

meant to say and could make a fair guess at her mother's reply. She could already hear the exchange:

"*And how did you find Monsieur Barr-rantes, Fleur?*"

"*Not quite so irresistible as you or he thought, Mother.*"

"*Mais – pourquoi pas?*"

"*Mais pourquoi?*"

"*Ah, là – quel dommage . . .*"

She would not place the call. The relationship she enjoyed with her mother had forever been one based on knowing rather than on confiding. Why then should she wonder at her mother's temerity in sending her a prospective lover? What the world took for the French affinity with romance was the world's mistake – Fleur knew it was all a matter of practicality with them, her mother no exception. Annette was well aware that her daughter was restive, that she had been born restive and would always chafe against restraint, however reconciled she might seem to the bit in the bridle of circumstance. So Fleur's very practical French mother had simply selected this personable foreigner for her *divertissement*. Very well! If he had a disposition to be entertaining let him do his best, but Fleur was in no mood to be easily amused. His best would need to be remarkable before she would even notice.

Lodging this ultimatum in the back of her mind, against the need for future reference, Fleur went up to the nursery. She had promised to take Kat to Hatchards – how that girl loved books!

The same morning began for father and son with an offer from the elder Mont to help the younger with his week-end's preparation. The offer was sincere but might not have been so prompt had Michael known that the subjects in need of attention were Latin verse translation and quadratic equations.

"You're on your own with the maths, old man," Michael said, "especially if I'm to keep my shoes and socks on."

Mont minor seemed unbothered since numbers held no mystery for him. In fact, if his report cards were to be believed, Kit was in most subjects an 'apt pupil'. By this his parents understood that if no subject fired him to an access of zeal then equally none gave him any great trouble. The boy – though boy, officially, he would be for only very little longer – had what his masters at Harrow called a *facility* for his lessons, though they never referred to any show of enthusiasm.

The Latin poet was Virgil whose expelled and exiled Trojans, despite the vicissitudes of the seething main, had managed to find the shores of Alba Longa in good time for the end of term. With two chairs pulled up to the desk in the little study, and the text of the *Æneid* open before them, the tenth and future eleventh baronets pored over the knots in the sixty-odd lines of the Mantuan's epic which Kit was required to turn into good prose copy by the following Monday.

In truth it was Michael who did most of the poring. He recalled committing vast tracts of the Eighth Book to memory for a speech day at Winchester when he was about his son's age and, looking at it now, recognised the verse still, but remembered also that he had never been sure of its translation.

Kit called out the vocabulary he did not know – of which there didn't seem too much – while Michael thumbed through the pages of *Cassell's Compact*, whose Latin to English section appeared unhelpfully more compact than those of his own day.

Unsure of something, Michael referred back to the text:

"I know I'm a duffer, but who's speaking here? Is it Æneas or king Evander – Æneas, surely? He was always going on about his fate."

Kit, whose case endings were a little fresher than Michael's, saw that it was Evander and made a note in his exercise book to this effect without troubling to correct his father. Economy of gesture was fast becoming the chief principle guiding his behaviour in matters that were of limited importance to him.

Standing under a massive Gaugin, too large by half for their modest hall, Michael opened the late morning post as he waited for Kit to find his blazer, prior to their leaving the house for what was now agreed by both parties to be a well-earned lunch. With no paper-knife to hand he was discovering the inverse mathematical proportion between the weight of a sheet of writing paper and the importance of what is written on it. Invitations! Michael was not known for uncharitable thoughts, but several passed through his mind as he dropped the stiff cards one by one with their envelopes back on to the salver on the coat sarcophagus, where they lay like fancy confectioner's wafers. The very quality of the paper they were printed on began to give him offence, and yet he was honest enough to own that he was himself wholly a product of the way of life which engendered this response – rather the total lack of one – to the present brooding crisis in the nation's and perhaps the world's agenda.

Something made him pick up the last card again. It looked more official than the others, one of Fleur's charities perhaps – that would endow it with some credibility, at least.

The Dumetrius Gallery invites

then, in a careful, clerkish hand, their own names –

to a preview of its SPANISH EXHIBITION
*at the new premises in Burlington Gardens
on Wednesday, August 23rd, 1939.*

An asterisk constructed in the same close hand at the bottom corner of the card directed his attention to the back of the invitation. Michael turned it over; there, a second deliberate little star added—

'*To include small Goya from Forsyte Bequest.*'

Michael had a dim memory of the National Gallery – the public caretaker of that once private collection which was Soames Forsyte's gift to a grateful nation – sending them some paperwork in this regard earlier in the year. Fleur must have dealt with it for he was sure he had not. At his death, her father's collection had stood at over seventy paintings, some of them very significant pieces: there was a Maclise, a Morland, a Constable and two old Cromes; a Mauve and a younger Teniers; a Monet, a Turner, the Goya of course, and no less than four Gaugins. This one was all that Fleur had wanted to keep then, though her father's will had given her a free hand to choose any she wanted. And she had had the Goya copied, because of her Spanish room; but that was all.

Well, no doubt they would go to Dumetrius' exhibition, and see the old girl in her original black lace, amid her compatriot pieces. But whose Spain would they be seeing – Goya's? – poor Lewis's? – or General Franco's?

Michael looked again at the note. *Small* Goya. With this his native humour, that better and enduring part of him, returned – how old Forsyte would have loved that!

Kit bounded down the stairs two at a time, and after the exchange of a winning grin for a fond scowl, son and father left for a brisk walk to St. James'.

Chapter Seven

Lunches

After returning her daughter to the day nursery with what seemed a yard of books, Fleur was sharing a late-ish lunch with Dinny Dornford, Michael's cousin on his mother's side. She and her husband were spending the week-end in Mount Street with the Dowager, Dinny's Aunt Em. This arrangement in the normal way would not have been necessary; Dinny and Eustace had a perfectly adequate house of their own in Campden Hill. During the summer recesses – Eustace being a Member of the Lower Chamber, as well as the King's Bench – they shared Condaford Grange with Dinny's parents, and a constant flow of constituents. But during this particular summer, for the past two weeks, a firm of builders and decorators had been installed in the house in Kensington, and were presently less than half-way through their task of converting the attic there to a nursery floor. So, when Eustace had been required to come up on Friday for the midnight vote, and Dinny had a routine appointment in Harley Street first thing on Monday morning, they had found themselves requisitioned as house-guests for the week-end by Em.

The little restaurant was in North Audley Street, and had a front window imperfectly screened from the road by a row of conical bay trees in tubs. Dinny had asked that they did not stray far: her fourth month became her but she was finding the heat trying. She actually didn't feel like lunching at all, but her aunt had begun to cluck.

"'*Elderly gravida*' is her latest expression," Dinny said. "She read it in a stray copy of the *Lancet* at her doctor's. It's what I am, apparently, so she clucks. Did *you* know she was coming up from Lippinghall just to get the house ready for us? We shan't be staying later than Monday. She's a sweetheart, but I already long for the peace of Condaford. Mother isn't nearly so bothering."

For several years it had been a popular belief among the Cherrells – Michael's mother's family, spelt 'Charwell' – that Dinny and her husband Eustace Dornford, K.C., the Honourable Member for Oxfordshire East, were avoiding the start of a family. Alone in her reserve on this subject, Lady Cherrell – Dinny's mother – had not claimed the right to own an opinion. Having had three children herself, and now with Hubert and Jean announcing they had started a fifth grandchild, she was philosophical. At Condaford they had always marked Dinny for a wife and mother, and for a long while it seemed she would be neither, after her first love affair ended so badly. Then Eustace appeared providentially, when Dinny was at the 'now or never' stage with men. A baby, Lady Cherrell felt, would arrive by the same agency.

But the Dowager was a different kettle of fish from her sister-in-law. (It was often said, indeed, that she was simply a different kettle of fish from anyone.) She had no such scruples, and even if she had was constitutionally incapable of adhering to them, owing to her inconsequences. She held that the delay was *"somethin' chemical – Eustace's bein' Catholic, an' all"*, and usually found a way of saying so whenever she saw Dinny. Now that her niece's first pregnancy had stifled this pet observation she had taken up a new concern for Dinny's health, which being country-bred was never less than excellent. In fact the only threat to Dinny's health *à ce moment* was from the dust raised during the removal of covers from the drawing-room of the largely disused house, in which occupation she left her aunt directing the butler before coming out to lunch with Fleur. Hence clucking, as she put it.

Fleur was more direct in her observation.

"Well, seven years is a long time to wait for a first baby."

Dinny nodded, and surprised her cousin with her frankness.

"Yes. That was me, I'm afraid."

Fleur made a little frown with her eyebrows by way of offering tacit acknowledgement of the things that were understood between women. Perhaps Em was right.

"Oh, not biologically," Dinny said, in reply. "I just wanted to make sure."

"Make sure? Of what?"

"Of myself. And that I wanted Eustace for himself, and not simply for his capacity to make me a wife and mother."

Seven years to make sure! It was almost Biblical. And for no special reason at that moment, Fleur's next thought was that it was nearly twice seven years since she had failed to do the same herself, to Jon.

Dinny said:

"Tell me honestly, Fleur, would you have had another baby at my age?"

Dinny was all of four years younger than her cousin-by-marriage.

"If we'd wanted a third, I suppose so. But it was different with Michael and me – we started so young."

Fleur was reminded, and not for the first time recently, that there was once a time before she and Michael were started at all, when she had been younger still.

"Kit was a summer baby, of course," she offered, covering her tracks before Dinny could get scent of her mood. "It *is* so boring towards the end – but you'll have the autumn, that will help."

"Hum. It's never been my favourite season: more suited to endings than beginnings, I've always thought."

"Dinny dear, I believe you've got the blues. Don't worry, it's only the extra pounds – one feels awfully weighed down, but it ends."

Testing that overworked poetic device, the pathetic fallacy, the looming clouds which had been gathering steadily since one o'clock burst in a concerted silent instant and the street outside the window was drenched. The cousins watched the deluge while their waiter hovered. Dinny settled back into her chair and drew in a breath of the quickening air from the open window. Fleur thought she had never looked prettier, the silky bloom on her cheeks framed by her red chestnut hair, and that slightly far-away look in her blue eyes. Contentment was something!

"I love the smell of a good down-pour in London," Dinny said, "—diesel and apples!"

Fleur wrinkled her nose at the scent from the street. She had always preferred drought.

"That decides us," she said. "We'll have to order coffee."

54

Dinny chose *thé à la camomille*, feeling it would be more calming for the baby. Boy or girl, a calm child would be a gift of Grace in these times.

"Have you chosen names?"

"Not yet. I've always liked the Old Testament ones – Joshua, Rebecca, David particularly. Eustace wants something from one of the families, if it's a boy, but I expect that's the thought of war – securing the line, just in case. Unfortunately all the Dornford men have rather, well, noticeable names. His father is only an Arthur, but there are uncles Percival and Gavin—"

"The knights of the round table!" Fleur interrupted. "No Uther Pendragon, I hope."

Dinny smiled loyally.

"How did Eustace escape being brave Launcelot?"

"He was named after his grandfather. I think that's what he really wants for his own son."

"Well, Arthur is a bit dull these days, unless you're royalty – but less noticeable than any of the Cherrells'."

"No, ours aren't much better – Conway, Lionel, Hilary, Adrian. That's why I'm rather hoping for a girl. But either way we're far from a decision. How did you and Michael decide?"

"We both just liked Christopher. I wanted him solid, Michael wanted him enquiring; so Wren and Columbus seemed good examples. Catherine followed without much need for debate."

"Lucky! We've gone in for appeasement at the moment, but it can't last. Our latest 'Munich agreement' is looking shaky. I say I'd like a longer name we can abbreviate – like Kit and Kat; Eustace says he wants a name it can spell at the first go. If we have to go Biblical, he says, then it's to be no more than four letters complete, or he won't vote. That just about leaves us with Adam and Eve."

"Or Cain and Abel?"

"Or Ham and Shem – or Noah! Oh, dear," Dinny gave a little laugh, "perhaps we'd better stick a pin in the telephone directory." She sipped her tea thoughtfully. "It's not that Eustace is being difficult, poor lamb, only that he favoured '*Eastuce*' as an early variant of his own until he was encouraged out of it by his nanny. He doesn't want his child to go through that difficulty. He really is a dear."

55

Dinny smiled fondly and for a lingering moment Fleur envied her absolutely. Like herself, Dinny had not been allowed to marry her great love – in her case Wilfrid, that same Wilfrid who had known '*all the pangs and pessimisms*' of unrequited love for Fleur those years before – and this mutual status had formed a firm if unexamined bond between the two women. But unlike Fleur, Dinny had been permitted the chance to get over her broken heart before she married. That had to be the better way after all, to have the pieces all swept up instead of getting them constantly under foot!

"How is Eustace – at the House all the time, like Michael?"

"Quite a lot these days, or in his 'surgery'. He's committed to his constituents and naturally they're happy to take everything he's got."

"Michael's been quoting Wilfrid," Fleur said, and watched Dinny through her lashes.

"Wilfrid?" It was as if she had to retrieve the name from a high shelf in her memory. "Why?"

"To make a point about an old soldier, in a letter to *The Times*. You know Michael – always looking to build up a cause."

"And Wilfrid always looked to tear one down." Dinny smiled faintly, and looked out at the rain, thinning before a second fall. Perhaps she knew Fleur's eyes were on her – perhaps, too, she did not mind that they were.

Contentment's done that for her, too, Fleur thought – she's traded her sense of self for a sense of purpose in others. All the Cherrells had it, one way or another, that ancient sense of service. Dinny's father and her uncles, in the order she had named them, made between them a general, a judge, a reverend and a professor. And Michael had it, from his mother, a tendency to put others before oneself which, in all the years of her acquaintance with it, was still as foreign to Fleur as the alien corn to Ruth. And Dinny was a Cherrell of the first blood. She had lost her heart to Wilfrid, but in devotion to her husband had recovered her heart's-ease. Well – some could!

"We all admired how you got over Wilfrid, Dinny. Do you ever think of him?"

Fleur knew the question, and the preface she had given it, were mildly wicked, but Dinny's excessive equilibrium was not helping her own.

Again Dinny made the unexpected answer.

"Do you remember, Fleur – that time you told me you were 'inoculated' before Wilfrid?"

Fleur remembered perfectly. On the same occasion, she had said that if she ever told her story – the tale of her 'inoculation' – to anyone, then it would be to Dinny. But she had never again broached the subject. It was just as well so, since she was beginning to suspect her immunity was wearing off.

So Fleur only nodded, and looked at her cousin rather more broadly.

"I have to confess," Dinny continued, "I was all wrapped up in *my* first love and I didn't understand what you meant then—"

"But now you do?"

"Yes. Wilfrid – dear Wilfrid – inoculated *me*, you see."

"And Eustace?"

"Eustace got me germ-free, when I was over the contagion – when I was safe."

Safe! The word for Fleur had the whiff of carbolic about it. But on Dinny it sat like the shine on a new penny – something good and sound and real.

"Second loves *are* sweeter," Dinny added.

Fleur was unable to comment, having never had one herself.

"So, yes, I do think of Wilfrid – but I think of Eustace more."

Because a question would otherwise have gone begging, Fleur said brightly, "And I Michael. We've married well and wisely, Dinny – and two phenomena, to boot. Let's hope they'll both be 'kicked upstairs' soon!"

The rain stopped quite as suddenly as it had started and left the bay trees dripping darkly. Fleur paid the bill and stood with Dinny at the door, waiting to see if they would need the field umbrella their waiter was wielding behind them. The gutters were still running, but the air was noticeably clearer. Fleur waved the waiter away.

"I'll walk back with you," she said. "I haven't seen Em for weeks."

The dark blue glossy door at Mount Street was opened by the expressionless Blore, whose features inclined away from them like the weathered escarpment they so closely resembled.

"Mrs Dornford. Your ladyship. Lady Mont is upstairs."

57

Following the butler up to the still partly sheeted drawing-room, they found Michael's mother moving between islets of furniture like a stout wading-bird, rather curved about the beak and chest, and in fine non-consecutive feather.

"Ah, Fleur. Does Michael know we're *neutral* now at Lippin'hall? The council changed us. I've told them it's a nonsense – we can billet ten without havin' any in the house, 'specially now the gardener's a ratin'. The Merchants don't mind him bein' deaf in the boiler-room—"

Here she paused, to sway across the room with a sigh.

"It won't be the same, Boswell without Johnson. He won't roll the terrace on his own. It'd be gratifyin' to have a complete family – will you ask? Too much pressure on the ankles – Dinny, you must go upstairs!"

In Winifred's ground floor dining-room – no less elegant than her drawing-room but, to the eye of the purist, despite its marqueterie and buhl not quite so loyal to the French Emperor – every morsel of the cold pigeon fillets had been particularly delicious, as had the asparagus and the lobster mousse which preceded them. Winifred had the highest hopes for the summer pudding still to come. Keeping to the Heidsieck throughout had been an inspiration.

They had spoken so far of the Theatre – of the new comedy that had just opened at the Colony Theatre – it was *so* amusing; of Music – they were allies in detecting a definite return to melody among the newer English composers, Vaughan Williams set them such an example; and of Art – they deferred to each other, but no, it was true, a national collection should start with a grounding in the Renaissance or, really, where did one begin? And if Winifred did not for one moment let herself suspect that her guest was capable of making himself equally agreeable to others who might hold opinions at variance with or even in direct opposition to her own – well, in whose interest there would it be to raise her suspicions?

As the pudding came and went, fulfilling every expectation, Imogen's notion crossed her mind more than once. Yes; there *was* something – something *familiar* about him. And because it was a pleasant familiarity and posed no threat that she could see, Winifred was content to let it ebb and flow around her right to the end of the meal. Sometimes it was a look which stirred her memory, sometimes a way he had of holding his head, and sometimes nothing that she could isolate from his general manner, which was – of course, as she reminded herself – quite foreign.

"—It must be a little strange for you, nevertheless," Winifred mused, the Heidsieck completing the sentence in her head, and seeming to tie it in neatly with what went before.

"What is that, Mrs Dartie?"

"Why, being in England, and yet not knowing whether a person you might pass on the street – or even sit next to at the theatre – could be a cousin, or an aunt or uncle?"

Barrantes smiled suddenly, an ingenuous response it seemed, a smile which extended to his dark, watching eyes and lit them fondly. He dabbed his mouth with his napkin, which gesture might also have allowed him to cover the most revealing part of his expression. He placed the tips of his fingers into a little steeple on the edge of the table exactly before him, watched the careful action of his own hands as he did so, and then looked up at Winifred, not unlike someone who has teased a willing subject too well and for too long.

"I see I have misled you somewhat. I have not explained my situation properly, and – you are right – it is a little strange. But you see, Mrs Dartie, in fact I do know who my English family are."

"But you said that you didn't know them, I thought?"

"I meant by that – they are unaware of my existence, not I of theirs."

"Oh. I see," said Winifred, who did not yet but trusted that she would if she persisted in a straight line with her questions. "What was your father then, if I may ask?"

"Oh, certainly you may ask – and you may be sure I made my mother's life miserable with that question when I was young. She would tell me only that he was un pícaro."

Since it had never in her time been considered a fashionable tongue, Winifred had no Spanish; but the word, and the way it was said, suggested membership of one of the more distinguished professions. She repeated it aloud, and Barrantes smiled encouragingly at her attempt to match his accent.

"And what is that?" she asked.

"A rogue – a scoundrel, if you prefer."

"Oh," said Winifred, who had no preference.

"He died some years ago. My researches since, such as they have been, have led me to understand that by occupation he was simply a gentleman – and his family quite exemplary."

"Ah!"

This was more promising. She ought never to have doubted her first instincts in the matter.

"Then why don't you introduce yourself to them?"

His brow clouded briefly as he replied:

"Because I fear they would not welcome me."

"Oh, but I can't imagine, even in the circumstances—" Winifred was pleased at this phrase for with it she was able to dismiss at a stroke all of the troubling details he had revealed hitherto, "— I simply can't imagine that they would be anything but delighted to know you!"

The fond light in his gaze changed subtly to one of gentle gratitude. To Winifred, not looking for such a response as she waited for his reply, it only seemed that his eyes grew deeper, opening strangely and becoming darker than before. Very slowly he raised one hand from the table. When Winifred asked her last question she had made an unconsidered gesture with her own hand which half reached out to him and then stopped, out of the ingrained courtesy of a hostess to a guest. Now Barrantes laid a warm, smooth finger on the back of that thin hand, with its web of blue veins. When he spoke it was with a hushed and solemn gravity.

"Tell me, my dear Mrs Dartie, in all sincerity; in the circumstances – *would you?*"

Turning out of the oyster-bar in Duke Street after a splendid 'three-courser' which he had not so much savoured as wolfed, Kit matched his father's casual step up the short stretch to Piccadilly, the glow of his share of a bottle of best house champagne expansively upon him. His actual birthday was not for another five weeks, just ahead of the end of term, but (as he had pointed out to the Guv'nor yesterday evening, and in letters beforehand) this was his last long-weekend *before* then. Michael had seen the logic of his son's argument and that it was specious, but conceded the point. For Kit the old man's standing a bottle of 'fizz' held the impress of a rite of passage: he felt pleasantly, not to say properly elevated, admitted now into that greater body of existence where men were without let or hindrance simply men, and all others were saps. In fact the budding disingenuousness which would serve him so well in his new-found land of manhood had already played its part in their choice of hostelry. Knowing his father's fondness for fish – a form of protein which in the general way Kit could not abide – he saw two clear advantages in acceding to the proposal of the Duke Street establishment. Firstly, there being no 'r' in the month, he was running no risk whatever of being asked, by way of initiation, to share a neighbourly plate of those raw molluscs which so disgusted him. Secondly and far more significantly the place was known to sport champagne as its chief beverage, and so Kit considered the small compromise of having to tolerate an area of smoked salmon with his scrambled eggs to be far outweighed by the access it afforded to 'fizz'.

As they crossed to the north side of Piccadilly, Kit cast a wary quarter-eye over the meandering, doggedly patient queue for the Summer Exhibition outside the Royal Academy. Usually he would have feared for a dose of culture – mandatorily prescribed on week-ends out to take the edge off his enjoyment – but not *this* week-end, surely? Not when a chap almost turns sixteen! Michael caught his son's expression, which for all Kit's mastery of the adult mien spoke a thousand words, and laughed genially.

"*Nil desperandum!* I haven't the stomach for it myself, and besides—" Michael squinted up to the sky where the morning sunshine had been ousted over lunch by a sullen mass of cloud. "We'd never get in before this lot comes down. I'd guess we've three minutes at most – what say we give your grandmother the chance to remember your birthday?"

Quickly they threaded the Arcade and half the next street up, until without sound or sign the heavens broke. The awning of a little gallery two doors away took them in before they had a dozen round splotches apiece on their jackets. They found they were sharing their bolt-hole with a small dog and a large woman, the two figures joined by a lead. Michael tipped his hat and there four souls stood in a perfectly proper English silence as they waited for Nature to expend herself.

61

The dog snuffled the air with a nose which was too short, while it swept the pavement with a tail which was too long — betraying the unintended union of a pekinese and something able to clear a garden wall — and looked solemnly at the rain falling in liquid rivets. Staring out, its reflective boot-button eyes expressed the only sensible sentiment:

'*Summer!*'

Chapter Eight

Afternoons

Probably it was his earlier dealings with Æneas which brought Michael to renewed thoughts of Wilfrid, whose *fidus Achates* he had always been. Or perhaps the brackish, musty smell of summer rain stirred a connection somewhere in his mind. Wilfrid who had loved and not been loved by Fleur those years ago. Wilfrid who some years later loved and *had* been loved by young Dinny, though sadly to his no greater contentment. Wilfrid Desert, the restless, questing poet who eventually found everlasting peace in the murky embrace of a river in the Far East. Michael only then realised they were standing opposite Wilfrid's old rooms off Cork Street, in the same spot where he had once before taken such scratch shelter, haunted by ungallant suspicions of his wife and best friend. Who had them now? he wondered as the rain fell, that little set of rooms where the future of their three lives had been played out like a thin drama in as many acts. Act One: Boy meets Girl (Girl is already Married). Act Two: Boy meets Girl again (Girl considers leaving Husband). Act Three: the First Kiss (followed shortly by the Final Embrace), Girl stays West, Boy goes East. Curtain.

Whoever the present tenant was Michael wished him an uneventful lease.

The awning above them creaked under the onslaught of a fresh cloudburst. A summer rainstorm, the surest way to be soaked to the skin – no break in the cloud, no chance to make a dash for it without a ducking. Kit was peering out at the street, his face screwed uncharitably against the weather as though it had consciously defied him. Reluctantly Michael nudged his arm, and indicated the door behind them.

63

"Looks like we're down for some culture, after all. Bad luck!"

Inside the gallery, which Michael did not then recognise, the comfort of being out of the rain was smaller than he might have expected for the six shillings their rescue cost. He consulted his catalogue with failing cheer.

"'This gallery is proud to present major works by the Russian artist-in-exile Vladymy Suslov, whose radical approach to line and structure, banned in his native Leningrad, places him in the van-guard of Neo-Formalism . . .' – oh! dear me. What price Art, eh? Come on, let's get our six bob's worth. Consider it an exercise in character-building!"

Following the majority of other visitors – some twelve in all – they began their circuit from the left and progressed clockwise.

Michael had been to a thousand such exhibitions in his time – and had paid lip-service to all the contemporary theories. The prevailing tone of satire in the post-war years, the dissonance of the machine age, the madness of art reflecting the greater insanity of our times, the liberation of thought from form, and so it went on. But something in him, in his nineteenth century roots perhaps, had never quite 'bought the line' that all art was just sentimental-ism until abstraction, until the Great Escape from Form. When the fashionable gallery talk was of tension, contrast, counterpoint and all the other disembodied notions which were tossed about like so many shuttlecocks, he had always wanted to voice the one unutter-able heresy – what about Beauty? Looking at Suslov's pieces, and not without a certain appreciation of what they offered, Michael knew this remained a good question. Beauty – where *was* she these days, the poor girl? Lurking nervously behind the gathered skirts of Hope and Faith, as far as he could see. At this, Michael laughed at himself. Was he such a 'grundy' at heart? But surely, he thought, surely it all had to come to this, hadn't it? We've lived in fractured, fragmented times for so long, appeased our baser selves piecemeal for twenty years. Faith has been replaced by analysis, Hope supplanted by living for the day, the moment. We've lived this way so long there's almost nothing of substance left; we've atomised ourselves bally near to extinction. Modernity is on the brink. So — nothing for it but to re-group. The backlash against *laisser-aller* was inevitable, so why shouldn't it start now? White *versus* black once more, the forces

64

of light *versus* the power of darkness. Truth and Beauty (there she was!) *versus* the unimaginable alternative. Get back to the *substance* of things! Begin the Great Return to Form!

In the absence of a revelatory fanfare Michael pursued the circuit, Kit bringing up the rear.

As they took in each canvas, Kit maintained a glassy silence which, in a contemporary, his father would have found disconcerting. But the young chap didn't seem sulky about it – rather he had the air of one in whom a fresh capacity was beginning to unfold. At the back of the gallery they reached the centre-piece of the exhibition, a canvas quite two-thirds larger than the next largest there. Michael watched his son as he stood before the picture. Kit narrowed his eyes as he gave it a hard, measured look, and drew in a narrow breath, in all like someone trying to pin down an evasive smell.

Kit said at last: "It looks like a diagram of an atom."

Michael looked again at the canvas. So it did, in a sort of way. And indeed – now he noticed the title, *The Final Analysis* – that was one way of approaching an interpretation of the work. Yes – maybe this Suslov saw it too – the imminent and necessary end of the present way. Hm—! Did the boy have an eye? It was said ability often jumped a generation: Old Forsyte's eye for a picture knew no parallel.

"I think you should buy it, Dad."

Michael cocked his head in surprise.

"Do you! Why?"

Kit gave his father a look he usually reserved for his maths master, the Venerable Smudger, who always made him explain the workings of self-evident answers.

"Buy it now, keep it in the attic for twenty years, then bring it out again as a lost masterpiece. They'd be bound to go for it – the saps."

They covered the rest of the exhibition in the same silence as before, except that Michael had the sense of having been poked rudely in the stomach by something. Perhaps it was not only talent which jumped the generations? Well — time would tell!

At the last offering, an adventurous triptych which required the observer to walk around it for maximum æsthetic benefit, Kit caught sight of an oddly familiar figure, one which he recognised immediately yet did not know. It took him a few seconds to realise that the little figure flitting between the paintings at the far end of the gallery was the batty-looking old girl from the park – whom he had taken for the grandmother of that young girl and her brother. Yes, it was her, he was sure. Kit looked around to see if the granddaughter was there too. He couldn't see her, and when he looked back the old lady herself had disappeared. What a rotten throw to have a relation like that! Completing his turn around the triptych, Kit found he had lost his own relation for the moment. Where had the Guv'nor got to? Ah! — he was standing by the door, beckoning. Good show – he'd had enough!

On their way out Kit stopped by the door, not because he had room for one more *oeuvre*, but because another unexpected thing caught the corner of his eye. In a side window was a little picture, a small pastel framed in silver, resting on a plain wooden bracket.

"I say – is this a relation of mother's?"

Unsuspecting, Michael stooped for a closer look.

The pastel was of a boy aged about eight or so, with shining eyes and hair, standing by the banister at the top of a stairway. He wore a linen sailor-suit and a frown, the latter suggesting indecision about his mode of descent and hinting that the banister might win the day. Michael thought it a pretty piece and its title, *Awakening*, very apt. Then his eye lit on the artist's signature: *Jolyon Forsyte, RA*. It was dated 1909.

"I didn't know there were any artists in the family," said Kit flatly, as if people had been keeping things from him.

"Neither did I," Michael confessed. Hadn't there been a Jolyon among the old Forsytes? But he had been in tea. Good Heavens! – a sideways thought accosted him on his blind-side. This was June Forsyte's gallery – of course it was! The very place he had first seen Fleur, first met his future father-in-law and first encountered, as it were, the rest of his life. And he just now had calmly walked around when at any time its proprietress might have tapped him on the shoulder . . . a quick shiver travelled the length of Michael's spine. He had never experienced anything but discomfort in the company of that little aged cousin of Fleur's, and had no desire to renew their

66

long-lapsed acquaintance. Involuntarily he cast a glance back into the gallery, steeling his expression. Was she there? Should he even know her again after so long?

Kit was asking about the pastelist:

"Did Grandfather collect him?"

"I don't recall that he did, no."

"Then I expect he wasn't any good."

They stepped from under the awning on to the freshly-dried pavement. Michael decided a sharp change of direction was indicated: there would be other occasions when his mother could cross her grandson's palm with silver. *What price Art?* was a question he wouldn't ask in jest again. They returned to Piccadilly and spent an additional penny on an evening paper, with a view to finding a 'double bill' to round off the day.

June Forsyte was there, it so happened, but Michael's nerves were redundant, for even had she seen him it was unlikely she would have recognised his features since her eyesight over any distance was getting bad. Out of vanity, which in June's case was only her adamant self-sufficiency, she rejected the idea of wearing spectacles. Imagine all that fuss of going to a doctor and then to an optometrist and what-have-you, when there was so much work to be done! Implicitly agreeing with the philosophy that there is no fate insurmountable by scorn, June had learned to screw her face up into a particular type of squint which seemed to accommodate the problem of focal length reasonably well. It was not a very difficult change to make in features historically given to impatience.

In any case, she had for most of the day been walled into a cramped back room where every Friday afternoon she irritably re-worked the perfectly competent arithmetic of her part-time accounts clerk. That this was Saturday put her in no better temper. It was very nice to see the children yesterday – she had enjoyed her walk in the park with her niece and nephew tremendously – but that sort of thing put one behind so! And Suslov wasn't doing at all well. June thought the gallery-going public simply hopeless: why couldn't they recognise his talent and snap it up while they were able! In twenty years they would wish they had! No doubt they would prefer that hateful Socialist Realism whose state-enforced strictures her Russian had been obliged to flee in order to preserve his singular genius for the benefit of mankind.

As the rain began again to drum its tattoo on the tar roof over this rear extension that was her office, June tilted her decided chin upwards. Her orangey-white hair wobbled and a satisfied smile suddenly linked all the countless tiny lines on her face. That was good – nothing was like a brisk shower for turning Philistines into Art-Lovers!

Young Catherine Mont – Kat for short – was, though she hadn't yet the expression of it, caught in the horns of a dilemma. Always a child who seemed content with her own company, she had been left alone perhaps more than was advisable for the proper bending of a young mind to conventional patterns of thought. Though she had been passably fond of one or two dolls, and loved her old bear, she received most toys with veiled and silent disappointment that they were not books. The disappointment was contagious – givers could see that their gifts, often brought back from foreign travels or obtained at great cost, were received politely but without that ingredient which enabled the giving to be its own reward. In this and other small ways over the years of her short life, the child who never troubled anyone came to be thought of as 'rather difficult'. The more she took to reading the more she was left to it, and consequently it had become the greater part of her world. It was in this world of escape, of loves and deaths and dramas, that her dilemma dwelt.

Because Finty did not allow reading at the table, she had mooned her way through lunch that day not knowing whether she ate cabbage or spinach, or both, and after being excused got down from the table and raced back to the source of her quandary, which lay open on the window-seat in her room. There she sat now, easily an hour and a half later, cross-legged like a Turk, ensconced with the book, and was still without a solution to her difficulty. What troubled her was this. She had completed *Pride and Prejudice* last week-end, and had followed it with *Jane Eyre*, which she finished only this morning, while waiting to be taken out to the book-shop. She would have finished it yesterday, but her secret vigil on the stairwell, to see the last of her mother's powdery, glittery, bright-voiced guests leave the party, left her too tired for reading by her little torch. They were

68

only her own relations, she knew, except for the tall dark man; but with the exercise of a little imagination – and she had so much – they were easily transformed into foreign princes and undiscovered gypsy kings. Her first misgivings came to her that morning. Now she was quite far into *Wuthering Heights* and only just beginning to perceive the enormity of the problem. How, just *how* could she possibly give herself up to its hero – a process she found absolutely necessary with every book she consumed – without breaking faith with either of his two predecessors? How commit to the dark and brooding Heathcliff and not lose Mr D'Arcy or Mr Rochester? And *worse still*, if that were possible, how could she ever match herself to Elizabeth, *and* to Jane, *and* to her own namesake, Catherine? Why couldn't someone tell her? Why wasn't there a set of instructions at the front of the book? – or a work of reference on the subject? It was all *very* difficult. And worrying as only she at the burdensome age of ten was able, young Catherine Mont – while the heavy summer rain wept against her window – continued with her reading, perplexed, absorbed, engrossed.

When Fleur left her cousin and mother-in-law, she intended to strike off down South Audley Street and walk home across Green Park. Goode's window might be worth a look too, as it was on her way; South Square was in sore need of a new breakfast service. She turned at the corner and quickly became aware of the appeal of a slim, dark figure on the opposite pavement, walking unhurriedly in her own direction, the ferrule of his closely furled umbrella tapping a light accompaniment to an elegant step. Her senses registered pleasure at the line and grace of the figure before her brain could over-ride the connection . . . It was Barrantes, of course. He smiled when he saw her, and transferring his umbrella to his left side raised his right hand deferentially, asking, as it were, for permission to interrupt her plans. The man was persistent as a shadow! Yes, that was it – he was like a tall evening shadow, or a finely cut silhouette; sleek, elaborate and yet secretive, revealing nothing of inner detail. Fleur watched as he crossed the road to her. She suspected him, on slight evidence backed by unfailing instinct, of being one of those people who had a capacity for turning up – never inappropriately, never where there was no welcome and never outstaying the one he found. But – he *would* turn up. She would have to look out for him in future!

"Lady Mont." With what Fleur already thought of as his customary slight bow he took her gloved hand – how careful he was to return only the light pressure she gave his! "This gives me an unexpected chance to repeat my thanks." Even his *bel canto* voice had a lyrical appeal.

"You have no need, Señor Barrantes—" Fleur replied, rather more abruptly than she had intended.

"Ah, my flowers were delivered?"

Indeed – they would shortly run out of vases at South Square!

"Yes. They were charming."

"As was the evening."

Fleur wanted only to continue on her way, but her way was also his and so they fell in step and walked abreast on blanched paving stones now just marginally less dusty than before the rain. He seemed content with their silence, their two matched footfalls and the light tip-tip of his umbrella in between. Fleur did not share his easy contentment, and soon his unfaltering composure began to rankle. She endured the implied intimacy of this situation for a few more paces before saying:

"Tell me—" at precisely the moment her fortuitous companion said:

"I wonder—" at which point they both stopped walking. He dipped his head again; nothing rippled the clear surface of his composure. "I am sorry. Please—"

Fleur was not at all certain what she had meant to say next, her first purpose having been simply to break the silence, so she said:

"No, really. What was it you were wondering?"

"It will seem presumptuous on my part."

"Let me be the judge of that." Fleur instantly knew she would regret this phrase, which she had meant only as a check. Whatever he said now, she was bound to accede to it.

"I was wondering if I might ask your opinion of something I saw this morning. It would take you only a little out of your way — but I forget myself." By the rigour of his sudden frown it could have been true. "You will have another appointment."

70

"No," Fleur replied, far too quickly to allow for good judgement, but desiring to contradict straightaway any notion he might have of her. "Not immediately."

"Excellent!" he exclaimed, and brought the tip of his umbrella to the pavement with a swift click. At this, Fleur understood that she had played her hand about as badly as it was possible to. The sensation was a new one to her.

Barrantes touched her elbow lightly and guided her across the road, where they took Hill Street and headed eastward. After Hill Street, they crossed Berkeley Square, let Bruton Street lead them into New Bond Street, and Clifford Street into Cork Street. All the while neither uttered a word to break what other pedestrians must have taken without a second glance for the silent concord of long-standing acquaintance. Their four heels and the tip-tip of his umbrella executed a rhythm between them, to which accompaniment Fleur walked in a kind of conscious trance. She had never, before him, met anyone who so matched her in social dexterity. His poise, grace and manners, his charm and – above all, she was sure – the agility of his wits were all so very much the equal of her own that she found herself effectively neutralised. She recognised in him an opponent, but also a creature of oddly kindred mettle. At the extreme edge of her consciousness she began to see something forming, just as the dark silent rain clouds had crept over the horizon earlier to pose their stealthy threat to the day. She had had the inkling of it the evening before and was now sure that he was implicitly aware of their perfect likeness in this regard and, what was more, that he was actually offering her a master-class of some strange sort. The idea was fanciful! But there it was, she could feel it: his unimpeachable discretion towards her was her greatest proof! And a fatalism which at any other time Fleur would have considered a dangerous indulgence came to her as an encouraging second for a fight. Would she take him on? In a world of lost possibilities, was there another way for her energies to be engaged? 'Mother knows best!' *En avant!*

In this spirit Fleur discovered she was safely able to register almost no surprise when she recognised the place to which the Argentinian led her. Like a patient recovering from anæsthesia, she knew she was cut but felt no pain at the realisation that they were

71

standing in front of June Forsyte's gallery, the place where she had first met Jon.

Barrantes approached the smaller of the gallery's two windows, whose side panels formed an abrupt funnel into the doorway; with an open palm he beckoned her to join him there. Standing of necessity close to the Argentine's side, since the funnel was not spacious even at its widest point, Fleur looked at the small pastel on its rest in the window.

"I imagine this must be a relation of yours, Lady Mont," he said. "Jolyon Forsyte."

She saw the artist's signature, that surname which was formerly her own, and the date. And she heard the echo of a young man's voice in her head, speaking words she knew by heart, for that was where they were long since written.

'Forsyte? Why – that's my name too. Perhaps we're cousins.' It was the first thing Jon had ever said to her.

"Yes," Fleur heard her own voice answer distantly, though it seemed she spoke without meaning to. "A cousin of my father's."

And then a second interpretation of the Argentinian's words came to her in a sharp ricochet off the glass barrier between herself and the picture in its silver frame. 1909. The little boy in his sailor-suit looked about seven or eight, just her own age then. She stared at the young face under its mop of sunny hair. There was surely no room for doubt – and in that narrow entrance where she stood with a tremble beginning in her knees none for pity either. Involuntarily, Fleur pressed her fingers to the pane. She wanted so dearly to reach through and touch his hair, smooth his frown, that early showing of his lion-cub look – for the boy could only be Jon!

"It is an enchanting piece, I think," Barrantes said. "The artist shows a devoted eye – a rare quality. The little fellow is so intent!"

Yes — *so he ever was.* How this foreigner knew what to say!

As her own devoted eye nearly betrayed her, Fleur leaned towards the pastel until her forehead just met the window. The cold contact snapped her back to her former watchfulness and instantly she straightened her spine. She saw Barrantes' image in the glass watching her, waiting motionlessly, silent as a cat. She turned to him and smiled efficiently, her voice as clear and her eyes as cool and unyielding as the window-pane.

"Isn't he just! I believe he must be my second cousin, Jon Forsyte, though I did think his father was only known for water-colours."

"There! I was certain that you would know its history—"

Breaking off suddenly, he urgently thrust the gallery door inward upon its hinges with his umbrella, and held himself against the opposite window, back to the glass, as a large woman bearing a small snub-nosed dog on her arm passed between them through the tight doorway. Once out and under the awning, heedless of anything but the sky to which she presented an untrusting face, the woman turned with audible dissatisfaction towards Piccadilly. Barrantes disengaged his back but maintained his grip on the door.

"Now I am decided," he said.

"Upon what?"

"Upon purchase!" and repeating his beckoning gesture with his free hand he remained with remarkable elegance in this extended position, until Fleur had no choice save a quick lie if she was not to enter into that place where the tenderest scenes from her past were framed and hung. So easily could she lose any of her court cards to the lowliest of his trumps!

"I can't—"

"It will take only moments."

"I need this confectioner's—"

"Then I shall see you there!"

He took a step to the door, moved his free hand to an area of his waistcoat which might have covered his heart, and with the slightest dip of his forehead towards Fleur slid without another word into June Forsyte's gallery.

Chapter Nine

And an Evening

It was in this way that Fleur returned to South Square in the late afternoon bearing an armful of devotion wrapped in tissue and brown paper, and a head full of new discontentment parcelled up with old thoughts freshly disturbed. Going into the confectioner's she had hoped to dodge the Argentinian before he could reclaim her company. But, true to his word, his transaction in June's gallery took him only minutes, and as Fleur paid for two separate half-pound bags of caramels – one for Kit to take back to school as tuck and one for him to share with his sister – she did not need to turn her head to know that Barrantes was waiting for her again, outside this second doorway. If she could only label him fulsome! Had he been *de trop*, she could dismiss him with a word or even with a look. But he was neither of those things nor anything like. He had taken her no more out of her way than he said he would; his behaviour toward her had been impeccable throughout; his approach deft and well-considered. And yet – or, perhaps *so* – she was beginning to find his attentions maddening!

Outside the confectioner's they once more fell into step, continuing down Cork Street in the now high sunshine. She must lose him soon! He carried a wrapped rectangle under his arm, from the neat crook of which his umbrella now depended.

"So you bought my cousin's picture?"

"I did. And I am told I have a bargain – it appears that your relation is a rising commodity."

"Really?"

"Indeed. The proprietress of the gallery told me so herself. She is even planning a retrospective of the artist later this year."

Hnh! June. Not seen since her last break with Jon, and not by any estimate missed in the interval. Fleur was sourly proud of instincts which had stopped her going in.

"So I am now in possession of an original 'Jolyon Forsyte'," Barrantes said.

Each time he spoke that name, Fleur felt her nerves stretch a little tighter.

"Though, of course," he continued, his smile becoming an odd little frown, "I could never consider myself its rightful owner."

They were approaching the next corner. This must be where she secured her leave. Fleur so focussed on this objective, that when a figure coming out of the back gate of Albany tipped his hat to her and seemed about to speak she quite unwittingly cut him cold.

The figure walked away but only so far, before he stopped under cover of an awning and watched as the woman, whom he knew, spoke to a man, whom he did not.

"I hope this indulgence of me will not have made you late for your next appointment."

"Don't consider it; but I'll take a taxi from here, I think."

She would be away in seconds. Barrantes had already raised his free arm. A cab, just turned out of Savile Row, was drawing towards them, all its windows down in a vain attempt at convection. The Argentine opened the door, held it, and shut it carefully behind her as she sat down; the black leather of the seat was hot through her dress. Fleur leaned forward to instruct the driver and found her face close to the Argentinian's as he stooped next to the open window.

"Thank you for your time, and for your help," said his lips six inches from her own. While he spoke it seemed that a transparent hood, as that sometimes seen in reposing birds of prey, lifted from his eyes. With a quiet urgency he added, "Please, you must let me—" and through the window he passed the rectangular package.

Before Fleur could voice her objection to his gift she reached out to it so that it should not fall and, as soon as she did, felt its weight transferred to her own hand. The next instant Barrantes had signalled to the cabbie. As she was driven off into the line of traffic – Jon's picture lying in her lap – she saw the Argentinian present her a final solemn bow.

That last knowing image of Barrantes held stubbornly to the

75

outskirts of her thoughts as Fleur prepared to dress for dinner with the Messengers – Vivian and his young second wife Nona, whom they were meeting at *Monseigneur's*. But the pastel – in its new place at the front of a Pembroke table of her grandmother Emily's, which already held a dozen or so other family likenesses – was her only clear point of focus. With her back to her dressing-table she sat and stared at it, legs entwined, arms wrapped about herself, with an absorption not less than that of a Hindu priest for his mandala. She held a brush in her hand but had yet to put it to her hair. Not until she heard Michael's footsteps coming down from the top floor did she apply the first brush stroke: by the time he had paused in his dressing-room and passed through into the bedroom, it might have been her only occupation.

"All quiet on the Western Front!" Michael exclaimed. "Nothing better than a pound of finest caramels for sealing the mouths of babes and their brothers – and Finty's disapproval improves their flavour no end."

"Kit knows he's to keep one bag for school."

"'Too late!' cried the watch."

"You indulge him, Michael."

"Do I? Perhaps. No more than he indulges me, I think. Ho—! I know this young fellow—!"

Michael stepped directly over to the pastel and Fleur caught her breath, so audibly to her own ears that she feigned a knot in her hair. It was impossible! How could Michael know?

"We saw it in the gallery today," he continued cheerily. "What a coincidence you should buy it."

"— Yes." It seemed the simplest answer – but when was Michael there? Stupid question: clearly, before she and the Argentine. "I passed by after leaving Em's," she said. A lie nearest the truth was always the easiest to commit, and stay committed to.

"We played you Box-and-Cox in that case—" Michael picked up the pastel, heavier than he expected in its silver frame. "Kit and I stopped in there on our way up to see her. The choice was between two varieties of immersion, Modern Art or the rain. On the whole, I reckon our son and heir would have preferred a good ducking."

Now he saw the piece again, Michael realised it really was quite fine, full of light and expression and with a certain – what was it? – a devotional quality, maybe?

"Hmm. Jolyon Forsyte – there's a name to conjure with!"

Fleur continued with her hair brush.

"Wasn't he one of the 'Old Forsytes'?"

Even after nineteen years of the closest association with its intricacies, Michael had still to be taken through a fully comprehensive course in Forsyte family history, an omission which any soul less generous than his might have taken for deliberate adumbration.

"No," Fleur replied evenly. "The next generation, my father's and Winifred's."

"Still around?"

"He died some years ago – I believe."

"Kit spotted the name; he was asking if his grandfather collected the artist. Do you think he has an eye?"

For her own besetting reasons Fleur thought the piece perfect, exalted, and continuing to misconstrue her husband's words answered with convincing dispassion.

"Oh, the little boy is done sweetly enough – wouldn't you say? Look at that frown."

She had done not much else since she unwrapped it.

"Yes, he's caught the Age of Reason all right! I meant Kit, actually. He came out with some things at the gallery; made me wonder whether he might go in for collecting."

"Well, perhaps he'll take after my father – who knows?"

This had rather been Michael's conclusion.

Knowing full well she was larding her deceit Fleur added: "He looks like Kit used to, don't you think, in his sailor-suit? That's why I noticed it."

Except that, like his son, the boy in the silver frame was fair of hair and eye, Michael was not struck by any particular resemblance, no more than that seen between distant cousins, but he was ready to accommodate the distortion of a mother's partial eye.

"Now who indulges?" he said, kissing her forehead.

He replaced the pastel carefully among the other varying resemblances on the table and Fleur, in another existence, might have wept for the innocence of his heart. How her hair shone!

77

Turning back towards the dressing-room, Michael shuffled off his jacket and examined the cloth; the light worsted was not noticeably distressed by its sprinkling of rain. Then he used a mild oath with great vehemence as a sealed and stamped envelope fell to the carpet from an inner pocket. His letter to the newspaper – all day he had meant to post it and instead had brought it home again. What a duffer he was getting! Then, as he picked up the envelope, a compensating idea occurred to him. There was a simple way to make quick amends.

"I might go and take a squint at old Lewis, you know," he said to Fleur, and he sat down on the corner of the bed to think it out. "I could pay him a call at the Mission."

"What for?" Fleur asked, and heard the harshness of her words. Why did Michael's concern for people, for things, for life, always provoke her to such cynicism? She covered it quickly:

"I mean, what more can you do for him?"

Michael shrugged his shoulders. "Show I care. Buy him a meal. Put a fiver in his back pocket. It's not much, but damn it, one can't just stand by."

"No. You couldn't. You have a capacity for commitment – for devotion. It's one I've never developed, it seems."

"Oh, Fleur, that's a nonsense."

"Funny; Em used that expression today—"

By his stricken face Michael looked ready to run his own mother out of town for the very suggestion.

"— Oh, not about me. She's keen to billet evacuees at Lippinghall but it's not a reception area for them. Did you know? She says it's a nonsense and wants to take ten."

"Wouldn't she! And half of Bethnal Green too, if she were allowed!"

"But *that's* devotion, you see. Wanting to do things for people when you don't have to. I don't, do I?"

"At the risk of sounding stuck in the family groove," Michael responded sweetly, "I repeat, *nonsense*." She wasn't serious, was she? If so, this was a worrying sign, and but one of several he had noticed lately. He watched her move listlessly to the window and kneel on the striped satin cushion of the chaise beneath it. The streetlamps just starting up in the square cast a sallow light over her expression, and showed her eyes strangely blank. By heaven, she was serious! Certainly he must be slipping in his avowed task of keeping her buoyed.

"You won't see it, will you, Michael?"

"What?" He came and sat by her and took her hand. "That you're strong and vital, and bright as a diamond—"

Fleur snatched her hand away: "And as hard?"

"Dear girl, now *you* don't see." He dared not reply to her tone; he must give jollity another try. "What about your charities?"

Fleur lowered her lids and raised her eyebrows, a little facial shrug revealing her French heritage, which seemed to say: 'One does what is expected of one.'

Michael moved to where he supposed was surer ground.

"And what about that young man—" he indicated the pastel with a nod of his head and consequently missed her wince, "the eleventh baronet? – and his sister? You're devoted to them – I see it daily."

"But they're part of me, Michael. All I've ever been is devoted to myself. I suppose I'm too much of a Forsyte to be any other way."

Michael took quick stock of the debate and the direction towards which it was heading. Well, was there any gainsaying her? Had she ever shown him any of this disputed commodity? Hand on heart, he was unable to say that she had. But that had not been 'the deal', as the American cousins would say. From first sight of her – in that same little gallery off Cork Street – he had been desperate, half-crazed to make Fleur his own. In the end he had only made her his wife. *That* had been the deal. Fleur evidently saw the path ahead, too, for suddenly and impatiently she drew the curtains together. Behind them Big Ben began to pound out the early, unfashionable hour for dining.

Chapter closed – for the moment.

"Dinny sends her love – she's quite blooming, of course."

The blank look in her eyes was gone – but for how long, Michael wondered?

"It's the Condaford air," he replied. "The Cherrells should start bottling it – it'd make a handy second string for Eustace if the voting public were ever to come to its senses and chuck him out."

Jollity, jollity! But at least she was smiling now.

79

Chapter Ten

Winifred Visits the Past

On the morning of the following day, at the hour agreed between them in a quiet moment at Fleur's memorable supper party, Mrs Winifred Dartie and Sir Michael Mont were to be found sitting in the back of the former's motor car, a fashionable landaulette kept closed despite the good weather, as it swept majestically toward that least likely of Forsyte destinations, a North London suburb. Given the choice Winifred would not have made this particular journey on a Sunday, but it was Michael's best time for it, and this was the delivery of his favour to her.

"I do hope this isn't a great bore for you, Michael."

"Not at all."

"You understand why I couldn't ask anyone else – Val or Imogen, or Fleur – I didn't want the fuss. They'd be bound to think I had a reason."

"Quite." Michael noticed the corner of Winifred's eye and realised his monosyllables were not pressing his sincerity upon her. "Honestly. It'll be an education for me, Aunt Winifred, I assure you."

"Oh, it will certainly be that. After all, it's where they all are—"

Winifred recalled with a little private start that this was not at all true, 'they' being the 'Old Forsytes', that astonishingly tenacious generation prior to her own. She knew very well that of those ten brothers and sisters, only eight now remained together, albeit in perpetuity, in the suburb to which she and Michael were currently being so smoothly conveyed. 'Old' Jolyon, the eldest male, and Susan, the youngest female, had chosen to take their eternal rest elsewhere. Susan, the widow of Hayman, a man of Woking, had inexplicably chosen cremation and the dispersal of her ashes outside that town, at *'that last great station on the railroad of life'*. As for Uncle Jolyon's final lodging, in the churchyard at Robin Hill, by that house . . . Winifred brought herself out of her reflections with a slow shake of her head.

"— and where I shall be soon, I dare say," she concluded.

"Aunt—!"

"It's very sweet of you, Michael, but it's only the truth. I'm nearly eighty-one, you know, and getting to be a very old woman indeed. Of course, that isn't really so old for a Forsyte – my father lived to be ninety, and so might Soames have but for that ghastly fire. I might get there myself, but if I don't—" Winifred made no attempt to finish her construction, but stared out with renewed disapproval at the passing local architecture.

"I understand," Michael said. "A sort of insurance against the worst coming to it."

"Exactly. And if we have this war – we *are* going to have it, I suppose?" She saw her nephew shrug his shoulders diplomatically. "No, you're right, don't tell me. Well, whatever happens, I'd rather be safe."

"I remember Fleur's father once telling me it was his experience that the contingencies *not* provided for were those which happened."

Winifred huffed in agreement. "I can't see that he was wrong, though I imagine he didn't mean to be quite so right with regard to his own last circumstances."

The final mile or so they travelled in silence, their minds no doubt turned both to the same subject. To Michael, who was natively possessed of an ironic eye, it had always seemed the supreme irony that one so careful in every way as his late father-in-law should have died in such a freak tilt of fate.

In the fire that started mysteriously in the picture gallery of his house at Mapledurham, Soames Forsyte had saved his daughter's life – and sacrificed his own – by pushing her out of the path of a falling painting, sustaining the worst of its impact upon himself. By this single act, Soames had rallied reserves of strength, courage and personal disregard such as he had never known himself to possess, save perhaps once before. That he who had been first the slave of Beauty and then her cruel master should ultimately be vanquished by

81

Art, her eternal lover, was the larger ironic structure which Michael, for want of a complete schooling in Forsyte annals, was unable to perceive. He knew this much, however: that the painting which struck the mortal blow was a Goya copy Soames had commissioned because of its likeness to Fleur. To die by a copy to save the original! That was insurance for you – but what a premium!

The driver was slowing. He pulled to a stop and dutifully opened the rear door. Michael helped Winifred out.

"Well. Here we are," she said as she straightened up, the effort awakening a twitch of lumbago in her lower spine.

They had arrived at Highgate Cemetery, where Victorianism and its staunchest proponents, the Forsytes, lay buried.

"'There sat the Shadow fear'd of man; Who broke our fair companionship—'" Michael quoted. "Cheery soul, old Alfred."

"Wasn't he?" Winifred agreed dourly. "And to think Victoria never realised he was writing about another *man*."

With a smile at his aunt's surprising worldliness, Michael offered his arm and together they stepped through the yawning gates.

When the London Cemetery Company was founded towards the middle of the last century it had been at the very cutting edge of Victorian entrepreneurialism. To deduce from basic evidence of the growing secularism of the age that for upwards of two hundred guineas one's fellow citizens would prefer to savour their immortality *during* their lifetimes was a stroke of business genius which fully deserved the fortune it brought in tow. Thus had Highgate Cemetery become the final bastion of upper-middle-class values. Surely, the carved granite vaults proclaimed, the over-fed marble cherubim trumpeted, the sad stone angels prayed, surely those so well presented here in death must be guaranteed the best of anything still to come?

Insurance again! and Michael considered whether the god Mammon might not have begun life as an actuary.

There was an oppressive dankness to the place which the mid-morning sun seemed unable to shift, though it played brightly on the columns and statuary and relief. Michael could feel the chill of the earth penetrating his shoe-leather – was it truly the coldness of death in the soil? Ah! — just the bre‸e up there on the hill, too exposed to hold the warmth of the day to itself. He flexed a shoulder-blade, the one away from Winifred, to dismiss a shiver.

In the Circle of Lebanon they came to the Forsyte vault. A lone cedar braced against the wind stood sentry nearby; sparse clouds like hares' tails scutted in the fast sky overhead. The construction owned a solidity which seemed drawn from the very essence of those whose name it bore. It looked to Michael like nothing so much as a ready-made annexe awaiting installation to a gentlemen's club. So it was, in a way. A club which required of its members only two things – permanent election and an unredeemable joining-fee. Tall, ugly, individual and massive, with fewer scrolls and folderols than many, it bore on its face a single central wreath in stone above the stark words: '*The family vault of Jolyon Forsyte: 1850.*' Seeing it, Michael was possessed by the notion that he had never paid this family the admiration which was its proper due. He saw now that the regard in which he had held his father-in-law should be accorded to them all and to all their forbears. To make a family something from nothing – no royal patronage and the gift of lands to lean on like his own lot! – nothing but hard work and application. Fleur had told him once that the earliest Forsytes were yeoman farmers. No wonder they were strong and tenacious, grown from the land. Yeomen to gentlemen within two generations – some harvest that!

Michael felt a small movement at his side; it was Winifred taking her hand from under his arm. He understood the gesture and hung back as she completed the last few steps alone.

Because she was born into a time and class which kept women at home while the men buried their dead, this was Winifred's first sight of her family's vault. She was at once surprised and impressed by its massive plainness. So – this was where the Old Forsytes, as they had even in their own lifetimes been known, were laid to rest. Ann, James, Swithin, Roger, Julia, Hester, Nicholas, and the 'baby', Timothy, were all entombed within. Of the next generation, her own, Winifred had already lived through the funerals of too many – her cousins George and Francie, Young Roger, Young Nicholas and Euphemia, and her sisters Rachel and Cecily. And of course, her dear brother, not lying there but at his own choice beneath an old crab-apple in the churchyard at Mapledurham. Soames! He had once seemed the most invincible Forsyte of them all.

Winifred stood quite still as the minutes passed, feeling far more alone than at any time in her life. They really were all gone, all those characters who had made up so much the greater part of her life; and the Age – her Age, of gowns and carriages, feathers and lace, of dances and gaiety and youth – it was gone with them. She tried to think of the last occasion when all these names had been assembled alive. Could it be as long ago as her own wedding? No, surely not? It must have been— And then she remembered. It was Uncle Jolyon's 'at home' for his granddaughter June, to announce her engagement to the young architect Philip Bosinney. What a coil had proceeded from that fatal event! It had been the very beginning of it all.

Winifred had seen enough. Though she would endure much before admitting the fact, her strength was not now what it used to be – and suddenly she felt it sapped to the quick. She returned to Michael and for a while they walked the grassy paths without speaking, her hand again within her nephew's arm, leaning now perhaps a little more heavily than before.

"I wonder—" she said at last, and they walked a few yards further before she continued. "I wonder how it all might have been if Soames hadn't made that first marriage."

By some stray prescience, Michael had guessed that he might be making a voyage of discovery in accompanying Winifred into her family past, but even on such sacred ground he had not expected a revelation. Since the day in that little gallery when he had first encountered this happy breed, Michael had felt like a blind beggar in the halls of Forsyte history, forever obliged by his handicap to keep to the walls, skirting the occasional great piece of furniture, knowing he could be tripped at any minute and having always to guess at the unseen centre from the lie of the perimeter. Now it seemed his sight might be partially restored by this most chance of digressions.

Michael had only once before heard mention of 'that first marriage'. When Fleur had re-encountered her great love (he never thought of the cousin as her first love, since he knew her never to have had a second) he had sought the truth of the situation from the one truly open-hearted Forsyte he knew. But June – the Forsyte whom he had thought that description fitted – had given him only the bones in the cupboard. Her open heart had not extended to relaying her own details, and without them the story was incomplete, unfleshed.

She had told him how Fleur's father had once been married to the cousin's mother, and that the marriage was not a success.

With her customary briskness, June had added:

'— *Imagine forcing yourself on a woman who didn't want you.*'

Because June's character was so habitually abrasive, and because his own was not, Michael had failed to appreciate her full meaning. She was always caustic in her opinion of people she didn't like, and so he had supposed from what she said that the position of his father-in-law, *vis-à-vis* his first wife, was only something like his own with Fleur; that is, not always a union of mutual and equal desire.

So Michael knew of the skeleton in the Forsyte cupboard, and of its bones he had a fair idea; but of its flesh, and of the passions which had once overmastered it, he was innocent as the day. Perhaps Winifred could offer a more generous outline?

Phrasing his question as if there was little of interest left for him to learn – a knack he had acquired in Parliament – Michael asked:

"Was that very long before he married Fleur's mother?"

As her nephew had intended, Winifred accepted the question at its face value, and replied as if he had somewhere skipped a chapter.

"Oh, my heavens, yes! They were married for seventeen years."

Here Michael felt the first small prickle of sickly anticipation at the back of his neck. He knew he was heading at last towards some patch of enlightenment, but was suddenly fearful to lose the familiar darkness of his long-kept ignorance. Seventeen years! No wonder it had gone so deep! He and Fleur had been married only two years longer. But the comparison was inept – they were content. That is, he was – but she—?

"Not that they were together for more than the first three—" Winifred went on, "or was it four? Irene left him, you see. But Soames wouldn't accept it. For a long while he believed he might get her back."

Like father, like daughter, was Michael's only thought. Anxious of his catch, he warily kept his line afloat.

"They didn't get on?"

"You mean, didn't she manage to cope with my brother?"

85

Michael was about to protest that his question carried no such overtone, but Winifred patted his arm comfortably.

"Oh, there; I know perfectly well how difficult Soames must have been to live with. I doubt I should have said that while he was alive, but – well, there it is. My mother was devoted to my father, and that didn't prevent him from being a distinct cross for her at times. And Soames certainly wasn't unlike Father."

"Perhaps she – Irene, I mean—" the name, which before today he had only ever heard June pronounce, sounded awkward to him in his own voice, "perhaps she simply wasn't capable of devotion." Recalling his conversation with Fleur he added, "Not everyone is."

"Ah," said Winifred sombrely and paused on the path. "If only that had been how it was. Poor Soames. I think that was truly the worst part of it for him. You see, she *was* such a devoted wife when she married again."

Michael's pessimism outran him; would Fleur be a devoted wife, if she—?

"But it all turned out for the best, don't you see?" Something which remained in Winifred of the mother caused her to offer comfort, but it was neither a fully conscious nor a fully operative impulse, and sadly missed its mark. "Soames met Annette, after all."

"And so John and Fleur were born," Michael said softly, still mentally mis-spelling that name. He spoke virtually to himself, his focus now a hundred yards away. Under his breath he added: '*From out the fatal loins of those two foes*—'. Her father's true love was to be the mother of Fleur's own! Poor star-crossed lovers! He could hear again Fleur's plaintive appeal to him one night before they were married, before he thought he stood a dog's chance with her:

'*Come again when I know I can't get my wish.*'

He had discovered years ago what that wish was – to be allowed to love and to have that love, her cousin John. Then June had supplied the last remaining piece. The reason why that love had been denied her. Now he had the whole story – or so he believed. And it was — well, not comedy.

"Yes," Winifred insisted. "It was the beginning of — it all." She had been about to use the expression '*the family feud*', but thought better of it. She was not a woman to use an impassioned phrase when an unimpassioned one would suffice.

86

Winifred was continuing; Michael reeled back his concentration.

"We were all very happy for Soames at first. Irene was a sensitive, artistic little thing, I thought. Certainly, he tried his best to give her everything she wanted, but she didn't seem to *want* anything at all——" Here Winifred pulled an upturned expression with her mouth, corners drawn down, which prompted all the other powdered furrows in her face into immediate mimicry. This fact – not *wanting* anything – to so devout a Forsyte as the sister of Soames was alone enough to substantiate the charge '*artistic*'. "He even had a splendid house built for her in the country, to try and make a new start."

"I gather it didn't work," Michael suggested.

"Hardly. Irene misbehaved herself with the architect."

And with this summing-up of the effect of passion upon human nature, Winifred unconsciously revealed the full extent of that emotion's absence from her life. The hope that she was the one to revive history's dead bones was likely to be stillborn.

To Michael, the mention of a house signified nothing, as this was another area of family history in which he was untutored. However, it came to him as no surprise that his father-in-law had attempted to shore up a failing marriage, only one institution after all, with another, that of property. Here Michael was closer than he could have known to the truth of the matter.

To Soames, that arch-Forsyte, the given facts of the case, as it presented itself in 1887, were not so much that marriage and property both were institutions – though naturally they were – but rather that his wife and his house were both his property, and it was upon this premise, legal and true, that he had decided, those many years ago, to act. And to the shade of Soames Forsyte it may have come as some small comfort that among those now present at Highgate some fifty years later, only one – and that one not of the living – ever knew the exact nature of the extreme action he had taken.

Winifred had not quite finished her tale.

"Soames was so bewitched by her beauty he didn't seem to notice what was going on, or to care if he did. And she *was* so beautiful. She still is, I understand, though she's nearly my age."

Winifred said this with a touch of injury in her voice, as if age, being naturally an accelerating object, ought by now to have made up the gap between herself and her former sister-in-law. To stand as her final exposition, she said:

"No. It was a poor match from the start. Irene was too sensitive, *too* artistic for Soames – for any of us, really. But of course, with cousin Jolyon it was altogether different, since he was a painter himself. He was in the Academy, you know."

Michael had not known, until then, and now alerted to the endless connection of things his thoughts raced ahead. *Jolyon Forsyte, RA.* The pastel! Then surely – the boy was John – and Fleur kept it in her room!

Returned to Green Street, Michael politely declined first his aunt's invitation to stay to lunch and then her offer of the car to take him back to South Square. It would do him no harm to walk, he said. What he did not say was that his initially unconsidered favour to her in fact had cost him dearly, and he hoped by walking and keeping his own company for a little longer to be able to digest the details he had swallowed. Had it been a more regular occurrence he might have noticed that this feeling accompanied all his discoveries about the collective Forsyte past.

Turning from Winifred, Michael smoothed his jacket in a reflexive gesture, as if his indigestion was of the stomach and not of the heart. His hand passed over the outline of something rectangular. The letter! He took the envelope from his pocket, its brown penny-ha'penny stamp franking his guilt, and slipped it into the box at the corner. Lucky now to make Tuesday's edition. Poor Lewis! Poor lovers! Poor all!

Winifred received Michael's kiss on her cheek and watched him go. What an agreeable fellow he was – and such a steadying influence on Fleur, after all! Before going in to a solitary luncheon – where she may once or twice have recalled her companion of yesterday – Winifred Dartie admitted to herself that the expedition had unexpectedly left her quite revived, the act of passing a job-lot of her troubles over to another being wholly unconscious. She felt she might almost have been to a spa rather than to a graveyard. With a glow of satisfaction not induced by thoughts of chilled cucumber soup she saw that lying on the console table in her

88

hall were three calling-cards. Ah, but none of them belonged to that charming Argentinian; it was too much to expect him to call again so soon. Just one from Lettie MacAnder, to let her know that she was up in Town again for the season, another from 'very young' Roger's youngest, Grace, who had less than delicately scored her sisters' names through in pencil, to indicate she had called by herself, and a third from St. John Hayman. That young fellow was a card himself, but awfully amusing. Well, she was sorry to have missed her callers, but she was glad to have paid her own call on the Old Forsytes. Really, she felt quite invigorated. It was remarkable – sea air itself could not have been more stimulating! And then a passing thought made her smile. All three cards had been left in the *morning*. Imagine – what *would* Aunt Ann have said!

To overcome the common misunderstanding that a Forsyte outside of London is the equivalent of a fish out of water, the student of Forsyteism should note that there are in fact pockets of them to be found in favourable habitats throughout the country. For example, there are any number situated on the South Coast. Not actual named Forsytes of course, those being, in almost all particulars[1], wedded to the nation's capital and to their own invested therein, but Forsytes in the general sense, members of that cautious and long-lived breed who, having nurtured their nest-eggs in the jungle of the city, migrate in reduced family groupings to the milder climate and kindlier environs of the sea, where in addition to five per cent they can accrue any amount of fresh air for their money. It would, indeed, be no exaggeration to say that between Eastbourne and Hayling Island the coast is nowadays fairly awash with Forsytes.

It was for this reason that Miss Elsie Smither, late of Green Street and formerly of "The Bower" (Timothy's) on the Bayswater Road, had been happy to retire there, after her useful days in service had expired.

Sitting at her window, a little bow with leaded panes – such

---

[1] *The notable exception to this rule being Thomas Forsyte, youngest son of 'old' Roger, who had gone to live in Jersey to avoid the indignity of taxation, and left there indignantly when the island began to talk about taxation of its own. He lived subsequently at Bournemouth.*

a nice feature! – Smither watched the light fail over the horizon. The sunsets they had here, it was fairly a privilege to watch them! In the seven years she had been retired to the coast, and had her little *maisonette* in 'The Elms' (oddly named since there were none, only a stretch of overtrimmed privet in front and a wild-set bramble behind), Smither had never ceased to wonder at the colours the sun could cast over the waters, the reflected glory of which she could see from her window, nearly, but not quite, overlooking 'the front'.

The day had passed quickly, which made a nice change. It was a shame not to be able to get out to Church anymore, but the truth was she hadn't really felt right since she got up. Not unwell, exactly – just not *right*. *Woozy* was how she would describe it, all swimmy, like those times when she and old Jane, the cook at Timothy's, would have a sweet sherry at Christmas! Funny how it had grown so dark, and for June – was it a storm, perhaps? Nothing like the coast for a good storm! Made you fear for your chimney-pots, some of them did! And it was getting chilly, too – a sure sign of rain. Smither pulled up her best tartan rug over her arms – Miss Winifred's own special retirement present to her it was, and from Asprey's, too! She would make the best of it and have a nap – only forty winks – until supper, and maybe by then the storm would have passed. Fearful dark it was getting!

In a dream of heart-warming clarity and detail, Smither seemed to see the whole parade of Forsytes pass before her as she had known them, each one performing a little dumb-show of his life just for her special benefit. She saw her first day at the big house on the Bayswater Road, when Miss Ann took her in and trained her to be a lady's maid. Every morning for nigh on twenty years she had helped the old lady with her attire, and with all the other 'necessaries' of that ancient toilet, which she didn't like to name, even now. Miss Ann had her pride, and Smither had always turned her back to her mistress at certain moments – such as when she put on her false curls – to spare it.

That big house in Bayswater – she wondered who it belonged to now? Shame it had to leave the family, really, but there it was – the younger ones wanted new places of their own. It was natural. Smither seemed to see everything which had ever happened there all at once, like an advent calendar when all the windows are open.

There was her first big occasion, Mr Timothy's fiftieth it had been, when she was allowed to bring in the tea. Then she remembered them all being told of old Mrs Jolyon's dying. Ever so sad the old gent was, when he came round to the house again, it coming so close after that business with young Mr Jolyon, who ran off with that foreign governess. Now that fair broke Miss Ann's heart, so it did. He was the first of all the children, you see, so he was bound to be her favourite, being the eldest of the next generation, so to speak. Miss Ann had seen him as the promise of the future. Smither surprised herself with this formulation. 'The promise of the future'. Yes, that was exactly right. But Mr Soames had quickly become the old mistress's next favourite. Such a responsible and accomplished gentleman he had been – but what a terrible way to go! Miss Winifred – Mrs Dartie, that is – she would have missed him all these years. She had been ever so good, taking her into service again after old Jane died in . . . what was it – '25? – or was it '26? Young Miller was at Green Street now. She had trained up nicely . . . ever such a careful girl, quick but reliable . . .

Here Smither's dream drifted back into half-conscious reverie. Remembering Mrs Dartie put her in mind of her will. It was a daily comfort to her to know it was safe with Young Mr Roger – Very Young, she should say – and that everything was settled. That business with the 'certain item' had been on her conscience these many years . . . It was good to know that it would go back to the family.

Opening her old eyes, Smither was disappointed. It mustn't have broken yet, the storm, it was darker than ever. Ooh! – a sudden apprehension misgave her – perhaps she had slept past supper-time, and it was the night already. Well, you never knew how long a good nap would take you. Old Mr Timothy used to swear by them, and he lived to be over a hundred. Smither reached unsteadily for the cord of her reading lamp at her right side. By the ochre light it cast she turned her face to the clock on the mantel. There it was! Nine o'clock already, no wonder it was dark! But so cold still she would have to set the fire. How long was that nap then? Lawks, whatever would Miss Ann have said? *Smither, you're a good girl really, but so* **slow** *– what a time you take over things!*

Smither began to get up, with a tremendous creak of corsets, but fell back into her chair at the attempt. Ooh, dear — she must have been sleeping all awkward because her left side felt funny, sort of numb and tingly at the same time. Pins and needles, she guessed, and just in the way of needing to put on the lights and set the grate. Still, the warden would be along in a minute or two. He wouldn't mind rubbing her wrists if she asked him, that always did the trick. He was a helpful sort of a chap, Mr Furlow, though she didn't like him always saying there was going to be another war this year, even if he was an old soldier. Smither didn't like to contradict a person, but she knew in her bones there wasn't going to be another war in her time. That nice Mr Chamberlain would never let it happen, she was certain. His father had been a good sort, too . . . Smither felt a yawn coming on. Perhaps she could just finish her nap until the warden came. But it was so chilly!

As the clock over her mantel chimed its tinny quarter-hour, Smither, surely the most faithful of all servants to the Forsyte family, in whose service she was proud and happy to have spent sixty years of her life, from girlhood to old age, resumed her nap and in so doing took that last ferry across waters unseen, if not unimagined, from her bow-window at 'The Elms'. The exact moment of her passing on that cloudless June day was recorded, had there been ears to mark it, by the last chime of the quarter before noon.

At nine o'clock that evening (Smither's old eyes had previously confused the big and little hands, just as she had mistaken the twilight of stricken vision for the fall of the day), the warden of the little set of 'old folks' cottages' in the cut just off the front opened the back door and called his habitual "Halloo!"

Not receiving his customary "Oh, it's *you*, Mr Furlow!" (he was her only visitor most days) he proceeded cautiously, like the old soldier he was, through to Miss Smither's little sitting-room.

There he found her in her old wing armchair, nicely tucked up under her red tartan blanket, head a little to one side, eyes closed. Another person might have thought she had just fallen asleep in her chair, but not Albert Furlow. Being an old soldier, he had seen it all before and knew the signs, even by the low-wattage light of the standard lamp. It wasn't so much that she looked pale; old folks, even on the coast, often hadn't much colour. Nor was it the stillness of her which alerted him; again, he knew that old folks (he was himself not quite sixty) could sleep sometimes without hardly seeming to breathe. No, it was something else; something that he had noticed first in Ypres, when his best friend took a sniper's bullet in the back one morning at dawn, and then quite a bit in this last line of work. No, it was Albert Furlow's experience that folks never looked quite so peaceful when they were asleep, as they did when they were dead.

Chapter Eleven

Michael Takes a Squint

After the pronounced comfort of his aunt's car it required no changing of inner gears for the aristocrat who possessed both feudal lands and a social conscience to hop on board a number 6 motor-bus at Piccadilly Circus and sit democratically in the sun on its top deck while that conveyance carried him to the far reaches of Hackney. Indeed, there was something temporarily purging to Michael's personal and professional worries in the laboured chug of the engine, in the long accommodating route broken by unhurried stops and starts, in the neighbourly jostling of passengers on the cue of the bell, and in the constant chirruping of the conductor.

'*Room for ev'ryone on top! Mind the step, grandma! Hallo, littl'un, got your ha'penny? Hold tight!'*

Ding-ding!

By the second stop on the Caledonian Road, Michael had decided it was the Eighth Wonder of the World: a Sunday afternoon 'bus-ride in London – and in this direction not a Forsyte for miles!

On the seat beside him was a derelict copy of one of the more cheerful weeklies. It was folded open at a page given half to news items – as opposed to the more frequently occurring gossip, recipes, household tips and competitions – and half to a political cartoon. Michael picked it up.

'*Three die in Gas Explosion*', '*Dog saves Boy from Canal*', '*Meningitis fear in London Borough*' – on more distant inspection this turned out to be neither the borough he was going to nor the one he had left, but another further east – '*Summer Temperatures – on the way up!'* . . . and so on. The stuff of news and news of stuff! Michael glanced at the cartoon, then glanced again because

94

it struck him as surprisingly good. The artist had drawn the Prime Minister and the German Chancellor as boxers in a ring. The referee was holding up an arm of the little Austrian, who stood victoriously in his shorts and peaked cap in the centre of the canvas, while a worried second – a fair likeness of the Foreign Secretary – fanned a sagging Chamberlain with the Munich Agreement.

The caption read:

'*Chamberlain on the ropes.*'

He's got it in one, thought Michael. That's just exactly where the old man is – and the rest of us with him! But for the world he wouldn't have such an understanding disturb the happiness of his fellow-travellers there about him on the 'bus. Not for all the tea in china, Michael decided, as he re-folded the discarded copy of the *Sunday Blackguard* and slipped it to the floor.

Alighting at something like a High Street, Michael realised he hadn't his exact bearings. He was about to stop a friendly native of those parts and ask for directions, with wampum if necessary, when he saw the one sign he required. Monstrously out of place in the tired leafless street, overlooked by dusty and unkept windows of ugly shops and pubs, an immaculately black top hat passed him by and underneath it, on a face barely rougher than a girl's, a quite daunting expression of *hauteur*. Below the face shone a stiff collar nearly too white for the unshaded eye to behold, and below that, a waistcoat of dazzling heliotrope. A set of perfectly pressed tails completed the *ensemble* from the rear. In all, it was a vision known nowhere else in the civilised world – an Eton senior in full 'Pop' on his way to do his designated good deed for the half. '*For Charity shall cover the multitude of sins,*' thought Michael. And *how* – he and I both! He turned on his heel and followed the youth at a distance, sorry to acknowledge that for all his socialist sensibilities he still needed 'one of his own' to show him his way.

Inside the Mission, Michael found not Lewis, but images of him in a variety of sizes and conditions, scattered singly or in small groups throughout the hall, all wearing to one degree or another the threadbare uniform of the Brigade of the Down-and-Outs. Other copies, conscripts and no doubt some volunteers, filtered in behind Michael. The creeping aroma of soup on the boil, cutting a stealthy swathe through older smells of unwashed bodies, cheap tobacco and thin disinfectant, told him he had arrived at a good time to stalk the original.

"Know a chap by the name of Lewis?" Michael asked the nearest man, seated on a spindly bentwood chair, who broke into a startling coughing-fit as he made to answer. Red cheeks blew out under yellow whiskers, tendons stiffened above a heaving chest, and all the while not a single sound issuing from him.

Attempting to spare the man's lungs and the chair any unnecessary strain, Michael added helpfully:

"An old soldier."

"Ain't we all, guv'nor?" came at last his short-winded reply, as the man wiped spittle shakily off his chin with the back of his hand and then indicated the far end of the room, neither gesture managing to dislodge an improbable length of ash from the end of his home-rolled cigarette.

In a high-windowed corner Michael found Lewis at a trestle, one wiry arm supporting his head, reading. Approaching, Michael saw that the book was a public library copy of *Homage to Catalonia*.

"Good man, Orwell, isn't he?"

Lewis looked up quickly with his hunted rabbit's eyes, and scrambled to get up. Michael stopped him from rising to attention.

"Don't! I'll join you." And hitching his trousers he sat down on an empty chair. "What do you make of him?"

Lewis folded over the top corner of his page and creased it purposefully with a blackened thumbnail before closing the book.

"Gets a lot of it right, sir, I'll give 'im that. But the way I see it, e's got no faith."

"I imagine Spain knocked it out of him – didn't it you?"

"Not a bit of it!" cried Lewis, fiercely. "Begging your pardon, Captain, but no. It was the battle we lost out there, not the war."

He reached under his chair and dragged up an old canvas hold-all, and slotted the library book into a pocket at the back. Then, as a second thought, Lewis showed the ruck-sack to Michael, smiling over the worn-out remnant of an old pride. The canvas, like its owner, was thin and faded, bleached by the sun of fierce days and the cold of desperate nights in Spain; but the whole was nonetheless recognisable as a British Army kit-bag.

"Pack up your troubles, eh, Captain Mont?"

Michael smiled back his best supportive smile. They had tried!

"Got somethink in 'ere you won't 'ave seen in a while, Captain. Bit of a mimento from the 'Un."

Lewis opened the bag and brought out an object swaddled in hessian. He balanced its weight in the palm of one hand and unwrapped it with the other, an old pirate showing his treasure.

Michael looked into Lewis's palm as if he might see the future there. In a way, he supposed he did. Before it was fully uncovered, he saw plainly what the object was. In the calloused hand lay a small German pistol; a Mauser. As Lewis removed the last end of sacking, three cylinders tumbled from its folds and struck bare boards with the ring of hard metal. Michael started. Lewis gave him a bright look as he picked up the bullets.

"Don't you worry, sir! Gun and ammo separate in barracks at all times!"

"I'm glad to hear it," said Michael, collecting himself quickly. "But do you think you ought – in here, I mean?"

"Now, sir—" Lewis looked at him as he had often done in France, usually when Michael questioned how a boiled egg had been obtained, or a clean collar, "don't you trust old Lewis better than that?"

He undid the safety catch and held the handle up for inspection.

"See this?"

Michael looked gingerly down the barrel, and at Lewis's grinning face at the sharp end.

"Quite safe, sir! See? —'ammer spring's gone. Gerry must 'ave 'it 'is 'ead with it – clean broke!" Lewis gave a hard chortle. "Like me, eh? Never did 'ave the price o' gettin' it mended prop'ly. Shame, really – lovely piece. Collector's item, they call it."

It looked new-minted in his custody, Michael observed. What did it mean for him, that it was so lovingly kept? A touchstone to the only reality which had never let him down? What a shocking testament to our times! Lewis began to polish the pistol on the sacking, falling into the easy rhythm of a long-time professional. The action seemed to make him reflective. In truth both men stared at the gun as their natural focus.

"I reckon it'll come to a 'ead before the end o' the summer

– don't you, Captain Mont?"

Michael repeated his parliamentary shrug of earlier in the day.

"I'm afraid one's running out of hope that it won't."

"Got to, a'n't it? Never should 'ave stood down on the Sudeten, sellin' out the Czechs like that."

Michael was not sure he disagreed. When last year Chamberlain announced to the House – after reading Lord Halifax's note passed to him by Sir John Simon – that he was going to meet Hitler at Munich, the Member for Mid-Bucks had tossed his order papers in the air with the best of them. Even old Queen Mary, up in the distinguished visitor's gallery, had smiled. Relief from imminent peril never did make for good judgement directly after – or how else could sane men have concurred with the dismembering of that previously sovereign country? And when Chamberlain returned with his bit of paper, like Moses down from the Mount, Michael had so *wanted* to believe . . .

The two men sat in the quiet of common understanding for several moments, until Lewis spoke again.

"No – should 'ave come to it *last* year," Lewis said at last, as if he had heard Michael's thoughts and agreed. He sniffed like a watchdog at the approach of dawn. "Can't say I'll mind when it does – soldierin's the only think I ever made a go of. Be good to see 'em on the run this time; them Blackshirts beat us in Spain, but they won't do it again. No, by the Lawd—! The Russian'll stop 'em good this time, you see if 'e don't, sir."

Michael, aware that the negotiations with Russia were far from settled, was less ready to agree with this, although he was prepared to accept Lloyd George's odds of ten-to-one against war if the Russians came to terms. Perhaps the old soldier was right – his testimony from Spain was first hand, after all. But Lewis sounded more determined than a man truly confident. His conviction possessed a feverish edge. As he spoke he was all the time polishing the gun under its length of sack-cloth, till he made it shine with the gleam of his own determination.

"How are the rations here?" Michael asked.

"Not bad, sir. Lot o' soup, but mustn't grumble."

"I thought I'd find a pub – do you know of a good one around here?"

"There's the Ship of Hope on the far corner."

Yes, of course! – wasn't that always where it was!

"Care to join me? My stand."

"Very kind of you, Captain Mont," said Lewis, which was the exact thing Michael had hoped he would not say. He repeated himself. "Very kind."

Within the hour the best victuals that the licensee of the above could provide had been consumed by both men, though in more appreciative portions by the one than by the other. Choosing his moment, Michael took out his wallet and found one of his cards. He held it out to Lewis.

"Keep this somewhere, will you? Just promise me that if things don't turn up for you in the next few weeks, you'll give me a call."

Michael had no idea what he would do when the call came, and it required all his political training to keep this doubt from his expression.

Lewis took the card and nodded, blinking his rabbit's eyes, visibly touched.

Hesitating for a second out of decency he knew he was about to breach, Michael reached into his wallet a second time and withdrew a banknote. Lewis recoiled when he saw the fold of white paper.

"Won't you let me?" Michael pleaded gently. "You saved my bacon a dozen times, and frankly it would help my conscience."

"You a'n't any need, Captain Mont!" Lewis flared like a cock standing its corner in the pit. "You did your bit, same as me – you got no need for a conscience. If you made a go of it after, then good luck to you, sir, I say. It's the system's as being at fault, not you."

To Michael's ever-raw egalitarian sensibilities this absolution was a blow to the head, and his hand holding out the money fell flat to the table top. After a few seconds he drew his other hand over his moustache and by the action pulled a deep frown over his face. He sighed, looking at the banknote and knowing that there was nothing further worth saying. As the frown deepened to a dreadful seriousness, Michael looked at Lewis for a long time, until at last he simply said:

"Please."

Lewis understood the request for what it was, an order.

"If you insist, sir."

He took the five pounds from Michael and folded it once more, carefully, before tucking it with the card into an inside pocket of his jacket. Once it was secured, Lewis withdrew his hand and gave the pocket a single, acknowledging tap, as if the transaction had set a gentlemen's agreement between them.

"I'll put it against somethink really useful, Captain Mont. You can be sure of it."

Chapter Twelve

A Death in the Family

"Here we are!"

"Are you published?"

"I'll say – top o' the page, an' all! They've even put Wilfrid's stuff in italics."

Fleur finished her eggs without relish – the new cook was developing a heavy hand with the salt, and she made the first mental note of the day to mention it later; there were early appointments which would stop her saying something directly. She took up her coffee cup.

"Read it to me."

Michael straightened the page of the newspaper with a crackle and read as Fleur sipped her coffee.

"'*From Sir Michael Mont, Bart., M.P., (Con.), Mid-Bucks.*' – Lord, how they love a good title!"

Michael infused his own words with that skilful degree of mock-seriousness which had for so long kept him sane in politics.

"—'*Sir,*
'*I had occasion recently to encounter a man I knew in the War, who served under me in France. The meeting was not auspicious as I came upon him begging for coppers in the street. He was reluctant to tell me his story for, remarkably, he still has some pride remaining to him, but after hearing it I felt obliged to put pen to paper, though in hope of what end save simple record I am at a loss to know—*'

"Pompous ass," Michael interjected.

"— '*This man has selflessly given his all for the sake of his fellows not once, as many of us might claim, but twice over, since he has just lately returned from Spain, where he fought bravely, I have no doubt, but on the losing side. He returns down-and-out, without home or job, and with little left to keep body and soul together save hope and meagre charity.*

'*We have long since given up the notion of a fit land for heroes to live in, but surely we can none of us survive with dignity if what remains is a land unfit even for the simple sustenance of mere mortal men?*' "

Michael sighed briefly.

"Then Wilfrid, and—

'*I remain, blah, blah.*' "

He laid down the paper, and stared at it ruefully, wondering whether he ought to regret more about the letter than his alliteration.

Fleur said: "Well, you've done your bit now."

"Have I?"

"Haven't you? You've already been to see him, and now this. You said yourself it was all you could do."

"I know. But to do all one can isn't to do all one should."

"Michael, you sound like a rather bad school motto taken from the Latin."

The scold was only light, but Michael decided quickly that in this case discreet agreement was the greater part of valour.

"Don't I! Comes with the territory, I'm afraid. It's all that my-friend-the-Honourable-Member-ing across the floor – makes one often wish for a toga."

Fleur replaced her cup and put her napkin on the table.

"I must make a start. That cook is too liberal with the salt."

Michael had thought it was just his porridge. He felt the lightest touch of her lips on his cheek, inhaled the quick freshness that her movements released from the fabric of her dress, and followed her with his smile as she left the dining-room. It was good of her to listen, to keep showing interest, though probably, given the dappled pattern of his career, it cost her the same effort every time. From Foggartism[1], his first abortive cause in Parliament, through slum clearance, and pacifism before it was respectable, through a motley assortment of committees to the present moment when he could not have told where he stood, Fleur had always been there, at his side, championing and consoling by turns. By whatever standards their marriage fell short in private, Michael knew it outstripped all comparison professionally and in public. For this much he was sincerely grateful – to ask for very much more would have seemed greedy.

In the few minutes it took Michael to summon a fresh pot of coffee to the breakfast table and to scan the major news articles of the day Fleur had already left the house, for he heard the click of the front door as he finished the leader and reached for the sugar-bowl. That made an early start, even for her, but she had mentioned something the previous night – some appointment he recalled vaguely, and was instantly ashamed of himself for not remembering exactly, for being too wrapped in his own considerations. He must do better. With characteristic self-depreciation Michael had always believed that if ever he should bore Fleur then the basis of their marriage would be severely compromised. Lately he knew he had been pushing his luck in that subject. His own first mental note of the day was to deduct himself a House point for inattention during class. Wake up at the back, Mont major! He stirred his coffee determinedly and returned to the newspaper.

Perhaps it was the earlier act of looking for his own name in the paper which caused Michael to see another's so clearly. His eye, as seemed lately to be its habit, caught the name *Forsyte*, on this occasion printed in heavy capitals. And it was in the 'Deaths' column!

His first understanding, imperfect and confused, was that he should know who this person was, and in his prevailing frame of mind Michael reproached himself for not recognising the first name. A second and more complete understanding crept upon him like the ghost at the feast when he moved his eye over the details.

'FORSYTE, Anne, née Wilmot. On Sunday, June —th, at Green Hill Manor, Nr. Wansdon, Sussex; suddenly, aged 34 years—'

---

[1] *The political philosophy of Sir James Foggart, whose central thesis advocated child emigration to the Dominions. See his book, 'The Parlous State of England' (pub. Danby & Winter, 1924) for further details.*

Thirty-four – Fleur's generation! Was this the death of a cousin? Then, unbidden, the picture came to him of a slim, dark-haired girl with the eyes of a water nymph and a soft, hesitant accent from the American South. Dear God, Anne Forsyte! John's wife – it must be she! Michael continued to read, with something like the warmth of incipient panic building in his hands as he held the paper needlessly closer. Yes, there it was—

'Beloved wife of Jon Forsyte and adored mother of Jolyon and Ann.'

Two children – a boy and a girl, like themselves! Michael's heart went out, but at first only into the void of his own damnably insufficient memory. Now he tried he could not bring to mind the details of the man's face, the face of Fleur's beloved cousin – of whose name he now had the correct spelling – except that it had been fair and handsome with early signs of the family chin, though no less fair for that. If Michael had been inclined to find himself an excuse he might have allowed that the memory, which would accompany him to his grave, of Fleur's own face when she knew she had finally lost her great love would be enough to expunge the details of a good number of others. Still Michael felt inadequate to respond. Fleur's loss had been inconsolably her own, but the cousin's loss had been necessarily Michael's gain and so his heart went out. To lose Fleur all those years before, and now to lose a wife! How could sanity bear it?

His nerves flinched as the telephone rang in the drawing-room. He raced to answer it as if the worst of the calamity had somehow yet to befall.

"My dear, have you seen *The Times*?"

It was Winifred.

"I have – but Fleur hasn't."

"I should have known earlier myself but for Val and Holly being in France. Val called me just now – they're coming back today. What a dreadful business – a riding accident of all things. The poor girl was younger than Fleur!"

Michael allowed his aunt's irony on this last point as unintentional in the circumstances.

"Shall you tell Fleur?" she asked.

"Rather than have her read it, of course. But she went straight out – I don't know that I'll see her before she sees it herself."

Winifred's voice seemed far away at the other end of the connection.

"Ah – such a coil!"

"Will you – if you're speaking to Holly – please convey my – our deepest sympathy?"

"Yes, dear boy – I'm sure it's all any of us can do."

In Winifred's concluding remark Michael found some trace of comfort for his own case. Perhaps it was as simple as that. They would all be sorry for those immediately affected, Fleur no less than any, and after a little while the living would go on. *Fin d'histoire.* Wishing hard that it might be so, Michael nevertheless made it a point to misplace the newspaper in his study before he left for the House.

Winifred remained for some time after the connection ceased with the telephone in her hand. In the normal way she was not one vulnerable to the fancies of superstition, but the conjunction of this sudden death – as yet barely explained to her over a bad line from France – with her own visit to Highgate on the same day was not readily dismissed. To say the least, it seemed to her more than an unhappy fortuity, and actually rather ominous. For the first time that she had consciously experienced it, something of her father's nervous pessimism overcame her. It would be too bad if that old business, between her niece and Young Jolyon's boy – which was how she still thought of Jon, though his father had been dead almost twenty years – if it should all start—! No, it was impossible. Fleur was too sensible, Michael too devoted to her, their children too important to them both. And it was to be hoped, Winifred thought genuinely, without a trace of malice, that the boy had been fond of his wife – too fond to have any other than a downcast eye for the foreseeable future. That must be how it was. She was old and getting foolish in her imaginings. Not seeing the family trait in herself, Winifred supposed this was what they called being in one's 'dotage', taking fright at unlikely possibilities – and she all her life noted for *sang-froid*! But still, she didn't like the coincidence of events, and wished that the significance, if there were any in it, might point elsewhere.

She started like a spring lamb when, as she replaced the receiver, the telephone rang again, arresting these reflections abruptly in mid-thought.

"Aunt Winifred?"

"Who's that?" Expecting to hear Val again, she could not immediately identify the voice of the man who spoke to her.

"It's Roger, Aunt. Are you all right?"

The speaker was 'very young' Roger Forsyte, necessarily the eldest son of her late cousin 'young' Roger, and the present and only family member in the firm of Cuthcott, Kingson and Forsyte, solicitors and commissioners for oaths.

"Oh, Roger. Yes – I'm well—"

"You sound rather shaky – are you sure?"

"*Yes.*" Winifred would *not* be the object of fussing.

"Only I've a little bit of bad news here for you. I wondered whether it was wise to telephone – perhaps I should call round?"

The newspaper – Roger would have seen it, of course.

"Don't worry – I knew it already. You saw *The Times*, I suppose?"

"— No." Roger's voice carried a doubting note. "Who put it in there, I wonder?"

"Why, her family, of course!" Winifred was prepared to be excessively irritated. Roger was usually so astute; he must be over-working himself.

"But Aunt, there were none – that's partly why I'm calling—"

Because the alternative was to become lost in a vexing confusion which she felt at that moment would be unendurable, Winifred rallied that old quality of coolness under agitation and interrupted her younger kinsman.

"Roger – Roger!"

He was silenced.

"Will you simply tell me – *whom* exactly are you talking about?"

"Smither."

"Smither?"

"Your old maid—"

"Yes, yes!" Vexation upon vexation! And Roger usually so sensible. "I do know, dear boy. What about her?"

"She died, Aunt. At the weekend – on Sunday."

Winifred held the telephone a little more tightly to her ear. A phrase of her father's came to her, one she had never before felt herself moved to use. Faintly, at the other end of the telephone line, Roger heard her say: '*There – I knew how it would be. . .*'

Fleur's day necessitated an early start, so many appointments clamoured for her attention in its course. None of them *mattered*, of course – not at the level she so craved for something to absorb her – but she was passably grateful that they promised to engage her energies for the larger part of the day.

The first appointment was one of two charity meetings scheduled for that morning. This charity – founded to help babies in Eastern Europe – had needed to convene an 'extraordinary' meeting at almost no notice for the purpose of discussing the situation in Czecho-Slovakia, if that was what the country was still to be called. (No one present seemed quite sure on this point, and the Secretary was given a directive to record this in the minutes.) The babies with whom they were actually concerned were in Rumania, but apparently some Slovak mothers, not unreasonably, were taking their own infants over the borders, thereby putting an even greater strain on resources. Everyone at the meeting seemed to feel the immediacy of the situation as a personal affront – it really was too bad of the German Chancellor to encroach on to territory they considered practically their own. Surely the Government should have done something in the Spring? Fleur sharply resented the eyes which were turned to her. She was not the only Parliamentary wife there; Emily Gore's husband was in the Lords and in one of the Ministries . . .

Yet Fleur wished, as she watched her fellow committee-women around the table, that she could feel as they felt about the iniquities of lives not their own. Some of them had the true light of zeal in their eyes. Commitment! It was all wash!

Then came a fitting for some autumn suits – a hot and horrid business, where the light-weight wool rubbed through her underlinen like sack-cloth, even without ashes.

The second charity meeting, this one closer to the 'home front', was the quarterly review of finances for her rest-home for women in Dorking, started when a tendency to charitable works proved a reliable way to use up her spare energies left over after running her kitchen during the General Strike in '26. At this meeting Fleur boxed the ears of the committee – verbally at least – over the state of their ledgers, a treatment of which they were not entirely deserving. In her present temperament she was loathe to have anything, however innocently, remind her of the year of the Strike. As if she wasn't presently reminding herself of it enough! She had found Jon again that year, 'fresh off the boat' from growing peaches in North Carolina, with his young American wife on his arm. She had so nearly kept him, too, despite that girl. And then there was the fire at Mapledurham, and her father's death because of it, when she had made him her promise as he died – a promise like a small child's—

'*Yes, Dad: I will be good!*'

Commitment! Wash!

In the late morning she called on Winifred. Mrs Dartie, she was told in confidence by Miller, was at her hairdresser's.

She lunched at her club, the '1930', where she had occasion to speak to no one save the porter and the steward, and read a copy of the *Daily Mail* between courses.

After lunch she walked up to Goode's, where she decided on a new breakfast service, some Christening silver to be kept for engraving against the birth of Dinny's baby, and a whisky decanter for Michael's agent, who was retiring next month owing to a condition of the liver which made the gift – Michael's suggestion – all the more certain to 'come in handy'.

As she turned her key in the latch at South Square, intending only to change from a hot dress into a cool one, and kick her heels for an hour before leaving for her next appointment, Fleur was surprised to find the door being hastily opened to her from the inside.

Timms bobbed nervily to her mistress, and then bobbed again in the direction of the drawing-room.

"Mr Bar-*hantes*, ma'am," Timms said, remembering the 'aitch' she had heard in his name, if not its exact location. "He called three times before, and looked so earnest I hadn't the heart to turn him away again – begging your pardon, ma'am." Timms bobbed once more.

This admitting of a caller, however persistent, in her absence, was against Fleur's explicit instructions for the running of the household. But she could see by his cards on the salver that the Argentinian had indeed called before. There were his two cards, one for her, one for Michael, each with the top right-hand corner turned neatly inward. How very correct of him – it was almost quaint. But three times – he was keen! There was also a telephone message, she noticed, in the maid's school-girl hand: '*Mrs Darty Rang, but will Ring Again.*' She took in all this at a glance and nodded once to Timms, who scuttled off, grateful to be merely dismissed.

Fleur removed her hat and gloves unhurriedly and laid them on the coat sarcophagus while Gauguin's dusky women, never adorned by such items, looked on. Touching her hair in the tortoise-shell mirror, Fleur saw them over her shoulder, reaching languidly for the easy fruits of their island life. So they might; theirs was a simple world, where only the imperatives of existence applied – see, do, take, have, *hold* – and where conditional tenses were unknown. She had reached out, not once but twice, and had grasped — ah! shadow, not substance! Well, no matter – now she had a languid hour herself. And idly wondering what the Argentinian's next manœuvre would be, and how she would counter it, she went into the drawing-room.

"I wanted to offer my services to you," he said, the moment Fleur let herself into the room and he saw she was alone. He stood by the window and his face, eloquent and grave, had a beautiful radiance suddenly in the sun-lighted room. In surroundings so given up to modernity, he might have stepped from an altar-piece by El Greco. "If there is anything at all I can do, you need only ask."

Fleur looked at him blankly, an unsympathetic cast over her face, set up against his stealing attraction. He had picked the wrong day to win her by servility.

"And, for what they are worth," he added, "I tender my sincere condolences."

Condolences? For what? No one had died.

"Your condolences?" she repeated. "Why?"

"Ah – *Madre de Dios*—" he said in a low voice, his eyes cast sideways and darker than ever with what seemed a very real concern. "You haven't heard!"

"Heard what? Tell me, please."

"It was in the newspaper this morning; I imagined—"

"Tell me!"

"Your second cousin, Jon Forsyte—"

"*No!!*" Her voice only whispered the word – it was her own heart Fleur heard cry.

"— his wife has died. Anne Forsyte died on Sunday."

'*Anne Forsyte died on Sunday.*' Those simple, unadorned words rattled chaotically in her head like tame birds startled in their cage, each one making more clamour than the last as they raced in wild, conflicting paths, breeding greater confusion among themselves in so doing.

"—I never for one moment thought – that you would not know," he was saying to her as she sat down on the sofa. She had done so involuntarily; Barrantes had steered her to it. Now he sat beside her, sideways on, half kneeling on the carpet – deferential as ever.

"I didn't – I hadn't heard." Fleur was really quite calm in herself, now she realised her heart and senses were untouched by this information. But her quick brain buzzed. No use trying to see what it meant – and it surely must mean something to her own case – with this fellow sitting by her now. She must get on her own to think.

"I am so sorry," he said gently.

She saw from his 'seeing' expression – heavy lids and thick, dusty lashes suspended a little higher over his great dark eyes – that she had let something slip in her reaction. The news had clearly affected her – no use to pretend otherwise, he saw too much always; but how to explain why she hadn't known?

"Thank you. So am I, for my cousin. Our two families don't see each other very much – but I know he'll be hurt badly by the loss."

Another lie nearest the truth, and she was indeed sorry for Jon's hurt – but for his loss?

"Is there anything—?"

"No—" Cut him off before any further explaining fell due, it was the only safe way. Fleur got up swiftly – though the Argentinian seemed to be first on his feet. Such constant anticipation, without any display of speed or effort – it was unnerving!

"I must make some calls, now I do know. I am grateful to

you, Señor Barrantes, for telling me this; and I appreciate your concern."

She extended her hand, and let him hold it briefly. He looked this time not at her, but at her hand in his and replied:

"It is nothing, but it is sincere."

Another inclination of his head and he was gone.

Chapter Thirteen

Fleur Continues to Think

When the trim shadow of Alexander Barrantes followed his elegant substance from Fleur's drawing-room, he was no sooner out of her sight than completely out of mind. All that was left from his visit was the news he had brought with him. As the room regained its quietude, Fleur threw herself into one of the deep-sided bergères, arms and legs at disregarded angles, chin thrust forward on a knuckle, and let her quick mind make all the running.

That girl, Anne – Fleur recalled her name here as the merest formality – who had won Jon simply because she herself had lost him, was gone, dead. It occurred to her that she did not know the cause of death. After a few moments she concluded that of the possibilities only two – accident or sudden illness – were at all likely. She would quite simply have got wind of anything else, any long-term problem, at the supper on Friday: even Holly's discretion could not have disguised something of that order. And Holly and Val had left for France on Saturday morning; so their departure would have temporarily cut off Winifred's line to events at Green Hill. With this fact in place Fleur brushed aside the tiresome possibility, stemming from an old habit within her family, that something might have been kept from her.

As if it were a gun-dog, she let her mind corner its quarry, single-purposedly flushing out the essence of the issue from a dense cover of secondary considerations. And the essence of the issue was Jon, her one and only ever quarry. Accident or illness was an insignificant detail; what mattered was Jon's response to it. Since it must have been sudden, shockingly so, Jon must be reeling from the blow. He was sensitive, deep-feeling, loyal – for this purpose Fleur disallowed the word loving – and would be raw from his loss, one from which it would take him surely a long time to heal. He would have Holly to help him, of course, when she returned – Holly and Jon were close though they were only half-brother and sister, and Wansdon was only a few miles from Green Hill. Winifred's line of communication could also serve as her own, Fleur reasoned; through Winifred she would be able to keep *au fait* without betraying too great an interest.

It was only at this point that Fleur began to understand how great her interest was. She repeated her first thought to herself; *that girl was gone.*

Something quick and exciting jarred her nerves at this understanding. Did this mean that Jon might somehow become available to her again? Dared she think it? Like the promise of a view at the summit to one starting on the foothills of a mountain, it seemed a hazy, distant prospect if it was in any way a possibility. Long-term strategy, so prized by politicians and diplomatists, had never been Fleur's strong suit. Her skills lay in the tactical playing of the cards in her hand, and quickly now she reviewed what they were. She saw that her highest cards were in the suit of her own immaculate conduct since the end of her affair with Jon. She had given unstinting support to her husband's passage through Parliament; as a skilful hostess she had established an unshakeable position for them on the ever-shifting sands that were called Society; and she had delivered a second child – all these facts were of high face value. Even her promise to her father on his death-bed, even this she counted as telling in favour of her hand. But above the value of these cards, alone or combined, lay the fact that no one, so far as she knew no one at all, would expect her to play a single one of them, even if they went so far to suspect her of still wishing to be in the game.

This determined review, and its not unfavourable outlook, prompted Fleur into action. She would telephone to Winifred, whose earlier call must have been in this regard. But first she needed to see the newspaper.

A quick search of the drawing-room, the hall and the Spanish dining-room told her that the newspaper, which Michael always left in one of those three places, had been removed.

Fleur rang for the maid, who was still flushed from her mistake over the Argentinian. No ma'am, she had not removed the paper. Timms bobbed and left the room tight-lipped, so containing the expression 'give a dog a bad name' until she was downstairs and could say it safely to the cook.

Fleur absently chewed the side of a finger. This meant Michael had taken *The Times* with him. Since she knew that a second copy was delivered to his office in Westminster she concluded he must have seen the death notice and was trying to keep it from her. It *was* tiresome, this habit of everyone's! Well – she would adopt it herself!

Glancing at her watch Fleur saw that her hour, which had proved anything but languid, was up. She went upstairs, swiftly changed dresses, retouched her hair and face, paused in front of the Pembroke table and left the house again – and all the time she was thinking, thinking, thinking.

"Hello?"

"Winifred – Fleur. Isn't it awful news about Jon's wife?"

She was not to know it, but Winifred was hearing Fleur's 'Charity' voice, much practised that day: calm, concerned but not overtly troubled, daintily sympathetic but only in a limited, business-like way. Winifred, like many an initially unwilling sponsor before her, was both reassured and persuaded by its tone. Fleur was a sensible little thing, after all!

"Yes, my dear – and so sudden."

Fleur wondered, no more than politely, whether Winifred had the details of it – she herself had only seen the newspaper.

This was timely. Winifred had just spent an hour talking on the telephone to her son, who was just back at Wansdon.

"—They were travelling all day, you know, and Val's leg gets so bad. Well – it seems she was thrown from her horse; it shied at something and Anne fell awkwardly. There was internal bleeding, I understand."

"Horrible!" This was Fleur's first involuntary remark.

"The only mercy was that she wasn't out alone. Young Jon was riding with her, and carried her back to the house. *Can* you imagine?"

Fleur said she could, and this was true.

"Val says he always thought her hunter had a flighty look in its eye – but there we are. Poor young fellow."

Fleur agreed; there they were, and poor Jon. And this was where the conversation might naturally have ended, if Winifred hadn't thought to add:

"Still, it will be a help to him, having his mother with him again."

It struck Fleur's ear ajar to be told this one ordinary fact. It was as though a half-forgotten spectre had been raised to rattle its chains once more – chains of old ownerships that had barred her way before. The spectre itself bore the beautiful face of Jon's mother, Irene, her own father's unhappy first wife and the living reason why she and Jon did not marry.

"I thought she was in Paris?"

"Val and Holly brought her back with them. Holly and she went directly to Green Hill—"

She has come back to claim him, Fleur thought, and to make sure I can't.

Winifred was running on.

"—Dear Val will so dislike being on his own at Wansdon, but he understands, of course."

Fleur matched her, keeping up that charity tone.

"Of course. What flowers, do you think—?"

But her thoughts were far, far away.

During a solitary supper Fleur only toyed with eating, turning her thoughts around her head as the food around her plate. Moving then to the drawing-room, she watched the sunset fail beyond the garden in the Square, and heard Big Ben, more times than she wished to count, tolling the knell of lost hours by their quarters. For a short period the servants busied about across the hall, clearing away food and turning off lights. There was even a muffled ring of laughter, at a shared joke; they believed their mistress to have retired for the night.

In the unlighted drawing-room Fleur witnessed first the outlines of objects becoming indistinct, then their forms, which seemed to shift and float, dark shapeless things hovering among pale. Even the doors of the room melted away and became only another part of insubstantial walls, closing in, receding, shifting, grey, black, grey.

In a dream she had had as a girl, there was always a door she must find but could not. In the darkling room it was the same. Fleur allowed herself to cry once, silently.

Chapter Fourteen

Michael Begins to Wonder

Michael had never quite taken to clubs – though he was himself considered immensely clubbable – and had lately come almost to detest them. Possibly all those years spent in that ultimate club at Westminster had cost him the taste. Or, with his ironic eye, perhaps he saw in their imperturbable inertia a microscope-view of what ailed a whole nation, and read on their walls the overdue obituary of a whole way of life. When he was still a sucking publisher he had passably enjoyed his time at the Hotch-potch, amid a batch of his contemporaries, all politico-literary 'movers-and-shakers'; what Wilfrid used to call 'the inky set'. But his membership there had lapsed with his own youth. Now he belonged to the Remove, where his late father-in-law had put him up, in a rare act of open approbation which Michael had felt under obligation to accept. Nothing about the place sang its merit to the baronet's ears, and his continued subscription rested on the single benefit of its seeming always able to offer a useful selection from both Chambers, day or night. In most other respects he considered it wholly a dud.

'*It's the Land of the Dozing Dead*,' was Michael's thought that Tuesday evening, as he crossed the Doric-columned portal. Passing his hat to the porter, he wondered what was the real difference between this establishment and the one he had visited at Highgate on Sunday, and whether there was a prize for spotting it. Not the *décor*, and certainly not the conversation. Scrolls, friezes and plinths abounded; here was a laurelled general, there an old bishop next to a fallen king – and those just the statuary! Every emblem, in fact, of that ridiculous grandiosity which bespoke the all-male preserve. The neo-classical nonsense of it all!

He had come in search of Abercrombie, the Member for the batman's home patch, but found the trail cold.

"Mr Abercrombie was certainly here yesterday, Sir Michael – all evening," the porter told him.

"Old Percy? In his cups!" another member confirmed, collecting his own hat on his way out and overhearing the name.

When Michael pursued his enquiries in the library he learned the general belief, which was that tonight the awesome Mrs Abercrombie would have requisitioned his company, in order to enlarge upon his headache. No one considered him up to a second escape.

Coming down the grand marble staircase, Michael was blamelessly passing a fellow club-member, when he felt his arm seized. He turned instantly, imagining he had dropped an item and was being alerted to it. But the grip on his forearm tightened, and felt moreover as if it was meant to hurt. He looked up at a spare, pinched face, a little older than his own and vaguely reminiscent of another he had once known. On it an habitually austere expression was disturbed by a concentration of anger in the eyes.

"Mullyon!"

It was Wilfrid's older brother Charles, now acceded to the Hampshire seat and Cornish title of their late father. He stood one step above Michael and, already taller, used the position to its full advantage, leaning over him as he spoke.

"How dared you!" came a harsh, meaning whisper.

"How dared I *what*? My arm – please!"

Michael had his arm flung down so that the socket jumped.

"That was a damned disloyal stunt! Can't you let him rest in his grave?"

"What 'stunt'?" Michael replied stonily, but knew that he must mean his letter, and the lines he had quoted.

The scene on the stair was already drawing the attention of three or four upturned heads, previously downturned over the tape machine in the hall below.

Michael added quietly: "I fear your manner adds nothing to the ambience of our surroundings."

"You openly associated Wilfrid with those filthy communists!"

This Desert, perhaps a little over fifty, spoke too haughtily for his own demeanour, which was startlingly overwrought. His quintessential Establishment features had clearly taken a knock. "*Here's another 'on the ropes' over something,*" Michael thought; but he stood his ground.

"I sincerely doubt Wilfrid would have seen it that way," Michael said simply, "or have cared—"

"He would have despised you for it!"

"I disagree."

"He was my brother—"

"And my best friend!"

This provoked a subdued snarl above him on the stair.

"If your own sympathies lie with the Bolshies, that's your business, I suppose – but on my family's behalf I demand you make a retraction."

"If you continue to make free with your allegations I may demand one myself," Michael replied.

Glancing down, he saw that one of the upturned heads was Abercrombie's, just arrived, a witness to the whole scene. Turning back to the new Lord Mullyon, seeing again the angry flecks in his eyes, it became Michael's intuitive understanding that the episode was a small part of some larger narrative, as yet undisclosed to him. Whatever its origin, the man's anger was top-heavy for its attribution.

"I intend to make you pay for this, Mont."

"As you wish."

His accuser continued to hold Michael's eye fiercely for a tense moment, then fled up the staircase like a thief in the night.

The incident at the Remove was quite enough to occupy Michael's thoughts until he let himself into South Square twenty minutes later. Then he recalled the first alarm of the day, and wondered whether, or what, Fleur knew. The hall was lighted in its usual way, by two sconces either side of the door, which was how Fleur always had it left when she retired before he returned from late sittings. But as Michael placed his hat on the old sarcophagus he had the sense that there was an extra quality to the silence, as of something hanging, ready to fall, or burst, or perhaps both. At first he passed by the drawing-room, then went back and looked through its half-closed doors, into unlighted emptiness beyond. His sense of a mood dependent upon discovery increased, as his eyes adjusted to the gloom. Yes, there she was, just a paler shape set into the dark nothingness of the unlighted room. Then she must know! He went to her.

She sat in the corner of the sofa, quite motionless, like an unarranged mannequin. She barely glanced at him when he dropped to a crouch by her side.

"I'm sorry!" were the first words Michael could think to say to her. So he was, but for what? For the loss of a relation by marriage she barely knew and could never have liked? Hardly that. Was he apologising for having married her at all, when her only wish had been to belong to another – and for remaining a constant reminder that she did not get her wish? Was he apologising for tying up her life so that, now her beloved cousin was free, she was not? Michael did not know. But he *was* sorry.

Fleur half turned her face to him. In the dismal light it looked ghostly, her eyes darkened smudges set into a mask of ivory. Impossible to tell if she had been crying, though his feeling was that she had.

"Yes," she said at last in a small, distant voice. Michael waited in case something should follow, but that was all. The silence and darkness consumed her again and, rising, he withdrew.

Out in the hall, in the small glow from the sconces, Michael stood once more before the Gaugin. So often he only passed it by, catching its colours in the corner of his eye before leaving, seeing details of an arm or waist upon returning. Now he felt himself wanting to ogle it, as one who had paid for his entrance ticket to the exhibition long ago, and was over-due the sensuous promise of the piece.

Like all great works of art it cast a changing reflection in the eye of each beholder, who discerned in its beauty the significance of different things at different times. When it first came to them it had represented a continuity of some sort after the sudden death of Fleur's father. The uncompromising, substantial female figures, their skin brown and warm, their expressions immutable and impassive as they reached up easily for ripe fruits on laden branches, offered then a conscious affirmation of life, or so Michael had thought. Now as he stood before the great canvas, so powerful in the poor light, he was uncertain. Even the title of the painting seemed suddenly to pose a new riddle.

'*D'où venons nous, que sommes nous, et où allons nous.*'

It might have been another exercise from his son's preparation. Where we come from, who we are and where we're going – *discuss* with reference to the end of peace for our time! And it could every bit as well apply to themselves, of course, to his relationship with Fleur as it had changed and, he hoped, matured since that awful time.

When he heard the story of the affair between his wife and her cousin Jon Forsyte, Michael's first and overwhelming response was to think '*poor girl!*' and to want to comfort her. He knew, after all, that he had only picked up the pieces of her heart when they married, and was more than willing to repeat the process had she wanted him to try. But Michael's offer of help went unrequested and so, by that pride which assails even the most selfless, unvoiced. He was left to look on, while this broken creature he loved so dearly went to ground, to lick her wounds, and ache in private. He remembered how she had kept to her room for three days after her father's funeral, emerging wraithlike, her skin translucent as alabaster. He knew it was not just for her father that she mourned, but for the loss, twice over, of her great love. The sobs he had heard coming from her room at night rent him apart – it was the sound of hope being smothered in a pillow.

He never ceased to love Fleur, as much through that awful, silent period as when he married her. And he knew he loved her still, though whether for her beauty, her strength or her wit, Michael, lacking the judgement of Paris, could not have begun to tell. But the constancy of his heart could not prevent a change being wrought in his soul.

Once he knew that there had been an affair – and it was Holly who had confirmed this when he had summoned the courage to ask her outright; Fleur had never spoken a word on the subject to this day – once he knew that everything which could have happened had happened, Michael began to experience an altogether unlooked-for sense of freedom. As the full impact of the knowledge bore in upon him, it was as if he had been disburdened of a weight he had borne for the longest time – like Atlas, a weight he had never thought to have the chance to set down. But after a while, also like Atlas, the absence of his burden brought him anxiety, not relief. Though no longer a tenant at will in the affairs of his own heart, the sense of equality between himself and Fleur which had not been there before left him oddly ill at ease. Surely his own increased freedom unavoidably implied the same for her?

In the ensuing thirteen years Fleur had never once shown him cause to doubt her renewed fidelity, nor had he looked for one being hidden – but of the true contents of her heart Michael's current knowledge was as slim as it had ever been.

'*Il y a toujours un qui baise, et l'autre qui tend la joue.*'

With Michael that was no longer quite the case. But how it was with her, all in all, he simply didn't know.

In that long-harboured spirit of loss and yearning, which in good times seemed only like the distant dawn, just beyond the horizon, and in bad like the phantom need to stretch a severed limb, Michael threw the bolts on the front door and, replacing the sconces with a light on the half landing, went upstairs.

Chapter Fifteen

June

While the summer was bestowing its green and luscious favours without condition upon a whole hemisphere, it was an ironic detail of the season that June Forsyte had repeatedly encountered all the most trying events of her life in or around her own month.

She had first become aware of the love affair between her 'little' brother Jon and Fleur – the daughter of her cousin Soames, progenitor as June saw him of the worst of her own misfortune – in this month in 1920. In the same month in 1926 she had been made aware of the rekindling of this love, burning with a fiercer flame in maturity; and the final calamitous ending of it all had come at the end of that same short, hot season. And forty years before that, the same month had seen the 'at home' for her own engagement at her grandfather Old Jolyon's house in Stanhope Gate. How proud she had been then! — so full of her fiancé, the young architect Philip Bosinney, whom the family had been summoned to meet. How splendid and uncompromising Phil was! —and how shadowy was the smile on the beautiful face of her best friend Irene, wife to Soames, when June had introduced Phil to her. A year later he was Irene's lover, not her own.

Some and none of these historical details flitted through June's mind as she had seen to the locking up of her little gallery late on that Saturday afternoon. She was not constitutionally suited to dwell on the melancholy of lost opportunity, and so focussed instead on its injustice. It was not often that she recalled these events, but that day for some reason – perhaps it was seeing someone buy that pastel of her father's – fragments of them had returned to her. When she did remember, it was with a surge of anger, whose flame burned strongly

still in her heart though its colour had faded to a pale trace in her hair
– righteous anger that young people should ever be resisted in their
search for happiness. The connection with the month, and whether
it was coincidental or accursed, never occurred to her. Nor did the
fact that the month this year had advanced into its second week
without the slightest hint of anything untoward, suggest itself to her
as a sign of trouble building over the horizon, a cue for providence.
It was not for nothing, after all, that her name was Forsyte.

So as June boarded the 'bus at Hyde Park Corner that would
take her home to Chiswick, nothing out of the ordinary run of
disturbances was irritating her. Always, at this mid-point in an
exhibition, she despaired – of selling enough of whatever latest
phenomenon she was promoting to make an impact, but not so
much that the taint of commercial success might attach itself to the
pure produce of genius. It was also a source of continuing annoyance
that her assistant at the gallery was such a persistent half-wit. The
'bus was hot and June's pet grievances, which she obstinately fed
and watered, made her hotter still. She tapped an unaccompanied
boy of about her nephew's age, sitting in the row in front of her,
firmly on the back, and directed him to open a window. The boy,
whose first thought was to cheek the "bossy old bird", had second
thoughts when he looked over his shoulder and caught the expression
in June's bright-burning eyes. It put him in mind of the ill-tempered
terrier which lived next door to them in Hammersmith; he opened
the window. June thanked him briskly and fanned her face with her
gloves.

As the park slipped away and Kensington Gore became the
High Street, June wondered if she ought to think about giving up
the gallery. This was another of her cyclical debates with herself,
which occupied her periodically, which were solved by her after
a lot of serious thinking, and which returned only when she had
quite forgotten her own line of argument. The vehicle chugged
rhythmically along its route, and June's hat above her arrangement
of silvery-orange hair kept time with the turn of the engine. At
Hammersmith the boy surprised himself and June by tipping his
cap to her as he left the 'bus. His seat was taken by a shop girl
with an anæmic face and wispy hair; from her sigh, this was the
first time she had been able to sit down all day.

In the early 'twenties June had once gone so far as to sell the gallery, and managed reasonably well for a time to continue her efforts in aid of genius from the studio in her house, 'The Poplars', in Chiswick. But the longing to throw down the gauntlet to the world over its æsthetic assumptions crept insidiously back to her, until finally she had to admit that there was no better means for her end (that is, for thoroughly blacking the eye of established taste) than the outright ownership of a gallery. And the means *to* this means arose providentially, out of the end of the affair between Fleur and her little brother.

Amid the *débris* at the precipitate end to that romance, which included three broken hearts, many shattered hopes and a good deal of roughly shaken faith, were two portraits commissioned from Harold Blade, the 'Raphaelite' and June's then current prodigy. One was of Fleur, the other was of Jon, and in the aftermath these remained in June's possession at 'The Poplars'. A third portrait, or rather the first in order of painting, was of Anne, Jon's wife, and had gone to their home at Green Hill before the worst began.

So, in a sad parody of what might have been, these two lovers had lain next to one another, cheek silently upon cheek, against a back wall of June's studio for nearly a year, and might have remained there for many more had not fame posthumously sought out the Raphaelite. At the time of his glorious demise he was in America, whither he had sailed after a final electrifying row with his patroness. On the eve of the opening of a first modest exhibition there he had preserved his liver at the expense of his life in several quarts of high-octane 'hooch' alcohol, thereby proving indisputably the truth of June's last words to him, which were that he was an unfit vessel for his own talent. The exhibition was a sell-out.

When notice of his unfortunate *succès* reached her, June set about removing all traces of the painter from her studio, with the ardour of a new verger rooting weeds from a graveyard, and found that she had no less than four Blades in all. The other two were smaller studies he had executed (appropriate word! for the Raphaelite's style was not kind) of herself and her maid. Unfeelingly she dispatched them all for sale at Jobson's where, through the agency of that firm's North American associate, they fetched an emotional sum in closed auction. With this windfall, June sought to buy back the lease of her old gallery from the intervening tenant. The price he demanded was no bargain, and this could not have pleased her more. To have the old place back, and to see the smile come off that fellow's face when she agreed to the first sum he asked for, were worth a king's ransom. And so, in this way, the Raphaelite's fall from grace enabled many others to follow the path to obscurity upon which he had so miserably stumbled. In his departure from this life Harold Blade had become, as it were, the patron saint of lame ducks.

It was therefore the case, when she arrived back at 'The Poplars' that evening, that nothing save a considered understanding of the repeating patterns of her own life – an achievement, after all, not reasonably expected of a Forsyte – could have alerted June to the fact that she was little more than twenty-four hours away from news of her next mid-summer tragedy.

And that news, which came over the telephone from Green Hill on Sunday, brought about a disturbing clash of emotions within the breast of June Forsyte, in the heart of her whose spirit had been, one way or another, at war with the world and its unfeeling ways for more than fifty years. Usually emboldened by the prospect of a fight, June was currently in possession of a conflict which, for once, she did not quite like to own. For once, her feelings misgave her and she was unsure of what she felt. Unquestionably it was tragic, *senseless* and tragic moreover, and June had all her life been the owner of an angry sensibility over lives taken young. But somewhere in her adamantly selfless little soul she made contact in the following few days with another notion, no less fervent, which sounded to her inner ear like a whispered word: '*Rejoice!*' And here was her conflict, for this new pain which was sharp was nevertheless sweet.

Jon had called her on Sunday – Holly was away, and his mother still in Paris, so June was the only one to whom he could immediately turn. She had arrived directly, going the whole way to Sussex by taxi-cab, not waiting to pack but ordering sufficient of her things to be sent after her to allow for a long stay. All other considerations she instantly set aside. Her assistant, previously not trusted with anything of consequence, could manage the gallery; Suslov, the genius-in-exile, could manage himself; any other lame ducks could wait.

And now as June helped her brother hold these two young scraps of humanity, one or other of them, hour after hour, alternately shivering or sobbing in her lap, something within her parched breast quickened and blew, like the sweet, tender flowers of her own month. The terrible sadness in which they all were steeped fell as rain upon her barrenness. Her nourishment was simply *their need of her*.

Need! To June the word was a sacred trust, and precious as myrrh. For once in her long life, here was true need of all she could give!

Chapter Sixteen

On Forsyte 'Change

'Very young' Roger Forsyte, a man of slightly thinning hair and slightly thickening waist, plus a limp gained during the last war, and a habit for snuff developed after it, was in fact not very young at all but nearly fifty. What hair remained to him was still faintly sandy, and his grey eyes, set above rather hollow cheeks and the family jaw, were still clear and shrewd. He was the present and only Forsyte in the firm known as Kingson's – properly Cuthcott, Kingson and Forsyte, solicitors and commissioners for oaths – but was fortunate to be also a man of much warmer character than those who had preceded him in the position.

Before its merger with Cuthcott, Holliday and Kingson, the family firm had originally been Forsyte, Bustard and Forsyte – though if any man set eyes on Bustard in his lifetime, he never spoke of it. The two original Forsytes were James and his son Soames, but at the time of the merger – 1900 – James was long retired and not expected to last the year; Cuthcott and Holliday were merely long dead. After debate as to which of the dead or dying should be included among the living, the title was formally reduced to just the three names, one Forsyte, as ever, standing for all. Soames was only the sleeping partner, moreover, as his own divorce that year had left him with little choice but to retire from the law. To go on seeing all his clients, people who had known him as a 'long-headed chap', an astute adviser – after the public humiliation of the case of *Forsyte versus Forsyte and Forsyte* – no!

Roger, this second cousin of Soames, had always harboured a soft spot for the old fellow. 'Uncle' Soames hadn't been the most lovable of men, but he had been solid, and adhered to the letter of the old values. The older Roger became himself, the more he respected the Victorians and their ways. In fact it was precisely this deep-felt respect for the ways of his elders which had occasioned his present journey, taking him into the mouth of Mansion House underground station somewhat ahead of the end-of-day rush that afternoon, exactly a week after he had broken the news of the old servant's death to his aunt. In his coat pocket was a parcel, and in that parcel was an old white lacquer box, the precise origin of which was to him completely unknown. All he knew was that the box – which was very old indeed, and appeared to be warped shut by damp and age – was the only item specifically mentioned in the last will and testament of Miss Elsie Smither, late of 'The Elms', Eastbourne, and was the old maid's bequest to her *dear, kind mistress, Mrs Winifred Dartie*'. What Aunt Winifred would make of it he had no idea, but Roger intended to execute his duty faithfully by delivering the box.

Being trustee to all Forsyte retainers, and therefore acting in this matter for the maid as well as for his aunt, Roger had also been required, under the terms of Smither's will, to put the rest of her personal effects up for sale, and to donate the proceeds to the Hampshire Rescue Home for Unwanted Animals. When he made the trip to Eastbourne, Roger needed only to take one look at the nature of the 'estate', by that time packed into fewer than half a dozen cardboard boxes by the warden, before he tipped the man five shillings to cart it all to the nearest charity shop. Back at his office in Old Jewry the following day, Roger wrote a cheque for fifty pounds of his own money and sent it in Smither's name to the Rescue Home.

Coming down from the top room at Asprey's that same afternoon, and intending not to miss a stroll across the pale green carpet to that establishment's antique jewellery department before leaving by the Albermarle Street door, Celia and Cecily Cardigan were met by an apparition. Surely—? Why yes! —it was! Over there, leaning gracefully against a counter in the very department they were heading for. None other than Señor Barrantes himself, not seen by either of them since that first brief introduction in Green Street, now over a week ago. What luck! And they had just enough time to go over to him and reintroduce themselves without being late for tea at Grandmama's. What a wonderful piece of luck!

Leaving Asprey's by the revolving door into Bond Street, Alexander Barrantes stood on the well-swept pavement and toyed with the idea of calling in at Mrs Winifred Dartie's house before returning to his hotel. Several heads turned as they passed him by, but the Argentinian, who knew better than anyone the power of his own appeal, paid them no attention. When at last he turned right towards Park Lane and his hotel, instead of left towards Green Street, there was a smile on his face as inexplicable as a cat's.

It was George Forsyte – the sardonic, the droll – who back in the old eighties had coined the expression "Forsyte 'Change". It was quickly taken up as a *mot*; after all, wasn't Timothy's where the family came to trade in tale and tattle, to speculate upon the value of rumour and allegation, which could rise or fall on the turn of a whisper? George was such a jester!

Now, fifty-odd years after George's coinage, and Forsyte 'Change transferred from Uncle Timothy's on the Bayswater Road to his niece Winifred's in Green Street, it befell the lot of the grandson of George's cousin, St. John Hayman, to continue with this (largely self-appointed) charge of drollery. He had been looking to coin a *mot* of his own there for as long as he could remember.

This thin, and rather gangling scion, also named St. John, after his grandfather (his father, named Gerald, having been killed in the War before he was born, and his mother never forgiving the fact) was there now – exactly one week after his great 'Aunt' Winifred had received news of those two deaths on a single day.

Prior to that conjunction of events, St. John had believed that Fleur's mysterious Argentinian – whom he had not yet managed actually to *meet* – was set to scoop the headlines on the *Forsyter Arbendblat*, as it were, for some time to come. Not so now; Barrantes had this last week been relegated to page two. This caused St. John some real difficulties. He had lost his best subject for witticisms in many a month – the best, in fact, since the cast had been taken off great Aunt Winifred's big toe after her last fall – and he was feeling the want of it. It was dashed difficult to find the fun in a funeral, particularly a funeral one hadn't been obliged to attend. It was also, he reflected, dashed difficult to feel sorry for a chap you'd never met; but, yes, he supposed he was. Awful bad luck, for a fellow to lose his wife like that. Shouldn't happen to a dog. She had been an American, St. John had heard – for St. John, by one means or another, tried to hear everything. And this was rum, too, how the unseen cousin had acquired an American wife, when no Forsyte to his knowledge had ever sought a spouse outside of London (and *hardly* ever outside Mayfair). The fellow was going off to America himself, they said – shame they'd never meet now. Hmm, it was *all* rum, St. John concluded; how such a stir had arisen from the death of one whom by all available reports none of the regulars on Forsyte 'Change except the Aged Aunt had ever met.

But this item of news, as it was hashed and re-hashed over the week, had unexpectedly opened up for St. John new avenues of scope. It had led his Great Aunt to let slip one or two previously withheld details of the great 'family feud' – and that *was* fun! Not yet was it a new font for his humour, but definitely it promised. The generations above his own, the 'oldies' (an expression which actually originated with him, but not one he could use creditably on the 'Change), they were fearfully close about that old business. However, St. John meant to find out more, and get to the bottom of the *casus belli*. It had to do with Cousin Fleur, and also with old Uncle Soames, *R.I.P.*, that much he knew – and it involved an almighty row between them and this cousin's side of the family. Hum! – here was meat! Years ago, after hearing a whisper about 'grand passion', he had once asked the Great Aunt, straight out, what it was all about. He saw his mistake immediately when she became, as he put it, 'all *bouche pressée*' over the subject.

St. John had acquired his own peculiar kind of bluff subtlety since then – there were more ways than one of skinning that particular rabbit!

From this example, the diligent student of Forsyteism will be able to derive a reliable template for the working of Forsyte 'Change, and may begin to see why, in its contradictory way, it was such an unstoppable mechanism. For on one hand it was believed that there was a definite advantage of collective security concerning certain secrets which lay stored, as it were, in the vaults of family memory.

But, on the other, the chief result of this squirrelling away of old events, year after year, decade upon decade, was that even at the most modest rates, compound interest had necessarily to accrue. It was, in fact, a living demonstration of the possibility of perpetual motion.

Now St. John's rather high-bridged nose was a-quiver at the unmistakable scent of scandal buried deep in the memory of the generations above his own. It was treasure-trove he meant to unearth at the first decent opportunity. The present was not the time however, as his Great Aunt, the most likely source of further information, was not in the room. She was in bed with her foot, Miller had told him when he arrived for tea (did this augur the return of the cast?) but would Mr St. John stay in any case, as the macaroons were ready. St. John said he would, and did. Until that great archaeological find – the remains of the family feud – he would content himself with steering a return to the story of the Argentinian visitor, which he felt sure he could wangle given half a decent chance.

To this end, 'Gwendolen' and Cecily, as he guessed they might, gave him his first firm opening in a week. Tea was very nearly finished and he was just debating whether to 'light up' or tackle the penultimate macaroon when the girls swept into Winifred's drawing-room. St. John sprang up from the giltwood piano stool, his cup held jauntily aloft, to receive their air-blown kisses.

Celia sat down on the edge of one of a pair of marqueterie chairs and helped herself to the cake which until that moment had seemed to have St. John's name on it, and passed its last neighbour on the plate over to Cecily.

"Fresh tea please, Miller," she said.

St. John hid his disappointment over the macaroon with great gallantry. He had barely seated himself again, and found a cigarette, when Cecily said archly:

"Guess who *we've* been talking to in *Bond* Street?"

"Yes, do guess, St. John," said Celia, her hand carefully covering a mouthful of desiccated cocoanut. "You never will."

"Ah! — what mystery have we here?"

St. John put his cigarette to his lips and with his free left hand reached under the piano lid behind him and tickled a high, suspenseful trill from the keys. This made the girls laugh; as always, Cecily laughed more openly than Celia. St. John drained and replaced his tea-cup before adding:

"Tell me, then, before I die from suspense – who?"

"Guess!"

"By the glaze in your eye, dear heart, I should say it was Ronald Colman. Is he shorter in person? One does hope. Tell me I'm right."

"You're stone cold, St. John – guess again!"

"No – be fair, Cessy," Celia said. To St. John she added, "Actually, you're quite warm."

"Oh, Celia—"

Cecily gave her older friend a pout she had retained from the nursery, which said she was spoiling her trick. Celia replied to the look.

"*You* were the one who said he looked like a matinée idol."

The pout was replaced by a rather too winsome blush.

"Oh-ho!"

St. John scented big game, and puffed eagerly. It was true he had not met the Argentinian, but since his every detail had been repeatedly relayed by the two Cardigan girls, St. John was sure to a safe bet that he had *seen* him – outside Albany, walking with Fleur, and she looking as if they had just had 'words'.

"You don't by any chance mean Cousin Fleur's South American friend, do you?"

"We do!"

"Umm?" St. John said appreciatively. "Bond Street, you said?"

"In Asprey's."

"Buying pearls!" Between them they recounted their tale.

Umm, St. John thought again. That was a jolly little tid-bit. Was there a love interest for the Argentinian? That would be worth sniffing out. His acrobatic mind soon began juggling the pieces.

Cecily sighed.

"What I wouldn't give for pearls like those—"

"What you *wouldn't* give would be exactly what was required, I should think."

"Oh, Celia – that's dreadful of you!"

"Really, Cessy dear, you're such a child."

And you, Celia dear, are getting to be quite a cat, St. John thought. *Ummm.* He juggled another thought: Cousin Fleur was still quite a looker, wasn't she? – and not exactly *devoted* to dear old Michael.

"When was this, pray tell?" he asked, feeling there were ducks about that he needed to get into a row. He screwed out his cigarette in a small soapstone dish.

"Just now."

"And you went up to him?"

"Of course," Cecily said. "We went straight up and said 'hello'."

This would not have been St. John's first move. He would have kept surveillance going for as long as possible, and moved in only at the most awkward moment for the party watched. In the business of news-gathering he had the instincts of a professional.

"And did he look caught out?" he asked hopefully. "Red at the gills, and covered with confusion and all of it?"

"Not a bit!" said Celia. "He kissed my hand."

"Mmm! – mine too. And I said, weren't those pearls absolutely exquisite – and just *guess* what he said to that!"

St. John had had enough of guessing for the moment, and wished simply to be told. Cecily caught the lowering of his eyebrow and began with—

"He said—" when Celia, who had a small talent for mimicry interrupted.

"He said – '*Yes, they belonged to my mother*—'!"

At this St. John's eyebrow raised itself again.

"Hum!"

"We didn't believe him for a minute," Celia went on. "He was obviously buying them, and we caught him red-handed."

St. John doubted this judgement.

"How d'you know he was buying them? He might have been trading them in!"

"Oh, we *know*. We know because of what happened next."

"Well – what happened next?" St. John pressed her.

"Well – he bowed beautifully – and we left."

In reply to another fine angle of her cousin's articulate brow Cecily pleaded, "It would have been too obvious to have hung

134

around – but I did catch what he said to the assistant when he thought we were out of hearing."

"What did he say? And don't make me guess!"

"He said—" This time Cecily gave way to the superior ability of her friend.

"*I should be most grateful if you would have them wrapped and sent to my hotel.*' There!" And the two girls once again set each other off into a round of not-so-dainty laughter.

St. John liked the sound of what he heard – not the laughter, but what it had followed – he liked it enormously. You did well, young Coz, he thought. Here was another promising tale – he didn't know but he would have to investigate the business of these pearls for himself.

"I wonder what Grandmama will make of it," Cecily said.

"Oh, I shouldn't tell her, if I were you," St. John said quickly. He couldn't have these two frightening the fish away before he got to the pond himself – oh no!

"Why not?" asked Celia.

"Why—" St. John scratched around his brain for an instant reason, "—because it's her birthday soon. Who's to say the pearls weren't for her?"

It had been the least likely thing he could think to say, and the Cardigan girls were agog at the possibility. St. John pressed ahead while his iron was hot.

"No. I really think you shouldn't tell her about it—"

"Not tell whom about what?" said Winifred, who came into the drawing-room at that moment, helped along by Miller at one side and a swan-handled malacca cane at the other.

"Auntie!"

Winifred's question was temporarily buried beneath a rush of enquiries after her health in general and her foot in particular. She eased herself into her chair and St. John brought up the footstool.

"Thank you, St. John. Fresh tea, Miller. I thought there were macaroons?" Miller left. "You were saying that you weren't going to tell somebody something," Winifred said again, suspecting it was she who was not being told whatever it was.

"Yes, Auntie dear – *you*. Not tell you that I've discovered your secret!"

135

"*My* secret? Whatever is that?"

St. John regained the piano stool.

"That you've been keeping company with a tall dark stranger, that's what."

"Ah – you were talking about Señor Barrantes? I should have guessed. I hardly think he qualifies as a stranger, St. John. Fleur's mother knows him."

St. John made no reply to this: he had once heard tell about her, too.

"He's certainly tall and dark—" Celia began.

"And *so* handsome," Cecily finished. "When can we come to lunch with him, Grandmama?"

"Yes," St. John added. "You know, you mustn't keep him all to yourself, Auntie. Lunch *à deux*, and all that. People *will* start to talk."

"Oh! —St. John, you are a dreadful tease."

So he was, and not one to give up a good subject, either.

"Well, I say; it is a bit racy, after all, isn't it? You can never be too careful with these foreigners, Auntie. I should say not!"

Winifred scowled fondly at her 'nephew'. Really, he did talk such nonsense – but he was so amusing.

"He might even be after your jewels – you'd better look out."

At this expression of his own, a phrase from a song came to him. It had been all the rage a couple of years ago, and was splendidly appropriate for the present moment. He turned on the piano stool, found the pedals with his feet, and flipping open the lid began to pick out a passable Latin rhythm on the pearly keys of the little upright Grand. With his head thrown back he began to sing to his own accompaniment.

> '*Look out for your wife!*
> *Look out for your girl!*
> *Look out for that guy!*
> *Look out for his eye –*
> *Aye-aye-aye-aye-aye!*'

By now St. John had found his key. The verse came to him like a dream.

> '*He's got hair without a kink in it –*

Flashing eye and what a wink in it –
Si,si,si – that South-American Joe!'

South American Joe! Just the ticket for the Argentinian. By
George – for of course it was indeed by him – St. John believed
he might finally have coined his *mot*!

Winifred and the girls were such a responsive audience for
this spontaneous entertainment that St. John broke into a second
chorus – and in such full throat that Miller had quite to shout to
make herself heard above the music.

"Mr Roger Forsyte, ma'am!"

St. John looked towards the door and paused after *'wink in it'* –
on the very hip of the rhythm – to continue brilliantly after Roger
said:

"Don't let me stop the fun. They charge you ten-and-six for
this at the Palladium!"

After she learned of Anne Forsyte's death, Fleur had decided to give
Green Street an extra wide berth. Later, when things settled down,
she would probably find reasons to go there more often, and so keep
her ear to the ground about developments at Green Hill. Many times
she had to fight the urge to pick up the telephone and place a call to
Sussex. It ought to have been so simple, to convey her sympathy –
or even a very little more – but she knew, of course, that it was not.
No; for the moment, she was determined to show every sign of not
caring a fig. But what she was determined upon, and what fate cast
her way were, as ever, two very separate commodities.

That same day of St. John's musical inspiration – which could
not have seemed more different in the unpeopled quiet of South
Square – Fleur received a letter by the late afternoon post. She
knew the hand, and took it directly upstairs to read in her little
room at the top of the house, a room not quite a study, which
in a grander time might have been called her *boudoir*. Creature of
instinct that she was, she sought this privacy, though she was alone
in the house. She sank onto the day bed there, expectancy fighting
fear in her heart as she tore open the envelope. While the afternoon
poured high summer's honest sunlight over her shoulder, she began
to read.

'Dear Fleur,

'God knows these are not easy letters to write, but they must be written and I am beginning to find that there is a sort of comfort in doing what one must. I wanted to thank you – & please, will you thank Michael for me, too – for the flowers. It was a kindness I shan't soon forget.

'As far as forgetting goes, I don't much. Never a day has passed but I have remembered you dearly. Yesterday I spent a selfish hour secretly listing all the people who have really mattered to me in my life, and there, as ever, you were. Do you remember, when you said that Michael was the best man you knew, and I said that Anne was the best girl? Well, we were right. With all my heart I wish nothing but happiness for you and Michael in the years ahead.

'It's America for us now, as soon as everything can be arranged. Anne's brother Francis needs us, and we him. If the children like it, we might 'settle', as they say.

'God bless you, Fleur, and keep you always
       'Jon.'

America! Land of opportunities – for another! He had gone there once before, immediately after his father's death, immediately after he had first given her up. His meaning was plain. Jon was also a creature of instinct, though, unlike herself, one of conscience too, and America was his instinctive retreat. When that girl died she had thought — but thinking, like wishing, never made a thing happen. If Jon had only stayed in England – who knew what might not have been possible?

Fleur heard a sigh and discovered that it originated from within herself. It was no good — she knew — no good to have a heart. The pages of the letter slipped to the floor with a soft rustle, like the first dead leaves of summer falling onto grass. She was unaware she had let them go.

Chapter Seventeen

Willow & Ash

The London Social Calendar – to which all Forsytes are indentured from birth – contains no event more enthusiastically attended by them than the Eton and Harrow cricket match. Royal Ascot, Goodwood, the Regatta at Henley and even the Lawn Tennis Championship at Wimbledon are all guaranteed their presence in consistent numbers, but still the edge of their eagerness is unequivocally reserved for 'Lord's'. And here now they all were assembled, on a mid-July day of cloudless perfection, to look at each other, and to sniff.

Unlike the other sporting fixtures of the Season, this was not and never had been a top-class event as far as the standards of the game were concerned. It was also the only really significant social event quite unattended by royalty. But then the cricket was the least of it, and this was without doubt the one gathering whose importance for the Forsyte not even royal patronage could enhance.

Why were Forsytes so devoted to it? Few had actually been to either school, only a few more had children there, leaving most unable to claim any relative who had been – ever. But the prescriptive right to attend at Lord's was derived from sources more intense and powerful than old school loyalties, more driving than any shallow preference for keeping company with members of the Royal Household. It did not even depend on an understanding of the game. No — Forsytes were there because this event was wholly of themselves; all on the ground and all in the stands were of themselves; and if there was a royal absence here today it was registered by the crowd in a carefully oblique satisfaction, which amongst lesser folk might have been identified as distinct smugness.

Let racing be the Sport of Kings, for cricket was the Sport of Forsytes!

E-ton! Har-row! Put your back into it! You're supposed to be batting, man — not digging a trench —! The customary barracking issued from the free seats in Block G at the Nursery end, and the whole crowd was in fine feather.

The two schools exemplified all that the Forsytean way of life implicitly embraced. Winchester, Stowe, Marlborough, Rugby and their fellows – it scarcely mattered which – those private centres of post-preparatory education (by some twist of the language called Public Schools when they could hardly be less so) were the hot-houses of Forsyteism in all its various flowering and non-flowering strains. In them were all the essential characteristics of the species induced. Fortitude, self-reliance, propriety of conduct, moral and behavioural standards and, above all these things, the very *tradition* of these things itself, and the security it ensured.

Tradition! Security! With one exception, there were no more sacred words in the whole Forsyte canon.

So here they all were. The pride of the English Establishment, lay and religious, civil and military, peers and commons, most still with their silk hats – grey, for the Season – many with their wives and children, and under a sky of cloudless blue every one of them looking brighter and sleeker and glossier than ever.

E-e-e-ton! Har-r-o-o-o-w!

The attendance that day was already being estimated in the early editions of the evening papers at ten thousand, a capacity crowd. Seasoned visitors might have admitted an extra gaiety in the crowd, a deliberate brightness, a topped-up measure of high spirits. It was as though by some mass intuition those gathered at the ground in St. John's Wood that day knew this to be the last show of its kind – for a while at least, and perhaps forever. Beneath the encircling blue stillness of the sky the crowd seemed caught under glass, like specimens in a bell-jar, unaware of their artificial preservation. The more their noise grew, the more it became indistinct, as a great murmur in a vacuum.

By one o'clock Winifred's party, like so many others, had picked itself up from the Grandstand and was heading for the Nursery

Grounds with a single objective raising the atavistic instinct of the pack – *lunch!* It was a shame, Winifred thought to herself, that Michael had felt he couldn't get away – the outing would have been a fillip for him. Still, they would have been an odd number with Señor Barrantes' coming along – and he certainly looked the part, quite dashing in his nice grey hat!

Winifred's club was the Bedouin, which she had joined at its inception after the War because its name intrigued her. Not that it summoned for her as it did for some members images of duney landscapes and Nilotic dawns, for Winifred was resolutely un-travelled; but she was convinced that any club so named would go far and it was best to join early while one could.

Between his contempt for the familiar tales of his elderly cousin and his impatience to see the game continue – it looked as if the right team was going to win at last this year – Kit's restive disposition put him in the lead as the party headed towards the Club tent. Perhaps if he watched for his moment he might be able to slip away from the rest of them after lunch and wander off alone for a spell. He had it in mind to make for the dressing-rooms and have a few words with the two of the team who were in his House. He hoped to be bowling himself next year, so they were bound to let him inside. Turning in at the grassy stretch which separated their tent from its neighbour, he saw a small figure leaning in an odd, huddled way against a fold in the canvas between two guy ropes. Hearing someone approach, the figure turned and Kit recog-nised him instantly as the boy in the Park – not because his appear-ance was so remarkable, since it was not, but because Kit's immediate verdict on his character then was so utterly confirmed by the smeary features before him now. What a spectacular sap this boy must be – he was crying! Only girls and babies cried in public! What on earth did he think he was about? Kit himself had not cried – in public or in private – since his seventh birthday. The sight now of these very real tears induced a sudden feral triumph which warmed his blood, though he would not for his life have been able to say why this particular boy's misery was so pleasing to him.

The little scene which followed was over in less than thirty seconds. Kit heard footsteps running up behind him, and this again was reminiscent of the Park. Kit turned and there was the girl, the boy's sister who had fed the birds and his own dog – but how changed she was! Her colour, her eyes – she looked as if all the sun had been drained out of her. She almost ran into Kit before she saw him.

"Oh!"

She stopped half a pace beyond him. Her dark eyes stared at him without sign of recognition.

"Hello," Kit said, knowing that whatever the details of the situation were they made this greeting senseless.

The girl's expression shifted momentarily, as a well-rehearsed effigy of a smile passed over her face.

"Oh—yes—from the Park—"

She was cut off by a voice calling her from a few yards behind them both. Kit and she and the boy all turned in a crooked line.

Kit saw a tallish man with fair hair and so much the same expression as the girl that he must be her father.

"It's all right, Dad," she said, sounding now suddenly grown-up, "Jonnie's here."

As soon as the man saw his son he ran to him, passing Kit without a glance. The girl followed, and the solemn little trio moved off together towards the main gate. On this occasion, though curiosity made him look, Kit knew there would be no farewell wave.

Fleur was only a few paces behind Kit, and behind her and to the side walked Barrantes with Jack Cardigan who was telling his 'best-ever' cricketing story, the latest in a generous line of statistics and anecdotes with which he had been subduing the Argentinian's ear since the start of play. She could hear Jack's reedy voice – what a terrible dullard he was, and how beautifully the foreigner bore him! She looked over her shoulder and Barrantes' dark eyes were already there to meet her own. He never missed a trick! Jack didn't notice, and she smiled non-committally and made a show of looking round them to see if Imogen and Winifred were in the rear. There they were, close in some serious conversation, comparing the cost of their dresses for the Season probably. Turning back Fleur quickened her step when she saw that Kit had not waited at the corner – she would remind him of his manners.

As she turned on the path, she saw not Kit but a figure that made her heart lurch in her breast — Jon! The face not seen for thirteen years, except in dreams, but his face as she herself had never seen it – gaunt, harrowed, sick with worry. To see him again under any circumstances would have been a shock, but this sighting had twice the effect on her, for she had expected him to be already in America. His letter had given no date for his going, and Fleur had assumed he meant to leave immediately. Seeing him standing there, she was assailed by a sudden wave of longing, a tide of forgotten feeling which swept over her and drenched her with a yearning to go to him, to be at his side, to soothe, to help. There he was, dear Jon, hurt and in need – of her!

Scanning the field with his deep-set, worried eyes there was a moment when Jon looked right at her, and Fleur felt an exquisite stab of pain as she realised in that same moment that he did not see her. It was not herself for whom he looked, so anxious, expectant, with such urgency and concern in his eyes. This simple detail impacted itself upon her the length of her body, and took the wind out of her senses. Years of allowing the world to see only what she wanted it to see in her face fell away in a second . . . She heard him call "Anne!", the name of his wife, that girl who had died, but Fleur was beyond hearing. She could only see and feel – Jon, and a pained and dreadful darkness which seemed to well up from her core . . .

Fleur was aware of an arm under hers, holding her firmly and supporting much of her weight. It was the Argentinian, of course. She had been on the brink of a cold faint, and he had caught her and pulled her back. And as Fleur turned her face to him those dark eyes were waiting for her – passive, absorbent, all-seeing. She looked away and took a deep breath of air which felt like the first in a long while. She glanced swiftly about her. No Jon in sight. An empty world again. Barrantes' grip relaxed though he still took her weight. What had he seen – Jon? or only her own reaction to him? She knew that he had seen how she must have looked in that moment. Had he read her feelings? By his very touch she knew he had – damn him for his perspicacity! Another swift survey told Fleur that no one else shared this understanding. Kit had gone on ahead, and Jack's attention had been claimed by his wife and mother-in-law. By whatever chance they had clearly witnessed nothing. Only Barrantes' stolid silence at her side remained to unnerve her. Why didn't he speak? It was as if he knew it all. Still with his arm under her own, and with no word passing between them, Fleur allowed the Argentinian to take her inside the tent.

At the table, as the women were finding their seats, Jack Cardigan – who, lest it be forgotten, had once bowled for Harrow – was reaching the end of his last fable.

"—So you see," Jack snorted, "the batsman didn't stand a chance – because the last ball turned out to be a *googly*!"

Barrantes, who had listened throughout with what seemed to Jack to be sincere attention, said,

"I *see*!"

He continued to look sincere as he held Winifred's chair for her and then added thoughtfully:

"And what, if I may ask, *is* a googly?"

The question was so exactly timed and weighted, and contained just the right hint of apology for extending the licence to use Jack as the butt of family humour to himself, that even Jack had to laugh – if only to demonstrate his own good sportsmanship. Fleur smiled compliantly, but felt Barrantes was covering for her, allowing her time to be certain of her composure. Learned in the hard school, her self-possession was usually as reliable as her wardrobe, faultless on every occasion – but this time it had taken a bad knock. She was at once grateful to the Argentinian and yet more wary than ever of his unerring perception of her needs.

"Yes, Jack," said Winifred as the laughter died away, preparing her face with a frown of concentration, "what *is* a googly? I know you must have told me before—"

"And he will again, Mother," Imogen said, settling her *embonpoint* on the chair which Kit, idly following Barrantes' lead, now held for her.

"Ah! A googly!" cried Jack blithely. "It's really very simple, but that's the genius of it. It's an *off*-break bowled with a *leg*-break action!"

Succinct as a line from Tacitus, Jack's description was tailored to leave space for an explanatory mime, which he provided directly in

144

elaborate slow-motion.

"Do you see?"

"Yes, dear," said Winifred. "I'm sure we do." She patted the seat of his chair. "Señor Barrantes' head will be spinning with it all." And afterwards she muttered, "I'm not certain mine isn't."

Jack sat down.

The Argentinian was the last to seat himself. As he attended to the arrangement of his coat-tails, he said:

"Not in the least. I am grateful for such a patient explanation of the game. Particularly the last detail about the concealed delivery—" He looked up and swept the completed table with his elegantly ingenuous gaze, ending with Fleur who sat opposite him "—that was most useful."

If Fleur had been burdened with less placid female relations than Winifred and her daughter, the silent but palpable communication which passed between the Argentinian and herself at this point could not have arrived without interception. As it was, it seemed to her that Barrantes was toying with their impregnable dullness, and was deliberately risking their observation of him as a bored cat might watch mice at play. Moreover it seemed that, with the arch of his fine brow, he was inviting her to join him in his sport. Fleur's own brow flexed at his daring. He should be careful not to toy with her sensibilities in the same way – the distinguishing line was a fine one!

Sitting uncommunicatively as the others chattered around him, Kit gave up wondering why the boy had been crying, and what it had all been about, and shifted his guesswork to the contents of the first course which had not yet arrived. He hoped it was not fish.

Had he been without the concrete excuse of an arm's length of papers to read, Michael would not have felt himself above the expediency of fabricating one. He knew that Kit resented his begging off at the last minute and quite rightly too, for Michael was always the first to see another's side of things. And Fleur – that little flat look in her eye again told him everything he needed to know about her feelings. But for all his genuine companionability Michael was first the obedient slave of his principles, and to spend time – even if he had it – at such frivolous social pastimes in these worried days seemed to him perilously near to taking up the fiddle while Rome burned.

With his wife's parting words still in his ears – the courteous but brittle advice that he would have to take himself out for lunch as she had given the servants the day off – Michael made his way up to his study. He took off his jacket, dropped it over the back of his chair and sat down with the first report open before him.

So far – so good, but concentration proved a wingèd beast for Michael and for the first hour did little more than ruffle the pages in front of him with its feathers. The White Monkey met his eye more than once and seemed to know he had no heart for it. He stuck at his appointed task and not with any great faith in his own efficiency, but gradually the papers and files changed from a tall pile on the left of his desk to two piles of moderate height, one on each side. Sensing modest achievement, Michael declared 'all out' for a late lunch and went down to the kitchen with the rough plan of a sandwich forming in his head. After discovering pigeon pie and an opened bottle of claret at the front of the larder, Michael soon parted faith with that nobleman's celebrated invention. He made up a small tray and carried his pilferings upstairs.

Dreamy and contented after his pigeon pie, Michael took a stroll out in the sunshine. Finding after a while he had wandered to the Embankment, he sat down on a bench facing the river. How readily worries were pacified by a full stomach! Eyes screwed tight closed he turned his face up to the sky, where the sun shone gloriously. The heat on his skin almost made him shiver. Then, as he somehow knew would happen, a figure approached from his left. Like Diogenes, Michael wished the fellow would stand a little less between him and the sun for a cold shadow fell across him. He opened his eyes and the shiver seized his whole body. It was Wilfrid! As true as day – Wilfrid! Older, drawn, deathly tired, down and out. *You too, old man?!* Michael wanted to say, stupidly, but astonishment had frozen his tongue. How was it possible? Wilfrid had drowned in the East years before. Michael tried frantically to remember if they had ever found the body, or had the authorities only deduced the accident? He couldn't recall the details, but they had made certain, surely?

And now Wilfrid was trying to tell him something and Michael was desperate to listen, but some idiot had chosen just that minute to test the air-raid warning sirens. He would lodge a formal complaint in the House! Wilfrid! — dear God, man, don't go—!

Michael awoke suddenly, with a ringing in his ears.

Chapter Eighteen

'Hair and Spirit'

A distant bell had roused Michael from his reverie. It rang for some time before he realised it belonged to his own front door, and had to continue ringing until he recalled that he was the only person in the house to answer it. At first he felt inclined to ignore the demand. Vivid images from his dream were still floating through his mind, beckoning, as if there were things they had yet to tell him. As though interpreting his wishes the bell stopped, and after a moment Michael set another file on his blotter, but found his concentration was not improved, Wilfrid's spectral face seeming to weave about in the space before him. He had just understood the file's title page when the bell resumed its peal. Conceding only a polite urgency, Michael took his jacket from the back of his chair and went downstairs.

Smoothing his collar as he opened the door, he found himself confronted by the slight but upright figure of an elderly lady. She was dressed in an oddly fashioned frock-coat and clasped a great shapeless hand-bag in front of her. She pointed her decided chin at him and smiled confidently, a combination of gestures which made her hat – clearly a matching piece for the bag – teeter precariously. She gave it no attention. Her eyes, screwed into a fierce squint, were fixed on Michael.

His first thought was that she must be a charity-worker making speculative house calls and he was about to reach into his pocket when the little *ancienne* used his name.

"Hello, Michael."

Her smile wavered only slightly as Michael, stumped for the appropriate response, kept his grip on the door and waited for understanding to dawn.

It was then that he remembered the chin.

"Good Lord! Cousin June?"

Since Michael found himself temporarily rooted to the spot, his aged cousin-by-marriage was forced to ask if it was convenient for her to come in. Michael nodded dumbly and stood aside; June entered the hallway like a sudden draught in the still afternoon.

"I didn't telephone first. I never do."

"It's quite a surprise—" Michael managed at last, hoping his tone was even. He was truly confounded by this sudden and actual apparition from the past treading so closely on the heels of the one in his dream – for the moment, neither seemed the more or the less probable, "—after all these years."

"Yes. I expect it is." Her smile was perplexingly confident. "No, thank you, I'll keep my coat." Michael had made the only other gesture he could think of, after closing the street door behind him. "I find I feel the cold these days."

He opened the doors to the drawing-room and again she passed him like a little gusting breeze. Her hair, which Michael remembered as a fiery red with random streaks of white, was now only the palest remembrance of orange. It was pinned up in a haphazard arrangement under her hat, causing this item to tremble with each decisive little step. 'All hair and spirit', James Forsyte, Fleur's grandfather, had once called her, and had not meant it as a compliment. Now it seemed that those features, correctly identified as her strongest, were all that survived, all others having been worn away in that long unequal contest with the elements which had been her life. For Michael, not insensible to these suggestions, the image she conjured was that of a storm lantern guttering valiantly on its last inch of wick.

"Fleur's not in, I'm afraid. She's at the Eton and Harrow match with our son."

"I know."

Michael blinked.

June continued: "My father would never miss it, especially when my young brother was alive."

Ever the charity scholar in such matters – recent revelations at Highgate notwithstanding – this last reference left Michael frankly baffled. Surely Jon was her brother? June seemed to expect his

149

confusion and sense it without looking at him. Her eyes were occupied in earnest scrutiny of the Piet Mondrian over the mantel.

"Holly's brother; he died in the Boer War," she said matter-of-factly, and then in the same tone, "Holly told me Fleur would be going to the match."

Michael understood from the jumble of family connections that among them anything could be found out by any member who was so motivated. Now, he wondered – what could be the motivation of this grizzled firebrand? She had squared herself in front of the painting and might well have been challenging the piece to defend its own æsthetic.

"And anyway, it's you I've come to see. That's good—" her chin indicated the Mondrian. The expanding geometric shapes of the painter's vision seemed to Michael more desperately in search of the edges of the canvas after this pronouncement. "I see Fleur is as modern as ever. One wouldn't expect her to change – except with the times."

Something in his visitor's tone made Michael suspect further characterisation of his wife's nature was on its way. He frowned quizzically in anticipation, but none came. June seemed to have finished with that line of comment. Because he could think of nothing to say himself, he offered her tea – he had heard a noise just before shutting the double doors and now realised it had been the maid returning. June accepted, and took her chin on a tour of the drawing-room while Michael rang the bell for Timms, who appeared briskly, bobbing a curtsey to the back of the unknown elder, and left with her master's instructions.

Michael found himself taking up a position by the hearth, and this made him feel he was somehow standing guard. Of their own values, perhaps? Protecting the *lares et penates* of South Square from the swooping visitation of this unlikely little avenging angel? It was his dream still, making him fanciful! June completed her inspection, and returned to the de Stijlist; her fierce blue eyes were aimed directly above Michael's head.

"That *is* good. His work is so fearless, though, of course, he's not right at the edge anymore."

Michael recalled the 'Neo-Formalist' he had seen at her gallery,

150

and wondered whether to be already over the precipice was any better.

The tray of tea was brought in and June, perching weightlessly on the edge of the sofa cushion, busied herself over it with the proprietorial assurance that was native to all her line.

The frown removed itself but the accompanying quizzical expression endured in Michael's faunish features, on his brow and on the tips of his ears. He stroked his moustache and watched June pouring tea. The more he stared at her, trying to pierce the web of lines which veiled her face, the more this aged sprite seemed fundamentally just as Michael now began to remember her. He recalled exactly this air of determination about her from their previous meetings, which had always been uncomfortable though thankfully few. In Michael's mind the image of the lantern gave way to that of a small terrier attaching itself remorselessly to his trouser leg, and a smile wandered over his face. He baulked it by giving undue care to receiving the tea-cup she offered up to him.

"Thanks. I saw your New Formalist's show the other day. I imagine he's pretty much in the front line."

"Indeed he is!" June's voice rose tellingly in triumph. Of all her innumerable lame ducks – as her grandfather had originally dubbed the artists she sponsored – Suslov had required the greatest investment of her belief to date. "What did you think of his work?"

Michael heard the ring of pride commingled with challenge in the question. Considering what indeed it was he did think, and how he might best express it to the artist's own patron, he made the mistake of drawing breath before answering. June was at his heels almost before he spoke.

"I thought he was rather—"

"Please don't say *interesting*! It's always what people say when they don't like a thing but think they should."

"I was going to say 'fatalistic', actually."

"Ah!"

"Except—"

"Yes?"

She *was* a terrier!

"Well, somehow there's too much energy in him to convince one he's resigned to it all."

For once June tucked in her chin.

"Forgive me. I'd forgotten you're the one who has feeling. But you're not a Forsyte, of course, so why shouldn't you have?"

The old lady sipped her tea and looked pleased with herself.

"He paints in a trance, you know," she continued. "It's his route to the unconscious mind. Oh, he's absolutely right – it's the only way. He's challenging people *really* to see the truth, in all its unadorned simplicity. That's why he called his masterpiece *The Final Analysis*." She added almost gaily, "He's a genius!"

History had not kept an exact tally of how many of June's lame ducks had laboured under this title, but their names were legion. Suslov was merely the latest and therefore to June automatically the brightest star in the infinite firmament of her belief.

Michael feared they might be heading towards a detailed appraisal of the Russian's unique talent, and attempted a change of gear.

"I'm afraid my son said it looked like a diagram of an atom," he offered, and there was an impish light in his eye, but June didn't see it, and simply over-rode him in her bulldozer manner.

"Exactly! The elemental truth! There's no discovery in science that art hasn't expressed first." But then she looked queerly at Michael. "Your son is shrewd. Perhaps you have another connoisseur in your family."

That this was Michael's own suspicion was more than wild horses could have driven him to confess. Visitor and host took the next moment to sip their tea.

Mention of the unconscious made Michael think again of Wilfrid.

"I used to have a friend – a poet – who would have taken up the challenge of your painter. He was a great champion of the cutting edge of truth. I think he believed that's all there was."

"Ah! — a true poet. Did you fall out?"

Michael first took this for an astounding piece of intuition. Then he realised June had only picked up his use of the past tense.

"He drowned – in a river in the Far East. He believed he was following his destiny, living by his truth. Of course, he died by it too."

"I'm sorry."

Then the old lady raised her chin with a quiver of a different kind of pride, her eyes fixed on a point somewhere in her memory.

"A thousand years before you were born, I knew a brilliant young architect who believed that beauty was a truth worth dying for."

"And did he follow his destiny?"

She barely spoke the word.

"Yes."

June looked again at Michael after a moment, her expression greatly softened, and he was moved to respond with a smile of ordinary sympathy, though he did not know for what.

"Well – I didn't come here to discuss my exhibition, though it's been very—"

"Interesting?"

The little lady approached a smile of her own. It was more a re-arrangement of musculature than anything arising from within, but it served its purpose.

"I like you, Michael. I did from the start, and could have wished your path had been easier. Your gift is for comedy and goodness knows there's been too little of that in our family."

Michael was suddenly mindful of the notice in the newspaper. He studied his tea and removed a microscopic piece of leaf with his spoon.

"You heard about my brother's wife?" June asked him.

He looked up, solemn-faced.

"Yes. I'm very sorry."

The old lady held his eyes with hers until he added,

"We both are."

"Thank you," she managed to say, and then her rage overcame her. "Oh, it was all such a dreadful waste! She was barely thirty, still a child—!" June's gaze flew around the room, as if seeking refuge from its own fury. "It — it was just a pointless riding accident."

"Ah," Michael said softly and nodded. What had stopped him from saying 'I know'?

"It's frightening—" June admitted quietly, her outburst spent; a little shudder rose from her core, "—our father's first wife, my mother that is . . . well, perhaps you don't know, but she died in the same way. It's a horrid notion to think one's fate may be predestined."

Michael nodded again and fell to scrutinising the hearth. Then in a flash of comprehension he understood why she was there. He knew now without a doubt what was the purpose of this seemingly capricious visit. The certainty of it set his features into an uncharacteristically grim mask. He braced himself for the inevitable attack on the flank he had so generously exposed to her advance.

"'*Omnipotens fortuna et ineluctabile fatum*'," he found himself saying aloud, as if to fill the boding space between them.

Looking up, he discovered with a jolt that June's burning eyes were already upon him, and saw that she was even now trying her best to judge the right moment. He knew her to be famously unequal to the task.

"Virgil," he continued passively. "My son's Latin prep." Here Michael's smile made a noble last stand. "Æneas laments his inescapable fate."

There was a further interminable moment's silence. He waited patiently.

"Are you and Fleur still happy?"

There it was!

"I believe so," he said.

Despite his determination not to be provoked Michael's tone was clipped, almost harsh. He added:

"I know I am."

"Oh, don't be defensive, please," June cried. Hastily she replaced her tea-cup on the tray where it made a small clatter of silver and bone china.

"I don't mean to be hurtful, my dear. I only want to stop anyone from being hurt again. My little brother is so—" now they were unoccupied her hands fluttered about each other like birds in a snare, "—so vulnerable now. I only wanted to say that Fleur mustn't—"

"Mustn't what!" Michael momentarily lost all guard of his voice.

"Interfere. Or help. It would be the same thing, don't you see?"

Michael was speechless. The better part of him wanted to put this intolerable bluntness of June's down to her age, but another part remembered that she was known for never having been any different. What had his father-in-law called her so many years before? A hornet? A gad-fly? Certainly she vexed his patience now,

154

like some persistent insect about his ears, all the more irritating for buzzing closest to his own edgy misgivings. Only consideration of her age checked Michael's next remark. He had been about to ask that she mind her own business, though evidently she thought this was what she was already doing. Instead, he provided her with a brief statement of events.

"When we heard we sent a wreath. It was from both of us. If you must know, Fleur was worried even about that – she was wary of having her sympathy misconstrued. Plainly she had every reason to be cautious."

June gathered up her great purse and stood.

"I'm sorry. I didn't mean to upset you, and you're right to defend Fleur. She's your wife, after all."

This was hardly the retraction Michael could have wished for at that moment, but her plaintive tone undid his intention to say something further.

"I'll go now. Don't mind me – only I have to say what I think!"

The old lady raised her face a final time and Michael saw that her eyes were shining fiercely with tears she forbade to fall. She turned and moved stiffly to the drawing-room doors. Michael moved to follow but she checked him with a small gesture of her hand.

"You needn't see me out."

She paused holding the door, and for the first time during this strange visit June spoke to Michael with her face turned deliberately from him.

"I believe you discovered your destiny a long while ago, Michael. I only hope Fleur has found hers."

She slipped from the room, with an agility born of her spirit not of her years. Michael heard the street door open swiftly and close.

"June?"

When Michael told Fleur of the visit that night, he saw her chin snap at the name. She looked up from idly buffing her nails as she sat at her dressing-table, but not to look at her husband. The name was rather tossed back to him over her shoulder, a thing unwanted.

"What did *she* want?"

155

It was axiomatic among Forsytes – even of Fleur's generation – that people did not go anywhere without wanting something for their trouble.

Michael told a good lie.

"To thank us for the wreath."

Fleur said nothing. She already possessed the only thanks she wanted.

"And to see how we were, I think," he added.

"Hnn."

This quick little noise was about the most disturbing Michael could have heard. It sounded dangerously like the echo of an old bitterness and what she next said confirmed his unease.

"And how are we, Michael?"

Fleur was surprised by her own recklessness, but the taste of something sour remained on her palate from the afternoon. She was aware she was looking for something to spoil.

At her question, Michael hung his head and stared at the carpet, a quite spontaneous gesture for he knew she didn't see him in her glass.

"That's always been for you to say, Fleur. You know that."

He moved to the bed and sat on its edge, still studying the carpet, forearms on knees, until the colour of the weave began to throb before his eyes and he had to switch his attention to an invisible place in the palm of one hand. Fleur continued with the nail buffer for a little while, and then replaced it on her table. Did she really want to hurt Michael? – any more, that is, than she was already considering? For a moment she had no answer. Touching the corner of one side-mirror she moved it on its hinges until she could see the bed. Here was her answer, if she wanted to acknowledge it. There was a doleful appeal about him, though her husband's fairmindedness was such that he intended none. He looked like a dog waiting to be whipped, actually like one expecting nothing else and wanting it over. Had she so accustomed him to it? Moved by an impulse she knew was not guilt and hoped was not pity, she went over to him. Kneeling on the carpet between his legs, she pressed her cheek into his shoulder, her face away from his. He didn't hold her at first, but when she put her arms around his waist he relented. His touch was light, fastidious – resolutely non-proprietorial.

"You're the best man I know. I've always believed that."

"But for you?"

Her pause was only momentary, while she cleared her mind of a useless vision.

"Of course."

She felt the hot exhalation of held-back breath in her hair, heard the short, barely voiced gasp of relief which escaped with it, and allowed her husband to hold her closer than in a long while.

Lying with her head on Michael's shoulder as he slept beside her, Fleur wondered, only for a passing moment but for the latest of times countless as the stars, why it was that this man in her bed, whom she could not fault, had never yet been able to supplant the one in her heart she might never have.

Part Two

Chapter One

Drifting

The summer wore on, usually fine, sometimes cool, and as if it had been any other year Forsytes all over England were set on making the most of it. In London the Royal Parks were full of them, at the shadier, fashionable hour. Later, in the evenings, theatres with the hottest seats in town, and restaurants with the coolest saw their patronage continue, and even increase. Later still, night clubs entertained until dawn, packed to the rafters with clients who had discovered that the best way to banish fear for the future was to live today as if there might be no tomorrow. And when not in London, those Forsytes prudent enough to have made alliances with the landed classes above them, or who owned land themselves (very few, since they had always considered property outside the Capital a dangerous investment), spent their time seeking diversion in houses large enough to billet whole streets in the East End, without considering themselves at all privileged to do so. After all, the drive down was *so* tiring!

But what of the 'possessive instinct', that tell-tale appendage by which all Forsytes are identified? What had become of it? Should it not have roused them to the barricades, as it were, to man the defences of their nation, surely any citizen's greatest possession, against an horizon that was dark and threatening storm? Not a bit of it! Their instincts, possessive or otherwise, were intact. Why, for what purpose, by way of income tax and other excesses of the Exchequer, did they keep a government, if not for the express one of sorting out such foreign business? *And* an army, older Forsytes would add here – remembering the Boer War and possibly the Sudan – eating its head off! No – let every man stick to his business. That was the way!

With more than a touch of that old quality – which had earned their forebears the right to the (purchased) family motto, 'For Forsite' – they saw no sense whatever in barking themselves while they kept dogs, and even less in poking their heads over the parapets of the social stockade while others were paid to risk theirs first!

In the words of the novelist and visionary, to the question 'Whither Forsytes?', the answer amounted practically to this:

'—Drifting with the rest of Mankind, towards Catastrophe.'

After her 'near miss' at the cricket ground, Fleur removed to Lippinghall with her daughter and the nurse. Kit was to follow at the end of term, and Michael would join them directly the House rose, which was likely to be in early August. Fleur was appalled by a detail which greeted her upon arrival. Michael's mother, once deciding to circumvent local bureaucracy by the time-honoured expedient of ignoring it, had by unknown means procured a family of five from Shoreditch to fill the gardener's cottage by the back meadow. Fleur instantly proscribed the area to the eleventh baronet and, in particular, to his sister – even though the family in question were not due to arrive for three days. Her injunction met with proportionate resistance; five persons born within the sound of Bow Bells held an infinite intrigue for one raised within the sound of the Division – and perhaps the reverse applied also, had anyone troubled to ask. It was no matter either way, as Fleur was deaf to protests from the ranks, and in this had an able lieutenant in Finty, whose wrath toward the lower orders of microbes – known to thrive and for the most part originate in the East End – knew no bounds or quarter.

"Don't you think they *might* be?"

Kit ignored the question. He sat with his back against the crook of an old willow, whose trunk stretched out like a twisting Tantalos across the gravel-bed of the stream, and wished his sister into another county. The day was warm and hazy, and he did not feel like an argument.

"Buy *why* can't they be?" she persisted. "*I* think they are – I'm sure of it."

"Oh, don't talk such rot, Katty."

Kat ignored the answer. Sitting cross-legged on higher ground above the willow, she wiped a strand of coppery hair from before her eyes, and under the shade of her hand looked across the water. She watched the cows idly grazing on the far bank, the forbidden back meadow, and tried not to look as if she was craning for a glimpse of the occupants of the gardener's cottage beyond.

There were four children and their mother. This she knew, for she had managed to count them as they arrived. The chance for observation had happened while she was taking Tigger out on one of her nature walks, the trail of which went along the tumbledown wall of the kitchen garden, passed through the plum orchard and came out at the lip of the meadow, where a flat wooden bridge spanned the stream. With a bundle of miscellaneous sticks and branches under her arm, she stood unseen at a break in the blackthorn hedge, the hedge itself obscured by a skein of white bind-weed, and watched them dismount from a very old van. She later heard Blore refer to the vehicle to Mrs Blore in the kitchen as a 'gypsy chara', and from this small seed, her conviction had grown. There was one boy about her own age, two little girls a bit younger, and a baby who toddled about like a drunken sailor when he was allowed down from his mother's hip. '. . . *And their names were Flopsy, Mopsy, Cotton-tail and Peter*,' Kat thought to herself as she counted them out. But the mother looked so tired, and the children were all so thin! Except for the baby, who was remarkably featureless, they all had dark eyes and hair, and skin which afterwards she wished badly to think of as foreign-looking, but which more properly appeared as if someone had dusted them lightly in cocoa-powder. That had been her only sighting of them so far. Even when she gave up pretending not to crane, and stood up on the bank, Kat could see none of the new tenants now.

Tigger, who from time to time was troubled by unseen tenants of his own, fell suddenly into a fit of scratching, working with his back leg until that limb became a blurr. This rout proving ineffective, he rolled onto his back, squirmed vigorously like a maggot in the rough grass, belly to the air, and then just as suddenly stopped, sat up and sneezed. Eviction was secured.

Above the water, midges were gathering for the last part of the afternoon. Kat had long ago noticed how they always managed to appear just before tea-time all through the summer. From nowhere, a light eddying breeze got up for a few seconds and blew a fine down towards her from the willow; from the cow-parsley, which she had never yet seen a cow eat, the smell which reminded her of dusty cupboards drifted to her over the stream.

"Mightn't they be?" Kat urged gently.

"No! They just need a bath, that's all." Saying this Kit sighed ominously and, leaning farther into the curve of the tree, shut his eyes, so signalling that he did not expect to be disturbed again.

Kat settled her focus on the little roof and chimney, all she could see of the cottage, from which woodsmoke was now drifting crookedly upwards into a peach-coloured sky. She was not her mother's daughter for nothing, and a fancy, once taken, was ever in danger of conversion to an *idée fixe*.

They *are*, she thought, and it thrilled her to be so certain – they're a family of gypsy princelings, with a fairy carriage disguised as an old van, and all living in that little cottage, just over the stream from here!

When Michael Mont stared out from the south window of the Jacobean wing at Lippinghall, all overhung in that part with a wisteria almost as ancient, he was not like the baronet

'*Whose eyes . . . saw from his window nothing save his own,*'

but like the rector, who characteristically

'*—lean'd not on his fathers but himself.*'

Indeed, so heavily did he lean, that Michael had just that moment assessed himself a thoroughly second-rate substitute for his own late father, whose likeness upon one of the walls he had spent some few minutes contemplating before arriving at his conclusion. Being one of those sons who are lucky enough to find in their fathers both friend and mentor, Michael sadly missed Bart's quick mind and attentive ear at times such as he now found about him. And were there ever such times?

Coming in tired and hot from a 'surgery' in his constituency, he had thrown some cold water over his face in a downstairs cloakroom and passed into the empty library. At that room's great window he now stood, rolling the last of an early scotch-and-soda over a small piece of ice left at the bottom of his tumbler, and staring out.

Even simple events that day had demonstrated to him his continuing need of Bart's irreplaceable function. He had listened in awe to his own platitudes spilling out at the questions brought to him. Yes, he agreed that there was a great need for *a . . .* ; he was sure the council could be prevailed upon to attend to *b . . .* ; a petition for *c . . .* ? — yes, of course he would sign! And so on, through the alphabet of wants and dissatisfactions from which his constituents spelled out their daily lives. But how to answer them honestly, when his pressing conviction was that none of these things would matter within the space of a few months, perhaps within only a few weeks? Bart would have known, or at least would have made his only son feel less of a clod for not knowing himself. Ah! — *the last of all the Barts was he!*

Michael remembered once, in his school days at Winchester, writing to ask his father's advice on an essay for which he felt a substantial lack of enthusiasm; its subject concerned the history of warfare. Bart had written back to suggest he begin with the observation that wars were very often initiated in the autumn.

'*Because of the harvest, my boy – armies march on their stomachs. Vive l'intérieur!*'

Bart had cited the Boer War, the Russian-Turkish War, and the great battles of the Crimea – Alma, Sebastopol and Balaklava. It was a persuasive theory even then; and, five years too late for inclusion in his essay, the Great War itself had been declared in August.

Well, they were into August now!

He heard the long-case clock on the great staircase striking the hour between late afternoon and early evening. Behind him, Blore announced in tones which were his own peculiar mix of the epic and the familiar that Mrs Val Dartie was telephoning to speak to her young ladyship, who was not in the house at present. (Although his mother was happy to be known as the Dowager, so freeing the title in its simple form for Fleur, Michael had noticed it was an arrangement Blore could never bring himself to confirm.)

Did the master wish to take the call?

165

"Put her through, Blore!"

Michael finished his watery scotch and picked up the telephone. He had not spoken to Holly since the night of the supper party, and wondered whether he shouldn't straightaway offer some passing phrase over the death of the cousin's wife those two months before – she was Holly's sister-in-law, after all. As always, his sense of the pitfalls on this terrain gave him pause. Of late, his only relief from worries over the international situation had come in contemplation of worries about the domestic one. The death of Anne Forsyte had resurrected a quality of bright but brittle sufferance in his wife toward himself which was reminiscent of a time once before —

The telephone line opened against his ear.

"Holly? Ah! – Fleur's out – you've got the lesser half, I'm afraid."

Holly must have read his mental hesitancy, for she made the first attempt to bridge things over.

"A jolly nice half, I think."

"Thanks! —perhaps you'd care to move to my constituency?"

He heard a little friendly laugh down the line.

"I was told your constituents are very faithful to you."

"Oh! they are. I believe they give me their votes as a kind of penance, you know – then pack me off to Westminster to sing in the wilderness."

"But without the jug of wine and loaf of bread?"

"For those I go to my club!"

How easy she was to chatter with, this gentle cousin of Fleur's. She had a way of making the unconsidered moment seem something of value. A nice woman! Michael asked what he could do for her.

"Val and I were thinking we should get back into circulation a little – after our recent times here."

Michael paused briefly and then said:

"I know it can't have been an easy time for you."

"Well, mine was the least part of it—"

There, out of nowhere, the suspected pitfall loomed.

Michael said quickly, "Yes; of course—"

and then leaped across the chasm with—

"How is your brother? Is he bearing up?"

"I think so. Drawing strength from the good years, he says."

"Like Pharaoh."

"Yes. America suits him, I believe."

"Ah."

Michael had not known that the beloved cousin was abroad. Did Fleur know? If so she had not mentioned it – but then, why would she have? He was not likely to be on her list of confidants in this matter. Taking a ready guess he asked:

"Does he intend to settle out there again?"

"That seems to be his plan."

Rather than repeat his previous monosyllable, Michael said nothing. A warm wave of gratitude ran through him towards this gentle, soft-spoken woman, who without knowing it had taken away what he was ashamed to acknowledge as the greater of his two besetting worries. Into the gap which followed Michael sent a little charitable wish that the cousin's bad years – spent safely an ocean away from Fleur – would be fewer than seven.

Holly was continuing:

"Now, we just lately discovered that Alexander's birthday falls the day before Val's. Val found out when they went to Lingfield last month and both bet on a horse called 'August Boy'. They'll be thirty-nine and fifty-nine together – the week-end of the 25th – so we thought of making a house party of it. It won't be terribly grand, but if you and Fleur could stand the backwaters of Wansdon, we'd be delighted to have you come down."

"A jolly nice backwater, I'm sure!" Michael returned gladly.

"That's two weeks from now. It's probably rather short notice for you both, but if you could ask Fleur for me – Alexander is rather more Fleur's guest than ours, after all."

"Of course. I'm sure we'll be there. It sounds splendid!"

Michael hadn't meant to agree so swiftly. Their invitations always went through Fleur, she kept the master diary. But it just seemed so natural to concur with Holly – and besides he felt such a debt of gratitude to her for the information about her brother that he would at that moment have done anything she asked. Not knowing his wife's very real dislike of that place, having never been told the reasons for it, he was confident Fleur would agree the date.

Wansdon on the 25th, then – they would in any case be going up for the Dumetrius show on the 23rd – and Dinny and Eustace were due down for a quiet week-end the week before. Yes, it was all still so 'jolly nice' that Michael wondered, as he replaced the telephone receiver, whether the one anxiety remaining to him was not simply a mental delusion of his own. The perceived threat to his marriage had proved only a false assumption based on his inaccurate reading of the facts of the case. One telephone call had put him right on that. It would be facile to imagine that the German problem could be settled over the telephone, but perhaps the conclusion he had come to consider inevitable was just another inaccurate reading? Surely the PM would never have proposed that the House rise, if the worst case had been the likeliest? And yet—

And yet there was Winston's speech last week, in reply to the PM's proposal. Like Bart's theory, it had been persuasive. With many of his colleagues, Michael had been surprised to find himself increasingly in agreement with a fellow member whom previously he had considered unreliable, not to say unsound. But this time he couldn't well see how anyone might disagree with the assertion that this was, at the very least, 'an odd moment', as Churchill put it, for the House to declare that it would go on a two months' holiday. It would be harvest-time soon!

He poured a second measure of scotch, and this time overlooked the soda. Glass in hand he returned to his post at the window, and resumed his contemplation of the nearest available horizon.

Winifred, who never left London unless it was absolutely unavoidable, had the same day quite happily accepted Holly's same invitation to go to Wansdon for the week-end of the 25th. The chief, in fact the only reason for willingly pledging herself to seventy-two hours' worth of undiluted fresh air was that one of the other guests was to be the person whose company over the last few weeks she had come so particularly – and so unexpectedly – to enjoy.

Dear Señor Barrantes. '*Perfectly delightful*' had been her first description of him, and it remained to this very moment how he seemed to her, as she once again sat across her Louis-Quinze table from him in the downstairs dining-room in Green Street the next day. For it happened that the lunch which first arose by accident had become a weekly occurrence. Not intentionally – on Winifred's part at least – but by a sort of pleasurable drifting into the habit. Every Saturday throughout the summer, Alexander Barrantes – who, it may safely be supposed, did not want for appointments – forsook all others and kept himself wholly unto Winifred and her luncheon-table. By whatever chance, he always arrived – with an apology for his timing – at just the hour when a late glass of sherry meant an implicit invitation to stay on. And Winifred, not quite deliberately we should say, never greeted him except with just the same degree of surprise and delight that had come to her on his very first visit there. At first they continued to talk of events in Town, of shows and exhi-bitions – even of the occasional book. They talked of every separate thing that, when combined, made up that conglomerate item called Society which still, at eighty, Winifred so adored. But gradually, as her visitor's spell worked upon her, mesmerising her native caution and putting it quite to sleep, Winifred began to speak more freely of matters closer to home. She shared with him memories of her father and brother, of her life at Park Lane before she married, and, once or twice (without referring to any of the grubbier details) she mentioned Monty. It seemed to her altogether such a natural progression – and this nice foreigner was so attentive!

"Oh, you'll certainly enjoy Wansdon, Señor Barrantes," she con-cluded, having just told the Argentinian all – all she knew, anyway – about the stud farm throughout an excellent fool. "I'm so glad that you and Val have become such friends. I couldn't wish for anything nicer."

"Nor could I, Mrs Dartie. I almost feel – that I have found a brother in him."

Winifred smiled contentedly. Yes, everything about him was so perfectly delightful. She noticed, however, that a look of mild perturbation had arisen momentarily on his face – he was scanning the table with a slightly worried look.

"Was there – something? Do tell me."

He looked up at her.

"I wish —" He stopped and his glance fell, as though perceiving the enormity of what he wished.

"Yes? Anything, Señor Barrantes. What is your wish?" Winifred offered an indulgent smile and an encouraging tilt of her head. She had only this morning been thinking what extra *bonne bouche*, savoury or sweet, she could provide for the meal that might please him. If it could be found in the kitchen, he should have it!

"Only this," he began again. "It would be a great honour for me, Mrs Dartie, if you—"

He looked up at her, and as he did so Winifred felt an odd, unfamiliar twinge beneath her ancient bosom.

"—if you were to feel able to call me by my given name."

His sincerity touched her almost tangibly. Winifred gave an inner gasp of delight. It was exactly the sweetmeat she could have wished for herself.

"Very well — Alexander."

How nice it felt to say his name aloud, and not just silently to herself! She added, in as matronly a voice as she could then manage:

"And I do hope you will call me by mine."

As if he were performing a sacrament, Barrantes lifted her hand from the table and held it to his lips; while Winifred watched, entranced, he kissed it chastely, and most solemnly. How warm and soft his kiss felt to that thin, veined hand! He looked up at her as he withdrew his lips and his dark, deep eyes seemed to open completely for a long moment, as though he were laying bare the contents of his spirit thereby as an offering.

"—Winifred."

At the sound of her name spoken by this singular, beguiling stranger, whom she felt she knew, perhaps not wisely, but so very, very well, something in Winifred's aged heart swelled tightly, and a tear squeezed its way into her eye. The tenderness of the moment was quite beyond anything she had known in all her long life.

Chapter Two

A Quiet Week-end

When she heard the tyres on the gravel, and 'Uncle' Eustace's trademark 'toot-to-to-*toot*-toot' on the horn, Kat twisted round in the window-seat of her little bedroom where she had been reading since her nursery tea with Finty, and was thrilled to see the car approaching between the pollarded willows along the curving Lippinghall drive. She raced downstairs and reached the car just ahead of Blore. This action was in highest breach of MacFintlock canon law, but she was prepared to risk excommunication for the price of being first to greet her favourite 'aunt'. In Dinny she had the only person she knew of in her family who shared her colouring. Aunt Dinny had exactly the same bright auburn hair, and this to Kat was an immeasurable comfort. And although her aunt's skin was creamier and not so pale, and her eyes the Cherrell family blue, not ice-green like her own, she nevertheless felt an affinity with Dinny that she felt for no one else in the world. Somehow, and it was probably because of the colour of her hair, she knew that Dinny always *understood*.

"You look nice and cool, darling," Dinny said as the girl opened the car door for her. "Have you come to help me?"

Kat was amazed. She hadn't seen Aunt Dinny since the beginning of June and the transformation in her size was astounding. Trying not to look at 'that bump', as she afterwards thought of it, Kat offered her thin white arm.

From the rear of the car, Blore produced a modest suitcase and valise. He asked stoically, "This is all the luggage, sir?"

Eustace had jogged around the bonnet to receive a good kiss from Kat and to take his wife's other side.

171

"That's it, Blore. We travel light these days."

"Except for me!" said Dinny, and Kat loved her even more for making her laugh and letting her help all at once.

"So what do you make of it?"

Eustace took his time in answering. With the precision of a man who might have bet a few pounds on the outcome, he wrinkled his sun-tanned brow and seemed concerned solely with measuring the lie of the lawn with his mallet before lining up for his next stroke. He and Michael were playing blue against red, and Eustace was bent on thrashing his host before tea. Bracing his ball with his foot, he drove it soundly through the next hoop, skewing Michael's, which had lain almost contiguously on the other side.

Eustace knew that Michael's question did not relate to the game. He took off from Michael, sending him into a nearby flower-bed.

"Croquet!"

Eustace's following stroke put him a yard from the winning peg and well ahead.

"Nothing good," Eustace said at last. "The old boy's right, you know, but no one believes him with his record. The cabinet think he's simply 'crying wolf'."

Michael sighed. Somehow it relaxed him to hear his fellow back-bencher voice the essence of his own views in such completely 'off-duty' surroundings. They had both read extracts in the newspaper from Churchill's address to the United States last week.

'*Holiday time, ladies and gentlemen!*' he had begun, his irony about as subtle as a landfall. '*How did we spend our summer holidays twenty-five years ago?*' he had asked and answered himself saying, '*Why, those were the very days when the German advance guards were breaking into Belgium and trampling down its people on their march towards Paris!*'

He was a wily old fox with a speech!

The hush that the Right Honourable Member for Epping had said was hanging all over Europe, now gathered over Michael as he took his turn 'from the rough'. In a spray of pink geranium leaves, his ball gained about eight feet, and in the wrong direction.

"Oh, bad luck!" Eustace called charitably, and with his own next shot was pegged out. With his light hazel eyes smiling, he added: "I say, you're not planning on joining the Reserve are you, old man?"

Coming unexpectedly upon the boy from the cottage that afternoon, on a solitary ramble before tea-time, Kat had to admit, the nearer she got to him, that there was a deal of truth in her brother's reference to his personal hygiene. He did have rather a smudgy face – and goodness, his knees—! But these details, she reflected, didn't necessarily stop him from being a foundling prince. This was the very point made in most of the authoritative texts (*Wuthering Heights* being one); that as foundlings they were unaware of their descent, and were often raised by poor people.

The boy lay on his stomach, heels kicking the air, looking down into the water from the flat wooden bridge which spanned the twelve feet or so across the banks of the stream. How lost and lonely he looked!

Under any circumstances, it would have been Kat's last impulse in the world to disobey her mother – but in this instance she was trying especially hard to execute her mother's stricture to the letter. The back meadow was barred, and she did not question it; but the boy was on the bridge, so it should be all right to talk to him there. Confident that she was not disobeying her mother, and thinking only that she should not break an even more important rule which had been dinned into her since the cradle – the code of hospitality – she walked quietly up to him and said:

"Hello."

The boy scrambled up, raising a spurt of yellow dust from the bridge. Facing Kat at a defensive angle he cried:

"I weren't doin' nothin'!"

"Oh! I'm sure you weren't."

"I was just watchin' the tiddlers!" He thrust his hands into the pockets of his great shorts, which started at his chest with a rope belt, and finished at his knees with double turn-ups. His expression defied her to contradict him.

Kat seemed to know that 'tiddlers' were the little fishes her brother used to net, and nodded agreeably.

"What's your name? Mine's Catherine."

"I'm Pete!"

173

Kat was enchanted. *Flopsy, Mopsy, Cotton-tail and **Peter***, she thought again. She wondered how they were all settling in at their new burrow.

"I expect you're missing your home?"

The boy looked at first as if he thought this a trick question. But something in her face, a sincerity, transparent as her skin, put him at ease.

"Me? Not likely! Better than an 'oliday, this is!"

The boy seemed to speak always in sturdy exclamations. Kat liked him, even though she wished he would wipe his nose. She sat down on the flat boards of the bridge, her legs over the water, and the boy did the same.

"Where do you usually go for your holiday?"

"We go 'oppin'!" said the boy, with special emphasis.

Here Kat wondered whether she had heard correctly. She understood about fallen 'aitches' in front of words, and that one should never draw attention to them, because their owners didn't know any better than to drop them. She also understood about neglected 'g' endings, for her Grandmother Em always ignored hers. Aunt Dinny once told her, in fact, that her grandmother had gone to a school where picking up a 'g' was actually *worse* than dropping an 'aitch'. So she *thought* that what the boy had said was that they went *hopping* for their holidays. And this to Kat was *quite* an extraordinary statement. She had heard of walking holidays, and climbing holidays, and even hiking holidays – but a *hopping* holiday – that was something wondrously new!

"Where do you hop?" she asked, trusting the question was not impolite.

"Dahn in Kent!"

The boy sniffed knowledgeably at this point, which was a mercy, since Kat was finding it hard to keep her focus away from his top lip.

"Myke a bob or two at it, an' all!"

Kat could barely contain her need to hear more – she could almost have hopped herself in her enthusiasm for this wonderful new pastime.

"Do a lot of people hop for their holidays?"

"Not 'arf! We all goes – even the byeby!"

"Your baby! But he's far too young to hop with you, isn't he?"

Wonder upon wonder – a hopping baby! But the boy was shaking his head, as if he had expected her to know better.

"When we're out 'oppin', we put 'im in the bin," he explained. Seeing Kat's eyes widen further he added, "'E don't mind – 'e likes it!"

The girl was lost for expression. It seemed the perfect height of adventure.

Both children stared silently into the stream for a while, swinging their legs in no particular rhythm, oddly comfortable in each other's company.

"My dad, 'e used to come with us, but 'e's a soldier now."

The boy sniffed again, and Kat sensed what he was going to say next.

"I – I 'ope 'e comes 'ome soon." He scraped a dirty hand across his eyes suddenly.

"I'm sure he will," Kat said gently, seeing he was trying not to cry. She found her handkerchief in her dress pocket, and offered it to him. The boy took it, blew his nose ferociously, and handed it straight back to her. The gesture was so swift, and so much of a piece, that despite a natural fastidiousness she automatically accepted the transaction. The same impulse of sympathetic politeness, which had led her to walk up to him in the first place, ensured she could do nothing else. At least that stemmed his problem!

There was a part of the garden at Lippinghall Manor known as 'the refuge', by virtue of its being so sunk within a border of yew hedges that it was possible to be there and to have no view of any other part of the house or grounds. On days of light breezes afternoon tea was served in its lee; this in contrast to days of no breezes, when the terrace was used, and days of howling winds, when this ever-moveable feast was held on a tiger-skin in front of the great fireplace in the hall.

It was here, where the sun was warm and bees hummed high and low among the hollyhocks and asters, that Fleur and Dinny were talking quietly about nursery colours. They had just agreed that blue was restful as long as it wasn't cold, when Kat ran up, anxious not to have missed any of Dinny's news and full to the brim with her own.

"Hello, darling," Dinny said to her. "Come and sit by me, won't you? I haven't had a proper chance to see you yet."

The girl moved towards Dinny until Fleur said:

"Hands, Kat! Have you washed?"

Kat was so anxious to be with Dinny, and not miss a moment of sitting beside her over tea, that, in an unthinking instant, she did something she would never have dared had she allowed herself even one second's thought; she lied to her mother with a quick nod of her head.

"Good. Then please take this plate to Aunt Dinny."

Blore brought up the samovar, a treasure supposed to have been rescued by the Mont who had been an Admiral, though no one knew quite how.

Michael and Eustace arrived next, Eustace flush with victory; Kit sauntered not far behind.

Michael pulled up a chair.

"Where's the Dowager?"

"Unknown," Fleur replied. "Last seen stalking black-fly among the zinnias."

"She shouldn't be hard to spot," Dinny said. "She has Poll on her shoulder."

"Kit, go and find your grandmother."

Kit made no immediate movement to that end; as Fleur turned her eye on him, there was a squawk. Em appeared, swaying slightly, wearing the green bird like a corsage.

"Full house!" said Michael, and gave her his chair.

"The black-fly are distressin'," she said. "They multiply faster than Boswell can divide. He just can't manage without Johnson."

"Shouldn't that be the other way around?"

"He wouldn't have had to manage without Hogg. Hogg was his own age. But your father *would* hold out till he got a Johnson, and now he's a ratin'. Sit on the back, Poll, and I'll find you a cracker."

"I always saw Bart's point," said Fleur. "And there would have been no point to Boswell and *Hogg*."

"Now Boswell's pointless on his own," said Michael. "How things recur."

"Haven't your new-comers anyone who could help him?" Dinny asked. "They might like to feel they're contributing."

176

"There's a boy. Only Kat's age, though – not up to the diggin'. Anyway, they're barred. Paradise is a walled garden. From the Arabic. Blore, is this the caravan?"

"The lapsang souchong, my lady."

"Awful smoky. Ask Augustine to make me some nice Indian in the Old Worcester, will you?"

The butler withdrew.

"Blore's too old. It's a blessin'."

"Barred?" Dinny asked, holding on to Em's previous thread.

"By me," said Fleur. "It sounds harsh, I know, but the possibility of disease is too ghastly. Evacuation is fine in principle, but none of it's been thought through. Don't fidget, Kat."

"You're way ahead of the Government there, Fleur," Eustace told her. "They've no contingencies for cleaning up the city kids before they evacuate, because first they'd have to admit there *was* a health problem."

Em began feeding bits of water-biscuit to the parakeet.

"Amazin' how they survive."

"The kids?"

"The Government. Don't these people vote?"

"Vigorously, Aunt, but hardly ever for their own good. Besides, nothing meets all eventualities better than a head in the sand. You agree, Michael?"

"I'm afraid I do. It's all 'us' and 'them' in the poor areas. They still think Parliament is for 'them' – 'us', that is. So what can one do? Percy Abercrombie swears that in his patch they still sew them into their clothes for the winter."

"Mediæval!"

"Just so. Ditto sleeping eight to a room. Nothing changes."

"If nothing changes, Michael, how can things recur?"

"You've a head, Fleur! Tell us, Michael – it's a poser. Here's Blore bringin' the Indian."

Chapter Three

Forsyte Bequest

To ask that heady metaphysical chestnut: 'What price Art?' of any Forsyte would be to ensure the impatient answer: 'Why, what it will fetch – of course!' It was almost a principle with them that there was little purpose in enjoying – far less in owning – a work of art unless and until its value was established. For them, 'What *point* Art?' was the real poser.

Dumetrius in his time had operated this principle in profitable dealings too numerous to list, particularly with his own cherished example of the species, the late Mr Soames Forsyte.

"*Now – there wath a man who knew the prithe of a picture!*" he would always say.

Dumetrius had died in the winter of the previous year – with a caution on his lips concerning the uncertain price of Expressionists, a phrase he had hitherto avoided. It was Dumetrius *fils* who now owned the gallery, who had negotiated its move from Suffolk Street to the new premises in Burlington Gardens, and who for the last year had masterminded the Spanish Exhibition for its formal opening. To this younger Dumetrius the name Forsyte had been spoken, it seemed from the cradle, in hushed and reverential tones (couched in the family impediment) and thus passed down into legend.

So it was in this traditional way that the son of Dumetrius greeted the daughter of Forsyte as she arrived with her party for the opening, in the early evening of August 23rd.

"Ah! Lady Mont—" Dumetrius in his glossy suit clasped his hands together in a knot of fingers, and tilted himself over the knot as he approached Fleur, "—thuch a pleathure!"

Fleur's group was smaller than she had intended. Michael was

178

there, as was his mother, making between them the whole sub-scription. All Fleur's other invitees – Winifred, the young Cardigan wives, and St. John Hayman – had for one or another reason fallen out. It was not that presently she missed the company of any of them, especially not the last three who had been asked purely so that they couldn't say they never were; but their absence from her arrangements exposed the constraint of larger circumstances, over which she knew she was not mistress. Ever a social creature, she found that the new steps to put the nation on a 'war-footing' were pinching her toes. Having a child with what appeared to be the influenza in the nursery at South Square also did not help her timetable.

When she spied Dumetrius approaching, Fleur – who at present had no good will to spare – continued to hold her catalogue with both hands, to avoid having one free to take his. She despised him for no particular sin save that he was obvious; she thought it a cardinal fault. But Dumetrius, who was only obvious when he chose to be, was also quicker than Fleur gave him credit, and divined the temperature of his reception before he came to a halt in front of her. So he kept his hands in their knot, and offered the tilt in their place.

"Thuch a thucthess!" Dumetrius extolled. "If I may venture to thay tho, Lady Mont, your father'th picture ith the linth-pin of it all! Our other Goyath would be lotht without it—"

Fleur offered a cold smile at this – she knew very well, as her father had known too, that it was considered to be only a 'small' work by the artist.

"Well, I muthn't antithipate for you – I thall allow you to enjoy your own thircuit!"

Dumetrius departed, none the worse for his exposure to Fleur's sentiments towards him; he had in any case spotted another party of dignitaries coming in behind her.

Michael's eyebrow shot up as Dumetrius hurried past them out of hearing.

"I thay!"

His mother turned from staring after the dealer's back.

"Awful annoyin', speech affectation," she said, and took her lorgnette from her bag. "Should have been a Velasquez."

179

Their first few minutes of quiet contemplation as they moved among the pictures were enough to tell them that, whatever his personal shortcomings, Dumetrius plainly knew his stuff. This show would put his new gallery on the map. The layout of it was intricate, with opaque partitions and pastel-tinted flats making perhaps a dozen separate areas for exhibition. The extra space was used wonderfully well – and with enormous imagination – to create a combined sense of immediacy and yet perspective. While avoiding the more obviously representative pieces, Dumetrius had managed, in the assembling of some forty works, to capture that evasive but evocative spirit which is the essence of any country's identity.

They passed through the first room slowly, saying nothing, for to pronounce on anything too soon would seem glib. These were in any case only early altar-pieces, all by minor and mostly nameless painters. There was one, of five tablets remaining from eight, by an artist known merely as the *Master of Sigüenza*, which depicted variously St. John the Baptist, St. Catherine, Salome and Herod. Next to it was a more modest arrangement by *An Anonymous Spaniard*, showing scenes from the New Testament. Others, not very different, followed.

The next room, really only a little annexe about ten feet square, was given over to Ribera. In it were pictures of three saints. Fleur knew, without consulting her catalogue, that the artist had been accused of copying the darkness of Caravaggio, and she said so. Michael and his mother said 'Um' and 'Ah' respectively, and they all moved on.

Via an open corridor offering several minor infanta by Velasquez, a brace of popes by Leonardo (Jusepe), and a still life of onions, salmon and a dog by a pupil of the Toledo school, they entered the Goya room.

"Here she is—" said Michael, as he saw the rather raddled dame in her profusion of black lace scorning him from the first wall. All three stepped up to the painting, unconsciously erecting a barrier around it against other gallery-goers, who may not have taken the precaution of having Forsyte blood in them, or in their partners.

Michael read aloud the little plaque at the bottom of the frame.

"'*Doña*— by Francisco de Goya, courtesy of The Forsyte Bequest.'"

"Gratifyin'," said the Dowager, the first to comment, tilting back her head and looking through her glasses.

"Yes, it is," Fleur agreed at last, surprised that this was what she felt herself. "My father would have been proud."

"She looks one or two husbands younger in the flesh," Michael said to Fleur. "I'd forgotten."

"No happier, though!"

"I imagine she feels the want of your dining table," Michael offered. "Without that she can't preside."

"We were probably a comedown for her. Father bought her from Lord Burlingford's estate in 1910. Goya was out then, but father believed he would come back."

"Remember him well," said Em to this last. "Difficult sort – no charm. Married a French girl."

After a moment's calculation, Michael and Fleur both realised that this characterisation referred in no part to the late connoisseur, or even to the late artist, but wholly to the late duke.

"Uncle 'Cuffs' bought his Purdeys," she added, as if this detail were sufficient to raise a reputation from the mire.

"Well, I'm glad we've only kept her copy," Fleur said. "She should be on view."

Michael then turned to the second wall and saw suddenly a vision from his own youth.

"Fleur – look. It's your Vendimia picture."

Fleur turned herself and a wholly ingenuous smile alighted upon her face before she could do anything to discourage it. The young girl, whom in her youth she was supposed to resemble, smiled back at her from the frame, a basket of grapes balanced jauntily on her head. In that unthinking moment Fleur remembered having a fancy-dress made to look like hers – grape-coloured like the vintage, with the bloom of velvet in its skirt. She had only ever worn it for Jon. A snatch of a poem ran through her mind —

*'Voice in the night crying, down in the old sleeping
Spanish city darkened under her white stars!'*

The unguarded smile closed to one of polite appreciation when she heard Michael tell his mother:

"We saw her in the Prado on our honeymoon. Fleur's father had her copied because of the likeness." And then he turned back to Fleur, as she knew he would, adding, "You know, darling, I can see it now. You're awfully alike still."

"Dear Michael," Fleur said, commanding a tolerant tone. "Parliament hasn't done you a bit of good – you're still the world's most ungifted liar."

"No, he's not all wrong," corrected the Dowager. "There is a touch of you in her, Fleur – perhaps in the past a bit more, but there's somethin' there."

"The resemblance was only ever passing," Fleur said. "And now it's firmly in the historic tense. Another country, as they say. Let's move on."

The third wall was given over to some cartoons, which were dark and rather difficult in their subjects, and to another large oil. Fleur affected to study them in order to lead a movement away from her lost youth on the previous wall. But her mother-in-law, usually so ready to leap-frog across topics, held tenaciously to her thread. When she might have been supposed not quite safely out of hearing, Fleur heard Em say:

"Copied, you say? Michael – wasn't this the one that fell on him?"

Fleur passed into the next room, and knew that Michael was sufficiently aware of his mother's special talent for elliptical *gaffes* that he would detain her over the remaining Goyas for a decent period.

Michael took his cue in his own domestic drama like the ageing *jeune premier* he felt himself increasingly to be. There was no point in remonstrating with his mother; she could never see where she had said the wrong thing, and invariably meant well by her infelicities. It was his own fault if anyone's; he should simply never have remarked upon the second Goya. Heaven knew, if he didn't, that between their honeymoon – when he had slept on a Spanish sofa for the first fortnight – and her father's death when Fleur had kept to her room for three nights and days, it was not a painting to which fond memories were attached.

Allowing his wife to go on ahead and get her space, Michael kept his mother's attention on the drawings. They shouldn't be

182

too long, though. He knew Fleur wanted to get back to check on Kat – they had brought her up with them after she had developed an achy cold at Lippinghall. It would probably pass in a couple of days, but Reardon in Harley Street was rather more reliable than old Catteridge in darkest Bucks. Also he needed to get to his club to catch up on the situation with Russia – Parliament had been recalled over it for tomorrow.

His mother was demanding the English of an inscription on one of the cartoons. *Por Liberal.* It was of a figure chained to a fence. Michael found the translation in his catalogue.

" '*For being of generous spirit*'," he said.

"Religious?"

"Ironic."

The other sketches were of assorted madmen in a selection of Bedlams. Grim stuff! — but as nothing compared to the force of the final oil, as Michael turned to face it. It was *The Third of May*, the artist's searing realisation of the terror of the military firing-squad. In a night scene composed in equal parts of stark fear and raw brutality, one figure in white was luminous against the darkness of the hills and town beyond. Kneeling on the bloody killing ground, arms flung wide in desperate appeal, his eyes bulging with terror, the man about to be shot was captured by Goya's extraordinary talent in the last moment of his life. And the man, for Michael, seemed to bear an uncanny resemblance to another he knew – he might have been Lewis' twin. Michael's original question was answered. This was Goya's Spain *and* Franco's – and Lewis had been in the thick of it for three years. Would he have been better off going out like this poor brute? — better off not seeing his comrades beaten?

And suddenly Michael wondered how Lewis would take the news, when he heard that Ribbentrop had shaken hands with Molotov in Moscow . . . He became aware that his mother had his arm – he was glad to go!

Turning alone around the next corner Fleur came upon a portrait by El Greco – *The Unknown Knight with his Hand on his Heart*. More accurately, she came upon the upper half of him, as that unidentified gallant was partly obscured to her by the back of another, whose tailoring she recognised instantly.

It was the Argentinian. As she had thought before – he *would* turn up!

Fleur stood a few feet behind him, a little to the side. He had not yet seen her, and it amused her to have the upper hand for once.

The Resurrection, and the *Coronation of the Virgin*, also by El Greco, were placed side by side on the wall opposite. In them, long-limbed figures stretched gracefully towards the heavens, bending limpid eyes upon each other from divers clouds. Michael and his mother went up to them without noticing the nobleman and his two admirers.

"Ah – bone structure!" said the Dowager, again putting up her lorgnette. "Pleasin' legs, too."

"Heavenly bodies indeed," Michael agreed. "And what eyes!"

Barrantes meanwhile, still observed by Fleur, had turned at Michael's voice. Fleur stepped a little further to the far side of him, and put herself behind a pair of elderly American women, so that she might remain seeing but unseen. At first she expected the Argentinian to go up to Michael and renew his acquaintance, but instead she saw him cast his eyes about the room. Well, well — was he looking for her?

After a further few moments of appreciative lingering, Michael and his mother moved on, evidently assuming her to be ahead of them still, rather than behind.

Not finding in the room her whom he evidently wished to see, Barrantes pivoted back to the painting, and discovered Fleur standing between himself and it.

A look of humorous surprise came into his eyes, as he saw her. Without consulting the picture, he put his hand to the same region of his own breast as the knight's. She had caught him out, and he was acknowledging the trick as won by her. Fleur found this immoderately pleasing. What was it that made her respond differently to him now? Something about him – his smile, perhaps – seemed, oh, more open, less cat-like somehow. And he had 'turned up' at a good moment. If he chose to be diverting now, she might well allow his overtures.

Fleur returned his smile. "You are always ahead of me, it seems. We weren't due to meet again until the week-end."

"A wonderful bonus!"

Nothing was said for a beat or two. A little stand-off was taking place. The American matriarchs passed them in the interval, and could be heard saying "*My!*" in close harmony as they turned into the next chamber.

Barrantes said:

"I saw your father's *Doña*, Lady Mont—"

Fleur held up her hand in not wholly feigned horror.

"Please, no more Goyas! And no more titles – around Michael's mother I always feel I'm usurping that one. Shall we be on first name terms?"

"Nothing would please me more," he said simply.

She did not let the Argentinian see, but Fleur gave him next what two previous generations of Forsytes would have labelled an old-fashioned look. Who knew what pleased him, except the games he played, and his own gamesmanship in playing them?

"Well – Alexander," Fleur said, voicing the first question that came to her as they continued along, at a significant tangent to the route taken by her relations and the Mothers of the Union, "you have yet to tell me how you know *my* mother."

"Well – Fleur – did she not tell you herself?"

He knew how to fence. Fleur smiled pleasantly and parried.

"No – she didn't. But then, I didn't ask. Now I confess I'm curious. She did say she thought you were a financier of some sort, but that can't be right."

"Oh? What makes you think she is mistaken? Why should I not be a financier?"

"Because you don't look like one."

"Do I not?"

"Not faintly."

"Hnh! Is that right? How remiss of me."

"Yes, I'm afraid it is." Fleur undid his tease by confirming it. She would match him, point for point. "Quite hopeless, in fact."

"Ah," Barrantes seemed to ponder his failing for a few paces. "But might not a person of subtlety manage to seem other than he is?"

"A person of subtlety would soon see that among the English subtlety got him nowhere. Certainly nowhere in making money.

You see, in this country we like foreigners to appear exactly what they are. Our most important national characteristic couldn't survive otherwise."

"And what is that?"

"Hypocrisy, of course."

He laughed.

"Then how should I look, Fleur – to best capitalise my appearance? Tell me, and it will be remedied at once!"

Fleur realised she was actively enjoying their joking conversation. She liked him far better today for some reason. Now – why? Was the change just in him – or also in herself?

"Well, for one thing, you seem — oh, don't look at me like that, there isn't a compliment coming."

His expression was exemplary, except for the tiniest flicker in his eye.

"I never doubted it. But go on; I seem . . . ?"

"Well, if you insist – too much 'a man of the world'."

"Do I? And that is incompatible with an interest in finance?"

"Only with a professional one."

"Ah!" he laughed again. "A trait which I am afraid I inherited from my father."

"Was he a financier?"

"No. But from all accounts I gather he was most definitely a 'man of the world'. His only interest in money was to buy one thing."

"Which was?"

"Personal gratification."

And before Fleur could think how decently, or at least discreetly, to ask him what, if any, of that commodity he had so far found for purchase in London, he spoke again, upon another subject.

"Oh, do look, Fleur – that woman sitting in front of the Magdalen. . ."

Fleur turned in the direction he was facing, but at first could not identify whom he meant. There were several people, including the two aforementioned matrons, between themselves and the un-finished painting – clearly a study for a *Noli me Tangere*, with Mary completed but Christ left as a shadowy outline. Barrantes also had the advantage of his height over Fleur.

". . . don't you think she is beautiful?" he continued. "She might have been Titian's '*Heavenly Love*' in her youth. Ah, she has turned away . . ."

Fleur was about to say that she couldn't see anyone to match his description, when the next moment that section of the gallery cleared, as the two matrons moved along to "*My!*" at the Resurrection. Across the open parquet floor, Fleur saw at first only another back – of quite an old woman, if the colour of her hair was a reliable indicator. It was silver – not grey or white, but pure silver – and fastened in a soft *chignon* at the base of her neck. The back itself – in a dress of not quite blue, and not quite mauve, the colour of delphiniums – was strangely flexible for one so old, not resting against the velvet banquette, but upright, and swaying slightly as she gave her face to the other Mary. If the word had not seemed inappropriate for her years, Fleur might have thought her almost willowy. Certainly her poise was elegant, and would have graced a woman half her age.

"Strange—" Barrantes was saying. "I have seen her once before today; in Paris at the Opera. She was sitting quite alone in a box: she looked so lovely, and so very sad. I was with your mother, who seemed to think she should know her, too. I remember we marvelled at her beauty . . . Look, Fleur, she is turning back!"

The woman rose slowly but effortlessly from her seat, and half turned towards them to leave. It was then that Fleur recognised a profile which, in all the years that had passed since she last saw it, time seemed not to have touched. Another quarter turn and there was that face, still passive and irresistible as it had been then – immovably passive in its resistance to Fleur's own wishes, and irresistible in its power to overcome those of Jon. For this was his mother, Irene, who stood moments more before the Magdalen and then, without seeing either of her observers and therefore unaware of the admiration of one of them, left the room.

Fleur realised stonily, as she watched her go, that for once in her life she wished someone dead. Here was the woman whom her father, despite himself, had loved until the day he died, not even then understanding what it was in her that baffled his hatred. Looking at that light figure moving away now, Fleur believed she might succeed where her father had failed. That time had dealt so indulgently with this woman seemed the bitterest of ironies. She herself had wasted so much of it, after all, in longing after that which only this woman's existence had barred to her. And to see her here, amongst all these pictures of Spain! Irene had taken Jon there all those years ago, in an attempt to make him forget her. Fleur felt a little thrill of bitter victory, when she remembered how that woman's strategy had also known its failures . . .

"Do you know her, Fleur?" Barrantes asked, at her side. Perhaps he sensed something – he had that capacity, she knew.

"Yes," she replied simply, her hatred wishing to find expression. His eyes were upon her, waiting to be told. Could she bring herself to tell him? So often we choose strangers for our most private confessions, and Fleur was in that second as close as she had ever come to revealing the knotted secret with which her past was tied and bound. Why shouldn't he know? *Pourquoi pas?*

"She was once married—"

Like the cue of the old comedy, Michael, with his mother on his arm, appeared on the other side of the room. Em waved.

"—to a distant relation of mine."

Other, more immediate ties had prevented her from telling her secret. The moment passed away utterly, and Fleur dealt instead with protocol.

"You must meet my mother-in-law, Alexander. Em, this is Señor Barrantes, a friend of my mother's from the Argentine."

"How d'you do," said the Dowager. "Handsome woman. Didn't know she was there."

Remarkably for a novice, Barrantes followed her construction and answered fluently.

"I came to know Mrs Forsyte when I was living in Paris, Lady Mont. But I am from the Argentine myself," and he bowed over her hand.

"Spanish speakin'?"

He nodded. Em gazed back at him for a second, then tapped his forearm with her long-stemmed glasses.

"Then tell us about these fellers."

And, with no more elaborate preamble than this, Fleur's group which had been three, and then two, became four.

He was knowledgeable and urbane (to borrow adjectives from

188

Winifred Dartie), light, humorous and discursive all at once. No visitors could have wanted a more felicitous guide than Alexander Barrantes provided to that little party, as it moved through the rest of the exhibition.

There was a lone Picasso there, a blue period of course, set next to a single Miro which did it no favours. The Argentinian passed it by with a light 'tsk, tsk.' Fleur consulted her catalogue, and saw the owner was listed as one '*Alexander Barrantes, Esquire*'.

Thus escorted, they went the whole course without flagging. In the final room, on a wall by itself, *El Jalaleo*, by John Singer Sargent, captured the last of their attention with a twirl of scarlet hems.

"Ah! The talk of the Paris *salon*," Barrantes said admiringly.

"Mmm," Fleur found herself agreeing with his tone. "And such marvellous movement. You can almost hear those skirts."

"And yet there is a sort of suspension about it, too, I feel," he continued, full seriously, and seeming to be lost in the picture before him. "Almost a passion-in-waiting."

Fleur avoided anyone's eye.

"Passion-in-waitin'," Em repeated thoughtfully. "Just right!"

Chapter Four

Attributions of a Dartie

Winifred Dartie, though only a few weeks from her eighty-first birthday, was not in the habit of lightly missing social engagements. In fact she would as readily have been parted from her social diary as from her own life, of which the former had forever been the guide. So in having to excuse herself from Fleur's group to the gallery – her toe had flared up again, after she had ill-advisedly tried to shoo the cat from a ledge on the landing – she felt a terrible deprivation. It was not missing the exhibition of 'the Forsyte Goya' which brought this great sense of loss – she had seen her brother's picture last in the National Gallery in '27, when his collection had gone there, and had never particularly cared for it. Rather, it was what her absence implicitly allowed for: the possibility that her grip on life, and on its events, might not now be as firm as it once was. Than this admission Winifred could envisage no greater horror.

Her current deprivation was set to double, furthermore, for having finally declined the gallery with good grace – the better to spare her toe for the week-end at Wansdon – Winifred had just that afternoon seen her doctor. His best recommendation for the whole foot was total immobility for another week. He left his patient looking much like a child who had lost a sixpence and found a bad penny in its place. Once the doctor had gone, Winifred summoned Miller and, over all sensible protests, insisted she would sit downstairs. There she sat in a brown study, holding on tightly to the ivory swan's head of her cane, as if by squeezing it she could strengthen her grip on life. In this position she was found by her son, who had called in between his tailor's and his club.

Winifred held up her powdery forehead, to be consoled with his kiss.

"It's a great bore, Val," she said, looking up at him from her chair as he stood with his elbow on the mantel. He checked the ormolu clock against his own hunter, and found it slow by two minutes. Next to the clock he noticed a white lacquer box he had not seen before. "Old age is the very pest."

"What did the quack say?"

"Not very much——" (Considering his fees, Winifred would have preferred him to be rather more verbose – she was presently paying him about two pounds a word.) "——except that these fractures seldom mend reliably."

"I could've told him that much! In a horse you have to have it——" Val glanced at his mother and decided not to continue. She wasn't likely to take the comparison too well, especially being already so long out to pasture. "Still, it's too bad, all the same. Holly was looking forward to having you there this week-end."

"I know, dear. It *is* too bad. And now her numbers will be out – will she be able to get someone else in at such short notice?"

"Oh, she probably won't bother. It's only going to be family on the first night, anyhow — and Alexander, of course."

"Yes," said Winifred solemnly, regretting her future loss as if it was already a present hardship, as real as her toe. "I shall miss it all terribly."

"What's this——" Val picked up the lacquer box and turned it in his hands, "——something new?"

"No, something rather old, actually. But what it is, I've no idea. Just a little box, by the look of it – Smither left it me in her will."

"Can't get it open – must be warped inside. I suppose you've tried?"

"Everything, dear boy. Miller even suggested steaming it in a *bain-marie*. I didn't let her, of course. No, it's just an old lacquer box – but rather pretty, don't you think? It even looks quite valuable. I must find a proper home for it – upstairs somewhere. It can't stay on the mantel for ever."

Val replaced the box on its temporary shelf.

"Poor old Smither. She was a good sort."

"Yes. I was touched when Roger brought it over." Recalling that day put Winifred in mind of something. "By the way – have you heard St. John Hayman's *mot* for Alexander. No? It's rather wicked. He got it from a song—" and she told her son his young kinsman's coinage.

Val laughed when he heard.

"South American Joe? That's pretty good. I'll bet Alexander wouldn't mind it himself. We're having supper at my club tonight – I've a mind to tell him."

Winifred caught the jocular lift of her son's eyebrow, and realised he was only teasing her. It was then that the drawing-room door, previously not quite closed, opened fully and Miller announced:

"Mr Barrantes, ma'am."

Barrantes stood with an irreproachable expression secured over his elegant features. He had spent the previous minute outside the door, with a smile in his eyes, and a finger to his lips, with that gesture restraining the maid from announcing him until her mistress had finished the tale of his *soubriquet*.

"Alexander!" cried Winifred delightedly, as if her sixpence had been suddenly recovered, or a thre'penny piece at least was within sight.

"Hello, old man," said Val genially. "We were just talking about you."

"And I of you." He went directly over to Winifred and knelt on one knee at her feet – or rather at her foot, which was propped on a cushion above the footstool. He took her hand, and held it in his. "I saw Fleur at the exhibition just now, and she told me you were in some discomfort. I am so sorry."

Winifred found this little display enchanting, which of course was its chief purpose. Really, he was quite a courtier – almost like a knight of old!

"Bless you, dear boy. Oh, it's nothing really, but it does mean I shan't be joining you all at Wansdon this week-end."

Barrantes' face fell, not excessively, but with enormous eloquence. Seeing his expression offered some recompense to Winifred for her pain and privation – it was bitter-sweet to know that her disappointment was shared.

As for Val, if he had not seen for himself that the object

of this speaking disappointment was his own mother, he would have supposed the Argentinian thwarted in love. He felt a fraternal impulse to say something consoling.

"I was going to drive Mother down myself tomorrow, ahead of everyone's arriving on Friday. If you've nothing on, why don't you come with me? We could get in an extra day's riding."

"Oh, yes, Alexander, you must. That's a splendid idea, Val. Now, you two, I must get up to my room, or I shall be paying that doctor twice over for the same opinion. Ring for Miller, will you, Val?"

Barrantes was instantly at her side to help Winifred from her chair, while Val reached across the fireplace to the bell. As Val straightened up he brushed the edge of the little lacquer box with his shoulder and it fell to the hearth, striking the fender on its way and breaking open upon landing there. From the sundered lids onto the fireside spilled something which might once have been organic and grey, as if perhaps a small animal had been trapped inside prior to their final closing.

"Great Scott!" said Val. "What the devil—?"

He looked to his mother for explanation, and found her staring hard at the contents of the box which lay immediately before her. So intent was her stare that Val said nothing more, and none there moved. This *tableau vivant* was interrupted when Miller came into the room, uncomprehendingly, as she heard her mistress cry:

"Aunt Ann's curls!"

The 'Iseeum' had changed remarkably, almost indecently, little since the day Val Dartie first crossed its threshold as a newly elected member nineteen years before. Then George Forsyte had been the guiding beacon of its Committee, steering in all points of taste, from plain matters of kitchens and cellarage to the sometimes ticklish subject of membership. Like the smell of a good cigar his influence lingered there now. Avoiding French and other modish influences, which George thought trashy, steaks and cutlets were still served as if *blue* could only ever properly refer to one's University colour. The furniture and arrangement, comfortable, unpretentious, and of an undetectable era, were still much as George had known them. Even that *ignis fatuus*, the stand against the newly rich, had wavered there later than many places, and still today the club resisted election of most of the 'frightful ticks', as George would have called these sons of industrial potentates, *et al*, now admitted by such previously respectable places as the Hotchpotch and the Aeroplane. Respectable they may be, but they had suffered for want of a George Forsyte to advise them.

The truth at the 'Iseeum' was no less than this – that over his forty years of assiduous attendance there, George had become an institution within an institution, sitting in his perennial chair by the bay window and noting with his humorous eye the decline of men and things outside his jurisdiction. George Forsyte – the sardonic, the well-groomed, the droll; inscrutable to all – save possibly his bookmaker; deliberately unmarried but only incidentally unsurvived – and these seventeen years dead.

His one remaining distinction, as yet unsung in these chapters, is that he was the person responsible for bringing Montague Dartie into the family.

Val steered Barrantes to his own usual table in the smoking-room, a small distinction which befitted the family tradition, and sent their liveried attendant to bring whisky and soda for two.

Barrantes seemed pleased with the place. After showing a well-mannered interest in the details obligatorily trotted out by members for first-time visitors – numbers, dates, historical figures, and so on – he asked Val if his father had belonged.

"For about thirty years, until he died." With a rueful grin Val added, "Though I believe some of his accounts survived him."

Two tumblers of scotch were brought, with a siphon on the side.

"Just a smidgeon, Perks. That's it. You knew my father, didn't you?"

"Yes, Mr Dartie; I *did*. —Sir?"

Barrantes declined soda.

"How would you describe him?" At an involuntary but well-covered facial twitch from the man, Val added, "Don't worry – you can't slander the dead!"

"I shouldn't dream of it, sir. Mr Montague Dartie, I should say, was a *sporting* genn'lman, sir. Particularly, I should say, on the *turf*."

"Tip you any winners, did he?"

"The occasional one, yes, sir."

"But more often not?"

"I believe he always *thought* they were winners, sir. I should say he had an *appreciation* of horses."

"I'm sure he did! O.K., Perks. That'll be all."

"Thank *you*, sir."

The man withdrew, and Val laughed heartily.

"There you are, Alexander. If you want to know anything about an Englishman, ask the man who serves him."

He took a mouthful from his tumbler and went on, less light-hearted.

"Do you know, I imagine there must have been times when my father would have confided his every thought to someone like that chap, over his snifter in this place. Yet I doubt if *I* ever really knew him."

Barrantes' frown was brief, but expressive. Val was encouraged to continue.

"He once made me ashamed of him in public."

Encouraged by the glass in his hand, and the companion at his side, Val related that incident of forty years ago, outside the Pandemonium Ballet, when he had seen his father with 'that Spanish filly' on his arm. At last he swallowed another mouthful, as if it might remove a residual taste.

"What did you do?" Barrantes asked, "—when you saw him?"

"I cut him dead. I guess I was a bit of a young prig in those days, but even so — It was frightful: — for mother, for all of us. I wonder you weren't better off not knowing yours."

To this, again, the eloquent foreigner made no reply. In any case, Val's expression had already changed.

"Look out – here's a young cousin of mine. He's an awful idiot, but he might make you laugh—St. John!"

Chapter Five

Departures

Though she had once sworn they would be required, it was not wild horses but mere dint of circumstance which drove Fleur to make that return journey to Wansdon, to the chalky sweep of the Downs where her one great passion had its nativity.

Still unforgiving of Michael for accepting Holly's invitation, her irritation toward her husband hardened into a lump of anger toward the world around her as she steered her car through London streets clogged with end-of-week traffic. She was glad a sitting in the House about that Russian business meant Michael was taking the train down later – it would have been impossible to be civil to him from the passenger seat! Gradually, the rattle and press of town gave way to the apple-pie order of the suburbs. Villadom! – where every squat two-storeyed 'semi' seemed to own the same patch of lawn in front, edged by lengths of the same low brick wall, and linked with identical sun-ray garden gates. Every building and street Fleur passed she disliked more than the last, though whether for itself or for where it was leading her would have required another to say. She drove on, hating it all.

Eventually 'A' roads became 'B' roads, and 'B' roads became the winding lanes of Sussex. Yet far from relieving her mood, the high green hedgerows with glimpses of rolling unharvested fields beyond served only to channel her anger. To Fleur it was as if everything in the world was set on leading her back to that place. As signs for Wansdon appeared this feeling had lodged solidly in her gullet, as something which refused to go down.

Needing to draw second wind before facing Holly and the tiresome prospect of play-acting through an entire week-end, Fleur drew up in a wooded lane, banked on one side by an orchard and on the other open between the trees to fields. Succumbing to the tug of a habit she had all but lost, she rifled the glove compartment until her hand lit on a packet of cigarettes. They looked old and dried-out when she opened the packet – she could not remember buying them – but there was a lighter in there too. She took them with her out of the car and found a gate.

Leaning on the gate and puffing smoke at first blue, then grey as she regained the old habit, Fleur focussed on the stale taste of tobacco on her tongue as a necessary prelude to thinking about nothing. Above the field in front of her a skylark hovered high over its nest, delivering a song like a tune played on a penny-whistle. The repetitive trill was a further strain on nerves already stretched tight. Without meaning to, she had driven faster than was wise, once getting through the city. A glance at her watch told her that if she kept to this pace she was set to arrive early. Of all things hateful about this unwanted week-end that would be the worst, to be the first arrival, to have to endure tea and small-talk with Holly, whose eyes she anticipated watching her for signs of the very feelings she would have to cover. No – tea and sympathy would be unendurable. Better to dawdle now and arrive late, after Michael's train if possible, and lose herself amongst the other guests. People were always less intolerable in groups.

Who had Holly said would be there? Fleur checked them off as she recalled their names. Apart from herself and Michael, and of course the Argentinian, there were to be four others, and probably an unknown fifth brought in at short notice to take Winifred's place. Jack Muskham was one of the four, she remembered – he was a cousin of Bart's with stables near Cambridge and whom Val knew through the horse connection. Michael would be sure to get easy mileage out of him. Then there was a couple who were from the farm next to Wansdon, but she failed to recall their hyphenated name. It had sounded Scottish, or old Irish – the Somebody-Fearons, or was it Somebody-Ferguson? They were likely to be tedious, but at least wouldn't be house-guests. The fourth was a woman writer, Evelyn Halley, a friend of Holly's and someone Fleur knew by sight from her club. Her books were autobiographical novels, about growing up in China during the Boxer Rebellion . . . oh! but that could be

Rosamund Hall! Fleur sighed the last of the smoke from her lungs. Altogether, she supposed the company could be worse – but for all the tea in China, that expression which Michael overused, she would *not* be early! She discarded her cigarette, which had done its job, then lifted the hasp from the gate and idly took a little stone path through the orchard.

As she followed the path, the smell of sweet cider stole up to her on both sides, from wind-fallen apples rotting on the grass. With this scent in her nostrils and the late afternoon sun on her neck, Fleur found her mood was pleasantly elevated after a few paces, though quite why, since she had long hardened herself against Nature's fickle lure, she could not have told. Perhaps it was just this easy – to catch a mood and run with it while you could. Somehow she was not convinced, but if this frame of mind could only accompany her through the week-end, it would be a mercy.

But the quality of this mercy was indeed strained – rather than drop as gentle rain it disappeared like vapour when Fleur saw where the orchard path had taken her.

The orchard ended at a hedge and another gate, and beyond it a garden began. A short lane led to an old house, then on to straw yards and farm buildings sloping up the hill behind. The house was prettily gabled, and between its gables was red with a covering of Virginia creeper. Through the hanging russet strands it was possible to see that the house was shuttered. Perhaps it was the way the leaves glowed in the low August sunshine which first stopped her. Or perhaps the connection came when she saw the house was closed and empty. Why had she not recognised the place before? She had been there only once, but once had been enough to last a lifetime. Here at this gate she had stood and opened a letter from Jon, which he had left in his place when he ended their affair. She had ever held it to be his one cowardly act – to tell her in that way, not face to face. It had been when he was deciding whether to buy this very farm, Green Hill, which just now she had recognised too late. Standing at the gate then she had read the note, and afterwards had slowly torn it into tiny fragments and buried it in the hedge. Now, as with everything else, she remembered each word.

'Last night Anne told me of her own accord that she knew what

198

*had happened. She told me, too, that she is to have a child. I have
promised her not to see you again. Forgive me and forget me, as I
must forget you.'*
  'Jon.'

In an instant of wretched recollection, Fleur realised fully that
in the thirteen years which divided that moment from this she had
done neither. She turned from the gate and fled to her car.

On the same Friday afternoon, at about the time Fleur was negotiating her last suburb, an Inspector of Police, holding his trilby
by the brim, stood stiffly in the hall at South Square, looking as
though he feared he had not scraped his shoe leather sufficiently
well before entering. This was only illusory, of course, for he was
scrupulous in such matters. Moreover, he had had occasion to
enter a great many 'toff' houses in his years at the Yard, and
was no longer awed by them. But this one had a detail he had
not encountered before, which the second he saw it underlined the
one essential truth of his trade – that there was no telling with
people. Trained in observation, his eye first noted the Gauguin,
and then utterly avoided it, an achievement seldom realised in
that spot. *Nudity!* – his studiously averted stare seemed to say,
underneath eyebrows like disapproving thickets – and *dusky* ladies,
too!

Timms had gone to fetch her master, who now came unhurriedly
down the stairs ahead of her. Having just returned from the House,
this was his first chance to read the newspapers in any depth – they
were full of Ribbentrop's success in Moscow, yesterday's bombshell
– and Michael had hoped not to be disturbed until he left for Victoria
station.

As the baronet took the last step down, the policeman put a
broad hand into his breast pocket and withdrew a white slip of
card. He consulted it before speaking.

"Am I addressing Sir Michael Mont, M.P.?"

"You are."

"Is this your card, sir?"

Michael looked at it.

"Yes, it is. May I ask how you came by it?"

"It was found on the body of a man who took his own life. A foreigner, we think."

Michael looked again at his own name printed in copperplate, but without seeing what could be the connection.

"I'm afraid I don't understand."

"Neither do we, sir, as yet. He was found at the Cenotaph this morning. Blew his brains out sometime during the night, if you'll excuse my saying—"

The inspector dipped his head towards a spot behind the baronet's shoulder, and rotated his hat in his hands. Michael half turned and saw a corner of a starched pinafore. The maid had failed to remove herself from the hall – the sight of such an important policeman 'mesmerising her right out of her proper senses', as she afterwards told the cook.

"That will be all, Timms – thank you," Michael said over his shoulder. Once hearing her hurrying away he turned back to the inspector. "Yes – I heard something about it earlier, at my club. Who was he?"

"I'm afraid we don't know that either. Unfortunately, there were no other identifying items on the body. I wondered, perhaps, if you might come with me now, sir. It could help—"

"Yes, of course."

They drove to the mortuary in a mutual silence which divided the two men quite as well as any tangible difference between them. The inspector's was the equable silence of a man who was trained to do a job and who was doing it. The moment was no more and no less solemn for him than any other he had spent in the execution of his duties – he could certainly think of worse trips he had made in his time. Michael's silence was entirely the converse of this. One possible explanation of the card had begun to occur to him. And if his worst – and the more he thought about it, his only – guess was correct, then he had done anything but his duty. The suspicion clung to him like a stale smell, all the way to the police mortuary.

In the pallid light of that place, the inspector fixed his measured policeman's stare on Michael's face and drew back a precise corner of the sheet, as if it was all part of a ritual procedure. He's done this before, naturally, Michael thought – spare my soul, but I haven't!

200

Leaving the inspector's gaze on him, Michael followed the sweep of his arm down to the dead man's face.

He had known and yet not known what he was going to see. Now there was no doubt left to him. It was Lewis; less recognisable at first because his hunted rabbit's eyes were closed and sunken into the face which even under bare mortuary lights still bore its weather-beaten tan. A small brown entry-wound at the right temple betrayed Lewis's method. A stained forage cap, replaced at a careful angle by some pair of hands through which he had lately passed, covered who-knew-what horror beneath.

Michael could only think: Poor devil! He saved my hide a dozen times or more, and I couldn't shift myself to save his.

The inspector drew the sheet down the length of the table and Michael saw that, true to the last, Lewis had died as a soldier. His slight frame looked like a tailor's dummy, lying stiffly as it were to attention, in the last uniform he was to wear – a Spanish militia-man's full outfit. A zipper jacket, with a grubby neckerchief stuffed into one pocket; a Sam Browne belt with water-bottle, tin pannikin and serrated hunting knife attached; then corduroy breeches and, below, one heavy-duty marching boot – the other presumably lost somehow in transit from the Cenotaph, leaving one thin bare foot to poke miserably up from the end of the sheet.

Michael knew now that at the back of his mind this had been his fear all along. He recalled the gleam in the batman's eye when he had said:

'The Russian'll stop 'em this time – you see if 'e don't!'

To Lewis's threadbare existence, sustained chiefly by that feverish belief, the Ribbentrop pact must have dealt the mortal blow.

Still with his eyes fixed on Michael's face the inspector said: "We were thinking he must have been some kind of foreigner, sir, because of his clothes. Perhaps you've had your wallet stolen lately, for the feller to have 'ad your card on him? We'll put him down as unidentified in the report if—"

"No, Inspector," Michael replied tersely, changing up to the higher gears of rank he seldom engaged. "This man was neither a foreigner nor a thief; and I can identify him. His name's Lewis. Lance-Corporal Lewis, Ronald Arthur, formerly from Mile End, and late of—"

Michael gave his own Company and Regiment.

"He fought at Amiens and Arras, and was decorated for it. Perhaps you could put that on your report – for the record."

The inspector shuffled his feet on the cold flagstones, and waited for his acknowledged superior to continue in the same well-understood tone. Michael pressed his lips into a rueful line. No sense in taking it out on this copper, who's only doing his job. If only I'd done mine!

"The Army would account for his making a neat job of it, I suppose," the inspector offered, and nodded respectfully towards the dark circle of the wound.

But for the sanctity of their surroundings, Michael would have whistled. Oh, quaint irony that! A lifetime spent fighting the good fight had ensured just one thing: that this old soldier knew how to make a 'neat job' of self deliverance.

The inspector sniffed solemnly before drawing the sheet back over the slight still body. An impulse to pursue a question mark in his mind, the notion to find out something further, led Michael to ask:

"Would it be possible — may I see the weapon?"

"Well—" the policeman held Michael's eye for a moment longer, while the late-grafted shoot of police procedure measured its strength against the tap-root of social advantage, and found itself out-classed. "Well, I don't see there's any harm in it. We'll make it 'off the record', though – if you don't mind, sir."

That's his little jibe back at me, Michael decided. Well, why not – what is it all to him?

From one of a row of lockers on the other side of the room, the inspector produced a cardboard box, and stood it on an empty table. The box had once been the home of six dozen cans of pilchards, but now was more than adequate to contain the residue of the batman's life: just the old kit-bag, and his 'civvy suit' bundled tidily with string. Michael wondered pathetically whether the library book had been returned.

The inspector dug into the box, withdrew a pistol, and handed it to Michael.

"There you are, sir."

"But surely . . .?" Michael began.

"Don't you worry, sir—" The policeman offered assurance with a cautious smile, misunderstanding the baronet's hesitation. "It's been unloaded all right. Didn't recognise it myself, never having been in the armed forces – turns out it's an old German piece from the War. Quite safe now, though."

Feeling a queasy sense that what he was hearing and seeing now he had heard and seen before, Michael held the Mauser which had been so dutifully polished by its last owner. For a second time he looked down the barrel, then worked the loading mechanism. The hammer spring had been repaired.

For a few moments more he remained simply puzzled. He remembered Lewis saying,

'Never did 'ave the price o' gettin' it mended prop'ly.'

Then, with a creeping, sickening certainty, he realised where Lewis had got the money for a repair. That fiver! His own cursed hand-out!

'I'll put it against somethink really useful, Captain Mont. You can be sure of it.'

Had Lewis meant to do this all along? Or had that cash given him the idea? Had his own money – his guilt, no less – been instrumental in this act? He feared it was so. How effortless his part in this tragedy had been – and he had thought he was helping! Dear God—! was there any good in money while the want of it was so pernicious?

Outside again, with the sun on his back, Michael gave vent to a long shiver – a physical cold absorbed from the mortuary and the moral chill of many years' standing coming together in one deep shudder from his bones. For a moment he thought to go back and tell the inspector to keep him abreast of his investigation. If there really was no family to be found in Mile End, he wished to be told. Having failed him in life, the least he could do was stand by Lewis in his death. Even if hallowed ground was out – and Michael imagined the fact could scarcely trouble that disturbed spirit further – there must be some decent last billet to be found for an old soldier. For it would have taken a harsher judge of his fellow men than he to rule that Lewis had not died in battle. Michael decided it was more than he could stand to enter that place a second time. He could telephone just as well from his office. That thought put him in mind of Wansdon – he should telephone there, too, and say he wouldn't be down until tomorrow, if at all.

Turning with shoulders hunched and head down, he set course for the House as if into the North Wind. Tracking instinctively by paving stones and lamp-posts, like a dog finding its way to the last place it was not whipped, Michael saw no one whom he passed on the streets, for his conscious mind was lost to visions . . . He saw instead Wilfrid's face, near death, above a white sheet in the military hospital where they had both lain as casualties . . . then the face became another's, suddenly animated, taking on the desperate expression of the man in the Goya, *The Third of May*, only to be overlaid itself with the batman's gaunt, lifeless, wind-tanned features . . . the rebel's white shirt and Lewis's mortuary pall and the infirmary sheet over Wilfrid winding together, round and round . . . it was all one, all one dire, shameful, mismanaged pig's breakfast – and he part of it. Yes, unequivocally, he part of it — Michael was looking to find himself no quarter. Fifteen years spent as close to the helm of the ship of state as made no difference, and all for what? Just to save his skin and damn his conscience? Was this peace with honour? A peace which literally – *quite* literally – was not worth the paper it was written on?

As he reached Parliament Square, a sensation overcame him from which he had so long been estranged that he could not immediately tell its name. By the time he entered the Lobby he knew what it was. By Jove—! it was decision!

Chapter Six

Native Heath

"*Curls?*"

"That's right. I thought it was a dead squirrel at first."

"Oh, Val, you're teasing!"

"Scout's honour."

Holly was torn. She knew her husband's word to be unimpeachable, but after almost forty years of marriage she also knew the kilter of his sense of humour. She looked at him through the mirror of her dressing-table, as he stooped behind her to check his tie. His expression, though reversed in the glass, seemed to her perfectly serious.

"But what did your mother say?"

"She didn't. Just stood, transfixed, and stared at the floor. I thought she was going to pass out, to tell you the truth—"

"Goodness!"

"—Then she clutched her hands together and cried '*Aunt Ann's curls!*' Sent a shiver up my spine, I can tell you. I'm not much used to Mother being delicate."

Holly still wasn't sure that she understood.

"But what exactly were they – these curls?"

"That's the rummest part of it. It was simply years ago – I mean, Aunt Ann died in 1886."

"Yes, I remember my father talking about her when Jolly and I were little. I never met her – or any of the 'Old Forsytes' apart from my grandfather."

"I did," Val said emphatically, "all of them. Mother would insist we went to old Uncle Timothy's once a week to pay our respects. Aunt Ann was the oldest of the lot. She was thin as paper, but with a *look*—"

Val set his own face into 'a look' at the recollection and Holly, still viewing him through the glass, could see for a moment how he must have been as a little boy, being made to plant the ritual kiss on his great-aunt's cheek.

"I reckon they were a different breed, you know," he said.

Holly mimicked his expression until he saw what she was doing.

"Not very different, perhaps," she said, and reached above her head and put her hand to his face.

Val smiled sheepishly. She could still catch him out, this wife of his – she kept him on course, steering with her gentle reins!

"Tell me about the curls."

"Well, we were all a bit surprised really – Mother had thought it was just an empty box, you see. Alexander took it in good part, but he must have thought it was pretty odd. They used to be all the rage, apparently, these hair-pieces – back in the days of reticules and furbelows. All the old ladies wore them – at the front – to make it look like they still had the full set under their bonnets. So Mother was saying, anyhow."

"And the maid had kept the curls?"

"Must have. All these years, too. Just so no one would find out the old girl's vanity. Can you believe it?"

Holly grew thoughtful. Yes, she could believe it. A small, selfless act – strictly speaking, perhaps a dishonest one, but whose whole intent was to protect the vulnerability of another. "I think it's rather a dear little story. Just think how it must have weighed on her conscience to have stolen from her mistress."

She got up from her dressing-table. The sympathetic frown over her mild, still pretty features vanished with a comic lift of her eyebrow.

"Did your mother say what she was going to do with the – bequest?"

"She most certainly did *not*!" Val laughed.

He put his hands on his wife's waist and drew her to him, the woman he had loved since she was a girl, and who had kept the Dartie in him 'on the straight and narrow' without ever making him feel the bit.

"That definitely comes under the heading of women's talk: you can ask her yourself if you've a yen to know."

He kissed her forehead and Holly pushed him away gently.

"Come on then," he said. "The chestnut mare and the black stallion will be wanting their hay."

For several minutes, Holly and Val believed themselves to be first down into the drawing-room, which was only as they intended it should be. A light breeze from the rose-garden played with the curtains at the open French window and filled the room with a soft, powdery fragrance. The memory came to Holly, as it often did on these balmy evenings of high summer, of their farm in South Africa. It had been their first home together after they were married – as babes, it seemed to her now – and where they had lived for twenty happy years.

Holly had never regretted the remove back to England. It had allowed her to be at Robin Hill again, to be with her beloved father during what was to be the last year of his life. And of course it had meant she could finally come to know her then nineteen year old baby brother, Jon, who had proved something of a darling. If only some portion of her own happiness could have been his – she would have surrendered it gladly.

There were still times when she could scarcely believe that she had now lived nearly another twenty years in this perfect condition of heart and mind with Val at Wansdon. From the first she had fallen deeply in love with the view from her windows over the South Downs, and on this dark, velvety evening she traced with her mind's eye every detail of its chalky outline. It had become her native heath, and she loved it too profoundly for words. They were suited, she and Val, to each other and to the life they shared, and Holly considered every moment of her life to be blessed. And Jon was back in America now – would he find some blessing of his own there? Holly wished fondly and very specially that he might; dear Jon!

As a barely conscious projection of her reminiscences, Holly's left hand sought out her husband's right ear and gave it a gentle scratch, while he poured a glass of ancient sherry for her, the last of his grandfather's pre-historic store brought out for the occasion.

As she received the glass, Holly thought she heard the whisper of quick voices borne in on the breeze. Turning to the French window, she saw Fleur come in from the garden.

The moment Fleur caught her cousin's eye she smiled brightly: "How one takes the flowers of England for granted! Alexander is lost in admiration of your roses, Holly. You must name them all for him by daylight."

"I shall put you to no such trouble," said he, suddenly appearing out of the shadows behind Fleur and following her into the room, his expression seamless. "A rose can be no more fragrant because one has its name."

"I believe Shakespeare shared your sentiment, Alexander," Holly said.

"I wonder he didn't mean to say 'rosé'," said Val with a grin, and the conversation was comfortably turned. "Have some sherry."

Because she had bathed and dressed quickly, it was in fact Fleur who found herself first down. She was unaware of her continuing haste. All she knew was that in making this return journey into the heartland of her own past she had committed a terrible folly. Since she arrived, and had learned of their diminished numbers in the house that night, her unease at being back at Wansdon had grown with each passing minute, until now she felt like a wild creature tethered to a stake. Unable to tolerate the empty drawing-room, or perhaps her own company within it, she passed through the French window and began to pace the avenues of the rose-garden.

She sought air and space but found neither. The turns of trellis and iron-work were close-set with climbing roses, the enclosed air dense with their endless scent. In a deepening sky, the newly risen moon slanting through leaf and thorn kept track of her as she wheeled aimlessly, and distracted her will to have a mind clear of all its precious, painful, useless memories. Here, on just such a night, she had given her heart, and received another's in return. Here, in evening air like this, swollen tight with scent and promise, she had surrendered her senses. In a sky as inky and as bright she had found her lodestar. It had been her one object of pursuit ever since.

With these memories and their fellows endlessly turning, she paced on. Then, at a particularly heady junction, she stopped.

One luscious bloom hung low from the arch above her, bowed by the weight of its own aching loveliness, like a manifestation of those very memories. The moonlight seemed to sink into its folds, and Fleur reached up to it, drawing it down to her, as if she too might lose herself within it.

A whispered cry escaped her before she knew she spoke:

"Oh, Jon!" and she drew a draught of the unbearable sweetness into her body.

It might have been seconds or minutes that she stood in this way, with the cool petals pressed to her lips, breathing their scent, until a voice at her side said:

"The smell of moonlight!"

Her exhortation to Jon on that first evening – all but the very words!

She let go the rose with a start. It sprang away to its former loft, as startled as she. Something soft fluttered to the ground in front of her, and Fleur saw that it was a single petal, shed like a tear. She turned her face to the speaker, her composure quickly recovered. The roses, and she, would keep their secrets! Alexander Barrantes presented himself with the slightest bow, inclining his body minutely towards her in his perfectly poised way.

"Forgive me. I did not mean to surprise you."

He seemed sincere. What was it about him that she found so infuriating? And so enticing? This fresh irritation from an external source came to her aid, and Fleur succeeded in holding his eye evenly.

"Nevertheless."

He took the barb elegantly with the least nod of his head, and moved to a section of the path where the moonlight fell untrammelled by the crossing of lattices. He held his face up to the moon, his eyes closed, and Fleur could not stop herself from watching him. He possessed beauty to a degree hitherto unknown by her in a man: even that he clearly knew this to be so could not dent its fascination for her. He began to speak without altering his pose. The effect had a seductive incongruence.

"One scents legend in the air here, amongst the hills," he said languidly and, just perceptibly to her, his nostrils flared. "I understand there are ancient earthworks nearby."

As one might answer an enquiring stranger Fleur said, "Yes

– Chanctonbury Ring," but still she looked at him through her lashes.

"So I read," he replied.

"You are invariably well informed."

"Not one part so well as I should like—"

He opened his eyes unexpectedly and Fleur could see he knew that she had been looking at him the while. Neither so much as blinked. Quite casually he returned to his original position at her side, reached for the rose above her and broke it off, turning the bloom slowly by its stem, running his hand over it as if it were a sentient thing.

"You see, knowledge is my sworn pursuit – my grail, if you like – holy or otherwise."

Fleur wished she could be scornful, but he was clearly serious.

"You consider yourself a knight errant?"

"Perhaps."

This should not pass unchallenged.

"Then tell me; what is it you seek to know here?"

"You had that answer from the first. I wanted to meet your family."

"Well, now you have – all of us."

"Not all, I think."

If he waited for Fleur to confirm or deny this last, he waited in vain. She only said:

"Do we make a good study?"

"The best – of course, the very best!"

"Oh? Why is that?"

"Because you are each so unaware of your own nature. Oh – I mean no disrespect to you, to any of you. Far from it – it is a quality I could wish for myself."

But I suspect that you don't, Fleur thought. She said: "So, you think we all lack self-awareness?"

"To varying degrees, yes."

"Rather a sorry failing, isn't it?" she said, after a short, mirthless laugh. "And our name Forsyte!"

He tilted his head, acknowledging her point as one he had already seen. There was one obvious question which was left hanging, and Fleur could see she was expected to ask it. Despite herself she said:

"Then I suppose I must ask you – what is it you believe you know of me?"

"Ah," he said wistfully. "Of you, Fleur, I know only a little."

"That's a pity, in a way – for you, that is. You know the danger of a little learning, Alexander – 'drink deep—'"

"'Or taste not—'!"

The words sounded to Fleur like a hungry whisper. He was looking at her over the rose, which he twisted from side to side on its stem, as a cat might flick its tail. There was that in his expression which she would rather not have witnessed. She turned away from him, and set her own face to the creamy moon, hard and bright – she as much as it.

"Now I have a question for you, Fleur."

He stood close behind, and spoke over her shoulder. A little *frisson* passed through her, from the sensation of his breath on her skin, but she did not turn.

"—You must tell me: am I to be '*el Caballero de la Triste Figura*'?"

"The knight with the sad countenance? Why ask me?"

"Because it is for you to say – I think you know that."

Fleur knew it too well. She had known it from first sight of him.

"Then yes," she answered. "If your happiness depends on me, very probably you are."

Where his words had been warm at her neck, there was now something cold as the moon, but soft and yielding. Fleur identified it too late to resist its effect. It was the rose – he was stroking the rose against her neck!

"It is not possible—?" he asked slowly, as slow as the trail of the swollen bloom over her skin, "—not possible at all, that you are a lady with a token to give one such knight?"

"If it were," she said, and heard conviction faltering in her voice, "this would be the last place to secure it from me."

"Ah. You have memories here. I sensed something of this from your mood before."

Fleur turned with a snap, freed from his spell by the one thing strong enough to wrench her away – the purely reflexive dislike of having her behaviour characterised. His intuition continued damnable, but she believed him to have made his first wrong move.

211

"If I have," she said coolly, "they will remain my memories."

She took a step back from him, to sever the contact completely, but instead the lowest-growing roses took his part and brushed her calves with their cool, silken heads.

He mirrored her movement with his maddeningly impeccable manners, and remained silent for some moments.

"I have no wish to intrude upon your past," he said at last, almost commiseratively, with a brief lowering of his dark heavy lashes. "*Noli me tangere*. I remember the painting."

Fleur held his eyes once more. There were no identifiable depths in those dark pools! Sensing danger and exhilaration in equal parts she turned on her heel and went indoors.

Chapter Seven

Another Country

During the five minutes which followed, the conversation in the drawing-room proceeded a little too gaily to convince any of those who conversed that he, or she, was entirely easy in the others' company. During the five minutes which followed these first, however, the tenor of the room palpably relaxed, for by that time James Forsyte's sherry had worked its treacly spell over the unintended quartet dispersed upon Holly's comfortable sofas and chairs. For a man who never entered a room without introducing unease, it was an unlikely legacy. In this expanded spirit they soon went in to supper.

After those moments in the rose-garden, and the possibilities which lingered in their silences, Fleur intended that conversation in the dining-room should sparkle. Magpie-like, she seized upon anything which showed even a faint glimmer to her quick bright eyes below their pale and glancing lids. Across the table from her all the while, Barrantes' eyes in the candlelight were like dark gems.

A concerted laugh went up when the pudding was brought in. Holly had arranged for a *bombe* to be made in the shape of a horse-shoe. A *compôte* of summer fruits was served with it. Their glasses raised, brimming with the sturdy mousse on James Forsyte's '95 Cliquot, which Winifred had sent down ahead of her for the occasion, Holly and Fleur toasted the health of the 'August Boys', and wished them many happy returns.

"You must make a wish, Val," Holly said. "And you, too, Alexander."

"Hmm — Well, any nag that looked as good as its odds would do me!" Val laughed.

"Alexander?"

"Ah – I am afraid I must disappoint you all there."

"Oh, why?"

"It's worth a go, old man."

Fleur said,

"Don't say you haven't anything left to wish for, Alexander?"

"Oh, no; I have many. And I wished for one of them. But surely you know, Fleur – if I tell my wish, it cannot come true."

Alone with Holly in the drawing-room, Fleur stood by the open French window and sipped her coffee from a tiny flowered Limoges cup. The breeze had died, and rose-scent hung in the air like a dusting from a powder-puff. From where she stood her view of the downs beyond was pricked out in silver-point by the high full moon. There was no noise until an owl called from a far away roost.

"That's our barn-owl," Holly said, coming up behind Fleur, and looking out at the night. "It's his hunting call."

"Well, he has a hunter's moon to see by tonight."

"Yes. Poor mouse!"

Holly returned to her chair. After an interval Fleur said:

"Did Alexander tell you I've acquired one of your father's pictures?"

The eyebrows above Holly's pretty features arched enquiringly.

"No. Which one do you have?"

"Oh, not an important piece, probably. Just a small pastel."

"I didn't know there were any."

"Perhaps there's just the one."

"How interesting – what's its subject?"

Fleur looked over her shoulder to speak. She wished to see Holly's face as she told her.

"Jon."

"Oh."

She was rewarded with a glimpse of a startled flicker, which vanished as Holly's expression quickly regained its calm.

"Yes," Fleur continued brightly. "Aged eight and in his sailor-suit – he looked a darling even then!" She turned back to the dark hills. Somewhere out there that house stood shuttered and empty. For some reason she thought to ask, "Is Jon's son like him at all?"

214

"A little – but rather more like my father, I should say. There's a quiet tenacity about him."

"Isn't there about all of us?"

Again Fleur looked over her shoulder. Holly returned her gaze steadily, without altering her mild expression, but said nothing. There was something in her manner which successfully defused all attempts at confrontation.

"I met your father once," Fleur continued, her tone a little less bright as she remembered the occasion. She began slowly to move along the walls of the room, trailing a hand over the smooth surface of each piece of furniture she passed.

"When was that?"

"When Jon took me to see Robin Hill. I remember he talked passionately to us about Art and Beauty."

Holly looked to one side and the light in her grey eyes, not visible to Fleur, grew misty.

"That was like him. He practised one and—"

"And married the other?"

"Worshipped the other, I was going to say. But, certainly, he believed my step-mother to be very beautiful."

"Yes. My father thought her so, too."

Fleur returned to her corner of the sofa. Seeing now the kind smile which faced her, she felt suddenly remorseless. It was easy for Holly to be gracious – she had got her wish!

"Do you know, Holly, I believe you're quite a marvel – you're the only one of us ever to have broken through."

"Broken through – what?"

"Why, the family feud, of course! The enmity between your father and mine, and their fathers before them."

"Oh, that – it's old history, surely?"

"But powerful. It stopped Jon and me from marrying, after all. Perhaps we should have gone out to South Africa, like you and Val—"

"Fleur—"

"—and all because of her."

"I don't think that's fair to Irene," Holly said. "An unhappy marriage must be a dreadful thing – for both parties."

"So it must. Though not worse than seeing the one you love

215

married to another—" Fleur caught herself, and lifted her voice once again, "—as my father had to. But, as you say, old history – you and Val have been happy enough for all of us! Now, do tell me – is Jon settling in?"

"He seems to be."

"How long do you think they'll be in America?"

"Jon says it's for good—"

For good! Then it really was all up! Fleur had hoped for any other answer. Though he had said practically as much in his letter, she had somewhere in her heart continued to hope that his stay out there would perhaps be only an extended visit. Now the stark hopelessness of it all bore in on her, and seemed far more profound in this place where the first promise of things had been born. Her commitment, over all those long years, to memories, to wants and dreams, had been ultimately for nothing.

Holly continued: "I think Jon believes that England never really needed him. He says that in America it doesn't matter whether you're needed or not, you can still make yourself useful."

"He tried that before," Fleur said, out of bitterness she no longer troubled to veil.

"Well, he's going to try again. Of course he feels that he should never have come back. He's given instructions for the sale of the farm."

"What about his mother?"

"She's in London now—"

This much Fleur already knew.

"—and I imagine she'll follow whenever Jon sends for her."

"Then she'll have him to herself again. I knew she would."

Another interval passed.

"You know, Fleur," Holly said quietly at last, "sometimes it's better to let go of the past – to let it die."

Advice, however well-intentioned, was at this moment more than Fleur could stand. It burned like acid in her blood.

"Tell me, Holly," she said very directly, and a sharp light danced in her eyes, "did you like my father?"

Holly hesitated. "I – never really knew him. Our paths didn't cross very often."

"But surely there was every opportunity – once you were back

216

in England?" Fleur felt merciless. "You married his nephew, after all."

"Yes. That's right, I suppose. But, Fleur, some things don't—"

"Exactly!"

She snapped out the word, and Holly was clearly shaken.

"You see," Fleur concluded simply, "it's in us all!"

Chapter Eight

Dreams

Long after the house had retired, Fleur sat in the corner of the window seat under the open casement in her room, not daring to lean out into the night for fear of drowning in reminiscence. The moon had only grown in brilliance — how cruel its beauty to a heart such as hers, so long denied, so long kept waiting — wanting!

To her inner ear Holly's soft words returned:

'Sometimes it's better to let go of the past – to let it die.'

Fleur heard their wisdom echoed in the long sigh of the night, a sound composed of all things tender and passing – the rustle of a swallow's breast over its nestling young, the fall of rose petals in the garden, the lost flutterings of a moth at the window.

Here, in this very room nearly twenty years before, her passion had staked its relentless claim on her life. Then, as tonight, the moonlight fell in silvered squares through the casement onto the counterpane; then, as now, an owl hooted in the distance, solitary and forlorn. Was it the same bird? — who knew how long was the life of an owl? Nearer – then or now? – one of the horses stamped its foot at a mouse in the stables, and sent a muffled snort up through the sweet, still, scent-laden air. Here, now, a moth was beating powdered wings against the closed side of the casement, seeking a path to the moon, blinded by the one thing it sought.

'—let it die!'

To Fleur's weary heart it was all one long continuum, she now knew. Jon had been there always. Was she brave enough, bitter enough, tired enough to concede? What did it matter, after all, to keep faith with — a shadow? *Yet it had been real!* So real she could still feel that kiss, still see herself, wearing her *Vendimia*

218

dress, skirts outheld, standing before Jon; he looking up, adoring, saying:

'*It's a dream!*'

and she replying:

'*No, I'm real – feel!*' and then that kiss, which seemed to steal her soul away.

Reaching for the clasp, Fleur opened the closed side of the casement. On weary wings, the moth staggered away into the night.

A soft scratch at her door, as if a cat wished to be let in, made Fleur start from her window seat. How long she had been sitting there she did not know. The moonlight had crept over the counterpane and now lay in a long tranche across the carpet, falling just short of the door which, without creak or portent, opened slowly before her eyes.

"Who—?" she whispered, and hurriedly pushed back a lock of hair which had fallen across her face as she turned and rose.

As the door was checked softly to, she heard that dark voice, now inside her room, answer from the blackness simply:

"I!"

With the moonlight full behind her, Fleur unwittingly presented a celestial figure to her visitor, haloed all round with mercurial rays, as if she had been borne in on moonbeams. And he, just a section of the darkness, a personification of the night, was waiting for her in the shadows.

Barrantes approached and stood silent before her in the moonlight, in all his dark, slim perfection. His hair, brows, eyes, the silk of his dressing-gown, all possessed a deep inky sheen, like the waters of a midnight river – the River of Forgetfulness!

In the silvered stillness of the room Fleur seemed to hear another sound in the night, a soft, urgent rhythm, and found it was her own pulse racing at her temples. Did she imagine there was any but one reason for his being there? His anticipation, as ever, was immaculate; his presumption absolute; his intuition — uncanny. He had surely been a step ahead of her all the way, and now was there to face her at the natural end of that path. Did she even care? What did it matter? Oh, what did any of it matter?

'*Pourquoi pas?*'

He took another step toward her, and very close murmured:

"Do you wish me to leave?"

Commitment! Faith! The luckless message in a bottle, which no one would ever read! At last the image broke into fragments and drifted away; with it went the last vestige of her resistance to his ineluctable power.

As one wishing finally to be shaken from a recurring dream, Fleur replied desperately, yet in a voice so whispered it barely touched the still air around them.

"No – stay!"

Suddenly his hands covered her face, her hair, while his body pressed close, warm, the length of hers. That scent – it surrounded her, smothered her, possessed her senses, as she had known from the first it must.

'Let the past die!'

With the guilty greed of apostasy, her lips sought his.

Fleur passed what remained of the night in dreamless sleep more satisfying and sound than any she had known for many, many years. How sweet it was she realised only when an urgent tapping threatened to snatch her from its embrace. She fought consciousness to stay there, wrapped in that honeyed forgetfulness of want, but the tapping became insistent; someone was outside her door. This understanding wrenched her quickly from the arms of sleep; and then finding that there were no other arms around her in the bed, Fleur first believed the noise to be her dark visitor of the night returning. Only hearing her own name, called from the other side of the door, prevented her from calling his. It was a woman's voice — Holly!

The door opened and in the uncertain half light of pre-dawn Holly's head appeared, followed by Holly's body, wrapped in a neat, plain dressing-gown of dove-grey. A grey figure in ashen light, she was frowning. Fleur sat up in her bed. The warm bliss of oblivion had left her utterly, and in its place came the chill expectation of discovery. What had happened?

As though seeing the question in her cousin's eyes, Holly answered.

"Michael rang – just now. I'm afraid it's your little girl: she's running a bad temperature. Michael thinks you should go back directly."

All Kat knew for certain was that she was cold. Outside, where she stood and shivered, the wet wind howled and lashed the night into a frenzy. Inside, she could see through the window, they were all laughing and talking around the fireplace, warming themselves and sharing smiles. It was strange that they should all be there, for Kat could find no way in for herself. Every time she tried to make them hear inside, every time she tried to shout at them through the window, the wind only wailed louder and drowned out her own cries. Oddly, some of them even seemed to know she was there, for occasionally one would turn and smile at her and, lifting an arm, wordlessly invite her to join them. Even *he* beckoned once. Then Kat screamed all the louder, but still no one heard. He shouldn't stand so near the fire, it wasn't safe! Even when she could see that he was burning, burning horribly, being consumed by flames twisting and turning about him, even then it still seemed to her that no one chose to hear.

Having been reassured by the doctor that his younger child had 'just caught herself a summer chill – nothing at all to worry about', Michael fell into a fitful sleep in which he dreamed of Fleur, dressed in the deep black of mourning, standing before the Cenotaph, upon which monument his own name was engraved.

He was roused from this uncomfortable dream – which might have owed something to the fact that he had fallen asleep in the old campaign chair in his study – by the stern hand of Finty attempting, as it seemed to Michael, to dislocate his shoulder.

"Sir Michael! It's Miss Kat, sir – she's taken for the worse!"

Michael was already on his feet and out of his study, turning the tight corner to the landing, and taking the last half-flight of steps up to the nursery in threes. He took only a single glance at the sight before him, which far surpassed the darkest worries he harboured – which any parent harbours – concerning childhood illness. His daughter lay with her thin white arms outside her sheet, her hands desperately clutching and unclutching, it seemed at nothing. Her small face, usually so pale, was red and angered as a new-born's, her auburn hair clinging in dark curls to the sweat on her forehead.

"Kitten!" Michael whispered, using his old nursery name for her. Just then, as Michael stood looking at her, she whimpered dreadfully. Fearful of losing his wits before he could sensibly request the right number, Michael raced back down the stairs and to the telephone extension in his study.

He was told the doctor would arrive within twenty minutes. His only other thought was to telephone Fleur.

Chapter Nine

Awakenings

The telephone line at South Square was engaged when Fleur tried to place a call after getting up and pulling her things together. While she was dressing, Holly brought her up some coffee which she did not touch. She left Wansdon with almost no ceremony and the least *devoir*, neglecting to return her cousin's sympathetic smile as she got into her car. Coffee and sympathy – she would have neither!

She drove as quickly as before, this time quite conscious of her speed, holding for the most part to the top of the camber. Save for a milk-cart or two and some slow farm vehicles, the roads were empty before her. It was a quarter to five o'clock when she left Wansdon, less than half an hour after Michael's call came through. For another hour the light continued grey and leaden, and Fleur kept her headlamps on as she drove, the lonely road slipping swiftly under her car, the cat's-eyes blinking.

It would be an exaggeration to say that in this fortuitous escape she thought of nothing but her child. Kat had had bad colds, even the influenza before, and was prone to the most dramatic of the available symptoms. Her constitution was sensitive, but not delicate – usually she was miserable for a few days, but there was never any danger. Besides, with no more details than those conveyed to her by Holly, Fleur knew it was futile to speculate. Should that have been enough to stave a mother's worries? Who can say how such a moment would take her? Certainly, Fleur's mind was as fully occupied on her drive back as it had been on the drive down, but, as has been said, with more than one occupying subject. Her night visitor taxed many of the miles under her spinning tyres. From his visit she was herself still spinning. Was that how a lover was acquired? Without negotiation

223

or terms – without overture or prelude? It was a gain, overall, she supposed – though it had been she who surrendered, for what seemed long hours. In that time she had experienced intense pleasure, but no joy; afterwards, there had been great relief but no real contentment. It had been – like falling, and somehow not minding to fall.

'*Between the stirrup and the ground, she something lost—*'

But what had she found? Fleur drove on without incident or accident, nearer the city passing empty buses just out from their depots, early delivery vans and commercial travellers beginning the new day. What did it hold for her? As the light rose fully over a waking city and its yawning inhabitants, she crossed the river at Westminster Bridge and so came to South Square.

Timms opened the door to her, and Fleur saw immediately from the maid's face that there had been a development for the worse since Michael's call.

"Oh, madam!" Timms cried, the instant she saw her mistress, her hands clutching her apron. "They took her to the clinic, Doctor Reardon and the master. Oh, madam – the doctor thinks – it might be meningitis!"

At the clinic in Harley Street, upon whose highly polished corridors white-starched nurses trod with noiseless shoes, Michael sat by himself in a small waiting-room, staring fixedly at a clock on the wall. It too was without sound, no tick betraying the stealthy progress of the hands across its face. All was hushed and pendant, even time seemed caught hanging, suspended like the dark heavy leaves of a large aspidistra which was the other silent inhabitant of the room. Only the hard leather chesterfield squeaked spasmodically as Michael crossed and uncrossed his legs against its studs. He had given up pacing, remembering how he had paced a similar floor when his daughter was born in this same hospital where now she suffered he dared not think what. To see a young child, wrapped in a blanket, being bundled into an ambulance in the small hours of the morning is a particularly dreadful sight. To be the parent watching it happen is perhaps the one thing worse. Now, at bay in the restraint of that spotless and barren room, Michael felt the want of useful purpose corroding his power to endure the waiting. For lack of other activity he fell to examining his own conscience.

Was there something more he could have done? Some overlooked symptom he should have seen? The pædiatrician had told him there was not, that the disease they feared had taken hold of Catherine was frequently mistaken for influenza, even by the medical profession. Apparently so. Michael nevertheless looked to find a contributing fault in himself. He was diligently occupied in this search when the door opened and, looking up, he saw Fleur standing in the room. She looked strained and sleepless. It was barely two hours since he had telephoned to Wansdon; she must have driven like the wind.

"No news yet," he said tenderly, answering the bleak enquiry in her eyes as he went to her. "They've put her in the isolation ward." He took both her hands in his, prising them gently from their unconscious grip around his own wrist. Summoning a half-smile he added, "They're just being cautious. I know they're doing everything possible for her."

Michael felt her flinch as he said this. Her arms recoiled to herself, where previously they had reached out to him, and her eyes dropped beneath their white lids. Did she blame herself? She surely had no need – for, as ever, Michael absolved his wife entirely. No one had known any better to act differently; not even the doctors. They moved together to the chesterfield, and sat side by side on unyielding leather.

Fully expecting their shared anxieties to draw them automatically closer in that proximity, and open to being leaned or cried upon at will, Michael was saddened to find only that he felt strangely separated from Fleur. It was due to something in her, that much he could tell. There was a steeliness under her pallor, a resistance to being comforted that he could not comprehend. She had simply shut him out. And at that realisation a greater sadness worked its way into him, like a slow narcotic administered under the skin – an understanding that if they were to be married for fifty years he would never know his wife any better, or be closer to her privy self than he was now.

An hour passed, during which different nurses looked in to offer beverages and found them in much this same attitude, together and yet so very much apart. One of Fleur's hands lay still between Michael's two, but without any significant pressure on either's part. It was as if she had forgotten it was hers. At the end of another half hour the waiting room door opened again, and the specialist appeared in the doorway.

"Lady Mont?"

Fleur stiffened. Michael stood, keeping his hold on her hand, and braced himself to be strong enough for two – if there was need!

The consultant stepped into the room, a small, neat man with very pink hands and face, and over the rest of him that species of high gloss which seems naturally to accompany an advanced medical salary. At the corners of his mouth a smile hovered for a moment without conviction, then dispersed before reaching his eyes. He turned his neat back to them and seemed to take enormous care with the elementary task of closing the door.

Oh! dear God, Michael thought suddenly. *This is how they tell you it's all up — with the world shut discreetly away!*

The consultant turned back and approached with the precision and gravity of an undertaker. Michael could feel Fleur's hand moist within his; he held it tightly.

"Your daughter," he began, looking at Fleur, and again the unconvincing smile hovered. "Your daughter has a very grave illness. If your husband had not acted so swiftly, I doubt—"

Within his own, Michael felt Fleur's hand shrink to a little closed fist. She was stung, he knew – how dared this man patronise her! Michael felt a rising urge to knock that smile and the rest of the sentence out of him. He checked himself, and interposed, asking:

"Is it meningitis?"

"It is. Our initial diagnosis was correct—"

Hang the man – he seemed almost pleased!

"—therefore the polysulfamide has been all the more effective through being administered at the earliest moment. The patient's response—"

At this stream of words Michael's restraint finally gave way. The fellow was a mountebank! This was not the time for a self-congratulatory speech – they needed the simple facts!

"But she is out of danger?"

"The child remains extremely unwell – but I think we can safely say the worst has passed."

"Thank God!"

"And your own good judgement, sir. You may leave knowing you have probably saved your daughter's life."

"I should like to stay." These were Fleur's first words – it was as if she had returned to the scene from a distant place.

"Of course. There can be a room for you, if you wish."

The consultant bade them good morning, and left the room, taking the same extraordinary care with the door as he opened and closed it for the second time.

A few minutes later, Michael took his own, strange farewell of Fleur in that barren little room. They exchanged sketchy arrangements; she would remain at the clinic until they allowed her to bring Kat home; he would send the maid along with whatever she needed for her stay. It was all very functional and controlled, until he went to kiss her good-bye and, in the second before their lips met, she suddenly opened the expression on her face. In that moment, before his own were shut, Michael thought he saw in her eyes a terrible plea for forgiveness. When, after that unelaborating kiss, he drew away from his wife, her face was once again closed to him.

He left her sitting in the corner of the chesterfield, with a crumpled look to her which he doubted a change of clothes could remedy.

As he passed through the reception area – in its design nearer to a small hotel lobby than a hospital – Michael noticed a man of about his own age sitting in a corner there. Both his elbows were dug into the arms of his chair and, in this position, he held his head in both hands. His face was covered by fingers which seemed to clutch at his dark and rather curly hair as if they feared his head would otherwise fall to the floor. Distress expressed itself in every angle of his body, though the man sat silently, and very still.

Poor devil! Michael thought. He's going through it! As might have I – but for God's good grace.

By whatever unconscious promptings these chances are made to occur, the man looked up momentarily as Michael walked past him.

"Michael?" Ingrained behaviour brought the man unnecessarily to his feet.

"Eustace! What—?" Michael instantly saw the answer to that unfinished question in his friend's face. "My God—! not Dinny?"

Eustace nodded in a way which became a sort of compressed shudder. He staggered slightly, swaying on his feet with the effort of keeping himself reined in.

"Thanks, old man," he said, as Michael put out a steadying hand. "I believe she's comfortable for the moment – they tell me she'll sleep for most of the day."

"What happened? Did she fall – what?"

"We thought it was a chill at first . . ."

Was it possible? Of all the awful chances that would be the worst. As Eustace continued, his voice unsteady as his legs, Michael heard how Dinny had not felt well since getting back to Condaford from Lippinghall. A chill seemed to turn into the 'flu, and then they feared it was something different again.

"I'm only glad we weren't still down at Condaford . . . Came up for the Russian business, like yourself, I suppose . . . Dinny was so pleased they'd finished the nursery in good time, you know. . ." He was almost rambling at this point, speaking lightly as if of the weather, while his hands shook in front of him, like an old man's to the rhythm of his pulse.

In all this, Michael realised there was one thing Eustace was not mentioning.

"And – the baby?"

Eustace looked down and shook his head, and this also became a pinned down shudder. Eventually he answered the question, speaking so quietly Michael only just caught the words.

"She doesn't know yet, you see."

Michael renewed his grip on his friend's arm. Eustace continued to stare at his shoes for a moment and then, looking up pitiably, spoke in a voice that might have come from the confessional.

"I wish I knew how I'm to tell her, Michael. She – we've – lost our son."

Chapter Ten

A Moment of Disbelief

The funeral for Dinny's baby – who in the short minutes of his life had been christened David Arthur Conway – was held at the Catholic Church in Mayfair, on Friday, the first day of September, 1939. Interment – with only immediate family following on – was to be at Condaford.

The coffin was tinier than Michael could have believed, had he not seen it with his own eyes. A little polished box almost lost in a sea of flowers upon which it seemed to float. A work of perfect miniaturisation – it might have been a casket fashioned for a doll.

Michael cast a heavy eye over the congregation. What a *dies malus* was this! In the front row was Dinny, pale and brave, with an expression of quite dire composure on her face. Her chestnut hair was swept up, out of sight under a hat whose short veil framed her sweet, sad face. Next to her, Eustace held her hand in his, their fingers laced and resting on his prayer-book underneath. He stared resolutely ahead at the stained-glass window, through which the morning sun fell in patches bright as gemstones on the little bier. On her daughter's other side, Lady Cherrell could be seen lifting her own veil and dabbing her eyes periodically. The General, Dinny's father, patted his wife's arm, and once in a while cleared his throat.

Then Michael took in the rest of his uncles sitting on the next row, grim as a rank of soldiers awaiting the last post, the best men in the world: Adrian, Lionel, and lastly Hilary, wearing his clerical bib. Hilary would conduct a second service at St. Alice's, where the body (Michael faltered at the thought that it was a baby, so tiny and new) was to be interred. In the row behind this, Dinny's brother Hubert

229

sat between his wife, Jean, and his other sister Clare. Tony Croom, whom Clare had resisted marrying for eight years now, thus sensibly retaining him as her friend and lover, had decided it was better for him to be left out of the mourners.

Without craning, Michael could not see many of the Dornfords, but he had no need to look. They can only be like ourselves, he thought, mired between incredulity and grief, and wondering how best to get from one comfortless bank to the other.

In their own row, to Michael's left, his mother had opened her own personal prayer-book, which she had brought with her to supplement the Catholic text. He looked over at the page she was reading. It was the morning prayer:

'*Give peace in our time, O Lord.*'

Oh, Lord, yes — in our time, please! Michael held his face up to the vaulted ceiling, and found the movement helped his eyes to clear.

At most there were thirty people in the church, all Cherrells, Dornfords, and their immediate partners by marriage. This intimacy of the gathering seemed to help a little, since no brave faces had to be found from reserves of courage already depleted, to greet less familiar friends. By some close instinct, both families were dressed in mourning so uniform it might all have been cut from a single roll of blackest cloth. In the whole church, no one wore so much as a buckle or brooch which caught the light; all brightness seemed absorbed, save where it fell on Dinny's baby's bier. Except there, everyone and everything seemed subdued under a pall of the most formidable restraint.

At first Michael wondered whether this effect was not partly due to the Catholic church they were in, which to his own laxer Anglican perspective gave off a sense of striving for higher order, demanding greater ritual. Michael recalled his father's funeral, the last he had attended, two years before. Then, a sort of sombre merriment had infused the ceremony, as much of Bart's own character as the sobriety of the occasion could properly license. But when his eye again came to rest on the little coffin, bathed in coloured light, Michael understood that in this case their surroundings could have no bearing on the scene. This restraint, which gripped every one of them there with the same steely hand, was a response only to the enormity of the situation. It would doubtless be maintained at Condaford. Each individual was simply at a loss how to react *at all*. How to mourn properly a life completely unlived? How to say anything of consolation? How begin any part of the long process of grief?

The priest and altar boys appeared. The congregation stood, a border of black around the bier. From an organ behind and high above, a plaintive chord sounded. The choir took up their first line.

Oh, Heaven! Michael knew he had not to look at Fleur or he would be lost. Already his eyes swam. What must she be thinking? Six days before, it might have been Kat—!

In its opening verse, the choir reached a last note of soaring delicacy; it was so terribly painful, so inexpressibly sad, to think that here was such loveliness waiting to bear a little lost life over the river!

Out of the corner of his eye Michael became aware that Fleur's hymn-book was trembling. Gently he slipped his own down onto the rest in front of him, and without turning his body put his hand under hers. More steadily now, together, they held one book between them.

Chapter Eleven

Fleur's Next Step

In the week between her instalment at the clinic and the funeral, Fleur kept always within calling distance of her daughter's bedside, for the remainder of the week-end in Harley Street and then – when the crisis was pronounced fully over by two specialists – in the darkened nursery at South Square. For all of that time, the part of her which had so long ago become mistress of the task of womanliness took over her every thought and action. When the child opened her eyes, it was Fleur she saw, bending over her bed, smiling, cooing, comforting. When medicine was required, it was Fleur who administered it, providing encouragement and then congratulations once it was taken. She knew every small fluctuation in her patient's temperature, and made the nurse keep strict notes of all solids and liquids consumed. If Kat slept poorly, Fleur slept not at all; between Monday and Thursday she did not set foot from the house. And on Friday, after that dreadful funeral, she was almost glad to be back at her post. In short, she was considerably more of a mother to her daughter during her seven days in purdah than she had been at any time since the child's infancy.

On Saturday, after a light breakfast taken late in the nursery (with jokes about elevenses at Rabbit's house) from a tray on her knee – followed by two chapters from *Emma* – Fleur left a kiss on her daughter's nicely warm forehead and allowed the nurse to persuade her to take some air. A proper walk, she was told firmly, would do her the power of good.

"Yes, Finty," Fleur said. "I believe you are right. Perhaps I'll take lunch at my club."

On the way down from the top floor, she stopped at her room

to change. It was only when she had changed – into a suit of russet and gold which looked particularly well against her hair – and while she was applying a little colour to her lips, that she saw in her looking-glass the hard set of her mouth beneath the fresh tint of salve. It was then she realised why she re-dressed herself – it had not much to do with her club – and for whom. That subject, which had turned in her head so many ways on the drive up from Wansdon, genuinely had crossed her mind not once in the whole week which followed. Now, duty done, and as she scrutinised her own face in the glass, it returned, but as nothing so mobile as a thought. Rather it appeared as a straightforward imperative – a plain need – to know how things stood.

Outside, Fleur walked towards St. James's Park, passed through it in the space of a few dozen lungs-full of fresh air, crossed the Mall and entered the Green Park. There, in the broken shade of a tall lime tree, some of its leaves already lost to the approaching Fall, she sat down on a bench.

All around her, young couples were out – made up of those lucky enough not to be required by their shops and factories on Saturday morning, and of others not lucky enough to be required at all. They strolled arm-in-arm, or sprawled out on the grass, idling contentedly in this perfect specimen of the days which bridge the two seasons; end days of summer, whose strength was failing gradually with the leaves on the trees, and whose warm breath was tinged with coming chill. Fleur breathed deeply but unconsciously of that prescribed fresh air. She crossed her legs and let one shoe slip from her heel, rocking it slightly from her toes as she sat thinking upon her bench. As for her fellow citizens, they were as insignificant as the piece of purple chocolate wrapper discarded on the path at her feet, which she actually noticed rather more than them. It was as well so, for these young people were undeserving of her scorn for their simple contentment. Instead, unseeing, Fleur sat contemplating the grass on the other side of the path in front of her, and the next step she would take upon it.

Her club was five minutes away, the Dorchester rather less. Where had her feet been taking her? Moved by an impulse she had not yet properly examined, Fleur sensed she had been making straight for the hotel. Continuing to sit motionlessly, except for the slight rocking of

233

her shoe, she faced the impulse square on. In the normal way – she supposed there was a normal way in these matters – she ought to have telephoned from the house, when Michael left that morning and the servants were busy. But to do so had seemed somehow demeaning. Barrantes had telephoned there several times during the week, but always his enquiry had been about her daughter's health, and the maid had been directed to answer all such while Fleur was occupied upstairs. He had sent round a selection of baskets for the recovering child – one would contain crystallised fruits, another chocolate animals. No communication had been persistent enough to come directly to her. This was evidence either of his capacity for discretion, or – and this was Fleur's worst suspicion – that he had no need to communicate with her. If the latter proved to be the case, she had no intention of playing the woman wronged; she simply needed to know. If the former was true of him – it was the more likely, after all, given what she knew thus far of his character – if she had actually acquired the Argentinian as a lover, then the need to know was still greater. Arrangements must be made – careful arrangements – he would surely realise that. As things were at present, she felt as if she had merely been granted a kind of access to him which was solely his to dispense – easy access perhaps, but without right of way. This alone was intolerable to Fleur; the Forsyte in her was used either to privation, or to ownership outright.

In the lobby of the hotel, Fleur went straight to the reception desk. She would ask for him, and get the clerk to say she was waiting in the reading room. If he was out, she would leave a note, on hotel paper. She hadn't thought what she would write in that note, but she was confident of her intention. In any case, the note-paper itself would say much of it for her.

"Mr Barr-*antes*, madam?" The sleek-suited desk clerk replied to her enquiry in a tone carefully calibrated, like a universal spanner, to fit every need and occasion. His eyebrows slid effortlessly up his forehead as he glanced down the register in front of him.

Fleur suddenly saw the measure of what she was doing. There would be many encounters with desk clerks.

"A-ah!" he said, as he found in the register confirmation of that which his manner suggested professional duty required him

234

to know quite well beforehand. "I'm afraid Mr Barr-*antes* left the hotel this morning. For Southampton."

"Southampton?"

Fleur repeated the word unguardedly. There were few things she might have been less prepared to hear, or which could have stung her more.

"Ye-es."

The clerk produced a faint, overworked smile, and again consulted the register. Again he looked up, as if no more than mildly sorry to deliver details which clearly carried further barbs with them.

"I have here that he sails *today* for Buenos *Aires*. There's no *forwarding* address, but his ship seems to be *The New Tusca-rora*."

Fleur stared back at him for a second.

"Didn't he—" she began, and then recovered the appropriate voice. "Was there any message?"

"May I take the *name*, madam?"

She gave it.

"No-o. I'm afraid *not*. Nothing for *Mo-*ont. There was a *par-cel*, I believe. It went a little while ago; *one* moment—"

With a sudden burst of animation he brought his hand down on the bell, then snapped his fingers at one of three bell-boys who all turned smartly at the ring. The boy came over to the front desk at a trot.

"Name of the *par-cel* that went just now; delivery for suite five-oh-one."

The bell-boy looked as though the question made no sense to him whatever. The jaunty angle of his green pill-box hat belied the ingenuousness of his face. Then his blank expression shifted upwards a little.

"Darcy," he said loftily. "Green Street."

The clerk dismissed the boy with a second snap of fingers and, turning back to Fleur, seemed to be sincerely sad for her loss. For with thirty years of service behind him, he could recognise a potential client when he saw one. As though already mourning tips that might have been, he said:

"I'm very *sorry*, madam."

Winifred had taken enormous care with her dress that morning, as was evidenced not only by her more than usually fashionable appearance, as she sat in her drawing-room at Green Street, but also in the discarded pile of unsatisfactory outfits remaining upstairs on her bed, which Miller had yet to replace on their hangers. That job could wait till the afternoon; presently she needed Miller to run errands. There were several items she had just that morning thought to incorporate into the luncheon, and had dispatched the maid to get from Fortnum's. That store was quite a blessing at times, and so convenient – only down the road!

It was now perhaps half an hour away from the time – that unappointed, yet strangely fixed and sanctioned moment – when she expected to receive her habitual Saturday visitor. Dear Alexander — how she had missed him last week-end! Winifred looked at the great ormolu clock, under its glass cloche on the mantel, and for a second her confidence misgave her. What if—? But no! — she rallied that quality of the blood for which she was renowned, and was quickly reassured. It was only because she had missed so many things lately – seeing her brother's Goya at that Spanish exhibition, and the week-end at Wansdon which had claimed her treasured private lunch-partner as well – that she was fearful of further deprivation. She was being foolish – he would come!

Yet there was an agitation within Winifred that morning which refused her best efforts at composure, and kept her old eyes never more than a minute or so on any other object in the room before tweaking them back to the filigree long-hand of the mantel clock, arrested ever nearer to its shorter companion at that appointed hour. It was not to be helped; she knew she would have no peace until he came, and then none really until she told him what she had quite decided to tell him the moment he was comfortably seated. This business about his English relatives was too frustrating – for *him*, that is, of course – and should be settled. What was more, Winifred intended to settle it herself. Why, there was next to nothing to it. Alexander must simply tell her their name – and since they would naturally be a good family, she would practically be bound to know them, or of them, at any rate – and she would then do the rest. She would intercede on his behalf and, through her own good offices, bring about an introduction. It was as simple, she believed fondly, as that. She felt sure Alexander would be sympathetic to her plan, perhaps even grateful for it – he clearly wanted to know these people or he would never have got Annette to introduce him to the Forsytes in their place.

'*They are unaware of my existence*—' Winifred remembered his saying that time she had first entertained him, '*not I of theirs.*'

She admired his discretion in this matter – it was so characteristic, not to wish to intrude – but she had ever held it possible, in some instances, to be too discreet for one's own good. And in the great good which she intended to do here she was not wholly – in fact, hardly at all – disinterested. Once Alexander got to know his English relatives, he would wish to see them often, and they him. And that might mean – she hoped dearly that it *would* mean – that she would see him too, whenever he came to London. It would be nice, so nice, to know she could look forward to seeing him again, on something like a regular basis, after this particular stay of his was over.

Twenty minutes to twelve! Miller ought to be on her way back by now; she was a good girl, and could be relied upon to be quick. Getting up from her chair, a residual twinge of lumbago rising with her, Winifred decided she would check the dining-room a last time, in case Miller had been over hasty with the settings. It was important that everything was 'just so' today.

In the dining-room, Winifred stood by the window and surveyed all that she was mistress of, and all that she had been mistress of for sixty years. Was it so long! It seemed not possible, but was true; fully sixty years had passed since she and Monty began their married life here in Green Street, in this ever-fashionable town house. The late summer sunlight which now filtered into the room cast over every object a golden glow, as if each were alive with her memories. Upon the table, crystal goblets which had been a wedding present from George refracted the light on a hundred tiny surfaces. They had been a set of twelve, she recalled, in a blue satin box, of which these two were all that remained. The old Worcester service had come from Uncle Jolyon on the same occasion – how well that had lasted! On the credenza, in a silver ice-bucket – young Nicholas' gift – an imperial pint from the last case of her father's Clicquot was chilling nicely. Indeed all around her, from every surface, the stuff and fabric of Winifred's life as a Forsyte – as daughter, sister, niece and cousin to that great and sometimes happy breed – glowed back at her, and seemed to set the room humming with recollection. If only — if only Monty hadn't been such a clown! But for that – and his episode with the Spanish dancer from which his spirit never completely rallied – she might still have him with her today—

The door bell rang, bringing Winifred back to the present tense in a small panic. Alexander was early – and Miller was late! Underneath the heavy lace at her bosom – lace being *couture* again that season – Winifred's heart beat with unreasonable speed. For a moment she thought of summoning the cook, or her driver, to let him in, but decades of social propriety soon quashed that notion. It absolutely wouldn't do – and especially not for Alexander! No, there was no choice but one – and, when she thought about it, it was rather a jolly idea, after all.

The bell rang a second time and, for the first that she could remember doing such a thing, Winifred, smiling radiantly, went into the hall to answer her own front door herself.

Her smile fell when she opened the door not to her special guest, but to a young boy in green livery, who looked as if he had come from one of the hotels in Park Lane.

"Package for Darcy," he said, touching his cap. With his other hand he was holding out a long slim parcel to Winifred.

"Do you mean Dartie?" she asked, hesitantly taking it. She was without her reading-glasses; it seemed to be her own name written on it, but in a hand she did not know.

"That's it," he nodded.

The boy lingered on the step, expecting a consideration for his trouble. He received instead an unconsidered thank you as the old lady shut the door upon him.

Winifred took the unexpected delivery with her up to the drawing-room, where she found Miller filling a decanter and setting sherry glasses on a tray.

"Ah — there you are!"

"Yes, madam. I did hurry, madam, but there was a terrible rush at the counter."

"Quite," Winifred said absently, turning the parcel over in her hands. "Tell me, Miller, was I expecting anything today?"

"No, madam."

"Are you certain?"

"I'm sure of it, madam. Nothing. Except for Mr Barrantes, of course."

Seeing that she was not required to say anything else, Miller left her mistress standing in front of the fireplace with her package, and slipped nimbly from the room.

Winifred was in two minds about opening the parcel, Smither's bequest having damped her enthusiasm for surprise gifts. Yet something about this delivery, something in its timing, piqued her. She glanced at the clock. Very nearly twelve – if she didn't open it now she would have to wait until Alexander left. And more because she couldn't bear the thought of having anything distract her from his company than from a real desire to know its contents, her aged hands sought to untie the bow of string around the package.

Surprisingly, string and paper came away easily, and Winifred was lost for somewhere to put the wrappings out of sight, until she popped them behind the fire screen. She found she was now holding a long, flat box, done up in thin ribbon, under which a fold of note-paper was wedged. She took out the note-paper, not stopping to read it, then slipped off the ribbon, and carefully opened the box.

Inside, nestling on a bed of white velvet, was a strand of pearls.

"Oh, good heavens —!" Winifred gasped aloud. "But they're exquisite!"

She had never seen such pearls – at least, not since her own, just as fine, were appropriated by her husband. It must be a mistake. The delivery boy must have meant Darcy after all. Snapping shut the box, she found her reading-glasses and unfolded the note.

The first words she saw were those embossed at the top: **The Dorchester** – Alexander's hotel!

With that same unreasonable acceleration of her heart starting up again, she began to read, and as she read, she seemed to hear that dark, charming voice in her ears.

'*My dear Winifred,*

'*How it distresses me to leave you like this! I would have stayed, were it possible, but events in the world – of which you will soon be aware – have served to make a necessity of my departure. My sadness in going is all the greater because there was so much still for us to talk about, so many confidences left to exchange.*

'When we first were introduced I said I felt that I had somehow come home – I fear you thought me fanciful then! I trust you will believe my sincerity now, dearest lady, when I write that in meeting you, and in knowing you, it is indeed my heart which has found its home.

'I suspect you think me fanciful still! If this should be the case, then I can only hope that as time passes you will remember me fondly whenever you look at these pearls, which, accompanied by my love, I beg humbly to return.'

'Alexander.'

Return—! At that last word, Winifred's knees buckled beneath her, and she dropped into her chair. She looked again at the letter, and again read its final line. *Return* the pearls? But how, if they were indeed hers, did Alexander come to have them? Monty had given them to that Spanish dancer, when he had gone to — Oh! dear heavens, then that would mean—!

Again she heard his dark voice, saying,

'It is my father's family I have not known, since he did not marry my mother—'

It was not — surely it was impossible? She felt her heart squeezed within her breast, at the chance that what was impossible was nevertheless true. Winifred removed her glasses and put a hand to her head to fight a feeling of giddiness which rose up as contradictory sensations tumbled inside her. To recover suddenly something so long lost – lost utterly, beyond hope of retrieval – and at the same instant to lose something so entirely unhoped for, and so newly found – it was almost too much to bear. Her good sense, so long the flag-ship of her constitution, foundered utterly, assailed by this notion amidships. She watched her resistance sink without trace. Her heart had raised its colours — she wished to believe.

'They are unaware of my existence, not I of theirs.'

Winifred recalled how Alexander had seemed all along so strangely familiar to her. Imogen had thought so, too, at that first evening at Fleur's. But if – *if* it was true – why hadn't he said something to her, made himself known to her for who he truly was?

*'Tell me, my dear Mrs Dartie – in the circumstances, **would you?**'*

Is that what he had meant then? Were the relations he had never met themselves? It seemed fabulous, an invention of her own deepest and most foolish longings, and yet — here were these pearls, which he said he returned.

As quickly as her thin trembling fingers could comply, she sought to re-open the box. Taking them from their bed of velvet, and letting the box fall to her knee, Winifred held up the pearls between both hands. The sunshine through the window, that mellow, evocative light so conducive to memory, so capricious with longing, played upon their lustre as they shook gently with the tremor of her fingers.

As her heart was seized again by the significance of that one last word in the note, Winifred's pale eyes swelled with tears, and she knew beyond any doubt that these pearls were her own.

Chapter Twelve

. . . And the Nation's

Stepping out from the hotel, Fleur returned smartly to South Square, her pride piqued to the marrow. A whole brood of feelings churned around inside her, each vying for supremacy over the others. She felt cheated; she felt abused; no less than either of these, she felt foolish. And, somewhere deep in what remained of her heart, she also felt disloyal. For so very long she had been faithful; faithful to Jon's memory, to her love for him, and to the sweet lost promise of what might have been. Now she was left with the distasteful fact that the man she was prepared to throw that loyalty over for had deserted her.

Obeying that automatic and not uncommon instinct to spread misery around, Fleur instantly set about finding fault with the household. Within the hour its habitual air of serene order was transformed to one of haste, bustle and mute irritability. She checked the blackout curtains, which had been stitched on to the lining of every drape, and was vexed to see that the needlework was exemplary. She changed the menu for lunch in the nursery, and invented one on the ground floor; she directed the removal of the television cabinet – useless now that the Corporation had stopped broadcasting – to limbo, or an attic if one was found first; she discovered dust in corners where hitherto none had existed, and disliked the arrangement of ornaments which had been unchanged for years. After all of this, furthermore, she felt not one whit better.

She went upstairs to her bedroom, taking the newspaper with her. There, sitting on the little pink-and-white chaise under the window while waiting for her newly ordered lunch to be prepared, she began to read on the front page how German troops had yesterday crossed the Polish frontier. Absently she took a cigarette from a box on the Pembroke table – she had returned to the habit under the stress of the past week. She struck her lighter, and inhaled. Grey smoke threaded the space between herself and the eight year old Jon. She continued to read – half-digesting other articles about the situation in Europe, Sir Nevile Henderson's intercession with the German foreign minister, and Mr Chamberlain's speech to the House – but failed to be distracted by her own device. She impatiently turned to an inside page, re-folding the broadsheet for closer examination, and was not satisfied until she found the Argentinian's name on the passenger list of the *New Tuscarora*. There he was – and there was the gong—! She dropped the folded paper onto the striped cushions, mashed her cigarette in an ash-tray, and went downstairs.

Michael felt he had been through more than a day of it, too. The mood of the House began as one of nervy anticipation and grew to an agony of suspense as the hours passed. Wound tight as jockeys at the starting post, Members waited all day for the flag to fall. The invasion of Poland in the small hours of the previous morning had removed all possibilities save one. Between pacifists and imperialists, appeasers and polemicists, there was now a common bond, a universal sentiment – simply *'Let's get it over with!'* When the Prime Minister appeared in the Commons that evening the tension was like an electric charge running through the assembly, packed hip to haunch on the green leather benches of Barry's fine gothic chamber.

But as Chamberlain embarked upon his speech, it seemed that what they were hearing – what the PM was leading up to pro-posing – was simply a second Munich. The Government would do nothing, he declared, until Henderson had received a reply from Ribbentrop. The Germans were to be given a last chance to with-draw. A ripple of incredulity, rising to anger, went around the Chamber. Was Poland to be made dispensable as Czecho-Slovakia had been? Surely not? Surely he, even he, knew that the time had come? *He's missed the pitch of the hall*, Michael thought to himself. *The old man's off by a mile.*

When Arthur Greenwood – acting Labour leader since Attlee's illness – got up to reply, there was a moment's silence before he reached the dispatch box. Little Leo Amery, sitting along from Michael, shot to his feet in that second and cried out:

"Speak for England, Arthur!"

Michael's heart was in his throat as the cry was taken up across the House.

Greenwood spoke robustly, saying he was gravely disturbed at the delay. He reminded the Prime Minister, to a rumbling chorus of '*hear, hear*', about the country's treaty obligations towards Poland, where a state of war had existed already for a day and a half. Michael could see Chamberlain, below him, shift in his seat, and then confer with Sir Kingsley Wood. There was a hush all around, which remained until Greenwood concluded:

". . . I wonder how long we are prepared to vacillate, at a time when Britain and all Britain stands for, and human civilisation, are in peril."

At this a concurring surge of voices went up, as loud on Michael's side as anywhere, his own voice among the many.

Chamberlain made a forceful denial of weakness, but when the session ended it was known that many members of the cabinet were in mutiny. They demanded, and were to be given, a further meeting at Downing Street.

With his raincoat collar turned up against a light rain, Michael negotiated his way home later that night by the low beam of a small pocket torch, which he used for only seconds at a time, and then extinguished. It was the second night of the blackout and, on a route he would have known blind-folded, he found himself stopping at corners to check his bearings, like a timid traveller in a strange land. His eyes as yet unaccustomed to the darkness, familiar things seemed to him both larger and smaller by turns. Quite modest buildings loomed out against the sky, and broad pavements narrowed to thin paths – a couple of times he almost turned his ankle on a kerb-stone. *This is the way!* he thought. *We'll all die under buses before Hitler gets us!*

At the corner of their square – he *believed* it was their square – he tripped over something lying in front of a house gate. Michael put his hand down and touched a cold, damp pelt. He snapped on his torch, and saw at his feet the body of a dog. Its dead eyes glistened at him dully in the feeble light – it wore no collar. Poor beast – the first casualty! Michael dragged it gently to the gutter. With any luck it would be gone by the morning.

On the safe haven of his own doorstep, Michael reached into a pocket for his latch-key. Then it seemed, from nowhere, a phosphorous bomb had been dropped – at his back suddenly the square danced in high relief. He turned his face to the sky. Lightning! The air sang with a static charge. Barely a breath apart, an almighty thunderclap cracked angrily overhead, racking the sky, letting fall a storm of Old Testament proportions.

'*And the first heaven passed away . . .*' Michael said to himself, glancing momentarily at the uproar, and slipped quickly inside.

The door was barely shut behind him, and he was only half out of his wet raincoat, when a warm body in a soft wrapper flew into his arms. Fleur! — She hated storms!

"Oh, Michael — hold me!" He was grateful to oblige, wrapping his arms around her as she pressed her face into his neck.

"Hey there—! Let's get you back to bed. It won't last long, old thing. The wardens will soon remind God there's a blackout!"

Upstairs, they huddled together on the bed, Fleur with the covers drawn around her, Michael sitting next to her on the quilt. With every successive roar of thunder, each one sufficient to raise the dead, she crushed herself a little further, and a little more desperately, into his shoulder. Michael could have wished the storm to endure all night, but after several intense minutes, and whether owing to any persuasion by local air-raid wardens, it passed on, moving to another borough, to rattle other windows, and frighten other folk.

In the strange, tense lull which followed, Michael felt obliged to loosen his arms around his wife. Fleur, regaining her own calm, pulled silently away. After a little while she asked:

"I suppose that's it?"

He knew she did not mean the storm.

"It appears so."

"When?"

"They say the PM will speak tomorrow morning – a radio address."

"Good," she said simply.

Michael slid from the bed and in the more familiar darkness of his dressing-room began to undress.

"So what happens now?" Fleur asked finally, after Michael had relayed everything he had witnessed in the House that day. They lay in bed, back against front like spoons, her head on his arm, both facing the window that Fleur had opened on to the clearing night. The moon had returned, paler after her drenching, and dipped in and out between tail-ends of cloud.

"I wish I could say I knew, but I don't – no one does for sure. There's still a chance that we'll call Hitler's bluff by declaring – it may come to nothing."

"Or everything." She had heard the phrase 'total war' whispered around.

"Yes. I'm afraid that is a possibility – although a remote one at the moment. The safe money's on it all being over by Christmas."

Fleur dismissed this last statement with a quick shake of her head. It was as if she had staked all she owned on the longer odds. When in her life had she not?

"Will there be air raids?"

"Possibly—"

Michael felt a quick flinch next to him. The feel of it against him stung like a slap on the face. Clearly she wished him to tell her something definite, however bad, but there was little he could truthfully say, other than that hackneyed exhortation to 'wait and see'. In any case, he knew it was beyond her nature to comply.

"In fact they're expected momentarily," he decided to confess. Later he could tell her about radio location, and the coastal defences. For the moment all he added was, "It's one thing old Anderson got right – at least we've the shelters for those."

There was no other woman before whom Michael would have spoken so forthrightly. He shifted his arm under her as she turned onto her back and stared up at the ceiling. In a passing trail of moonlight he caught the light in her eye. It seemed to crystallise then, and stamp her features with a new kind of determination. This was evidently what she needed to hear!

"The children shall stay at Lippinghall," she said. She spoke evenly, with little more inflexion than she might have given to a troublesome shopping list. "Finty can go down with Kat tomorrow."

She paused. Michael sensed the tension in her and knew she was thinking through the new situation, sifting out the details relevant to herself.

"There must be something I can be needed for here in town," she said, and now he heard the lift of urgency beginning in her voice. "Can you find me something, Michael? Something real?"

By Heaven — she was determined!

"Darling, if that's what—"

"Yes. It is what I want. I must *do* something this time, Michael, or I shall go mad. Kit and Kat will be fine with your mother. I must stay here, where things matter."

Michael could have said any number of things, not least of which that as her husband he forbade her to put at risk the one person he held dearest in the world – namely, her own. But the certainty that nothing he might say would make any difference – would in any case come too late to influence a decision already taken – kept him from speaking his mind. Instead, in a voice that he wanted to be encouraging and with a smile which, though invisible, tried not to be regretful, he said:

"Then we'll find you something – something *real!*"

Her hair was suddenly against his face, and her arms were squeezing him, hugging him tightly around his neck. The embrace lasted only a few seconds, but in that time Michael may well have fallen in love with her all over again. And the world well nigh lost—!

After Michael fell asleep, Fleur slipped from her sheets and went to the little striped chaise beneath the window of their room. There she sat for long hours, watching the freshly cleared night sky, and trying to see into a future which was lying beyond its dark veil.

So, here it was. War. Her first response, carefully hidden from Michael like so much of what she had been feeling in the preceding months, was a bitter one. To commit herself to perfecting a life she had not wanted for nearly twenty years and be rewarded only with another war was a body-blow to her inner composure, to that part of her from which she derived her very sense of self. She might as well have held out for Jon in the first place – steeled herself to face the threat of ruin after, bold with victory – as well as suffer so

247

much the same fate now. After all those years of compromise in a life of constant substitution, and despite her early discovery that life was by no means fair, this struck her as a new and monstrous injustice. Which way now? Was this the end of it all, or just the new beginning of something far worse? Was the crisis of her own drama deepened or resolved by this greater play? Could it be any easier, now that the worst seemed set to happen? She felt as if the whole of her existence were on the brink.

Leaning from her open window Fleur stared out into the remains of the night and waited for dawn – the first of war. She had taken up a cigarette but for a while forgot to light it. It hung unconsidered between her fingers. There was no light outside. The stars, consenting or not, had vanished, drawn over the horizon by the moon. Inexhaustible darkness stretched out before her and for long minutes seemed to take her soul with it to the borders of existence. What was a life, that it could matter in this nothingness? In her own void there had been only one anchorage, one sure, fixed point, one pole-star. Like the sky above her, she was without even that now.

Michael stirred in his sleep, and she turned at the noise. The room at her back was unlit, and its small darkness seemed no more welcoming than the huge abyss before her. For some little time she thought of nothing, was aware of nothing, except her own mortal self and its balance at the window. Desultorily she picked up the lighter, and toyed with it, striking it aimlessly, the cigarette still unnoticed between her fingers. By the yellow flare from the flame she saw the newspaper lying next to her on a cushion. She picked it up, folded as she had left it before lunch, and in the way that a tongue will seek out an aching tooth she sought again, by the arc of light cast by the little flame, the passenger list of the *New Tuscarora*. There was his name – he had sailed that afternoon! Well, he had been distracting for a while – as her mother would say, *ah là . . .*

There, suddenly, was another name – further down the page in the same column, at the extreme edge of the yellow arc. The flame jumped in a puff of air from the window and for a moment, as her eye lost its place, Fleur believed herself prey to hallucinations. Hastily, she moved the quivering light down the page. It was not another departure she had noticed but an arrival – on the *Ile de France* from New York. Yes, there it was – in plain print!

'*Mr Jon Forsyte and family . . .*'

He had returned! But — why?

Something came back to her then – something Holly had said at Wansdon.

'*Jon believes that England never really needed him—*'

Could it be he now believed that she did? It must be so – why else would he return so soon, and bring his children with him too? It was the war, Fleur was certain, this hateful, threatening war which had brought him back – to England – and to her!

She snapped shut the lighter and let it fall with the cigarette to the chaise. She turned back to the open window, the paper held tightly to her, barely breathing, not daring yet to think. For a moment she feared nothing had changed, that nothing could make a difference. All seemed still and dark as before. And then – slight and sudden – Fleur felt the shift. Hesitant at first, then with growing conviction, the blackness shrank back minutely from its furthest limit and she saw the beginning of grey appear, and, beyond the grey, the thinnest promise — light!

She had witnessed it – at the same second in the ether as in her soul – the almost imperceptible return of perspective, a frail but renewed sense of shape, of the place and proportion of things, of everything which had for so long been lost to her. Thinking was unnecessary now, as now there was no alternative left to consider. Only one thing remained to do. To take up the fight! To have and to hold – or lose forever – her heart's one desire!

The air had grown brackish and chill with the breeze off the river. Beneath her thin wrapper she shivered – but her spirit was resolute.

'*No retreat, no retreat, they must conquer or die who have no retreat!*'

Silently Fleur closed the window on the shifting tremulous dawn.

Book Two

1940–1945

Dark Clouds

---

*'Here and here did England help me –
how can I help England?'*

Robert Browning

Part One

Chapter One

A Present from the Past

On the evening of his thirty-ninth birthday, Jon Forsyte realised quite suddenly that he had learned to live with the fact of his wife's death, and this came as something of a surprise to one who had also learned, many years earlier, not to expect too much from his life.

For the weeks immediately following that riding accident the summer before, the knowledge that Anne was dead would creep up on him at every unguarded moment. Like the worst-imagined monster of his childhood, it would spring out from dark corners and set him shaking. In the night he would wake, sweating, from dreams in which he tried to carry her to safety – her body broken in his arms, his feet weighing like lead and moving so slowly he might be wading through treacle. Such was the strength of these visions that upon waking he instantly doubted the evidence of the empty bed beside him. Those moments at night were not the worst. Worst were the fragments of days when he forgot about her altogether. Waking, as it seemed, from these moments filled him with a panic he had never known before. Only once perhaps; an experience he had while flying – initially a skill he had mastered for spraying crops, and latterly his chief recreation – when his engine cut out, and his heart seemed to go into freefall with it for long seconds, until he got both restarted.

Anne's accident was almost a year ago, and during the interval the seasons kept the only calendar for the lives lived at Green Hill. Christmas, Easter, the children's birthday, Anne's soon after, were all occasions to be negotiated, endured for others' sakes, not enjoyed. For Jon, a spectral absence pervaded each day, feast and fast alike.

Now his own birthday – not an event he was previously given

to marking overmuch – was upon them, and reluctantly he now realised it held no fears. It seemed as if all his grieving, while by no means over, had at last brought him a kind of peace. This, when he did realise it, troubled him quite as much as anything. It was a thing he had not expected – and as yet, also a thing he did not know he wanted. For Jon was a man possessed of a conscience.

He had loved his young American wife for many reasons – because she was dear and kind, because she had given him children and because she loved him – but mostly he had loved her because he owned a conscience.

His father had once reflected that a man should be born old with the full wisdom of age and, growing young, take that wisdom with him into all the possibilities of youth. It seemed to Jon that his own youth had been harried with problems. It was fully twenty years since he had known a life without care; twenty years to the day since he had first met Fleur, his unimagined cousin, in June's gallery. From that encounter first love had blossomed, only to be blighted by a quirk of family history. Then his dear father was lost too soon and his beloved mother widowed in consequence of the same detail. A second love, new-found in America, had been hurt by his own treachery with the first upon their return to England; and now that second love was taken. Recently Jon had more than once allowed himself to wonder what his life would have been, had he and Fleur— But twofold guilt 'cut in' on his wonderings. He had no right to imagine Fleur out of her life, nor Anne out of his own!

On that May evening, with the scent of summer's approach on its breezes, Jon stood by an open window in his bedroom with these inner shadows reflected in the grey of his deep-set eyes. His outward occupation, however, was the arrangement of his tie before a cheval-glass. He had agreed to have a supper that night, for the combined households of Green Hill, Wansdon and – if genius permitted – Chiswick also. The habitual accoutrements of what he once overheard described as his 'rather tweedy' middle-age – pipe, reading-spectacles, jacket of the aforesaid cloth, twill trousers and brogues – lay discarded in his dressing-room. He had bathed and dressed with more than usual care, and believed himself to be very nearly looking forward to going down. They would be seven, all immediate family: it would be quiet and comfy and, better than either, not difficult. Unlike this tie!

There was a light knock at his door.

"Yes?"

"May I come in for a moment?"

Jon found a smile for his sister as she stepped into the room. Holly saw quickly, in the dim focus of his eyes as he turned, that it was mostly a technical accomplishment.

"Sorry," he murmured, as he turned his shirt-back to her again, to continue with his tie, "I can't ever get this thing straight without a mirror."

"Let me—"

Holly crossed the room, setting down a small morocco case on the ledge of a tallboy before taking up the two jumbled ends of black silk beneath the points of her brother's collar. Jon jutted his chin in the prescribed manner, while she inspected his handiwork so far and set to work improving it. For a few moments the ritual of tying was conducted as if it was the sole object of their concentration.

"Is everybody down?" Jon asked his sister, over her head.

It was a dry bone of a question, she noted; polite, but hollow and brittle. Holly decided a buoyant note was required of her.

"Just Val and June so far, I think," she answered. "I left them on the stairs looking at your Stubbs. June was explaining that he didn't actually paint *horses*, so much as the socially relevant *image* of a horse, dictated by the values of the times in which he painted – or something like that! She's really a marvel at seventy, don't you think?"

"Yes, she is."

No change there – Holly maintained her tone.

"It is sweet of her to make the journey, after all. She hates to leave the gallery."

"Yes."

"Apparently, she's between geniuses at the moment."

"Ah."

"So it's a good time for your birthday supper—"

Holly saw her brother's chin jut up another inch.

"Is it?" he replied, and Holly heard faintly for the first time the arousal of conviction in his voice.

She had completed a satisfactory bow, and raised a small sallow hand from the knot to his face. But Jon turned quickly away. The gentle touch of his own hand, which put hers from him as he turned, told her he was reluctant to be brusque; but it was a clear gesture.

Jon moved to the open window, and gave his face to the pink and purple evening. He put one knee on the settle under the window, and leant his knuckles on the sill. Watching from behind, Holly saw his shoulders rise expansively in a single deep breath. On the warm air, the heavenly mixture of apple-blossom and woodsmoke reached her, and tweaked her heart. She picked up her package and joined her brother silently at the window.

Outside, the light was caught in exact balance between day and night. The evening seemed leant on an easel, its colours muted pastels, the shadows just charcoal smudges from an artist's thumb. The view beyond the garden on this side of the house was continuous orchard, the source of that aching under-scent, the apple-trees smothered in a surf of their own blossom, rippling towards the blurry mid-distance. Far beyond, with stilly mists between, the roll of the Downs appeared no more substantial than a cloudbank.

The ticking of myriad slight insects, and the drowsy cooing of doves which had once been Anne's, formed all the sound for a while, until Holly said:

"It *will* get easier, Jon."

"Perhaps it shouldn't get easier. Perhaps — I don't want it to."

Half-brother and half-sister lapsed into a further silence as unevenly matched as their parentage. To fill the void, other species joined the doves in evensong, piping from scattered roosts. Only a blackbird broke from the chorus, and swept low across the lawn calling recklessly. Unseen somewhere below on the terrace, a game of tag started up suddenly between the twins. Two young voices, remarkably alike, rang out in contiguous laughter and then as suddenly subsided, as the pursuit continued inside.

"I remember when Jolly and I were children," Holly said, "and we couldn't get our way over something, Dad would say, 'If you don't face it *now*, little ones, it will only seem bigger and worse when you *do*'—"

Jon smiled in surprise – the great gap of years between his

two sisters and himself allowed him rather to think he had been his father's only child.

"He used to tell me that, too."

"Did he?" said Holly fondly. "Well, he was right, you know. Sometimes it's the only thing one can do."

"I reckon Dad was always right. Oh, but Holly, I thought – I thought I had faced it – Anne's death. I thought I'd faced up to it completely. But—"

"And you have, Jon. You've done admirably, everyone says so. I rather think," there was a delicate understanding in her voice as she went on, "—well, that all you haven't faced is yourself. You can't go on atoning for something that wasn't your fault."

Jon instantly hung his chin. As usual, Holly had spied the tender truth of his situation, and found the gentlest way of expressing it. He nodded guiltily into his chest. Holly returned her hand to his cheek, and he let it stay for a while.

"I've been thinking about Dad a lot, lately," Jon said at last, casting himself on to the settle. "He went through it twice . . . oh—!" he nearly sprang up again, "I — mean—"

"It's *all right*, Jon."

Holly sat down beside him and briefly pressed his hand, her warm gaze unwavering. It was easy to forgive this allusion, which in part was to her own mother's death. She understood her brother well enough – it had been only an unthinking reference, not a thoughtless one.

Jon looked glumly into his hands, no happier for his absolution.

Holly had been waiting for her moment. This seemed as good as any, and she lifted the box from her lap.

"Now, I know you said you didn't want to be given any presents—"

"And you promised!"

"Yes — but this is different. I've been wanting to give it you for a while—"

She held the old square morocco covered box out to him. Jon took it tolerantly, and in the hope that it contained nothing extravagant. He could feel Holly's eyes on him as he removed the lid.

Inside, with its perfect circumference snug against faded velvet, lay an old gold hunter. Jon took it out, and held the ancient watch

259

in his palm. Its worn casing felt smooth as butter. He guessed it had a meaning, but could not tell what, and looked up enquiringly.

"It was Grandfather's," Holly said quietly.

Jon squeezed her wrist with his free hand, and she went on.

"He left it to Jolly, and then it came to me with his belongings when—"

She paused to overcome a catch in her throat.

"—when he died", Jon said, as quietly, "—the year before I was born. Oh, Holly – surely you can't bear to part with it?"

"Well, I shan't be, if you'll have it, Jon. I've wanted you to for the longest time, but there never quite seemed the moment. If Jolly had lived, it would probably be his son's by now. So, you see, you must have it – it's only right."

Jon's heart sank under the weight of the gift, unwanted but beyond refusing. Jolly – his father's first son! His own brother, never known, who died in the Transvaal during the Boer War. Jolly, short for Jolyon, whose death had freed the family name for himself, and whose feeble substitute Jon now more than ever felt himself to be.

Here was the essence of what he had so long been feeling. That from as far back as he could remember – actually from his birth, it would seem – he had been caught in the middle of events that were neither of his making, nor of his mending. More and more he felt the net of circumstance everywhere around him. *If Jolly had lived—*. Well, perhaps that would have been a good thing all round! Jolly's son could have taken the name as well as he – far better, probably.

He looked up at Holly, feeling an ungrateful cur to have such mongrel feelings, and yet not at all sure he was wrong. He managed to force thanks into his eyes.

Holly felt her own begin to swell, and some of the pink of the sunset rose in her cheeks. Her blood instinctively retreated from that frail barrier ahead, so important to Forsytes young and old, which divided what was felt from what was shown. She retained the moisture behind her lashes by looking down at the watch, as it lay across the flat of Jon's palm.

"I never thought to wind it, do you think it will still work?"

Jon took his cue – not caring either, to breach that too-familiar dividing line. He held up the watch in his palm almost to their eye level and, very gently pressing the pendant, released the lid of the casing.

The aged mechanism, which had never yet failed its duty in more than a hundred years of service, remembered its charge. With pearl-white face tilted up to the next Jolyon Forsyte of the line, and thin black hands closed at twelve o'clock, as if in prayer before a requiem, the repeater began to strike. Echoing from the ages, its mellow note sounded solemnly in the room, and through the open window drifted away on sweet air into the unknowable future.

Chapter Two

The Past in the Present

In the drawing-room, beneath a portrait of her mother by Harold Blade which it was said she resembled, young Ann Forsyte sat back on her stool at the piano and, as the last note of a Bartok rhapsody took wing from under the slant of that instrument's glossy black lid, allowed a first smile to light her face. She swept her long hair back over her shoulder; she no longer wore it in a golden plait, but loose under a pair of tortoiseshell combs, and it had fallen forward during her playing. Running a hand over these quickly, to make sure they were still in place, she stood to a hearty round of applause from her audience, divided between two long sofas either side of the broad fireplace. They were hopelessly partisan, of course, being just family – but how sweet they all were to be so encouraging!

A kiss first for her grandmother, for turning the music perfectly, and then a special birthday hug for her father.

"Ann, darling, that was marvellous!" he said, standing, and she went over to his wide open arms.

"Happy birthday, Daddy!" she said, squeezing him hard. "You said we weren't to give you presents, so that was the only thing I could think to do instead."

"It was the best present ever."

She hugged him quickly a second time, then went the round of the others. Her brother, rising after his father, made do with a knowing tilt of his elbow against hers, and a sidelong look. Being a young fellow in his third 'half' at Eton, such demonstration was enough; anything more would have been silly and superfluous, particularly between two who were so close in height and feature, and in understanding. He scowled at her from copies of her own brown eyes, and Ann knew his congratulations were sincere. She wrinkled her rather sudden nose at him in return.

Her aunt and uncle each pressed a hand in sequence, and kissed a cheek.

"I do envy you, Ann. I was never one part as good as you. You make it all seem so effortless."

"If you get any better, you'll have to start charging admission. Five bob for a good seat in the stalls!"

"You have real talent," said her other aunt, from the opposite sofa. Somehow the compliment came over rather as a caution. The girl went over to her, and looked down into fierce blue eyes which squinted up at her through a veil of wrinkles. "I hope you intend studying seriously one day."

"Oh, I'd love to, Auntie June," she replied, and dipped down to place a kiss on the tilted cheek, "if I ever dreamt I was good enough."

"I'm sure you are, child," June answered imperiously, and turned to look over the back of the sofa. "You teach her, Irene: you must think—"

"I think," Irene said, taking the music sheets up in her arms, "that Ann has a long while before she need do anything seriously." She walked around the front of the piano to where a case lay open on a little table, and laid the music inside. "As long as she enjoys her music, I've no doubt it's a possibility, one of many—"

"But you were happy at the *Conservatoire*, weren't you?" June persisted.

Ann alone saw a brief shadow pass across her grandmother's face, still so very lovely despite her age, at this reference to her early days in Paris. The sight of it made the girl wonder what – apart from her study of music there, which was inconceivable – had been its cause.

"Yes, June – you are right, of course!" Her smile was soft, but her look was impenetrable. "But you'll allow me to be indulgent and wish Ann many times my own happiness, won't you?"

June could not think what properly to answer. A servant appeared and Irene continued.

"Now – if we are all ready – I'm sure supper is, too!"

She turned her smile to Val, who offered his arm readily, and together they led the way. Jon took in his elder sister, and Jonnie his remaining aunt. Ann followed behind them, a half skip lifting her step, her unoccupied hands entwined at her back, and left her mother's portrait to preside over the empty room.

With this particular seven around the table, the meal was rather more animated than it might have been, say, had they been minus the Chiswick contingent and only six.

June was in fine form, and before the main course was served had put her foot irretrievably into several subjects.

The conversation began innocuously enough, with Irene asking Holly how her work as an auxiliary nurse at the cottage hospital was coming along.

"Oh it's great fun – though the equipment has advanced quite a bit since June and I did our training for the Transvaal."

"I'm glad to hear it," said June, her spoon suspended over her soup. "Do you remember those ridiculous 'sterile' procedures they taught us? I'm certain they didn't make a scrap of difference out there."

"But these new drugs we've got now would have, I'm sure, June. They'll save thousands of lives this time."

"I dare say the lack of sub-tropical disease in darkest Sussex helps, too. Hey—!"

Val already knew that Holly forbade him to tease June; under the width of the table her toe against his shin was an unnecessary reminder.

"Tell us about *your* search for war work, Val dear."

"I thought you were all-fired to join the local defence when it starts?" Jon asked.

"I *was*, but I scotched that."

"Oh, really? Why?"

"I didn't reckon my leg would be up to the drilling, even without a rifle. And besides, I saw our fellows yesterday. A couple of antique generals polishing their shot-guns, waiting to go over the top. They looked a dreadful lot of — old soldiers."

Val had been about to repeat his original complaint to Holly, that the *avant-garde* of what was likely to become the Local Defence Volunteers were '*a dreadful lot of old women*', but her toe gave him another prompt.

"Isn't that the whole point?" Jon asked, aware of the traffic under the table. He laughed. "Anyway, you're one yourself!"

"You're caught out, Val, admit it," said his wife.

"O.K." Val smiled sheepishly. "But I don't see your tin-hat hanging around, old man."

"No; but it may come to that. I'm having no luck with anything else."

"Where have you tried?"

This was a sore point with Jon. Too young to be conscripted in the last war, and practically too old to volunteer in this present one, he was nevertheless determined to 'do his bit'. Government restrictions, he had discovered, seemed devised not to let him. He avoided looking down to the end of the table where his mother sat, since it was a matter that for several reasons he had not yet discussed with her.

"I offered my services at Mastonbury, but it was no go."

Almost as soon as that first air-raid siren had sounded, mistaken though it was, it had occurred to Jon that his own aviatory skills might be put to better use than averting the not inestimable threat of black-fly and bark-beetle. Without happening to mention the fact to anyone, he paid a visit to RAF Mastonbury, and had privately nursed the grudge of his rejection ever since.

"What – not even the Reserve?" asked Val. "Surely you're not too old for them?"

"It's not that. This 'reserved occupations' business is the problem."

"But you've got a farm manager," Val protested.

"I told them that, but it wasn't any use."

Jon might have added that with the situation in Europe growing worse he fully intended calling on the Station Commander again, in the hope that things might have changed to his favour.

"I even suggested they might use me as some sort of flying instructor."

"And they turned you down for that, too? They must be cracked."

"The COC quoted King's Regulations at me, and suggested I try the Air Transport Auxiliary out at White Waltham. Flying planes between factories and bases, that sort of thing."

"And did you, Jon?" asked his mother.

She had always managed to know when he was keeping something

265

secret. Between Jon's brows a crease set in, as if to defend himself against the unspoken accusation which hovered in her dark eyes. It gave him an expression which someone he had once known called his 'lion-cub' look.

"I plan to," he said, "but I may have missed my chance there, too. It seems they drew up their register of pilots holding private licences at the end of last summer, when – when we were away."

The 'lion-cub' look set a little deeper over his features, as if he had just then become aware of the cage closing around him. In a second unwitting echo of that other person, he added,

"I must do *something* this time."

"It isn't your fault you weren't old enough for the last war, darling," Irene said.

"I wish I had been. Everyone else has managed to contribute at some time, except me. Val fought, June and Holly were nurses, and—"

Jon stopped short of saying, '*and Jolly gave his life*'. That old habit among Forsytes, still active on both sides of the family, of not telling things, had extended to the next generation concerning that short life and death, as well as certain other matters. Consequently neither Jonnie nor Ann knew of their lost uncle.

But ancient secrets, as history has shown, are never invulnerable to detection. June's foot, in any case, was already in position.

"I'm *glad* you were too young last time! And thank Goodness the children are too young this time – that's all I can say," she said, and her head quite shook on her thin little neck with the strength of her feeling. As everyone else around the table began to believe she had finished, she went on. "Just think, if Jolly had been a year or two younger—"

Jon looked quickly at Holly who was sitting between the children – her chin dipped fractionally – and then to his mother, whose eyes met his. Val looked into his soup plate.

June took no notice of the expressions flying around her. It only remained for everyone to wait for the inevitable next question, which came in seconds from the very youngest there.

"Who's Jolly?"

"Do you mean you don't know?" June demanded of her nephew. She swept the table with an accusing chin.

266

"Oh, what is it about secrets in this family!" she cried. "I've never seen the use of them – they only make things worse! The truth never hurts one!"

"Other people's truths never do," Irene said quietly.

June caught another impenetrable look from her old friend at the end of the table and subsided, biting her lip. Jonnie repeated his question, and both children were suddenly alert with interest.

"Well – there was never—" Jon began, struggling to know what to say for the best.

It was Holly who poured oil.

"He was my brother."

"Another uncle!" exclaimed Jonnie, astonished.

"*Was* your brother?" Ann asked.

"Yes," Holly said evenly. "I'm afraid he died in the Boer War."

"Oh." The girl's face showed instant sympathy. "Where you injured your leg, Uncle Val?"

"That's right." Val tuned his reply to the tone he had heard in his wife's voice. "We joined the Imperial Yeomanry together."

Ann was always a sensitive child, and felt the need to say something consoling. "Gosh – then you must have been great friends."

This was the way with June's particular talent. By putting her foot so adamantly into these things, it was as if she cleared a path for others to follow. Now it was Val's turn to struggle, as he remembered his old adversary. How he had wanted to break his nose for him! He nearly had, too!

"Well, we — we were all cousins, of course. I say – turbot – terrific—!"

That might well have been that, as the fish came and went, and a saddle of lamb – that peculiarly significant Forsyte dish, over which many notable scenes had been conducted in the past – was brought in. Even so, *per se*, the lamb might not have been enough. June's infectious influence was the deciding factor.

"It's a funny name," Jonnie said at last, just when the conversation might have been turned for good.

"Short for Jolyon, of course," June declared simply.

Jonnie, as at least four adults there anticipated, was aghast.

"But that's father's name! And mine!"

"Jolly died before your father was born, darling," said his grandmother, in that calming way of hers which usually worked with him. "Grandfather and I both wanted the name to go on."

On this occasion, the boy was only somewhat reassured.

"Oh."

Again the conversation might have been diverted, since enough thought was being given to achieving it. But June was on her mark for one final insertion.

"So, when you marry and have a son," she added, cheerily, "he can be the next Jolyon, you see?"

June was confident that this last contribution had brought the subject of her opening to a comfortable close, and indeed the talk moved on while vegetables were distributed. Only the twins continued to consider what she had said, sharing many thoughts in their silent closeness.

In adjacent rooms each child sat at an open window framed with creeper, looking up at the stars in the still warm night. The two windows shared a little mock balcony, just deep enough to hold a trough of flowers between them. They had debated for a while what other family secrets might yet be hidden from them, but the nature of the subject soon defeated speculation. A minute or so of companionable silence followed, until Jonnie suddenly asked his sister:

"You won't ever marry, will you, Ann?"

"I don't think so. That is – I don't know. Would you mind terribly?"

"Oh, yes – terribly. You wouldn't want to *really*, would you?"

"I suppose I might, if I loved someone enough."

Jonnie fell silent again, but a mood that was not so companionable bristled from him. He plucked at a polyanthus in the trough.

"You might find someone yourself, you know," Ann suggested gently.

Jonnie shook his head. Somehow it was not quite a childish gesture.

"No."

"You always say that, but I don't see how you can possibly know. It's so many years away for both of us. How *can* you know?"

Jonnie looked at his sister as if it was already a betrayal to ask. "I just do."

Downstairs in the drawing-room, in a tableau replicated the length of the country, the voice from the wireless-set held its listeners captive with the news – much iterated that weekend amid bulletins of the German invasion of the Low Countries, and the continuing air battle over France – that the King had received with regret the resignation of the Prime Minister, Mr Chamberlain.

His Majesty, they were told by the disembodied voice, had asked Mr Churchill to form the new administration. Mr Churchill, furthermore, had accepted.

Chapter Three

Bosinney's Monument

That his injury gained in one war had barred his participation and probably saved his life in the next, seemed to Val Dartie not the sort of equation upon which a gentleman could properly take his debts on that account to be settled. Having met the first and missed the second, here was a third opportunity to serve afforded him in his lifetime. Like the majority of his compatriots, reading daily and listening nightly to the ominous news from France, Val felt the instancy 'to do his bit'.

He had first thought of Local Defence but, as he had said at the week-end, didn't fancy having to rub along with the old generals. Probably he had encountered too few of them while serving in South Africa. It was true, in any case, that his leg was not up to the drilling. In fact, anything that required much mobility off a horse was out; that old injury, however out-dated its merit, meant he was no longer reliable even for driving any distance. What he wanted was something active – but sedentary. Aware of the contradiction, he continued to scout for a cause – 'like the dowager with the heirloom no one wants', he told Holly – until his keen eye eventually alighted on the Observer Corps. Two-thirds through his sixtieth year, his eyes were still sharp enough to spot a fox at a hundred yards and this was what gave him the idea. Accordingly, on the Monday after Jon's birthday supper – where, thanks to June, so much that was previously closeted away had been so healthily aired – Val asked his wife if she would drive him into Horsham in order that he might volunteer.

"Is that O.K.?"

"Of course." Holly watched as her husband ate his breakfast

with his customary relish, and wondered how much longer they would be able to get kippers. "I don't have to be in London until about twelve."

"What about June? Isn't she anxious to get back?"

They shared an expression which indicated June was always anxious to get somewhere.

"Twelve *is* June's time for being there – I can collect the supplies for the hospital at any time. So you may as well cadge a lift, too."

Val nodded over his napkin.

"Consider it cadged!"

"But, Val, I've just thought – how will you get back?"

"Take the train as far as it goes, and then walk the rest, I suppose."

Their local line took the easiest route through the Downs, shunning the incline wherever possible, though catching a good many little villages 'on the flat', as Val described the Vale of Sussex, as if desirous to make up for inadequacy elsewhere. The branch line from Horsham stopped short of Wansdon, and their old manor-house nestled higher up the hills on the north side of the village, by a long way further than Holly thought good for his leg.

"It's nearly three miles – do you think you ought?"

"Well, if it gets too bad, I'll start thumbing."

"You could 'phone and ask Ives to pick you up from the station in the van."

"Not likely! Can't take a good stableman away from his duties. I've had to give him a pay-rise to keep him from signing up, as it is. I'll be fine, don't worry."

Asking Holly not to worry over her husband, even when the request came from the man himself, was quite as pointless as asking a whelping bitch not to lick her pups. Worrying for Val, her dearest friend and companion for more than forty years – managing his life for him, but so gently that he need not notice the fact unless he chose to – was by now a deep instinct with her. Without children of their own (her decision, since they were second cousins) all that was nurturing in Holly had devolved upon Val. Rather than betray her concern to its object, she looked down and stirred cream into her morning coffee. They would never be without that ingredient, surely, with so many dairy farms around!

*

271

From Horsham, with June now beside her – and with the discreet pressure of Val's hand on her arm and the brush of his moustache on the corner of her mouth still lingering sensations – Holly turned her car towards London, and the westerly borough of Chiswick. Her route lay through Reigate, Croydon, Kingston and lastly, before crossing the river by Chiswick Bridge, Richmond. On a day already guided by instinct, Holly found that the nearer she took her vehicle to the river, the more the old home of her childhood was in her thoughts. Robin Hill! Not seen since – since when? Since that time when Jon had first brought Anne to see the place, after a lunch at South Square; when Fleur had come along, too. So many years had washed the sad memories of that summer all but away. Too many years! And a fanciful little indulgence began to hatch in her heart. She became aware of it only when she noticed a new construction on Richmond Green. It was a municipal air-raid shelter. The sight of it jarred Holly's long-stored memory of the place, as she drove past.

There was the turning ahead. Robin Hill within three miles! Had it changed? Holly glanced towards her passenger, looking for evidence of recognition. It had been June's home for a while, too – she might have mixed feelings about being so close.

Her sister's caution was redundant. June sat oblivious to location. Like all other pointers of social convenience, road signs meant nothing to her. In her own way, perhaps, she had been admiring the scenery thus far. Holly hoped so, but it was difficult to tell. These days, a little fiery scowl had become the chief fixture of June's face, through which all other expressions must take leave to pass. It was true to say that not all succeeded. Even when she did smile at something, it was not a reliable indicator of approval.

"We're in Richmond, June," Holly ventured. "Hasn't it changed?"

"That ditch doesn't help. We must be near Robin Hill."

Dear June! She scattered so much buck-shot whenever she opened her mouth, one sometimes forgot that not all of it landed painfully. Now; did that mean she *would* like to see the old place? She waited for a moment, but June said nothing more. Holly gave her the benefit of the doubt – probably she wanted to get back to Chiswick – and returned to her own thoughts. A traffic-light barred the way on to London, and its red light gave her pause. Was there any particular reason why she should want to look at the old place now? Holly searched her brain and found none. Red and amber; but was there any reason why she should not? They would be past the turn soon.

"June, dear?"

"Mmm?"

"Do you have time for a very small *détour*?"

"I think so; it's a pleasant day to see places."

At this sanction, and barely half a second before the green light showed, Holly put an arm out of her window and indicated an imminent turn. Then she changed the signal into a little wave, to show the driver behind her she was sorry for changing her mind so late; he immediately regretted that he had applied his horn. Turning back around Richmond Green she made for Robin Hill.

"Men!" said June irritably, at the noise. "They can never make up their minds!"

Such memories! Even the old road out was instantly familiar to Holly, so many times had she taken it by carriage or on horse-back in those old days. She felt akin to every tree along the way. Would the house be so unchanged, after all these years?

Seeing the main gate open when she reached it, Holly realised that part of her had hoped it would be shut. Slowly, respectful of that all-important lapse of ownership, she drove her car up the curving gravel way, lined on the house side by a screen of poplars, and approached like the uninvited visitor she was. She kept her window down, and listened for voices over the rhythm of her engine. She heard a cuckoo call mockingly from the walled fruit-garden, but nothing else.

Then, suddenly, the poplars fell away, and on the crest of the hill she saw it. All of a piece and in a single moment, the majestic white rise of the house was before them.

In the bonny spring sunlight, which by late morning was streaming on its face, Philip Bosinney's masterpiece wore its first half-century with beguiling charm, and without a wrinkle on its white-stone complexion. Sun-blinds down like lazy eyelids, and drawn at the same slant and in the same hue as its green slate tiles, the house seemed caught basking in the day's glory and its own, while to the side the old oak, its guarding spirit, stood solidly by.

Holly drew up a little way short of the front aspect, parking discreetly under a low-hanging yew, out of sight of the windows.

While June stayed in the car, her expression becoming oddly vulnerable as she stared ahead through a windscreen quite obscured with over-hanging branches, Holly walked up to the door and knocked.

How strange! — to bid for entrance into this place which had once contained the entirety of her life. But better to ask for permission to look around than be discovered in mid-circuit. Receiving no immediate or even interim reply, she stepped back to scan the windows for a face appearing at any of them. None did, and no sound came from within. From the wall of the fruit-garden, or a place near to it, the cuckoo repeated its private joke.

"No one's home," she called to June. "Shall we walk around?"

After their modest tour around the place, past what had been Old Jolyon's fernery and then Irene's rose-garden, now badly overgrown, they came to a halt at the rear of the house. On the very edge of the garden, by the old oak which no longer carried a swing beneath it, they stood together for several minutes looking out. Before them lay the meadow, falling first away towards the coppice where the larches grew untended, and then in the distance growing shimmery and blue with ten thousand bluebells. At their backs and brooding in the sun lay the house, the font of Forsyte song and story.

Holly sighed contentedly. This was the *mise-en-scène* of her childhood, her only remembered home for all her life before Val.

"It *is* a wonderful place. So peaceful — so — timeless."

June replied rather sharply.

"The product of genius is always timeless."

June gripped her handbag more tightly to her flat little bosom, and rocked on her heels. For her the house held another story altogether. While Holly remembered early days with her father and grandfather, the names of horses ridden and loved decades ago, and the moment when she received Val's first kiss, June's thoughts had gone back further still. She had been thinking of the architect of the house – literally the genius of the place – to whom she had been engaged those millions of moments ago.

Aware of some of this detail, Holly sensed there was a tender memory to be soothed.

"What was he like, June? I've never known."

"Phil? Oh! he was — splendid!"

Her small figure rose shakily on tip-toe as she announced this, like one craning for a glimpse of a passing hero.

"He didn't care a fig for convention, or for what people thought of him – he didn't care for anything except his art!"

In this, June had re-written history somewhat. There had been a time when Bosinney cared — *loved* — so deeply that he was prepared to lose everything – his art, his career, and June too.

"He created a monument here," she declared, turning back to the house.

"To Art and Beauty."

"Yes! Phil worshipped both."

This second declaration seemed to have brought her too close to the primary material of past events for the comfort of her own revised version. Her scowl intensified in a brief spasm, and then seemed to pass away altogether.

Holly said:

"Grandfather loved this place, and father, too. I sometimes wonder – if only Dad hadn't died so suddenly, it might still be in the family."

"Yes, it's such a shame—!"

Holly took this as fervent agreement with her own sentiments, until June flew on—

"Such a useless shame – Jon and Fleur *should* have lived here!"

Holly's eyebrows lifted involuntarily. She had assumed it to be a given wisdom that *that* marriage had never taken place.

"Surely you don't think Jon would have been really happy with Fleur – do you, June?"

"Has he been really happy without her?"

June's scowl returned, as she squinted furiously up at the four ivied corners of the house in front of her.

"In any event," she continued passionately, "I think he ought to have been allowed to try. They both ought to have had their chance!"

Holly made no direct answer to this. She knew too well that she had been allowed hers, and that her every happiness flowed from it – as Fleur herself had not shunned pointing out to her the last time they met. June, too, spoke as one who had been denied. But then, there had been more parties to the drama than just those two young lovers, and Holly began to put their case.

"I know Father was against it, June, before he died. And Irene—"

"Irene should have put up with it!" June cried, and stamped her foot. A trace of something forgiven, but never forgotten, quivered in her voice. Holly knew there was nothing else she could safely say.

The cuckoo piped again in the silence, like a needle stuck on a gramophone record.

"That bird repeats itself," June said impatiently. "Shall we go?"

On their way down to the road they saw a van, newly parked half-on, half-off the gravel at the foot of the drive. As Holly drew level with it before turning onto the road, a young workman got out and touched his cap to her, taking her car for one belonging to the house. He then set about nailing a pole to the gate-post.

As driver and passenger both looked left before their car turned right, they caught sight of a sign fixed to the top of the pole.

In bold black letters, beneath the name of a well-known London agent, was the inelegant but not inaccurate phrase –

IMPORTANT FAMILY HOUSE
FOR SALE

Chapter Four

The New G.O.M.

For Fleur, whose nature forever chafed against restraint in any form, the sight of the end of what they were calling the 'phoney' war, in that eventful spring, came as a blessed release. As with the breaking of rain before a storm – much as she hated storms – the oppression of waiting and wondering was lifted, along with that terrible feeling of being held down which above all she could not endure. There had been a point, some six months ago, now, when Fleur felt she might well shoot the next person who ventured to tell her it would all be over by Christmas. She wanted it to come – long-lived and hard-fought if necessary – and she wanted to be at the centre of it when it arrived. Nothing less, nothing short of total immersion in the 'war effort' would be enough to absorb her.

By Christmas however, so far from being all over, 'it', in fact, had not even begun. As usual the season was spent at Lippinghall, with Michael's mother, and his sisters Flora and Celia, back from their outposts in India and China with their respective families. There Fleur found herself marooned for two weeks on a sea of optimism and good humour which, of all their party, she alone had to dissemble. Deprived of due cause to shoot the next person, though many times tempted, she had borrowed a Purdey and shot spinneys with Michael instead.

Beginning in the new year, and continuing through a horrid snow-bound winter into the spring, she undertook an early campaign – restricted to a border skirmish, and hopeless as it turned out – to induce her mother to leave France. Annette would have none of it. France was strong, the French stronger, her *Armée de l'Air* invincible: she would remain. In all fairness to her, Annette

277

had wanted to return there when the first war was declared, not caring to be *dépaysée* while her '*pauvres*' suffered. But Soames had put his foot down, insisting her place was with her husband and child in England, and left her the option of knitting socks for soldiers. Now for this second engagement she was home, and meant to stay – *à l'outrance!*

The telephone conversations Fleur had therefore to conduct with her mother were profoundly irritating, since she had no love of showing concern for people who took none for themselves. Her irritation was compounded by poor and nowadays increasingly intercepted lines to Paris.

The latest of those exchanges, on that same Monday morning in May, was no better than usual.

"But what if France *doesn't* stand firm? Michael doubts——"

Fleur was interrupted by a sharp sound on the line. At first she took it for another of many mechanical distortions; then she understood it was a hiss from her mother.

"Tch! Michael — is an *Englishman*. All Englishmen doubt the French; and do you know why, *chérie*? Hmm? Because secretly they all admire the Germans."

Annette did not actually employ this last noun. She used the words '*les Bosches*' with an adjective after the definite article, and a tone resonating centuries of Frankish discord. She added:

"*We* have always seen them for what they *are*."

"Perhaps so. But there's simply no reason in running risks with your life over ancient history——"

"Do you think not?" her mother purred. "You surprise me, Fleur."

"I wish you would see sense."

"Tch! There is no sense in my being in England. Your father stopped me from returning the last time, when there was no danger at all. As always, he was concerned for his *pr-r-operty*."

Such disdain in a simple roll of the tongue!

"But if France *is* in danger this time?"

"Then I would not wish to be safe in England. *Cela va sans dire*."

"Well, I want you to know it's a tremendous worry."

"There is no need. That was always your father's way, to *r-r-ride* before the hounds. It did not imp*r-r-rove* him."

There was another indeterminate noise on the line, after which Annette's voice continued slightly ameliorated.

"But nothing has happened yet; there will be time for worry when it has. Be practical, *chérie* – remember, you are half French!"

It was in the frame of mind hereby engendered, and not assuaged by the prospect of a working lunch, that Fleur stepped out from her shining front door at South Square on a mission to disband one of her charities. She felt sufficiently uncharitable for the task.

The fine May morning greeted her instantly – bright, clear and altogether bobbish – and brought her close to losing hold of her mood. The gardens were thick with outer greenery, though through the border of railings and climbing roses it was just possible to see where the lawns and flower beds had been divided up into strips for vegetables. She had instructed the cook to have peas and runner-beans put in theirs, since broad beans were forbidden. And a raspberry cage might do well in the sun. The trees were untouched, mercifully, those tall friendly planes with dappled trunks and leaves like great hands. From their shade this morning that unendingly cheerful London refrain of sparrow and starling sang out at her. For once it seemed appropriate, and did not grate on her nerves.

Fleur stood on her threshold and for a moment almost forgave her mother's intransigence. Such weather beggared belief in a war which had as yet been barely evident on the worst of days. But, as with the spring, it was a delusion to think it might last. How lucky her mother was, to see her path so clearly: France for the French, the French for France – *et à bas les autres!* A comfortable and self-perpetuating balance – which her daughter had not inherited.

Fleur struck off towards Piccadilly, her face pleasantly shaded beneath the brim of her hat, and her legs agreeably warmed through their 'nude' silk by a waxing sun. She submitted to these sensations as she walked, taking note of the brisk traffic – human and machine – which passed her on the city's streets. There were some uniforms about, but not so many as before the Expeditionary Forces went out. Many people carried their gas-masks, but quite a few did not. Fleur, mindful of her husband's public position, always took hers, in the calf carrying case she had had made for it. There seemed fewer private cars about, but many more taxis. Some had been attached to the auxiliary fire service and carried ladders on their roofs and towed pumps on trailers behind. Shop fronts looked a little less opulent, but in these parts that was managed chiefly for appearance's sake. Rationing, by and large, was still something which affected other people – though petrol at one-and-ten a gallon was a shock all round. The most obvious changes were the air-raid precautions; rough St. Andrew's crosses on every window, and an abundance of sandbags. Fleur frankly doubted the efficacy of either measure. Would dexhoid tape really prevent the glass from flying when the raids came? — and surely a sandbag could kill you as well as a brick? She tilted her head up and saw in the distance the one other inescapable detail. The barrages – great balloon shapes like sheep tethered on the horizon – signalling that the first danger would indeed come from the sky. She dismissed a shudder and walked on.

Though Fleur absorbed her surroundings through her conscious senses, her inner self acknowledged them only as a corollary to her main cause. These early details of the engagement without served only to strengthen her resolve for the one within.

When Mr Chamberlain declared the country at war last September, Fleur had made a private declaration of her own. In the odd hiatus that followed it had not been possible for her to act on it, any more than it had been possible for the country. But, like the nation, she had at least mobilised her resolve. Being a child of the century she was a weather-vane for its every mood. Now there was a new PM, and Fleur was beginning to feel that the battle, and the plan for winning it, were drawing closer.

They might know something of Mr Churchill's strategy concerning Germany that afternoon – Michael had obtained gallery passes for her and Winifred to hear his first speech. Fleur's own strategy, meanwhile, was nothing like so near to hand. All that was certain, was that it concerned Jon. After a scare that he might emigrate last summer, he had come home to stay. This was the first point in her favour. Jon was widowed furthermore, another convenient detail, and from all accounts she could obtain – no more than the odd unguarded word from Winifred passed on from Holly, but enough – he looked set to remain unmarried. Instinct, her only ally in this engagement, told her there would never be a better moment to put her war-plan into action. For that was what she had decided upon – nothing less than full-scale war.

Fleur was set to go 'all out' to regain Jon, even if it took her years.

The charity – the one involving Rumanian babies – was briskly wound up. Since the Axis they had been able to do very little of any use, and that with less efficiency than justified the continued raising of revenue. People would want to concentrate on domestic causes now, Fleur reminded them.

Emily, the over-thin and impossibly elegant Lady Gore, offered a glassy smile at this, and Fleur just managed to catch the words,

"*Some* of us have never concentrated on anything *else*."

The last note taken down in the minutes was a unanimous motion that existing funds, and any which might come in subsequently, were to be passed to the Red Cross.

Going on directly to Parliament Square, with ideas about a replacement *cause* forming sketchily in her head, Fleur sought her aunt in the Lobby, that lofty purlieu, and found her scrutinising a likeness of Gladstone. Winifred was dressed entirely in shades of lilac, and wore a sort of pill-box hat with a veil over it. Fleur thought she looked a little more like Queen Mary every day.

"Ah, there you are, dear! We used to call him the Grand Old Man," she said, nodding at the stucco effigy. "I was just remembering how your father made a point of coming here when the fellow moved the Home Rule Bill in '86."

"Was Father interested in Ireland?" Fleur thought it unlikely.

"Oh, no, dear – of course not. But your grandfather had got him a pass, and Soames knew he'd have a fit if it was wasted. They say Churchill is in the same mould. Of Gladstone, I mean – not your grandfather. What does Michael make of him?"

"That he's a good talker, and it's obvious he was after the job. Michael abstained in the vote after the Norway debate – he wanted Halifax – but he says they'll all rally now."

"I should hope so! There was no question of it in the Kaiser War. Lord Kitchener was such an inspiration; although I suppose this chap followed him at the War Office, after all. Here is Michael!"

Some years before, Fleur had encouraged her husband to give up formal dress in the chamber and lead the way in lounge suits. Today in common with many in the House – never slow to perceive history in the making once it was right under their noses – Michael had returned to his tail-coat and winged collar. She had forgotten how smart he looked in white piping.

The Member for Mid-Bucks greeted first his wife's aunt, then his wife. Fleur pressed her cheek into her husband's kiss. She found it easier to concentrate on other matters when she was kind to Michael.

"What was it Disraeli said of him, Michael?" Winifred asked, indicating the statue again, "—about his being drunk all the time?"

Michael's brow wrinkled for a second or two, then cleared.

"Oh! yes— '*A sophisticated rhetorician, inebriated with the exuberance of his own verbosity.*' "

"That's the one. And was he?"

"Permanently tight, I believe – come and hear another!"

Escorting them to the gallery, Michael took Fleur's arm and said, "Are you missing your babies now, old thing?"

"Rather – and on the scout for another *cause, célèbre* if poss., but anything hearty will do."

Hearty it needs must be, she knew, for her own heart would be occupied elsewhere – for the duration, if not longer.

· "I'm certain anything you take up will become celebrated. I'll keep a look out for a good'un."

Fleur tucked her head towards him. How sweet and loyal he was. Oh, well!

The gallery was ridiculously packed, but they were in a good row. Making space for her aunt on one side, Fleur had almost to sit upon the knee of her neighbour on the other. The man looked like a magistrate, or a bank manager, and she perched on the very edge of the bench so as not to appear to be encouraging him. She looked down and found as much of a jam below. All across the Floor there was a distinct buzz, as of something marked out in formic. There was a palpable sense, if not yet of direction, then at least of moment. And by all accounts, the man of that moment had just taken office.

From so high above the chamber, Fleur's view was at a distorting angle. Each person there below seemed all head, like a peg-doll – and some of them every bit as bald! While the Speaker gave the order of the day's events, Fleur sought out the newly elevated Rt. Hon. Member for Epping. When she had first seen him he had just rejoined the Conservatives and was Chancellor – and Michael

282

was making his maiden speech! There he was, sitting behind the despatch box. Her immediate impression of the man now, as he sat with his hands closed over his waistcoat, was that he had all the appearance of a rather cross Toby-jug, with those scowling eyes under sprouting brows, and a defiant jaw lodged between the peaks of a too-high collar. What a face—! He turned in his seat to speak to his neighbour on the front bench, and under the effect of this animation the likeness, to Fleur's mind, passed from the aforesaid jug to Tweedledee. Next to a mirror, she thought with a smile, he could be Tweedledum, too, and irreverently recalled:

'*Tweedledum and Tweedledee agreed to have a battle—*'

Well, there seemed a 'good'un' coming!

The business of the day was got underway. Mr Eden was fielding questions about enemy parachutists, and how they were to be tackled. Fleur watched as the heads bobbed below, up and down like organ stops.

"*. . . Will he consider the immediate formation of a voluntary corps composed of older, responsible men to be armed with rifles and Bren guns and trained for instant action in their own localities, in case of raids?*"

The questioner sat down. Mr Eden bobbed up.

"*This matter has been receiving urgent attention in the light of recent events . . .*"

Mr Eden sat down. Another questioner bobbed up.

"*Will he look into the precedent of the last war, when a voluntary force was organised?*"

Mr Eden bobbed up. The questioner sat down.

"*I am aware of this precedent . . .*"

Fleur scanned the back benches and found Michael, squeezed on an end. He twinkled a quick smile up at her, which she returned. Then Winifred spoke at her ear.

The Member for Mid-Bucks, having caught his wife's eye, returned his attention to the Floor. Yes, they ought to get a move on with Local Defence. If we don't authorise it, it will happen anyway, and anyone with a pop-gun will be out for glory. From the other side someone shouted something along the same lines.

"*Let us arm everybody! Let us all have arms?*"

Eden was getting a hard time from across the Floor, but handled it with suavity. It was *de rigueur* for the Left to mistrust that combination of good looks and a pleasant voice in ministerial office; Michael tended to agree.

Another question:

"*Does the right honourable gentleman realise that his supporters in this House do not seem to think he has the capacity for the job?*"

It's in the air, thought Michael. All we want to know now is who can get the job done. On that score Chamberlain lost our confidence rather before he lost his own; Amery did well to quote Cromwell in the debate last week –

'*You have sat too long for any good you have been doing. Depart, I say, and let us have done with you. In the name of God, go.*'

In other words, will those who can, do – and will those who can't, kindly close the door quietly behind them on the way out! Well, Chamberlain clearly couldn't – and so he went. But when the white smoke went up and it was Churchill, Michael still had his doubts. Well – they would see!

Hullo. The new PM's in the dock. Here we go—!

When Winifred spoke into her niece's ear it was to say:

"Did I hear you're looking to start up a new charity, dear?"

"That's right. I've given up Rumania; it stopped being any use to anybody."

To Winifred the idea that Rumania could *ever* have been any use to anybody was clearly a novelty.

"And what are you looking for now?"

Fleur pursed her lips and gave a little shrug. At her other side, the bank manager felt the movement, and smiled appreciatively.

"I don't know exactly," she said. "Something that matters on the 'Home Front'."

"I wonder, had you thought of nursing?"

Fleur had not, and perhaps something in her expression indicated as much to her aunt.

"I don't mean yourself, of course. I thought of it because Holly's become an Auxiliary – she trained in the Boer War, you know. She says they're going to be frightfully short of beds, particularly for convalescence, if things get worse in France. I thought of your rest home in Dorking."

Fleur quickly sifted the notion through a variety of filters in her brain, and found no trace of interest in it. There was something altogether too wholesome in nursing; it would only make her more cynical. And another rest home would be just that. What she needed now was something entirely new.

"I suppose it's a thought, Winifred," she said, by way of dismissal, "but what I really need—"

But there was no time for exposition. The Prime Minister of three days had risen to the dispatch box. All murmur subsided; the House and gallery gave their undivided attention.

Having received His Majesty's Commission only on Friday – Mr Churchill said, in his gruff, singular voice – he would not address the House at any length today, as much remained to be done in the forming of his new Administration.

"... it must be remembered that we are in the preliminary stage of one of the greatest battles in history ... I would say to the House, as I have said to those who have joined this Government: 'I have nothing to offer but blood, toil, tears and sweat.'"

'Michael's right,' Fleur thought. 'He is a good talker; he'll make them rally.'

"We have before us an ordeal of the most grievous kind. We have before us many, many long months of struggle and of suffering. You ask, what is our policy? I will say: It is to wage war, by sea, land and air, with all our might and with all the strength that God can give us..."

Fleur stiffened in her seat. Quite unbidden, a tingle rose at her neck. It seemed suddenly to her own purpose that these words were directed.

"You ask, What is our aim? I can answer in one word: **Victory** — victory at all costs, victory in spite of all terror, victory, however long and hard the road may be; for without victory, there is no survival."

The words rang in her ears as the speech continued below. Fleur looked to Winifred, who through her veil was applying the tip of one mauve finger to the corner of her eye. Yes, that last phrase went home with everyone. Even the fellow on her other side had sniffed, and made it an excuse to reach for his handkerchief.

'*Without victory, there is no survival*—' Fleur repeated the words to herself like a mantra, and was insensible to much of the continuing speech, and even to the bank manager, until the Prime Minister concluded:

"*But I take up my task with buoyancy and hope!*"

Something fluttered inside her suddenly. The possibility of things – of everything – returned to her, with those few deft words. She looked quickly down. That was it; the PM had resumed his seat, and others rose to take up the debate. Good – she had heard enough! Fleur touched Winifred's arm, and got up. As she edged along the row, the bank manager let out a muffled squeak.

"I'm so sorry," Fleur said sweetly. "Was that your foot?"

They left the gallery, and Michael, waiting for the vote.

When they were outside again, Winifred said:

"Well! That was certainly rousing stuff. I think he'll be very effective, don't you, Fleur? Perhaps we've got a new Grand Old Man."

Dispatching her aunt into a taxi, Fleur walked back to South Square. There was an hour or two before Michael would be home. With her own house to herself, she would order tea, and think.

Chapter Five

Kit Misses 'Bill'

Within two hours, Michael Mont and Eustace Dornford were walking abreast in the general direction of South Square. Michael was making for a certain still well-stocked drinks cabinet of his acquaintance located in those parts and Eustace for the underground station, where the Circle Line would take him home to Campden Hill.

The difference between the back-benchers was not great, but was never more noticeable than when they walked side by side, for in a man's step his soul and spirit may be gauged. Both men were a shade less than tallish, and a few well-carried years short of fifty. Eustace was dark, Michael fair, but both were greying at the temples and on the upper lip. Eustace was the more athletic-looking of the two, having been a Blue at Oxford; Michael was still trim. In his politics neither was that dyed-in-the-wool, hearts-of-oak species of Tory to be found commonly in any of the southern constituencies of England, of which their contiguous two were typical. In fact, each considered the other quite the best type of Tory available; that is, hardly a Tory at all. And yet there *was* a difference as they walked along. Somehow, in Eustace's step there was something straighter, more targeted; in Michael's there was something less so. The difference in all was perhaps best compared to that between a pointer and a retriever. Both dogs will locate and fetch, serving faithfully; but the pointer seems always to know in advance where the quarry will be – a retriever is best trained to wait, and watch it fall from the sky.

Of the two, Michael was the only one aware of this shortfall, since it resided within himself. He had his own opinion as to the cause. What he lacked was certainty, and that in turn, he knew, was occasioned by an absence of faith. Eustace, he saw, possessed a faith that would see him into the millennium and, because of it, his sense of certainty – his belief in what were the sure determinants of life – had shifted over the years probably rather less than the continental drift. By contrast, the beliefs of the tenth baronet were ever the proverbial sands upon which the wise man did not build. Though he knew he possessed a good heart, his seemed far less reliable than many he knew. It was the very mechanism that stirred the waters of his conscience, made him question himself constantly, and kept him forever from the solace of faith. And when he first entered politics it had failed him altogether. But for the misgivings of that organ, he might actually have been a Socialist.

This, ultimately, was the difference; it lay between what was, and what might have been.

"—I don't see what you're worrying about, Michael. The old war-horse is saddled up again, and by the sound of him today he means business."

"That's precisely what I worry about. He might well be carried away by the vigour of his own rhetoric, but I'm not sure I want him to take us along too."

"Just what we do need someone to do. Given that we didn't start this show, we'd better see that we finish it. They'll all rally now, you'll see. There simply isn't a better man than Winston for winning a war with words."

Michael shrugged. If that were all it took.

"Can you honestly imagine Halifax holding the floor today?" Eustace asked. "'On the whole, er, I rather think that, ah, all things considered we perhaps ought to try and, er, win, what?' Disaster!"

Michael walked on, still demurring. It was plain that Eustace had converted. Faith, after all!

"I wish we knew what kind of a strategist he'll make. 'Victory by any means' – does that allow for the possibility of a cease-fire, I wonder? Or for a negotiated peace?"

"Michael, dear fellow – don't say you're still hankering after appeasement?"

"Good Lord, no! We gave that the old school try, and it failed miserably. No. It's just that I—"

288

Michael dug his hands deeper into his jacket pockets for a few paces, and tried to nail down his anxiety.

"I suppose the last war left me a little sceptical about rallying cries, that's all. And I rather think it left our new leader champing at the bit."

Eustace clapped a hand on his colleague's shoulder and laughed.

"I do believe you are that rarest of political birds, Michael – the born back-bencher!"

Michael raised a smile.

"Then kindly show respect for a dying breed. 'They also serve' – who only stand and wait to be called!"

They reached the parting of their ways a little before the turning into South Square.

"Come in for a drink – Fleur will love to see you."

"Thanks, old man, but no can do. Dinny's got your mother coming for supper—"

"Ah—then you'd best stay 'one under'. You'll need to keep consecutive. Give my love to both!"

As he watched his friend cross the road and walk away, Michael thought; He's the genuine article, old Dornford – the true believer. As for me – I'm the perennial trier. 'Have-a-Go' Mont's my name! But what's my game?

What-ho—!

Michael turned his corner and put one foot directly into a skillet. A mound of kitchen utensils glinted dully at him in the late sun. As he withdrew his foot, Timms appeared bearing three pans and a roasting-tray. She bobbed at her master and dropped a lid. Michael bent to pick it up for her.

"What's this lot in aid of, Timms?"

"It's the WVS. Thank you, sir."

"Is this their stuff? I know we're supposed to dig for victory, but I rather draw the line at cooking for it."

"The 'aluminium drive', sir."

"Oh, of course. Out of the frying pan, and into the Spitfire!"

The maid put her load by the rest of the stack. From her apron pocket she produced an egg-poacher and some spatulas. Michael watched, quizzical and a little forlorn, as if he were witnessing the end of breakfasts for the duration of hostilities.

"Lady Mont did say these could go, sir. There's still the ironware."

"Until the Navy needs more battleships. What then – eh, Timms?"

Timms did not know what to answer; she wasn't sure if she had been contradicted.

"Cook says the ironware's best for the Aga."

"If cook says it's for the best, then the Admiralty must look to its own galleys. Carry on!"

The maid bobbed again and bustled back, telling herself she never fully understood the half of what the baronet said to her; though Tilly, their kitchen-maid, who had been at South Square for donkey's years before her, said that she should have heard the *ninth* baronet, old Sir Lawrence – *he* talked like a riddle-me-ree!

Timms turned down into the little alley by the side of the house, some half a minute ahead of her master. She was searching her pockets for the key to the back door, when she heard a footstep behind her. As she turned, a hand was clamped not too roughly over her mouth.

"Don't make a racket, Timmy!" came a quick whisper.

As the hand was removed, she turned to see a familiar face, and on it a smile that had won her before.

"You wouldn't want to give me away, would you?"

Timms recovered herself, and huffed.

"Give you away!" she whispered back. "Why I'm sure it's true no one would have you if you were wrapped!"

"That's a girl! Do get a move on and let me in!"

Hearing mention of the WVS, brought Michael back to wondering what Fleur would do for a new cause. The Woman's Voluntary was the obvious choice for her talents, but he knew she wouldn't touch them with a long pole. She was a chief in all such matters, not an indian, so unless Stella Reading was prepared to hand over her head-dress Fleur would not go near. If he was honest he also knew they were a bit on the homely side for her. She would want something more stylish, he was sure; with his half-French wife it was always – '*le style est la femme même*'.

But she needed *something*, and that quickly, to put her at the eye of the coming storm. Michael was not among the husbands who believed their wives wanted charitable occupation for safety's sake. That whole line of thinking was on the scrap heap these days, it belonged in the last century. Modern women owned themselves, but somehow with Fleur that had never seemed quite enough. She needed to be right at the centre of things and have others around her, in order to shine. When she was without constellation, Michael knew from old, her energies turned inwards and burned her up. Without a single practical notion how to help her whose star already shone brilliantly at the centre of his own universe, he decided he must see what he could do.

Michael heard the telephone bell ringing as he let himself inside; Fleur was taking the call when he entered the drawing-room. He was surprised to see his mother on the sofa. He leaned over and kissed her cheek.

"Hullo there! – I thought you were at Dinny's."

"I am. She's doin' the tombola. I'm puttin' you down for buried treasure."

Her son, still leaning over the sofa back, caught up with her meaning after only a second or two. War or no war, the marquee season was upon them. Each spring, for as far back as he could remember, the villages of Broad Lipping and Lipping Minster, (known collectively as the Lippings, near Folwell, Bucks.) pooled resources for their May Festival, and with much bunting and general to-do set out their stalls on the wide acres at Lippinghall Manor. Fleur called it the *fête* worse than death.

"Ah. Good show," he replied, lying heartily. "Anything for a cause. Whitsun, isn't it?"

"I left Kat makin' streamers with the nurse – Poll was unmakin' some of them. Will Kit be down? He might like a shy."

Michael thought not, but kept his opinion to himself.

"Fleur was sayin' she needs a charity. Should be plenty goin'."

"There are, but it's not that easy. She needs something she can really throw herself into. She's looking to start up a proper outfit, a brand-new war charity."

"Her aunt suggested nursin'. Not everyone's talent, I'd've thought."

If this was his mother's peripheral way of saying that Fleur's nature lacked the Nightingale component, then Michael was rather

291

in agreement. He abstained out of loyalty and moved to the drinks cabinet in search of the gin. Passing by, he ran a hand over his wife's elbow as she stood at the telephone. How pretty the least part of her was!

Fleur put the receiver down.

"Darling, that was Nona. She and Vivian want us to meet them directly at the Savoy for their celebration on the 31st, and not at theirs beforehand."

It really was just as well he had married a social creature. If he were ever left to rely on his own endeavours, that whole world would pass him by. Michael remembered the Messengers' celebration only as something he had almost not remembered at all.

"Right-o. Only I think I've forgotten what we're supposed to be celebrating."

Fleur smiled back at him; rather fondly, he thought.

"No you haven't – they've not said. It's all a mystery until we get there. Nona rang because the youngest little 'Message' has just come down with the mumps, and she doesn't want us exposed."

"Michael's safe," said Em. "Flora gave him hers."

Fleur threw herself into one of the bergères by the hearth, and to Michael's following glance looked a little abstracted for a moment, until her expression cleared.

"Mix me a 'Special', will you, Michael? I need something with a 'kick' in it."

Three 'South Square Specials' soon took effect. Even Em achieved a certain degree of consecution while she stayed with the day's natural topic.

"Lionel and Adrian were at Harrow with him, of course. Waitin' for greatness to be thrust upon him even then, the Judge says. Eustace is keen, considerin' Halifax is Catholic. The cocoanuts will be hard, though."

When the telephone rang again Michael answered it.

"You don't suppose a marrow-shy would do, do you? Boswell's always got plenty under glass."

Fleur suggested various alternatives to her mother-in-law, and listened to her husband with one ear.

"Yes, this is he," she heard him say, and then there was a long

292

pause. From his wrinkled forehead it was clear he was being given something in great detail.

"I see," he said at last. "You've made quite sure? Of course."

There was another pause. Fleur saw her husband's expression change from grave attention to a graver acceptance.

"I appreciate that," Michael said finally. "I assure you, we will."

He replaced the receiver without a 'good-bye' or a 'thank you'. He picked up his cocktail glass and refilled it from the shaker. Fleur raised an eyebrow at him.

"That was Kit's headmaster."

"Is he ill?" she asked quickly.

Michael shook his head.

"No. He's not ill. He's absconded."

Fleur could only repeat the word.

"Absconded?"

Michael swallowed some more 'Special' and nodded.

"It seems he missed roll-call. The master sent a prefect to search the usual hide-outs. The boy thought to look in Kit's locker, and found he'd cleared it out."

Fleur looked quickly at her watch.

"So he's been gone for an hour?"

Michael shook his head again.

"He had a period in House before; that makes it nearer two."

Fleur was suddenly furious and worried in equal parts, but the fury was uppermost.

"Did they say where they think he's gone?"

"Heading this way, probably. Apparently most escapees make for home."

"The idiot."

With this observation standing, Fleur stared fixedly into the hearth and offered nothing more. Michael drained his glass.

"Uncle Cuffs missed 'bill' once," Em announced, in case it might console. "Went to Ascot for the Gold Cup. Came in last and got rusticated. Find me a cab, will you, Michael?"

Michael forced a quick smile, and showed his mother out.

"If he pitches up at Campden Hill, or Mount Street even, you might send him here with a flea in his ear," he said, as he put her into a taxi.

"Worryin', all the same. 'The hour of thoughtless youth', an' that. Bound to turn up safe and sorry."

As he returned to the drawing-room, Michael realised it was not for his son's safety that he was worried; whether he would be sorry remained to be seen. Concerning the hour of youth, he was confident that Kit would do nothing thoughtlessly. Whatever his son's motives, Michael was certain he had acted quite deliberately, not on impulse, and *that* understanding was what worried him. With only another year before going up to the University Kit had given his academic career a serious winding.

Fleur was following this line of thought, too. As soon as Michael reappeared she said:

"He'll be expelled for this."

He sighed heavily. "He ought to be, Lord knows. Maybe I can pull a few strings."

"Not unless he has a good reason."

"If they can be reminded he's really a Cherrell and not an errant Mont, his reasons might not matter so much to them—"

"They matter to me," Fleur said. "If he can't answer for himself, I shouldn't want you to help him."

Michael could not keep his surprise at her tone from his face. Fleur saw it, and answered impatiently.

"If he chooses to act irresponsibly, he must take the consequences. He's made his own bed—"

Fleur had never intended to finish that old saw, which her practical nature had always seen as self-evident, and nothing more than an expression of the harsh reality of life. Nevertheless, it was finished for her, and in a voice that sounded suddenly older than when she last heard it.

"Don't worry, Mother. I intend to sleep on it, too."

Fleur twisted sharply in her seat. Michael looked to the doorway.

Having silently come through from the kitchen, Kit had been listening in the hall since his father returned to the drawing-room. At his mother's last words, he appeared in the open doorway and spoke with a casualness that was not wholly affected. He had answered his mother, but held his father's eye.

"You'd better come in and account for yourself," Michael said. "If you can."

Kit stepped into the room and stood at the far end of the sofa. He saw his father move to a predictable position at the centre of the hearth-rug. Well — he had expected pi-jaw!

"You realise, I hope, that you've put everyone to a great deal of trouble?"

Here it came! Kit nodded idly, not quite insolently, and let his gaze slip to one side.

"Yes."

"Please have the courtesy to look at me when you answer!"

Kit straightened up. The old man was plainly in no mood to be messed around.

"I just left the school," he said simply. "That's all."

"Evidently – with consummate ease, it would seem. Your head-master telephoned a few minutes ago to let us know. Do you imagine it will be as easy to get you back in?"

"I don't see that it matters much, either way."

"I beg your pardon?"

It was Kit's turn to sigh deeply. The old man was beetling. Oh, well – nothing for it, except just to say.

"I'm not going back. I've joined the RAF."

There was a moment of terrible silence, after which Fleur snapped crossly.

"You're not old enough."

Kit gave back a little facial shrug, a gesture he had learned from her years ago.

"I told them I was eighteen. The recruiting officer didn't seem to care, anyway."

Kit saw his parents look at each other for the first time since the beginning of this catechism. Then his mother turned back to him, but said nothing more, and eventually dropped her eyes to the floor. His father only scratched his head.

Fleur got up to leave the room. Kit stood back to let her pass, which she did without looking at him. At the doorway she only half turned to say:

"We'll talk about this in the morning; your father and I are dining out this evening. You'd better go and see if cook can feed you."

*

That night, as Fleur combed out her hair, Michael took slow turns on the carpet behind her, his hands thrust into his trouser pockets. He had removed his dinner jacket and loosened his tie, but the rest of his undressing was suspended while he paced.

"*That* won't help, Michael," Fleur said, watching his image move between the three parts of her dressing-glass.

"I wish I knew what would."

"You'll simply have to take him back to the recruiting office tomorrow, and explain it to them."

"Explain what, though? Explain that our son lied to get into the forces?"

"Yes. Of course."

"Well, I'm afraid that's just what I don't think I can do."

"Why not?"

Fleur put down her comb, and turned on her stool.

Michael stopped pacing, and looked back at her. He could see in her eyes that she didn't begin to understand. He sat down on the edge of the bed. When Fleur asked for the second time, he tried to explain.

"Because I am quite certain he would never forgive us – me, in particular – if I did."

Fleur made a little scornful noise in her throat, and returned to her dressing-table.

"Is that all? You'd rather I never forgave you if you don't?"

Michael saw an icy patch ahead. As driving manuals always suggested, he proceeded with caution.

"That isn't what I mean, Fleur—"

"Then what do you mean, Michael?"

From a crystal jar she began applying tiny amounts of vanishing cream to the already invisible lines under her eyes.

Michael ran a finger over his moustache, and began again on another tack.

"The Air Force is going to bring in cadetships for boys over sixteen in the new year. If he still wants to join up then – as I'm sure he will – there'll be nothing we can do to stop him."

"Then he can wait."

"Can he, do you suppose?"

"He'll have to, if we stop him now."

"I'd have hated it, if Bart had tried to stop me."

"That doesn't apply, and you know it. You were of age."

"That's what I'm saying – he will be, shortly."

"So until then we do nothing to stop him? How can you possibly want him to go out—"

"Of course I don't want him to go out, Fleur! But the worst of the air battle may well be over before he's trained, and with any luck—"

"Luck! Is that all it comes down to?"

"Yes! I'm afraid in time of war that's pretty much all there is."

"It *is* what you want, Michael!"

"No, Fleur! I want him safe – Kat, too – all of us, out of this awful business. But what you or I *want* doesn't come into any of it. We'll just have to face it—"

"—Oh!" she cried, and suddenly screwed her hands into little fists and rolled up her eyes to the ceiling.

"Fleur—!"

Michael moved to put his arms around her but she shrugged him off. In that brief touch of her shoulders he felt tension quivering through her. He assumed it to be remorse. Poor heart, he thought. Kit's a part of her; she solemnly wished him his bed to lie on, and now her wish is granted. Then in one of her mirrors he saw her close her eyes and set her face into an unexpected but not unknown expression, and Michael realised he was quite wrong. It was not remorse which set her quivering, but anger. Her son had colluded with events; he had crossed her will; and her husband had taken his part.

Fleur only resumed her combing, saying nothing further, while Michael began unbuttoning his shirt, as a pronounced silence fell between them.

Chapter Six

June Contributes

Within thirty seconds of Holly leaving her at 'The Poplars' on that Monday afternoon, June knew that she had made a mistake. Holly had asked if she wanted to be left at Chiswick, or taken into her gallery in Town. June thanked her and declined further transport. She was tired, she said, and the gallery would wait until tomorrow. Within a few moments of being alone, however, she knew neither of these assertions was correct.

It was not actually the case, of course, that any genius would go in peril of his life or livelihood, for want of her alms or sustenance, not to say her critique, if she did not attend the gallery until Tuesday. Seriously to think such a thing, besides, flew in the face of her own cant, which held that the very stamp of genius was its ability to withstand privation. No; what was the case with June was that after a week-end with her extended family at Green Hill her little house and studio in Chiswick seemed suddenly vast and empty. To see everyone busy in fighting the good fight and be unoccupied oneself was to this passionate little soul nothing short of purgatory.

She went out to the gate in case Holly should have stalled her car, or otherwise stopped, but the street was empty as the house. June flitted back inside, and spent some further moments looking for things to do. Save gathering up her post she found none. Nothing looked the worse for her absence and nothing much seemed sensible of her return. Even the maid Trudi was 'off' until the evening. Without a current genius – Suslov having returned to Leningrad in a fit of patriotic outrage over Operation Barbarossa, and new genius seeming in as short supply as anything else these days – she scarcely needed a maid at all.

Standing in her little meal room, June had an awkward sense of being in the centre of a vacuum. It was not as if she possessed a cat.

What was also the case, was that she fretted about the old house at Robin Hill. Before today she hadn't given the place a thought in years, but seeing it again had kindled a strange feeling of loss in her. Yet it had never properly been her home. Her attachment to it was as the greatest product – and the last – of the young architect she had once loved. Phil! It was more than fifty years since he died. For June Forsyte – with her father's tenacity and her grandfather's devotion to helpless things conjoint in her fiery nature – there had never been another love. Impossible — after Phil!

Perhaps unconsciously, in giving unflagging aid to wave after wave of yet-to-arrive artists, she sought still to find some spark of that flame which had been Bosinney's bright genius, taken from the world and her too soon. If only — it was rare for June to use this construction in any context as it unsettled her, but no other here applied. If only Phil had remained in love with her, as she had with him, and not fallen oceans deep instead with Irene. If she and Phil had married then Irene – she felt sure – would never have left Soames, would probably have given him the son he so long demanded of her. Then what trouble might have been prevented down the generations . . . Then — oh! Here was the most disturbing part yet – Jon might have been *Fleur*'s brother, not her own! How awful – imagine him called James!

On the point of removing her hatpin in front of a round dim mirror of elderly glass, her thoughts were interrupted as she suddenly saw a very sad and unexpectedly old woman staring back at her from the misty depths of its disintegrating glaze. Momentarily unnerved at this vision, she barely noticed when her doorbell rang. It was rung with a diffident pressure that raised only a small sound, and when a second followed, scarcely more demanding, June went out into the hall, thinking it was Trudi returning without her key. She opened the door crossly.

"Julius, *gnädige Frau*."

It seemed that a parcel of about June's height, but with a felt hat on it, had spoken. As she watched, a figure not very much taller, if substantially wider, and standing behind the parcel, raised itself up from a comically low bow.

"Julius," said the man again, alternately crushing and stretching the hat between his hands.

Nothing else was said by either party for several seconds. Since Trudi was an Austrian and had been in her employ for two decades, June had come to know the sound of certain words of German. She had never thought to *apply* them, naturally – but she could recognise one or two when they were used.

June made a meaningless gesture prior to speaking, and the man copied it hopefully. This rather threw her off what she had intended to say about his having the wrong address, and left her with only the standard Forsyte protocol for dealing with foreigners.

"Do you speak *English*?"

Another approach might have elicited what little he had from the man. All he offered to June's interrogative was further distress to his hat, and upturned hang-dog eyes staring out from an expression pathetic with apology.

"*Nur etwas – leider!*"

June's impatience at his failing in her language made him spare in the use of his own. When she clucked her tongue and frowned more intensely, the man reached out to her imploringly with the tortured piece of felt.

"*Ich heise* Julius," he repeated, so earnestly that the circlet of dark brown curls around his otherwise shining head stood up like ruffled duck feathers. As June began to shut her door in his face, sheer desperation drove him to cry—

"Julius, *gnädige! Kunstmaler!*"

This last was the one word of German June knew beyond any misunderstanding. Her soul would probably have translated it if he had spoken in Sanskrit.

"*Painter?* You're a *painter!*" she cried, while the man nodded furiously. "Oh, don't stand there like an idiot – come in!"

June had made no small amount of progress in the language by the time the maid returned at five o'clock. The man was a painter in oils – '*ölmalerei*' had become clear when he produced a well-used palette from his parcel. His Christian name was Abram – or rather it was not his Christian name, since even June could hazard a guess at

'*Jude*'. Each diligently excavated fact was followed with little claps of joy from the old lady, and a great smile from the artist. Once Trudi was able to interpret for her, June learned further that he was not in fact from Essen but simply hungry. The maid brought him bread and cheese and a glass of wine, explaining in her own heavy accent—

"It is what he asked."

June waved away the explanation. She would not have balked at giving him caviare had there been any in her kitchen. Her little face was set in a sort of fierce rapture, like that more commonly seen on Byzantine martyrs. Before her was the greatest treasure life could offer – genius had found her once again.

The next morning, with Julius equipped with fresh oils and canvas in her studio and Trudi on orders to provide for his least whim, June re-jammed her hat-pin, gathered up her bag, her gas-mask and an umbrella, and left for Town. Purpose and passion had been renewed in her veins at a stroke by the arrival of this new lame duck. A letter from Boris Strumolowski, the lamest of many years past and long-since comfortably established in Paris, was found to be waiting in the post delivered to the empty house that week-end. It was typical of the impassioned Slav not to consider entrusting his letter to Julius himself. It was sent to introduce the German painter to her, and served to explain why he had repeated his name so often on the doorstep. With Trudi's help, June had got his whole story out of him over the course of the evening. Now she had a fight to win, aid to seek, support to gain – now she had a *battle* on her hands. Life was once more joyous.

June's invigoration did not permit her to wait for a 'bus. Whoever coined the phrase '*there'll be another one along in a minute*' had clearly never lived in Chiswick. She took the two hundred yards to the underground station in a personal best time, moving rather like a hornet's nest on castors, and bought a ticket at the window.

On the platform wall she saw a poster whose legend ran:

'*Careless Talk Costs Lives*'

June squinted at it scornfully. What a ridiculous caution. Why on earth would she want to talk to any of the hordes – smelling of their

301

cooked breakfasts and sucking on their boiled sweets – with whom one was forced to rub elbows on the underground these days? It was unimaginable! She narrowed her terrible gaze to the bottom corner of the poster, and saw that responsibility was claimed by the Ministry of Information. Hnh! It wasn't at all informative – merely fatuous and annoying. A complete waste of effort, and very indifferently drawn. It was a waste of paper, what was more. On that score, if the train she wanted had not pulled into the station at that minute she might have taken a decision to write in to someone about it. Instead June stepped briskly into a carriage, took an empty seat, put her bag and gas-mask case on her lap and brought the tip of her umbrella down smartly on a particularly tender corn belonging to the man sitting next to her. As he raised himself in mute protest, June nodded to him and consoled herself with the thought that, war or no war, manners in this city were not entirely dead.

At South Square, breakfast was an edgy and subdued affair. Kit had the rest of the week to himself before he had to report and was the only one who ate with appetite. Fleur had nothing to say to her son, and refused to meet her husband's eye over the table. Michael felt there was a good deal he could have said to either of them, had the other not also been in the room, and so was forced to keep the silence. '*Per ardua ad astra*', he thought. 'Through hard knocks we shall see stars!' By nine-thirty Michael thought it for the best that mother and son not be left to stew together, and took Kit off to his tailor's to see about a uniform. Fleur took a cup of coffee into her drawing-room.

There she stewed by herself for a good hour, but not over Kit. She had given up that subject, over which she recognised she no longer had suzerainty, and returned to one wholly in her own domain.

The time spent thinking over her coffee-cup brought Fleur to a remarkably clear understanding of her situation. If she really meant to have Jon, to get him back in her life once and for all, then what she must do was simply present him with an entrance to it through which he already wished to pass. Yes; simply said. Yet, the more she thought about it, perhaps not so difficult to do. As she had already decided, her own life was her best camouflage. No one would suspect her of hidden motives, if her every move were

302

public. All would be convinced this time – among them, Jon himself.

One thing was clear: her first approach to him must be direct and open. He had shied at a liaison the last time, because of the secrecy and duplicity involved – even though she had offered to take the burden of arrangements upon herself. It was not in Jon's nature to submit to anything mean, or hole-in-corner; that wretched conscience of his had proved unconquerable to her best challenge. Now her quick brain perceived the obvious answer to this problem: it was to play his integrity to her own advantage, to use it as the very lever with which she would prise open his resistance.

Once this understanding was secured, other details – which only months ago had seemed impossibly out of reach – fell obligingly into place. Her search for a new 'war charity' was the perfect chance. Of course! How elementary solutions were — once you had them! She would devise a charity – Winifred's suggestion would do as well as another, offering beds for wounded soldiers or something like – and go to Jon, among some carefully selected others, for help with it. Surely he could not refuse? He was wealthy; it was unlikely he had less from his father than she from hers. And if, as she suspected, his present circumstances prevented him from taking active part in the war ... how grateful she was to that American girl for leaving him a widowed father, and a farmer, to boot! Yes; he was bound to want to contribute. For his contribution she would see that he was made a member of the committee or, if that was too much for him, just to have him listed as a benefactor would be enough. With his conscience, and the right balance of worthies signed up before him, he couldn't possibly decline. He would be on board, and that was all she needed to proceed.

And once she had him on board? Well, there was the duration of this otherwise purposeless war to see what could not be made to happen.

The doorbell stirred her from her thoughts. Her coffee was cold, her resolve much the same temperature. The caller overtook the maid before she was properly announced.

"Miss June—"

"*June?*"

"That's right, my dear. May I come in?"

Since June was already in, Fleur made no answer. The maid

went away, and the two cousins faced each other. June Forsyte, of all people – she looked ancient! Fleur decided not even to try and think when she had last seen her. What trouble had she brought with her this time?

"Well, child," June began brightly, "I'm very happy to see you again. It must be years."

Fleur made an expression of agreement which fell rather short of a smile. June was undeterred.

"This is a pretty room; I thought so last time."

"When you came to find out how we were?"

Fleur gestured June to sit. June took the barb with a little tilt of her head, and sat.

"I was only worried that Jon shouldn't—"

"—Shouldn't have me chasing after him the moment his wife died. Wasn't that it?"

"I haven't come here to fight with you, Fleur. I was always on your side, you know."

"That's comforting. Then why have you come, may one ask?"

June was nettled, but swallowed on her rising resentment and remembered her purpose.

"It's Michael I want, really. I have a German refugee staying with me – a Jew. He has a child already in England, and I've said I'll help him to trace her."

"I believe you'll want the Refugee Children's Movement, in that case, not Michael."

"I've already seen them this morning. They mentioned his name – he's on the Commons' Committee, isn't he?"

"Yes—"

June seized her chance and went on quickly.

"All Julius knows is that she was taken in by a family somewhere in the Chalfonts – and that's in Michael's constituency."

June stopped there, confident she had recovered lost ground.

Fleur smiled thinly. She had no real stomach to spar with June, it was only residual aversion which made her spiteful.

"Well, Michael's out all day. Shall I tell him about it when he comes home?"

"Yes. Thank you. That's all I came for."

June rose, and Fleur found the dignity of the little upright figure strangely affecting. She followed her to the door, wondering if there was anything conciliatory she might say finally. She could think of nothing – nothing that would have been honest, anyway.

It was June who made the effort, but with only her usual success.

"I expect your boy will be going off soon. There seems no end to it. This dreadful business!"

Fleur pressed her lips together, and tipped her chin upwards in a species of nod.

"Jon's is far too young, thank Goodness."

The mention of the name that was never very far from the front of her thoughts led Fleur to consider she might be throwing away an opportunity to learn something new. It was worth one shot.

"Jon will want to do his bit, I expect."

It landed, but only just.

"Naturally. But as a farmer and a widower, of course—"

Of course. Nothing new there. Fleur nodded blandly again with her chin. At least that girl's death had kept him safe!

"As a matter of fact, we were just discussing it this week-end."

This was more promising. Fleur took an easy guess, and asked: "You were down at Green Hill?"

Hearing how June rattled on by way of an answer, Fleur believed at first she had overshot her mark. But the rattle soon struck a note of interest.

"Holly drove me back yesterday, or I should still be changing trains! Transport is so unreliable these days. We came back by way of Robin Hill. Oh, it's such a shame. It's quite empty, you know, and up for sale."

Fleur had not known. And save by June's unwitting contribution, perhaps she never would have.

"I do hope someone buys it," the old lady said feelingly, "and puts it to good use again. It was a happy house, after all."

On the verge of remembering that her description did not fit the whole history of the house by any stretch of imagination, June found the street door was already open in front of her. Uncertain she had been wise to stray into this last subject, she said a hasty good-bye, and hurried off along the pavement.

305

For some time after her uninvited cousin had vanished at the corner, Fleur continued to stand at her door, staring up at the tall trees but not hearing the birds.

Chapter Seven

And Jon Wants To

It was mid-week before Jon could find a free morning to visit Mastonbury again. By that time he had heard of Val's success with the Observers and was beginning to despair that, like the previous Prime Minister, he too had 'missed the bus'. Why, even June had a new genius on her books, Holly told him. So he felt a sorry chump indeed as he left the base empty-handed a second time. The COC had told him again; he would have to settle for putting his name down at White Waltham, and hope they could use him as a ferry pilot. What had they taught him when he was a child? That the winning wasn't important, just the taking part – if only!

When his car stuttered to a halt about a quarter of a mile along the main road out of Mastonbury, Jon was prepared to take it as a metaphor. His drive to be part of the war effort had just about run out. With the hood down, it needed only to rain . . .

His head had been under the bonnet for several not very constructive minutes, when he heard a voice behind him say:

"Need any help, sir?"

Jon straightened up, wiping his hands on his handkerchief, and saw a young airman standing by the edge of the road.

"I'm pretty good with engines."

"I know I'm not," said Jon, wondering if he himself was good with anything at all. "I'd be jolly grateful if you'd take a look."

The young man removed his uniform jacket and side-cap, tossed them on to the passenger seat and ducked a fair, tousley head under the bonnet. In less than five minutes the engine was coaxed into a response, like an unwilling horse in the hands of an experienced groom. Jon sat behind the wheel, where he had been applying or

307

relieving the clutch as he was asked. The airman let down the bonnet with an expert's lack of flourish, and recovered his uniform.

"Better keep her turning now, sir. She should get you back if you haven't too far to go."

"What about you? Are you going into the village? The least I can do is give you a lift."

"I was heading for the 'Forrester's', actually. My gang's off until seventeen-hundred."

He looks barely old enough to order a pint, Jon thought, and he's already flying fighters over France.

"Get in, and I'll take you. My name's Forsyte, by the way."

"Thanks! Pilot Officer Roberts, R.D. Call me Bobby – everyone does!"

Each made to offer and then withdraw a hand badly stained with oil; they laughed together when they realised the embarrassment was mutual. Still sharing the joke, the young fellow clambered into the passenger seat and Jon nosed his vehicle back onto the road.

'For the want of a nail, a shoe was lost.' Thus runs the nursery tale, to teach small children how an action, or the want of one, may have consequences. For want of whatever minor engine part – or for want of its services – Jon's car did not reach The Forrester's Arms on that occasion. Not far before the turning for Green Hill, but still a good mile and a half from the desired hostelry, it went into a second collapse.

Another check under the lid confirmed a poor diagnosis.

"Sorry I can't get you to the pub," Jon said, and took his pipe from the glove compartment, preparatory to getting out.

"That's O.K. But what about you, sir – how will you get home?"

"I am home. My farm's Green Hill, just up there. I'll send a van back with a tow rope."

Still sitting behind the wheel, Jon struck a match and drew on his pipe. Through the first billow of smoke he saw the young officer look in the direction he had indicated, then turn back and scratch his chin.

"You know, we could probably shunt her ourselves."

Jon smiled at the suggestion.

"It's not called Green *Hill* for nothing."

"I'm game, sir."

Jon puffed more smoke. Yes, you are, he thought, as he looked into the face of this young fellow who stood by the car, hands on hips, side-cap tucked into his lapel, and fair hair in disarray. You certainly are. And it seemed to Jon that he saw something of himself looking back at him.

"Right you are!"

In war-time, as those who survive these periods confirm, a certain phenomenon occurs in human relationships. A force of acceleration takes hold, so that minutes may have the value of hours and days the impact of years. Previously reticent individuals find themselves talking freely; life histories are exchanged in a single conversation, life-long attachments made in an afternoon. It is as if the physical economies imposed by war cause equivalent retrenchment elsewhere, and this holds true even among Forsytes. And of all things to become dispensable, caution – that hitherto enshrined quality, by which in time of peace the race is recognised – is usually the first.

Jon Forsyte was experiencing this phenomenon now, as others of his family would before the end of hostilities. In return for his help with the car, he had persuaded the airman to stay for lunch, and lunch had drifted into further conversation over coffee in the garden. He proved to be an open-hearted, likeable young fellow, given to raking a hand through his hair whenever he contemplated his own opinions on a subject, and listening intently to Jon when he expressed his. He was rather diffident in some ways, and altogether quieter and more thoughtful than the figure Jon had imagined of the typical cock-sure young flyer.

Jon wished he was one of his fellows at Mastonbury, and when he said as much, Bobby replied:

"I expect you played your part in the last war, sir."

"No. I'm afraid I didn't. Believe it or not, I wasn't old enough."

"Well, not to worry, sir. Farming keeps us all going!"

There came a point, while they had been talking about the farm, when Jon thought he saw the airman stifle a yawn in his throat.

"I imagine you're rather short on leave these days."

"Pretty much; especially since things started looking ropy in

France. I don't mind for myself, but it's hard on my family."
He tackled his hair and looked thoughtful. "If we'd had the full twenty-four hours off today I might have tried to get home."

"And where is home for you, Officer Roberts?" Irene asked.

"Richmond, ma'am. Just outside, actually."

"Really?" said Jon, surprised. "Where exactly?"

He gave the location of a row of cottages by triangulating them between a church and a war memorial. Jon knew the area instantly.

"That's extraordinary. I grew up two miles away, at Robin Hill."

"That wonderful old place?" The airman raked his hair again. "I always thought it belonged to a peer. Oh! – that is—"

Jon laughed, and began to fill his pipe.

"Don't worry, that's not me. He bought it from us in 1920."

"Golly. The year before I was born. You must have been sorry to leave it."

Jon smiled and bit down on his pipe-stem. Irene said softly:

"Tell us about your family."

"Oh, there's just my mother and sister, and me. My father died a couple of years ago."

"I'm so sorry."

"Thanks. It was tougher on my sister than me. She's only fifteen now."

"Is she like you?"

Bobby's face lighted up.

"No! I should say not, lucky for her! She's a real red-head, and quite a looker already—"

The flyer looked to the horizon as something caught his eye. All three turned to watch a squadron of Hurricanes climbing in 'finger four' formation from Mastonbury in the distance. They might have been a dozen starlings, and Jon watched them as he always did, with a guilty twinge that he had so far made no contribution of his own.

It was time he went, the airman said, and thanked Irene. Jon walked with him down to the gate.

"Well, thanks awfully, sir. That's quite topped me up; you've been jolly kind."

"Not at all. You've cheered me up, too. Perhaps you'll come and see us again, next time you can't get home."

"Really?"

Jon smiled and nodded, and tapped out his pipe on the gate-post. The airman dug up his hair again.

"I'll be back like a shot, in that case. I'll give your tractor the once-over, next time!"

Jon laughed, and when they shook hands, he felt as if he were saying goodbye to a version of himself.

Fleur did not get around to telling her husband of June's request until he came home on Wednesday evening.

"Julius, she said? It has the advantage of singularity, at least. I'll put some feelers out at the week-end – get someone to check the missing lists."

"I may be on those myself this week-end," Fleur said after a pause. "I've an idea for my new charity; I might go for nursing after all. Anyway, I want to 'check out a few leads', as they say in the films."

Michael looked at her, but she didn't seem to want to elaborate. Kit was off on Friday; he supposed it was more urgent now than ever for her to find occupation.

"Don't we have tickets for a show tonight?" she asked.

"'*Idiot's Delight*'. According to the reviews it's exactly that."

"I was thinking – you ought to go with Kit, and take him for a meal afterwards."

"Perhaps I can get us an extra ticket—"

"No. There's no need. I'll be happy here."

It seemed to Michael as if she might be something like happy with her own company for the evening, or at least content to dispense with his. She had been pale lately. If she could find something to absorb her, it might restore her colour.

"O.K. I'll go up and tell him."

Michael left the drawing-room and began to walk up, aware of a tug of disappointment. Over what? Hadn't he been looking forward to the play? — or was it just the necessary proximity to Fleur he was anticipating? Ah, he was the idiot, all right, and she his delight — but what was hers?

311

Chapter Eight

On Forsyte 'Change

With all around her disposed to service, it was Winifred Dartie's conviction that to carry on as near to normal as her existence hitherto was the most patriotic duty of which she was capable. She recalled Uncle Timothy's map during the Boer War, and how he kept all the flags in their latest positions of battle, and knew she was not up to the same. Having to read and digest all the news columns as well as the society ones, even with the pages reduced as they were, would make reading the paper rather a bore. Besides, the wireless did it all for one nowadays, and offered music afterwards; only yesterday there had been some very nice Paganini variations, and a little Grieg.

She stood by the window in her drawing-room looking out into Green Street, while her hand sought the strand of pearls at her bosom. Absently, she began to tell them, one by one, as if they were beads on a rosary. The action brought a similar comfort, as she contemplated the quiet street. Strange – if one didn't know, one couldn't really guess there was a war on: there was nothing to tell by, in this view. Only, perhaps, the crosses on the windows, but here done so neatly that one soon stopped seeing them. As Mr Powell had said last Sunday – Winifred had taken to 'catching' the occasional sermon – they were like the marks the Israelites made on their doors to ward off the Angel of Death. It was a comforting thought, in its way.

Inside the house Winifred herself had made various alterations in the cause, and took a small pride in their being achieved as tastefully and discreetly as possible. There were the black-out curtains, of course, none of which was too obtrusive save for the one over the fanlight in the hall. That was an eyesore, but couldn't be helped. Then there was the major re-arrangement of the cellars, so that the staff had their own shelter at the rear, and Winifred hers at the front. Remembering her brother's advice during the General Strike, she had also put by a lot of non-perishable goods in the larders. There was a stirrup-pump in a cupboard on every floor – oh, and lines painted to a height of four inches around the inside of all baths, to save water. This last idea she had from Fleur, who had done it at South Square as soon as war was declared. What was it Michael called them? — her Plimsoll lines!

She heard familiar footsteps, not quite as brisk as usual, on the pavement below, and looked down to see the top of St. John Hayman's head. Jolly! Company for tea, and St. John could tell her all about the show he had promised to take her to tomorrow night. She had forgotten what it was, but remembered it sounded amusing.

When Miller brought St. John up to her, Winifred saw at once he was not his usual self. She dispatched her maid to the kitchen, to find some macaroons.

"Ah, St. John." Winifred received his kiss, and thought he did look rather glum close up. "So nice to see you, my dear – how are you?"

St. John sat down on her little gilt-framed sofa, not on the piano stool as was customary. He raised a smile, but one that drooped a little at the edges. He didn't even light a cigarette.

"Oh, I'm fine, Auntie. Fine, I suppose. Heard any good jokes lately?"

Winifred was taken by surprise. In all her long life, she had never before been asked this question, even by St. John. But then St. John was always saying surprising things. Then she realised that she *had* heard a joke lately, and that it must be a good one because it had made her laugh. Perhaps it would cheer him up.

"Well, yes – as a matter of fact I *have*. Jack told it me. Now, let me see—" Winifred drummed her fingers on her chin while she got it straight "—ah, that's right."

She failed to suppress a gurgle at the memory of how it went, then began to tell the joke, conducting herself with a finger as she went along.

"A man walks down Piccadilly, and another man stops him

and asks: 'Can you tell me what side the War Office is on?' and the first man says—"

"'Our side, I hope.'"

"Oh!"

"Sorry, Auntie – that one's got a beard on it."

"Jack said he'd just heard it from one of the other wardens."

St. John made no reply, except one eyebrow moved upwards in a tired sort of way. The maid brought in a tray. Winifred was just thinking that once Miller had set it down and gone she would tackle her young visitor on his mood, when the doorbell sounded a second time. The maid went out again and returned with the Cardigan girls, who entered puffing slightly, Cecily first, then Celia. Stairs were not conducive to their condition, which was seven and eight months pregnant respectively.

"Ah, tea!" Celia said, rather as if she were in a corner-house. "Good-oh, I'm gasping."

She eased herself down onto a high-seated marqueterie chair, and dropped her bag to the floor.

"You've taken the best chair," Cecily complained. "The others are all lower."

"Well, you're shorter than I am. Use a cushion."

Winifred was beginning to wonder if there wasn't some infection about. St. John's mood seemed to be upon everyone. She directed him to bring a cushion for his cousin. Cecily sat down upon it on another chair. When all were settled, none seemed the least bit inclined to make conversation.

Miller came and went again, leaving more china, and an extra pot of hot water. Winifred began to pour.

"How's the war production going, then?" St. John asked at last.

"Oh, dry up," Celia said. "You should try it sometime."

"Not my style, dearest," St. John answered.

That was that for a while.

"How are you both getting along?" Winifred asked the girls, as neither seemed willing to volunteer the information.

"Auntie!" Cecily said, casting a look towards St. John that indicated it was a strictly women-only subject.

As the tea-cups went round in silence, Winifred thought to tell her big news of the week.

"Have you heard? — young Kit's joined the Air Force."

No one had heard. No one seemed very bothered.

"He'll look very smart in that nice blue of theirs – it will bring out his eyes so well."

No one disagreed. Celia only added,

"John says all the worst bounders join the RAF."

"I'm sure Kit won't associate with any of them, dear."

"I didn't say he would! Only that John says—"

"Yes – yes, quite!"

Freshly baked macaroons followed upon the heels of the tea-cups. One might have heard a crumb falling. Driven to an uncharacteristic attempt at irony, Winifred said,

"Well, this *is* jolly!"

There was only another pause. St. John was frowning at an inward understanding. Celia stared ahead blankly. Only Cecily seemed to be thinking of something to say. Winifred smiled at her, encouragingly.

"I had a letter from James today."

A break-through! John and James were in the same battalion of the Expeditionary Force in France – a letter was promising.

"How nice, dear. What did he say?"

"Nothing much."

"Oh."

St. John snapped: "I'm not surprised. Joined-up writing was never his *forte*."

Cecily gasped.

"That's very mean of you," said Celia, in defence of her brother-in-law.

"No it isn't. It's only the truth. No wonder it's turning into a dog's breakfast in France with idiots like your two directing traffic."

"St. John, really!" said Winifred. "What *is* the matter with you today? Are you liverish?"

"Not in the slightest! Absolutely nothing is the matter with me!" And he got up from the sofa and took his cup and saucer to the window, where he presented his back to the room.

Winifred was starting to miss her earlier solitude, when Celia said slyly,

"I know what's up with him. You went to the recruiting office today, didn't you? Don't deny it, I remember you told us last month that you had an appointment coming up. That's what it is, isn't it!"

"You never mentioned anything about it to *me*, St. John."

"I wanted to surprise you, Auntie, and—"

"—And they surprised you instead," Celia went on, sensing tender toes ripe for treading. "What happened, St. John – come on, spill the beans – didn't they make you a general straight off?"

"Oh – dry up!"

Celia and Cecily went off into a peal of laughter.

'Spill the beans'? What extraordinary expressions young people used nowadays. Winifred felt she must assume command of the situation before it disintegrated any further.

"*Did* you, St. John? Did you go today?"

St. John nodded, and his cup and saucer rattled faintly in his hand.

"Then tell us, dear boy, for heaven's sake. What rank have they made you?"

"Head cook and bottle-washer," Cecily offered, and the girls went off again.

St. John rose majestically above the giggling.

"I have no rank," he said.

"No *rank*?" Winifred asked, confronting the frightful possibility that he might have been made a non-commissioned officer. "What do you mean?"

"Exactly that, Aunt. I haven't a rank because they won't take me. I've been passed unfit for active service."

The girls sobered. Winifred brought a hand up to her mouth. Perhaps the Angel of Death was hovering after all. St. John turned to face them with a strained dignity in his bearing.

"Good gracious – my dear. Are you unwell? Sit down, do."

Both girls rose instantly – as instantly as they were able – to usher him back to the sofa. Cecily offered him her cushion. St. John manfully refused.

He took a deep breath, half of another macaroon, and explained.

"C-3. That's what they said I was."

"Oh—"

"Came as an awful shock, I can tell you."

St. John let himself receive comfort on all sides.

316

"Yes, dear, of course it must have. But are they saying you're ill? Whatever is wrong?"

"Amongst other things, epistaxis, genu vagum and otitis media."

St. John rolled out perfect Latin, as it had been written down for him by the army M.O.

"Oh! *dear* boy. It sounds dreadful. What *is* the matter with you?"

The three women watched as St. John took the rest of the macaroon. St. John was being so brave, so calm. St. John would tell them in his own time. They hung on his reply.

It came at last.

"Nose-bleeds, knock-knees and a tin-ear."

There was no sound for some seconds. It was Celia who broke ranks first, sounding as if she were politely trying not to cough. Cecily hadn't the control of her older friend, and a tiny squeak of a giggle escaped her. Celia waved her to stop before it was too late, but the time for containment had passed. Then Winifred succumbed, and all three gave way.

"Poor old St. John," Cecily said, as she paused to draw breath, "—you sound even too decrepit for the Local Defence!"

"Perhaps not," Celia said. "They can always use him for target practice—"

And off they went again. St. John remained above it all. He reached for his cigarette-case. He would wreathe himself in smoke until they had come to their senses. And he would find a way to fix Celia Cardigan's cart for her another time. His Aunt seemed finally to have rallied her sense of propriety, and was offering consolation.

"Never mind, dear. You can always be a warden, like Jack."

Hnh! Too little, too late. St. John was not to be consoled so easily. He struck his lighter, and inhaled.

"Put that light out!" Celia cried.

St. John felt his dignity was suddenly beyond retrieval, and took another macaroon.

Miller announced Mr Roger Forsyte, who surveyed the scene that met him in Winifred's drawing-room.

"I don't know – I always miss the good stuff here. What's the joke this time?"

Miller couldn't say, and those who could seemed not in a fit state to explain. 'Very young' Roger sat down on the piano stool and rested his brief-case on the lid. He applied some snuff while things calmed. Eventually all eyes were dabbed, throats were cleared, fresh tea was summoned and produced.

"Now, Roger, what's your news?" Winifred asked.

This triggered Celia and Cecily again, but only passingly, as both were too tired to laugh much more. They soon subsided into sighs. Celia held her side. St. John sniffed and drew on his cigarette.

"Oh, nothing too dramatic. Martha and the girls are doing the Women's Voluntary, and I've become a warden—"

Roger saw his young cousin shoot a barbed glance at Celia Cardigan.

"I haven't said a word," she said. "Is there any more tea? I shouldn't have laughed so hard after those macaroons."

Roger got up to pass her cup to his aunt, and back again, then returned for one for himself.

"That must be interesting, dear."

"Yes; it is rather. We do all kinds of stuff besides patrolling – first aid, fire control, traffic diversion, all sorts."

He caught another look from St. John, who said acidly:

"Wot larks, eh?"

St. John got up then, and set a peremptory kiss on his aunt's cheek.

"You're not going so soon, are you?"

He had decided he would, feeling there was only further irritation to be got for his money if he stayed at Green Street.

"'Fraid so, Auntie. Just popped round between goes in the oxygen tent and the old iron-lung. Thanks awfully."

With the air of one who by some curse was destined never to be around when the really interesting beans were spilled, St. John offered a brave sufferer's smile at the doorway, and left.

Winifred took two seconds to recall what they had been talking about.

"Oh, yes! Well, I'm sure it's a great comfort having sturdy, dependable fellows like you and Jack out there at night. Even if we don't get any raids, there are so many houses left empty in Town nowadays, you know, and the police can't be everywhere. Lettie MacAnder in Berkeley Street has been away since Christmas, and Fleur's mother-in-law is hardly ever at Mount Street, she tells me."

318

"Yes," Roger said. "It's the same near us. And Fleur will be gone soon herself, I imagine."

"Oh, I don't think so. She's happy enough to go down to Lippinghall at the week-ends, but she has too much to keep her in Westminster during the week."

"But she's leaving Westminster, I thought?"

"Roger, dear," said Winifred roundly, "why would you think that?"

Roger's shrewd grey eyes narrowed briefly. He was clearly about to put his foot into something. He looked across the room for assistance, but despaired of finding any. The two Cardigan girls were talking closely together about something else. He had Winifred's sole attention. There was nothing for it — the brick was dropped.

"Because she's asked me to negotiate the purchase of a house in Surrey for her – that's why."

Hearing this Winifred stiffened at the neck. She had been told nothing of any prospective move by her niece, and therefore said:

"Don't be ridiculous, Roger."

"I'm afraid it's true, Aunt. I shouldn't have said anything, I can see that now, but it is true."

"But she hasn't mentioned a word of it to me."

Roger lifted his eyebrows sympathetically.

"Surrey, did you say? Where in Surrey?"

"Near Richmond, I think."

Winifred frowned. It was not the most felicitous location. The house Soames had built for that first wife of his was near Richmond.

Roger was anxious to right his mistake. He reached into his brief-case.

"You may as well see the prospectus, now I've let the cat out of the bag. Here you are."

Winifred reached for her reading-glasses, and took the paper from him. She read out the agent's hyperbole, mostly to herself.

"'. . . an imposing family residence of great character and originality. Built in 1887, the house is of two stories designed in a quadrangle around a central courtyard enclosed with a glass roof, allowing for maximum benefit of space and light, and commanding fine views over Richmond and the surrounding countryside. . .'"

For once, the details were not hyperbolic at all, but exactly described a house she hadn't seen for simply years – not since just after the General Strike, she remembered – and hadn't thought about for every bit as long.

"Oh, my stars—" she said to Roger, looking up at him over her glasses. "It's Robin Hill."

"That's it."

"But Roger, don't you—"

"Roger—?"

"Hmm?"

Celia had cut in. How irritating of her; Winifred was in limbo until she could pump every last detail out of her nephew.

"Did you say you were learning first-aid at the ARP?"

"That's right. Splints and bandages, pressure points, the works."

"Anything about delivering babies?"

"Good Lord, no!"

"Ah—"

Celia stood with difficulty; she had gone quite pale. Cecily helped her up, and was flushing.

"—In that case, could I ask you to go outside and get me a cab? I think I'm having my baby now."

Chapter Nine

Return of the House

When Fleur said his name the following night just as he was about to join her in bed, Michael was alerted by an odd tone in her voice. It was as if a door somewhere was shutting, with him on the wrong side.

"Michael, I've decided to buy Robin Hill for my new charity – Jon Forsyte's old house out at Richmond, do you remember?"

Michael could hardly forget. So that was what she had been planning! Was this better or worse than his imaginings? He had never seen the house, but he had seen Fleur's face that time she suggested they all go there, when Jon Forsyte had brought his young wife to lunch at South Square. Another man, who loved her less, might have called the expression sly – but Michael could never be another man. He was prevented from checking for the same expression now; Fleur had turned to put her book on her bedside table.

As though she had heard his thoughts, she turned back and presented her face. It seemed blameless, very frank.

"It's just perfect for what I need, and I can get it for a knock-down price – the owner's decamped to Switzerland. You don't mind, do you, Michael?"

She had started and finished with his name, but still Michael had the feeling that he was being carefully excluded.

"If it's what you want, Fleur," he said neutrally. "Of course not."

"I didn't think you would – you're too sensible. It's not as if I were planning to buy a farm on the Downs, after all; then I'd expect you to be jealous. Put out the light!"

The light in question was also on her table. In stretching over

321

to it he reached her shoulder first, and his capacity for analysis evaporated. Had she meant it to?

Two weeks later, as he sat with his aunt-in-law in the back of his own car heading towards Richmond, Michael felt this faculty returning. Fleur seemed to have laid all her cards on the table. She had urged him to make the trip out, to see her newly acquired premise. Directly he agreed, she suggested her aunt might want to come as well, and so it was arranged. Fleur said she would take the train down in the morning, and they could drive down and collect her later that afternoon. Michael supposed it was natural Winifred would want to 'take a lunar', as used to be the phrase; but was that the only reason why Fleur wanted him accompanied?

Fleur was expecting them at four, and they left Green Street with enough time for Riggs to proceed comfortably. Winifred did not like to be driven in excess of thirty, even on the open road. Something Winifred said on the way triggered his further unease, though not immediately. First she told him rather more than he needed to know about Celia Cardigan's new baby: a boy, and her own first great-grandchild. Then for the next mile or so out from Mayfair, she delivered a review of the last show she had seen.

"St. John took me to see the *most* ridiculous person at a place called the Hippodrome the other night. Now; what was the fellow's name? Ah, yes – Max Miller."

"There's a funny thing!" escaped Michael before he could think better of it.

"How very odd," said Winifred, looking at him roundly. "That's just what that fellow kept saying."

Michael pulled his moustache.

"Only it never was – funny – at all," she went on. "I can't imagine what everyone was laughing at."

"I believe he's rather an acquired taste."

"His clothes certainly are. I shouldn't have had them for curtains. And he spoke so quickly I couldn't understand one word of what he said."

Which was probably just as well, Michael thought, or St. John would have had a deal of explaining to do. Miller wasn't billed as *The Cheeky Chappie* for nothing.

322

"I thought he might be quite promising at first. He said he got all his jokes from the Blue Book."

The baronet's eyebrows shot up.

"I don't think he meant the social register, Aunt!"

"Then what did he mean?"

Michael passed on explaining.

"And there was one very peculiar moment when he looked straight at me – St. John insisted we sit in the front stalls, which was tedious of him. This ridiculous man looked straight down at me from the stage, and do you know what he said?"

Michael knew, but restrained himself from chanting. He let Winifred repeat the comedian's words, which she did exactly, but with a deadly timing that was all her own.

"He said – '*Take a good look, lady, there'll never be another.*' Extraordinary!"

They passed a news-stand where the latest figures of the evacuation from Dunkirk were posted.

"Will they get them all out safely, do you think?"

"As many as humanly possibly, I've no doubt. But ten divisions will take some carting – and they won't refuse French troops who want to come."

"The French," said Winifred, without elaboration. Michael supposed she held with the orthodoxy of opinion on the subject. "*We* can organise, though."

Can't we just, thought Michael – *after the event!* After nearly a year of national lethargy and inertia, it was marvellous to see how resourceful and energetic a people could be in the grip of real crisis. We've found our direction at last – pity it's backwards! Heigh-ho!

"Fleur has a gift for organisation," Winifred added after recalling her niece was half French, as if to establish the ascendancy of Forsyte blood over the Continental type which also ran in her veins. "I think this home is an excellent idea. Has she picked a Service?"

"I don't think so yet, though she'll need to decide before she registers. I imagine the Army is the obvious choice."

Winifred sighed strangely.

"I *think* her father would have been pleased with her decision."

"The Army?"

"No, no. Robin Hill."

Michael sat up a little straighter in his seat. What could she mean by that? Why on this earth would Soames Forsyte have wanted his daughter to own a house which once belonged to the man who had stolen his first wife from him? Michael remembered his father-in-law as having many difficult traits, but low spite was not one of them.

"Yes, I think so," Winifred repeated to herself, with greater conviction.

They were crossing the river by the Albert Bridge, and the sun on the water attracted her attention for a moment or two. Still looking out she resumed with another little sigh.

"I'm sure he would have liked to see it returned to the family."

Her explanation made even less sense to Michael than his own guesswork. He was such a flea-brain on this subject!

"I thought he didn't consider that side were 'family'?"

"That's what I mean, dear boy. He'd have wanted it back with Fleur."

"I'm sorry – back with her?"

"Of course."

"I don't follow you."

Winifred's shoulders moved first at this, up a little, before she turned round in her seat to face Michael. Her encounter at the Hippodrome had left her ill-disposed towards jokes.

"Are you being serious?"

She saw instantly that he was. Winifred shook her head and tutted. She had always thought the hegemony concerning family secrets was oversubscribed.

"Has no one ever told you? Robin Hill was Soames' house. He built it for Irene when they were married."

Her nephew received this new piece of knowledge in silence, and for the next mile or two turned it over in the same way. Like an urn dug up from antiquity, the broken fragments of the story he had never quite been told were beginning to take shape. He recalled another conversation between himself and his aunt, which occurred one breezy Sunday last summer at Highgate Cemetery.

'... *Soames tried his best to give her everything she wanted* ... *He even had a splendid house built for her in the country, to make a new start.*'

324

'*I gather it didn't work.*'

'*Hardly. Irene misbehaved herself with the architect.*'

Michael spent the rest of the journey attempting to appreciate the finer points of suburban architecture, and the innate joys of corporation planning. He failed abjectly, but considered it worth the try. Anything was better than pursuing the line of thought opened up to him by this latest revelation. Where, oh where, was it written, that in car rides with Winifred Dartie he should have his sensibilities turned over with every mile?

Since his scare last summer – when Anne Forsyte had died suddenly and the terrifying spectre of Fleur regaining her lost love was raised up before him – Michael had come to feel increasingly calm about his marriage. He knew that Jon Forsyte had returned from America at the start of the war, but Fleur seemed 'O.K.' about it. He had noticed no overtures from her towards 'that side of the family'. To his almost certain knowledge she had not seen Holly since the week-end at Wansdon when Kat was so ill, and he knew she would never volunteer for the company of Jon's other sister, June, even though it did seem it was impossible to avoid that little woman from time to time. It had therefore become Michael's sincere belief that his wife no longer desired to make headway across those waters. Was he now to think she had only been becalmed for want of opportunity?

It was too much to contemplate with Winifred beside him, and Fleur ahead. They were already through Richmond!

For all his jumble of feelings towards it, Michael was yet too honest a man, owning too fine a sense of beauty, not to be impressed when he saw Bosinney's house for the first time. Naturally, he did not know to call it Bosinney's; having always thought of the house as Jon Forsyte's, he had just learned a fortnight ago to call it Fleur's – and only today to call it her father's. Despite his determination to banish its every trace from his mind, one thought recurred. When Fleur had first fallen in love with her cousin, it was over this house that she must have expected one day to be mistress.

From deep in the bright spring greenery, a cuckoo called. They found the front door was already open, and without knocking they passed through into the inner courtyard.

Winifred was seeing the interior of the house herself for the first

325

time. So this was where Irene had lived all those years – with cousin Jo, not with Soames! Her intuition for fashion identified an elegance about the place, though it was quite empty of effects (the peer was resident in Switzerland now, she had read). It had distinct charm, which Winifred grudgingly attributed to the influence of her former sister-in-law, rather than to the skill of the architect. Since Bosinney had been prey to that charm himself at the time of his commission, Winifred may not have been altogether mistaken.

They found an agency secretary using the telephone in what had been a study, and Michael asked if she knew the whereabouts of her employer. After ending her discourse with a supplier of some sort on the other end of the line, the woman told them she had last seen Lady Mont an hour ago, in the garden. Winifred and Michael were about to re-cross the court to the garden doors, when Fleur suddenly appeared from that direction.

"My!" said Winifred, without really knowing she had spoken.

The exclamation exactly met Michael's first response, too. If he had ever thought his wife pretty – and he could not recall a moment since he met her when he had not – then he saw now, as if for the very first time, that she was beautiful. The change was brought about by the expression which lighted her face. Her cheeks had high colour, her eyes had a dreamy shine in them, and her lips were parted in a smile. It was an expression of joy, pure and unclouded, which Michael had simply never seen before.

Fleur stopped in mid-step when she saw her visitors were already arrived. She glanced swiftly over her shoulder, then raised a hand to check the colour in her cheeks, and let it continue up to where a strand of hair had fallen over her forehead. As she did so, she modified the open smile which had given her face its glory.

"There you are! I ran all the way up from the coppice in case you thought I'd gone. Shall I show you round?"

When earlier that day Fleur had first crossed the portals of Robin Hill, knowing herself to be mistress of the place at last, her face had shown no expression at all. She had been quite alone – she had made sure she would be. Roger had wanted to meet her there with the keys, in case there were problems, but she insisted he deliver them to her at South Square. There would be no problems, she told him.

It was as well there was no witness as she stepped into the inner court; the rush of memory nearly disabled her, but she commanded her senses to hold. Here she last stood twenty years ago, bidding a strained good-bye to Jon after taking tea with his parents that time he had brought her to see where he lived. Even then she had known there was something between their families which threatened to bar her from him.

'*I should like to see where you live, Jon,*' she had said to him, cautioning – '*I wouldn't come to the house, of course.*'

She remembered how Jon had gazed at her, enraptured.

'*Splendid! I can show it you from the copse, we shan't meet anybody.*'

They had come unexpectedly upon his mother, sitting on the fallen log in that coppice. Awkwardness and tea had ensued. That woman was châtelaine then – but Fleur had the keys now, and gripped them tightly in her hand. She felt her victory – hollow as the house – echo around the empty hall. The pleasure of it was a hair's breadth away from pain.

She looked in at the drawing-room. Here she might have presided for all those years. Here she had presided, in dreams.

'*Ah, how lovely to see you – you know my husband, Jon, of course—*'

She passed to the foot of the staircase, hesitated, and went up, her heels ringing on the steps. Among the bedrooms, instinct, keen as any blade, brought her straight to the master suite. She saw her own hand, pale, ghost-like, open the door, and felt her fantasies gust in ahead of her. Louvres were closed to at the windows, breaking up the sunshine into thin bars; Fleur breathed deeply, as the dust resettled against these slanting beams of light, and took her bearings. Like the rest of the house, the room was quite empty. Phantom patches on the carpeting were all that was left to show where furniture had once stood. A chest, a dressing-table, a couch, a chair; the bed. For Fleur it was furnished with a thousand imaginings, with scenes consummated through twenty years of lost, sad wishing. Here, in dreams, she and Jon had — might have — *would* have— When the room became blurred, she did not at once realise it was because her eyes had filled with tears. When she did realise, she turned on her heel, and ran back down the stairs.

By the time the temporary secretary she had engaged arrived, Fleur had launched herself into a fit of measuring, sizing and checking which lasted well into the afternoon. Finally leaving the woman in the study to decipher a notepad filled with pot-hooks, Fleur took herself outside into the sun.

Gradually, possession, that genetic material occurring in the bones of Forsytes, warmed her flesh quite as effectively as the Whitsuntide weather. She stretched indulgently, like a creature that had quartered its new territory. Her mind was still ticking off practical items from her list as she wandered from the terrace on to the grass. She would keep the agency woman on for the moment. Tomorrow she would set her to engage an advance squad of cleaners, ahead of decorators and fitters, so that she could see the full extent of what needed to be done. And she must get a gardener – this lawn needed rolling!

On the edge of the lawn she stood looking out, drawing strength from the sun and air, her feet up to the ankles in clover. Inevitably her eyes were drawn down towards the coppice. The larches had grown tall with neglect. Strange – she owned every one of them now. And the fallen log, where she had finally claimed Jon as her own – body and soul – was it still there?

The cuckoo resumed its hollow peal, like an ancient watch repeating. It beckoned from that direction. Fleur followed, and found her heart.

Chapter Ten

Serendipity

A telephone call that morning, at about the time Fleur took possession of his old home, summoned Jon to Mastonbury. The COC, his adjutant said, would like a word.

The word was not the one Jon had allowed himself to hope for on the way. Wing-Commander Welling looked up from a letter he was writing as Jon came into his office. He put down his pen and took his half-lens glasses from his nose.

"Ah, Mr Forsyte. Thank you for coming in – do sit down – we want your field."

Jon sat.

"My field?"

"If you don't mind – there'll be compensation. We've always been a bit cramped here, and we noticed your field at the back of us was fallow."

Through the COC's window, Jon could see the airstrip stretching out against a backdrop of woodland. Green Hill lay beyond, the two establishments meeting across a stretch of common pasture to the north.

"We're hemmed in on this side, you see. It would help us tremendously to have it. Save cutting down the spinney, and with the common thrown in we'll be able to take our corsets off properly."

"Yes," Jon said, and managed a brief smile. He knew he must sound flat. "Anything that helps, of course."

Welling shuffled the papers on his desk.

"I know you'd prefer to take a more active part, Mr Forsyte, but believe me, this *will* help. The traffic's pretty heavy at the moment – likely to get heavier, too – we need all the space we can get. One

329

of our flyers crashed just this morning because he came in too short on a damaged wing – we can't afford that happening again."

"No," Jon said. "Of course."

"We'll consider it settled, then? There'll be paperwork, there always is these days—" Welling put a hand down on the pile of papers – "one sort or another. But if you're agreed—"

"Yes," Jon said. "Of course."

"—Excellent!"

Welling replaced his half-lenses and returned to his writing; Jon realised the interview was over. Apart from the technical transaction, it was as if it had never been. The adjutant appeared, as if by conjuring, at the door.

"Thank you, sir," he said, speaking *sotto*, as though normal volume might remind his senior officer that Jon was still there. "I'll show you out."

He ducked into the room and held the door open. Feeling like a fifth wheel awaiting a puncture, Jon rose to leave. On an impulse not to go without making some gain for his journey, he asked the adjutant:

"I know one of your flyers. Could I leave a message for him?"

"Certainly, sir. No problem. What's his name?"

"Roberts. He's a young pilot officer—"

Jon felt a shift in the atmosphere at once. The adjutant was no longer looking at him, but over his shoulder at his Station Commander. Behind him, Jon was aware of the senior officer's attention once more. He heard Welling repeat the name.

"R.D. Roberts?"

Jon turned.

"That's right."

He saw the Commander pick up the letter he had been attending to, and watched as his eyes came up to meet his own.

Jon drove towards Richmond believing there was no reprieve for one such as himself. The young airman – who in a different world might have been his son or brother – was dead. At nineteen, his life was over before it was even half begun. At more than twice that age, Jon felt the usurper.

Upon hearing the news at Mastonbury – Welling had been

330

writing the very letter he now carried in his breast pocket – Jon begged to be the one to break it to the airman's family. It was the least he could offer to do. After making the appropriate noises about 'channels', hemming and hawing over procedure for a few moments, the COC agreed. Perhaps he saw the field slipping away if he demurred.

Jon drove stolidly on.

'*There's just my mother and sister, and me—*' Jon recalled Bobby saying at Green Hill. *Bobby*. He hardly knew him. In any other situation, they would have yet to arrive at first name terms. In any other situation, the young fellow would have still been alive.

He reached the first point of triangulation within the hour. At the war memorial, he stopped his car and got out. He could see the church spire off in the distance, poking up at the end of a curving avenue of old limes. As he remembered the location from his youth, the row of cottages should be a quarter of a mile or so further to his left. Jon investigated the road on foot, and found there was a turning beyond the memorial, tucked behind a stand of beeches. A sign said '*Acre Lane*'. A good bet for Pole Cottages, the address on the envelope he carried.

Jon walked back to his car, wishing he had his pipe. As he got in, he saw a cyclist come out of the turning, and take the corner in his direction. It was a young girl, not very much older than his own daughter, wearing a light cotton dress – pin-striped in pale blue and white, perhaps a school uniform – and a straw hat, with her hair tucked up into it, tied under her chin with a broad ribbon of the same blue.

"Oh, excuse me—!" Jon called, waving as she approached.

The girl stopped her bicycle, putting one foot on the ground and hopping along until she drew level on the other side of the road.

"I'm sorry to stop you," he said. "I'm looking for Pole Cottages – are they the way you've just come?"

The girl gave him a puzzled look, as if she may have mistrusted his motive for asking her. Jon felt he could hardly justify his question with its real reason, and did not feel up to invention. He could only hope his expression was honest.

After submitting to her scrutiny for a further few seconds, Jon was relieved to find he must have passed the test. She twisted in her saddle and pointed to the turning.

"Go up there until you come to Perch Row, on the right. You can't miss it."

"Thanks. Thank you very much."

The girl smiled briefly, but her original expression remained in her eyes. As she cycled off again, down the road behind him, Jon restarted his engine.

There were no surprises waiting for him at the end of his journey. After fifteen minutes, no longer, spent inside the last of the little row of cottages, Jon was everlastingly grateful to that much-derided native quality, the stiff upper-lip. He was in no doubt that Mrs Roberts, a pleasant-faced, fair haired woman between his own age and Holly's, would give way at some point, but not before he left. She thanked him for coming, for his trouble; she thanked him several times, in fact. Jon replied on varying occasions that it was no trouble, no trouble at all, the least he could do. If there was anything else—? He was thanked again. He took out his card, and left it with the letter, which lay, returned to its envelope, on a dresser.

As Jon stepped from the front door onto the garden path, he saw the girl again. Her face bore the same expression; only one thing about her was changed. Her cycle was there, leaning against the fence, and she was just unlatching the gate on her way in. She stood aside on a little patch of front lawn as she saw Jon come out of the cottage. Behind her sloped a range of blue early summer flowers, carefully tended: delphiniums, scabious, pansies, lobelia. The blues of the flowers, the blue of her dress, and of the ribbon on the hat she now held in her hand, seemed all to serve only one purpose – to emphasise the glorious red of her hair as it fell about her shoulders.

Jon held her eyes – another, paler shade of the surrounding colour – and hoped his expression was still as trustworthy as she had found it before. It was impossible to say anything. His guilt alone, as he saw her eyes grow larger with intuitive realisation, was inexpressible. He latched the gate softly, and regained his car. Within two miles, he knew he could drive no further with any proper attention to the road. He found a lane he used to know as well as any part of himself. Parking by a hedgerow, he found the path he had

332

taken countless times in years before, and more than once in recent months, and started up its gentle climb. When he saw the larches, he felt safe. He sat down on the old log – mossy now, fallen away in places – and let his thoughts and feelings tumble out.

When Jon turned his head at the quick snap of a twig, he was roused suddenly from ghostly memories by a waking apparition which made him start up from the log.

He saw a light figure standing under one of the larches; one hand was keeping aside a low-hanging branch from its face, the other hand was held up to open lips. As the breeze soughed through the coppice, it seemed a tremor ran from the tree through the figure. Against an arbour of young green leaves, under patchwork sunlight which fell through them, Jon saw chestnut hair glinting brightly, a strand of it falling across a pale broad brow, above widely spaced hazel eyes that were strangely lit and dancing with mute expression. Beneath, when the hand was slowly withdrawn to sweep the fallen hair away, he saw the lips, still trembling, part again, as if they might speak his name. Instead, he only heard the breeze sigh above them, and his own voice, strained and low, before he even knew he spoke.

"*Fleur!*"

When the figure did not answer, Jon felt himself plunge deeper into unreality than before. Fleur — *a vision, or a waking dream?* The poet in him was willing to believe the presence of either.

"Fleur — is it really you? Say something—!"

Jon watched as a visible effort of will passed like a cloud across the clear dark eyes.

"Do you want me to?" she asked faintly.

"Yes!"

The breeze sighed again; perhaps she sighed too.

"I'm glad. I couldn't at first."

"Nor could I," he confessed. "I thought – it was enchantment."

"Perhaps it is."

"We should have expected it. Enchantment's only natural – in this place."

She nodded, a little startled, her eyes becoming clouded a second time. Jon was fully as surprised at himself. It was the shock of seeing

333

her that had provoked his candour. *This place*. It was where they had last met, where he had last held her, where they had finally become lovers, body and soul. How strange to see her again, here, now.

"How strange—" he repeated, and realising it was the first time he had used the phrase aloud, continued "—to meet again like this."

"Like the princes of Serendip."

"Yes."

"Do you wish we hadn't?"

The speed of her question prompted him to another confession.

"No!"

Why was it so? A year ago he would have felt guilty just to own a thought about her. But a year ago there was Anne.

Fleur was watching him, her eyes once again clear as a bird's.

"Do you?" he asked back.

"No."

When she shook her head, her hair caught the broken sunlight and gave off deep red glimmerings. It was exactly the colour he remembered. Everything about her was as he remembered, every detail. How little she had changed – it *was* enchantment, just to look at her, in this place!

"It's impossible I haven't seen you for fourteen years—"

He hardly knew he had kept count until then.

"I've seen you," she answered.

"When?"

"Only once."

"But where? Why didn't you say—?"

"It wasn't the moment."

Clearly it was that now. Neither said so; there was no need.

Jon passed a hand up his forehead to his hair. And then he smiled. Neither of them had, so far. He saw her face soften as she watched him, as if it were really he who was the vision.

Stepping forwards cautiously, she came towards the log, hovered for a second, then seemed to take a conscious decision to sit down upon it. Jon saw what she intended and automatically made way for her to sit. Then he succumbed to his next natural impulse – and sat down beside her.

334

Fleur! the warm scent of her was like a piece of summer itself. Suddenly Jon was desperate to know what had brought her there, but didn't see how he could rightfully ask. It was impertinent, since he had no right there himself. And he felt she was still unnerved, still cautious. Small wonder – he could hardly believe his own senses.

"I suppose you're wondering what I'm doing here—" he began.

He ran his hand up his brow again and scanned the edges of the little clearing around the log, looking at nothing, trying to see his own reasons more clearly. It was like being in a confessional booth, with the larches closing around them.

"Actually I've come here once or twice – since—" he stopped, faltering as he groped his way out of the construction— "when I've wanted to be alone, and think about things."

He brought his hand down from his brow and gave a small laugh, half nervous, half a sigh.

"I expect I ought to have got the owner's permission first."

He looked back at Fleur, and was rewarded with her first smile. In a moment her hesitancy had gone.

"Don't worry," she said, her voice still small, but steady; she touched his shoulder lightly. "She grants it you now."

Jon believed his face must reveal him an idiot, as he felt understanding creep slowly over his features. Did she mean—?

The answer came without his asking:

"Yes, Jon. I've bought Robin Hill."

What enormous impact the least item can have, if its arrival is truly unexpected. When Jon heard those few extraordinary words, time seemed to buckle under him for the moment. Present and past seemed caught on a carousel that was turning around the two of them. Memories, visions, reality – no one part seemed more immediate than another. It was as if she had said:

'*The past can change – look, I've changed it!*'

Again she answered his unasked question:

"Not to live in."

"Oh!"

Jon was ashamed at the relief he felt, hearing that. He hoped she didn't detect it, but he couldn't help himself; he *was* relieved. What potency there was in old possessions, old ownerships!

"I'm starting a convalescent home for wounded servicemen."

"Oh – how marvellous of you!" he stammered, and was all the more ashamed of his mean-heartedness. It was like her to do something, to organise, be practical and get things done. What could he say was his own contribution, after all? And not for the first time that day Jon 'thought more meanly of himself, for not having been a soldier.'

"I'm doing my bit, you see, Jon. I was determined to do something."

"Yes – it's like you to know how to help, to do something." He snapped up a blue-flowered weed growing between his feet. It made him think of the cottage garden, and the young girl's face as she stood among the blue flowers there. He turned it abstractedly in his hand. "I wish I had your – your certainty about things."

They were both looking at the weed in his hand. Jon cast it away when he realised it was a wild forget-me-not.

"No one seems to want my help."

His sentence hung in the air, until Fleur said softly:

"I do, Jon," and when he looked up at her, doubting her meaning, she added firmly, "—as long as you're serious."

Her eyes were scanning his. There was a stern little frown over her brow. He felt she knew everything he was thinking – if only he knew himself!

"Look, Jon, if you really want to help, I can use you. If you'll put the past aside, I will too; then perhaps we can both make a contribution."

With that little speech she had taken a weight from him. He might never have found the words himself, and the chance would have been missed. How capable she was, and sensible! Fleur!

"Oh, yes – do let's, Fleur – tell me what I can do."

"Well, I'm registering Robin Hill as a war charity and I need a board of governors willing to contribute. I can manage the initial amount myself, but there'll be equipment to buy, salaries, running costs. I've got a couple of people on the board already; I'm looking for two or three more. The work-load won't be heavy – only a meeting every quarter, and odds and ends of things – but the contribution I'll want from you will be—"

She mentioned a round figure. Jon thought it reasonable, and said so. In truth he would cheerfully have paid twice the price

336

for the amount of conscience-salving it promised to purchase him. Robin Hill a convalescent home – that was something!

"It all sounds splendid," he said, when he had heard her out. "God knows, there's already a need for these places." He thought suddenly of one beyond help, and added, "Especially for airmen."

Fleur's face took on another little smile.

"My home *is* for airmen."

Jon smiled back at her, but before he could look in her eyes, she got up. He followed.

"I'll have the details sent to you. Of course, you can always back out once you've read them—"

"No – don't worry!"

He wished she hadn't thought him capable of backing out. He meant to be as good as his word.

"Well," she said evenly, "that's settled then. I must get back—"

She indicated the direction of the house.

"So must I," he said, nodding the opposite way. "My car's down in the lane."

Fleur was holding out her hand to him. He took it; her grasp was light, firm, unmeaningful. Despite himself, Jon felt a little pang when she let go, that it was nothing more. So – they really had put the past aside! She moved away from him with a quick, light step. When she was under the same larch where she had first appeared, she turned swiftly and said:

"*Au revoir!*"

Before he could reply, she was gone.

Chapter Eleven

'Guilty'

Sitting beside her aunt for the return journey, with Michael 'up front' next to Riggs, Fleur kept the conversation going at a great rate on her plans for the house. She debated how many convalescing airmen — now she had decided on a service — she could take comfortably; what ratio of resident staff they would need; what degree of medical supervision. While she kept up this patter, her mind raced along its own track, speeding on. Seeing Jon had left her light-headed, exhilarated, as if she were breathing ether. Having him there, as it were in her hand, dropped by Providence, had been an experience of sheer and singular joy; having to leave him, letting him go whence he came, reassured by her performance, now brought her absurd anxiety. Ought she to have left him with some hint, some token of what was possible now between them? Had she let him go *too* certain of his safety? Between Richmond and Chiswick she believed she had utterly lost her chance; between Chiswick and Hammersmith hope returned and she was again convinced of her success — and so it went, from borough to borough. She might as well have plucked the petals of a daisy for augury. Chattering blithely the while, and inwardly turning her chances over and over, Fleur did not notice how the back of her husband's neck reddened periodically, nor how the points of his ears, when she waxed her most enthusiastic, could be seen just slightly to droop.

"I knew it would be a tonic for you, dear," said Winifred, comforted by this new animation in her niece, "especially with Kit going off so suddenly. I haven't seen you so fired over anything since that canteen of yours during the General Strike."

When they left Winifred at Green Street and returned to South

Square, Fleur went straight up to her bath. Michael turned into his study, ostensibly to look at some papers. The hinges of his campaign chair creaked as he dropped into it; for the moment, he felt thoroughly sorry for himself. Of all the disturbing incidents of that little excursion, his aunt's last comment was perhaps the most troubling. Yes, Fleur's present buoyancy was *just* like her mood during the General Strike; and he fell gloomily to contemplating the chain of events which had started then.

From above his desk, with the rinds of a stolen fruit in its articulated paw, the White Monkey looked at him with an expression of high irony in its near-human eyes. Michael avoided its gaze for a while, preferring to continue nursing the spectre he was none too sure he hadn't raised himself. But then he looked back. Yes, you're right, he thought, addressing the creature. I'm getting to be a suspicious beggar, and it won't do. First I worry that she hasn't a good cause, then I'm frantic when she has. You know the answer, don't you? No prize worth the capture!

By the time he went into his dressing-room, he could hear Fleur's voice in the next room. She was singing in her bath!

Heads turned as they entered the Savoy. Fleur was a vision in deep red: her dress, her lips, her hair – all set against the creamy white of her skin and of pearls at her neck and wrists. She was irresistible! Having her on his arm, Michael felt his heart swell. He could not have been prouder if he had been sure she was dressed solely for him.

They found the Messengers already at the bar; Vivian was mixing his own cocktail, after his particular habit, and Nona was counting olives after hers.

"Now that's what I like to see," said Michael as they approached. "The aristocracy applying itself to what it does best."

Nona kissed him sweetly, a slim, blonde little thing in a blue shift, ten years younger than Fleur, and the mother of four to date.

Vivian raised an eyebrow meanwhile. Ancient Anglo-Irish blood was piqued.

"Just limbering up at the bar. *Noblesse oblige.* Fleur, you are a dream, my darling."

He held her at arm's length to admire her with heavy lidded

eyes, and then kissed her with his rather fleshy mouth. Michael noticed he kept his eyes and lips open slightly in the process – he was an awful old *roué*!

"Have one of these," Vivian ordered, pouring viscous green liquid from a shaker into four conical glasses. "No olives, Nona, they'll clash."

"What *is* it, Vivian?" Fleur asked.

"Ask not for whom the Bell's tolls. My latest creation, and not for the faint-hearted. I call 'em Spit-fires."

Fleur only sniffed at her glass, and pulled a little *moue*. Michael sipped gingerly, and winced.

"Dear Lord! – there's a bit too much fire in it for me."

"Ah – so not enough spit?"

Michael sputtered. Fleur said:

"Vivian, you're dreadful. I believe you set us up for that."

"Michael's the third he's caught today," said Nona. "He's far worse than any of the children."

They ordered real drinks from the barman. On the other side of the dance floor, a well-known, dark-haired crooner began singing a verse which sounded suspiciously like Shakespeare to an 'up-tempo' setting. Michael cocked an ear.

> *'There was a lover and his lass,*
> *with a hey, and a ho,*
> *and a hey-nonny-no—'*

It seemed an unlikely combination, but Fleur's foot was already tapping.

"I know they reckon this chap can sing anything," he said, "but can it really be the Bard?"

"Should ha' heard his last number," said Vivian. "'*Blow, blow thou winter wind*' – and they say there's a war on!"

They laughed above the beat of the ten-piece band and moved to a table. Their cocktails arrived.

"So what are we celebrating tonight?" Fleur asked. "Tell us so we can drink to it."

"Excellent notion. Raise your glasses, people, if you will, and repeat after me: '*Parce nuntio*—'"

"Parquet what?" queried Michael, his glass suspended.

"'*Parce nuntio, Domine, ad laborem tuum*'," Vivian intoned. "My family's ancient and venerable crest – mock it at your peril – and now inscribed over the newest, and I may say hottest publishing house in Town. I thank you."

Michael and Fleur still did not drink, but exchanged a mystified glance.

"*Do* humour him," said Nona tolerantly. "He's just coughed up *une jambe et un bras* to buy out Compson Grice."

"At Danby and Winter?" said Michael incredulously. "Good Heavens, my old firm – whatever for?"

"For the purpose of selling books, dear fellow. Should ha' thought that was obvious, even to a baronet. Drink, damn you."

They drank. It was always difficult to tell when Vivian was being serious.

"But you don't know the first thing about books," Michael resumed.

"Correction. Don't know the first thing about *anything*. Frankly, it was getting dull; or I was, same difference. They brought me up to do nothing – I thought publishing would be the next best thing."

Michael could not help but laugh.

"That's one way of approaching the business, I suppose. But have you really bought all their list? Penniless poets, earnest essayists—?"

"—Monotonous monographists, the bally lot of 'em. Dead wood for the most part, same as everywhere. But Messenger has the answer. *War memoirs*, old darling – and yours is going to be one of the first. Shall we dance?"

Husbands and wives paired off onto the dance floor. To the tune of '*One Morning in May*', Fleur and Michael got into a quickstep.

"Do you think he means it, Michael?"

"With Vivian, who knows? There may be something in it."

"Hmm. '*War Diaries of a Back-Bencher*.' It sounds promising."

"Subtitle: '*They Also Served*.' Well, he's spent his life trying to lose his inheritance – it'd be rude to try and stop him now. Perhaps I should ask for an advance!"

They took another fast turn around the floor before the song finished. Michael was about to lead her back to their table, when Fleur said:

"Let's stay for one more number."

Michael was happy to consent, and happier still when a change of tempo was announced.

"Here's a slow foxtrot, ladies and gentlemen," said the singer, in his quick, eager, slightly accented voice. "I'd like to dedicate it to Mr Hitler – it's called 'Guilty'." A ripple of laughter went up from the floor. "And don't worry about air-raids, either – I haven't had a hit in years!"

Another laugh subsided as the violas took up the refrain, and the crooner took up the verse in his inimitable way.

> *'Is it a crime? Is it a sin?*
> *Loving you, dear, like I do—'*

Michael listened to the words of the song as they moved together across the floor.

> *'If it's a crime, then I'm guilty*
> *– guilty of loving you.'*

With Fleur in his arms, and their bodies close in slow rhythm, Michael finally let go the last of his fears. He turned his face into her hair, deeply inhaled the scent of her, and smiled.

With her head tucked into her husband's shoulder, and the firm grasp of his arm at her back, Fleur also heard the words of the song. She too began to smile.

Part Two

Chapter One

'They Also Serve'

Spirits at the Remove had risen lately; in keeping, the wine committee had authorised the release of its last reserve of cognac. It was a week since Paris was liberated and the Allied armies were surging at last across France and Belgium towards the German and Dutch Frontiers. It was also – unimaginably! – the fifth anniversary of the declaration of hostilities. Since Fleur was out at Richmond, at her home for airmen, Michael had taken a late lunch at his club. He took a glass of the brandy, but did not drink to the toast which was being offered.

"Unconditional surrender!"

Michael would as soon drink to the likelihood of good weather. Fuller details were just coming out concerning the von Stauffenberg bomb plot which had failed to kill Hitler at Rastenburg, and it was Michael's unpopular opinion that with Allied help for the anti-Nazi movement inside the Reich, this present anniversary need never have been reached. He had been barracked for saying as much in the Commons' debate on the subject, and was tackled again for repeating himself now.

Abercrombie was the most scathing.

"Bloody irony – you pacifists want to let the 'good' Germans hang on to the Ruhr, so they can prepare for World War Three!"

Was it worth the effort of replying? The brandy decided for him.

"Do you suppose there'll be Germans of *any* persuasion left if we don't offer them terms?"

This was tactically unsound, as Michael realised the second he heard himself say it. It allowed for several cheers, a cry of "Damn' right – get 'em all!" and another of "Pastoralisation!"

When he went on to assert that reducing Germany to agri-
cultural status was actually an economic aim, and therefore not
a legitimate war one, he was told he had the wrong end of the
stick. Sinews stiffened with cognac, Michael pursued his point: had
anyone considered that Britain's supplying Germany with all her
industrial goods after the war was presently seen as the preferred
way of paying for the Beveridge plan? One member suggested that
his views were demented. When another declared that he must be a
Socialist after all, and that his membership there was the thin end
of the wedge, Michael realised he had quite missed the pitch of the
hall.

All the more convinced that he had hold of the right end of the
stick, whether or not it was also the thin end of the wedge, he
signed for his meal, got his hat and raincoat from the porter and left.

Unsure of his own worth at the best of times, Michael knew for
certain that he wasn't worth his salt if he felt unable to speak his
mind, inside the House or out of it. But speaking fell short of acting,
and as a back-bencher his scope for the latter since the country had
been at war was hopelessly limited. The independence he relished in
peace had become a millstone during the hostilities. He considered
how he would put this latest encounter down in his memoir – which
he had kept faithfully to date – and then wondered whether he would
bother at all. Whether the entries were made in their reinforced
basement at South Square, or on his knee during any of the duller
debates in the House, the process of keeping this detailed record of
events, and the minutiae of his responses to them, served chiefly to
help him feel more keenly the inadequacies of his position. In the end,
criticism was no substitute for service. It might be an eye-catching
title for the book but the notion that 'they also serve' went down
uneasily as a placebo for real contribution; perhaps it would make
for a perfect ending both ways if he resigned his seat?

And so, turning this latest dilemma around and around in his
head – whether to stay or go, and which action would better serve
the country and his pronounced sense of duty towards it – he set
course under a cloudy sky for South Square. Fleur would be back
by now; he would talk it through with her.

As Michael turned into the square he was distracted from these
wheeling thoughts by the sight of a large black staff car standing at

the kerb, directly in front of his own door. His first guess raised an alarm – would they send a car if something had happened to Kit? No, he was calmed by a second thought – a telegram was always the first thing, and Fleur would have called him, or sent someone round to the club.

Drawing level with the driver's window, Michael was further reassured by the sight of a young WAAF seated behind the wheel, and occupied in knitting something that might soon be a sock on busy needles with bottle-green wool. From the corner of her eye she caught the baronet looking at her, and quickly slipped the work down to her knee. Michael saw her stifle what he thought was rather an engaging smile as she straightened up in her seat. Turning her head to him she touched her cap, and he saw under it a wisp of the brightest red hair, bar none, that he had ever seen. She removed the smile from her face but it was still in her eyes. Certain now that she was there on no terrible mission, and unduly pleased to encounter a pretty girl of playful spirit towards the end of an otherwise disenchanting day, Michael smiled back at her, and tipped his hat by return. She nodded and turned back to face the wheel. Michael took the steps up to the front door in pairs, and let himself in with his latch-key.

On the marble sarcophagus in the hall, where with more than usual end-of-day thanks he relinquished his own hat and raincoat, he saw another's there before him. A peaked cap lay on top of a macintosh. The colour of both articles placed their owner in the American Army, the shoulder badge indicated he was a Lieutenant Colonel, and the spread-eagle on the cap badge told he was a flyer. So translating all the available signs, Michael decided Fleur must have brought back a visiting 'high-up' from her Home.

He opened the drawing-room doors to see his wife talking to the rest of the uniform by the fireplace. In the moment before she noticed him, Michael had the feeling he might have walked in on something. But Fleur saw him almost at once and said:

"Ah, Michael – you're home. Look who's here!"

He looked, at a uniformed back which turned unhurriedly into a uniformed front. The face, when he could see it, with its mild intelligent features and wistful dark eyes, was lodged so far back in his memory that Michael barely knew from which file he should try to retrieve it. He moved forward automatically. The face smiled at him respectfully, the uniform stiffened, and a hand reached out and firmly gripped his own.

Something in that odd mix of deference and confidence gave Michael's memory the necessary prod.

"No, surely—? It can't be!"

The hand gripped his more solidly still, and a confirming voice spoke in a quiet American accent, which Michael recalled being from one of the southern states.

"It surely can be – and is."

He remembered the young man who had come to stay, years ago, and felt suddenly much older himself.

"Good Lord — Francis Wilmot?"

Francis Wilmot, brother to Anne Wilmot; Anne Wilmot, late wife of Jon Forsyte; Jon Forsyte—

"Lieutenant Colonel Wilmot now, Michael," Fleur corrected.

"Yes – I saw the scrambled egg on your cap. You're over here, are you – for the duration?"

"Fresh off the plane today—"

"—And due to have supper with Mr Winant tonight, so we mustn't keep him."

"Oh, well – I see." Michael remembered liking the fellow while he had stayed that time, if he was still leery of the connection which had brought him to them. He said, honestly enough, "You'll come and see us again, though?"

"As soon as I see the chance for some free time, I'll be honoured to come calling."

"Good show. I'll see you out."

Michael went out into the hall to pick up the Lieutenant Colonel's macintosh and hat, leaving Fleur to let her cheek be kissed in farewell. He heard the American say something to her briefly, but could not make out what it was. When he opened the street door, he saw that the girl had resumed her knitting.

Chapter Two

Over Here

One overcast day in the early autumn of 1924, a young man in his mid-twenties had descended from a taxi onto the broad well-swept pavement of South Square, inspired with a certain uneasiness as he looked up at the first English house he had ever proposed to enter. His skin was pale, his eyes and hair dark, and his appearance so mildly American that the honest cockney driver had distinct qualms about asking for twice his fare.

When, upon the exact stretch of pavement at a little before four o'clock on this present afternoon in September 1944, there stood a man in the early part of well-trimmed middle-age, he might have passed for the father of the above. It was twenty years later almost to the day, and to the first glance of his matured eye – for it was the same man – nothing about the scene had changed but himself.

The double-fronted house, with its bright windows and shrubs in boxes lining white steps up to the broad front door, seemed wholly unaltered. The trees at his back were as tall as ever, and the birds hidden in them gave off the same chirrupings. Time, that waits for no man, seemed to him to have overlooked this one scene from his past; and then the bell on the Parliament clock began to chime. Its stately boom made the only break in the familiar leafy quietude of the square: *two — three — four —*

The man heard it and remembered. Change, in fact, lay all about him, and left a broken trail in every direction he cared to cast his eyes. On his route into town from the aerodrome there had been the chastening prospect of bomb craters and ruined homes to either side. He was grateful to have come in that way; he had heard that the east of the city, by the docks, lay in devastation.

Even in this sheltered square he had only to look over his shoulder to see where railings, sent for scrap, were missing from the central garden; he had remembered it laid out to lawn and linked with a chain of flower-beds, alternating yellow chrysanthemums and purple daisies. Now – strange! he looked again to be sure – it was given over entirely to vegetables. Yes, plainly, there were heads of cabbages in neat rows – of all things! He knew something of the 'austerity measures' in operation here from his briefing, but somehow the notion of a humble cabbage growing in a neighbourhood so privileged as this — well, it was an education. He clucked softly to himself at the sight and adjusted his gaze once more.

Beyond the dappled trunks of massive plane-trees and visible through their waning autumn foliage, he saw with a pang of sadness the twenty-yard gap in what until the Blitz had been a row of Queen Anne town-houses. To lose such antiquity at a stroke! Why, in the Carolinas, we weren't but Crown Colonies ourselves when they were built, he thought to himself, marvelling the more at a nation whose tenacity was fostered from roots so deep in history that his own seemed scarce those of a green sapling. He appreciated then, as perhaps never so fully before, the very real grit possessed by this little country whose people had endured five long years of war, nearly two of them quite alone in the whole world. *Sand* was his word for it – that quality he admired above all others. How inadequately he had understood that back in '24, on his first visit! And it seemed to the man, his realisation coming upon him in a sudden moment, that he had been a boy all his life until the start of this war, or at best until a very little before.

The chance observer (that pet of the novelist), had he also witnessed the first scene, would have found his own comparisons between youth and man disadvantaged by the fact that the dark hair, starting now a little higher on the forehead, and eyes, if not precisely darker then deeper-set than before, were at present obscured by the glossy peak of an olive-coloured uniform cap, which shade agreed with that of a uniform macintosh. There was a resemblance between earlier and later selves, but one clouded by experience, as if a ghost of some past event had walked through the man, and its reflection been caught far at the back of his eyes. Absolute confirmation that the two disparate ages were those of the one man

350

came only when, looking back towards the house, he could be heard to murmur in his quiet 'southern states' accent – "It surely is," just as he had that time before.

Francis Wilmot was unaware he had repeated himself. He turned round to the car which, unlike that first taxi, still waited by the kerb at his back with its engine turning, and spoke to the driver. She was a young woman also in uniform, though hers was of the native shade of blue.

"I don't rightly know how long I'll be. Just wait here for me a whiles, will you?"

The young woman had quickly learned, in this first day of her temporary assignment, how to overcome the smile which orders so sweetly spoken naturally induced. She nodded efficiently and, checking the hand-brake, shut off her engine. It was only when she saw the American officer admitted inside the house that she reached into a bag lying on the floor of the car by her feet, and withdrew a roll of knitting.

Timms – these days entirely unawed by the greatness of the persons who appeared in relays before her on the doorstep at South Square – placed the peaked cap and macintosh all but nonchalantly on top of the coat sarcophagus in the hall and showed the American officer into the drawing-room, asking him kindly to sit while she took his card up to her mistress, not long back from Richmond.

Francis Wilmot, preferring to stand, gazed wonderingly around him. He had expected, in the way a dreamer expects upon finding himself returned to a familiar scene, to see a room which seemed to shimmer with hues of sub-gold and silver. His memory was of Fleur's 'bi-metallic parlour', of its glass lustres set daintily upon skeletal gilt furniture, its pictures of flowers adorning gold-panelled walls, and of a wondrously soft silver-coloured carpet beneath a high silver-coloured ceiling. Though the room as it appeared now hardly represented a rude awakening, it was so different in every particular from its former self that Francis suddenly doubted the original had ever been reality.

Allowing the 'Deco' to remain long after the height of its fashion all through the early years of the war – when the appearance of austerity had seemed nothing short of a patriotic duty – Fleur had only that summer begun to change the livery of her drawing-room. Raised in material abundance, she naturally abhorred the utility

351

regulations which were imposed, and yet she was obliged to be mindful that her husband belonged to the body which had imposed them. The challenge of getting a first-rate job done in the worst of circumstances and without too great ostentation had piqued her proper sense of the bargain. Having transformed the house at Richmond, where she spent most of her days, she was determined to do the same to the drawing-room in Westminster to which she returned at night. Besides this, the Normandy landings had brought fresh hope for the future in their wake, and she wished to act upon it. Covering her bets for that future, uncertain as it continued since Arnhem, she had looked to the distant past and chosen a theme from antiquity – not what merely seemed such to a near-colonial eye, but true Classical Antiquity, authenticated by several raids on Jobson's where she discovered ancient artifacts, amphorae and so forth, could be picked up for a song. As Michael put it, the War had knocked the bottom out of Greek vases.

The final execution was remarkable. The walls had been marbled in a shade of antique amber, and linked top and bottom with a Greek-key design in gold. Fluted *trompe-l'oeil* columns appeared to hold up the ceiling at each corner of the room, and at either side of the fireplace, which itself was now set with twinkling blue-green mosaic. For upholstery and drapes, Fleur had commandeered a bale of green slub satin, shot with blue, which her mother-in-law had remembered buying before the war, for Mount Street, and then forgetting once it started.

A Persian carpet, there being no such item as a Roman one, was borrowed from Lippinghall, where the Mondrian, with her Fragonard and Chardin and other treasures, was stored. Jobson's had also offered the chance to come by some pre-Raphaelite paintings, all suitably neo-classical studies (chiefly evocations of mythological characters in different stages of undress) and these now hung in their places.

So it was in this room that Francis now stood and, for several minutes, silently marvelled. Turning full circle and looking finally at a portrayal of Psyche, caught fresh from her bath and hanging demurely above the fireplace, Francis spoke aloud again, saying to himself softly:

"I believe I must be in the Palace of Minos."

Behind him he heard a bright, bell-like voice reply:

"Then I must be Ariadne — or is it Europa? I always forget."

He turned and saw Fleur, dressed in a suit of palest eau-de-nil *crêpe*, dark chestnut hair swept up to frame the lovely, creamy face he had remembered so well. Her lips smiled at him, warmly he seemed to think, and from where he stood the light in her dancing hazel eyes appeared to do much the same.

"Ariadne herself – why, Fleur!"

She came over to him, hand outstretched. He took the hand.

"Dear Francis—"

She let him kiss her cheek, which he would never have presumed to do had she not tilted her face up to him. He noticed a remarkable absence of lines there, except for the tiniest spider's traces beneath and across those so-white lids. Two decades lay as reverently upon her as his own kiss.

"This is a jolly surprise – how long have you been over here?"

"Not quite a day. Forgive me if I'm a little cock-eyed still from the flight, but I so wanted to stop by."

"How sweet of you to make us a priority. You certainly don't look cock-eyed – you haven't a crease out of place."

She sat down and gestured Francis to follow, watching him the while. Well! — Francis Wilmot. He was the person farthest from her thoughts when the maid brought up his card, as if from a stranger. He still seemed the least likely to expect in uniform. Those mild brown eyes were no more direct than when she had last seen them; and his voice with its soft accent and unexpected cadences seemed inappropriate for command.

"Well—!" Fleur said finally, having watched him sit with her head tipped to one side, like a bird. "Once one gets used to the uniform, I think I should have known you anywhere. Can it possibly be twenty years?"

"Not twenty months, Fleur, to look at you."

Francis could think only how fine she was still – as if painted by a master herself. He continued to look at her and added softly,

"You're quite unchanged."

"Ah, that Southern charm. I'm positively ancient these days, and Michael is Methuselah."

"Is he still a politician?"

"For his sins; and still trouncing the Government for theirs from the back-benches."

"My—"

There was silence for a few seconds as each continued to absorb details of the other's face, though with unequal degrees of scrutiny. Tilting his head back and rather to the side, in a way that Fleur remembered his having, the American looked again at the room about him, turning the same adoration on it that he had lavished on Fleur's face.

Fleur continued to watch him however, her white lids covering the larger part of her gaze.

"It's stupid of me," he said. "I was expecting your gold and silver room. But this is lovelier still."

"Thank you. Michael calls it 'early Æschylus' – but I rather prefer your first description."

"The pictures are enchanting – but don't you fear for them?"

"The raids, you mean? It has rather been dive-bomb alley around here, so I suppose one should. My father would have had a fit to see them still hanging. The whole of the National Gallery is in a Welsh cave now, his bequest with them. But one's nerves pass the point where fits are possible any longer."

She sighed and the American noticed for the first time the little dark patches under the inner corners of her eyes.

"We've the flying bombs now, first the ones, then the twos – had you heard?"

"The rockets – yes, I heard. You've all been safe here, I hope? I saw the other side of the square."

Fleur tapped her head.

"Touch wood. The windows go periodically, and we had part of a nose-cone through the roof in the Blitz, but that's all so far. Michael uses it for a paper-weight."

The American clucked softly again.

"It must all have been a great worry for you – for everyone."

"At first. But after so many years of it, well, perspectives change. Mine have, anyway."

Her face became hard for a moment or two, and Francis felt as if he were seeing a private thought – an inner determination of some kind which had momentarily escaped her control – appear

354

too near the surface. He watched as an odd little smile softened her features as she continued:

"Eventually one becomes inured to the consequences of things."

"I guess it's a natural defence mechanism."

"Perhaps that's right."

Fleur lowered her dark lashes briefly before continuing:

"The last time I saw you, you'll remember, you were battling with your own 'defence mechanism'. You had just decided not to die of pneumonia."

"A decision I owed to you. I never have forgotten your kindness during that time—"

"During that 'fool business'?"

This had been the American's own phrase for what had preceded and almost certainly induced the pneumonia – his ill-matched attachment to Marjorie Ferrar, Fleur's quondam friend, by whom she had been taken into court for calling her a snake of the first water, in response to being called a snob and a nobody in her own parlour. Fleur resurrected the expression deliberately; the sight of this visitor gave rise to recollections of that long-past but not wholly faded slight.

"Yes," said Francis, with a disarming candour she had not expected, "—and I was the fool. I'm indebted to you, Fleur. You quite saved me."

"For the skies, it seems," Fleur replied, deflecting the historical subject she had raised herself. Her eyes were nowadays set only on the future; the war, and that very private resolution of hers which had made it endurable, had seen to that. "I had no idea you were in the Air Force – and such a high-flyer, too." She tapped her shoulder, to indicate the insignia on his own. "Colonel isn't it?"

"Only 'light'," he said, the same candour now weighted with a touch of homespun bafflement.

"Congratulations – tell me all."

"Oh, there isn't so much to tell. I managed to get in six months' basic flying last time around – so I was ahead this time, is all. Now they've given me a ground job over here."

"I'm sure you're being very modest. When did you join up?"

"Five years ago now."

"How admirable! Straight after war was declared—"

"Actually, straight after my sister died."

355

Fleur had overlooked this earlier event. His simple and unmeaningly spoken statement brought her face to face with an issue which – between her study where she received the card, and her drawing-room where she received its owner – there had been no time to process. To compose her face, after seeing that her unexpected caller was the brother of Jon's dead wife, had taken all the time there was! Later, at her own leisure, she would consider this new turn carefully, sifting from many possibilities any mote which might be grist for her own mill. For the present, she decided to follow the lead given by her guest.

"Five years!" she repeated. "We were all very sorry. It must have been a tremendous shock for you."

Fleur's tone, whilst delicate and persuasive – that 'charity' voice of hers – might yet have been asking after a stray kitten. If her visitor was sensitive to this nuance, it brought no hardening of his expression; none, at least, that she could detect. It was in any case difficult to see where it might have rested among such open features. Instead, Francis tilted his head up in that sidelong way he had, and looked at Psyche for a moment, in whose pale face he might for a second have hoped to catch the fleeting likeness of a wood nymph, and be reminded of the vanilla scent of her hair. He took a silent breath, not quite a sigh, and looking back to Fleur said,

"Sometimes it seems only a moment ago."

"I'm sure. She — you were very close, of course."

"It's kind of you to remember. I know Anne admired you greatly."

Ah! Here was the first riddle solved.

Fleur continued to scan her visitor's face from beneath gracefully suspended lids. Like his quiet voice, the American's pleasant features were without the least detectable semblance of irony. To Fleur he seemed like all his breed – all that she had ever met, and those were enough – with nothing secret about his face, nothing whatever kept back behind the eyes. Such openness! It was a way of living she considered insupportable. So, no conclusion but one then; Francis knew nothing of Jon's infidelity to his sister. Plainly – for Fleur would surely have read its understanding in that guileless face – Anne Forsyte had not told her brother about it. Or, if Francis did know of the incident from whatever source (grudgingly she admitted it possible that Jon had confessed after his wife's death) then clearly he was unaware that Fleur had been, as lawyers tended so euphemistically to put it, 'the other party'.

So Fleur responded with a light smile, which was carefully shaped not to carry any further import.

"Will you stay for supper? I know Michael will want to see you."

"I'd be honoured, Fleur, truly. But I have to be at Grosvenor Square this evening—" Francis pulled the edge of his cuff back with a straight finger and glanced at his watch. "In fact, I should be making tracks."

Fleur stood, and the American followed promptly, as before.

"Grosvenor Square – at the Embassy?"

"That's right."

Fleur's initial understanding of her visitor's rank was instantly augmented. Surely it was not every American officer, certainly not every Lieutenant Colonel, who was required to dine with the Ambassador?

"Then Mr Winant's gain is our loss. But you'll take a 'rain-check', as I believe you say?"

"That's what we say, all right – and I surely will, if I may. Perhaps I might call you when I'm settled in?"

"Please do."

In place of the farewell niceties which would automatically have followed, Fleur decided she would risk stirring the waters once.

"Have you seen Jon?"

"Not yet. I'm due out at Green Hill tomorrow."

"He's helping me with my convalescent home now, you know. Give him my love, will you, and tell him I'll see him at the next board meeting?"

"Ah – then I'll be sure to."

Fleur had never doubted it. She ventured a second stir.

"Will he marry again, do you think?"

It was a straightforward question, except from one who had first meant to marry him herself. Its answer was a few moments being fashioned, clearly going through careful stages in formulation, like a laboratory process going on under glass. Fleur kept watch for any clues to its final composition. In a face so unguarded there were surprisingly few.

At last Francis said:

"I don't guess I'm rightly in a position to comment, Fleur—"

He paused, and because his reply seemed complete Fleur thought she would have to settle for a non-answer to her enquiry. She ought to have expected his discretion – and perhaps he was reminding her of it. But then, quite unprompted, he continued his construction:

"—but it seems to me that Jon is the faithful type, if only to memory."

This quiet opinion – so respectful of all parties, so absolutely sincere – secretly thrilled her. Francis did not know of her affair; that girl had not spoken of it, she knew now for sure. But more important by far, she knew that Jon had also said nothing, despite every opportunity. He had kept faith!

Before Fleur could assimilate this new detail – and find where it fitted into the overall picture her private resolution had so determinedly framed – she became aware that her husband had entered the drawing-room.

When the American had left, and they were sharing cocktails, Michael said to Fleur:

"You know, it isn't every half-colonel who gets his own driver and who's asked to dine at the Embassy."

"So I thought. What do you suppose it means?"

"There's only one thing it can mean, my love. Our Francis, or his desk-job at least, must be quite a bit special."

Chapter Three

And Over There

The drive down to Green Hill the following morning was one Francis Wilmot had never taken until that day. When he was last in England his sister and new brother-in-law were still farming peaches back in North Carolina, and Francis had no occasion then to venture into the country, save to leave and regain his port of entry. He hadn't even seen Paris. 'That fool business' with Marjorie Ferrar, and his illness after it, had detained him in the capital. Now he was embarked on his first visit to the house where his sister had spent thirteen years of her life, it struck him as a peculiar irony that he should go there only after her death. Though he knew not a yard of the way to Sussex – could barely have told which point of the compass he required to set him in the right direction – yet a familiar hand of emotions was raised in him as his car passed between heath and fold, between farmland and meadow. From the moment he left his own country for England, he had in his heart covered the same journey a thousand times.

His arrival at the farm was a scene he anticipated with equal parts of longing and dread, whose balance within him seemed to shift and sway with every mile gained. The weather had cleared overnight, and this perfect specimen of an English autumn day – with a strengthening sun in a crystal sky, and a shimmer over everything – offered no hiding place for a faint heart. As bright as the shine on an apple, it simply defied contradiction. Francis 'eased down' in the back seat and tried his best to succumb; but his feelings remained contrary.

His driver was handling the car confidently, and had covered the whole distance so far at the top range of the permissible limits.

359

Since there was as yet little chill in the season it was possible to travel comfortably with windows down; the American welcomed that homebound wash of air, rich, crisp and chaff-laden, from newly harvested fields on either side. The countryside looked to him like nothing so much as an old quilt, worked in pieces of velvet and cord; brown and russet, red and tan, all stitched over with green and gold.

Just when he arrived at this observation, those tiny patchworked fields would disappear behind such high hedgerows that the lane became a veritable tunnel of dark greenery, thick with rosehips, and blackberries swollen with rain. Often the bushes themselves were tucked behind tall dried-out heads of dead cow parsley bristling on to the road. Francis asked what this plant was called in England, and was told. He thought the answer oddly prosaic; he had known it all his life by the much finer name of Queen Anne's lace. The hedges and fields ran on. When on a close bend a shower of sparrows was startled from a thicket, and fluttered up in a dusty sweep over the car, Francis was surprised – he had thought them to be only town birds. And when he noticed a single bird, of about the same size as the sparrows but with a proud red breast, adamantly standing its ground on a gate-post as the car passed at the next close turn, he realised he had seen a robin – but a creature a third the size of the ones he knew from home.

This was the dual essence of everything about him, and everything within, the familiar and the strange, and with each extra mile under the wheels these qualities rotated and set his heart churning.

Nothing of this struggle made its way through to the surface of Francis's appearance, however, and his driver – the same young WAAF, whom he was thinking of getting permanently assigned – was not the first, nor even the youngest, to be misled by his seeming equilibrium. All she knew was that she was driving her new officer down to the country where he had relatives. She could not have known, on such short acquaintance, that there was at the core of Francis Wilmot, as there had been in his sister, a well of deep quietism, not springing from undisturbed waters, but simply so far beneath the surface that nothing could ever be seen above of any disturbance below. The only exception to this was perhaps at the very back of his eyes, where to the rarely perceptive that ghost could be seen to hover. By this detail of character, that which was merely silent and reflective in Francis was often taken for evidence of peace and tranquillity, and dealt with as such. It was a family trait; because of it, Wilmots were born into the world to be its comforters, not the comforted.

"You seem pretty familiar with all the twists and turns here, Penny." (Francis had lastingly endeared himself to her by asking her permission to use her given name.) "Do you know these roads?"

"Yes, sir. I grew up in Surrey."

"That's around here?"

"The next county north – we just came through it."

"Ah."

Francis caught sight of Penny's nice oval face through her rear-view mirror and saw that his geography, or lack of it, induced a smile. Much of what he said, he noticed, had this effect on her. It was a sweet kind of smile, though.

"Does your family still live there?"

In the mirror he saw her smile fade quickly. From her voice he would not have known the difference.

"I don't have any family, Colonel Wilmot."

The use of his name was just enough to indicate he should drop the subject.

"I see," he said, indicating compliance. "Well, you certainly drive like a native, that's for sure."

Some yards ahead of them a cart pulled into the road from a farm gate and halted, straddling both lanes. Penny slowed the car to a stop, and slipped up her hand-brake. The horse clipped the road surface with a front hoof, as if marking time at a known pause. Its driver whistled tunelessly.

After a minute of silent waiting, Francis asked:

"You don't suppose we're here for the duration, are we?"

Penny shifted round in her seat, and faced Francis over her elbow, the same pleasant smile restored. What a pleasant face altogether, he thought, and smiled back, admiring the spark of good-natured humour which seemed always ready to quicken in her. It was that red hair!

"I expect he's waiting to pick up some farm workers for their lunch."

361

"Off to the nearest public house?"

"The farm-house, more likely. Either way, they won't want to be late, and he doesn't look the sort to be early."

"Why, Penny, you are quite a country girl, aren't you? I hadn't realised."

To this she answered quickly, with just a touch of injury in her voice.

"I hope I've picked most of the hayseeds out of my hair, Colonel."

Francis almost 'bought it', but he caught the lift of her brow in time.

"Well, I guess that puts me in my place, doesn't it? — Looks like I'm the hayseed around here. There go your farm workers, right on time."

Some ten or a dozen young women appeared then, in a noisy, laughing, striding *troupe*. Land-girls in their rather school-girlish uniform of fawn trousers, white blouses and dark sweaters. Some had tied their sweaters around their shoulders, others had their hair wrapped in bright scarves. After a morning's work all seeming as fresh still as the new-mown hay. The boldest of them had brazen blonde locks which spilled out of her red bandanna and fell cockily over one eye – in a manner that could have been natural, but was more probably borrowed from a certain American actress. She spotted Francis in the back of the car and came over to him, a gleam in her eye.

Leaning an arm against the top of Francis' open window, and speaking loud enough to benefit her friends who were piling onto the back of the cart, she said:

"Hi there, Captain – how are you?"

Francis answered mildly: "I'm just fine, thanks."

"Hear that, girls? Says he's just fine."

A whoop went up from the others.

"Well now, Captain; if I wasn't a good little girl, I'd ask you for a light. Can't say I've ever been lit up by a Yank before."

There were whistles and cheers. The cart driver didn't even turn – no doubt he had been through all this before. Not so Francis, though he knew quite well what was happening. He even knew the English expression for it – he was being thoroughly 'ragged'.

"I've got matches, if that's what you need."

"Oh, you've got what I need, all right, Captain."

This drew another round of cat-calling from the cart, while the girl let Francis find a match-book in his trouser pocket. He held it out to her – one he'd picked up for a souvenir after his last meal off-base before embarkation – and she took it from him.

"Hmm—" she read the cover, and nodded with exaggerated consideration. "Well, it's not Sardi's—"

There was more laughter.

"—but thanks, anyway."

"You're very welcome, I'm sure."

"I'm sure I am. Trouble is, now I haven't got a cigarette."

"I can't help you there – I don't smoke."

"That's O.K., Captain – neither do I!"

The girl strolled back to the cart to great applause, like a boxer returning to his corner after a knock-out, and blew a kiss to Francis over her shoulder as she was helped up.

The cart driver, once he was loaded up, pulled over to the side – perversely, since it was a thing he could more easily have done empty than laden – just enough to let Penny slip back into gear and drive on. All the girls blew kisses and waved as the car passed.

In the mirror again, Francis saw the laughter in Penny's eyes.

"Does it suit me, would you say?"

"What's that, sir?"

"This egg – all over my face."

"I dare say it's all right, sir, if you've got the coupons!"

Before he knew it, Francis was laughing with her.

Strange and familiar – the land, the people, their language and humour – like something he had always known, yet nothing like at all. And, suddenly sensing that the worst of the tension in him had gone, he began laughing again.

Chapter Four

Rencounter

Between young people things happen quickly. Between young people in war-time even that pace is accelerated. Ann Forsyte, at seventeen years and some few months, was of a prime age to experience this phenomenon at its maximum velocity. As to the identity of the speeding item particular in her case, she wondered, she suspected, she speculated and, in this order, finally she hoped – it was love.

Intuitively guided by that old superstition in her family – that it was the airing of feelings which killed them – she told no one. Not even her brother was admitted into her confidence, though if she had wanted a better way to alert him to the situation, she could not have found one.

That morning Ann slipped away as soon as she could after her piano practice, checking first that no one – particularly Jonnie – saw her leave. Knowing she had barely two hours before her uncle was due, she went quickly along the lane, down through the orchards under trees that were laden and nearly ready for picking, apples first, then plums, until she came out at fields where the barley stubble had just been turned in. Skirting these, keeping to the grassy edges, she came to the perimeter fence which marked out what was once another of her father's fields, but these last four years given over to the air-base at Mastonbury.

As she drew nearer to the assigned place – where the fence left off and a stretch of woodland began – she felt her pulse quicken with anticipation. Funny! – even a month ago, she would have felt this way over her uncle's arrival. But now there was a young man—

Each time they met – there had been only some three times after their first encounter, over not quite as many weeks – it was always just there, by the break in the fence, under a leaning crab apple. Always she felt this flutter, between her ribs, right from the first . . .

Ann remembered the day in August when she had first seen this young fellow. She found him in uniform sitting at a distant end of one of their orchards, with his back against the trunk of one of their trees, and munching blithely on one of their apples, which may or may not have fallen into his hand. It was a scene of such out-and-out coolness, that Ann had been intrigued from the first instant. Keeping the trees between them, she stole quietly up towards him.

Then a spotted dog appeared, from wherever it had been foraging, and ran right to her. It sat directly at her feet, flicking its whip of a tail and staring up.

The young pilot saw only his dog chasing off.

"Come back, you hound!"

Then he saw Ann.

"Oh, hello there. Who are you? My dog thinks he knows you."

Ann failed to suppress a small laugh.

"I live here," she said. "At Green Hill Farm. Are you from Mastonbury?"

"My squad's just transferred there. These apples are good, have one—"

She laughed again. He *was* cool!

"So they're recruiting dalmatians now? As under-carriage dogs, I suppose?"

He gave her a smile then – and, somewhere in the very middle of her, she knew she was hooked.

"I sneaked in to escape my relations for half an hour, you won't give me away, will you? My guv'nor served with the Station Commander last time round and decided to pay me a visit. Just like it was a new school, you've no idea. He's even brought an aged aunt and the dog with him. The dog's the only one worth talking to, honestly. His name's Tigger, mine's Mont, Christopher – Kit for short."

"I'm Ann," she said, and would have gone on to give her own surname too, except that hearing what the dog was called had reminded her of something – a vague notion of familiarity she couldn't quite recall . . .

Now as she ran, it suddenly occurred to her that she still hadn't offered her surname. Funny how it had never seemed to matter. Kit and Ann had more than happily sufficed. Perhaps she would ask him today—

—He was there! She saw his pilot's uniform as he leant against the tree-trunk, and her heart tripped. She loved the look of him, that languid control, that assurance he had – like a tawny cat, stretching himself. He always leant against the same tree, copying its swaggering angle. She ran over the last fifty yards, her sun-coloured hair spinning out behind her.

"You're late," he said, his face stern as she ran up to him. Then he smiled and Ann knew he was not really cross. He could smile so beautifully.

"My practice went on for ever—"

"What was it – ballet?"

"Piano!" He always teased her about something. She wrinkled her nose at him and he caught her by the waist. Did he mean to kiss her this time? She intended to let him, if he did. Ann looked into his eyes, cool and blue, but couldn't read what was in them. Ah! — he was letting go.

"Come on, let's walk a bit," he said.

They followed a bridle path up towards Chanctonbury Ring. At the top of the hill, with the ancient beeches whispering in conference at their back, they sat down on sun-warmed grass. Kit leaned back on his hands and turned his face up to the sky. Ann sat forward, looking out. On such a crystal morning the view stretched for miles around from this place, high up as the sky-larks trilling over their nests. Half-way down on this side lay their farm, looking like a toy farm-set Jonnie was given once and long since left to gather dust with her dolls in an attic. She could see the house, its covering of creeper making it seem a little red building block. The village of Wansdon lay away to the right, in the dip of the vale, with the river running through it like a silver thread. The whole of the county seemed stretched out at their feet, running away to the shimmering band of the channel in the distance.

"I love this view," Ann said. "It's so – oh, I don't know how to say it – so over-the-hills-and-far-away. Do you know what I mean?"

366

"I know what you mean exactly. It's the best of England up here. Down there it's no good, when you get up close. It's best to stay above it." He took in a deep lungful of air. "That's why I wanted to fly."

"I wish I could fly."

"Didn't you tell me your old man had a kite – couldn't he teach you?"

"Yes, I suppose he could – but I don't mean fly a plane. I wish I – I wish we could just take off from here – and fly!"

"What, like Peter Pan and Wendy – off to Never Never Land?"

"Oh, yes!"

He laughed.

"You *are* a kid, a funny little kid."

He made a billy-goat noise at her and lay back on the grass, knees up, his hands behind his head, and his cap tipped down to his nose.

Ann turned to look at him. When she saw he couldn't see her, she leaned back on one elbow. He mustn't think her forward, even though there were times she truly wished she were!

After a while in which only the breeze and a few late wasps stirred, he suddenly asked:

"Would you really take off, if you could? Travel, I mean; see the world?"

There was a semi-serious note in his voice now, and an ever so slight challenge, to which Ann felt she must rise.

"Certainly."

"Live abroad even?"

"Yes. We nearly went to live in America once, but it didn't quite happen."

"Why not?"

"Oh, the war. My father thought he ought to be here; you know, help the effort."

She heard Kit snort under his cap; then he tossed it to one side and sat up.

"You wouldn't have caught me coming back, not for this damn' mess."

Ann imagined at first he was just being modest about his own efforts – flyers were like that, always down-playing things – but he sounded even more serious when he continued.

"I reckon this country's just about had it."

This notion sent a cold ripple running through her.

"But we're going to win, aren't we?" she asked quickly.

"That – yes," he said, sounding oddly off-hand. "Now the Yanks are doing it all for us. But it won't make any difference. England's dished."

She supposed it was because he saw so much of the worst of it, from the air.

"People will pick up the pieces again when the war's over, you'll see."

"Not me. I shan't hang around to see. I'll be off the minute I can."

To Never Never Land with his shadow, Ann thought, and something sank inside her. He was so decisive – she was sure he meant to do it.

"Where would you go?" she asked. As if it mattered!

"India. Straight into the Indian Civil, get to know the territory for a couple of years, then maybe buy a place out there."

"Oh," she said quietly, "it sounds wonderful."

"Don't you think so?"

"Yes."

He turned and looked at her over his shoulder.

"Fancy tagging along?"

Ann made no reply. He was teasing again, and she wished he wouldn't.

"Ah, so that was all just a line, was it?" he asked, mocking her still. "About wanting to fly away and live abroad?"

"No, I meant it. It's just that I know you don't."

Ann sat up straight and dusted grass from the skirt of her dress, preparatory to going. It was no use to stay any longer. She started to get up, but suddenly she felt his hand around her wrist.

"Please don't joke about it," she said, and looked down, trying to loose her hand, but he only tightened his grip. With his free hand he held her chin up so that she had to meet his eyes.

"When you get to know me better, little Ann of Green Hill, you'll realise I never joke about anything. I laugh a lot, but I'm always deadly serious."

He freed her hand. Her wrist tingled where he had held it. She saw him reach inside his jacket.

"Here." He held out a little flat box to her. Ann was by now thoroughly confused, and made no move to take it. "Go on, open it. It won't bite you."

Ann took the box and did as she was told. A diamond pendant lay inside, the size and shape of a single tear-drop. She lifted it from the velvet and held it up by its golden chain, thin as a whisper.

"Sorry it's not a ring," he said. "I got it because the chain made me think of your hair. If you put it on we can be engaged."

Ann could not speak. He took the chain from her and opened its tiny clasp. She turned her neck to him, and swept up her hair in shaking hands. She felt the pendant fall under the neck of her dress, and drop cold towards her breasts, then move up again as he fastened the chain. Then she felt his lips at her neck.

After that first long embrace, during which it seemed to Ann that some part of her did actually take flight, then and there on the hill, she realised with a start she would be late.

"Golly, I have to get back!"

"Me, too. Too bad. Will you be at the match tomorrow?"

"Rather! Will you?"

"They'll have to tie me down to stop me – I want the first wicket. I'll see you there."

They got up, and dusted each other down. Ann let him kiss her again, briefly, before she broke away and ran all the way back to the house.

There was an unfamiliar black car parked outside the house when Ann reached the end of the lane. A quick thought ran through her head, and she tucked the tear-drop pendant back under the neck of her dress, where it had jogged out with her running, just before she turned in. Jonnie appeared in the front doorway. He was the only one who noticed her, and Ann avoided his eye. She could see some of her uncle's American uniform; he was bent over the car boot, removing luggage. Her father was standing by the car, but hadn't seen her. He was talking to a young woman in WAAF uniform. As Ann approached, she saw him pass a hand up over his brow, and heard him say:

"Well, what a jolly turn up – have you heard this Francis—?"

Ann saw her uncle put his head up from the boot. Goodness, he looked so much older than she remembered.

369

"What say there, Jon?"

"I used to know your driver's brother – he was a young flyer here at Mastonbury."

"Is that so—?"

Francis was suddenly looking in Ann's direction, and she saw him freeze for a second. Then his lips moved, not to speak to her, but as if he were repeating a rosary. Faintly she could hear what he was saying. It sounded like –

"Oh, my saints . . . my sweet saints . . ."

"Uncle Francis!"

Irene was playing when Francis came down that evening. There was no one else in the drawing-room; it was early yet and he had thought to be alone for a while with his sister's picture. A wood fire had been lighted in the broad hearth, and was beginning to scent the room with cedar.

A slow smile appeared on her face as he entered. Without looking up from the piano she seemed to know he was there, though Francis was certain he had made no noise. It was as if she had just *sensed* his being in the room. And the thought came suddenly to him out of nowhere, that it would be next to impossible to keep a secret from this woman.

"Do you mind?" she asked.

"No. No, please – don't stop over me. Grieg is wonderful."

"I thought of him tonight for some reason. Perhaps it's the logs burning."

She went on playing. Francis stood by the piano and watched her, the grace of her as she played, and thought what a beauty she must have been in her time.

When the piece was finished she looked up at him, smiling still, and Francis found himself saying,

"I hope you'll forgive me, Mrs Forsyte, but you are just more beautiful than ever."

"And you, Francis, are simply more charming. Tell me, is there anything you would especially like to hear?"

His eyes were drawn ineluctably to the portrait above the piano. He had something, that painter – Blade, it said, in the lower corner, but the name meant nothing to him. Whoever he was, the man had caught the spirit of the woods that Francis always felt was in his sister, the shimmery light that seemed to dart between the shadows in her eyes. He thought he saw it again this morning, when he first saw his niece.

"Chopin!" he whispered.

"Yes," Irene answered softly. She began a prelude. "Anne loved Chopin."

Francis listened with his eyes closed until he felt the constriction in his throat begin to ease. It seemed it took him a while.

"I see her in young Ann," he said at last.

"Do you?"

"Not in her colouring – Ann takes that from you, ma'am – but I still see it somehow, in her eyes. Something of her mother's spirit."

"Yes. Perhaps that's it. They were very close."

The prelude had come to an end. Irene folded her hands in her lap. She seemed not to want to play another piece. Francis went on.

"And Jonnie – I reckon he takes after his father quite a bit, now he's grown – especially around the jaw."

"People say he takes after my husband, too."

Since he knew Jon's father had died before any Forsyte had encountered any Wilmot, Francis could neither agree nor disagree with this. And anyhow, he had seen the lady's face when she spoke, and believed that to say a word further would be kind of akin to talking in church.

The appearance of his niece broke the hush.

"Why, Ann, how lovely you look – and I see you've got those ear-bobs on!"

"They're beautiful, Uncle Francis, really they are. Thank you so much."

Ann touched the single pearls at her ears, but was thinking of the single tear-drop beneath her dress, hanging above her heart. She had chosen a high necked dress to wear that evening so she might not have to unfasten the clasp of the pendant until she went to bed that night. She might not unfasten it even then.

"Well, it's sweet of you to wear them tonight, and your dress is so pretty. Could I ask you to turn around for me, do you think?"

371

What a sweetheart he was, Ann had almost forgotten. She twirled round prettily on her toes, and dropped a little curtsy.

Francis was shaking his head slowly as he gazed at her.

"My word," he said. "My word."

The expression, limited as it was, served to mask the silent longing that arose in him; that had arisen in him each time he saw his niece that day. How like her mother she was – and yet— A disturbing, Derby-dog of a thought crossed his mind, and not for the first time, but Francis once more shooed it away. It was not to be, this fond notion, and there was no good in supposing. Besides, the prayer-book was against him, and to a man who professed no religion, and who was consequently more religious than most, that was a barrier not to be surmounted.

"I'm sorry to stare," he went on at last, and no one in the world might have guessed there was ever any other thought between, "but I can't seem to get over how you've grown. You weren't but a little bit of a girl when I last saw you. It just doesn't seem possible."

"I think you'll find, Francis," Irene said, "that little girls have a habit of growing up. Especially when you're not watching them."

"I guess they do, at that. But they don't all grow into such beautiful young women."

Ann felt her cheeks glowing.

"Oh, there now, I've made you blush. That's the job of a much younger fellow than me. I should have quit while I was ahead. If there is a young fellow on the scene, Ann, you can tell him tomorrow and he can box my ears for me. How's that?"

Ann only smiled brightly and turned away to the fire where a log had begun to spit. She took a poker to it. Behind her, she heard her grandmother say,

"Don't worry, Francis, there's no young fellow. If there were I'm sure Ann would tell us all about him."

Grandmother and granddaughter had left the dining room, after a supper so 'fine and dandy', as Francis put it, that old family ties had become new ones before the arrival of the fish. Jon was heartily relieved. He had anticipated all kinds of awkwardness, and had experienced and witnessed absolutely none. In fact, it had all been – again, Francis' phrase – 'just peachy'. Now he took further delight in seeing his son and brother-in-law negotiate the etiquette of the port decanter.

"Is that so?" Francis said to Jonnie. "D'you mean it always has to go this ways around? Huh! Now why is that?"

"I haven't a clue, actually. Do you know, Dad?"

Jon could not say that he knew either. Francis held his glass up to a candle, and watched the crystal turn to ruby.

"This is certainly a fine old port, Jon."

"It should be," Jon said, as he tamped down his pipe. "My grandfather laid it down in eighteen-eighty-nine."

For Francis, the notion that one could drink such antiquity, and not be lynched for it on the spot, induced a glow all of its own.

"Are you coming to the cricket match tomorrow, Uncle?"

"Yes, you might like to, Francis. Our village v. the Mastonbury eleven, if the weather holds."

"Dad and I are both playing."

"Are you now?" Francis looked towards Jon, who was smiling crookedly as he held a match up to his pipe and kindled the tobacco.

"It's about the one bit of the war effort I'm up to," he said, between puffs.

Francis thought he could hear an undertone of some sort. He knew Jon had been doing some ferry-piloting, though only lately from what he said. And hadn't Fleur mentioned that he was helping her with a convalescent home? The American felt that somehow it wasn't his place to refer to that here. He thought to say something on a connected matter, something that he had been turning over on his way here, but then thought better of it. It would keep; instead he tilted his head back and said,

"Well, that sounds like something I shouldn't miss. Does the base have a regular team?"

"Not really – they just field whoever's around on the day."

"I have to tell you I don't know anything about cricket—"

"That's all right," said Jonnie. "The flyers don't either – it'll be a walk-over!"

Chapter Five

The Players Assemble

The Battle of Britain, the Blitz, the black-out, the buzz-bombs, the rationing of bacon and eggs, sugar and butter, and a thousand other body-blows of the last five years of war had passed into the community chest that was English folklore. There was hardly a citizen who couldn't point to a piece of shrapnel over his fireplace and say with conviction: *Missed me by inches!* Really interesting recipes for powdered eggs had come to assume the place in everyday conversation that was usually sacred to the weather. And without exception, every soldier who ever trained had at one time or another been billeted in a girls' school dormitory where a sign over a bell read: *Please ring if a mistress is required in the night.* Piece by piece, the flotsam and jetsam of war was being converted, like Chinese whispers, to the stuff of legend.

England can take it! ran the popular saying. Forsytes, too, on their highly adequate chins. Some things, though, were hard to take – and for Forsytes the closure of Lord's for the duration was one of them. For some, being denied access to that great sportsground, with its fine lawns smooth as a sultan's carpet between the stands, was simply a nasty blow, and rather below the belt. For others it seemed tantamount to collaboration.

Elsewhere though, the game persisted, trimmed back to its roots on village greens up and down the still leafy counties of an otherwise benighted land. As the visitors for the Wansdon *v.* Mastonbury game took up their positions on the field, Francis Wilmot was experiencing his first taste of the sport, sitting with Jon's family among some several dozen other spectators. Frankly, he was prepared to admit he was stumped.

374

"So, now, that's mid-off?" he said hopefully, indicating a region of the out-field that might have been at eleven on a clock face, with himself and Val at half past the hour.

"No, that's deep mid-on," Val Dartie explained. "Mid-off is over there, see the hayricks?"

"Ah."

At least Francis knew a hayrick when he saw one. He was still wondering how a shingled hut in back of where they were sitting, of the sort he might once have kept cattle-feed in, came to be called 'The Pavilion'. Or how another he would never have considered for even that lowly purpose was designated 'The Visitor's Room'. The field was pretty though, set as it was between the village church and a pair of 'real old' barns, and its being that mellowing time of year, and all the hedges berried and the leaves turning for the Fall. It was a pity there was no sun so far – that sky was looking dramatic in the distance.

Jon's mother and sister were sitting in the row behind.

"Do we know who Mastonbury are fielding?" Irene asked.

"I don't think so," said Holly, "just whoever's not flying today. It's cloudy, so that should mean they have their best to pick from. Isn't that right, Val? – Val?"

Val was continuing to pinpoint the distinction between mid-on and mid-off. Francis felt he was only continuing not to.

"Now do you see how it goes?" he asked the American.

"I *guess* I do. So, when each man on the field comes in towards the batsman, that makes him a silly – whatever? Is that right now?"

"That's right! Cover point becomes silly point, mid-off becomes silly mid-off, mid-on silly mid-on—"

Val felt that his pupil was at last making progress. The American continued.

"So mid-wicket becomes a silly wicket, and square leg becomes a silly leg. I get it!"

Val made an indeterminate noise.

"Don't groan, Val," said his wife. "You started it."

She leaned forward in her chair and tapped Francis on his shoulder. Unconscious of the distinction, he turned his off-side ear. Holly was amused to catch the tiniest wink from the corner of his eye.

"I think you should raise the white flag, while you can. It may be your only chance."

"Well, if you think it wouldn't be impolite—"

On the leg-side, Val said to Irene:

"Where's young Ann got to?"

"Still cutting sandwiches, I imagine."

"She'll miss the first over if she's not sharp. Forsytes at first and second bat – what a line up! I'll go and find her."

When Val had gone, Francis said:

"Your husband certainly knows his cricket, Mrs Dartie—"

"Please – call me Holly."

"Holly – I wonder he doesn't play himself."

"It's because of *his* silly leg. It's kept him from playing for forty years, and made him an expert overnight."

"Ah, I see. Well, for a game, he's got it pretty well in his blood."

"Oh, but cricket is far more than a game, Francis," said Jon's mother.

"It is?"

"But of course. Cricket is a metaphor. Surely you'd noticed?"

"I can't say I had, Mrs Forsyte. A metaphor for what?"

"For the way Englishmen believe the world should be run. Two teams dressed in immaculate white, both playing fairly by the rules and conducting themselves in an orderly and becoming fashion – and everything over for tea. An Empire was built on it!"

It was she who was joshing now, surely?

"But what happens if you don't make the team?"

Yes – he caught the teasing arch of her brow as she answered.

"Precisely!"

"Irene's right, you know, Francis," said Holly, in much the same vein. "It's a metaphor for how they think, too."

"And how's that?"

"Oh, like schoolboys! —Here's Val!"

Val regained his seat.

"Ann's on her way. Look out – here come the noble batsmen!"

From behind them, Jon and Jonnie came out of the pavilion, each in flannels, shirt and buckskin boots of a white which seemed astonishing for such an overcast day.

"Good man, Jon! Jonnie! Don't they make the flyers look a left-over bunch? Where's their bowler?"

Father and son made their way out on to the pitch as a pleasant ripple of applause went round.

"Should we cheer?" Francis asked.

"I think just clapping for now," said Holly. "We'll keep the cheering for the first boundary."

The applause died away as the two batsmen reached their wickets and the field, spectator and player alike, applied its attention to the business of the day. The one exception to this was the visiting batsman.

"Well – *he's* a cool customer, I must say," said Val, watching as the Mastonbury bowler sauntered in from the outfield where he had been leaning against a hayrick at the long-off boundary, his school cricket-cap pulled over his eyes against an imaginary sun. "Who does he think he is?"

As though by way of answer, the young flyer got lazily up, dusted his flannels, strolled back onto the green, and passed his cap to the umpire, revealing the back of a tawny head. He then took a few seconds as it seemed to screw the hard ball, red as an apple, into the palm of his right hand, and, turning back to the pitch, ran at a steadily increasing rate that ended with a little insolent skip, towards the wicket.

It was Holly who first understood, but she found herself so taken by surprise that she couldn't touch her husband's shoulder in time to stop him from saying what she knew absolutely he was about to.

"Great Scott!" Val exclaimed, leaning forward in his amazement as his wife's hand reached out towards him from behind. "It's Kit Mont!"

Ann Forsyte was then returning to her family from the refreshments tent – which the ladies there believed would be too small if the weather did not hold – and was just close enough to hear her uncle's exclamation.

She was astonished. How was it that Uncle Val knew Kit, as by his tone he plainly did? She was about to come up and say something, to ask a fair question that would not reveal her own position, when she glanced at her grandmother and stopped short. Why should she look like that? Ann could make no sense of it. It was as if her uncle had named a murderer.

She saw her aunt put a hand on her grandmother's arm, in the way people do when they want to offer comfort, but her grandmother only stared ahead. She was staring at Kit. The puzzle deepened when Ann heard her American uncle say, quite pleasantly:

"Really? Do you mean Fleur's son?"

"Er – that's right, he just got transferred to Mastonbury." The girl saw her aunt tap her toe under the seat of Uncle Val's chair as he spoke. "Ah – better concentrate on the game now, old man."

What was it that everyone knew and she did not? Her grandmother might have been a statue.

"Ann dear, there you are," said her aunt when she saw her, sounding quite as if nothing had happened. "Come and sit by us will you? – there's a chair here."

Ann shook her head, and offered a quick, nondescript smile. She set her face to the field, feeling suddenly a little sick. Her plan had been to introduce Kit to her family at tea – as a friend only, of course, the pendant was still a secret. Now it seemed they all knew him anyway and, except for Uncle Francis, were not happy that they did.

She remembered then how she and Jonnie had found out about their lost uncle, Jolly, who had died in the Boer War. If Aunt June hadn't put her foot into it, they might still not know. What had she said afterwards?

'*Oh, what is it about secrets in this family!*'

Ann rubbed her hands over her arms. The memory of that passionate little outburst sent a horrid shiver over her. Yes! What *was* it? And suddenly the thought came to her that no one must know her own.

Jon's strategy for the game was clear in his head as he stepped up to the crease. He saw how the young flyer moved – confident, nonchalant, relaxed – and had him instantly marked for a smooth fast-bowler. So, on the first delivery, Jon only padded up and offered a dead bat. The ball trickled forward and the bowler picked it up. They exchanged glances from five yards; and Jon knew he was right to be cautious. The fellow had a glint of steel in his eyes.

On the second delivery, the young flyer began to show his colours. The ball seemed to veer in the air, as if it had a motor in it, and swung to leg. Jon got just a touch on it. Square leg trotted over.

The third ball pitched short and reared up savagely towards Jon's head. He made a quick choice and ducked. It flew over him, and when a lightning glance over his shoulder told him it had cleared the wicket-keeper's head too, Jon decided to take the runs. Jonnie approved, and said so as they crossed. They just squeaked in for two byes.

The good-natured crowd, nevertheless partial to the home team, appreciated this *élan* and applauded warmly. The bowler seemed chastened, and the fourth and fifth deliveries were both medium-pace balls – full-length and straight. Father and son managed six; one to the covers for two, and a boundary. The crowd responded heartily, Francis cheered, and the gods smiled.

Jon didn't spot that the sixth ball was far slower than any of the others until it was too late. He played his stroke too soon and had the singular pleasure of seeing the ball rise gently, and drop like a homing pigeon right into the bowler's hands.

"*Howzat!!*"

Jon turned on his heel, tucked his bat under his arm, and returned to the pavilion.

The gods were tired of their sport, even if the Forsytes were not. Jonnie notched up a scant eighteen, before Kit bowled him out and the sky opened. Spectators fled to the tents, players scattered between pavilions and under anywhere that was dry. In the flurry of activity Ann slipped away, and found Kit under a tree.

"Hello, you! How d'you like my style? They're going down like skittles. If this rain gives up—"

Ann could hardly think how to begin. She wiped the rain from her face, letting him go on for a few seconds, until she blurted:

"Is your mother's name Fleur?"

"Yes! Why on earth—?"

"Then my uncle knows her."

"Who's he?"

"Francis Wilmot. He's with the American Air Force."

Kit shook his head dismissively.

"Never heard of him."

"And my other uncle—"

"I thought we were supposed to be playing cricket, not Happy Families," he said. "And what's his name when he's at home – Mr Bun the Baker?"

"Don't laugh, Kit. It's serious. He recognised you straight away."

"Tell me his name, then, since he's got the advantage over me?"

"Dartie. Val Dartie."

Kit looked at her. As so often, Ann couldn't read what he was thinking.

"Val Dartie's my cousin," he said at last, "a first cousin of my mother's. That means we're related. What's your other name?"

When she told him, he repeated it immediately with a laugh.

"Forsyte! Half my relations are Forsytes! Well, what a riot – we are playing Happy Families, after all—"

"No. It's awful – that's why I came over. There's something wrong, I know there is."

"Like what?"

"I don't know yet. I saw—" Without giving an account of the transformation his name had produced in her grandmother, Ann couldn't properly tell him what she had seen. She realised already that, whatever was wrong, it centred around her. "I wanted to introduce you to them over tea. I don't see how I can now."

"Well, Val's all right. I only saw him a couple of weeks ago. The trouble must be with your lot."

This was already Ann's conclusion.

"It doesn't matter anyway – I can't stay to bat, so I shan't be there. Anyway, this rain looks like it's setting in – come here, you!"

In his arms, with his lips again on her neck, her cheeks, her lips, it did seem for a long moment that nothing else mattered. It didn't seem to worry Kit, but then she had noticed nothing ever did. Afterwards, without his arms around her, Ann was not so sure. But before she left to go back to her family, she insisted they agree quite solemnly on one thing. No one, family or no, was yet to know they were engaged.

Chapter Six

Celebration at South Square

The gathering of folk in Fleur's 'Grecian' parlour was a modest one, as befitted the season, the setting and the occasion. The season? It was an evening towards the end of October, when the last of a mostly reasonable autumn was showing signs of losing out to an altogether unreasonable winter. As for the setting, it was the one previously mentioned – the War, only a little further advanced. The occasion was a wedding anniversary; to their joint and several amazement, the Monts had been married for twenty-four years.

Having passed through 'paper' – (her flirtation with Wilfrid who was just then getting into print); 'sugar' – (her first attempt to regain Jon and not nearly as sweet as it might have been); and 'copper' – (the birth of Kat, plainly an influence on her hair); Fleur had drawn the line after 'tin'. Ten years of strict adherence was enough. Throughout the whole of the Thirties – hers and the century's – anniversary parties were out. With the War though, and their twentieth ('broken china', as Michael put it) falling in the Blitz, the event had crept back like a bad habit no one had the will to kick. A husband with a blameless past made the habit all the more grating, though Michael had actually made her laugh about this present one. There being no designated commodity for the twenty-fourth year, he asked would she settle for a double-twelfth ('silk and fine linen') and please accept two pairs of best winter drawers?

Fleur considered inviting twelve couples, but Michael pointed out a dangerous precedent. When it came to their golden wedding, they might peg out before getting through all the invitations. They finally agreed on eight *in toto* – a particularly modest number, since it included themselves. The other six were Michael's mother, Dinny

381

and Eustace, Vivian and Nona, and lastly Francis Wilmot, as he was personable and single and handy for Em. He was also one further connection to Jon, and therefore useful.

Since the inception of her Home, Fleur had seen Jon just a little more often than once a quarter. She had kept all their meetings strictly on a business footing – no lunches afterwards unless it was with everyone else, no special smiles or looks. It had not been easy, seeing him at her Spanish dining table amongst the good and the great who made up the rest of her committee, and treating him just like one of them. But she had made herself do it. He must be reassured this time. She was playing a waiting game – but she meant to win – however long it took. Besides, Michael's Uncle Hilary had a quick eye for nuances, and she had put him in the Chair. No, she would stay her hand a little longer; instinct told her it was her only way. Meantime, if she was not well-fed on Jon's company, at least she no longer starved. If she hadn't yet regained his love, she had his gratitude. That was something. And perhaps Francis was another card to play.

On second consideration, Fleur thought the American had changed much less than she might have expected. Now she had a chance to study him – six guests in the room giving her so much more time to think than her usual gatherings – now she could see how he moved, how he smiled and talked when he didn't know her eyes were on him, she was favourably impressed. He wore his age as well as his uniform. This was fortunate; it was usually far too easy to see one's own increment of age in the face of a long-absent contemporary. The gentle, wistful brown eyes she remembered, and the narrow, rather sudden nose, which features he had shared with his sister.

'*You were just too good to Francis. He always talks of you—*'

Well, she was out of the way— Francis turned his face towards her as this last thought crossed her mind, as if he might have heard its tread. Fleur was mildly disarmed to see that his expression didn't change a whit; in fact, she rather felt it was only her own which did. She went over to him, where he stood talking to her mother-in-law on the hearth rug and, for all she knew, to Poll, who was on her shoulder.

"It always was just the prettiest room, all gold and silver," she heard him say, with that hanging sort of lilt in his voice that his accent gave it.

"You go back to the bi-metallic period, then," Em said. "You missed the Deco. I never caught it myself. The Psyche's like Kat."

Fleur stepped in.

"My daughter, Catherine – the hair is anyway. She's only fifteen and rather thin at present."

"Fillin' out, though."

"I didn't know you and Michael had another child, Fleur."

This was promising. That girl really had kept quiet.

"After you, Claud," said the parakeet.

"So this little critter talks!"

"That's Michael's fault," Fleur said. "He will have the radio on in the country."

"Irritatin'," said Em. "The bird hasn't got a switch."

"After you, Cecil."

"Poll, you're rusticated. I'm puttin' you in the kitchen."

Em left with the parakeet.

"I believe I saw your son when I was in the country myself."

"Really – at his base?"

"No, on Wansdon Green. The village played the airmen while I was down there staying with Jon. Kit's a mighty fine 'fast-bowler', so I understand."

"Jon's been introducing you to cricket, has he? Did you understand any of it?"

"It's certainly a fascinating game."

"That's a nice diplomatic answer. But cricket's far more than a game, Francis," Fleur said, and wondered why the American tilted his head in that way. "It's our national character played out for all to see."

"I gathered something of that."

"What did you gather of Kit's character?"

"He was really going for it."

"He does; it's an infallible indicator. How was Jon's game?"

"I couldn't hardly tell. He was caught out in his first 'over'."

Timms passed with a tray.

"Did Jon tell you about my charity, too?"

"He certainly did. It's a wonderful thing for you to have got up, Fleur."

"Jon says so?"

383

"He says he wishes he had half your ability to organise."

That was what came from appearing business-like! Well – it was something that Jon found her convincing. So long as she hadn't convinced him *too* well—

"He had just become a ferry-pilot last time I saw him – is he still busy with it?"

"Not so busy as he'd like, is my feeling. He wishes he could do more."

Fleur learned this with interest. Perhaps she could devise more for him to do.

"Well, I couldn't have managed my home without his help. You must come down and see it for yourself. We have a couple of your boys with us at the moment."

"I'd like that."

"Good. That's a date then."

Fleur caught sight of her husband's face across the room, and saw that he was looking at her again. That was the third time she had noticed it – she had never known him so watchful of her as tonight. She smiled brightly and waved to him to come over . . .

The baronet had been lightly admonishing his publisher. He hardly knew he was also watching his wife. He had bitten down on the bullet when Fleur bought the cousin's old house, her father's house as was, for her convalescent home. She was occupied and happy; it was what he wished for her, and Michael felt in any case that it was not his place to cavil. One building or another, what did it matter? He had tried to persuade himself with this line of argument, and sweep the historical details under the carpet. But he was not entirely persuaded, and the details remained incompletely swept.

"Have you always wanted to own Robin Hill?" he had asked her once, in the still watch of a night without bombs towards the end of the Blitz. "I'd understand, Fleur, if you had. I only want to know."

Without turning towards him in their bed she had answered in the darkness:

"I suppose I have. I hadn't really thought of it before; but yes, I suppose so."

"Thanks – for telling me."

"Michael?"

"Yes?"

"Don't be too understanding. I'm not worth it, you know."

After that, he could never see his way to putting another question. He went out of his way not to be around when she had her committees at South Square, though she always told him he was welcome to sit in. Ironically, Fleur's openness was the very thing which troubled him most. Absence of evidence was not evidence of absence, though Michael hated himself for thinking so. He knew his uncle would have found a discreet way of telling him, if there was anything . . . and he despised himself all the more for feeling safer for the presence of a *de facto* spy in her camp.

And what was truly ridiculous was that, despite all his misgivings, he still liked what he saw of the cousin. Their encounters were mostly brief exchanges in the hall as he arrived and Jon left, or *vice versa*, but Michael couldn't mark him for the sort a wife-stealer was made of. Ah — but hadn't that been his father's talent, though . . . ?

"Vivian, you're stewed."

"No more than your breakfast prunes, old dear. Hardly so much these days. Had a brace of cocktails with some people first. Rather bad gin, rather bad people, but couldn't be rude. Who's the American Cousin?"

"Exactly that. A cousin of Fleur's married his sister."

Michael congratulated himself on his perspicuity. How very simple he made it sound.

"Where're they?" Vivian failed to find them in the room. "Ah!" he pronounced, opening a strangely lucid eye, "skelintons! Don't worry, dear boy – Messenger is the soul. Too many m'self. Look, Fleur wants us!"

They went over.

"Fleur," said Vivian, circling her waist, "I have spied the secret of your successful marriage."

"Through a glass darkly?"

"You keep Michael keen. He's been watching you all evening like a suitor on tenterhooks. Fabulous! Tell Nona, will you?"

"Francis, have you met—" Fleur gave Vivian his full title, because she knew it would annoy him and extricate her waist from his arm. "Vivian, this is Lieutenant Colonel Francis Wilmot, U.S.A.A.F."

"Your Lordship," said the American upon introduction, while

Fleur slipped away to talk to Dinny, avoiding her husband's eye.

"Lord, no!" said Vivian *con amore*, "—can't be doin' with it."

"My apologies; do I have that wrong?"

"No, too right by half. Makes me feel so damn' old. Listen, Wilmot – you drop mine, an' I'll drop yours. How does that sound to you?"

"It sounds pretty democratic, I'd say."

"Fine. Michael thinks the aristocracy won't survive the war, anyhow. May as well start now."

"Do you reckon not, Michael?"

"I do. This war's mixed people up too much. I don't see how they'll ever take to the old order again."

"Will they have a choice in it?"

"If they vote Labour in next time, they might well."

"That bally lot!" cried Vivian. "The stealthy rise of the underdog. Ghastly."

"Haven't the underdogs deserved a bigger slice of the pie for themselves, after the Hell they've been through?"

"You're a damn' socialist *manqué*, Michael, that's your trouble. Your bad conscience gets in the way of your better brain. The real Labour johnnies don't want a bigger share – they just want it all, too. Same as everybody. It's Nature. You've got your planned economy now, and everyone sittin' in the Lords – it's the most you can reasonably expect from one war. Where's that tray?"

Vivian turned to get a refill, and was claimed by Em.

"How's your glass?" Michael asked.

"Oh, just fine, thanks. This is a good bourbon you've got here, Michael."

"It should be – it's your own! We're both jolly grateful for that case you sent round today. But I meant to ask you; can you spare it?"

"Certainly, I can. I made sure to bring a few over with me."

"More than a few, I trust."

"Well, quite a few actually – enough for the duration."

Both men laughed.

"Now, tell me," said the American, "are politics more interesting or less during a war?"

"A bit of both, I think. One achieves far less than in peace, that's for sure, but that little seems much more important. Or it may be just that we've all become more adept at kidding ourselves to that effect."

"But the democratic process survives. That's an achievement in itself, surely?"

"Yes, it survives. We rather wheel it about in a bath-chair nowadays, but it hangs on."

"So is that right – what your friend Messenger said – is Parliament all sitting in the Lords now?"

"Yes, but that's not down to the democratic process, I'm afraid. The Führer forced our hand in the Blitz – the Lower Chamber's unusable. You know, I sometimes think friend Adolf's the best democrat of us all. He's done more for slum-clearance in five years than Parliament has in a century! Here's Eustace; he'll agree ..."

Fleur was talking to Dinny when she saw Michael leave the drawing-room.

"That's right. Francis' sister was married to my cousin Jon."

"Did they divorce?"

"She died just before the war. She was only your age."

"How terrible!"

Fleur nodded quickly, and made sure a little pained frown passed across her brow. Dinny had that quick Cherrell eye, too. Nona joined them, wanting to talk about the latest Revue. Where had Michael gone. . . ?

"Are socks awfully slow work?"

Penny Roberts got up with a start from the straight-backed chair next to the coat sarcophagus in the hall, and her knitting tumbled to the floor. Michael helped her pick it up. He felt a distinct draft when he was on his knees.

"I only ask because you were knitting one in that colour when I first saw you about six weeks ago."

He handed her a bottle-green ball, which had rolled under the sarcophagus.

"Thanks. It's another pair."

"A very sensible shade too—" And a good colour for her hair, he thought. That red! "—One can't have too much of it."

"I don't have any, actually; it's the same ball. I unravel it when I've finished one thing – and start another."

"Oh, I see." Michael didn't, in truth, but he found the explanation beguiling. "Well, I only wondered whether you'd find a cup of tea welcome. I'm afraid we'll be keeping your Colonel for ages yet."

"Oh, don't worry about me, please. I'm fine, honestly, and I'm sure everyone's very busy. I have my—"

"Your knitting — yes, I know. Listen, why don't you pop through to the kitchen with it and claim a cup that cheers? Through the doors there, and first right. You'll find a jolly cook who loves to nourish, and a parrot that does ITMA."

Michael held up a hand against the young driver's next demurral, and was rewarded with a friendly smile. What a face! he thought, as he watched her take the turn to the kitchen. I'd almost rather follow her for a chat over the purl and plain. But back to the fray. . .

"How're your other diaries goin'?" Em was asking Vivian as Michael passed them, coming back into the room. "Michael says he's keepin' up."

"If he isn't I shall want to know why. They're middlin', Em. Had a sub-lieutenant lined up, but he went overboard."

"Ah."

"There was a rear-gunner, too."

"What happened to him?"

"He caught some flak."

Em paused, swaying slightly, then said: "You're setting' me up, Vivian. Fleur said you would—"

The drone of the siren started suddenly just then. Everyone stopped to listen, but no one moved. Their reflexes were confused. They heard only the second of the two calls which had become so familiar, and it was shriller than usual.

"That's odd," said Michael. "No air-raid first?"

"What does it mean?" Fleur asked. "We can't possibly have missed one."

"Intoxication at the Observers probably," said Vivian.

"But listen," said Dinny. "It's coming from below, not above."

They all listened again.

"Poll!" said Em at last. "I forgot. He's learnt the all-clear."

Chapter Seven

Hunter's Moon

Putting on galoshes and a heavy coat against the damp and cold, Ann Forsyte declared she was going for a walk before the light failed completely. Her grandmother looked up from her *petit point*, as the girl stopped in at the drawing-room to let them know. She felt Irene's eyes on her. Ann looked at her father, who only poked his head above his evening paper, and said over the top of it, rather abstractedly she thought,

"Don't go far, darling. It'll be dark soon."

She set off through the empty orchards, with her coat buttoned right to the neck. Only her hands were exposed; she had forgotten her gloves. She pushed one hand into a pocket, and with the other held her coat collar tightly under her chin. Above her the sky was already turning from blue to pale violet. Through bare dark branches she could see the moon, white and full and already quite high. The air was still, and tingled against her cheeks. There would be a frost tonight. She walked on quickly under the trees, her galoshes pressing into leaf-mould underfoot, and soon came out onto the fields. The moon followed her.

There was Kit, waiting where the fence ended, leaning against the leaning tree as he always did. He looked immune to the cold, careless of it, with his arms tucked into the side pockets of his flying jacket, and one booted foot resting on a knuckle of old root.

"Aren't you cold?" Ann asked, running up to him, and putting her hands into his.

"No, but you are. Your hands are frozen."

His felt warm as toast.

"Cold hands, warm heart they say," he said, and Ann watched

389

entranced as he took both her hands and blew into them, then put them inside the pockets of his flying jacket. Then he put his arms around her shoulders and drew her close, tucking her head under his chin.

"Little cousin Ann."

This was a new tone in him, gentle, fond, almost tender. Ann breathed it in contentedly.

"It's funny to think we're already related," he went on. "If my mother's cousin is your uncle, we must be second cousins, or something."

"Twice removed, I think—"

He drew her closer.

"Not removed at all. Kissing cousins, in fact."

And he kissed her.

"Can't imagine why they don't like each other," he said afterwards; "not after that."

"They don't though, Kit. Whatever it is, it's serious."

"Have you found out anything?"

"I tried to pump Holly, but she only asked me why I wanted to know."

"Did you tell her?"

"No! We can't tell anybody until we know how things stand. Suppose they wanted me to stop seeing you?"

"Well – suppose they did? Would you?"

"No – but it would be dreadful, if my family hated you. Or yours me. They might put all sorts of pressure on us."

"That doesn't matter—"

"Oh, but Kit, it does. Of course it does—"

"Listen, listen; I've got something to tell you."

Ann held her breath. He had told her he would have, last time they met.

"The year I was born my grandfather invested a chunk of money for me—"

This wasn't quite the start Ann had hoped for, but she snuggled her hands deeper into his pockets to hear him out.

"He was a cautious old bird, and he made sure I couldn't touch any of it until I turned twenty-one. Well, I was twenty-one in July. Now it's come through; the paperwork's done and it's mine—"

In 1923, Soames Forsyte had seen that an initial amount of fifty thousand pounds was so astutely invested on behalf of his coming grandchild as to be virtually free from the ravages of taxation, and proof against any subsequent follies of government he might not live to oversee (such as produced the great Stock Exchange crash, and Britain's coming off gold). It was the product of Soames' highest calling – to secure capital growth, and thereby protect the future against its own worse nature. This forward planning now gave his twenty-one year old grandson at a stroke more than he, Soames Forsyte, left behind upon his own death, after a lifetime spent worrying over what calamities befell the misapplication of money.

The figure Kit gave to Ann – a girl who had never before heard anyone mention money so frankly, or even much at all – seemed utterly astounding.

"— My gracious!"

"A bit good, isn't it? And mine outright. So you see, there's nothing they can do. They can't touch us."

"Us?"

"That's right – us. Shall we get married? I do love you, you know."

"Oh, yes, Kit! Yes, please!"

"Let's then."

"When?"

"Whenever we want. How about the day the war's over? It's only a few months away now, everyone says so. We'll find a registry office and get married on the very day!"

Ann thought it all seemed impossibly romantic, and just all impossible, by turns. *Could* one just get married like that? And on such a day?

Then suddenly Kit lifted her up, and carried her around laughing. He was always so sure of everything. He would make it happen! As the branches spun overhead she could see the pole star shining in an indigo sky, and the man in the moon seemed to smile back at her.

"I've got to go home," Ann said, when her feet were on the ground again. "I wish we could just go in together and tell them."

All the practical problems were racing in her head now, but they would have to wait for another time.

"By the way," he said. "They're moving my squadron again, don't ask me why; over to Gravesend."

Gravesend! The name said it all! It was miles away – how would she ever see him?

"When are you going?"

"Tomorrow. Will you miss me?"

"Oh, yes, terribly!"

"Good."

"But Kit, it's awful – how will I see you?"

"Oh, I'll get leave, I suppose. And we can write. You will write to me, won't you, little cousin?"

She nodded quickly, blurted "Every day!" and bit her lip against the coming tears.

"That's all right then. You'd better get back, before they send the dogs out for you. And listen; no matter what, we'll meet on the day the war ends. Right?"

"Right—"

He wrapped his arms round her and kissed her again, then broke off suddenly, and started back across the field to his base, his hands in his pockets.

Ann felt the clutch of pure panic seize her as she saw him walk away.

"Oh, but where, Kit?" she cried after him. "Where!"

He turned round nonchalantly, and continued walking away from her, backwards.

"Anywhere you like," he called back, with a shrug. "I know; Piccadilly Circus – under the Eros!"

With a wide wave and a smile as broad he turned and jogged away towards the base.

Not long after his daughter left for her walk, Jon took a telephone call in his study. He had half – more than half – expected it, after seeing how clear the day had been, and that a full moon was on the rise. Francis had told him that would be the deciding factor. It was the first thing the American accent said to him now, as Jon put the receiver to his ear.

"Well, Jon – we've got our hunter's moon, I guess. Are you ready?"

"Yes."

"Good. Can you drive over to Kingston, and meet me at the factory? You know where that is?"

Jon said he did; he had ferried new planes from there several times. They agreed a likely time for his arrival, and that was that. For several seconds after the click Jon listened to the empty line singing vacantly at his ear.

"Who was that telephoning?" his mother asked as he came back into the drawing-room.

Jon stood by the piano.

"Francis."

He saw an expression of alarm pass fleetingly across her eyes; then it was gone.

"On that matter you told me about?"

"Yes."

She looked at him, and he held her eyes in a way he hadn't for years.

"I have to go."

"I know, Jon. I know."

She looked away then, and seemed in search of a colour for her embroidery.

"I'll be back before morning; don't worry."

She nodded, drawing a thread.

He thought to go over to her – she seemed suddenly grown old, sitting in that corner of the sofa by the fire – but there was something untouchable in her; a private centre of hard-won sanctity to which he had never been permitted access. He decided just to leave.

As he reached the door she suddenly cried "Jon—!"

He turned. She held a hand to her throat, then let it drop to her lap.

"Take care, my darling – won't you?"

His last image – which stuck obdurately in his mind as he drove off onto the moonlit road – was of her lovely face bent over her embroidery-frame, with a furrow of pain between her eyes that was placed there by himself.

"Where's Dad?"

Ann thought her grandmother was looking strained when she first came back to the drawing-room, but she sounded quite calm when she spoke.

"Seeing Uncle Francis. They arranged to meet in London tonight."

"Did they?"

Ann was fairly certain it was the first she had heard of it, but said nothing. She took it as a further sign that she lived among people whom she loved, but who nevertheless kept things from her. She sat down where her father had been sitting, and picked up his newspaper. Her grandmother, across the hearth from her, went on sewing.

The girl idled through a few pages, reading half an article which seemed to confirm what Kit had said about the war having only a few more months to run, then put the paper on a cushion to the side of her.

"Does Uncle Val have a cousin called Fleur Mont?"

It had been easier to say than to think about saying. Her grandmother continued with her needle a while before answering slowly, "Yes."

"Isn't Aunt Holly related to her, too – and Dad?"

"Yes, they are. Distantly. Ann dear, why do you ask?"

"Because Aunt Holly wouldn't tell me either."

"And what made you ask her?"

"Because of the cricket match. Uncle Val recognised—" she nearly tripped herself up then, "—the bowler from Mastonbury. And Uncle Francis obviously knew his mother."

In the course of this exchange her grandmother's tone and manner had not altered. They might have been discussing the weather. It remained unaltered as she looked up from her work once more.

"And from that you deduced they were all related?"

It was almost more than the girl could do to hold that steady, unblinking gaze. It resisted all penetration, its passivity made it untouchable. But she must break through this resistance!

"No," she answered. "Kit told me."

Ann had heard of people turning white when they received a great shock. Now she witnessed it. Her grandmother hadn't moved, or flinched, and the expression on her face seemed as composed as ever. But in that moment her colour drained quite away.

"What is it?" the girl cried. "Why don't you like them? Why won't anybody tell me—?"

"If you were to say why you wanted to know, perhaps it would be easier for you to find out. Secrecy often meets with secrecy."

Ann felt herself flush, felt her cheeks burn hot with frustration as she looked into those dark eyes opposite, set into a face still and pale as milk. She tried to draw a deep breath, but the tension in her was more than she knew. She found the air would only come to her in sudden, shallow little sobs.

"Because – we're engaged – that's why. Kit Mont and I – we're going – to be married!"

Jon drove full of a churning mixture of hope and apprehension. To be doing *something* at last – something *real!* All the years of lost chances and self-reproof seemed to have vanished in the night air. The road was like a photographic negative in the moonlight, stretching out in clear lines ahead of him. He had no need for a map – though he could have read one under this moon – and hardly missed the absent road signs. This was what he was *meant* to do. Francis had called it a mission – to Jon it felt just that. Whatever the details turned out to be – his guess was a covert flight to France – he would have done something in this damned war – something that mattered.

He was nearer to Richmond before he realised he had come the long way about for Kingston. Old habit, he supposed, with Robin Hill so close. Then the siren took up its wail, that familiar banshee stalking the night. The lights were already strafing the sky in the east. Local dogs began howling with the starting up of guns in Richmond Park.

Jon drove faster. He was no distance from the factory, only a few miles. Nothing would stop him getting there, not even an air-raid, which for all he knew was directed at the very place. *The Forsyte will always get through*, he told himself and smiled grimly, leaning into his wheel.

He picked out a strange noise just then, far above the register of the guns, a sort of high whistling, growing closer. He leaned further forward and looked up through his windscreen. The lights were intersecting overhead, the guns pounding; there was nothing to do but drive on. He just barely noticed that the whistling had stopped when his ears were filled with a sudden rending, as though a mile of calico had been ripped in two. The shock of the sound ran right through him, and made him swerve across the road. He was the only idiot out anyway, so it didn't matter. Jon was still congratulating himself on a near-miss, when everything in his line of vision seemed suddenly to turn a brilliant white, as if a flash-bulb had gone off in his face. Then the road imploded in front of him. He swerved again, but a tree beat him to the verge . . . He felt an impact, but dimly, like landing a punch with a numb fist, as he remembered doing once as a small boy. . . Then the blackness returned, a different blackness somehow, creeping in at the edges of everything . . . filling his eyes, his head . . .

Chapter Eight

Voice in the Night

All the convalescing flyers were back inside after the raid; the all-clear had wound down, and no one was hurt. 'Another batch of V-Twos,' seemed to be the consensus, falling somewhere between Robin Hill and Richmond. In the words of Mr Eddy, the porter-cum-handyman whose claustrophobia kept him out of the shelter, it had been 'better than a Brock's Benefit.' Well within the hour the house had regained its night-time quiet and order.

Fleur was on the point of leaving when she heard a fresh commotion in the covered court. She had just called Michael to tell him she was on her way home, putting on her coat and hat as she spoke to him, and was smoothing on her gloves and giving way to a first little yawn, when she heard the ambulance bell.

She left her office, which had formerly been Young Jolyon's study, and found her matron remonstrating with an Auxiliary driver at the open front door.

"What's the matter, matron?"

"I've told him, your ladyship, but he insists—"

"An' I've told 'er, there's no place closer," said the man, assuming his previous point had been made loudly enough to be heard by all. The cold night air crept in around them.

"He's brought a civilian here, a road accident he says—"

"But we're not a hospital," Fleur said to the man. "Can't you go over to Richmond?"

"I told 'er that five minutes ago. The roads're up all round – I can't get nowhere else."

"What about the Red Cross station?"

"I can get 'im to the Red Cross, all right, but it'll take us best part of an hour. I don't reckon this feller's got an hour in 'im without 'elp. 'E's bin burned, an' taken an 'eck of a crack on the 'ead, by the looks of it."

"But we haven't the proper facilities—" began the matron again, but Fleur cut her off.

"Bring him in," she said. "We'll do what we can."

Fleur began to unbutton her gloves as she went back to her office. She had learned that, however carefully she chose the people who worked for her, no one possessed a fraction of her clear-headedness in an emergency. She didn't doubt that half an hour of her time spent on the telephone would find and procure proper facilities somewhere within striking distance. She would give Dr. Truscott, her 'resident', a call, too. He only lived a mile away, and might as well earn his keep. There was no need to ring Michael again; she would be home before he missed her.

Truscott, responding rather to the tone in his employer's voice than to the nature of the emergency as she described it to him, arrived in under a quarter of an hour. Fleur sent him upstairs while she continued with her calls. As she thought, in less than thirty minutes she had found three places who would take the patient if she could arrange transport. When she got off the line, she began to put on her coat for the second time; then she saw Truscott standing in her doorway.

"How's the new patient?" she asked cursorily, picking up her hat and gloves.

"Poorly, Lady Mont. Very poorly. Are you not staying?"

"No. There's no need, is there? I've told Eddy to drive him over to the Red Cross station, as soon as you give the word."

"There'll be no question of that, I'm afraid. This man has severe burns on the upper chest and arms, and he's badly concussed. There's the possibility of spinal injury, too. I can't be sure. I certainly can't authorise that he be moved, now he's here."

"What are you suggesting we do then?"

"I've ordered the burns and abrasions dressed, and that he's made as comfortable as possible. What else — frankly, I don't know."

"Well then, surely we must try and move him? You could go along—"

"I doubt there's any point in trying. You see, your ladyship, it isn't that we haven't the facilities. Rather – there's very little one can do in such cases, whatever expertise is on hand. It rests with the patient – with his own strength, and whatever God he prays to."

Fleur saw the look in Truscott's tired eyes. He was a first-rate man or she wouldn't have had him, but this was not primarily *his* domain. He was reminding her tacitly of the chain of command. If a civilian was going to die there tonight, it was to be on her authority, not his. She dropped her gloves and hat back onto her desk with a short sigh, and asked to see the patient herself.

Nothing in her life had prepared Fleur for what she saw next. Afterwards she remembered that silent walk up the staircase at Robin Hill, unconsidered at the time, as a transition from one life to another. The doctor led the way, past other rooms where other patients lay asleep, or reading by small lights, or listening to the radio through headsets. It was in all respects an unexceptional scene, and offered no clues as to what was ahead. There was no chance for Fleur to prepare herself. She simply followed Truscott to a room at the end of the half-darkened landing, turned in after him and, when the nurse moved away, saw the patient lying there, bandaged, and tented between pale sheets.

It was Jon.

No answer came to her aid, to the rapid flux of why—? and how—? through her mind. There was no way to understand it – and, in another second she realised, no reason to. Jon was there, and needed her. That was all. She held tightly to the door frame at her back, watched stonily as Truscott made his methodical checks, swinging herself around into the dim landing when she felt she could stand to watch no more.

When, after some further moments, the doctor joined her there, Fleur made him deliver a minute account of everything. Diagnosis, prognosis, treatment if any; all that was wrong, and all that had been done and could yet be done to try and make it right. Not knowing whence the strength came to her, she listened, absorbing every detail.

It boiled down to very little over what he had first given her downstairs, when the patient was still just another casualty to her – barely that.

"We've done what we can, rest assured, what anyone could. All that's left now, is to watch – and pray."

Jon was dreaming and, strangely enough, some of the time he knew he dreamt. Some of the time, though, he felt he was only remembering, and it tried him not to be sure which was which. He had a memory of heat, and a dull sense now that he was hurt because of it. Silly fish!—he had got sunstroke again. Or perhaps it wasn't again at all; perhaps he had only dreamed he recovered. Was he still in Spain? Nothing was clear in his mind, but that might make some sense. In Spain, travelling with his mother, and wanting to be back in England with Fleur. It was all a hazy mess when he tried to sort it out, and his head and eyes felt hot and queer. The room he was in was too dimly lit for him to see anything very much, even the ceiling; he could only see the darkness above him, but it felt familiar. He made an effort to turn his eyes to the window, which was a mistake because when he did everything seemed to move up to meet him in a terrible rush. He only caught a glimpse of a great moon shining in a jet black sky, and then heard the sound of shutters being closed. Darkness drifted in again . . . His forehead felt cool now—if it would only last . . .

Fleur watched. From the second she began her noiseless vigil, the world and the war had ceased to exist for her. Hours or minutes might have passed as she sat by Jon's bed, it made no difference, for time had stopped too. She barely glanced up as the matron came and went periodically, only a little more when Truscott made his checks at larger intervals. This was her clock, their repeating the order of vital signs to her on the quarters and halves of hours. In between, in the long silent minutes of her watch, only her heart beat the seconds away. She would smooth down his hair, which was ruffled by his bandage. It was still so fair, and only slightly grey. His lashes were dark as ever. From time to time she would press her hand to his forehead. Once she pressed her lips there. When the first signs of fever set in, Fleur felt cold fear grab her heart; she could actually feel it tightening its hold with fingers of steel, stifling her breath.

Another conference on the landing. Truscott said he had expected as much, but offered no further remedy. They were doing all that they could. Fleur heard him out, tense with a sort of emotional blankness that kept her seeming outwardly calm, and feeling inwardly like something about to break apart. Part of her wanted to shake the man out of his professional implacability, wanted to strike him in her fury of helplessness and *make* him do more. Her good brain over-rode the impulse, and she merely asked that he go over the situation again, just to be sure. When, interrupting their talk, the matron came to say that Sir Michael was on the telephone, asking when she would be home, Fleur heard her husband's name as though it belonged to a stranger in another world. It took a supreme act of composure on her part to give any answer at all.

"Tell him I'm not coming home," she said, and realised she meant it in a way she could explain to no one.

The matron retreated down the hallway on soft heels, and Truscott gave his opinion again. It was as before, was given calmly, and remained hopelessly rational. Reckless with a desperation she could not show, hoping for any detail she might latch on to, Fleur finally asked for odds. Immediately, she wished she had not.

'*Fifty-fifty*', she was told, and then came the awful rider – '*probably rather less.*'

Fleur was 'staying with an emergency', Michael heard the matron say. He thanked her and put the telephone receiver back on its rest. Before he had time to feel sorry for himself, as he was rather tempted to lately in his new status of charity widower, the telephone rang with another call.

"Michael? Is that you?"

He said it was, but had no idea to whom he said it.

"Oh, it's marvellous! Simply marvellous – I just wanted to thank you."

There was no need, Michael said, and hoped to himself that there wasn't. Who *was* this speaking? He couldn't see a way to ask politely, while the voice rattled on in his ear.

"I knew we'd find her, and we have. And without your help in the beginning we never would have managed it. Michael, you're an angel, you know."

This he doubted; but at least the voice was becoming familiar. Michael had a mental flash of a handbag and a chin, and realised he was talking to June Forsyte. She had acquired an immigrant painter, at the start of the war, who was minus a daughter, he remembered, retrieving the details from a file in his brain marked lost causes. No doubt this determined little woman had struck a bargain with St. Jude!

"Please tell – er, Julius – I'm very happy for him. Was she living in my constituency after all?"

"No. We found her in Bristol, working by the docks. It was the only way she could make a living, poor girl."

Michael gathered her meaning after a second.

"Ah! Quite. Has she been reunited with her father?"

"Not yet. She's coming here tomorrow. I've told Julius she can stay until we find them a place of their own, until they get to know each other again. Then perhaps the girl can help in my gallery for a while. She's a pretty thing – only seventeen."

The old lady's voice was as passionate as Michael ever remembered it. It's her driving power, he thought; her motivating force. Every Forsyte he had ever known possessed one – in one form or another.

"Well, I'm glad it's all worked out."

"Thanks to you, you know. Good-bye."

Feeling a little less like an empty vessel than earlier in the evening, Michael took his hat and overcoat, and headed out into the frosted night to his club.

It was not fair. That was Jon's conclusion. Or he thought it was, it was so jolly difficult to know anything for certain, the way he felt, so hot and achy. It was so unfair that they should try and keep him from Fleur, when he loved her so. Fleur! If they believed two months in Spain was going to change how he felt about her – well, they were wrong. He had a poem for her. He seemed to have written it down in the moonlight, when he could barely see the pen in his hand and the words slithered off the page in silver ink. He couldn't find it now. If he could only remember it—! If Fleur was there, he would read it to her. *Sleeping Spanish city — voice crying —* what? What came next? *One bereaved.* No, no. Not that. *Bereaved* was wrong. *Deprived?* Yes, two syllables, short-long. *Deprived* was better, but still not right. *One denied! Denied* was right. If he died now, they would regret to their dying day that they had denied him

Fleur! If he could just see her again ... but it was getting dark ...
It didn't seem to matter anymore ... nothing seemed to matter ...

And suddenly Jon thought he heard an angel talking to him,
saying his poem, word for word—

Fleur had come to a decision. It was simply this; that since there
was nothing else to do, she would *will* Jon to pull through. What had
brought her here, to this fatal house, at this vital moment, if it was not
her will? Jon might have been lying dead hours since, on a stretcher
in that ambulance, if not for the circumstances *her* strength of will
had manifested. It was all of a piece, she saw it now. It was simply
meant to happen. She would save him. And, in saving his life, she
knew also that she would be saving her own. This was how it was
meant to be.

She leaned forward in her chair, kept the cold compress gently
touching his forehead, and looked into eyes she believed were not
sightless now, pouring into them from her own the will to live.
Several times she nearly told Jon that she was there, that she loved
him still, and would never leave him – but even now the knowledge
that there was no margin for error this time kept her cautious. At
one point he began to murmur something, but it was only babble
in his fever. Once – she thought – once he said her name. It was
too much; she had to speak.

"Yes, Jon, I'm here," she whispered, and through hot tears
added, "Don't leave me!"

Uncertain noises came back to her. Half-words, nonsense. Then,
clear as day, she heard her name again. Hope – on a knife's edge
with panic – teetered in her stomach. Fleur bent closer to Jon. He
must have strength! She was looking into his eyes when it seemed
to her the light in them went out.

She called Truscott.

What for? she wondered, as he told her what she knew he
would. High fever. Keep him cool. Pray. Pray! What use were
doctors? A priest might have had more sense.

She sent Truscott away.

As one twice baptised, in two languages, Fleur had no religion
save that of self-belief. She knew no prayers by heart, nor psalms,
or she might have tried one even so, risking its hollow echo in the
room. Then she realised she knew one verse better than anything

403

in the world. It was the poem Jon had written for her, and sent to her from Spain. To Fleur it was more sacred than any prayer. Softly then, slowly, she began to recite:

> *'Voice in the night crying, down in the old sleeping*
>   *Spanish city darkened under her white stars!*

> *'What says the voice—its clear—lingering anguish?*
> *Just the watchman, telling his dateless tale of safety?*
> *Just a road-man, flinging to the moon his song?'*

And here on the last line, through some quirk of her own need, she changed a word, and never for one moment knew she had.

> *'No! 'Tis one* denied, *whose lover's heart is weeping,*
>   *Just his cry:* How long?'

Chapter Nine

Visitation

When Jon's fever broke finally, in the last dregs of a night without hours, something in Fleur snapped too, and she felt suddenly tired to death. Truscott returned, and made his checks. Yes, he nodded, as if he would not have been surprised either way; temperature falling, vital signs stronger, a better outlook altogether. The patient, whoever he was – this with a half-quizzical look to his employer – was over the worst.

Fleur pressed the heels of both hands against her eyes to stave off the itch of sleep, and got up from her chair. Taking a last look at Jon from the door of the room she went downstairs, and found Francis waiting in her office.

"How long have you been here?" she asked dully, past the capacity for surprise, long past caring why the American should be there at all.

"Not above an hour or so. Your matron let me in. Jon's been here all night, she told me."

"Yes." Fleur looked at the American's face, but saw no demand of any kind in his open, serious features. "He had an accident."

"In the air-raid. I know."

Fleur only tilted her head for enquiry; she didn't care if it wasn't answered.

"He was coming to meet me, I'm sorry to say. When he didn't arrive I had to borrow a jeep and try and track him down. It took me the best part of the night."

She perceived an unasked question in what Francis was saying. Since the blame for Jon's being out rested squarely with him, Fleur made no attempt to ease its passage, but let him continue.

"His family were pretty well worried sick for him."

And why hadn't she let them know? Now Fleur could see the question hanging in the American's wistful brown eyes. She imagined he wouldn't like the honest answer, which was that in the whole long night it had never once occurred to her to do so. Nor another question – why Jon had driven out in the night to meet him.

"I dare say they were," she answered flatly. "So was I."

Francis received her answer with a little sidelong look, quite mild, and that characteristic backward tilt of his head.

"How is he now?"

"Pulling through. If you want to go up, you'll find my doctor with him. He'll put you wise."

Francis nodded silently, picked up his cap and gloves which were resting on the desk, and got up. At the door he turned round and said,

"I called Green Hill from here, Fleur; I hope you don't mind. They'll be over first thing."

Fleur gave a minuscule shrug. Francis seemed unable to leave the door.

"Was there something else?" she asked him, and watched him shake his head slowly.

"I guess not," he said, looking at her once more. "Leastways, nothing that won't keep."

She listened to the retreat of the American's light tread up the stairs, and then out of the distance heard another noise. Somewhere a foolhardy cock was crowing to an ashen dawn.

Fleur put her coat over her shoulders and passed through the covered court to the terrace, where she stood numbly looking out at the wintry grounds. It was just first light, and the lawn in front of her was frosted like a cake. There was no wind, nothing stirred. Only a pair of crows bayed intermittently from the top of the old oak tree, black shapes on black branches below a whitening sky. Fleur pulled her coat around her, holding the fur of its collar to her face, automatically wrapping herself against the cold she didn't yet feel. She actually felt nothing – just distanced from everything. It seemed she watched the scene, and herself, as if over her own shoulder. In all, it was perhaps the strangest hour of her life.

Is this how it would have felt, she wondered, had Jon belonged to her for all those years? How easily it might have happened this way. Had they lived together here, at Robin Hill, Jon might well have had his wish and gone to war; might have come back to her injured; might be lying upstairs, as now – only in their bed. Is this how it would have been, having nursed him through the night, to wait to receive their interlocking web of relatives?

'*Yes, do go up, Holly — Val — June, but only for a minute. I don't want him tired, now he's home!*'

Would his mother have come? Would that woman ever have set foot in this house while she, the daughter of her hated first husband, was mistress of it? Would she come even now?

Fleur began to feel the cold nipping at her cheeks, and at the tip of her nose, but she didn't move, and barely shivered.

She had meant to be shut into her office when they arrived, but lost track of time standing on the terrace. Hearing a car pull up at the front of the house brought her back to present reality, and she hurried inside, making for her room.

She was too late – and only half the way across the covered court – when she saw her, her shape, framed by the open doorway. Irene stood as though carved from stone, one gloved hand held to her heart, one foot poised on the last step before the threshold. She had been looking up into the court like one held under a spell, or like one casting the same. With a small turn of her neck, her dark eyes fell on Fleur.

Fleur returned her stare, but could not find the challenge she had expected in that inaccessible look, the equivalent of what she knew must be in her own. Rather the eyes she saw were filled only with a terrible passivity. That quality which had so confounded Soames Forsyte sixty years ago, in the days when he lived estranged with Irene, the creature of his passion, in their little house in Knightsbridge – that same quality of the nerves confounded his daughter now. What was she thinking, this woman, standing still as a statue on the steps of this house? — the house which her lover Bosinney designed for Soames — the house which finally was owned by Soames' enemy, Jolyon, whom she subsequently loved and married, and by whom she had her son, Jon? What sort of woman was she, who by her

407

great beauty had enslaved and ultimately destroyed every man who ever loved her? Fleur searched that face, still beautiful now, but found no answers in it. The woman offered no defence, no explanation, no challenge. Quite suddenly then, Fleur realised why it was so—

It's because this place is hers, she thought. It doesn't matter that I've bought it, it could never make any difference, because she *owns* it. As a wraith owns a castle, *this place belongs to her.*

For an immeasurable moment they stayed like this, fixed in unquantifiable relation to each other. Then Fleur took a step back towards the wall, and Irene passed silently by her and up the staircase, like a dream passing in the first light of day.

Fleur walked hurriedly to her office, not turning when she heard Holly's voice call her name from behind.

In the chair where Fleur had spent the night in watching, Irene now sat presenting much the same aspect of devotion to the patient, who remained unconscious, and therefore unaware of this critical substitution in *dramatis personae*. Ann hovered at the foot of her father's bed, feeling too desperately akin to Judas to look at him, while Holly and Val conferred with a senior nurse on the landing. The nurse relayed the events of the night, though only as she understood them since relieving the matron of her shift that morning. All she knew was what was on the patient's chart; that he'd had a terrible fever, brought on by his burns, but was now over the very worst.

When the nurse left them, Val said: "Well, I suppose we've got Fleur to thank for his pulling through—"

For this well-intentioned remark he received two communications – a quick, unsettling look from Irene, and then a little nip on the skin at the back of his hand from his wife's thumb. To the first he could attribute no just meaning whatever; the second told him that he was out of his depth and should best shut up. Ann's response went unrecorded; she stood at the window looking down at the lawn, where the night's frost was gradually receding in the path of a faint yellow sun.

From her office, Fleur heard the little group descend the stairs some three quarters of an hour later. For all that time she had remained in one position, leaning stiffly against the edge of her desk, a hand gripping the wood on each side of her like a vice. The visitors stood together in the inner court, but Fleur made no move to go to them. When she heard Francis join them, emerging from the day room – formerly Irene's drawing-room there – where she had heard him exchanging amiable small-talk with some early-risers among the men, Fleur moved to the half open doorway of her office, whence unseen she felt entitled to listen. She imagined their conversation must include her name.

Before making himself sociable in the day room, Francis had made sure to ask a few key questions of the matron. She was anxious to get off shift, since Dr Truscott had left over an hour ago and she did not wish to be taken for granted; but the American officer approached her with such courtesy that she hardly minded staying a few minutes more to answer him. When she left him, Francis believed he had a clearer picture of the situation overall than before. One phrase of the matron's was the most telling. When he asked if it was so, that Lady Mont had watched the new patient right through the night, the matron answered that she had, and added – 'she tended him like an angel'.

In the day room, where he had joshed two of the men about getting up a 'Paul Jones' once they each had a new leg fitted, Francis continued to piece the picture together.

He knew there had been something between Fleur and his brother-in-law right from the start. He hadn't been two minutes in Fleur's 'bi-metallic' parlour that first time before he knew they were – or that they *had* been – more than simply cousins. And he knew that Jon's mother was the rub, so to speak. What had Fleur said about her back then?

'Well, I hope she won't be jealous of your sister!'

That was it; and he remembered her tone of voice, and the hard set her face had worn for a few seconds after she spoke. Francis believed furthermore that whatever lay between Jon and Fleur before they made their separate marriages was still lying around when Jon came back to England in '26. He knew it for a fact; not from anything said by his sister, or by Jon, but rather from what neither of them said at all. After Anne announced she was pregnant in the Fall of that year, and they moved into Green

Hill, neither she nor Jon ever mentioned Fleur's name to him again.

So, as Francis saw it, it didn't take any rocket engineer to draw the proper conclusion about the present situation in the light of those two others. From two known points, he calculated the hidden third. And once he had it all worked out — why then, a lion's den wouldn't have got it from him. He owed Fleur at least that much.

Listening by her office door, waiting for him to 'spill the beans' on her, Fleur heard Francis say how he had taken the decision himself not to call Green Hill earlier in the night. They had all been too intent on Jon's welfare to place the call right there and then. Seeing how he had pulled through, it was for the best, he reckoned. He led them to the door, where they conferred once more, out of Fleur's hearing, and then he saw them into Holly's car. He went back into the day room for his hat and great-coat.

When Francis returned to the covered court, Fleur came out of her office, feeling she ought to say something to him. A simple 'thank you', if no more.

"Francis—"

She called to him as he reached the door. When he turned, she could see by his face that somehow he knew everything.

"Don't worry yourself, Fleur," he said gently, as he put on his cap, tilting his head back a little and to the side, as was his way. "Like I said – it'll keep."

Jon was removed in the afternoon. Francis had conjured an ambulance replete with medical attendant and a good deal of appropriate equipment, and, as Fleur watched, Jon was transferred with the utmost care on a stretcher to the back of it. After his eighteen hours or so at Robin Hill, she saw him whisked away – to East Grinstead, she was told when she asked, to the specialist burns unit – knowing for a certainty that he had never once been conscious of his surroundings or of her presence beside him in them. Her last glimpse was of his fair hair poking up through the bandages around his head, as the ambulance doors closed.

Fleur shut her office door on the cheery noises coming from tea in the day room. She rang through to Michael, but only reached Timms.

410

Sir Michael was out at the House, ma'am. Fleur left a message to say she would be back before supper. Next she made poor work out of a little bit of late lunch brought in to her on a tray. When the tray was taken away, she found a packet of cigarettes in a drawer and lit one up, barely drawing smoke. She leaned back in her chair, feeling inordinately weary. Within seconds she was asleep.

It was Fleur's turn to dream, and her dream, like Joseph's, was in two parts. First it seemed that her father stood before her, in the office there, lean and trim and grey, spare as ever. She smiled up at him, and got a frown back in return.

"It's a bad business," she heard him say. "Don't let them hurt you, child!"

Whether his warning was directed specifically at members of the other side of their family, or only generally at the Germans she couldn't discern. Then her father's shape melted away, as the first part of her dream gave way to the second.

In it, she seemed to be back at Mapledurham, that last dreadful night when she knew she had finally lost Jon. She saw herself pacing the length of her father's picture gallery, puffing abstractedly on her cigarette, trying to concentrate on the paintings, trying to feel — nothing! She felt herself give up the ghost she was chasing, felt herself surrender the shadow she had caught to its substance that had eluded her. She saw herself throw away her cigarette, three-quarters smoked, into a waste-paper basket by the writing bureau, and leave the gallery.

She was lying on her bed, asleep but fully dressed, when she heard her father's voice again.

"Get up!" he said, "there's a fire in the picture gallery!"

She awoke, startled and afraid, immediately remembering her cigarette. Was it possible—? Had she—?

Her father spoke once more; there was a dire urgency in his voice.

"Get everyone out of the house!"

Fleur felt a sharp pain in her hand. She was really awake this time. Her cigarette had burnt down to the butt between her fingers. She mashed it out ferociously and leaped up. Though she was awake she was driven still by the propulsion of her dream. Not stopping to know what she did, Fleur ran from her office into the court. She saw the porter coming up from the kitchen stairs and grabbed him by the arm.

"Quick!" she cried. "Get everyone out of the house!"

The man only stared. Fleur shook his arm.

"Quickly! Everyone!"

"But your ladyship—" he began, and then broke off. The sirens had started.

Fleur sat in the shelter next to the senior nurse on duty. On her other side lay one of their weakest patients on a stretcher. He was just a young boy, who had come in that afternoon at about the time Jon had left. Fleur held his head in her lap, and sang quietly under the noise to calm her nerves.

'*Auprès de ma blonde, il fait bon — fait bon — fait bon —*'

The young flyer's hair was like Jon's.

Her dream still disturbed her – was it only that? Just a memory awakened as she slept, or something beyond? She could not rid herself of the feeling that she really had seen her father. Could it have happened? Had he warned her? What place more likely for his spirit to rise uneasy than here? She might believe it now, though she had never believed such things before.

The young man shifted nervously on his stretcher.

'*Auprès de ma blonde, il fait bon dormir.*'

She felt, rather than heard, the next explosion, and tried to shield the boy's head from the judder of its impact through the ground. Long before the all-clear came, Fleur knew it was the house.

Chapter Ten

Certain Understandings

A new year, and the end in sight of what felt like a very old war. The member for Mid-Bucks left his club at a little after four and set course for home into a biting snow-flecked wind that seemed to want to blow right through to his bones. Fleur was expecting him, and he would rather be early than late. Now she was without the occupation formerly provided by her Home, he didn't think it fair to keep her waiting. He turned up his coat collar and walked off at a slant, securing his hat low on his brow and keeping his head down. It won't last, he thought. I'll be bare-headed before I get out of Pall Mall.

Michael made dogged progress eastwards along that thoroughfare until a spreading lake of wet snow at the next junction forced him to divert north to Piccadilly. Fearless explorer braves arctic wastes, he mused — but will he make it home for tea! The slush seemed deeper hereabouts, and he was aware of a certain seepage in his left shoe. That's only right, I suppose – aren't we all on our uppers now? A newspaper headline, soaked and torn in the gutter, caught his eye – *Allies Seek Unconditional Surrender*. That bannered slogan he found so uncomfortable looked to be a whisker away from a reality; but at what price? Just since Yalta the Red Army had reached the Danube, and the American cousins were on the Rhine. He could cheer heartily for their progress – but what about Dresden? That ghastly firestorm – in a city packed to the rafters with civilians, and refugees from the Eastern Front – had seared many a conscience. It was no salve to his own that he had seen it coming, or something like, as long as that single-minded banner flew. And now word was filtering through of conditions inside the camps. If the half of it was true, the prolonged

413

misery of those poor devils must also be put down on the great tally of the war. How inconceivable it seems now, he thought, that we weren't prepared to pay a fraction of this deplorable price six years ago to buy the peace. Well, it was a case of badly spilt milk, and would surely require a lot of mopping up all round. *This* had certainly better be the war to end all wars, or the next one will finish us off for good. With any luck, we'll lack the stomach and the nerves to go through it again. Meanwhile, one last test of a hard-pressed national constitution – a winter to end all winters! He trudged on.

With his line of vision limited to the pavement a few feet in front of him, and less than that above, he was encouraged to find a pleasing pair of legs walking two paces ahead in his own direction. 'Nude' looked so awfully chilly at this time of year, even above a pair of stout and practical galoshes. A rather better combination, he supposed, than less fashionable stockings and more fashionable shoes. Sensible girl! Michael slowed down to prolong his vantage, and anyway might have followed her to Billericay for what little stock he could take of his own bearings in the sleet. But conditions underfoot intervened. The girl slipped, stumbled forward, and fell onto her knees in the snow. Michael was obliged to perform a quick *entrechat* to avoid going down with her. When he offered a gloved hand to help, a fair-isle mitten accepted his support. As he braced his footing to take her weight – which was wholly inconsiderable – he saw a matching fair-isle tam-o'shanter drop to the ground between them. Michael stooped to retrieve the article, and was nicely surprised when he gave it back to a familiar oval face, now surrounded by a tumble of fine red hair gathering snow.

"Well — I seem always to be handing you your knitting. I didn't recognise you in mufti. Are you all right?"

The girl whom he knew only as Francis Wilmot's driver nodded with a quick little smile, and wiped a smudge of snow from her forehead.

"I think so." She checked her knees, and Michael allowed himself no more than a second to do the same. "Nothing broken anyway. Thanks for a nice helping hand."

She shook out her woollen tam, stretched it between both hands, but stopped short of putting it on when she saw how it was wet through.

414

"Better not," said Michael. "You'll keep drier without. Are you going far?"

"Only to Victoria."

"But you're soaked."

"Oh, it won't matter. I've a good idea I can dry out while I wait for a train – they take forever."

"Well, I've a better one. Join me for a cup of tea at that Lyons, and we can both send up steam over a bun."

Michael held up his hand as he had in the hall at South Square, and was rewarded with another smile of compliance. Placing a hand at her elbow he steered a cautious path to the next traffic-lights, and they crossed towards the tea-shop.

Inside, they were met by a living wall of heat, rising off the two dozen or so other bodies already availing themselves of the insulation to be had for the price of a cup of tea.

"Good-oh!" said Michael. "The fashionable hour."

"I should have brought my dancing shoes," said the young WAAF at his side, and Michael jollied her elbow in reply, as he saw a pair of Anzacs get up from a table for two.

"Here's a bit of luck—"

He waved his hat at their 'nippie', and she summoned them to take up the spare seats. Michael's was still warm.

"Yes, dear?"

"Two teas and matching buns, please. With currants, if possible."

"Yes, dear."

The nippie departed, reasonably true to her name. Looking at his young companion across the tiny square of table, Michael realised he hadn't an idea what to say to her – all the less when she smiled back at him. By Jove, though — that *was* a smile!

"It's rotten weather for leave," he began. "Or perhaps you're rather glad not to be driving in it?"

"I didn't want to take any, but Colonel Wilmot insisted I have a full week, starting today."

"That was jolly decent of him. What are you planning – a few days in the South of France? – a spot of gardening?"

Just when he was thinking there was nothing nicer in a miserable city that minute than to be sitting opposite this girl's smile, Michael saw her laugh sweetly at his asininities. Suddenly he felt himself ever such the tiniest bit smitten. For a man who had previously considered the whole of his heart to be happily consigned to his wife, it was quite a jolt. An incautious moment of elderly fantasy, he thought, and best gotten over in the next second.

The next second elapsed. Their attendant spirit brought two teas, much of Michael's cooling conveniently in the saucer. Buns followed.

"Does Victoria take you home?"

The girl shook her head and her gossamer fine hair tumbled about her shoulders.

"No, I'm going to see a friend in Sussex—"

"Ah."

"Well – not really a friend—"

Michael felt an inexplicable little turn of jealousy in his chest. Get a grip on yourself, Mont. You're already a sufficient idiot – there's no call to make yourself a prize one. He nodded in such a way as he hoped was suitable for his age and station. He wished it was Victoria!

"Someone you'd like to be more than a friend?" he guessed.

The girl tipped her chin up and down once, suggesting he was on the right track.

"But there's a problem?" he suggested.

Her chin repeated the move. So, Mont wasn't the champion idiot of the world then. Any brute who could fail to notice this girl's interest in him, and respond in kind, deserved to walk off with the gold medal – that or a white stick—

Michael's eyebrows rose involuntarily when he heard his last thought echoed.

"It's just that he doesn't see very well."

"So I gather," he replied gently, then wished he hadn't when he saw her flush.

"He was in an accident – it's affected his sight."

"Ah. I'm sorry."

"It's so difficult, you see – to know how to make contact."

Plainly, there was only one vacancy at the table – that of Dutch uncle. Michael unilaterally appointed himself to the job, knowing there could be none more qualified than he to advise. After all, who knew, better than he did, the feeling of being unregarded by one's beloved?

He held his quizzical frown, and set a crooked smile under it. It was all the encouragement she needed to go on. By the end of his cup, and three-quarters of the way through his bun, Michael felt he knew everything there was to know about this near-sighted Lochinvar in Sussex – everything except his identity, and he considered that none of his business. He could see her point, too. Wasn't most of the delicate work in courtships carried out by means of looks and glances?

"Here's a thought—" Michael offered, but stopped mid-sentence. "Do you know, I've just realised – we've been talking all this time and I don't know your name—"

"Penelope. Penny—"

"That's nice. Now, Penny – you say you're uncertain of this fellow because you can't be sure whether he's caught your expression – am I right?"

"That's it, really."

"And you feel it's not your place to make the first move?"

"Mmm."

"Well, had you considered that it might be exactly the same way about for him? Perhaps *he's* uncertain of *you*, for just that reason. If he's the decent chap you say he is, how's he to know, and not push himself on you?"

"I hadn't thought. Oh, I do wish it could be so simple—"

"How do you know it isn't – unless you give it the old school try?"

"But wouldn't you consider it — well, forward? Rather off-putting?"

Michael would have considered himself thrice-blessed, but didn't say so. Instead, he shook his head and smiled at her.

"Not nowadays. No. It's the one good thing that promises to come out of this mess. Women have drawn level, and I'm betting they'll stay there. Take a chance, Penny – and make sure he doesn't miss his."

Her hand was still grasping his across the table when the nippie brought their bill.

It had taken Fleur a while to recover herself, after those two last nights at Robin Hill. A good deal of thinking was required of her to decide whether she had gained or lost overall in the experience.

417

Either way, her nerves – perhaps for the first time in all the long course of the war – had taken a battering.

Unquestionably, the house was a huge loss. When she was first able to see the extent of the damage – on that second dawn, after another sleepless night, spent in seeing all her airmen moved safely to other establishments – she was surprised at the extent of her own shock. The house was little more than an open shell, still steaming, its inward structure ripped out through its back wall by the path of a rocket falling directly through the roof of the covered court. The old oak was down, and most of the garden was rendered a gaping crater, strewn with rubble. Part of the casing of the missile was lodged amid the broken beams – it was just possible to read 'Nach England' on its side. Bosinney's monument, which stood for nearly sixty years, had been destroyed in a moment. Fleur's dream however – her father's warning, if that was what it was – had kept everyone safe. Their only casualty was the porter, who one last time had refused to go down with them to the shelter.

And now she was without the Home, wasn't she also without justifiable means of seeing Jon? All the time he was being treated in the burns unit, Fleur paid him no visits; how could she, without risking another encounter with his mother, without betraying the real nature of her concern? Holly rang South Square regularly with bulletins of his progress, but Fleur found it hard to be grateful for this consideration. Presumably they deemed Jon safe from her depredations while he was in hospital! Now he was spending each week-end at Green Hill, Winifred had told her. No doubt his mother was on guard there, too.

Fleur sat over her tea-tray that wintry afternoon, absently drawing a spoon through the sugar-bowl as she reviewed her hand. Her fear was that she had waited too long to play her cards. Robin Hill had been her ace; the only extra card she had picked up was her vigil with Jon. What its value was, she couldn't yet tell.

She heard the front door open and close, and a man's light footsteps in the hall approaching the drawing-room.

"Hello! You're nice and early—"

She looked up from her tray expecting to see her husband back for tea, and saw instead the uniformed figure of her son.

"Oh – Kit."

"Mother."

"Have you got some leave?"

"A two-day pass. Thought I'd look in."

"I suppose anything's better than Gravesend?"

She held up her cheek and received a kiss. It was a perfunctory gesture from both parties. Since Kit had left school to volunteer in that first year of the war, and Fleur had tried to stop him and found she couldn't, a certain coolness had set in between mother and son. They had tested their wills on one another, and were now at a mutually acknowledged stand-off.

Kit moved on to the hearth, where a fire had not long been lighted. He tapped idly at the fender with his foot and gazed for a few moments into the bluish yellow flames. Then he said:

"I've been thinking about what I'm going to do next."

"Have you?"

Fleur knew her son. He was not seeking advice. It was only his way of telling her he had come to another decision she probably would not like.

"I reckon the war will be over soon, so I've decided—"

There!

"I'm going to try India. Go out with the Indian Civil, and then maybe get a place out there—"

Kit in India! The notion came too soon upon her present loss for it to register properly.

"I'm sure your father will know how you should go about applying."

She hadn't meant to sound so unconcerned, and managed a smile of a sort. Kit managed one back. It was as close as they were going to get.

"There's something else, too."

The thought ran quickly through Fleur's mind, whether her son hadn't in fact gone absent without leave, as he had that time before from his school. No; he loved flying too well. And it certainly wasn't money—

"I'm going to get married."

Fleur supposed after a second that she was only surprised he hadn't said he was married already. How distanced they had become from each other in these few years—

419

"Who's the lucky girl?"

"Someone you know already, I think."

"Really? Who?"

"Ann Forsyte – Val Dartie's niece."

Fleur stared at her son and could think of nothing whatever to say in reply. All the standard formulas failed her. How in the world—? The answer came – at Mastonbury, of course. The base was near Wansdon; somehow Kit must have met Jon's daughter while his squadron was there. Then a deeper realisation bore in upon her. Jon's daughter – and her son!

"I gather our side of the family doesn't get on with hers," Kit said.

Fleur made a small gesture, and might have offered a minor explanation – something about the Old Forsytes – to stave off any questions, but Kit went on.

"It doesn't matter; I don't need to know about it. We'll be in India so it won't make any difference. I just thought I'd let you know."

Fleur nodded, as inwardly she was beginning to absorb the meaning of it. So, that fatal passion – her father's for Jon's mother, hers for Jon – had infected the next generation. It was ironic – so exquisitely ironic, that Kit was to have what had been denied her. Imagine! Her son married to Jon's daughter. She and Jon parents-in-law. Jon's grandchildren hers too. The significance of it was stupefying—

When Michael reached home he knew as soon as he stepped into the drawing-room, and saw his wife and son together there, that he had walked into a scene. Fleur's eyes when he saw them looked uncommonly bright, even for her. Her expression was completely closed off, locked up in private thoughts. Kit only glanced at his father, then stared up at the Psyche over the fireplace, his elbow leant on the mantel.

"Hello, old man—" Michael said to his son. "We hadn't expected to see you for a while."

"He's brought us some news, Michael," Fleur told him, in a tone of voice he couldn't decipher. "I'd sit down first, if I were you."

Chapter Eleven

And Certain Others

Mending was a slow process. Jon had tried to speed it up, but discovered that any effort on his part only slowed the process down still further; Nature wanted things done a certain way, and he was forced to accede to Her wishes. It seemed a milestone in his progress when he was allowed home to Green Hill for week-ends. While there, he tried to be no burden to anyone, was tolerantly receptive of all gestures toward his comfort, and complained of nothing, not even his own very real pain. He spent his days in various chairs, holding open various books in front of him, while actually gazing out over the top of them through various windows. His eyesight was often patchy, in any case, since it seemed he had also obtained a skull fracture in the crash. He walked outside on occasions when the weather allowed – never very far, and with a slight stoop – along various garden paths. All the time he presented a pleasant outward aspect to his family and friends, when inside himself he felt he was little short of an absolute failure. At no point could he see his own performance for what it really was – probably the most heroic of his life.

Holly called in every day, frequently bringing June who was staying temporarily at Wansdon. Jon had been dismayed to learn that on the night after his own accident there had been another rocket attack on the area. June's house – then host to the reunion of Julius and his daughter – took a direct hit. Its mistress was luckily detained; first over a crisis at her gallery, where the plumbing had never recovered from the strike on the Burlington Arcade during the Blitz, and then on her homing bus which broke down at Hammersmith. She was the only member of the household not obliterated. Hearing of June's misfortune made Jon less pitying of his own. When they told him that Robin Hill had been destroyed as well, his feelings were entirely for Fleur. The house would be a dreadful loss to her, he was sure. He knew his own position on her Board had been not much more than a sinecure, though he would always be grateful to her for offering it to him; but for Fleur the Home had been a real cause. She had been there during the raid, he was told, and had got everyone down to the shelter just in time. How marvellous of her – to stay so cool, and not think of her own peril! He wanted to write to her, but couldn't yet manage a pen for the burns on his hands. All things considered, he would rather wait than get someone to write the letter for him.

Of his stay at Robin Hill, and of the vigil carried out by his bedside there, Jon knew nothing. German rockets might rain down upon the whole country, but the family mechanism among Forsytes for keeping secrets remained intact.

Francis 'stopped by' at Green Hill as often as he could, to see how his brother-in-law was getting along. He was due to be moved to France any day – it seemed he would get to see Paris after all.

"I let you down," Jon said, when they were first alone. "I'm sorry. It was my fault."

To which Francis replied quietly, and as sincerely as he had ever spoken in his life, that the fault, if anyone's, was all his own.

Jon insisted the young WAAF driver join them whenever Francis called. She always cheered him up somehow – and no matter how poor his eyes were he could always see her hair quite clearly!

Sitting in his grandfather's old leather armchair, Jon was watching the snow fall in blurry whirls outside the window of his second-floor study that wintry afternoon, when his mother came in. They were alone in the house. Jonnie was still away at school and Ann, who was now enrolled at the cottage hospital with Holly, had called earlier to say she would be spending the night at Wansdon. When Francis was down last week-end – his last before leaving for France – the young driver had said she would call again today, if she might, as she had some leave. It was sweet of her to want to, Jon thought, but she would never set out in such weather . . .

"Not reading, darling?"

Jon picked up an imperfectly disguised note of worry in his

mother's voice and sought to reassure her.

"Oh, I thought I'd just rest my eyes for a bit. I got through most of the paper this morning."

His mother pressed a hand to his shoulder as she passed him, by which he knew that he was unconvincing. She sat down on a chair opposite his own and folded her hands on her lap. Jon couldn't see the details of her expression, but something told him she wanted to talk. There was an uncustomary lack of quietude in the silence between them.

For a while longer they both watched the snow tumbling outside, then Irene said:

"Jon dear, has Ann said anything to you recently?"

"No. About what?"

"About—" Jon heard her take a light breath before continuing – "about her plans to be married."

"No!" Jon ran a hand up his forehead to his hair and smiled faintly in his astonishment. "She hasn't said a word—"

His mother's voice was strangely disturbed when she went on.

"Perhaps she wanted to wait until you were stronger – perhaps I should have waited myself, only I—"

"But why? I suppose it must all have happened rather suddenly, but it's splendid news. It gives me something to hurry and get better for."

He saw his mother press her hands together in front of her, and tilt her face up to the ceiling. He wished he could see her eyes clearly. There was something she wasn't saying, something which presumably had kept Ann from telling him herself.

"Is there anything wrong?"

He could feel his mother composing her strength before she answered him. She dropped her hands to her lap again and stared before her, as if she had just that moment resigned herself to an inevitability.

"Who is she marrying?" he asked, smiling. "Do tell me."

After a sigh he barely heard, Irene replied at last. Blankly, like one surrendering a last hope, she said:

"Fleur's son. Ann wants to marry Kit Mont."

Jon felt himself all but physically struck by the news. Of all things unimagined – unimaginable! – this was the last in the world.

Suddenly he realised how long it was that he had been away from his own home, how many weeks and months had passed with his taking no part in life at Green Hill.

"But how does Ann know him?" Jon asked, rather dazed, and feeling stupid for not knowing the answer. "Where did they meet?"

"Here," his mother replied slowly, giving the word an odd weight. "He's a pilot; he was at Mastonbury for a while. Ann told me she would meet him by—"

"—By the field," Jon said, in a flash of certainty, and saw his mother nod stiffly. "Well. Of all the things."

Fleur's son and his own daughter – what a twist! How old would Kit be now? Not more than twenty-one! Only two years older than he had been when he first met Fleur. Well, it was ironic. Suddenly then, Jon thought he perceived the larger picture. Perhaps this was finally the way to lay that old ghost for good? Fleur had begun the process when she asked for his help with Robin Hill.

'If you'll put the past aside, I will too.'

It was wonderful to think it might really be possible; to end those years of enmity and estrangement between the two sides of the family. Perhaps Ann's marriage was the thing that could bring it about. He wished it might be. If only his mother wouldn't be hurt!

"How do you feel about it?" he asked, and thought he saw her shudder slightly.

"My feelings are of no importance. My only concern is that Ann should be happy."

"Well, she – she must be in love with him. Have you met him?"

He was unable to see that there was a desolate little smile on his mother's face as she replied.

"No."

"I expect we'd better arrange to, in that case. He must get leave at some point, I imagine—"

Jon wondered what Fleur's son would be like. Strong and decisive, like her? Yes, Ann would love that in him. After all, he had loved it himself in Fleur! And if Kit took after his father at all, he must be a good-natured sort of fellow ... A thought occurred to Jon then. It was the one thing his mother hadn't said.

"Does Ann know anything about—?"

Before he could finish the question, Irene shook her head quickly and with some agitation. He felt a slight plea coming from her in the gesture.

"Well, why should she?" Jon said, to calm her. "It's all in the past now."

"Yes," she answered faintly.

And there it must stay, Jon added silently in his heart, with a passion he hadn't expected of himself. It encouraged him to speak more plainly.

"We mustn't stand in her way. It wouldn't be — fair — if she's in love with him. And if he's in love with her, well, he'll want to make her happy."

Irene made no reply, but Jon knew then that her eyes were on him again. He didn't need to see their exact expression; he knew what they were saying.

'*Whose son is he*—? *Whose grandson*—?'

As she passed behind him on her way to the door, she pressed a kiss on the crown of his head. He felt her breath trembling in his hair as she said,

"I shan't see her married, Jon. It lies with you. You gave your father his last wish. I shall always bless you for it."

Jon caught her hand and tried to bring it to his lips, but his grip was still poor. She slipped it from him and left the room.

The snow seemed to be falling harder now. It looked more like sleet, Jon thought, though it was probably just his vision getting patchy again. Certainly, the wind was stronger. He could hear it beginning to whip around the gables and across the yards. Forgetting the black-out for once, he had kept the curtains open in his study, and sat looking out still, as he had continued to do since his mother left the room. Beyond the light from his window the evening was black as a witch's hat, and no more charitable; not a night for even a fox to be abroad. Yet the storm outside contrasted strangely with the general lack of commotion he felt in himself. Jon had tried to find the high drama in the situation but had failed. He appreciated how it must seem to his mother, it was only natural that she be alarmed at first; but the greater part of him saw the situation from his daughter's point of view. If Ann was in love, then his chief concern was that she be happy – that she be allowed her happiness. What did his daughter have to do with that old business, after all? Nothing – no more than Fleur's son. It was sacrifice enough that he and Fleur—

Jon consoled himself with the thought that his mother must surely come round, when she saw how it was. She loved Ann as well as he did himself. Her fears were grounded in the past; she must see that the future was innocent of all save the faintest association with those old events. But her parting words disturbed him, though he tried not to think of them. Whenever he was troubled by anything it seemed his sight grew worse, and this had been the case since his mother left the room.

When Penny Roberts stood at the open door of Jon's study, after availing herself of hot towels and a hair-brush in Irene's bedroom, she was startled to see his hand reach out to her. He was sitting by the window with his back to the room, staring out through open curtains at the fearsome weather she had arrived in ten minutes before. He didn't turn towards her, but just reached out behind him in her direction. Penny was certain she hadn't made a sound on her way up the stairs, in case he was sleeping, and wondered at first if he wasn't simply stretching after a nap.

Then she heard him say her name.

"Penny—?"

"I was quiet as a mouse!" she said, coming up behind his chair. "How did you know it was me?"

Jon still didn't turn to her, but kept looking out.

"The snow-flakes," he said. "I can see every one of them quite clearly now. I knew it had to be you."

Penny summoned her courage, remembered the advice she had been given earlier in the day, and put her hand gently on his shoulder. She watched entranced as Jon took her hand in his poor burned own, and brought it round to his lips. In return, she bent and kissed the crown of his head.

Chapter Twelve

The Curtain Falls

April, and a cold spring ushering the end of war in Europe. *Any day now!* Everyone said it and, what was far more important, most believed it was finally the truth. *Not long now!*

Still Fleur stayed her hand. Jon was recovering; that was her chief concern for the moment. Only when she heard that he was permanently back at Green Hill, at the end of the month, did she decide to telephone. If his mother answered, so be it. She would have no hesitation, and some dark pleasure, in saying exactly what her purpose was.

'*Please tell him it concerns my son's wedding.*'

However bitter the news had first been to her, it would have hit that woman harder. Nemesis had claimed her own back. Fleur placed the call on the last day of April, the first really mild day of spring. She stood nervously by the telephone, and could hear her pulse tripping in the ear-piece as she waited for the ringing to be answered.

"Wansdon two-seven—"

Not his mother! A young woman – his daughter?

"May I speak to Mr Jon Forsyte?"

A hesitation down the line.

"I'm sorry, but he can't come to the telephone at the moment."

A bright voice, but there was a strained note in it. Perhaps Jon had relapsed—

"—I hope he's well?"

"Yes – thank you—"

That hesitation again, then the young woman went on.

"Could I take a message for him?"

Hardly. What was there to say? *'Tell your father it's about your marriage—'* Anyway, it was possible the voice didn't even belong to the girl. It seemed to Fleur that she might have heard it somewhere before.

"No. There's no message. Perhaps I'd better call again later—"

"I don't think so, you see—"

There was something wrong! What was it she was not being told?

"—I'm afraid his mother died during the night."

From where she had been standing by the telephone in her drawing-room at South Square, Fleur sat down abruptly on her sofa.

"Oh—" she managed to say, before she dropped the receiver back on its rest "—then I'm sorry to have disturbed you."

When she read Irene's death notice in the paper later that week, Fleur experienced again a version of her initial response to the news. A blossoming of wild hope like a flower in her heart, and yet at the centre of the flower – the indistinct threat of something dreadful lurking. It was like inhaling the scent of a rose while fearing to find a beetle inside. Death had beset the vital moments of her two previous near-victories. It was the death of his father which had driven Jon to give her up in the first place. Her own father's death had set the seal on her second surrender. Now came the death of the woman whom both their fathers had loved. Perhaps now the circle was complete. Was it too foolish to think—too futile to hope that it might drive Jon back, bring him full-circle in this sweep of fate? As Fleur saw it – and her father's blood in her directed her to think it was the only sensible way – all those who had ever stood between Jon and herself were dead. Their fathers, his wife, his mother – who was left to tell them no now?

Fleur possessed her soul for three more days. On the Monday after the date given in the newspaper for the funeral – at the church near Robin Hill, she noted with a sour smile – Fleur telephoned again to Sussex. This time she was sitting down. This time she was quite calm, and listened patiently to the ringing at the other end of the line. Fate had dealt her the upper hand. She would offer her condolences, her sympathy, her support; she would make Jon know she was sincere. After that she would ask how he wanted to proceed with the wedding arrangements. (Kit had not mentioned a date – she presumed the girl had one in mind.) Perhaps he wouldn't want to talk about it so soon – or perhaps it might seem altogether a relief. She would soon pick out his mood, and the details were unimportant either way. What mattered was that she should lose no time in re-establishing contact with him, now she had this perfect chance. She knew she had already regained his trust; on that basis she could play her hand to win. When they met in future it would be just the two of them, without a committee between. It was all she needed – to set the stage. The rest – she allowed no room for doubt – would follow.

At her ear a young man's voice gave the name of the house.

"Mr Jolyon Forsyte, please."

She had used his full name deliberately, to show deference to the circumstances. No false moves this time. It surprised her, therefore, to hear the same young voice answer.

"Speaking."

Of course – his son.

"Then I believe it's your father I want."

No deceit there! The young man replied:

"He isn't here."

"Can you tell me when he'll be back?"

"I'm afraid I can't. Perhaps my—"

Fleur had noticed another voice in the background, and now heard a rustle next to the telephone.

"Who is this, please?"

June! Fleur commandeered her charity voice.

"June? Is that you?"

"Fleur?"

"Yes – I rang to offer Jon my condolences. Isn't he at home?"

"No."

"Has he come up to Town? – if so, I—"

"No — that is, I doubt he has—"

There was something more agitated than usual about her ancient cousin's voice. Instinctively, Fleur exerted direct pressure on the point of weakness.

"Do you mean you don't know where he is?"

"Oh, my dear – it's such a worry!"

She had struck the nail on the head without trying. Fleur was gratified that her intuition was so sound. It was a sign she was right to act now. Getting June on the telephone was a stroke of good luck, too. Holly would never have broken ranks. She continued to press deftly.

"Whatever's wrong, June? You make it sound as if he's gone missing."

"No – well – not exactly, perhaps. It's just that he's gone off by himself, and taken the car."

Fleur didn't see what the fuss was about, until June went on.

"It's his eyes, you see. He can't always see very clearly nowadays – his sight comes and goes. He isn't supposed to drive—"

Before Fleur could contract any of June's alarm, her good sense cut in.

"Surely he wouldn't have set off anywhere if he wasn't sure about seeing properly?"

"Let's hope so, child."

"When did he leave?"

"About an hour ago."

"And he said nothing about where he intended to go?"

"Not to me. No." A compressed quality had come over June's voice in those last few words. "He told my nephew he wanted to be on his own somewhere for a while – to think."

Fleur was reassured. A fuss over nothing, and as likely as not generated by June. That little woman was the very spirit of disturbance.

"Well, I'm sure he'll come back when he has. Will you tell him I called?"

"Yes. Of course! Good-bye."

June's final tone was perfect – it was as if she had been accused of petty larceny. Fleur smiled as she replaced the receiver, and leaned back into the deep-sided bergère, crossing her legs and idly rocking one shoe on her toes. Good. That was an encouraging start, particularly getting June. What had she said the last time she was here?

'I was always on your side, you know.'

Fleur intended to see that she stayed in that self-proclaimed position now. She sighed a sigh that was as near to contented as was possible, given it came from one whose heart's desire was still

430

not within her grasp. But now — ah, now it felt within reach—

Her shoe fell to the Persian carpet as, suddenly, she sat upright in her chair.

'*On his own somewhere – to think—*'

She knew. She knew to a perfect certainty where Jon had driven. Resetting her shoe, she summoned the car to be brought round, and within five minutes was driving towards the place herself.

Jon had barely seen the road, as one or two travellers in the opposite direction had indicated with their horns, though his driving was on the whole no worse than some new recruit's to the Auxiliary might have been. He navigated by a sort of grim intuition, the long-suffering instinct of home. At the end of his journey, he parked at the top of the long rising lane, unlatched the gate, and walked up through the meadow – skirting the wood and coppice, already hazy with bluebells – and towards the church.

He tried to avoid seeing the house, and took a path which formerly would have served his purpose by offering a screen of poplars along one side. But he had not reckoned on the trees being down too. Unable to resist the urge to turn, he looked, and saw too much despite his eyes. Robin Hill was a ruin, only the broken hulk remaining of a house that was once his whole existence, which once contained everything he loved in the world. He hurried to the churchyard, and found again the little plot where his father and grandfather were buried, his mother now between them, the flowers on her grave, spilling on to both, still fresh and bright.

Standing alone before those three headstones, two weathered and moss-grown, one newly carved, where two days earlier he had stood with his son and daughter on either arm, Jon felt himself cast down into a bottomless well of grief and loneliness. He had lost the person who loved him best, and whom just then he doubted he had ever loved back as well as she deserved. At the burial he had felt less than he feared he might, just dull and empty, and was more concerned for his children than himself. Now the pain came to him, as real as any physical sensation of his recent past . . .

"How our sins pursue us," his mother had said simply, when he broached the subject of Ann's engagement that last week-end as they sat alone in the drawing-room.

431

"No!" he urged feelingly. "You never sinned – it wasn't your fault that—"

"Oh, but it was, Jon. It was my fault. I married without love, knowingly. That was a sin."

Jon shook his head, distressed by her words but more disturbed by her manner. She seemed to have become detached from her surroundings, remote from them and from him. As usual she had placed her embroidery-frame before her, but all evening, he noticed, she did not touch it. There was an unearthly calm about her as she went on.

"An unhappy marriage wrecks so many lives, not just those who live within its misery. I've borne much of the sorrow myself – as much as I could. Darling Jon, I'm so sorry that you had to be hurt by it — Can you ever forgive me?"

To Jon, whose pervasive conscience put him always in the guilty corner, the question seemed unanswerable. And the dignity and sanctity of her, so still and calm, sitting across from him by the fireside, seemed to put her beyond the reach of his assurances. At last she got up, and came to him; she kissed his forehead, and smoothed his hair the way she used to when he was a boy; then she went up to her room. It was his last conversation with her – if only he had known it was the last!

Standing in the churchyard now, Jon felt the tears heavy on his lashes. If there was a way forward, from this place in his life to a better, he didn't see it – and despaired of anyone leading him there.

When Fleur pulled up in the lane and saw there was already a car parked on the grass verge, she knew it was Jon's. Hunches — instinct — intuition! Her senses were alive with an inner certainty, a surety of touch that guided her actions and sharpened her wits. When she reached the coppice and saw it was empty, and the old log seat unoccupied, it gave her no more than a moment's pause. Briefly she considered going up to the wreck of the house to see if he was there, but thought better of it. This place – so significant to their lives, their love – this place of enchantment was where she would wait. It was impossible for him to regain his car without passing – and anyway – he would come! She sat down on the log, seeing the

details of everything around her in a perfect crystal clarity, sure —
sure as her life — that the hour was hers.

Before she heard any noise, Fleur knew he was behind her.
Rather the lack of sound, and the sense of a presence in it, told her
he was there. The copse fell silent suddenly, the birds were hushed,
even the breeze seemed to have died. She didn't turn instantly;
above all Jon mustn't think she had followed him. Instead, she
trailed her hand along the old log, as if in a moment of abstraction,
running her fingers over the striations on the bark. When in a few
moments she did turn from this attitude, her expression of perfect
surprise was not wholly feigned. She had last seen Jon bandaged
and unconscious from his injuries. She had expected when she saw
him again to see simply the old Jon restored. The sight of him now,
therefore, was a true shock. How different he seemed! Drawn and
damaged — hurt, she felt, in some inner place that might never fully
heal.

"I'm sorry," he said expressionlessly. "I'll leave you."

He was beginning to back away.

"No! Don't go," she said quickly, "—there's no need."

Jon kept his mark, neither retreating nor advancing.

"Sit by me if you'd like," she added, as though his liking to or
not was all the same to her.

The suggestion had just the right thrown-away touch. Like a
persuaded child, Jon came over and sat, elbows on knees, hands
hanging between, with his face set forward, staring out blankly into
the trees. The hush settled over them again.

"I shouldn't have been trespassing," he said, after a moment.

"You weren't," she answered. "You couldn't. History won't
allow it."

"*History!*"

Jon spoke the word in a sort of whispered hiss, and Fleur saw
him wring his hands, still staring out. A wood-pecker drummed
from somewhere nearby, a hollow sound. The beech wood rose
closely around them, empty as a church.

Knowing she must say something to keep him by her, and
that soon, Fleur said,

"I came here to be quiet – and to think—" and was rewarded
with a little flinch of surprise from Jon. As he turned to look at

433

her she continued, staring out as he had done, as if truly pensive, "—about Kit and Ann."

At her side he drew a deep breath.

"It's ironic, isn't it?" she said.

"Yes."

"Had you thought, Jon – they might have been—"

"Yes!"

Her next words, '—*brother and sister*', needed no saying. A quarter of a century before, her father had needed to say no more to his mother in the house that was now just a ghost behind them.

"We can't stand in their way, can we?"

"No."

Fleur thought this all the answer she was likely to get. She knew without looking that Jon wore his lion-cub expression, and that, she remembered, had always preceded silence. But this time he went on, and the words she heard set her trembling with fresh hope.

"No," he repeated, "this time there's no reason to."

"Your mother—?" she ventured faintly, bending up her face to him, respectful as one whispering a response in communion.

Jon nodded, and Fleur felt a shudder pass through him.

"She only ever wanted Ann's happiness."

"And yours."

"Mine?" Jon let out a sigh. "I've forgotten what happiness is, I think."

Here it was. The opening she had so long negotiated and contrived was here on a plate in front of her. For a second her nerve almost failed her. A wrong word now—

"You'll remember, Jon – if you give it time," she said, in a voice so light that it might have charmed the angels, "and if you let people help you."

She heard Jon give a little soft snort of contradiction. All the better if he saw no comfort ahead. She would be his comfort, his shoulder – arms, lips, everything – in his time of need. She needed only to say so; to make the offer; now.

"I could help – if you'd let me—"

To her heart's unbelieving delight he took her hand and held it gently between his. The breeze sighed for her, rustling the green

434

feathering of the trees above them. Each passing second marked an infinite moment of time. They might have been alone in the world.

"You've been a friend to me, Fleur," he said, and raised her hand to his lips.

Fleur watched, as if the process were happening before her in slow-motion, in every move exactly as she had hoped it would be, better than she had planned. She felt the kiss light on her finger-tips, and said,

"I could be more—"

She was watching him too closely, with too partial an eye, to see that he had not understood her meaning until then. The effect of her last words on him was startling; the transformation wrought by them in his features was total. He dropped her hand as if it had been a live wire, and started away from her, getting up from the log at a bound.

"No, Fleur!" he cried. "It can't start again – it mustn't!"

Fleur looked blankly around her, momentarily stunned.

"Mustn't?" she repeated after him in a daze, almost as though to herself. Then she stood, and raised her face up to him, her voice strengthening as she drew level.

"Mustn't? Who can say that to us anymore, Jon? We're the only ones it affects now. There's no one left to bid us no, if it's what we choose. Is there—?"

She saw something then, an extraneous thought passing across his eyes before he answered sadly,

"No. No one, I suppose. Just history."

"History?" This was impossible — they were going round in circles, almost literally as they moved about the copse — getting nowhere! "That old business between our parents, you mean?"

"Yes. It was there when my father died, and it's still there now my mother—" Jon brought a hand up to his face, and scraped it over his brow and hair.

"But it was always between them, not us," she urged. "And they've gone!"

Jon pulled at his hair and looked at her imploringly.

"Oh, Fleur, I know — but it's what made me give you up — what made me stop—"

"Stop loving me? I don't believe it. You can't look at me now and tell me that you ever did—?"

435

She forced him to hold her eyes, and at last he offered the least possible shake of his head.

"I knew you couldn't. Not here, not in this place. And besides—" she looked at him through suddenly lowered lashes, her head poised like a ballerina's, her chin tilted defiantly, "—you told me yourself that you hadn't."

She had played her best card. Had she judged it right? The rest of her hand would win or fold accordingly.

"I—?" he faltered. "But it was years ago—"

"No!" She cut him short and saw by his expression, by the confusion in his face, what she had long suspected. "They haven't told you, have they – about the night you had your accident?"

Jon had his back to one of the larches, as if he guessed a fresh onslaught on his conscience was coming.

Fleur sat down again on the log seat. As calmly as she could and faltering hardly at all, except towards the end, she related to him the circumstances of his return to his old home. When she had finished she knew she had gained considerable ground. Jon was plainly much affected. More than once he opened his mouth to speak, standing before her, but managed nothing. Fleur kept quiet. She would not help him this time.

At last he said,

"I wish I could repay you."

"Do you? If so, you can."

"But, Fleur, I owe you my life—"

"No, Jon. *You owe me mine.*"

There! She had said it. Four simple words that would stand between them forever — but as a bridge — or a barrier?

Jon hung his head.

"Yes," he said glumly. "I suppose I always have."

Hearing this she flew to him, and clung to his neck, pressing her cheek into his.

"Oh, Jon! Jon! It *will* work this time, it *will* — I'll make it, I promise—!"

Jon seized her hands and prised them from his neck, holding them down and away from him.

"No, Fleur!"

But she held on. They stood gripping each other's hands in a sort of struggle, like partners in a mad dance – she desperate for him not to break free, he desperate to keep his distance.

"Why?" she cried. "*Why?* Not that old business? You can't —"

"Yes — yes!" he answered fervidly. "Don't you see, it was always there – it's with us still – nothing's changed. My mother, your father—"

"But, Jon, it was fifty years ago — more. If he had been a murderer she couldn't have hated him so much—"

Fleur felt something in Jon slacken then, as if she had dealt him a blow and he was reeling. They held hands more loosely now, like a parody of simple lovers.

"What did he *do* that was so terrible?"

"Perhaps it would have been better if he had killed her," Jon said miserably. "Oh, Fleur, do you really not know? Tell me you do."

She shook her head and held on more tightly, moving her hands up to his shoulders so that he should not avoid her eyes. But it seemed he had no intention of trying. He was looking straight at her, deeply searching her face as he answered. She felt his hands under her own arms, holding her gently now, as though she might have need of his support.

"Fleur — he *raped* her — at the height of her love for the man who built this house. Just as she was going to leave him, your father raped her – as if she had been his slave—!"

Fleur screwed shut her eyes, and turned her head away from Jon's face in disbelief, clutching at the fabric of his jacket like a child hearing what it cannot bear to be told.

"No—!"

When she looked back at him, and saw his expression hadn't changed – except that he seemed more miserable, and sadder than ever – she knew it was the truth. The beetle in the rose! The ugliness of fact embedded in the beauty of truth. An ancient act of passion – reckless, violent, the one thing truly unforgivable – which had sewn its poisonous seeds before either of them was born. It was the wicked detail she had never been told. Wicked — and so unfair!

But still Fleur stood before him, holding on to his arms, as if she believed even yet that she might shake his conviction from him. Even now it was not in her to let go. Under the cloth of his

437

jacket his muscles slackened again in her grip. He dropped his arms, and she let them go. As her last, desperate point of contact she held his eyes, willing him to say something more, anything. At last he spoke, and she saw come into his gaze an expression so tender, full of such pain as she knew he could never inflict – not on her, not Jon – that for one deluded instant she believed there was hope still.

"Darling Fleur—" he began, but then faltered pitiably.

She saw a smile, so sweet, so tender, spread through his features, and she caught her breath, and held it as if defying her heart to beat. She looked at him through the tears standing in her eyes, and saw they were matched in his. When at last he spoke again there was a dreadful finality in his voice.

"—It's over. Really. You must believe me. It's all over."

Fleur ran down to the empty cars, stopping first at Jon's, not seeing it wasn't her own until she had opened the door. Dimly perceiving her mistake she pushed the door to with a dry sob, but had not the strength to shut it, and stumbled to the next vehicle. She got into her car, and sat leaning forward over the driving wheel, with a numb feeling in her limbs — and no sensation elsewhere save a dead weight of realisation in her chest. *It was over.* She was beaten in the very hour she felt closest to victory; from this defeat she knew there could be no rally. The hope by which she had eked out her inward living for so long was shrivelled to nothing inside her. After the performance of her life, the curtain had fallen. Lights out. No applause. Mechanically she started the engine, but still sat there — numbed beyond all sensation, pained beyond all feeling. A man on a bicycle passed and tipped his hat. Fleur did not see him. She saw nothing whatever outwardly, but only inwardly instead – from a focus of years – that it had *never* been possible for her to have Jon. That one possessive act of her father's had seen to it. It was too bitter to bear — but true. From the moment they met — in that little gallery belonging to June — this fatality was upon them — their stars were already crossed.

At last she released the brake, and drove wretchedly on. How she guided the car back to London, she hardly knew. Life seemed finally to have gone out.

Shut in the hall at South Square, Fleur stood with her forehead and palms against the cold painted surface of the door, grateful for a half second of any feeling outside herself. Gaugin's women at her back still reached languidly for their island fruit, the luscious apples she knew at last she would never eat.

A light noise behind her — she turned and saw Michael standing in the doorway of the drawing-room. There was something stricken in his expression — stricken yet so painfully sympathetic, as if in some way he knew her misery and was trying to reach her in it.

"Oh, my darling," he said, "you know it's over, don't you?"

Michael came towards her, for she found she could not move, and took her in his arms as if she had been an injured child.

"My poor darling — it's all over!"

A low moan escaped her and she was sobbing suddenly in his arms. With her chin cradled on his shoulder and his face buried in her hair, Fleur realised then her husband's meaning.

—It was the war!

Chapter Thirteen

Envoi

On the morning of the next day, disdaining a light drizzle and supported between the maid Miller's arm and her swan-headed cane, Winifred Dartie had traversed the length of Mayfair, from her house in Green Street all the way through the shored and pitted by-roads of that region to Piccadilly. On her way down she had been offered (and had refused) a nose on elastic, a policeman's hat, several flags, and a whistle that extended a red feather when you blew into it. Miller had even been kissed. These vicissitudes notwithstanding, they were now ensconced safely on Lettie MacAnder's doorstep at the bottom of Berkeley Street, from which vantage it was possible to see the crowd without having to be part of it. Lettie, being still in the country, would never know, and would be green besides to have missed it.

What a crowd! It was as if the whole world had turned out to celebrate, swarming from every street, moving and writhing in massed internal rhythm. Not a car or 'bus in sight, either; just this thronging mass of faces, hatless, open-mouthed, with teeth crooked or often missing, laughing and singing and going merrily nowhere.

"Shouldn't we be thinking of getting back, ma'am?" asked Miller, after five minutes. "It's a terrible crush, and your foot—"

"My foot – nonsense! I wouldn't miss seeing this for a king's ransom – nor should you. And we've an excellent position here."

So saying, she planted herself squarely in front of the maid, who was shorter than her by several inches. Below, and coming from a few feet away on the pavement, Winifred made out a shrill voice, which seemed out of place yet quite familiar, saying sharply to a reveller:

440

"Will you kindly *not* push!"

Looking down, Winifred could see a dreadful hat perched on a bundle of faintly orange hair.

"Good heavens – June? Is that you, dear?"

It was she. From her gallery off Cork Street, where with the help of her niece she had lately set up a little flat for herself on the top floor, June had made her way round by a different set of side streets, heading for the open space of the park, until the force of the crowd had jostled her down towards Piccadilly. Hearing her name she looked up.

"Winifred!"

June gained a foothold on Lettie MacAnder's steps and ascended to two below her cousin.

"Well," she said, looking up bluntly, "I never expected to see you again."

"Neither did I," Winifred answered truthfully and, after searching vainly for pleasantries, fell silent again. They watched the seething crowd from their separate steps for a while, until June said:

"Aren't people marvellous? All these years of hardship and misery – and just look at them now."

Winifred – who had just then been thinking that the war couldn't have been all that terrible for them to have so much energy left to celebrate with – decided it was simpler to agree.

"It's quite a sight, I must say."

By inference and with a look down the side of her nose to June she added:

"How are you keeping these days?"

"Very well, thank you. You?"

"Oh, yes."

There was another pause, into which the noise of the mob surged in a ragged chorus of 'When the Lights Go on Again', and then ebbed away and flowed on.

"I heard about—" Winifred began, just as June thought to say—

"Did you hear—?"

Both stopped short of saying their next word, 'Irene'. Winifred went on.

"I suppose she was eighty."

"Eighty-one."

"Um."

Being closer to eighty-seven herself, Winifred didn't know if this should be a consolation or not. She stole another sidelong look at her cousin. She must be seventy-five, if she was a day! But since the subject of family had been broached, Winifred ventured another item.

"You know about Fleur's son and that girl?"

"My niece, you mean – yes."

"I imagine she's a nice enough young—"

"She is!"

"Well, I hope they'll be happy. That old business – it's dead and buried now."

Winifred caught a fierce look from the corner of June's eye and realised her metaphor was untimely. They watched the crowd again for some moments; then June said suddenly that she must be going.

"As you wish, dear," Winifred replied, not sorry to see her go, though not seeing where even one as bustling and impatient as June could get *to* on such a day.

June stepped down onto the pavement, and within a few paces was lost in the crowd, hat and all. Winifred remained for some minutes staring after her cousin, or after her direction at least, wondering if what she had last said to her was really true. It had been such a coil, that old business; with Irene always at the heart of it, at the very centre of the family feud. And dimly aware of some Classical reference, about two brothers at war over the wife of one of them, Winifred stopped her mental peregrinations there, lest she recall too much about that old unpleasantness. Perhaps it *was* dead and buried now — perhaps—! And those two young people – Fleur's son and Jon's daughter – could get on with their lives. Still — Fleur's son and Jon's daughter, after all! Imagine what the Old Forsytes would have said about that!

And quite suddenly Winifred perceived, and for the very first time, a disturbing fact about herself and her cousin who had just left. She and June — it was they who were the Old Forsytes now!

When, some ten days earlier, her elder aunt had pronounced her intention of quitting her temporary base at Wansdon and setting herself up with a flat above her gallery in London, Ann had insisted

442

she be allowed to help. It is likely, since she was a kind-hearted girl, that she would have volunteered in any case. Aunt June was getting frail, though she would never admit to it, and was always taking on new schemes that threatened to be too much for her. But this was not any case, and Ann's motive for once was not altruism. London, which she hardly knew and didn't particularly like, meant only Kit, whom she loved. They had agreed to meet in Piccadilly Circus, under the Eros, at twelve noon on the day the war ended. She must be there!

So Ann went up to London with June, but had been there only a day when her grandmother died. For the following few days she gave up hope of ever seeing Kit again; it seemed not possible that life could go on as before. When, on the Monday after the funeral, the announcement had come over the radio-set at Green Hill – saying the war would be officially over the next day, Tuesday the 8th of May – it seemed to Ann that her chance of meeting up with Kit was over for good too. She had been listening with her aunt as her father returned from his drive; oblivious as ever, June instantly declared she wanted to go back to London. But her father looked so drawn when he came back, as if he had been through something terrible on his journey, that Ann wondered if she had the heart to say she was leaving again with June for a few more days. But her heart was what required her to go. Holly – on one of her supply runs – had driven the two of them down late on Monday afternoon.

After an uneasy night on an old divan in Cork Street, Ann spent the morning helping her aunt again, but full of a private agitation she couldn't confide, and worrying how she might contrive to slip away.

By half past eleven June's curiosity about the goings on outside got the better of her, and she suggested they go and watch the celebrations now that the drizzle was beginning to clear. Ann paltered, seeing her chance but having no excuse ready. She claimed a headache, and said she would rather go out later, when the weather might be brighter. This scheme nearly back-fired completely when June, alert to the possibility of a lame duck on her premises, offered to stay herself until such time as that might be. The headache had to be scaled down to only a slight one, and then converted sideways into not much more than a preference for spending a little time by herself, before June could be persuaded to leave. From the front window of

443

the flat, Ann watched her go – heading west in the direction of the park – and waited a full minute longer before she snatched up her raincoat and left in another direction – south, towards Piccadilly.

The people! It seemed impossible that the streets could hold so many without splitting at the seams or caving in underfoot. Swept along by the frivolous tide which met her on the pavement, Ann took an unintentional turn into Vigo Street and was momentarily lost when she came out on the broad curve of Regent Street. Then she remembered being taken to see the lights there one Christmas before the war. She took her bearings, turned towards the Eros — and found it wasn't there.

Craning over the shoulders in front of her she saw only a mound of sandbags, fifty yards away and covered with dozens and dozens of people. How would she ever find Kit in all those faces? Her heart sank, and its sinking must have had repercussions in her face, for she was stopped by a brace of young soldiers pressing in the opposite direction.

"You lost, lovey?" said one.

"You look lost," said the other.

She shook her head, but their attention was not so easily dismissed. When she tried to push past they barred her way, smiling, leering a little too, turning it into part of the great game of communality that was going on all round. But Ann wanted no part of it; she only wanted Kit. Ahead of her she saw a clock hanging outside a shop. It was past twelve already – what if Kit thought she wasn't coming? What if he didn't wait—!

"Please," she insisted. "I can't see—"

"Can't see, lovey? That won't do."

"Why didn't you say?"

And before she knew what was happening, let alone how to prevent it, she was hoicked between them onto their shoulders. Ann tried to get down but the squaddies held her firmly and – what was infinitely worse – began to carry her back the way she had just struggled to come.

"No — please!"

"Hey there, you louts!" cried a commanding voice suddenly from above her head. "Put her down – she's my girl!"

The soldiers, intuitively knowing it was they who were being

444

addressed among the merry thousands, turned in tandem towards the nearest lamp-post. Ann looked up, and saw Kit standing half-way up its stem. He might have landed that second.

"Oh, Kit—!"

"Bring her here, you men, and look sharp about it!"

After nearly six years of it, rank was second nature in the mob and carried even this day. The two soldiers simply passed Ann up to Kit, calling him 'Wing-Co' with a laugh and moving on.

Ann didn't know how she was managing to defy gravity – perched on that lamp-post, somehow on Kit's knee, and with his arm so tightly round her waist she could barely breathe – but she didn't care either. It was the nearest thing to flying, hanging up there, weightless, above the crowd. Kit was squeezing her closer to him, shouting in her ear over the noise.

"—We didn't make it to the Eros – do you mind?"

"No!"

"—And it'll take me a couple of months to get de-mobbed – before we can get married – is that too long to wait?"

"No!"

"—You happy?"

"Yes!"

"—Still love me?"

"Yes—!" And she kissed him in mid-air.

A MONT INTERLUDE
Summer's End

'—This young beauty, round and sound
As a mountain apple, youth and truth
With loves and doves, at all events
With money in the Three per Cents—'

Robert Browning

Summer's End

"Bye-bye, Katkin!"

Astrid's clear blue eyes were very nearly tearful, and a little pout almost overcame her lower lip before she ran on in her mile-a-minute way—

"Don't do anything I wouldn't do; or if you do, be sure and write me a nice long letter about it, telling *all*. Best hug!"

Kat hugged, and was hugged ferociously back. For a moment their two lengths of hair mingled over each other, clashing in a way that only the most committed friendship could allow; endless waves of dark auburn falling against straight 'carrot' with just a flick of a curl at the ends.

"Got your trunk all right, Miss Bigby?"

The porter poked his head out of the lodge and looked towards the two young women, as they stood each in the other's arms on the broad pavement outside the college main gate.

"Yes, thanks, Cornish – my brother picked it up this morning."

The porter hung in the open door of the small arched gateway a second longer than he might have, then touched a finger to the top of his brow, where rumour said there had once been a forelock.

"Right-y-ho, Miss. My regards to his young lordship."

He withdrew to his station inside the lodge. Astrid tapped her own forehead.

"—Oh, crikey; now that's what I call a really subtle reminder."

She dashed after the retreating porter, only pausing to find the zip-fastener on her clutch-bag. Half a minute later she was back outside.

"A little crawling to the staff never goes amiss – as my sainted grandmother would say. My last ten bob note, too. There goes the cost-of-living index."

"I suppose he did get Giles out of that scrape in Eights' week."

"So he did. I'll tell Giles it cost me a quid, and demand it back."

She slipped her hand through Kat's arm and nuzzled her cheek. Their two manes clashed again, like a pair of promising young colts out in the late afternoon sun. Standing shoulder to shoulder, as they looked north up the Woodstock Road, the young women were oblivious to how easily they attracted the casual glances of passers-by.

They presented an oddly integrated, and yet strangely unmatched pair. Kat was half a hand the taller, though it was Astrid who seemed the longer in the neck. (*Goitrey*, her grandmother Em had pronounced after meeting her.) Whereas Kat's nose was neat and straight like her mother's, Astrid's was perhaps a little too turned up at its tip for the democratic taste. Astrid's eyes were a clear, very demanding blue, and she was given to flashing them at every apostrophe; her mouth was thin, daintily formed, very English. Kat's eyes were ice-green, fringed with dark lashes, the expression in them questioning, and a little mysterious. Her mouth, not at all English, was a feature she would have changed if she could; full, rather crumpled and downturned, giving her a troubled expression in repose. She had been told there was a Rossetti she resembled. Both young women were pale-complexioned, a feature rather over-emphasised by the drama of their hair, but only on Kat did it suggest an inner delicacy. Finally, and to Astrid's lasting concern, Kat was utterly without freckles.

Undoubtedly, both young women had 'style', as a bloodstock expert would have meant the word, meaning good bones set under sleek flesh. This was particularly in evidence whenever the breeze pressed their full summer skirts against outlines of two sets of thorough-bred legs. Casual glances became momentarily less so.

They were waiting for Astrid's brother to circle round and bring about their final parting for the long vacation. Another two minutes went by and then Giles appeared, passing the Infirmary. He waved over the windscreen of his two-seater, and applied its historic horn as he saw them.

"Well, my duck," Astrid said with a sigh, as the car hove

450

to, "that was our last good term. We had the best time, didn't we? All play and absolutely no work. It'll be quite the other way around next Michaelmas."

"Hmm, yes. Depressin' – as *my* sainted grandmother would say."

Giles drove past them, still tooting, and reversed smartly into the vehicle entrance. He raised his long form from the low-set driver's seat in an athletic movement reminiscent of his recent triumph at the head of the river, and saluted extravagantly. The girls walked over to him, Astrid saying,

"I believe you've had the misfortune of meeting my brother, the Seventh Congenital Idiot of Pennycruik?"

Giles possessed milder versions of the family eyes and hair demonstrated by his sister; he also owned radically fewer freckles. He was four years older than Astrid, but only a year ahead in his studies – Greats, at Trinity – because of the War. Also because of the war, which had orphaned them in the bombing of the Café de Paris, brother and sister were bonded closer than twins and, as a natural consequence, were never heard to exchange a kind word.

"Hi there, Montie!" Giles delivered the best of his smile to Kat, then turned the withered remains on his sister. "Hello, sprog – got all your junk?"

"No, you have, unless you've lost my valuables since lunch."

Astrid's voice carried that tart edge of authority often allocated to female siblings.

In a truly awful impersonation of an American film star who had done him no harm and deserved better, Giles replied: "I'm your valuables, kiddo. Don't you forget it."

Astrid pulled a face as he leaned over to open the door for her.

"Sadly true," she replied, slipping down next to him. "An ill-favoured thing, but mine own."

Kat shut the car door. From the passenger seat Astrid said:

"Say you'll come and visit us *en Écosse*? We'll be there the absolute whole time, just us and the awful 'Uncs'. I'll only curl up with boredom if you don't."

"I'll try. We're in France for a while, I think."

"Crikey – *ready* money."

Giles was getting into gear. Astrid indicated the need for one last hug, and Kat bent down quickly.

451

"O.K., you two, break it up. Sure we can't give you a lift, Montie? Plenty of room in the dicky."

Kat declined the offer and straightened up.

"Thanks, anyway. My father's due in half an hour."

"O.K.," said Giles again, a little disappointed. "'Always willingly!'"

The girls looked at each other, and swallowed on lumps of rising emotion. They had been inseparable since Freshers', a two year span which seemed already a whole lifetime. With every successive term it became a little harder to leave, a little more painful to break that special bond. Only Giles' presence stemmed the tears.

"Ring me up anyway, will you? Promise?"

"Promise," Kat said.

"And please don't be too brilliant in your vac. essay. What was it again – '*Gloom in Hamlet*'?"

"'*Darkness and Light in Othello*' – cf. Wilson Knight."

"There, you see – you're being brilliant already— 'bye!"

Giles pulled away in a merciless burst of exhaust. Astrid blew a kiss, and Kat found herself waving to a boot and a spare wheel that were suddenly far off in the line of traffic.

Turning into the arch of the main gate, Kat walked back through East quad, where the bedding plants – mostly red and white geraniums, punctuated with clumps of Oxford blue lobelia – seemed now to wear a tired look. Her bags were all packed and waiting, her library books were all returned; there was nothing at all left to do but find a sunny spot in the main quad where she could while away her blessèd last half hour.

She passed by the window of the room she had chosen for her final year. From October she would have this view, east facing towards the lodge, as she worked at her desk. Astrid was right, of course. It would have to be pretty well all work, and no real play right through to Trinity, when they would sit Schools. And suddenly Kat smiled as she recalled Astrid declaring she would buy black lace foundations to wear under her subfusc— '*For luck!*'

As she passed under the second of the three arches which led to the main quad, Kat heard her name called. It was Cornish again, who came up behind waving a piece of paper, Chamberlain-like.

"Telephone message for you, Miss Mont. Just came through."
He passed it to her, tipping his theoretical forelock once more and
turning back.

It was from her father, written out by the porter as a single
construction in pencil. '*Two hour delay forgive tardy parent sups
on rout affectionate aged P.*'

So. Her last half hour was to be two and a half, perhaps
more. Too long just to sit, and Astrid had been the last and best
of her friends to leave. Besides which, Kat knew she possessed no
real heart to talk to anyone else – she was too full of goodbyes,
too aware that another year of her short tenure on this venerable
yet endearing place, which had so eaten its way into her heart and
mind, had passed away. *And summer's lease . . .*

What to do? Her room, denuded of all her things, was no
longer a refuge, and Astrid's stood empty next door. If she stayed
in college she ran the risk of being dragged into conversation with
any of the strays and stragglers who were staying up.

She determined to ride. Returning to her room, in Maitland, she
took her purse, her fountain pen and a slim volume bound in calf.
She might finish her diary by the river. Deciding against her hat, she
locked her door, retraced her steps on the faded salmon-red carpet
along the empty corridor and back down two flights of stairs. Once
outside she found her own bicycle among the serried rows standing
behind House, and left college by the vehicle entrance.

Bliss! There was a particular quality about Oxford, amongst the
very many otherwise documented, that was apparent only from the
vantage point of a sit-up-and-beg bicycle saddle.

The Cotswold stone frontages of St. Giles breezed by, biscuit-
coloured in the slanting sun. Past the Martyrs' Memorial – the
Muggers' Memugger, as her Great Aunt Winifred had called it on
her last visit, referring to some bygone jargon – Kat turned into the
Broad. One hand for modesty's sake on her skirt as she took the
corner, and with the sun at her back, she began pedalling on her
own long shadow towards the Sheldonian. There she would kneel in
a year or so – given a deal of assiduous application and a following
wind – a fully-fledged B.A. Hons. in a rabbit-trimmed hood. Then
she would know all that there was to be knowed!

The elongated faces of the Cæsars leered at her from their

pillars as she rode by. Clearly they disdained her frivolity; in life they might have admired her hair, flying out in the breeze, a bright auburn flag. She cornered again at the Bod., rode down Catte Street, dismounted to cross the High, then pedalled on down Magpie Lane.

At Merton Street she stopped on a whim, leaned her bicycle against a wall, and looked in at the gate of Corpus Christi. The stone pelican in the tiny front quad was quite alone in a miniature wilderness, though Kat could hear voices and a gramophone coming from a window above. At the mouth of the third staircase an undergraduate appeared, his gown draped over one shoulder and a knapsack slung on the other. She watched him hurry across the quadrangle, and disappear under an archway. Knox-Gordon, T.J.H., she thought; or Baguley, D., perhaps. Certainly not Ferrar, The Hon. R., since she had come to have reason to recognise him, and this fellow was quite unknown to her. Those were the names she had once idly noted on her way up to the top of that third staircase. Strange that she should remember these details equally among others far more relevant to that place which had been the setting for the first conundrum of the term . . .

Three days before the beginning of that Trinity term, in what was unofficially referred to as *Noughth* week, Kat had entered that staircase in Corpus, in response to a note she found in her pigeon-hole.

In a spiky, rushed hand, was written,

> '*Miss Mont,*
>
> '*I should like to see you in my rooms at C.C.C. tomorrow at 11 a.m., to discuss the coming term's work, and to introduce myself as,*
>
> '*Your servant ever,*
> '*Boyd*'

The single syllable was scratched into the paper, and underlined with a deep score from the nib.

Boyd. A.L., she recalled; Ph.D. (*Somewhere*); other letters (*Elsewhere*); Professor. Newly appointed lecturer and tutor in seventeenth century poetry; visiting on sabbatical from an American university, also with a monosyllabic name, which she did not recall. Smith, Brown, Jones – some such. The one word in advance circulation about him during Hilary had been *good*; but invariably it was coupled with a second – *difficult*. Forewarned, Kat had taken the precaution over the Easter vacation of looking up a monograph of his, the only piece she could find published in England, for exactly her present purpose.

'*Donne's Sensual Landscape*'. It had been altogether an eye-opener. She was prepared to describe it as 'frank and illuminating', if she needed a gambit in the first meeting. Then, after the esteemed visiting professor had dismissed her assessment with the politely veiled sneer she had come generally to expect from dons at the men's colleges, she would offer her own theory on the poet's '*new-found land*'. At twenty, Fleur's daughter was learning how to combat the instinctive prejudice stirred up in the brains and other vitals of the opposite sex, by the presence of an unequivocally first-class mind behind an indisputably award-winning face.

Passing *BAGULEY* and *KNOX-GORDON* and *FERRAR*, Kat reached the top landing. There two doors were cramped on either side of a narrow leaded window, deep-set into the cold stone wall; cool spring sunshine fell through it striking the boards at a lowish angle. The first door, at the very mouth of the stairs on the right, stood ajar. Upon her cursory inspection it proved to be an unlighted cubicle with a stained hand-basin and a rag of a roller towel above. She could dimly see where an inner door, also ajar, was marked with the tell-tale initials of the water closet. A slowly filling cistern rumbled in the darkness beyond. So much for sanitation. The other door, on the left of the little landing, must be the one she sought, unless she had mistaken the staircase.

The 'oak' to this second door hung wide open towards her, half blocking the thin light from the window. Kat pushed it to, so that she could read the name on the wall. Over a patch of blue paint slightly brighter and cleaner than the watered-down duck-egg of the rest of the staircase – indicative of how recently the present occupant had taken tenure there – a college craftsman had stencilled

455

PROFESSOR A. L. BOYD. Now that she had nearly closed the oak she could see a card set in the little brass slot in the green baize. The same fast, angular hand had written simply _BOYD_ underlined. The same nib had broken through the surface of the card.

A brief, shelf-lined passage led to the inner door. It too was open, though not sufficiently to let her see any occupant within. Kat knocked, with all the confidence of a second-year scholar who had already weathered several tutors, and was fully prepared to weather several more; then she waited. There was no reply. She knocked again. Still there was no murmur from within. Consulting her wrist she confirmed what she already knew. She was on time, and the professor looked to be late.

She heard footsteps on the stair and looked down into the well, expecting the American academic. A young male, plainly an undergraduate, was approaching at speed. Baguley, she wondered? He seemed unsurprised to see her on the landing. In fact he gave her hardly a second look before he ducked into the little cubicle and closed the door behind himself. She heard the inward door opening, and then dimly, a few seconds later, the noise that might naturally be expected to follow.

Disliking to wait for the flush, Kat entered the professor's dark-panelled set.

Her first thought was that she had never seen so many books not on shelves. They spilled from torn-open crates, as if essential volumes had been required from each one, and every time had to be wrested from the very bottom of the case. Opened boxes stood precipitously upon others still sealed. Some were not even proper packing cases, she noted, but corrugated cardboard boxes, with assorted unheard-of brand-names printed on their sides. Three boxes which formed a pile by the desk had evidently all once contained the same commodity – _Old Adam Fine Kentucky Bourbon_. This item was the only name she recognised, being the American whisky Colonel Wilmot had favoured during the war. She remembered the great stir it had caused when he brought a case of it to South Square, saying he had had a supply shipped over. When her father worried that the gift shouldn't deplete a limited stock, and asked how many cases he had brought with him, Colonel Wilmot replied '_enough for the duration_' and both her parents had laughed. When she was

456

told this story at the time, by Timms, she herself had not quite seen the joke.

For a fanciful moment, Kat allowed herself to wonder whether the printed name and helpful line drawings of bottles on each of those three boxes didn't actually signify their present contents, set as they were, she now clearly saw, quite separately to one side. It wasn't an unlikely indulgence, after all, for a man who could summon ten thousand words on the sensuality of Donne's *terra nova*. '*Malt doth more than Milton can—*', she remembered from somewhere. She sat down in a chair before the desk, where more books and papers were scattered, and settled down to clear her mind of all fancies save those of the metaphysical poets, for the few minutes she had prior to her tutor's arrival.

One by one the few minutes became many – twenty-five when she checked her wrist for the third time, and Kat began to wonder whether she had the wrong day, or time. She checked in her bag, and found the note. She was right on both counts. The professor, apparently, was not. There was no alternative but to continue to wait.

At twenty minutes before the end of the hour, Kat, who had been rather lulled by the silence of her vigil, became suddenly aware of a commotion at the foot of the staircase. At first her ears couldn't separate the layers of sound. Then, discerning that like ancient Gaul the noise was divided into three parts, she began instantly to analyse it. The first sound seemed to be the stumbling, clattering fall of a large person, with steel tips to his shoe-leather and perhaps wearing a great-coat, as something that flapped like a blanket had muffled the suddenness of his prostration. The second sound was unmistakable, however incongruous, and could only be the noise made by apples and oranges spilling from a bag and tumbling over the flagstones. Kat's instant mental vision – no doubt due in large part to the influence of the metaphysicals – was of an alchemist experimenting inexpertly with the trick of levitation, a conceit not entirely dispelled by the identification of the third sound. It was a loud oath, offered in tones which suggested familiarity with such, and with the implacability of the Gods imprecated thereby. It was all faintly ridiculous.

By the time these understandings had settled, the steel-tipped soles were already beating their advance, two-at-a-time, up to the top of the stairs. Kat's last fancy was that they sounded like seven-league boots.

Next she was aware of the sunlight dimming on the little landing. Kat turned her face expectantly, ready to explain her unauthorised entry, just as a figure emerged from the shadow of the short tunnel. She saw him silhouetted against pale sunlight, as it claimed the space between the doorframe and his outline and gave him the illusion of an aura.

"Ah," he said, in a voice that was deep and slightly hoarse. He cleared his throat. "Miss Mont, I presume. You are early."

"No—" Kat began, her explanation ready and marshalled, but he rode over her answer, by saying simply,

"Then I must be late."

He looked at her briefly, and Kat found she was unable to characterise the expression in his long, rather spare features. It seemed candid enough as he stood there, on the threshold, with that hint of an aureole around him, yet she could not be sure. There was a mocking glint, she thought, in his pale eyes. There seemed a challenge in them.

"'Tell him that wastes his time and me'—", he said, speaking the words clearly and precisely in his incongruous accent, then stepped into the room.

It was only then that Kat saw how immensely tall he was. He ducked automatically as he entered, evidently through long habit, though his head cleared the lintel with inches to spare. The panelled room, which previously possessed quite adequate proportions, seemed to shrink as he came in.

He began to move about the room, loose-jointedly on long strides, and was suddenly preoccupied with his own actions. Kat's guesswork about his clothing and purchases was uncannily accurate. Despite the month, he wore around his shoulders what looked to her like a Russian cavalry coat, made of dark grey wool cloth. It was lined with a dangerous-looking, dappled grey pelt that extended to the collar, which he wore turned up, so that it framed his head. Since his own hair was swept directly back from his forehead to his neck, and was also grey – that grizzled-worsted mixture some men have, which seems made up equally of separate white and black strands

458

– it was difficult immediately to distinguish where the two pelts met. *'Perhaps there is no difference,'* Kat heard herself think.

Under one arm he carried a torn brown-paper bag filled with oranges. He dropped his load on to the end of his desk, and began to shrug off his coat. He tossed the garment across a worn chesterfield under the window where it sprawled, lining outwards, like a half-tamed wolf.

Kat could think of nothing to say. And oddly, it seemed that he required her to say nothing. She felt it had ceased to matter whether she was in the room or not.

At last he sat down behind his desk. He leaned over the scattered papers and propped his head on a large, long-fingered hand.

"So, Miss Mont—" he said, casually taking up a stray pencil and trailing it across a notebook while he looked at her, "it appears I am required to tutor you in seventeenth-century verse this term?"

Kat nodded with a quick tilt of her chin. Her hair moved against her neck with the gesture, and she saw his eyes slip sideways.

Then he gave her that challenging look again, from far back behind his pale eyes. A faint smile accompanied it. He continued to move the pencil absently.

"You make me feel a fraud," was the next thing he said.

If this was his brand of donnish disdain, it was altogether different to what she had expected. It came without any of the usual cues.

He went on without changing his expression.

"I feel I ought to be offering you the pre-Raphaelites — your hair."

"Oh, that."

"Yes, that."

"It's been suggested before."

"I should have liked to be the first to suggest it to you."

Tossing the pencil aside, he leaned back in his seat and looked up at the ceiling for some moments. Again Kat felt him become preoccupied within himself. Then he looked at her again; the mocking light had drained away.

"Where shall we begin?"

Kat took this for rhetorical until he flexed his pointed eyebrows at her.

"With Milton?" she suggested. It was the safest thing to say.

459

"A cautious choice. The architect of verse — but what did he build? Perhaps you would like to tell me next week?"

Kat nodded again, and again she saw his eyes slip fleetingly to her hair.

He pushed himself up from his desk and crossed the room. She wondered if this was her cue to go; it was difficult to tell, and so she watched him warily, from under her lashes. There was an unlikely lubrication to his movements, despite the height and breadth of his frame. He managed to appear languid, casual, and yet from the first she had detected an urgency in him. It was an unsettling combination, and Kat wondered frankly if she could stand it for a term.

His clothes were the same jarring mixture. He wore a houndstooth-check Norfolk jacket with those obligatory leather patches at the elbow. Underneath was a thin sweater of a port-wine shade and under that a blue shirt indifferently ironed. A checkered bow-tie finished the outfit above, and there were green corduroy trousers and vast brown brogues below. It seemed impossible he had come by the *ensemble* accidentally, but equally impossible that anyone should have compiled it deliberately.

He opened a cupboard set into one of the long unladen shelves. Kat caught the glint of sunlight on glass and before she could properly decline he began to pour sherry into two tumblers from a half-full bottle. As he poured, a college clock somewhere, ahead of the many, began to chime the quarter before noon. There was a mirror on the back wall of the drinks cupboard, and through it she saw him cast a sidelong glance at her. Through his expression came her first understanding that she must look concerned. That crumpled mouth of hers was always speaking for her!

"Don't worry, Miss Mont," he said quietly. "The sun will be over the yard-arm by now – somewhere in the world."

He handed her a glass of unusually pale sherry. As pale as his eyes, she thought, and surprised herself.

"Not 'the clear spirit', alas," he said, and raised his glass solemnly, as if in apology.

He stood by the chesterfield at the window. Looking out, presumably over the stone pelican below, he began slowly, melancholically, but rather beautifully to recite:

> " 'Fame is the spur that the clear spirit doth raise
> (That last infirmity of noble mind)
> To scorn delights, and live laborious days—' "

He stopped to drain his glass. Without turning back to Kat he added:

"In any event, you'll be at my lecture on Monday, won't you?"

A little later, as she got up to go, she noticed the cover of the notebook on his desk. Looking at it upside-down, she saw there was a pencil sketch on it; the face of a young woman, with a full mouth, and pre-Raphaelite hair.

He never gave the lecture. In the small hours of the morning of the intervening Sunday, Kat had heard an ambulance bell ringing urgently in the forecourt of the Radcliffe Infirmary. It was not in any way an unusual sound, the hospital was next door to her college; but for some reason she had awakened at it, then passed back into sleep.

On the door of the lecture theatre the following morning was a notice which told of the suspension of the series entitled '**The Great Redemption/The Great Argument** – *An Interpretation of Paradise Lost*.'

> '*It is with regret that the departure from the University of Professor A.L. Boyd is announced, owing to the sudden onset of ill-health . . .*'

. . . Knox-Gordon reappeared and passed out of the gate, interrupting her reverie. Kat regained her bicycle and continued south, taking the dusty track by the side of Merton which led towards Christ Church meadow, and the river.

By the river Kat felt a growing sadness steal over her. All around her the term was near to winding down for good, and the best of the summer slipping away, its energy dissipated by those hundreds of departures in every college. What remained was the heel end of things, thin and worn down. Her diary remained closed – it was too real to record.

Fenced off in the meadow, cows munched on burdock leaves and flicked resignedly with their tails at tired flies. There were one or two horses in with the cows, looking under-exercised. The riverbank was overgrown with willow herb and tall nettles, the water greenish and low. A batch of ducks gathered at the bank when they saw her; Kat wished she had thought to bring a bun to feed to them. She watched them scatter in the wash of an overladen punt, as a party of House-men poled their way back to the boat-yard at Folly Bridge from a last debauched picnic after Schools.

Kat remembered how Astrid and she cheered themselves almost senseless that afternoon when the Trinity boat had stolen a march on the rival eight and slid to the top of the river. Giles waded back from his ceremonial ducking, grinning like a madman.

"All rowed fast, but none so fast as stroke," Kat teased him, but he was impervious with victory.

That night a pair of crossed sculls had been erected on the roof of Maitland. The rumour was circulating in Hall at breakfast next morning that a 'continental' (i.e. unexpurgated) copy of Lawrence's last great novel had been left there with them. The Dean promptly ordered it all down, and wrote in no uncertain terms to her counterpart at Trinity. It was only through the faithful offices of Cornish – who confirmed to the Dean that the oars had no distinguishing marks beyond Trinity colours on their blades – that Giles was saved from an automatic rustication. He had had the Bigby family crest and motto – *'Semper grate, semper gratis'* – set into the top of each shaft at the beginning of the year.

Having taken the longest way up to Folly Bridge, Kat continued in the manner of an army salute and took the shortest way down. She cycled along the Corn, glancing at shop-windows as she rode by them, repassed the Memorial on its lee-side, and was once more in St. Giles.

Passing the sign for the Eagle and Child, a public house better known by a much coarser name, she recalled the term's second conundrum.

One evening in Third week, Giles had summoned her to the 'Rabbit Room' there for a secret tryst. He was at sea over what to get his sister for her birthday, he said, and would Kat steer him with some suggestions? She offered a few, most having silk or sugar in them, Astrid's two favourite ingredients. Giles was profusely grateful, and went off to get their drinks.

In the 'Inkling' corner, a stall across from where they were sitting, a group of adventurers from the Debating Society held forth at one another. Kat listened to their banter with half an ear while Giles stood at the bar, waiting to order. At the centre of the group, evidently holding court, sat a brown-skinned, dark-bearded figure whose appearance immediately struck the eye. He was noticeable not so much for the cut of his suit, though it was a great deal better than any around him, nor for his grooming, equally superior to that of his companions, but for the swathe of immaculate silk wound above his head. The turban might have been moulded, it was so perfectly shaped. Beneath it his eyes glinted like jet. Kat knew him by sight. His name was Pravin, often called 'The Divine Pravin', a Christ Church man, apparently a brilliant lawyer, and president of the Union that term. He was also supposed to be a prince.

They were talking of India, trading anecdotes about the Raj as if it was a period already lost in the mists of time. The latest was one about a young English officer's wife who had misbehaved notoriously.

"Didn't your brother have some trouble in that department, Ferrar?" asked a young man who sat on Pravin's right. "They say the mems used to get awfully lonely up in the hills—"

The chief courtier, Kat thought, and licensed to snipe.

"Chuck it!" Ferrar said sharply.

Kat recognised him as the fellow who had made use of the plumbing at the top of Professor Boyd's staircase.

"Come, come," said Pravin, in the mannered, rather queanly way that had won him such admiration at the Union. "If dear Ralph declines to discuss his brother's domestic affairs with us, we should respect his discretion."

He paused and stroked his beard.

"In any case," he added, "my intelligence is that it was the young District Officer in the case who was to blame entirely. An appalling womaniser, one heard, from whose advances no memsahib, not even the fragrant sister-in-law of our noble friend here, was safe."

Ferrar had to appear grateful for this intervention, even though it was plainly vicious; to do otherwise would have broken faith with the group ethic of Pravin's omniscience. But Kat could see that he was roused. He replied not to Pravin but to the chief courtier.

"He tried to force her, if you must know. The bastard just about broke her arm before he let her go."

"I say! The Himmler of Simla—" some wit tossed in, from the edge of the group, and the chief courtier made the supplementary suggestion, *sotto voce*, that he believed it likely the treatment had been to the lady's taste.

Ferrar skulked away towards the bar, and brushed past Giles who was returning. Pravin tutted, as if the weight of the world's decline were on his shoulders. He seemed to ponder for a moment or two, stroking his neat glossy beard, then fixed his eyes on space, and murmured slowly:

> *"Said Mont to a fellow named Ferrar,*
> *'You've gone and made one blooming error.*
> *I'm no poodle-faker –*
> *If she likes it, I'll make 'er!*
> *Now, tell me, how could one be fairer?' "*

There was laughter, which Pravin accepted graciously, but as if it were nothing short of his due. The yogi had brought enlightenment to his faithful. Shortly the group left for Hall.

Kat experienced a shock at the sound of her own name. She had no notion of what was meant by 'poodle-faker'; Giles, who she believed must have heard the whole verse, either couldn't or wouldn't elaborate, other than to say it was probably British-Other-Ranks for something. The subject was dropped between them, and – significantly perhaps – had not been alluded to all the term since.

Now Kat cycled on, wondering whether it was something she could ask her father. But then, Mont was not such a singular name; at a pinch, it need have nothing whatever to do with Kit. He had left the Indian Civil Service six months ago, and had a tea-estate now.

Somehow, though her loyalty resisted, the suspicion recurred that it did have to do with him after all . . .

Stowing her bicycle 'for the duration', Kat finally gained the spot she had first intended two hours before – a bench in the main quadrangle, in a corner between the old lime-tree outside House and the roses trailing along the wall of the Library.

There she sat, and watched the light slowly fade in the square expanse of sky above the college buildings, while clouds tinged with pink gathered on the little breeze. As earlier in the day she had packed her belongings, so now she packed her memories, one snippet at a time. The thoughts came and went, came and went, in enchanted procession. Eventually they ceased, were all packed up, and her consciousness was made up only of the sounds and scents around her. The air was neither warm nor cool, but skin-temperature exactly, breathing over her in soft gusts, wrapping her in a balmy rose-scented oblivion. There was a distant train, a bell or two, church clocks chiming, and birds calling from outposts of roof and brickwork – pigeons on House, a song-thrush over Maitland, a magpie on Chapel. Mostly there was silence; she might be the last person in the world.

A timeless sense of peace washed over her, rising through her from the ground in a slow wave. It was a feeling nothing less than love. She loved this place, and her life within it. The stillness, the passion, the awakening it had brought her. It was so unutterably lovely, her life here, so inexpressibly precious to her, so exquisite, that in that moment of understanding she barely remembered to breathe.

The sunset began streaking pink over the chapel, then yellow towards Jericho; evensong bells began tumbling all around, and still she sat there. A lone magpie stalked across the grass. *One for sorrow.* Kat thought of the professor, and wondered passingly what became of him.

She turned at the sound of footsteps on the gravel path behind her.

"All packed up?"

Dad!

The magpie, his own peace irreparably disturbed, flew up to join his mate on the chapel roof.

A FORSYTE INTERLUDE
Torn Sails

'They were dangerous guides the feelings—'

Lord Tennyson

Torn Sails

It was raining steadily as the Orient liner came into dock, but to Ann Mont, wrapped in her coat and standing by herself on the boat deck, the weather seemed as mild as an infant's tears. The slate-grey sky, forecast to remain over Southampton for most of the week and not considered a particular feature by those just coming into focus on the quayside, was to Ann quite lovely and could stay forever. English rain had the quality of mercy in it.

Seventeen months had passed since her last sight of this coast. Since her marriage nearly seven years ago, on board a vessel not unlike this one, she had been back only three times; for her father's wedding in the spring of '46; for her brother's Olympian feat of graduating with a 'congratulatory' First in what he only ever referred to as *Jurisprudence*, at Oxford in '48; and two years later in the late summer of 1950, for no reason better than that she couldn't bear to be away any longer. She travelled alone on each occasion, for reasons which suited all parties. This time all parties knew that she intended to stay.

She breathed deeply, as the wind blew in her face. The sharp salt smell of the sea which had been in her nostrils for the last two weeks was gone, replaced by subtler, landward scents – the brackish savour of the wintry shoreline, of damp earth and rain-soaked branches, mixed up with the underlying diesel of the dockyard and railway. And there was Dad—! standing alone and rather stooped, waving his pipe in his hand from the dockside crowd. She looked for Penny, but couldn't see her; just her father. Ah — they were discreet people, her beloved family.

Ann landed in the usual hurly-burly of disembarkation. From the stasis of the boat, everything was suddenly a mad rush of porters and trunks, umbrellas and long-lost relatives. She found her own, and for some minutes stood wrapped in his arms, her face buried between his and the rough tweed of his coat collar. The rain began to run from the brim of his hat into her hair but she didn't mind. She was home.

On the drive back to Green Hill from the coast, little of any consequence was said in the car. This was partly due to the presence of the driver, even though he was screened off behind a glass panel, but mostly because the first thing Ann said to her father when she was able to speak was –

"I'm not going to say anything, Dad, and I know you wouldn't ask anyway – but I'm back for good this time. I love you terribly."

He took her cold, thin little hand in his own, lovely and warm, and held it on his knee. They drove on like this, saying nothing, feeling much, holding on hard. Ann set her face to the window and for many miles blotted up the rain-drenched images as they passed outside, like a plant starved of moisture.

Only once she thought to say,

"Why are all the bells ringing? It isn't Sunday."

It was not a thing she had noticed until they were out in open countryside, but it seemed every church tower was tolling.

"It's the King," her father said. "The King is dead."

Three weeks went by before Ann was led to elaborate on her situation, and even then it was not very much of an elaboration. She was talking to her step-mother, not to her father, and never intending to say anything at all. The two young women were alone in the kitchen, where they had acquired the habit of getting their mid-morning coffee, rather than trouble anyone for it. By 'anyone', was meant the cook at Green Hill, still the incumbent of Ann's childhood there, and a woman now approaching the age which immature judgement had appointed her then. An unspoken arrangement since Penny's arrival had relieved this good woman of the responsibility of lunch, and so, after breakfast and before preparations for supper, she kept generally to her sitting room. Today, since it was Shrove Tuesday, they would have pancakes for lunch and Ann was looking forward with almost childlike anticipation to helping her step-mother make

470

them. The kitchen, for all its size, was cosy, warmed day and night by an old black-leaded range set into the wall at one end. Outside, the day was cold and windswept, the orchards bare and haggard-looking. Inside, where they sat across the corner of a scrubbed pine table, the warmth was enticing, seductive, and conducive to the exchange of confidences.

"You and Dad seem awfully happy, Penny. I am glad."

"We are, Ann; we really are."

"It shows, especially in Dad. How are his eyes? He never talks about himself."

Penny gave her a mild look; as if to say it was a family trait.

"They're no worse, thankfully. Sometimes he thinks he sees better, but I think it's just when his surroundings are familiar to him. That helps."

"He spotted me straight away from the dock, so I thought perhaps—"

Penny smiled and gave a quick little shake of her head.

"I think he was looking for you with his heart, my dear. That helps too."

Ann looked at this bright young woman whom she could only see as a sister, never as a mother, and thought what a comfort she must have been to her father over the years of her own absence. Then Ann spent a moment considering what comfort Penny might yet have to provide, now that she herself was back and her troubles likely to follow hard in her wake. With that startling hair and the reassuring face framed by it, her father's second wife was also his second chance, his fresh start. Ann prayed nightly that she had not returned to spoil it.

"He worries about you, Ann."

"I know he does. I wish I could tell him there's no reason to."

"I think it would help if you told him a little of what the reason was. He'll never ask, you know, but he does want to help, if he can."

"I'm just afraid I wouldn't know how. After mother died, we got very close and I truly thought I'd always be able to talk to him, about anything. But now—"

"But, Ann, he hasn't changed, just because he's married again—"

"No. The change is all in me – since *I* married. Now I know there are some things I'll never tell another soul."

471

Ann felt suddenly tired, though it was only mid-morning. Since she returned, her sleep had been erratic, filled with all the maniacal bird and insect callings of the subcontinent which she had so often thought she would never escape. When she woke in the night here it was to nothing more abrasive than an owl hooting from the straw yards, or a mouse running behind a skirting – and in a bed blessèdly empty.

"I'll go up for a while, I think. I know it's pathetic of me."

"No it isn't. It's probably my coffee; I always forget we can make it full-strength nowadays." Penny gave her another of her quick smiles, but her eyes were worried. Ann knew she looked strained, and that she was still too thin. "You go up now, and I'll call you for lunch."

Ann was about to add something, but Penny read her thoughts and cut her off.

"I shan't say anything – don't worry."

In her room, the old room of her childhood, Ann lay on her back on top of the covers, and stared towards the window. No flowers poked through the soil in the little trough, and there were no leaves on the threads of creeper scratching against the windowpane in the cold February wind, but she wouldn't change one part of it. Inside, in this room, she was warm, snug, and safe. But for how long? The unspoken subject was no less real for her silence over it. How long would it be until Kit came back, and began to make overtures? How long before he began to circulate his own version of events? She knew him capable of doing both with great persuasion. That was always his chief talent. And if she was to be free from the nightmare of either of those eventualities, then she *must* talk about it – before a judge and possibly a jury, twelve burghers, 'good and true', to regain her freedom. The thought struck her heart like ice. She shuddered suddenly, and drew the counterpane over her. She would tell Jonnie; she could trust herself with him in a way it pained her to think she could not with her father. He could advise her as brother and lawyer both. She turned her face to the pillow; the decision brought a strange relief.

In a few minutes she was asleep, and dreaming of the cry of wild cranes in the northern sky over Simla, whose advent was always the herald of cold weather.

Under the convenient flag of seeing about some new dresses, Ann took a morning train up to London a few days later. Since it was a Saturday her true colours were suspected but – as ever – no one said anything.

Her brother had been at Green Hill for her first week-end, but had been too busy to come down again since. He had finished his articles at Herring's, and was now in possession of a junior partnership there. The law was something he was meant for, Ann felt. He had a great air of professional probity about him already, especially around his middle!

His flat was on the top floor of a nice old building in Sloane Street. It was up more stairs than it might have been – the cage lift for some reason rising no further than the fourth floor – but was also bigger than it could have been. Ann guessed her father was helping him with it.

"What do you think of my jolly *pied-à-terre?*" he asked her, as he took her coat and gloves. She intended keeping her hat, until a joshing glance from her brother's eye told her it would be old hat if she did. She was out of date, it was true; her manners were still tinted pale colonial. She had some catching up to do.

"More like a jolly foot-in-the-sky; don't you need oxygen up here?"

She went to a window and looked out through remarkably clean nets. The thought crossed her mind that her father had thrown in a charwoman with the lease. Domestic arrangements had never been Jonnie's strong suit.

"It's quite a view, though."

Jonnie stood behind her.

"Certainly is. Every last remaining bomb-site between here and Big Ben. On a clear day you can see Lambeth, supposing you'd ever want to. Now. Question one: fancy a sherry before lunch?"

Ann shook her head.

"Not yet. Soon. I want to get used to the altitude first."

She felt her brother's hand on her shoulder.

"Question two – I didn't get a chance to ask you at home – are you O.K.?"

"Yes and no to that one. I've stopped looking for ants in the

473

sugar, so I suppose I'm progressing, but I'm afraid it will take a little more than that."

"Can I help?"

"I don't know," she said, turning her head to him. "That's rather what I've come about. *Can* you?"

"*Ça dépend.* As your brother, of course, I'm licensed to break a few bones in a good cause. As a promising junior partner – well, you tell me."

It was exactly what she must do – Ann knew – there was no escaping it. She drew a deep breath and said,

"Question one: do Herring's handle divorces?"

"They do; and very capably. Question two?"

"Can I have that sherry?"

One hour and half a bottle of Berry's best *amontillado* later, Ann believed her brother deserved his partnership on the strength of his air of probity alone. He listened to everything she had told him – which was only the skim off the surface, but grisly all the same – without once altering his expression. Not the slightest lift of an eyebrow had escaped him, and the tone in his voice when he put a few supplementary questions to her, was unimpeachable.

"That's the potted version, anyway. Not nice listening, is it?"

"Not very. How's your appetite?"

Ann thought he put this question, as he had the others, in the light of what she had told him.

"Rather shaky still, but getting better."

"Good. If I offered you three courses and not a curry among them, could we continue over lunch? There's a jolly decent little place on the Square."

Spring came and went, summer blew along, and as every day passed Ann regained a little piece more of her private centre, of her inner calm.

Herring's were appointed to do the deed. Documents flew between them and Kingson's. Ann was disconcerted at first, when she saw their letter heading, but then was consoled as she realised there were Forsytes on both sides of the judicial line. Finally, papers were served. 'Mont *versus* Mont' was due to appear on the cause lists at the end of the year.

In all of it, Green Hill became her Xanadu, her pleasure dome, and not too stately, where nothing could touch her, and where any legal unpleasantness which needed her attention was always filtered through Jonnie. She knew it would have to be ghastly at some point, but not yet.

So meanwhile she walked, read, played a little, drove now and then over to Wansdon, helped in the orchards and on the farm, slept better, ate more and in general began to assume the appearance of a young woman whose life was gradually getting back onto its proper tracks.

In all her solitary ramblings across the farm, she only once went down to the place where the gap in the perimeter fence used to be. The field had been restored many years since, when the base was abandoned. The crab-apple tree still stood at a swaggering angle, as if bent into the character of its former companion.

Then suddenly she remembered being swirled around under a hunter's moon.

'*I do love you, you know.*'

It had taken her years of living out there with Kit, to understand this statement for the *hapax legomenon* that it was . . .

No matter now! Now she was back, and her heart and life were mending under an English sun.

So much so that when, at the end of August, her father suggested she might like to join him and Penny for the last Test at the Oval, she actually agreed to go up with them.

But her nerve failed her when the September morning arrived. It was mad even to think she could cope with cricket; the jollity of the crowd, the polite cheering, the niceties of the game. '*Play the game!*' She refused her father's best persuasion and offered her apologies instead.

"I'm sorry. Now it's come to it, I'd really rather not. You go – I'll be happy as a lark here."

"Let's run you over to Wansdon, then," her father said. "Holly will love to have you."

"No, Dad, don't trouble—"

"No trouble, it's on our way."

"Dad—"

"Jon—"

"Oh. Right."

Ann saw them to the car. As her father was getting in on the far side, Penny said to her,

"I'm afraid everyone's off at ten, because I was sure you were coming with us. But there's a mass of cold stuff in the larder, so don't starve, will you?"

"I'll have put on two pounds before you come back."

Penny got in beside her husband, and the car slid away.

Ann went back inside. She found the newspaper, got herself a glass of milk from the kitchen, and took both into the drawing-room. Wedging herself among the cushions at the end of one of the two long sofas there, the glass within easy reach on the unlaid hearth, she curled her legs up under her and began to read.

This was another thing which she had once thought she might never do again. Reading had once seemed to serve much the same purpose as etching five bar gates on the wall of a cell. Both activities marked the passage of time, neither helped it pass any the quicker.

At one time she believed she had read every title offered in 'Bell's Indian & Colonial Library', as supplied by Messrs. Thacker and Spink of Simla. From *The Girls at the Grange* to *Lost Man's Lane*, from *Miss Rayburn's Diamonds* to *The Indiscretions of Lady Asenath* (illus.), Ann had run the gamut.

'In a general way, Little Nina was far too nimble to find herself embarrassed by his amatory designs; but on this occasion she lagged . . .'

She began to fear the gamut had run her.

But here she was, in her English home, and Bell's Library, the old hill station and the new plantation were thousands of miles away. The Raj was dead. It, and the ghost of British colonialism which lingered on after had no place in her life anymore. In short, she was no longer a 'mem'. In fact, if this newspaper was anything to judge by, she was now a New Elizabethan! She read on – about the current total for the Somerset & Devon Flood Relief Fund, about Mr Eden's return from his honeymoon, and about a forthcoming challenge to the world water speed record – chewing happily on every word, and now and again sipping her milk.

She had just begun on the cross-word, and was thinking that she might soon see about some lunch, when she heard a car pull up outside the house. She got up with a knowing smile on her face. A pound to a penny it was Aunt Holly. Dad would have called in on their way up and suggested she ever-so-casually drop by.

Ann hurried to the door; she wanted to see her aunt 'caught out'. She opened it still smiling — and her smile was met by another. With a dreadful start, she suddenly remembered she had once thought it beautiful. In a strange way, she could see that it still was.

"Now, isn't that a promising way for a wife to greet a husband — were you expecting me, little Ann of Green Hill?"

Book Three

1952–1953

One More Affair

'Tis your slave shall pay, while his soul endures,
Full due, love's whole debt, summus jus . . .
. . . would this wine
Had washed all over that body of yours,
Ere I drank it, and you down with it, thus!'

Robert Browning

Chapter One

Face in the Fog

Towards the end of November 1952, on a fog-bound afternoon cold as charity, fifty minutes into the later of the two hours usually available for lunch, Catherine Mont – still Kat to her friends and family – buttoned everything it was possible to button about her person, left the change from two half-crowns under her saucer for the waitress who had served her a meal costing hardly four shillings, and prepared to exchange the warm haze of the tea-shop in St. Martin's Lane for the icy obscurity outside.

Before she got to the door, a cry called her back.

"Hey, miss—!"

She turned and saw the waitress waving a small book at her.

"Your boss'll be on to you if you forget the accounts!"

The book which Kat had left on her table was a little black ledger, bound at the spine and across the corners in bright scarlet and with a marker inside of the same colour, but it had nothing to do with her work or with accounts, though perhaps it had something to do with reckoning. She had bought it on an impulse at the beginning of the week, from a stationer's who was holding a sale of old stock. In it, on its blue feinted pages, she had begun to write; nothing very much, she was realistic enough to admit, or of any great significance so far, but it was a beginning.

Kat took it from the woman with thanks, and was glad she possessed her father's weakness of tipping generously. Her expression, on a face so wintry pale, with its accidentally sad mouth, and incidentally hungry eyes of ice-green, was such an odd combination of innocence and mystery, of need and yet self-sufficiency, that the waitress felt a twinge of guilt that she hadn't given the young lady

481

a larger helping of bread and butter with her order.

Tucking the ledger into her handbag, and her handbag under her arm, Kat thanked the woman again and left.

Despite her precautions against it, Kat gasped at the cold acrid air which lay in wait for her as she stepped out into the street. The noxious vapour, which had coiled itself like a serpent around the capital all week, was a creeping, cunning, almost sentient thing. It lay in banks at unexpected corners, gave way without warning, clearing completely in patches only to circle back and re-group elsewhere. To Kat it seemed as if all the exhalations of the vast grey city – from car engines and bus diesels, from the tall chimney stacks of power-stations and factories, from the shorter ones of terraced houses and gardened squares, and from the millions of lives moving *via* one or another, to one from another – had breathed life into a separate creation. Like the tongue of a patient, as her father believed, this current 'pea-souper' indicated the general health of the Capital. He was 'on to it', and was bent on getting 'Clean Air' through the House before Christmas.

Kat tucked her cheek into the trim of fur around the hood of her coat, and endeavoured to breathe through it rather than directly into the fog. The strip of dark mink – salvaged from a cast-off of her mother's – divided the two shades conveniently; the deep, poster-red of her coat, and the darker red of her bright auburn hair, worn twisted up in a French pleat.

She walked quickly northwards in the flow of afternoon pedestrians, moving between dim pools of yellow light from street-lamps haloed vaguely in the fog. By means of a little passage after the next theatre, where a new 'Who-done-it' had just opened to good reviews, she cut through to Charing Cross Road and then turned north again, following the strand of second-hand booksellers' which led to the offices of Messenger & Company, where since September she had laboured for her living under the catch-all title of Publisher's Assistant.

The grimy fronts as she passed them had the look of curiosity shops from a different century. '*Gibbon, Decline and Fall (incomplete)*', she read in one window. Then '*Whitaker – pre-War eds.*', and '*Picture Post – back numbers, all years*'. She supposed it was in the nature of the business that nothing was new, but it seemed symptomatic of the general malaise. An age, a system, a way of living – as all the pundits agreed – had ended with the war; the problem appeared to be that, so far, the new one had not yet begun.

In another window, which looked so impoverished it might have been gas-lit, was a sorry first edition, badly foxed, of *The Waste Land*.

'Well, Mr Eliot,' she thought as she quickened her step, already a good stride on her long legs, 'I'm sorry to tell you, but you're wrong. *November* is the cruellest month.'

There had been no real need for her to venture out from the ramshackle premises of Messenger's (*Parce nuntio ad et cetera*) on such a day. A supply of piping tea and biscuits – mostly plain, due to the continued fact of rationing, which like the fog seemed set to stay for ever – was always available in a back room on the half-landing. Kat had often made do with a mid-day meal of such; she was of slight frame, though quite tall, and could subsist on bird-like quantities without privation. But it was not hunger which had driven her out into the fog, only the general necessity of putting a little distance between herself and one of her colleagues – the young publisher she was assigned to assist.

Kat hoped she was wrong, but thought it unlikely. Giles Bigby, Astrid's brother, was getting a look in his eye. He was twenty-seven, four years older than herself, but to Kat he seemed a perfect boy. She liked him well enough, and he could even be amusing at times, but she couldn't bear the fact that he was — well — *interested*. Giles was a gentleman, of course – in point of fact he was a nobleman, a quite out-dated distinction in her view – and he behaved impeccably towards her whenever they passed in the cramped corridors at Messenger's, or when he came into the office she shared with one of the secretaries. Mercifully he was often 'out', though where he should be, as a very junior partner, except 'in' she didn't understand. But it promised to make things difficult if she couldn't sit down at her desk without feeling his puppy's eyes on her the moment he entered the room. Today he had been having a working lunch 'in' over sandwiches – and so it was she who was 'out' in this pall!

And here was Messenger's—

Pleasantly flushed from her brisk walk she stepped up to the entrance, a door flat on the street, letting the visitor directly up a rickety flight-and-a-half of stairs to offices which occupied the two floors above a bookseller specialising in political cartoons. As she reached her hand up to a button set into the jamb, to be 'buzzed up', the street door was flung in on itself, and Kat felt a jolt like a thunder clap as a vast figure issued suddenly from the darkened hallway and lurched past her into the fog.

She turned, as much from the force of the encounter as from any sense of personal affront, and stared after the man. He had stopped under the nearest lamp and was scowling furiously down the street, his coat unbuttoned, his arms hanging at his sides. For some reason to do with his stance, or perhaps his aspect, Kat felt that his focus was not on what he saw, though in any case the fog around him must have obscured his view beyond a few feet. From where she stood by the doorway, she took in the details of him. The sallow street-lighting, misted and shifting, made a portrait of his face. The bumps on his high forehead, the bridge of his nose, and the jut of his chin beneath a short grizzled beard were all highlighted in dull yellow. In contrast, cobalt and black defined his long cheeks, also bearded roughly, and the hollows of his eyes, where a white speck shone angrily in each. Expressionist, she decided fancifully. A sudden, dark, and difficult study. Was it Braque — or Derain he made her think of? In an oddly dramatic gesture, the man swept out an arm and placed on his head an immense hat – retrieved from nowhere it seemed in the fog – and his face was cast in utter darkness. If he had seen her at all, or been aware that he had almost flattened her, he gave no sign; again it was Kat's intuitive understanding that he saw nothing. She watched as he stamped off, his heavy loden coat flapping behind him, heels ringing on the pavement, his head held strangely high for one already so tall – almost tilted backwards – as if he was reluctant to take the path down which his giant's stride bore him.

Giles' voice, striking a mournful note, was the first she heard upon entering the front office. Giles himself stood alone in the centre of the floor like one confronted with the unthinkable.

"That's blown it! By Harry – I'll say!"

With one hand on his head, the other curled round a batch of papers, he evidently addressed himself.

"You clot, Bigby—" he went on, while Kat took off her coat. "You absolute clot!"

"Trouble at mill?"

"Merry murder! Struck down in my prime!"

"So was I nearly, coming up—"

"Oh, Montie! It's 'lights out' for me now, and that's for sure."

Kat had never cared for this nickname Giles gave her, which seemed to have stuck from Oxford, but he looked so baleful that she decided not to pick him up on it this time. She still had no idea what or whom he meant.

"Please make sense, Giles; I'm full of fog and someone just bumped into me downstairs."

"You mean you saw him — didn't you try to stop him?"

"No—" Taking off her gloves and putting them inside her coat pocket she moved towards the ladies' cloakroom. Giles sloped miserably along at her heels. "—Stop who?"

"The Great Author, of course."

This description was unenlightening. After fully two months in the profession, Kat understood its cardinal rule. Every author was considered great – if not by his publisher then at least by himself.

"His name is Legion, for they are many," and she nodded towards the sign on the door ahead of her, which signal Giles caught and interpreted just in time to divert from following her in.

Back at her desk – after running a comb through her hair and touching her lips with a pale salve – she saw that Giles was languishing still, seated at his in the connecting office. He leaned his chin on the heel of his hand, and stabbed at his blotter with the point of a pencil. Kat went through to him, shutting the door behind her.

"Since I'm paid to assist, I thought I'd risk asking – just this once, and not to make a habit of it. *What* were you talking about?"

Giles looked up bleakly.

"All my own fault – bad time to see him – lunch. Dare say he'd been through a couple of bottles of scotch already before coming here. Fellow was probably half-cut."

This made no more sense to Kat than before, but she let Giles ramble on.

485

"You see before you, Montie dear, an about-to-be ex-publisher. Cut off in an instant – and at the tender parts, too. A promising career is no more."

"Don't be silly, Giles. What never was can't be no more."

He was not reassured by her teasing, if he even noticed it.

"Blimey, though – what *is* a Bigby going to do?"

"A Bigby could start by telling his invaluable assistant which author he believes he's offended so irrevocably."

"None other than *Mon-sewer* Avery Lehrer Boyd. That's who."

She had seen the name before, on their list of new clients, and had thought nothing of it. Now a distant bell began to sound a faint peal of recognition in the back of her mind. The singular height of the man downstairs, and something about his face under the street-lamp, its absorption perhaps, began to connect with the name.

"Oh — not Professor Boyd?"

"The same," Giles confirmed. "Mad, bad Professor Boyd. Late of Brown, Oxford, and most watering-holes on the Left Bank. Lately late of Messenger and Co., it would appear."

He gave a grim little smile and began stabbing again.

Kat could barely credit the apparition in the fog as her former professor. Without the name she would never have thought to recognise him for the same man. She recalled the spiky hand which had scratched '*Boyd*' below a note to her at the start of her second Trinity term.

"I didn't know he was a writer as well."

"I wonder he knows himself, the way that fellow carries on. He's damn' lucky to have someone to publish him over here at all, after his continental stuff."

"Continental stuff?"

"Yes – you know." Giles hemmed. "The sort – they wrap in plain dust-jackets."

Here, for want of a certain ungentlemanly or possibly ignoble nerve, his explanation ground to a halt. He coughed in his throat a second time and looked hopefully up at Kat.

"Oh!" she said, in exaggerated understanding. "Do you mean the sort rowers have been known to leave on the roofs of women's colleges?"

"Um," said Giles bluffly. "Much like."

"Are you trying to tell me that Professor Boyd writes 'advanced literature', Giles?"

"Has done," he nodded. "For the last couple of years – in Paris."

"And that Messenger's is going to publish it?"

"Ah – no. The Old Man struck a deal with him to keep it clean — sort of 'morals clause'. He senses genius, and a quick bob or two if it can be kept in its cage. That's what the upset was all about just now—" Giles took a sighing breath before recounting the tale: "It was all going well over the ham and mustard, with Bigby proving his worth as a negotiator, when friend Boyd ups and decides he won't be dictated to about artistic content and refuses to sign his contract. Then of all things, he asks me what degree I've got – I tell him – and straight away he's quoting Æschylus at me!"

"Which play?" Kat asked, but Giles was beyond seeing the humour of the situation.

"*Prometheus Bound*, I think. First he asks me if I really want to put him in chains to write, and when I reply that it's not what I want so much as what the Governor ordered, he gives me one of his lunatic smiles and says 'To neglect what Zeus decrees is a grievous thing,'[1] and storms out. The man's a certifiable maniac."

Kat failed to suppress a grin. She had always admired swagger, especially the intellectual sort, and poor Giles did look so utterly adrift.

"Well, well. That's quite a leap from lecturing on Milton. *Est-il, peut-être, le Byron de nos jours?*"

"The Don Juan, more like. Little birds tell me his reputation is rather advanced too – *avec les femmes.*"

"Astrid and I had him for seventeenth century verse – or rather we were supposed to—"

"Of course — that's right. I tell you, Montie, no one thought he'd have the nerve to turn up again after that stunt of his at Oxford."

"What stunt was that? If I remember rightly, he wasn't there a week before he had to leave because he was ill—"

Giles smiled at her, with a glaze of superior knowledge coming

---

[1] Εξωριαζειν γαρ πατρος λογους βαρυ.

over his eyes. Kat took no exception to this, as she considered it part of her job to see it was not often occasioned.

"You bought the cover-story! He wasn't ill – at least not in the ordinary way. Fellow tried to top himself – a nifty cocktail of scotch and sleeping powders, they said. His scout found him and got his stomach pumped at the Radcliffe. When he came to the beaks sent him packing."

Kat listened, growing serious. She remembered the one time she had met the professor quite clearly now. He had seemed absorbed then; intense, brooding – yes; but no worse. What had brought him so rapidly to that ultimate degree of despair, she wondered? Then, out of nowhere, she recalled the lines he had quoted to her from *Lycidas*—and what followed them:

> '*Comes the blind Fury with th'abhorrèd shears*
> *And slits the thin-spun life.*'

"The thing is, Montie," Giles went on, with a tell-tale rise in his voice which would have alerted her sooner if she hadn't been lost for the moment in thought, "the thing *is* – I'm scuppered if he doesn't sign before the Old Man gets back tomorrow. And I was wondering – *Ars mulieris*, and all that – and your knowing him before. . ."

On the other side of Trafalgar Square from his daughter's workplace, Sir Michael Mont emerged into the fog from his own. Since turning Independent in the '45 election – and still failing to reduce his majority by more than a few hundred votes – he had been demoted from his office inside Westminster, and now worked out of a room in a building off Whitehall. The baronet did not complain. 'Independent is as Independent does', had become his motto, and to be away from the hub of things these days suited him nicely. 'Negotiating on the margins', he had decided, with more than a touch of ironic resignation, was his true *forte*. More than ever, as he neared the steep rise to sixty, he was what his friend and cousin by marriage, Eustace Dornford, had once called him – namely, that *rara avis* in politics, the Member who believed he could not eat his cake and have it too.

Towards the end of the War, he had come close to chucking the whole show. But once he realised that the gesture wouldn't matter 'a row of beans either way' – as he learned to say from a visiting American during that time – he had decided not to resign from his constituency but from his party instead. His change of parliamentary colours did not pass without comment, particularly from within his domestic corral. Eustace thought he was barmy to rock his constituency boat, but wished him well. His mother, growing sadly less elliptical with age, said he ought to consider endorsing permanently pressed trousers if he was returned, 'on account of you keepin' your seat so long.' His wife merely asked him, 'Independent of what?' For a whole Parliament it remained a besetting question.

Now, after two more elections, with the brief sun of socialism sinking in the west – more over Jericho than the New Jerusalem – and the G.O.M. reinstated at Number Ten, professions of 'consensus' politics notwithstanding, Michael at last had the answer. Independent of that lot, he decided, neither belonging to or supported by them, neither of them or with them, but now and forever wholly independent of the 'old gang'. Amen.

Trusting his ears to detect a gap in the traffic where his eyes could not, he launched himself across the road, aiming modestly for the other side – like the chicken! he thought – but only reaching the Cenotaph on its island in the middle. Hearing the rumble of a 'bus or two approaching, Michael paused there and waited for the dim shapes to pass. Feeling a chill across his scalp as he removed his hat, he fell into contemplation of the monument, or that bit he could see of it, and the bank of poppy wreaths left from Armistice Day on its steps. In the shifting fog the dark red flowers seemed to undulate faintly, like a slow tide of blood over the foot of the memorial.

'THE GLORIOUS DEAD'

he read on its face, and below looked ruefully to where there were now two sets of dates. He put his head back and peered up as far as he could see. The column looked as if it might stretch upwards for ever. So it could well. They might build it a thousand miles high, he thought, and still we'd never see it coming. More than forty million this go, nearly ten million last – on that ratio, how many yet to come?

A selfish and comforting thought passed through him – his son, at least, had been spared; his son, unlike so many poor beggars, had been allowed to carry on, and make a life for himself in the world. Then a less selfish thought, and quite discomforting, followed as a direct consequence of the first; that son had returned from the world and was now back in England to contest his wife's petition for divorce! It promised to be an ugly engagement, with rockets and incendiaries lined up on both sides. This will put the instinct for self-preservation to the test, he mused — how useful to have got one's hand in during the Blitz!

Michael became aware he was no longer alone on his island. A tall figure loomed out of the vapour and stood a few feet away at his side. The baronet made a discreet half turn, in the way of inspecting someone occupying the same pew in church. The man seemed absorbed in his own thoughts before the monument, and Michael respectfully resumed his eyes-front position. After a second or two he turned back. Some aspect of the man's image – other than his extreme height – had jarred in his mind. Now he saw what it was — the fellow had neglected to remove his hat.

"You'll not mind my saying, sir – but haven't you forgotten—?"

The newcomer looked round sharply from under a wide brim. There was such a defiantly interrogative expression in his eyes that it was Michael's immediate thought that he didn't understand English.

"—your hat?" Michael concluded, and made a small gesture with his own.

A slow look of understanding came over the man's crop-bearded face, accompanied by quite the most disconcerting smile. With a long arm he swept down his hat.

Michael nodded in acknowledgement. They stood in silence for a further few seconds, until the fellow at his side suddenly pronounced:

"No use to catch a physical cold as well as a moral one—"

Before the baronet could properly register his surprise, the man had reset his hat and stalked away, and the fog was filling the place he left behind him.

Chapter Two

Contracts

In the sheer intensity of his relief at her agreeing to make the mercy dash for his career, Giles had mistakenly pressed a note worth five pounds instead of one into his assistant's hand for return cab-fare to the author's address – a garden square in a once-fashionable part of South Kensington. Indeed, there could be no more reliable litmus of Giles' gratitude than the fact that he also said he wouldn't care if he never saw the change, though meaning from the pound.

On descending again to the Charing Cross Road at a little after four-thirty, Kat decided it was hopeless to attempt that method of transport, though she was in a position to offer the driver double or even treble fare. It was almost dark, and what traffic remained on the streets was struggling to keep pace with that on the pavements; if she took a taxi, she would probably have to walk in front of it. Ruling out buses for the same reason, she took the tube, and emerged from a crowded carriage at Gloucester Road just as an announcement was coming over the platform speakers. Through a mangle of electronic and cultural distortions she could just make out that the station was about to close, '—*d'yew-tew-de-ryle-men'-a'-Errs-Corr*!', by which she understood a train had come off its tracks at the next stop.

Asking directions of a news-vendor who was on the point of packing up to go home, Kat managed more by nerve than navigation to find the square. Its tall houses, all uniform high-Victorian, five steps up between two pillars and once quite grand, appeared now – even half hidden in the fog – to be in the last stages of gentility, their peeling stucco fronts and cracked paint-work standing illustration of what can happen when the trade and carriage classes merge. Examining alternate pillars Kat followed the numbers, which descended consecutively clock-wise from the southern corner. In the centre of the square, the dark gardens spread and stretched in the vapour like a magic wood; she kept them on her right and came at last to the mansion block she sought.

On a porch with no porch-light, she pressed all the bells in turn, prepared to say 'Flat Nine?' to any voice which answered. None did. She checked her watch by the street lighting. Ten minutes past five – not late enough for people to be home from their offices, far too soon for a wayward writer to be returned from wherever it was he went into the fog. She would have to wait, at least for a period, and hope not to freeze meanwhile on the door-step. Then behind her Kat heard a soft buzz and a click; someone was in, and had opened the door as an afterthought. She leaned quickly into it before the lock caught again and, saying 'thank you' to the panel in case her benefactor should be listening, went inside.

Finding a light switch on the wall, Kat saw that flats 1 and 2 were immediately ahead of her on the ground floor. She looked up the coiling stairwell and guessed that number nine must be on the fourth floor, at the very top. Seeing no lift, and certain the climb would be to no purpose, she pulled back her hood and went up.

A faint ticking accompanied her ascent. She didn't realise what it was until complete darkness fell upon her on the third landing. A time-switch! — only what she should have expected on such an ill-conceived expedition. Groping along the walls, feeling with both hands, it took her an anxious few moments to find the button. The light came on again, and the ticking resumed. She hurried up the last flight and didn't look for the door until she had identified the next button and secured another minute's electricity. Then she saw there was only one door on this last landing. It bore a brass nine upon it and stood ajar, open onto the hallway of a half-lighted flat within.

How things recur, was her only thought, and she knocked twice.

Recalling the circumstances of their first meeting, Kat less than half expected an answer, and after a full minute had received none. "Oh, well," she said under her breath, "here we are again—" and stepped inside.

A brief antechamber led to a large main room, which was all there seemed to be of what was plainly a converted attic. The artist's garret, she thought, and no less dismal than recommended in all the chief literary sources. A thin dado rail separated panelling of sorts below from distempered walls above; beneath a central paper-shaded light, the distemper was the colour of faded newsprint. A gas-fire was lighted too, set into the far wall, and hissed gently behind its purple-and-orange glow. The greater part of the room was arranged as an all-in-one parlour, with a dining-table – utility issue and covered with a dark brown chenille cloth – standing in the middle of the floor. One or two book cases – still remarkably free of books, she noted, though there were none in boxes either – a kitchen dresser with an ancient Remington and angle-poise on it, a broken-down easy chair with foot stool arranged before the fire, a standard lamp with a fringed shade, and a pair of bentwood chairs, one at the table, one against the wall, were all the other furniture she could see. Twisting round Kat noticed an alcove, up two steps from where she stood, in which it was just possible to see a wardrobe and the corner post of a brass bed poking out from the edge of a faded silk screen.

Those seemed to be the entire contents of the apartment, arranged with a sort of threadbare tidiness rather than for comfort, as if a negligible amount of living was conducted within its walls. Nowhere was there sign of the inhabitant, and Kat wondered whether it wasn't simply the man's habit to go out and leave his door open.

She twisted back as a sudden noise made her review this conclusion. From behind a curtain hung on a brass rail on the far side of the room, came the sound of glass breaking. The sound was followed by another – a loud oath – which took her back what seemed half a lifetime, to one fine spring morning in a set of rooms in Oxford.

The curtain was swept back on the instant, with a quick scrape of brass rings, and the professor – as Kat still thought of him – emerged from what looked to be a little kitchen. He was dressed in much the same haphazard fashion as when she last saw him; a little less colourfully, perhaps, in shades of lovat and sage, and indeterminately flecked tweed. He carried a box, full of empty bottles, hoist under one arm, and took two full paces into the room before he saw her.

Kat felt a nervous flutter start in her stomach as she met his pale eyes above the hollow, grey-bearded cheeks. She realised suddenly what a dreadful breach of civility she had committed – she had no invitation to call on this occasion – they were not in Oxford now!

"It was open," she said, aware she was beginning lamely. "I knocked—"

"Upon the moonlit door—," he said, his accent couched in the same deep and slightly hoarse voice she remembered. "And did you receive an answer?"

It was more than Kat could do to reply.

He scanned her face and then made a gesture of dismissal with his free hand, as if he considered the point not worth pursuing. He passed her with the box of empty bottles, and returned from the vestibule without it. Kat heard the door slam shut in the interval. Once back, he stood for some seconds staring at her again.

At last he said:

"I know you from somewhere."

"Yes."

"Another world, I would guess."

"I've come from Messenger's."

"Ah."

"Giles Bigby asked me—"

"—to try where he had failed?"

She nodded. "He feels he could have been more – subtle."

His sherry-pale eyes took on the challenging gleam she had first noticed in that book-crammed set at Corpus.

"Subtle he needs must be—"

He stopped, mid-quotation, and flexed his sharp eyebrows at her.

"—who would seduce angels!" Kat finished, as though it had been a tutorial after all, and was both relieved and startled when he gave a short dry laugh.

"I've never taught you, have I?"

He put the question rhetorically, and was already shaking his head before she answered.

"No."

"I thought not. Pity. I would have remembered you better if I had. Tell me your name."

"Catherine Mont."

A recollection of some kind passed briefly across his eyes.

"Well, Miss Mont," he said, spreading out a huge hand towards the table, "come into my parlour."

Before she could stifle the reflex, Kat heard herself add,

"—said the spider to the fly."

She was the more startled, and the less relieved, when he laughed again, a sort of deep chuckle, not wholly convivial. He indicated her coat, and Kat let him take it. He hung it carelessly next to his own loden great-coat on a hat-stand which, with his wide brimmed hat tossed above, stood like a guardian effigy of him by the door. Moving to the table he drew out the chair for her. She sat.

He left her then without another word, going to the kitchen. Kat used the interval to remove her gloves, and try to think what she would say when he returned. He came back presently – before she had made much progress in that direction – with two enamel mugs hanging from his thumb, and a bottle of whisky cradled in the same hand. Not an American bourbon, she saw, but a modest Scotch blend. '*Enough for the duration*', Kat recalled, and hoped he didn't intend either mug for her. He caught up the second chair with his other hand and carried it to the table, as if it had been so much matchwood.

There, opposite her, he seemed almost to implant himself, dropping on the chair in a heavy, jarring motion which Kat felt across the width of the table. As heavily, he set down the bottle and the two mugs – one black, one white, both indifferently chipped – heedlessly rucking the cloth.

Kat remembered Giles had thought him 'half-cut' two hours before; it was not her own impression now. He appeared to her quite sober, but every bit as unpredictable as one who was not.

"You've come about the contract, I suppose?"

"Yes. I'm sorry to disturb you at home—"

"You haven't."

She was unable to judge, from this, whether he meant that she had not disturbed him, or that this was not his home.

"—but the truth is that Giles – Bigby – will be in a lot of hot water with the senior partner if he doesn't have your signature by tomorrow."

Kat took the contract out of her bag and laid it, rather crumpled where Giles had clutched at it, on the table between them. Boyd snatched it up in a great paw, and gave it a derisory glance before dropping it again to the table top.

"He's a friend of yours – the sucking publisher?" he asked with his eyebrows once more arched.

"I'm his assistant," Kat offered, but since the eyebrows remained aloft she felt compelled to add: "We were at Oxford together."

"Oxford!" Boyd called out over her head, as if a light-bulb somewhere had just then shattered. "I was right – I *didn't* teach you."

"No," she confirmed. "Not quite."

He looked at her for another moment, as if estimating from her face what she knew of that episode in his life. From his face, she was unable to tell what he deduced.

"I forgot your name—" he said and, when Kat began to reply that it didn't matter in the slightest, continued over her, "—but not your hair."

Kat saw his eyes slip around her face for a second or two. She wished to deflect the compliment, if such it was, and said airily:

"Well, it was all of three and a half years ago. I expect I must have changed a bit."

"No. You, Miss Mont, are unaltered. My perception has changed, that's all. And this—" and he scraped his chin.

"Yes. I was – surprised – to see you bearded."

"Like the pard?"

"Mmm."

"But still full of strange oaths!" and he smiled, in such an open, disarming way, revealing nice even teeth, though rather long, that Kat found herself for the first time smiling back. She felt as if she had passed the first stage of some unintelligible test.

He seized the whisky bottle, which for a while he seemed to have forgotten, and began to twist its stopper. At first it defeated him; he adjusted his grip and started to pull again.

"Why do you work there?" he asked suddenly, when Kat thought he was giving the whole of his attention to the bottle.

Not wanting to encourage a return to personal terrain, she countered in a breezy, neutral tone.

"At Messenger's?"

"Yes. Why do you work at Messenger's?" he repeated deliberately.

Kat recognised this last modulation, as one belonging to 'the don who is about to spring a trap'. She determined not to fall in. This was not the moment to give the loyal speech in defence of the firm; nor to mention that her employer was also her father's best friend.

"Why does one work anywhere?" she replied.

"That's what I'm asking you." His tone was suddenly serious, almost – well, almost passionate, she thought, and his pale eyes seemed to have darkened. "Why do you work at all? You don't need to earn money, do you?"

What a mixture he was! Disturbing and disarming by turns – unconcerned one moment, impassioned the next – and never any explanation in between! Kat thought she would never have coped with it for a whole term – and wondered if she could cope now.

"Do you?" he repeated.

"No, but—"

Again he rode over her discomfiture, as if it was of no significance.

"You *see*, don't you?" he said, looking into her eyes, examining each separately, as if he might have discovered that they were of different colours.

Kat attempted no answer, because she had no idea in the world what he meant, until he added,

"Why don't you *write*?"

In a quick, hot burst of self-consciousness, Kat thought of her recent scribblings and suddenly felt he could tell. He was uncanny!

"You blush—" he added, in the manner of a connoisseur discovering the last bottle in a case to be even better than the first, "— you didn't then, I'll bet. A haughty lot, you Oxford women."

This also was true. She had never had this weakness at the University. Blushing was something the wider world of men had induced in her.

"What should one write?" she asked defiantly, willing the fire in her cheeks to subside.

"Ah," he replied, as if still savouring her to himself. "Old enough to know the question: too young still to know the answer. But you will know – I'm sure of it."

"You make it sound like the curse of the oracle."

"It is—"

He looked at her blankly as he spoke.

"—it's just exactly that."

Kat felt a strange moment pass between them. If she was honest with herself, she knew what he was trying to say – what he had in fact succeeded in communicating to her – though in language so new-coined it was still hot to the touch.

He addressed himself to the whisky bottle again.

"When did you start to write?" Kat asked him, seeing that the only way to keep her head above water was to go with the flow.

"You don't *start* to write," he said through clenched jaws, and Kat thought she had offended him, until she realised his expression was caused by continued resistance from the stopper. "You only discover that you — *are* writing!"

The cork gave way on the auxiliary verb, and the whole set of his body relaxed. He poured a practised measure into each mug, and placed one before Kat. She touched it politely with her fingertips, and straightened the handle to one side.

"What do you write *on*?" he asked earnestly, as if her answer would make all the difference to him.

Kat stared back.

"Hmm?" he persisted evenly. "Tell me. You'll have bought a bound note-book of some sort, I'd guess, and you keep it somewhere—"

He *was* uncanny! He might have been rifling through her handbag in front of her, looking for private compartments.

"I shouldn't think you're the scraps-of-paper type, you're too—" he looked at her over the rim of his mug, the black one, as he swallowed his whisky at one gulp, then put the mug down and bared his long teeth as the alcohol hit, "—fastidious."

He had found the adjective he sought for her.

"—Hmm?"

"In a ledger," Kat offered reluctantly.

"Oh, glory!" he cried, and laughed in his throat. "A great reckoning in a little room! You do write in your room, don't you? But not in bed? Tell me you don't write in bed—"

Just as before, when he had challenged her entrance and it seemed impossible to reply, so it seemed impossible not to answer him now.

"I have a desk."

"Ah. An *escritoire*, no doubt. Your *bonheur-du-jour*."

Did he mock? He was such a volatile concoction, Kat found she didn't know how to tell – and feeling that actually she would rather not know, she let her gaze drop to her hand where it rested, quite coolly she noticed, on the table by the white mug.

When he spoke next, she heard a smile in his voice, and a far gentler tone.

"An *escritoire* to a dealer, a desk to a young lady, and high tea to a termite."

A long pause followed.

"It's good whisky, isn't it?" he asked at last.

Kat had not touched the drink, had made no attempt to swallow her portion.

"Excellent," she replied, and looked up.

For the merest moment then, across his eyes, the veil lifted. It was barely perceptible, like the shutter opening behind a lens – less than half a blink and it was gone – but Kat felt the movement. As of an apostate drawing one inch back from the brink.

Fleur experienced equal parts of gratitude and irritation at the telephone when it rang in her still largely Classical 'parlour' a little later that same fog-filled evening. Irritation, because she believed she had been on the point of negotiating her son into a corner from which he would have no choice but to answer her plainly; gratitude, because of her suspicion as to what that plain answer would be.

She got up at the ringing, passing her son standing in his habitual attitude of self-possession in front of the fire, 'very young' Roger sitting in one less so, in one of the bergères, and the tea things on a tray. There were no pips to indicate a public kiosk when she lifted the receiver, as the caller had pressed button 'A' upon getting through first to Timms.

"Hello, darling – are you—? . . . No? . . . At Astrid's, ah . . . No, that's just as well . . . Yes, it's filthy, isn't it! . . . All right, sweetie . . . 'Bye!"

Fleur replaced the receiver.

"Kat can't get home in the fog," she said, more to prolong the break from the matter in hand than because she thought anyone would care to know. "She's staying the night with Astrid Bigby in Bedford Square."

"Well, it's good to hear you have one sensible child, Mother. One out of two can't be a bad average these days."

Fleur shot a clear glance at her son as she regained her corner of the sofa. This 'child' who spoke was rising thirty! 'Very young' Roger stared into the fire and wished he had his snuff on him. He had meant only to drop off some papers between stations on his way home to Hatfield, but had been diverted by the suggestion of tea. It was a mistake to have stayed; clients, whether family members or no, felt less free to snipe at one another when they sat in his office.

"I haven't said it's not sensible – what you propose," Fleur answered, "—just likely to be a thorough waste of effort, that's all. I don't see how you can expect to win a defence without grounds."

"I have grounds," Kit said placidly, "—or shall have soon."

"Which you won't confide to anyone, not even your Counsel. How on earth is he meant to prepare his case, if you keep him half-briefed like this?"

"That's his look-out – he'll be sharper at the crease if he thinks he's on a sticky wicket. Anyway, this Haberdasher is supposed to be hot stuff, isn't he?"

Kit glanced at his kinsman and solicitor, who took the cue.

"Oh, unquestionably. One of the top two 'silks' for the job," Roger replied, not adding the less favourable detail that Herring's had been able to retain the other, one Bowman, Q.C.

"Just as well; he looks an oily bounder."

"I won't disagree with you there, but he's effective in court. The fellow takes no prisoners."

Kit smiled to himself in a stilly way.

"I can't understand why you won't let Roger cross-petition, while there's still time," Fleur said, "for 'restitution of conjugal rights'. That's the happy phrase, I believe."

Receiving no answer, she added:

"She deserted you, after all."

'Very young' Roger swallowed on his lawyer's mission to explain the nice difference between 'desertion' and 'constructive desertion', *vide* the Matrimonial Causes Act, 1950.

500

Kit replied to his mother only after a while.

"She's still my wife."

It was an answer and yet no answer, and characteristically unimpassioned in its delivery. On the whole, Fleur would have felt better able to tolerate an outburst from her son than this continued 'cool'. But passion seemed beyond him — though, as she herself knew, there were many kinds. The passion to have, for example, was another.

"It's all in hand – don't worry, Mother."

But Fleur was worried, and resented the feeling, having developed a particular sensitivity to lost causes since the war. To have a son about to defend a charge of adultery in the High Court, armed with little more than what presently appeared a half-hearted apology, seemed only another.

Em came down just as Roger was leaving. She had been persuaded by Michael to sell Mount Street, rather than keep it under dust-sheets for ten months out of every twelve, and now stayed at South Square whenever she was 'up'. Fleur made the introduction.

"How d'you do? You'll need a muffler. It's these atom bombs they keep droppin'. The paper said we've been testin' ours. So unsettlin'!"

When, a few minutes later, the tenth baronet arrived home out of the loathsome pall, he found conversation between his mother, his wife and his son which concerned only the weather.

Chapter Three

Walk in the Park

After a night as conventual as any she had known Kat awoke – from a dream of Rochester sitting in his chair outside Jane's room – to an unfamiliar skylight and a familiar smell. Coffee! – boiling somewhere, and beneath its aroma the agreeable drift of bread warming. Under the influence of such stimuli her senses were roused rather before her brain. She thought hazily of Paris, where she had spent a year with her grandmother after coming down from the University; the countless cafés with their tables outside, all so similar yet each individual and memorable in some way, where every cup of coffee was as excellent as the last, and the croissants broke with a warm puff of air; the variegated *affiches*, newly posted or peeling; the funny little stalls for selling books; the pervading French grey of everything, even the sky—

Kat raised herself on her elbows with a start, her hair tumbling unrestrained over her shoulders. She was not in Paris with a grey dawn breaking through the skylight above – this was no *atelier* – she had spent the night between the posters of a brass bed in a converted attic in South Kensington! Remembering the blameless reasons for her sequester – the worsening fog; the impossibility of getting safely through it to South Square even though her former professor had offered to escort her there; the time it had taken them to grope their way to a little restaurant only two roads away for supper, where she had persuaded him to let Giles treat them out of his fiver; how it had taken them even longer to get back to the mansion block – these recollections slowed her pulse-rate somewhat. Realising it would appear inexplicable, not to say inexcusable, to a third party, Kat had tried to see her predicament

502

as 'just one of those things'; a one-off, extra-ordinary situation, to be handled expediently, and in an adult manner, of which last the covering telephone call to her mother – from a box on the corner of the square, since the garret was not 'connected' – had been merely one demonstration.

She slipped from the covers and dressed quickly behind the screen. Noiselessly taking the two steps down into the room she saw no one, but could hear kitchen sounds coming from behind the curtain. On the chenille table-cloth were their two mugs from the previous evening and the whisky bottle, whose contents had evaporated substantially since she last saw it. The armchair, she noticed, had a travelling rug crumpled upon it.

'Please don't worry, Miss Mont. It won't by any means be the first time I have passed the night in a chair . . .'

For some reason, it had not been difficult to believe that of him.

She returned from the bathroom – fortified by a surprising supply of hot water from the tap and fresh powder from her compact, the pleat restored to her hair – to find the table had been laid. The cloth was gone, and two places were set across a corner. In a small basket was a batch of brioches, and next to the basket two dishes with butter and jam. Kat smiled when she saw the little spread – got from where at this hour she couldn't imagine – so nicely French, in such a drab English setting!

"Good!" came a voice and Kat looked up to see Boyd, holding the curtain aside with one hand, gripping a coffee-pot in the other, and watching her with a smile of his own. "Not quite *Les Deux Magots*, but I'm glad it meets with your approval. Here! Let's have this while it's hot."

And with no further to-do, he began to fill her cup.

Much as during the previous evening, they fell to talking about Paris, exchanging recollections and observations of so many of the same places that Kat could only guess again how often they must have come within inches or minutes of meeting during her year there. For one so changeable, conversation with him was surprisingly fluent and easy.

"I sometimes wish I'd stayed on," she said, "with my grandmother, or perhaps in a little place of my own. I loved it so. Every day in Paris seemed – so immediate – like a new adventure somehow."

"That's because the French are practical and live in the present. They start every day afresh."

"Whereas the English are sentimental and live in the past?"

"It's the only safe place if you're that way inclined. Every day in London – seems a little more like yesterday."

It had been her own thought only the day before.

"Is that its value for you?" she asked.

"I couldn't tell you," he said, and his face clouded, only to brighten quickly when he added: "Maybe you could tell me – if you were to reckon it up in your ledger."

By the time their breakfast was over the morning was light. From the flat's small windows set under the eaves Kat could see the empty top branches of lime trees in the square, and a white sky beyond.

"The fog cleared in the night," he said, causing her to wonder whether he had occupied the armchair for the interval after all. She pictured him stalking the darkness like a wild beast. "Do you have time to take a walk in the park?"

Kat was caught out by the question and, to give herself a moment to think, glanced down mechanically at her wrist. Her watch had stopped; she had forgotten to wind it before getting into bed.

"I think so," she said, having no choice but to look up at him again. He appeared genuinely pleased by her answer, and she found herself adding, "Yes. I should like that."

The very last of autumn clung obdurately to Kensington Gardens. Starting at Palace Gate and turning east, Kat and Boyd walked side by side a conventional distance apart, under a crooked avenue of horse-chestnuts, the steel tips of his shoe-leather striking the path regularly in a way she now came to regard as oddly reassuring. Most of the leaves were down, lying in piles like wood-shavings on the grass, and here and there drifting across the path, while overhead a sprinkling of yellow-fingered hands adhered still to the ends of blackened arms spanning the width of the walk. Of birds and beasts, there were the hardy and homely strains – pigeons, starlings, sparrows and crows; some gulls too, swooping over the Round Pond, keening plaintively, a sure sign of a hard winter coming. A bold robin trilled at them from a corner of railing as they passed. On the ground, amongst the leaves, squirrels foraged for lost fodder, noses and paws down busily, tails up and twitching. A few early-risers walked dogs.

In a flash of black and white and mid-night blue, a lone magpie settled on the path in front of them.

"One for sorrow," Kat said, before she could think not to.

"No, no!" Boyd whispered to her suddenly, as if she had been a disheartened child. He stopped and tipped his hat at the bird.

"Good morning, Mr Magpie—"

The bird cocked its head and stared with one beady eye.

"—How's your wife today?"

Then Boyd touched her arm and indicated one of the trees. Kat looked round the fur-trim of her coat's red hood. From behind the chestnut bole, a second bird stepped out.

"Two for joy," he corrected gently.

Off to one side of them, near the padlocked bandstand, a black dog began barking at a crow perched low in a young rowan tree. The great black bird answered back indomitably from its branch, bark for bark. They turned to watch the spectacle.

"One begins to understand the adjective 'dogged'," Boyd said.

"Also the verb 'to crow'."

The dog persisted, but making no impression undertook jumping frantically up at the tree between barks.

"And the phrase 'feather-brained'."

"A metaphor unfairly drawn from birds, being most accurately applied to dogs."

Kat found they were sharing laughter for the first time; his laugh was milder than she had heard it before.

"It's the best way to enjoy a park, I think," she said, "— walking with a dog."

"Yes. A dog – or a lover."

The owner leashed the black dog, and the spectators walked on, Kat wondering what recollections – happy or sad – had prompted his last remark.

"My brother and I used to walk our dog here before the War."

"What sort of dog?"

"A dalmatian – called Tigger."

"Called Tigger?"

Boyd's mobile brows saw the joke; Kat was encouraged to continue.

"My brother chose him, so I was allowed to name him: English nurseries are notoriously fair. I was very young at the time – not up to seeing the conflict between spots and stripes. Poor old Tigger – he hadn't a brain in his head, but I did love him—"

Without taking a conscious decision to do so, feeling only that it was the most natural thing in the world, Kat began to tell Boyd all about her beloved animal – her chief companion in a too solitary childhood – and in the process revealing far more about herself to the astute listener than she would ever have deliberately intended.

"—He was fourteen when he died, and lame in one leg – it was just before I went up to Oxford. We haven't had a dog since."

Here Kat glanced up sideways under her hood and saw that Boyd was looking at her with a smiling, mystified expression. She stopped abruptly, and felt fresh colour rise in her cheeks. They had passed the steps of the Albert Memorial and reached Coalbrook Gate – she had been talking for a quarter of a mile!

"Heavens, I'm sorry," she said.

"Why?"

"For rabbiting. It's not something I do usually – I have a best friend who does it quite enough for both of us. You must be bored stiff."

Boyd shook his head and turned forward again, looking at nothing in particular in the park ahead of him.

"Not at all," he said. "I'm enchanted." He turned back to her and asked simply: "Which way shall we go now?"

"I'm afraid I'd better go down to the road," she pointed to Kensington Gore, "and strap-hang on a number ten to work. I'd love to go on walking—"

"So should I."

"—but I oughtn't to be late."

"No, of course," he said, more seriously. "You mustn't let me make you late – it isn't in my contract."

"Oh, my goodness! The contract—!"

He smiled again and put his hand inside his coat, withdrawing a fold of papers and handing it to her. To the question in her altering expression he answered:

506

"Signed, and dated for yesterday. You can tell your friend Bigby he's out of hot water."

"Thank you. I shall," and she took the contract from him. "He'll be eternally grateful to you."

"He needn't be. I doubt if I'll require his gratitude for that long."

He snatched down his hat and offered a hand. When she reached out, the hand closed round hers, enveloping it completely and pressing firmly, as if he might have wanted to take a cast.

Kat was uncertain what to call him, so said only:

"Good-bye!"

"Good-bye, Miss Mont."

All the way down to the bus stop, Kat felt his pale eyes following her.

There are occasions in every woman's life when what she experiences is so private and personal that its nature may be confided only to a mother, a best friend or a doctor. Ann Mont – still living exclusively as a Forsyte at Green Hill – was without any of these save the last, and he, being of the domestic variety and attending all Forsytes and Darties locally, met none of her present requirements. She set about remedying this in moments when she could use the telephone without the risk of being overheard.

So, having said casually over supper one night that it was too long since she had seen June, Ann let her young step-mother drive her to the station the next morning in time to catch the nine-twenty for Victoria. In a carriage taken up entirely by pinstriped brokers and befurred 'county' dames, she lodged her overnight bag between attaché cases and furled umbrellas in the overhead rack, and took a corner seat by the corridor. As the train rattled from the station, Ann could not shake the conviction that Penny knew her visit to June was a blind. The last thing she had said to her was,

'If you ever want to talk, Ann – in confidence, I mean – you always can, about anything.'

Ann had felt those blue eyes following her all the way across the forecourt . . .

At Victoria, the bustle of the city beginning the moment she stepped down to the platform, Ann felt her privacy return in the anonymity of the crowd. She was due to see June for lunch, but

507

had an appointment beforehand; so finding a taxi, she gave the driver the name of a well-known street and a number.

The metropolis, as it always did, seemed vast and unknowable to her, and she said as much to her cabbie. Remembering the fog which had so recently cleared and the income it had cost him, he replied feelingly that he knew exactly how she felt, and silently saw an opening to take the 'scenic' route.

Ann looked out of her window, seeing and not seeing much of what passed . . . Queen Victoria's Memorial in front of Buckingham Palace . . . the stately length of Pall Mall . . . the grand curve of Regent Street, under Christmas lights strung merrily between lamp-posts but not yet lighted . . . (here a cold glance over her shoulder to see the restored statue of Eros through the cab's rear window . . .) two elegant sides of Cavendish Square . . . then turning into the spotlessness of a street exclusive to one certain profession, and going all the way to a high number at the top.

Inside the discreet establishment at that address Ann gave her legal name, having no thought to do otherwise, and learned she was forty-five minutes early for her twelve o'clock appointment. Deciding it was better for her nerves to walk than to wait, she told the receptionist she would return just before the hour, then regained the street and followed signs she had seen for the Regent's Park.

In that wintry sanctuary, Ann soon felt calmer than on any part of her journey hitherto. Walking slowly, between freshly turned beds quite bare of flowers or leaves, she tried not to think of anything, least of all of her reasons for needing to undertake this journey in the first place. Since Kit's not wholly unexpected appearance at Green Hill on the day of the last Test Match – which visit she had so far mentioned to no one – her nerves had been ragged, her digestion and other regular functions in tatters. So – she would neither think nor feel, until it was all over. She sat down on a bench, huddling into her coat, and watched the gulls crying in the bleak sky over the boating lake in the distance, taking cold comfort in her solitude. But her solitude lasted no longer than five minutes. Absorbed in this self-induced blankness of mind and being, she felt a judder go through the bench as someone sat down none too daintily at its other end.

Ann glanced at the intruder across her up-turned coat collar,

508

resenting proximity in a park filled with empty benches. She saw a young woman, of about her own age and colouring, though coarser in every particular, sitting in a similar attitude to her own, wrapped in a rather overworn brown fur – beaver, or something like – and holding an equally overworked handkerchief to her eyes. Red nails on beringed fingers peeped from its folds. Taking in the details of this vision, Ann saw in a flash how the last few years of her life had affected her, how her experiences had hardened her to the abiding misery of the world. Only one or two years ago, her first and last impulse would have been to ask the woman what was upsetting her, and how she might help. But not now. As if to test her resolve at that moment, the woman let out a muffled wail into her handkerchief. Ann began to shiver. Closing her coat collar to her ears, she got up and headed back to her appointment.

Her hour, for which she paid fully in cash, lasted twenty-two minutes, at the end of which time, having heard the consultant pronounce what he believed to be the possible outcome of his several tests, and no more than she herself feared, Ann was informed by the nurse that her results would be sent to her under plain cover in a week or so. Afterwards, her coat clutched tightly to her once more, she stood on the pavement outside for a long minute, doubting she would ever feel whole, or wholesome, again. Understandings she had managed to blank out earlier, were revived. She felt suddenly how degrading it was, degrading beyond words, to have let herself be exposed yet another time to the vagaries of a husband she wished to be rid of, whom she wished now had never been hers. She shivered inside her coat at the memory of that fatal morning two months ago, when the fastest way to be rid of him then had seemed to be submission. *'Play the game!'* Well, she had – but for the last time. Her divorce would put an end to it. The thought of the case, just weeks away, was tolerable only for that reason – the promise of release. Speaking of it all just now to a stranger who happened to be a doctor, had been awful enough; to have to repeat the details before another twelve strangers, 'good and true', and a court full of gawpers, who might be anyone, might think anything — unhh! it was loathsome!

As Ann was standing like this, back to the railings and face set forward, looking at nothing, seeing only the dim general prospect of the future, an indistinct figure in brown crossed the road towards her. The figure, she saw, was that of her beaver-clad companion on the bench in the park; she was making for the same entrance Ann had just left. On the threshold, the woman hesitated, took a half step forward, hesitated again, then turned back and ran down the steps to the pavement. There she gave vent to such a burst of full-throated sobbing, that Ann felt it was altogether more than she could manage to walk away from the drama a second time.

She offered the woman her own handkerchief which, since she had resolved to remain stony-eyed herself, she knew she wouldn't need. Besides, she saw that it was one from the early days of her marriage, with the initials A.M. embroidered in one corner. She might give away every item she owned with that monograph! The woman looked at her from black-smudged eyes set into a face several layers deep in a modern product, whose advertisement promised 'That Natural Glow'.

"Try not to upset yourself, please," Ann urged her, uncertain in whose interest she spoke. "I'm sure you'll be all right."

The 'Perfect Peony' lips produced a thin simper. The nose blew into the fine linen.

"Thanks, love. I shouldn't make such a show of meself in the street, I know. It's just that I'm a bit nervous, what with seeing a new doctor, an' all. I've got him for an examination – Benyon, the bloke's name is – I don't know him from Adam."

Between renewed whimpering she had named the consultant Ann had just seen. Ann felt suddenly sorry for her – she looked as if the fee alone would relieve her of a week's subsistence, and her efforts at turning herself out for the location fell little short of pathetic.

"Oh, there's really nothing to worry about," Ann said, recovering some of the old urge to reassure, and then confessed, "He's perfectly pleasant. I've just seen him myself."

At this, a strange expression came over the woman's face, like a bird's sizing up a worm.

"Right-y-ho, love. I was hopin' you'd say that. Thanks ever so."

And pocketing Ann's handkerchief she trotted up the steps to the building and went inside.

Not taking the bus she mentioned, but spending the residue of

Giles Bigby's fiver on a cab, Kat had just time to stop in at South Square, change her clothes faster than she had ever needed to since leaving school, and get to Messenger's some few minutes behind the appointed time, but still – a crucial distinction – ahead of the secretary. She found Giles waiting for her on her desk.

"Well?"

He swung himself around to her as she sat down. His genial, sandy-complexioned face was balanced between hope and despondency.

"Well what, Giles?"

"Oh, Montie, don't torment a fellow. Have you got it?"

"Have I got what, Giles?"

"The contract!"

"Oh, that."

"Yes, that!"

"Yes."

"Yes? Seriously, yes?"

Kat produced the document from her bag.

"What — signed?"

She nodded.

"Dear girl! — whatever did you do to get it out of him?"

Suppressing the words *'may you never know!'*, Kat held out the contract across her desk, and Giles received it from her as if it had been a Dead Sea scroll. In a moment conjoint of relief and triumph, he pressed it to his lips.

"Saved! Maniac or no, the man has my unending gratitude."

"He's already told me he won't be requiring it. However, you should know, Giles, that *I* shall."

"Anything! Any time! Montie darling, I'm indebtedly yours!"

Blowing her a great kiss, Giles went into his own office and shut the connecting door – a thing he hardly ever did. After a while, blithe and tuneless humming could be heard coming from the other side of its rippled glass panels.

Kat smiled to herself. Giles was a harmless idiot, after all. And he could hardly suspect he was already obliging her with an alibi for the awkward circumstances of the night before. He and Astrid shared their flat in Bedford Square, and since Astrid was away 'on assignment' until Saturday, neither of them need ever know the service they had provided for her!

Her sense of achievement on both fronts lasted throughout the morning and into her lunch-hour, taken in her usual place.

When she returned at two o'clock she was told a delivery was waiting for her at her desk. Sitting down, she saw only a narrow cardboard tube lying on top of her blotter, her name and the address of Messenger's on its side. She rattled it lightly, but heard nothing. She removed a cap at one end and withdrew – a single white rose. She held it up by the tip of its stem. A rose – just out of bud, and white and fresh as a June morning – in November! She admired its perfection for a moment, held it to her nose and caught its scent – then realised who had sent it. She got up to go through and remonstrate with Giles, to put him back in his place before he got any 'ideas' about his indebtedness – fancy conjuring a rose, indeed! But the telephone rang on her desk, and she sat down again to answer it.

"Messenger's. Miss Mont speaking — hello?"

She heard nothing immediately, just the vacant echo and small cracklings of an open line at her ear. Then, quite distinct and very close, she heard a mouth swallowing, and a light intake of breath.

> *"The red rose cries, 'She is near, she is near,'*
> *And the white rose weeps—"*

Boyd's deep voice, already slightly cracked, was instantly recognisable down the line.

"*'She is late!'*" Kat replied with a little laugh, rather pleased to remember her Tennyson, and rather more by the cleverness of the professor's device. So the delivery was from him – he was the conjurer!

"Only four minutes," she added, "not enough to blot my copybook."

"Or your ledger?"

"That neither."

"Good. Will you walk with me again—?"

She hesitated, partly through not knowing what to answer, and partly since Polly, the secretary with whom she shared the office, had just returned from her own lunch-break.

But Boyd pressed her.

"—On Saturday?"

Saturday – already a busy day for her this week-end. She thought to suggest Sunday, but was reluctant to presume the right.

"I'm not sure – I—"

"Please – do!"

"Oh! — then yes. Where?"

Kat saw that her question put Polly on alert – she had found a reason to consult a filing-cabinet on the wall behind her.

"The Physic Garden – on the Embankment. At three?"

"Fine."

She heard another quick breath down the line.

> *"—The larkspur listens, 'I hear, I hear,'*
> *And the lily whispers, 'I wait.' "*

Kat heard a click, and the connection ceased.

Chapter Four

Meeting the Professor

Above her astringent *coiffure*, Astrid was wearing a hat like a geranium leaf – similar in colour and shape, not very much larger in size – and was still showing no inclination to remove it, though she had arrived at Bedford Square from the airport before ten o'clock that morning, and was presently, at noon, standing in her underthings. The intervening two hours had been passed in her bedroom demonstrating all her new acquisitions to Kat. Giles, possessed of second sight where his sister was concerned, was 'out'.

"Damask rose *is* your colour, Katkin," she sighed, holding an evening 'creation' of this shade under her friend's chin. "All you need is a knight-at-arms and a pacing steed – *et voilà* — *La Belle Dame Sans Merci*. It's that wonderful hair." And she sighed again. "Mine's a fright with it – I look like the Lady of Shalott – *afterwards*. Take it!"

Kat took the dress and held it up to herself in a cheval glass purloined from Giles' room, though there were already two large mirrors on the walls of Astrid's room, and more inside cupboard doors. Astrid was right – the colour did look well on her. Kat swayed to the side and the skirt moved after her with a pleasing swish.

"Do they really give you all this stuff 'with compliments'?"

Astrid had launched herself upon the tissue paper in yet another box.

"Absolutely! How could they expect me to write nice things about them if they didn't?"

How could anyone reasonably expect Astrid to write *anything*, Kat thought fondly, except by generous inducements of this perquisite sort? The sense of service which ran like a religion through one side of her family, and the sense of a bargain persisting in the other, had produced in Kat a kind of tempered application for her work. She was burdened by the belief that a fair day's effort was required for a fair day's wage, for only by that arrangement did she feel entitled to own her own thoughts in the workplace. It would have bothered her enormously if, say, for unlikely instance, Messenger's were to promise her a writing contract, or a library of free books, in exchange for commitment to her present position. Astrid on the other hand, her pedigree placing her higher up the social evolutionary scale in these sensibilities, would no doubt have taken both *and* demanded all her royalties in advance! A pretty face and figure, a smart title, and what others less partial might call a 'pushy' manner, were no bars to advancement in the age of the New Elizabethans!

"Look!"

Kat obeyed. Astrid had shimmied into a slim tube of pea-green which started snugly at her waist and ended similarly a mere twenty inches below, possibly not even that, and outlining every curve between.

"My dear — knees?"

"Dior, darling – isn't he fabulous! Short skirts are back for the spring!"

The two lunched at a little restaurant just eluding the shadow of the British Museum, across a window table so sun-drenched it was difficult to credit an outside temperature in the low forties. Dior was wise to wait for the spring before raising hemlines! Kat was happy to talk about Paris for the third time that week, though Astrid's part of the city was not the one she had shared with the professor two days earlier. Not for The Hon. Astrid were the populist delights of *le Boul' Mich'* and the Latin Quarter. *Pas du tout!* A room at the *Georges V*, and the very best *repas plus complet* that her Society magazine's expense-account would run to. No wonder her grand-mother Annette took to Astrid so – she was the granddaughter she never had!

"*Comment-ça-va, chez la grandemère?*" asked Kat.

"*Tout va bien – elle était très élégante, comme d'habitude, mais en plus de l'embonpoint, je crois . . .*"

"*Rao-orrw!*"

Kat responded to Astrid's last comment by setting her fingers into mock claws.

"I know, Katkins, but you needn't worry. It's missed your generation – and your mother's by the look of her – she's pure twentieth century. But your grandmother might have sat to Goya. Let's have pud – the mag's paying."

"Not for me, or I'll be 'ick. Not to mention fat and forty in seventeen years' time. Anyway, I have to be off soon."

Astrid pouted.

"Chucking me for a prior engagement?"

"An appointment."

"An appointment—?" Astrid's clear blue eyes grew large. "A date! Don't lie to me – I can tell by the sudden bloom on your cheeks! Who?"

"No one you know," Kat replied honestly. "Not a 'date' either, that I know of—"

"'Said she, feigning indifference'. Well, I go away for three days—! What's his name? Is he *indecently* rich?"

"Do you know, Astrid, they really ought to let you loose on the social column at your rag. You have all the spontaneous invention for it."

"Oh, I've told them that. So I have to keep in practice with my friends till they give me a shot. Tell me all about it at the theatre tonight – you're still coming, aren't you?"

"Of course."

"Goody-good. Just bring your out-door stuff and change at our place – I want to see you in that dress."

'*Alone and palely loitering*,' Kat thought, when she saw Boyd sitting in the little garden. He was hatless in the cold-hearted sunshine, but wearing the cavalry coat she remembered from Oxford. With the fur of the collar high at his neck, and his hair and beard still of so much the same grey, he looked more than ever as if he might have been growing from it, or it from him. He was staring out, towards the river ahead of him but, as before, Kat had the sense that his furrowed gaze was on something much further away.

She approached from the side, wishing not to disturb his reverie until the last moment, and sat down lightly a little away from him on the bench. He didn't move, and at first she thought him irretrievably locked in reflection; but after a while he turned himself sideways on the seat. Without preliminaries, and as if they had been conversing all along, he said to her,

"You were so right."

"That's good."

"Yes."

"About what?"

He looked hard into her eyes, then his face relaxed and he gave his dry chuckle.

"Most things, I would suppose. In this case, London – where each day seems a little more like yesterday."

"It was you who said that."

"It was you who inspired me. Let's walk!" He stood, and raised the crook of his arm to her. "—Miss Mont?"

Suddenly hearing Astrid's pronouncement tingling in her ears – 'A date!' – and continuing to resist its accuracy, she got up and slipped her hand tentatively under his arm.

"Thank you — Professor Boyd?"

"Technically correct, but – since I no longer actually profess anything, except occasionally my existence – a substantive fraud. Any of my names will serve."

Desiring to avoid the responsibility of selecting one at this stage of their acquaintance, Kat said instead:

"Neither of mine will, I'm afraid. They make me feel I've yet to leave the office. By a family convention I'm called Kat – will that do?"

He didn't answer, but tucked his arm closer to his side, drawing her hand with it.

He led her out of the garden and they crossed the embankment road by the traffic-lights at Albert Bridge.

"Battersea Park today?" she asked, seeing the tall point of the Festival spire against a rim of skyline already yellowing on the opposite bank.

"Yes – you were right about another thing, too."

And that, to her considerable surprise, was all their conversation throughout the length of the park. Kat walked at Boyd's side, still attached to his arm, and was generally composed from head to knees, but below there suffered a slightly spongy feeling in her calves, as if either the path was 'interior-sprung', or she had just stepped off a boat. He was such an indefinable combination of qualities that just the simple act of accompanying him was irresistibly piquant. '*Piquant* – adjective,' she thought; and to keep her head clear played a game she and Astrid had used on each other before examinations. '**One**; agreeably pungent or appetising. **Two**; pleasantly stimulating, or disquieting, to the mind or senses. *Piquancy*, noun; *piquantly*, adverb—'

They had reached the main road at the far end of the park, and stopped on the pavement, where they appeared to be waiting their chance with the traffic. Beyond the railway nexus, the power station lay like a great Victorian sofa-table on its back. Boyd took her across further minor roads, and at last Kat saw their destination – a hostelry, of sorts, though it smacked of the hospice too, where a last chance was offered to the lucky few, who might be unlucky yet. It was the Lost Dogs' Home.

Boyd walking ahead, they went inside, a certain amount of renewed barking attending the renewal of hope, however slight, which their arrival brought. Kat felt her eyes soon beginning to fill. Before they finished even one section of the wire run, where two dozen or more individuals had rushed up to them, the first tear had fallen. To be met by all those eyes, eager with inquiry, all those tails wagging in unified request — '*Take me! – me! – me! – me! – **me!***' It was too much!

"I'm sorry," Kat said, stopping to put a gloved finger to her cheek, and turning away. "I can't bear it."

"You're not alone," Boyd replied softly, and put his hand on her shoulder. "Neither can they."

"I just want to take them all."

"One anyway."

She looked up at him inquiringly. She had thought until then that this was just a destination chosen from caprice, in place of the zoo, or the waxworks, or any other featured site.

"You told me it was the best way to walk in the park," he said, "—with a dog. So here we are."

"Do you mean you're going to pick one?"

"No—"

"Oh."

She saw Boyd study her face – where she knew her eyes and mouth, particularly her mouth, betrayed her. She watched as over his sherry-tinted eyes came the same expression of mystified enchantment she had seen on their first walk to Coalbrook Gate.

"—not I. You. You're going to pick one for me."

"I've got some nice new pups, miss," said a keeper who came up to them at that well-judged moment. "Half Yorkshire, by the look of them, and half Cavalier. Nice mix."

Before her eyes, the man produced one of the same from his jacket pocket. The blob of black and tan fur shivered as he turned it in his palm.

"We've been rearing them a fortnight – five in all – proper handful, I can tell you."

Kat removed one of her gloves and put her little finger to the tiny muzzle. The pup began to suckle. Her throat tightened, but she knew it was out of the question.

"Someone will take them, surely? Darling little scraps like this?"

"I dare say so, miss. Most times we find a place for the pups. Most of them."

Nodding quickly, not trusting her voice, Kat turned back to the wire. Only three contenders remained there, the rest having conceded the likely advantage of the puppy's case over their own. One was a young Jack Russell, wire-haired, with two dark patches over his eyes, and over his back a tail curling as nature intended.

"He simply must be called 'Bandit'," she said, and tried the name.

The dog turned an instant somersault at the word, delirious with recollection of former status, his boot-button eyes gleaming. Kat reached involuntarily for Boyd's hand and felt hers squeezed in return.

"Who's this one?" he asked, taking her hand and holding it to the second nose at the wire.

A sturdy ginger mongrel, of parentage too diverse to calculate, stood four-square in front of them, its sabre of a tail flicking confidently.

"I don't think I dare guess."

"Dog number seventeen, miss," volunteered the keeper, who was still hovering behind. "They're all numbered, soon as they come in."

"Seventeen – lucky for some?"

The third dog was beginning to walk away.

"No, boy – come back," she called. "You're still in with a chance."

This dog, a blue roan cocker and rather old, made no move, but watched her steadily from red-rimmed eyes above a grey muzzle. Over its brow a long whisp of white hair stood up like a question-mark. At the other end, its docked tail was neither up nor down, but suspended – along with its belief.

'*Life passes me by*,' the expression seemed to say. '*Nevertheless – I remain.*'

"Knows his own mind, miss, that one. Number nine. Getting on a bit, but still hearty."

Kat looked at Boyd.

"You choose," he said.

She looked between the three dogs in an effort to be even-handed, but her heart had already chosen. Besides, the docked tail was fluttering.

"You probably want a younger dog—"

"You choose."

She took a deep breath and pointed to the spaniel. Boyd smiled.

"That's very charitable of you, miss," the keeper said. "There's not many folk who would take on an older dog. People don't usually like to give their hearts on such a short return."

Any return at all seemed worth the effort to Kat.

The standard fee was exchanged, a collar and lead being thrown in with the price. As they went out, the keeper said finally,

"Yes, I'm glad to see him taken – his time was up tomorrow, and it would've been a great shame."

In Battersea Park again, Boyd removed the dog's collar and lead and dropped both articles in a litter-bin.

"Aren't you afraid he'll bolt?"

Without answering, Boyd crouched down and held the dog's face in his hands – looking into its eyes, Kat couldn't help from noticing, in a way he had once or twice looked into hers.

The dog held the stare with its rheumy, pink-edged eyes for what seemed the longest moment, then glanced away. Boyd dropped his hands, and the dog lifted a speckled front paw. The transaction – whatever it was – was done.

With the light failing above them and a chilly yellow sun setting ahead, they retraced the length of the park, Kat walking again on Boyd's arm, and the black and white feather-haired dog – between excursions to trees – trotting at his heels.

Once more on the embankment at Chelsea, they found a bench and sat down to watch the western sky take on a greenish tinge as the sun slipped finally away.

"I have something I was planning to do this evening," he said, *à propos* of nothing out of the silence, "—but I'd drop it gladly, if you were free."

"I'm not – I'm sorry."

He continued to stare at the sunset.

"So am I."

He spoke so sincerely that Kat felt moved – uncharacteristically for her – to offer an explanation.

"I've arranged to go to the theatre."

"Ah. With your friend Bigby?"

There was a slight lift to his tone as he pronounced the name.

"With my *friends* Bigby. His sister and I are great chums – Giles just tends to hang around."

"Then he has more sense than I credited him."

The dog, who had been sitting at their feet and looking fixedly at his new master, shuffled his front paws anxiously and started up a sing-song whimper.

"He wants to be home," Kat said, "even though he doesn't know where 'home' is yet."

"But he believes, all the same."

"What are you going to call him?"

"You decide."

"No! Nursery rules! I chose him, you have to give him his name."

Boyd and the dog looked at each other. Kat thought – two grey muzzles sizing each other up! Which will win?

"Well," said Boyd at last, "he looks as if he might once have had tenure somewhere. Let's call him what they no longer call me." And he called to the dog. "Professor—!"

The heavy, black, drooping-down ears did their best to prick; the speckled paws shuffled more rapidly. The deal was struck.

"Shall we walk you home, the Professor and I?" Boyd asked her.

"I'd better catch a cab, and save some time."

Boyd flagged one down, and opened the door for her. Kat got in, and the dog made a good dash to follow.

"No, Professor – stay with master!" She shooed him out. "Good boy!"

Between them they shut the door quickly, to prevent the dog trying again. When Kat leaned forward in her seat and pulled the window down to say her good-byes, Boyd leaned in.

"What play are you seeing?" he asked.

"The new 'Who-done-it' at the Ambassadors."

"Ah," he said, and gave her another of his long, unaccountable looks. "Then I mustn't keep you."

"I've enjoyed our afternoon."

"Me too. I've no doubt you'll enjoy your evening every bit as much."

"I'm sure we'll see ourselves again—" Kat began, but stopped short. She had meant only that they were likely to run into each other at her office, but realised it might not be what was conveyed.

"We shall," he said simply, and smiled, "—sooner than you think. Good-bye, Kat!"

"Good-bye!"

Passing through the foyer of the theatre, Astrid had one eye on her reflection in each of a succession of ormolu mirrors.

"This cape's a mistake – I look like an Odeon curtain."

It had been Kat's thought too, but she didn't say so. Her own cloak was a simple affair in black velvet, its gold taffeta lining sitting very well against the 'damask rose'.

"*You* look perfect, darling. Doesn't she, Giles?" Astrid poked her brother.

"Um! Pretty as a posy!"

"Let us divest."

Leaving their cloaks at the room so designated, and Giles showing their tickets and getting programmes, the two young women sought their row.

"It's awfully good of your boss to pass round the 'comps' like this," Astrid said as they wove their way down the aisle.

"I thought so," Kat agreed, thinking in addition that it must be a Bigby trait to be perennially on the receiving end of such. *Semper gratis*, after all.

"I didn't know Giles was such a favourite."

"He brought off rather a *coup* this week – with a little help from another. The 'old man' was grateful."

Giles caught them up.

"E-ten, eleven and twelve — here we are."

Giles nudged his sister down the row first, in order to have Kat sitting next to him as he brought up the rear. His plan missed coming off as they all had to shuffle out again when a couple already seated discovered that they should have been in 'F'.

"Excuse us—! Sorry!—so sorry! 'Scuse us. Thanks—sorry!"

"We're an apologetic race, aren't we?" said Astrid scornfully.

"And so much to be apologetic for. That last was my toe!"

Giles gestured to his sister to start again down the row, but the shuffle had left Kat at the head of their party.

"No—oh! well—all right—"

Kat left Giles blustering in the aisle as she negotiated the lead towards 'E-twelve' just as the house lights began to dim. She had deliberately nipped in, seeing the Bigby strategy coming from afar, and avoided catching his expression now by looking out for feet and handbags on the floor. Poor Giles! If he didn't press, she might change places with Astrid after the interval.

Then she heard him exclaim: "Good Lord — I say!"

Something in Giles' tone made her look further along the row, rather than back at him. Standing up ahead of her in the falling light – from what she saw instantly was 'E-thirteen' – and looking inexpressibly distinguished with his grey hair above his dress suit, was Boyd.

In that moment of darkness before the curtain rose, she heard him say under his breath,

"—And nothing else saw all day long."

"Messenger likes his little jokes," Boyd whispered at her ear as the curtain fell upon act one, scene two, and a corpse.

"One ought to expect them," Kat replied, "but his trick is that one never does. How's the Professor?"

523

"Full of brains – the sheep variety – and asleep in the armchair. I told him to stay off the scotch. Bigby – we meet again—"

They joined the exodus making for the stalls' bar, Giles and Boyd pairing up a few paces in front of Kat and Astrid, whose blue eyes were still flashing from her introduction.

"My *dear*—"

"Yes?" Kat answered, in a careless manner she intended to maintain.

"—Why didn't anyone *tell* me authors could be so scrummy?"

Scrummy! Of all the adjectives Kat might have tried attaching to him, scrumptious was the very last. There was something about Astrid, for all her fashion-plate sophistication, which seemed frozen in the last term of the upper third.

"Perhaps because their advances are often less so."

"That's a handicap," Astrid admitted, but to Kat's ears sounded as if she were toying with how it might be overcome. "Are they always his age?"

"He is. Others needn't be."

"Forty-what? More?"

"I haven't an idea."

"Mmm. I'll drill Giles later. I must go and powder – warm him up for me, won't you?"

Giles was proclaiming sagely to his new client, as Kat squeezed through to them in the tightly packed bar.

"—Jolly good fun and all that, but it'll never run. Thrillers never do. We've ordered some fizz – will you join us?"

"With pleasure," he said solemnly. "Miss Mont!"

Giles went off in search of their ice bucket, feeling he was a mild cad leaving Kat to make conversation with such a tricky cove as that one. But still – she was capable!

"Well – *Miss* Mont," Boyd repeated with a twinkle, as they both watched Giles recede into the crowd.

"*Mr* Boyd," she returned, letting him know she was grateful for his return to formality in front of the others. Yet — what made him know that she had not told Astrid of their earlier 'appointment'?

For a short while he only smiled at her, but not in any way she found uncomfortable. In fact, she found the whole situation highly pleasing; as, it appeared, did he. She smiled back. There was suddenly

524

a bond of complicity between them, and it was, well — piquant!

"So," he said, "have you decided 'who-done-it'?"

"Not really – but I suppose it has to be the person-least-likely. That makes it the old lady who knits."

"Ah," he began fondly, "old enough—" and then stopped.

She saw him look over the cluster of heads to one side of them. The glittery, chattering crowd was parting like the Red Sea as Astrid swept towards them, with the distorted elegance of a mannequin down a cat-walk. Boyd turned back to Kat and resumed, dropping his voice to a conspiratorial murmur.

"Old enough to detect the formula – too young still to apply it cynically."

"Aren't you glad?" she asked, matching his tone.

"Oh, yes," he answered. "Eternally."

The white rose stood in a slim silver vase on a bureau and, next to it, the little red and black ledger wherein several more blue pages were now covered with its owner's forward-slanting hand. On an etagère nearby, a theatre programme lay upon the pages of an opened novel, just begun. Over the arms of a japanned chair on the far side of the room – once the day-nursery at South Square – the 'damask rose' dress tumbled in still folds to a green carpet.

Asleep in her bed, her hair spread out over her pillow, Kat breathed lightly as a child, and dreamed she was saving a grey wolf from the abyss.

Chapter Five

Answers

When the plain envelope arrived at Green Hill, bearing her married name and a London post-mark, Ann opened it and took out the letter before she realised fully what it was. Below the copperplate address on a single sheet, she saw two type-written paragraphs, the first beginning '*I am pleased to inform you*—', and the second '*However*—', and brought her coffee-cup rather sharply down on its saucer at the breakfast table.

"No sugar!" she said, to cover her reflex, and her father promptly apologised and passed the bowl.

Penny looked up.

"*Four* these days? The fresh air must finally be taking."

"Oh! — then I forgot to stir."

Penny was *too* quick! It was as if she had developed eyes for them both!

Ann joined her father enthusiastically in discussing the future of mechanical apple-pickers, and made sure she was not the first to leave the table. When Penny had gone – saying she would be out all morning, and leaving a kiss on the top of her husband's head – Ann slipped the letter into her skirt pocket, and went up to her room. There, at once taking out the letter again, she discovered it contained two details, one per paragraph. In the first, she was told that her initial fears were completely unfounded – hence '*I am pleased*—'. In the second she learned something which had never once crossed her mind, not even as the vaguest suspicion – something for which the consultant had tested purely on his own initiative, and only then as a perfunctory check. '*However*—' However—!

Ann sank to her bed, barely taking in the information and feeling suddenly faint. For some few minutes she simply sat there, with the letter on her lap and staring out of the window, where bare tendrils of creeper scratched aimlessly to and fro in the wind. It was half an hour before she gathered the wherewithal to go back downstairs, and watch her chance with the 'phone. Getting through to the clinic, she found the earliest appointment available to her was towards the end of the following afternoon. She took it, and next rang her brother at his office.

"Lunch tomorrow? You're in luck – Bowman just cancelled on me. Can you make it here for twelve-thirty? Jolly good!"

The offices of Herring & Partners being just off the Strand, lunch was at another of Jonnie Forsyte's many 'jolly decent little places', where he watched his sister order two courses and consume little more than her bread roll. To his inquiring look, Ann produced an apologetic smile.

"My nerves don't run to full portions at the moment."

"My tailor would wish such nerves upon me. 'I'm afraid we had best err on the side of charity with regard to the *waist*-coat, Mr Forsyte.' He can't resist a dig. I should introduce Bowman."

Ann brought to mind the figure of the 'silk' her brother had retained for her. He was a little bright button of a man, measuring as much around his circumference as from pole to pole, with a penchant for violet *cachoux* which he took periodically from a tin in his waistcoat pocket. His eyes, she recalled, were sad and oystery behind thick lenses, calling attention away from a nose and mouth which were shrewd and pointy.

She contemplated her brother's eyes and nose, copies of her own, above a well-developed first version of the family chin, and the early showings of a second. She wanted to ask him how what she had learned in that letter – if true – would affect her case. But all formulas for putting the question, even to Jonnie, deserted her. She hadn't yet told him of Kit's visit – how could she begin to tell him of its outcome?

"Is Bowman confident?" she asked instead.

"One of the great unanswerables. Sorry to play the cautious lawyer, but it's true. Yes, inasmuch as he wouldn't have taken on a case he didn't believe he could win. Yes, furthermore, because

Bowman's known especially for winning petitions from wives."

Ann listened fondly to her brother. '*Inasmuch as*', '*furthermore*' — he ought to take the bar himself.

"However—"

That recurrent word!

"However?"

"Well, for one thing, Bowman thinks the other side may have something up its sleeve."

Ann moved a piece of Dover sole around her plate.

"What makes him think that?"

"Because your case is pretty much as winnable as they come. I can see Bowman's point. The respondent accepts the charges, and the co-respondent practically helps him run up the flag, but still he defends. It makes no sense, unless they know something we don't."

And if they do, it still doesn't, Ann thought to herself.

"For another?"

"Then there are certain standard variables – if that wasn't a contradiction in terms."

It was, but described how Ann felt exactly – a contradiction in terms.

"Me, for one."

"'Fraid so. The jury must want to believe you, and they're notoriously fickle entities; so it's rather up to you to give them no chance not to."

"'Answer all questions clearly, and maintain a dignified composure.'"

"That's it. The ring of conviction."

"Mmm. Much like responses in church. How appropriate."

At the clinic Ann was shown into the waiting-room, though she had judged her arrival finely, wanting to spend no longer than was necessary on those premises. The consultant, it appeared, was running late. Passing over a selection of stylish society magazines on a central table, she picked up the only copy of *Picture Post* – 'now down to 4d!' – and sat in the corner of a long green chesterfield, one of three lining the room, and bearing as many other patients.

She flipped idly through the black and white pages – here encountering pictures of a pneumatic starlet getting out of a streamlined sports-car, there seeing underfed children playing in overgrown bomb-craters, and, scattered in between, 'Great Men of Our Nation – an Occasional Series'. From time to time she checked her watch. Then, from the corner of her eye, she saw a hand, set with peony-red nails and too many rings, twinkling at her. Ann looked up from her magazine and saw a familiar expanse of brown fur. Its inhabitant, evidently feeling more like herself on this visit than on her first, smiled broadly and came over. The chesterfield bounced as she sat down.

"Fancy seeing you again! You keeping well, duck? Come to see Dr Benyon, have you?"

Ann nodded obliquely, and was spared from having to engage in such diverting conversation by the appearance of a receptionist.

"Mr Benyon will see you now, Mrs Mont."

"I think you must have made a mistake," Ann concluded simply, after the consultant had asked her why she thought a second appointment necessary.

He sniffed over her case-notes, then peered at her through drooping lids, as if she must be something of a simpleton to question the authenticity of any or all of the two dozen framed gold-leaf certificates which covered his consulting-room walls.

"There can be no doubt, Mrs Mont. It isn't a very difficult thing to detect, after all. By my reckoning, your baby is due sometime in the middle part of June."

Ann reached Green Hill suffering the sort of embattled emotional turmoil which produces stupor. In her coat pocket was the letter, which she had twisted over and over on the train home, as if by some prestidigitation the type-written words might be shuffled into a different, more favourable syntax. Feeling cold to the bone she went into the kitchen, and was drawn to the old black-leaded range for warmth. She stood before it in her coat and gloves and hat, knowing herself on some core level to be impervious to its heat, and again took out the letter. She would burn it, and hope against hope that Benyon was wrong. If he was not, if the unthinkable was true — then at least the suit would be over before her condition became obvious. Kit should not know of it, would not be able to use it to keep her. Scanning that last, short, life-altering paragraph a final time, she stooped to open the door of the stove.

"Ann, my dear!"

She straightened up at the sound of her name and, keeping the letter at her back, turned to see Penny in the doorway.

Her step-mother came over to her, looking suddenly even younger than usual, her cheeks flushed like a schoolgirl's with a secret, her pale blue eyes shining.

"I told myself I was going to wait for your father to come in, but it's no use — I simply can't. It's too marvellous! Oh, Ann! Just when I'd almost given up hoping — it's finally happened – I'm going to have a baby!"

Ann submitted to Penny's embrace, too drained to attempt any immediate reply, and behind her back screwed the page of the letter into a tight, tight ball.

Chapter Six

A Family Affair

If men make buildings, buildings also make men. It was not for nothing – as it seemed to the baronet's ironic eye, albeit these days somewhat wrinkled about the edges – that the Court in which they sat had all the appearance of a public school chapel, done out in the regulation dark wood and 'Gothic'. Here we are, hushed like schoolboys, he thought, with our necks and collars as matron would wish them, doing our best to sit upright on hard pews, waiting for the service to start, not wanting to be here for a single minute longer than we have to and wondering if we've brought enough money to put in the box afterwards.

Michael examined the persons immediately around him in the well of the Court, looking for augury. Kit sat motionless, in a disturbingly casual attitude with one arm over the back of his seat. 'Very young' Roger sorted through some papers, while the slick and hawk-like figure of Haberdasher remained standing, hands tucked into the sleeves of his gown, elbows extended, surveying the court with a predatory eye. Michael saw that the Q.C., as one now must remember to say, had so positioned himself as to prevent Kit and Fleur having clear sight of the petitioner. Sign of a good tactician, he wondered? Or merely of one who liked to hold the floor? Michael himself, when he looked across, could only just make out her hair, which showed like spun gold beneath a navy blue *toque*. Next to her he could see the profile of a young man of her own age and colouring – her solicitor from Herring's, the baronet assumed, though he looked so like her he might have been her brother. The other 'silk', talking to them both, was a small spherical person in heavy horn-rimmed spectacles. As Michael watched him, he withdrew a little tin from his waistcoat pocket, and popped a pink pill from it into his mouth. Of those sitting beyond the young woman – his daughter-in-law after all, in this strange affair, though he barely knew her – Michael made no effort to gain a better view. He had no desire to risk meeting the eyes of Fleur's one-time – for all he knew, even now – beloved cousin and his second young wife, that sweet-faced driver of Francis Wilmot's! What a web it was – or, as he last heard Winifred Dartie describe the predicament, *such a coil!*

Thus situated – Forsytes to the right of him, Forsytes to the left – Michael felt the urge to shift in his seat. Succumbing to it earned him a sharp glance from his wife. He caught the hard little crease between her eyes and, so cautioned, sat still. Fleur had spoken fewer than twenty words to him since breakfast, but her face had done all the talking necessary in that time.

'*Baronet's Son in Society Divorce Suit*', ran the flyers on the news-stands, past some dozen of which the dutiful Riggs had managed to take them on their journey in. Fleur and Michael sat alone in the back of the car, Kit having elected to make his own way from his club, but the conversation gained no fluency from the respondent's absence.

"We should have Roger for supper tonight, if he wants it."

"Right-o!"

"Lippinghall Friday – Vivian and Nona arriving Saturday."

"Good!"

Fleur's manner was crisp but without animation. 'Dry-cleaned' was how she appeared to her husband. It was a mercy that the suit had come so near the holidays, so that she could immerse herself in the country while this affair – whatever its outcome – blew over in Town. After that – normal service to be resumed as soon as possible!

When, once, Michael looked at Fleur, as she sat with her face set forward as the car jogged along in the morning traffic, that same hard crease was fixed between her brows. The dark fur stole, which she wore swept across the shoulders of a severely tailored suit, and the short, speckled veil of her tilted, elfin hat, with its bright, cross-wise feather, gave her rather a foreign look. '*European Countess flies in for Son's Ordeal . . .*'

Her face was set forward now, too, and under the high ceiling lights her veil obscured the exact expression in her eyes.

At their backs, the buzz of many voices – previously signifying that the Court was filling swiftly, as the ripe scent of scandal in the making brought the pack out for the chase – subsided on the instant.

"Pray rise for Mr Justice Orr!"

The Court rose obediently, to sit again when Mr Justice Orr sat, lowering himself into his cathedral seat, red curtains drawn behind him and above.

'A stickler!' Michael decided quickly, judging the Judge by the lozenge-shaped half-lenses on the bridge of his nose. Half-lenses – he had found in his dealings with men of power – generally indicated a preference for the hard line, and the means of enforcing it.

The jury had filed into their two-ranked box.

"Mont *versus* Mont—"

Michael's hand was given a convulsive squeeze. Fleur — poor darling! And the thought ran through him – there was a time when it might have been us!

"—and Ferrar – wife's petition."

The spherical man – Bowman, Michael recalled – began to speak, in a high, pleasant voice such as might belong to one who spent his spare hours singing in a choir. The names and details of the 'parties', the places and circumstances of their marriage and cohabitation were given melodically, while the watery eyes swam upwards through thick lenses to the ceiling of the Court.

"Once discovering beyond suspicion of doubt at the beginning of this year that the respondent had not remained faithful to his marriage vows, the petitioner returned to England, seeking initially only the solace of her family. There, after due consultation and much heart-searching, she took the further step, resulting in the petition which the Court has before it today, for divorce on the grounds of adultery."

A noiseless but palpable thrill passed around the Court at the first use of that ever-titillating word. At the back of his neck, Michael felt the hairs standing.

Bowman gave an outline of the case. It seemed to Michael to be of the 'open and shut' variety. The faces of the jury, when he scanned them, seemed already to agree.

"Having once before forgiven her husband for transgressions which led to his being named co-respondent in 'Ferrar *v*. Ferrar & Mont', which case passed undefended through this forum in the spring of 1950, the petitioner subsequently found that relationship to have been revived in the summer of 1951. This situation culminated in events occurring in January of this year – to be given in detail later – which led the petitioner reluctantly to conclude that her marriage, in any meaningful sense, had ceased to be viable. It is upon this latter ground that the case is brought."

As though genuinely sorry to disappoint its vulgar curiosity, Bowman then told the Court that the above-named third party – formerly one Christabel Treffrey; still, by courtesy and in respect of her children, Lady Ferrar – would not be making an appearance before them. Her deposition had been received by Herring's, the circular Q.C. explained melodiously, and its contents were deemed to constitute an effectual plea of '*nolo contendere*' to the charge of the petition. By way of consolation he added that it would be read in full later.

"Mrs Christopher Mont."

The petitioner rose and approached the witness box; as with any audience whose appetite is whetted and whose seats may not be the best, the transition from prologue to scene one was used for the clearing of some throats and the getting over of various winter coughs in the back of the Court.

Beneath the high canopy of the 'box', a slight, still figure appeared. Dressed in powder-blue trimmed with navy, with her round hat set very straight above fine golden hair and her head carried erect, she seemed almost doll-like. The honey-coloured look Michael remembered from when he had met her those years before, was replaced by a porcelain paleness, against which her dark eyes were huge and unblinking. 'She looks as though she might break if you held her roughly,' was the baronet's first thought. His second was; 'The jury will see it, too.'

Bowman put questions, and received answers which elaborated his opening statement. His witness spoke in a quiet, clear voice, unwavering even when she was asked what her own relationship had been to the co-respondent.

"She was my best friend."

If it was possible to hear ears pricking, Michael heard them then. A sort of settling movement rippled through the jury, as they prepared to brace themselves for what might follow.

"And what, specifically, Mrs Mont, was the incident which brought about your final separation – the one occurring in January of this year?"

There was a pause before any answer came.

"I realised that my husband was continuing his affair with the co-respondent."

Bowman's eyes were fixed liquidly on the canopy above his witness's head. Her reply seemed to cause them great distress.

"*Specifically*, Mrs Mont."

Another pause, longer than before. Then:

"I discovered them in bed together."

A low expression of disgust, tempered with delight, escaped from the body of the Court. Mr Justice Orr peered out over the tops of his half-lenses, and it was quashed.

"*In flagrante delicto*, in fact?"

"I believe that is the phrase."

"And where, *exactly*, did this episode take place?"

"At our home—"

Bowman's eyes stressed once again the importance of his adverb.

"—in my bedroom."

Another murmur went around the Court. The Judge peered again. One juryman blew his nose.

"Were the respondent and co-respondent aware that you had so come upon them?"

"After some moments."

"And what was their response to being discovered?"

The petitioner could be seen taking a deep breath before replying.

"They laughed."

'*Good God!*' came a startled cry from the back of the Court. A worthy citizen was evidently appalled.

Here Bowman took a moment to wipe his spectacles on his gown, and reset them upon his pointed nose. By this action he seemed to readjust the focus of the whole Court.

"My next question will be as distressing to you as it is necessary to these proceedings, Mrs Mont. It is my duty to ask you – did this response mark the end of the episode?"

The small voice was further reduced on the single word of the answer.

"No."

"What then followed?"

"My husband spoke to me."

"From your bed?"

"Yes."

"Saying what?"

There was no reply. When Bowman seemed reluctant to prompt his witness further, Mr Justice Orr intervened.

"Did you hear the question, Mrs Mont?"

"Yes, my Lord."

Then please answer.

There was no reply.

"The Court wishes to be tolerant in these circumstances. Be so good as to repeat your question, for the record, Mr Bowman."

"My Lord." As if reprising the tune of a song, Bowman said: "When your husband spoke to you from the bed, what did he say – Mrs Mont?"

"He made a suggestion," came the answer at last.

"To what effect?"

"That I join them."

The Court gasped as though it had been one creature with many mouths, then fell into rapt silence.

"Finally, Mrs Mont, did you make any reply to this suggestion?"

The petitioner shook her head with sudden vehemence. It was all the more effective for being the first movement she had made.

"No. I ran from the house."

"Thank you."

Bowman, Q.C., sat down. From the witness box, the small, clear voice added:

"I should like a glass of water, please."

One was brought. In the interval, Michael felt a cold sweat had formed on his forehead. He applied his handkerchief, and saw his hand was trembling mildly. 'Steady, Barker!', he told himself, but his humour failed him. To have one's son proclaimed a sensualist

536

in open court — it was a shock! At his side Fleur still hadn't moved.

Haberdasher had risen, and was hovering. The Judge and he both waited for the petitioner to set down her glass. When she had, Mr Justice Orr said:

"Are you ready to continue, Mrs Mont?"

"Yes, my Lord."

"Very well. Sir Clifford?"

Haberdasher stroked his long, sallow chin, like an undertaker deciding whether or not a coffin was the right length. His voice, when he spoke, was in all points as lubricious as his appearance.

"Mrs Mont, this must be a trying time for you, so I shall keep my questions to a minimum. The Court understands that although you forgave your husband for his adulterous behaviour once before, you have not done so on this second occasion, with which we are presently concerned – is that understanding correct?"

"Yes."

"I should like, then, to ask you to clarify one point. When you forgave your husband's conduct, over the matter of 'Ferrar v. Ferrar and Mont', what form did this forgiveness take?"

The petitioner's dark eyes grew larger.

"I am afraid I don't understand what the question means."

"Ah, then let me rephrase it. When you had forgiven your husband his transgressions, was normal marital congress restored between you?"

"Yes."

"To the extent of sexual relations?"

"Yes."

"You are aware, are you, Mrs Mont, that such forgiveness in a marriage, as far as the Law is concerned, is seen as condonation?"

"Yes."

"And that such condonation – again in legal terms – restores the *status quo*?"

"Yes."

"Thank you!"

Haberdasher returned to his table.

"You have no further questions, Sir Clifford?" asked the Judge over his half-lenses.

"None for the moment, my Lord."

"Then I propose we break here for lunch."

Lunch passed silently. The afternoon session, devoted to the examination of testimony submitted by the co-respondent, and by members and former members of the native staff of the two households concerned, was concluded before four o'clock.

Kit returned to his club, but at least accepted a lift there. Roger excused himself from supper, but accepted tea. At South Square, their three-cornered conversation was kept on a deliberately inconsequential kilter, though Em's absence was felt, given it was her particular strength.

"How's Martha?" Fleur asked, pouring. "Still golfing?"

"Rather! No sugar, thanks. Nine holes every day, rain or shine – it's her grand passion. I'm by way of being a golf widower, you might say."

"My father took up golf when he was sixty-nine."

"Uncle Soames! I'd no idea he'd got the bug."

"He hadn't. It was only that Jack Cardigan gave him a set of clubs for his birthday and he couldn't stand to see them wasted."

"Ah! a family trait, that," Roger offered.

"Yes," said Fleur, and to Michael, taking his cup, her tone sounded a little flatter. "I can't say I'm fond of waste, myself. Have some more fruit-cake."

"Don't, Michael! Please."

He had intended only to console, putting his hands on her shoulders as Fleur brushed her hair in front of her three-part dressing-glass that night. Feeling her recoil from his touch, Michael withdrew his hands immediately.

"Sorry!"

Seeing the look of hopelessness in her eyes, as they stared into the central mirror – not seeing her occupation or her reflection, but just blankly staring – he was reminded of the real nature of the case. It was not Mont *v.* Mont she would have to endure for another day in the Courts, but Forsyte *v.* Forsyte. If Fleur had not been crossed in love, after all, before ever there was a Mont on the scene, those two would have been brother and sister, and this misery spared. Yes, it was a waste; an all-round waste.

538

"I wonder if Kit really wants us there at all," she said unexpectedly, presaging what had been her husband's next thought.

"Weddings and divorces," he replied with a shrug. "The invitations set the teeth on edge one way or another. I can't say I relish the idea of being 'in at the kill'."

"Kit still seems to think he'll win. I don't see how."

In her glass, her expression seemed to add, 'Or why.'

"It's an uncivilised business," Michael offered, "—having to lay bare one's private life."

"Or perhaps it's the only civilised one. Dirty linen exists, after all."

"In that case, the truly civilised way would be to have to air it before one married, and by mandate at every anniversary thereafter."

"In that case, my dear, who would ever marry?"

"I, for one!"

"Well," Fleur said, getting up from her table and turning with a sad little smile. "We can't all be perfect, Michael, can we?"

Feeling he had been somehow reproached with his own virtue, Michael made no reply, and slept that night in his dressing-room.

Chapter Seven

Polteed's Finest Hour

Going in past the flyers on the second day, Friday, Michael noted his overnight elevation to the peerage. *'Baron's Son Caught with Wife's Best Friend'*. This and the other made-to-measure headline, *'I Saw Him'* – suggestions of troilism being reserved for the Sunday editions – accompanied their silence to Carey Street. He won't find himself there, at least, Michael reflected, seeing the street sign as Riggs drew up; even if the Judge gives her costs on top of a settlement. Money's something, in a scrape.

As they filed in, Michael saw Fleur cast a lightning glance across the well of the Court before she sat down. After that single deviation she kept her eyes strictly forward, as on the day before. This time she wore a heavy, deep-coloured fur, and a hat with a brim, as though her previous outfit had left her too exposed, and she expected to be chilled to the bone during the remainder of the business. The petitioner, Michael noticed as he let himself follow Fleur's glance, looked more doll-like than ever, dressed in soft grey velvet that made her seem wrapped in mole-skin.

"If it please your Lordship, and members of the jury," Haber-dasher began, his voice sounding – if such a thing was possible – even soapier than the day before, "the accusations of adultery in this case are not contested by the respondent. His assertion is that his marriage remains viable, and his grounds for such an assertion are simply this; that his conduct on the occasion in question has, in fact and in deed, been condoned by the petitioner. The respondent will give his own sworn testimony to this effect, and I shall also introduce independent evidence in corroboration. I therefore call the respondent."

540

When Michael first saw his son in the witness box, he had the sensation of seeing a complete stranger standing there. A fair-headed young fellow of about thirty, keen of eye and chin, with a traveller's tan and the services of a decent tailor, he might have been any eager young buck, making good in the colonies and back for a spell of leave. The mirage passed, as the respondent leant one hand on the rail and assumed his habitual pose and expression – that 'sniff', originating with one born two generations above him, so passed down, genetically distilled, and emerging in Kit as a quality of mild but fixed disdain.

After scant preliminaries, Haberdasher asked:

"Is the affair between yourself and the co-respondent at an end?"

"It is."

"When did it end?"

"During the summer, before I came back to England."

"Is your wife aware of this fact, Mr Mont?"

"I've told her. You'd have to ask her if she believes me."

"Quite so – and therefore you do not contest the charge of adultery brought by your wife?"

"I'd have to be an idiot if I did."

A quick laugh escaped from the back of the Court. The Judge was 'on to it' with his lozenge-shaped lenses, and next turned them towards Kit. To no avail, Michael thought; I gave up trying that look when he was ten!

Haberdasher continued:

"Then – please tell us if you will – on what grounds do you defend this suit?"

"On the grounds that the '*status quo*', as you call it, has been restored between us."

The Judge's eyebrows moved upwards by a degree at the respondent's tone. He was unused to being reminded of his own Law in his own Court.

"Meaning full marital congress?" Haberdasher pursued.

"Meaning that."

"To the extent of sexual relations?"

"Meaning that too!"

The level of attention rose tangibly in the body of the Court. Day two might prove every bit as worthwhile as day one. Good show!

"Mr Mont, I now ask you to relay the circumstances . . ."

When Ann heard the question 'on what grounds do you defend?' she had no thought as to what Kit might answer. When she heard his reply, she had to swallow hard to stop herself from crying out 'No!!' She clutched at her gloves on her lap, and stifled the word in her throat. It was unthinkable that he would use that one lapse against her, just to prove his case. Why should he want to? What did he hope to gain? He knew she would never return to him. How could the mere technical fact of possession mean so much to a man? — But Kit was already describing that morning at Green Hill – while her father and brother and step-mother listened . . .

"And you did not resort to coercion in any form, Mr Mont?"

"I didn't need to."

No; it was true. She had seen her submission as a way of speeding his departure and – if she was honest with herself – as a sort of parting gift, a memento of those times before . . . something of the old urge to comfort . . . but nothing more. Surely even Kit could see that?

Jonnie had scribbled a note and put it into her hand. She looked down and read:

'His word against yours. Bowman will tackle on X.'

Kit was speaking again. Ann looked up and saw with a start that he was looking directly at her as his Q.C. put his next question. It was as if he knew what her brother had just written to her; as if he knew and was happy to play the game, confident of winning.

"So you believe that the marriage is salvageable for its own sake?"

"Yes," he was saying, fixing her with his steely grey-blue eyes, "and for the sake of any future child. I have reason to believe that my wife is pregnant."

"Thank you, Mr Mont!"

Ann shut her eyes as a chill seized her suddenly, turning hot and fluttery as she felt it rising up her neck and under her chin. She suppressed it with a quick shake of her head. He could not know. No one knew. No one else in the world; only she and that consultant. She had a vision of Benyon in the box, repaying his grudge against her for doubting his results, but dismissed it by recalling that his professional oath was on her side. Patient confidentiality – a doctor could be struck off for violating it. As to the oath she herself was

542

under — well, if they asked her she would lie. It was her only way out. Knowing the eyes of the whole Court were on her, Ann raised her own, and tried to set her gaze on a neutral point somewhere below the Judge's bench where there were no faces. On her lap, her hands plucked alternately at the fingers of her gloves and at Jonnie's note.

Haberdasher sat down. Bowman, having whispered something to Jonnie, was quickly on his feet, his eyes swimming towards the canopy.

"Are you aware of the consequences of perjury, Mr Mont?"

Haberdasher rose too.

"My Lord—"

"Yes, yes. Mr Bowman, it seems to me the respondent is quite well-informed as to these points of Law."

"As your Lordship pleases. Were there any other persons in the house at the time of this alleged reconciliation, Mr Mont, besides you and your wife?"

"Not that I noticed."

"So there were, in fact, no witnesses who could testify even to your presence at the house that day?"

"Only my wife. Unfortunately, there was no 'third party', on that occasion."

Another illicit laugh from the rear. Mr Justice Orr interposed.

"If you would kindly surrender the use of legal terminology, Mr Mont, to those qualified in its application—"

"My Lord."

"Mr Bowman—"

"I have no further questions for the respondent, my Lord."

Bowman popped a *cachou* and returned to his table.

"You may step down, Mr Mont."

... Ann felt her brother's hand on her arm, and Penny's on her shoulder. They believed her, and thought Kit the perjurer! What would they think when they knew it was all the other way about! She took a deep breath through her nose, and set her mouth into a hard line. It didn't matter — nothing mattered except to be out of this hateful place, and free! Afterwards she would make them understand, why she had lied, why she had needed to — afterwards. For the moment, and until this sickening charade was over, it was simply Kit's word against hers.

Ann knew vaguely that Kit's Q.C. had risen again, and that her own was locked once more in urgent consultation with her brother. She had lost the power to concentrate on what was happening. It was as much as she could do to hold on to that single thought, as she twisted Jonnie's note between her fingers.

'*His word against yours . . .*'

"I call Miss Olive Bletsoe."

There was a murmur from deep in the body of the Court as the next witness approached the box. Ann barely looked up, glimpsing a drab figure in brown standing under the canopy.

'*His word against yours . . .*'

Haberdasher drooled:

"Miss Bletsoe; you are an operative in the employ of the Polteed Private Investigation Agency[1], is that correct?"

"Yes. That's right."

"And your duties in that position are, I believe, generally those of surveillance?"

"That's it."

The woman's voice trilled out each answer in a set cadence, as from one who had been rehearsed in the art of giving evidence. The effect was to suggest some pert little town-bird had flown into the Court and settled on its rafters. Ann was roused from her study by a quality in the warbling.

"And, under instructions received by Polteed's from the respondent, you were one of two operatives directed to follow the petitioner, Mrs Christopher Mont, throughout the months of October and November of this year?"

"That's right. I was on the London end," chirped the witness, pleased to notice, as she gave her testimony from her notes, that her best side was turned towards the jury. It was clever, how they arranged these places! "Whenever she left home and went to the station, I'd get a call saying she was coming in, on such-or-such a train. Then I'd pick her up from Victoria."

"And how often did the petitioner come to London during that period?"

---

[1] *For earlier examples of the sterling work carried out by this firm, vide: Forsyte v. Forsyte and Forsyte (1900), and Corven v. Corven and Croom (1931).*

"Only the twice. Went to the same place each time, though."

"And where was that, Miss Bletsoe?"

"Harley Street."

. . . Ann was staring at the hand which held the rail of the witness box. The nails looked like little red berries, and she could see the flash of rings under the lights. She listened to the rest of the testimony – the times and duration of her appointments, the consultant's special qualifications, every detail – not knowing if the words were coming from outside or inside her head. The whole Court seemed ringing with the minutiae of her innermost life.

When her own handkerchief was entered into evidence, she would have left, then and there, if she could have trusted her legs to carry her.

Bowman had no questions and the witness was allowed down. Ann saw her brother look quickly across the well of the Court. Mechanically she followed his gaze, to where Kit's Q.C. was bent in close conference with his solicitor. She felt suddenly numb, and perfectly, perfectly senseless.

Haberdasher rose from the huddle.

"My Lord, in light of the evidence furnished by the last witness, I should be glad of your permission to recall the petitioner."

The Judge nodded and, eventually, Ann understood he meant her. She got up unsteadily, seeing Jonnie's hand under her arm, but not feeling it there. She left her brother and walked to the witness box, with no sensation of there being a floor beneath her feet. She might have been floating . . .

Upon hearing the girl at last answer, quietly and affirmatively, to the question, twice repeated like some terrible incantation, '*Are you, in fact, expecting your husband's baby, Mrs Mont?*', Fleur felt an unexpectedly sickening lurch in her stomach. Michael's hand reached across, but she drew her own away. She wanted simply to go. Getting up to leave, Michael rising dutifully at her side, she heard a dull thud and, almost on the same instant, Jon's voice on the other side of the Court crying,

"*Ann!*"

That inescapable name!

Fleur turned momentarily towards the centre of the commotion – caught in a blur the sight of Jon rushing headlong towards an

545

apparently empty witness box, glimpsed the pain and worry on his face – and, not wishing to see more, turned back.

The Judge was calling for an usher, maintaining the calm over a sudden rise of other voices in the Court, and explaining,

"—it appears the petitioner has fainted."

Fleur did not look again, but found the nearest door, taking Michael's arm to steady herself until they found fresh air, and Riggs, outside.

Chapter Eight

Country Retreat

Mr Justice Orr, speaking with the very real regret of a 'stickler' hoist by his own petard, announced to the jury the existence in the suit of that which he identified as 'an absolute bar'. Bending the words of a popular poet to fit the case, he explained how, on the part of the petitioner, forgiveness of evil done was not free – at least from legal consequences. He directed them, thereby, to deny the petition.

Michael, once seeing Fleur into the car and instructing Riggs to return his mistress to South Square, had gone back into court in time to hear this adjudication. Taking leave of Haberdasher, and turning a corner with his son and 'very young' Roger on their way out again, Michael was alarmed to come suddenly upon 'the other side' gathered in one of the panelled outer corridors. Kit looked directly at the girl, who looked away immediately and was shielded by her step-mother. Kit walked on, his expression revealing nothing, and when Roger drew his counterpart to one side, to exchange a few last words of business, Michael was left standing awkwardly in front of Jon Forsyte.

Two seconds passed, perhaps three, no more; chapter and verse was covered in that time without a word being spoken. In the faces of both men was the same mixture of sensibilities; something of recrimination, something more of regret and, deep in the eyes of each, blue upon grey, the recognition of the perfect irony of it all.

'*If not for you, then I—*'

'*If not for me, then you—*'

Winifred Dartie had the word for it – it *was* a coil! Michael gave the briefest of perceptible nods, and left quickly.

*

At Lippinghall, where through various routes the family was once more assembled by the cocktail hour, it was as if the divorce had never been – which indeed, by strict legal definition, it had not. This process of group apperception was secured largely by Michael's spending five minutes in his study at South Square before they left – a precaution while Fleur was changing for the drive down – to telephone down to his mother there, who he knew would be 'waitin'' for the outcome. He told her what it was, heard her pronounce it *'too frustratin''*, and then extracted her best promise not to refer to the subject – even by the most remote act of leap-frogging – for at least the ensuing seventy-two hours.

Kit went from the Courts to lunch at his club – where, in the spirit of the adage *'There but for the Grace of God'*, it was certain that no fingers would be pointed, though it was uncertain whether he would have cared if any were. (In fact, once it was bruited that he had won, an amount of *kudos* was silently awarded, as due to the man who had succeeded in putting his wife in her place.) He then taxied to Paddington, passably happy to join his sister on the four-twenty-five train, due to arrive at Pangbourne at a little before six, by which hour Riggs would be waiting to convey them over the last few miles to the Lippings.

Kat looked at her brother, who was lounging over two seats with the arm rest up as the train steamed steadily out of London; it was too early for most people to be out from their offices – her own release being due to Giles' continued indebtedness over that matter of the contract – and they had got a carriage by themselves.

"Is there anything to say?" she asked him.

Kit shrugged in the way their mother did, she noticed, a quick flinch of the shoulders coupled with a slower lowering of the eyelids. Very French, she thought; a neat, expressive gesture she had never mastered herself.

"Nothing much," he said. "Petition denied, that's all."

It seemed inappropriate to offer her congratulations, and so Kat just nodded, in a manner that was designed to let him know an evening paper had already come her way. He nodded back.

"They'll hold the juicy stuff for the Sundays."

A sharp rap at the door and the conductor appeared. They offered their tickets, and had them clipped and offered back. The conductor tipped his cap – mostly to Kat, since young gentlemen had not sprawled in his own youth – and passed on.

"Are you staying on for a while?"

It was odd, to be talking to her brother in these half-familiar, half-distant terms – as if they had been old college acquaintances accidentally reunited on the train.

Kit shook his head.

"Next boat out – leaving Sunday. I've booked Riggs to take me back to Town at first-light tomorrow, so don't forget to wish me a 'Merry Christmas' before you go to bed tonight."

"I won't. Do they know?"

"Just the Guv'nor."

Kat nodded again. Kit tells Father; Father tells Mother and Grandmother, making sure to inform each separately from the other. Then everybody knows; *et fin d'histoire*.

"When will you be back again?"

"Sooner than anybody wants me, probably," he answered, with a curl in one corner of his mouth. "I'll try if I can't get a decent price on the estate, and come back for good in the summer. Then—"

He stopped and looked out of the window, at the yellow lights of suburbia joggling past in the blackness beyond.

"—Then we'll see."

Over the rattle of the train, Kat thought she heard his sigh.

"I hope it wasn't gruesome for you, Kit."

Even as she was asking, she had the sense that it was not – that all along the experience had been no worse than irksome for her brother, and that other considerations altogether were what was really troubling him. He replied without immediately turning from the window.

"Consider it an exercise in character-building, as Dad used to say."

When he finally did look at her, he was smiling nicely, and Kat felt for a short moment that she had her big brother back, in a way she hadn't for years.

"A word of advice, Katty, if you're thinking of ever getting hitched—"

She raised her eyebrows to encourage him, and his smile broadened.

"—*don't*."

Conversation only once reverted to the topic.

"Perhaps he means to make a go of the marriage this time," Michael said later that Friday evening, when Kit and Kat and their grandmother had gone up, and he and Fleur were alone, watching the last log crumble to potash in the library fireplace, "if she'll have him back."

"She won't," Fleur returned simply, lazily lowering her lashes as she shrugged the answer.

Michael might have asked her why she was so sure, but the reflection in her eyes, when their lids were raised again, suggested that the mathematics of the equation were too tedious to relate to such a dunderhead as himself. He set about coming at the same point a less contentious way.

"Does Kit know that, do you think?"

"I can't think that he doesn't," Fleur said, and gave a little shake of her head as she considered the improbability of it for a moment. "He must know she's out of love with him – what he did or didn't do doesn't matter, after that."

"But plenty of marriages survive without romance, surely?"

"Only if they started without it. That way, there are no illusions. It's disillusionment that's so fatal."

In the fire-basket, the last of the log fell in on itself with a soft crash of embers, and Michael, watching its descent, had the uncomfortable feeling he was listening to the voice of authority. Was that how their union had survived these thirty-two years – because from the start it lacked anything so vital?

"Anyway," Fleur continued, with a sigh in her voice that indicated her tolerance of the subject was not without limitation, "it's only the child he wants. The twelfth baronet, after all."

"Good Lord—!"

The notion of a potential twelfth on the way caught the tenth of the line so completely by surprise that he sat up in his armchair, as if he had been slapped across the face.

"D'you know, I hadn't thought—"

Fleur got up from her own chair then, and through her dark lashes, this time lowered in nothing more significant than a yawn, it was possible to understand from the expression in her eyes that her husband's answer had caused her no surprise whatever.

But Michael was riveted by the notion. He had begun to turn over his earlier assumptions in the light of this new discovery. It made all the difference, of course; he saw that now. What would Kit do, if his young wife wouldn't return to him? What did the Law empower him to do, for that matter, if the child was an heir? Could a neck be in Chancery before it was born? It was a conundrum, and, to the best of his knowledge, not one which had ever troubled the Mont line before. He would consult Whitaker before he went up, or he would never sleep. His son's imperturbability in this affair must have come through the distaff side of his make-up!

He realised Fleur was leaving the room. She had finished with the topic, he knew. She couldn't influence it, and so she had simply let it go. It was her French blood, of course — that trait was pure Lamotte!

"—Is that really all he cares about, do you think?" he asked her finally, as she reached the library doors.

Again Fleur's shoulders rose minutely.

"The Miller of Dee, my dear. Don't be long."

By the time Michael rose from his reverie, the fire was out. He drew the fire-screen in front of the cooling ashes and, having forgotten Whitaker, went up.

When Kat came down to breakfast the next morning, a half hour or so later than her customary time and more than two after her brother had left for London, she realised the rôle of 'sole resident offspring' had been reappointed to her in the interim with something of a vengeance.

"Morning, everybody!"

"Morning, sleepy-head!" called her father from the sideboard. "Scrambled eggs, kidleys, or am I challenged for the last sausage?"

She rubbed her cheek against his as she passed, picking up his tone of only slightly over-done *bonhomie*.

"Kidleys, please, and coffee, if there is some. Mother—"

"Good morning, darling. Coffee here, hot milk on the end."

Fleur tilted up her face for her daughter's kiss with rather more commitment than was usual with her. Kat then passed to Em.

"Gran'—"

551

"Blore's just brought some fresh. His timin' – it's almost Swiss." Em patted her granddaughter's arm. "There – you kiss so nicely, Kat. I always expect to catch Augustine windin' him in the kitchen. Who's shootin' this afternoon?"

Fleur answered.

"Vivian will, Nona won't, so I suppose Michael's in and I'm out."

"Vivian?" Kat asked, directly she sat down.

"A busman's holiday for you, I'm afraid." Her father brought up her plate, sat down to his own, and then, as an after-thought, looked at her over his sausage. "You haven't fallen out with him in the office, have you?"

"No, not at all — but I've invited Astrid and Giles down this week-end."

There was a moment's silence.

"Coo Lummy!" cried her father.

"*Hay Fever!*" said her grandmother.

"You didn't tell me," her mother snapped, a little too readily for the well-being of the general mood.

"That's a *gaffe*, Kat."

"Mine, I'm afraid. Kat told me, when you were both in with Kit one time. I thought I'd mentioned it, but I'm slippin' these days. '*Ignorance is Bliss.*' Bigby, I forgot. So sorry."

"Jolly!"

So saying, the baronet thought for a while, working through the permutations to ask:

"How is Bigby's professional rating at the moment?"

"Quite high right now. He just helped secure a new American author, and was marked a gold star for his efforts."

"Thank Heaven. Does he shoot?"

"Like a native, Dad – the Pennycruik Moors—"

"—Ah, of course."

"Now I'm rememberin' — Uncle 'Cuffs' always went before the First War. They never re-stocked afterwards, and people stopped goin' between. Then there was the Blitz at the *Café de Paris*, and now they're all goin' to the National Trust instead. How'm I doin', Kat?"

"Spot on, Gran'. Burke's is not more consecutive."

The baronet's brow forwent some of its worry.

"Then that doesn't sound so bad. But, for pity's sake, Kat, do tell him not to bag anything Vivian misses. I don't think we should push our luck."

"Works' outin'," Em said. "Blore ought to get a charabanc!"

The Bigbys arrived some forty minutes ahead of the Messengers that morning, and, once the initial shock of a *de facto* 'Company week-end' was overcome, lunch was a noisy, merry business. With sinews stiffened by Augustine's renowned game pie and spirits raised by the good claret it demanded, the afternoon was spent in hastening dozens more little lives to their end in the spinneys of the Mont country seat.

Over tea, taken on the tiger-skin spread in front of the conflagration got up by Blore in the fireplace of the great hall, Michael asked about the latest Messenger signing. His own *War Diaries* had been a moderate success, but their sequel – *Peace Diaries*, recording his experience of opposition – was an immoderate failure, and remaindered after six months. When Vivian made no suggestions for a third volume, Michael felt he had not so much lost a publisher as regained a friend.

"I hear you've acquired a new American, Vivian?"

"New to me, anyhow; he's kicked around in other places. Avery Lehrer Boyd. Mad, bad and dangerous to know – but good for trade, I reckon. Wouldn't you say, Bigby?" Here Vivian turned magnanimously to Giles, who was on the point of accepting his third piece of Dundee cake. "Bigby knows the feller."

Giles considered declining the cake, then decided to take it, but to sit up a little straighter in his seat at the same time. He was about to say '*Kat knows him too*,' in the manner of pass-the-parcel, but realised it wasn't to his advantage to admit her assistance.

"Is he, Giles?" Michael asked.

"I'd say so, sir. The man's a maniac, if you ask me."

Since they had, this was taken as fair comment.

"'*Le Byron de nos jours*', Kat called him," Giles added, determined not to go the distance alone in this particular event. He glanced towards her, expecting her to look up at the mention of her name, but she was engaged in what he instantly identified as girls' talk with the Dowager and Astrid, and his host's and senior partner's wives.

"There you are," said Vivian. "Kat's got him in one. Wolf at the door."

"What's his story?" Fleur asked, turning on her chair and joining in. She was sitting between the two halves of the gathering, which against her best contrivance had fallen into men down one side and women down the other of the great hearth. Her interest in galleries and fashion in any case, the chief topics so far on the spindle side, was flagging. "Byronic types usually have one. 'A lady in the case', I imagine."

Vivian nodded over his tea-cup.

"Dramatic stuff, too. He's cagey, but I've pieced most of it together. Love of his life, an' all that. She died in the war – French girl in America, went back in 'thirty-nine – killed in the Resistance, some say. Boyd refused conscription after that."

"An objector, too?"

"Oh, if you'd met him, Michael, you'd expect it. Maverick streak and mad-dog eyes. The Yanks assigned him to the malaria project for the duration, 'long with the other conscies. Still gets bouts of it now and then – wallows – drinks too much – and the rest. In between he writes."

"He sounds a heretic," said Fleur, "or a candidate for *felo-de-se*."

"Bit o' both, I'd ha' thought, given his record to date. Not a bad mixture, when there's talent in with it."

"And is there?" asked Michael. "Does he write well?"

"Like an angel, as long as it's fit to print."

"Ah – quite. Well, I suppose today's literary outlaw is tomorrow's academician. Look at my old chum, Wilfrid Desert. He's been all but canonised in the twenty years since he died, yet they were asking him to resign from his club two before. But it does sound as if you've got your hands full with this one, my dear."

"Genius has its price. Fleur, darling, did Bigby leave any cake?"

As tea drew to a close people drifted away from the hall, singly or in assorted pairs, to gain the quiet of their rooms for an hour or so, and begin preparing themselves for the next round of socialising – the cocktails that would inevitably precede supper. Kat was one of the first to seek the refuge of her bedroom. She had listened greedily to every word that was said about Boyd, while appearing to have

554

no other interest than jollying her grandmother with accounts of the galleries she had lately been to – without mentioning whose company she had been to them in. She wisely let Astrid deliver the review of the play they had seen at The Ambassadors.

Despite this dissembling, her grandmother still managed to compliment her on the recent colour she had noticed in her cheeks. '*Becomin'!*' was her expression.

In her room now, too alert to settle properly anywhere, too full of interest in what she had just learned to pick up a book, Kat paced for some minutes and eventually cast herself upon her bed, so that she was lying on her back and staring up at a non-existent point somewhere in mid-space above her head and beneath the ceiling.

Maverick . . . heretic . . . genius . . . mad-dog eyes . . . felo-de-se.
The attributions she had heard ought to have startled her, ought to have made her reconsider her own view of the man, but she took them all as nothing but more fair comment, and some of them even as due tribute on his behalf. Hadn't she thought him an apostate herself? And her very first image of him had been in that wolven coat. The truth was that to have him considered all those things simply added to the general piquancy. *Agreeably disquieting to the senses* — yes, it was — more than ever! And as for the whisper of a great love lost—

Through her door she heard voices approaching on the stair, which had to twist past the little landing exclusive to her bedroom and its neighbour in order to accommodate the digression of architectural styles occurring in that wing.

She heard her mother talking with Astrid, and recognised Giles' rather heavy male footfall amongst the lighter female ones. When they stopped on her landing, she caught her name several times, first in her mother's voice. Kat lay still on her bed and listened.

"I make no apologies for putting you in the 'monk's cell' next to Kat, Astrid, because I knew you'd both be padding along the corridors for chats in the dead of night if I didn't. They connect through the dressing-room, have you discovered?"

Then in Astrid's own plucked tones.

"Yes, thanks — it's so lovely having a proper chance to catch up on everything in our jim-jams — it'll be just like college. Kat *never* stays with me any more, not since she started working with *Giles*."

Her mother laughed fondly.

"Oh, Astrid, you're like third-formers – she was with you only at the end of last month."

"I'm sorry – when?"

Lord! Here Kat could almost *feel* Giles look to Astrid, and heard the small but significant hesitation from her mother before she replied.

"On the last night of the fog – the twenty-sixth, wasn't it?"

"But I was in Paris on the twenty-sixth."

Her mother's tone changed narrowly.

"Astrid, are you sure? Kat told me she spent the night at Bedford Square—"

"Well, she—"

"She did, Lady Mont—"

(interrupting her — Giles' voice, at its most gallant pitch!)

"—but with me."

Now Kat knew both sets of female eyes were on Giles, who spoke stiffly.

"The fog was appalling – it was the only sensible thing. It was all perfectly proper, I needn't add."

Nothing from Astrid, and from her mother only,

"I see. Well, be down for drinks at eight, please."

Two clicks as Astrid's door opened and closed, while Giles and her mother continued up. Would Astrid come through directly? Now – what to say if she did? But she wouldn't come; Astrid's instinct would be to beard her brother first; and Giles, if she knew him, would fight his corner. Well, there was nothing to be done about it, one way or the other. If Giles stood by his story, she would have to talk to him. If he didn't — heigh-ho!

New voices on the stairs.

Her father and grandmother were talking now, and as their footsteps rose up towards her door, and before they continued to rise further up and away from it, Kat again heard her name spoken more than once, and again she lay still and listened. What she heard was at first only a re-working of what she had told downstairs to her grandmother, who was now telling her father, but getting the pictures in the wrong galleries. Then both footsteps and voices suddenly stopped.

"—Cheeks and galleries!" said Em, coming to a halt on a bend in the stair above her son, arrested by the tidal motion of her revelation and swaying gently in its surge. "Kat's in love—!"

When Kat heard her grandmother's latest pronouncement, carried clearly to her in her room, as all conversations were destined to be from that particular twist on the stair, by one of the stranger freaks of acoustical irregularity at Lippinghall, it caused her far greater sensation than any part of the previous exchange there.

Her first reaction was, '*I am?*', followed so quickly by her second, '*Of course!*', that it was as if the first had never been. During supper, it seemed to those watching her that she almost shone.

The house grew silent, or silent at least of human sound, since the building itself was never without noise, that organic susurration of creaks and shifts and settlings, from old timbers minutely shrinking and ancient boards easefully sighing, which was chorus to its age.

Lying still for a long while, listening to the tall-case clock ticking mustily through the spaces below, hearing one o'clock strike, and two, Kat felt the possibility of *une nuit blanche* approaching, and knew she would never sleep unless she stirred first. Astrid had clearly failed to corner Giles, for she had not come through, and must now be fast asleep next door.

Before the next quarter chimed Kat got up, putting her feet into slippers and her head and arms through a heavy sweater pulled from a drawer. Shaking down the rough woollen ribbing over the silk of her night-dress, she left her room and went downstairs, her step so light and swift – the house her intimate in every detail underfoot – that anyone happening upon her must have taken her for a spirit gliding. But no one did happen upon her and, unchallenged, Kat reached her destination – the little passage behind the kitchens, a corridor smelling of mildew and damp leather, and reserved for the comings and goings of shooting parties, which was known historically as the 'field entrance'.

There, in the dim glow of the pilot-flame from a gas boiler, by some tradition also lodged in that alley, she put her feet – slippers and all – into a pair of her father's wellington boots, claimed a waxed jacket and a scarf from a jumble of outdoor belongings on a row of pegs, then lifted the great latch of the door with both hands

557

and released the complaint of its old hinges upon the night.

Outside, the clear, moonless sky shed a dull lustre over skeletal shapes of shrubs and bushes. No breeze blew, nothing stirred, no creature broke the icy, graphite stillness but herself, as she stepped over grass, and gravel, and grass again, following no path but the capricious drift of her heart.

'*Kat's in love!*'

Would she have known but for that fortuitous piece of eavesdropping? It had seemed a fabulous suggestion but, like a hidden reflection, recognisable absolutely for one's own the moment it was revealed. She wandered on in the frosted light, warmed by her new knowledge, full of fresh awareness. In the grey sheen of the night now, she saw him everywhere — half-ambling, half-running towards her on long limbs, down the slope of the back meadow with the pewtery sky behind him, his wolven coat flapping open with his descent to the mercuric stream — walking towards her beneath the black fists of pollarded willows lining the drive, his heels crunching on the little stones — or standing quite still, waiting for her, a graven statue against bleached branches of wisteria criss-crossing the shadow of the library wing. All around her she conjured him, marvelling at his height, his grace, his wisdom; and at every turn the phantom followed her, and answered her beckoning.

As a little girl playing in these grounds, she would summon her own foreign prince in a fairy carriage – with high-stepping horses and attendant sprites in golden livery – to whisk her away and make her his princess. On foot and unattended now, as the fantasy matured, this dark challenging man took his place.

On the terrace, the house rising dimly at her back, she thrust her face up to the grey profundity above and breathed deeply, inhaling the cold mystery of the night until she was crammed with its secrets. Like a willing accomplice, the air surrendered its scents to her; pepper from the old limes, truffles from the oaks, the vague tang of citrus from the willows, all elements in that intoxicating musk which was the very breath of night.

At last she gave a long sigh, then stretched and smiled. In a sky made of polished slate – cloudless, moonless, starless; 'gin-clear', as her grandmother called such nights – Kat saw his face, asleep, or so it seemed, and kissed his eyes from afar.

Chapter Nine

Repercussions

Their founder and chief proprietor taking a forward-looking view of staff privileges (and of his own capacity for seasonal revelry), the offices of Messenger and Company were closed from this, the last week-end before Christmas, until the morning of the first Monday in the New Year. So, after that all-round instructive week-end, it was not until fully two weeks later that Kat encountered Giles again. It was longer still, of course, since she had seen Boyd, though only after her grandmother's revelation had she actually begun counting the days. From Lippinghall – *ultima Thule*, as it felt – she ventured to send a note to South Kensington, asking — suggesting — she might call and claim some tea on that day . . .

Going into her office on that Monday morning, with no mind for work and focussed only on the anticipatory tingle she felt in her stomach – a frothy feeling like the one that used to come after eating sherbet too quickly – Kat became aware of the shift in atmosphere almost at once.

First tackling the pile of correspondence waiting on her desk, she saw with a further unreasonable stirring below her ribs that Boyd had replied to her note. She recognised his bold, spiky hand immediately. His note simply said:

> *'I shall be found by the fire—*
> *'B.'*

It was as she was tucking the page carefully back into its envelope – for she wanted to keep both, liking as much to have her name written out by him as the communication itself – that

559

Giles appeared in their connecting doorway, and the air in the room went somehow flat.

"Giles — Happy New Year!"

He returned the favour, not in his usual hearty manner but formally, mumbling rather. He seemed, in any event, to be addressing his shoe.

"How was bonny Scotland?"

"Bonny — thanks."

Giles directed this at first to the filing cabinet, then to the secretary's yet-to-be occupied desk, and there the exchange lapsed.

"Good!" said Kat, after an interval in which she continued to smile cheerfully at him and he continued to smile obliquely at Polly's blotter. She put her head on one side, as if from an angle she might manage to peer around the corner of his gaze, but Giles only turned back into his office, studying the linoleum as he went, and shutting the door behind.

This state of affairs persisted through the morning. Kat soon came to realise that if she had disliked being Giles' idol in the old year, she disliked even more being his fallen one in the new. Finally accustomed to having his puppy's eyes always on her, to have them as assiduously averted was a whole new source of irritation. She decided on the direct approach, finding with Giles over the years of their acquaintance that almost any other was likely to be too subtle for him.

As the rest of the population removed for their mid-day break, Kat slipped through to Giles' office and discovered him standing moodily at his window, his hands together at his back as he gazed out at the broad tree-lined thoroughfare below.

To Kat he looked like one who had just lost a favourite pet. So he has, she thought — the custody of my virtue, as he thinks!

"Giles—"

"You ought to get some lunch," he said, not unkindly, but still at the window.

"I doubt I shall ever eat again, after two consecutive weeks at Lippinghall. Anyway, I've come to talk to you about something."

Giles' back stiffened perceptibly.

"There's no need!"

That timbre of the gallant, last heard on the stair outside her

560

room, had returned to his voice, and Kat was suddenly very cross. What right had he to presume this rôle for himself?

"There wouldn't be, I'm sure, except for your electing to play the pompous ass in all this."

Giles turned from the window in the best theatrical manner, as when the stage direction '*stifling his pride*' appears in the text. His pride was wounded, there was no doubt, and that on top of the very real hurt he felt in other emotional departments, and had nursed the length of the holidays at 'Castle Bigby', brought the heroic in him to the fore. He stood behind his desk, turning over a glass paper-weight as transparent as the effect he was after.

"Oh, do sit down, Giles — really!"

Kat pulled a chair to the front of his desk and, sitting herself, stared at him until he followed suit on the corresponding side.

"Now. I ought to be furious with you—"

He looked at her then for the first time that morning; not quite into her eyes, but at a point just above them on her forehead. In his amiable, gingery features Kat saw something of the expression he must have worn for his nanny twenty-odd years before – '*it wasn't me*' finely overlaid with '*I won't do it again*'. Resisting the urge to smile, because he was obviously used to the look gaining him a reprieve, she went on.

"—As it is, I've made allowance for the notorious inter-breeding which has gone on in your family down the centuries and instead I'm simply cross."

"Um!"

"As you may well say. First, I want you to know that I appreciate your leaping into the breach at Lippinghall – when my mother asked about the last night of the fog."

Giles looked as if he were going to articulate a second "Um!", but thought better of it.

"Astrid, I suppose—" he began instead.

"No, not Astrid; she hasn't said a word on the subject. I over-heard you talking on the stair. It was gallant of you to prop up my cover story like that – especially since it was you who put me in the position of needing one."

By the struggle going on in his sandy face, it was clear Giles had already used his best monosyllable, and was searching for a second.

"Ah—!" he said, at last.

"Now, further to that, will you please tell me why you haven't been able to look me in the eye all morning?"

She had expected him to bluster a denial, but Giles seemed unable to say anything else. Kat watched him, but he only stared down at his hands, strangled together on his desk, and appeared to be in some very real distress. The Englishman at his capable best, she thought, brought to a standstill by a log-jam of his own most cherished prejudices – namely, what a well-bred young woman should and should not do, and how a gentleman – or nobleman! – should respond. What swampy terrain the moral high-ground was – and Giles was already in it up to his knees! She wondered why she didn't find this all more comical.

"I see. Well, so that you know — and to stop you fretting any longer, Giles — here is the 'authorised version'. As you surmised, I spent the night at Professor Boyd's flat—"

Giles' front features stiffened as his back had done. The prig! Kat thought; by rights, I should leave him mired – he deserves no better. But she continued.

"As you kindly told my mother, the fog was appalling – it was the only sensible thing. *And* as you'll remember feeling the need to add – it was all perfectly proper."

"Oh! — I'm sure!"

The bravely borne tension was instantly gone, from his face and voice, and from his hands, which, but for her presence in the room, might have clapped. He looked, in fact, as if he had been just let off a detention. As I always suspected, she thought; a perfect little boy – and a cowardly one, too. How people let one down!

Giles reached out a conciliatory hand to her, palm down, across the desk, but Kat got up, holding his eyes with a very plain look, and walked to the door.

"Montie—" he began as she moved away. "I didn't—"

Kat turned round in the doorway.

"Oh, yes, Giles. You did."

She closed the connecting door between them and regained her desk, the disappointment she had felt at Giles' behaviour suddenly transferred to her own. And a keen awareness came to her then, that

562

she had breached some fundamental code of her own, in helping Giles to maintain his.

The trick with the outer door of the mansion block, which Kat had stumbled upon unwittingly in the fog that first evening, was that it could be opened simply by pressing the button for 'Flat 9'. It had been so rigged as a labour-saving device by the previous occupant of the attic apartment, who had enjoyed a nominal rent for equally nominal caretaking. Boyd had demonstrated the mechanism for her the last time she saw him, and had told her to make use of it whenever she called again. And when he added, as she left him, that his door was always open, she had taken away with her the fond hope that perhaps he meant the statement a little more than literally.

Well, here was the test—

Pressing that convenient button this present evening – after trading her lunch hour for an extra fifteen minutes off her leaving time – Kat entered the hall of the mansion block and attacked the coiling staircase at a sufficient rate to disguise the fact that her heart had been pounding since before she left the tube station.

Since his door was indeed open, she passed silently through the vestibule, and found him as his note had promised, in the broken-down easy chair beside a hissing gas-fire, one long leg — a length of herring-bone tweed and brogue-leather — raised on the footstool, one sprawled at an angle. Directly in front of the fire – close enough nearly to scorch in the orange heat – lay the speckled dog, 'Professor', on its side, like a tatted hearth rug in black and white relief, wheezing slightly. In the room's low light, coming only from the gas jets and the standard lamp behind his chair, she thought both occupants were asleep, until the dog's black tail began to flutter and its visible eye moved towards her.

Kat put a finger to her lips. 'Professor' seemed to understand, or perhaps had never intended making any noise. Quickly she left her coat and things on the hat-stand and approached the fire, dropping to a crouch by the dog's head and crumpling one of its heavy black ears in her hand. The wheezing became a pleasurable whimper.

"Shhh—" Kat ordered, barely whispering. "Master's sleeping!"

She felt an unexpected sensation then, of her own head being gently touched.

"There you are!"

She turned at the sound of his voice and, for a brief moment, her cheek came to rest in the wide palm of his hand. Her heart raced dizzily to interpret the gesture, until she saw that he had one of her hair-combs between his fingers – it must have become dislodged when she took off her hat. Stupidly disappointed but with enough sense left to cover quickly, she took it from him and slipped swiftly onto the footstool where his leg still rested.

"Happy New Year!" she said, smiling at him.

He smiled back, mostly in his eyes, and replied, "Tea?"

She saw the customary three-quarters empty whisky bottle and a tumbler on the carpet next to his chair. It was so strange how he seemed always to be drinking and yet never drunk – nor anything like.

"Not yet. I'll get warm first, please."

"Be my guest." And he removed his foot from the stool, and stretched.

The old dog stretched too, wondering whether it was a sign for a walk, and, finding it wasn't, turned onto his other side in front of the fire and settled down again.

"Over easy," Boyd said, and rubbed the toe of his shoe against the feathery flank. The black tail acknowledged the comment.

"How was your holiday?" Kat asked, turning her back to the fire and facing him. She saw his eyes slip quickly round her face, where – though she didn't know it – the unflickering light from the fire made a red aura of her loosened hair. Then he replied:

"How was yours?"

Twice he had deflected reference to his own part in the season; Kat took the hint.

"Mine was oddly eventful. Our secret is out."

"Do we have one?"

"The last night of the fog."

"Ah," he nodded slowly. "Bigby will have inserted his foot, no doubt."

She had told him who would be down at Lippinghall, first for that week-end and then throughout the holiday. It caused her a passing qualm – as it had caused her many more durable ones over the past two weeks – to think he had spent the whole of the time

564

on his own. Just writing, she imagined, and drinking. The curse of the oracle!

"Actually, he sped to the rescue of my honour."

"Odd enough to be an event in itself."

"And not without forfeit. Now I am popularly believed to have spent the night alone with him."

"Then all is lost save honour!"

Boyd chuckled drily in his throat, and turned to look at the fire.

"You mustn't be mean to Giles – he's quite harmless, you know."

"I know. I'd consider it the greatest sin – in anyone else."

He turned back, and the look he gave her then was thoroughly disconcerting. Vivian's label, '*wolf at the door*', came back to her as she looked at his grey-bearded face, at his grey hair swept back from his high, bumpy forehead, and into his spice-coloured eyes, where the pupils were dark pinpoints, fixing her. She felt he was willing her to venture the next step, to be bold enough to draw the next inference from the details given, her conclusion unaided, uncoloured by him; his tutorial manner was as challenging as ever!

"I think you should know there's another popular belief about me among my family—"

His eyebrows arched gently. In the unshifting firelight his eyes remained fixed on her own.

"Arising from the previous one?"

"Out of the same general process. I'm blessed with a grandmother who is one of the seven seers – and she's pronounced me in love."

There — she had said it! No going back now — but how to proceed?

The dog got up at this moment, and moved between them. As Kat had been the one to save him from his awkward predicament – on that cold afternoon in Battersea, which might otherwise have been his last – he had evidently decided the time had come to save his rescuer from hers. He put his grey velvet muzzle on her lap, and, with his forelock standing as a whimsical question-mark on the proceedings, looked up at her over the red rims of his eyes. Pointed towards Boyd, the stump of a tail wagged purposefully.

"Tea!" said Boyd.

This command not occurring in his vocabulary, 'Professor' would have remained in his position, since it was comfortable and got his nose stroked nicely; but his master was rising, and the young lady after him, and so he felt obliged to follow. Out—? No! To the kitchen — hurrah!

The kitchen was very narrow, no more than a little galley, and required two people to work in close proximity in order to produce a reasonable tray of tea. Boyd filled the kettle from the tap, set it on the stove and put a match to the ring underneath. The gas lit with a soft *whh-ump*. The two old enamel mugs were on a high shelf above the sink, and Kat half-hoped he would glance at her figure when she stretched up – perhaps a little more than was necessary – to get at them. From the corner of her eye she saw that he did not, that he rather looked away, as if wishing to avoid the temptation for himself, or the suggestion of compromise for her. In his silence he remained challenging – inasmuch as he required her to make any running – but had they left the tutorial yet? Nothing in his manner once suggested they had or ever would. What hope was there? In the learning of love she was only a postulant, while he — he was already an apostate!

She got the mugs, laid them on the draining-board next to an earthenware pot, and found a tea-spoon in a drawer. These necessary chores being accomplished, nothing was said for a while, as they waited for the water to heat, until Boyd asked:

"Being a seer — your grandmother — she's not often wrong?"

"Being a seer — not often, no. She divines by ellipsis – and tends to be infallible."

"Well – it's quite a pronouncement."

"So I thought when I overheard it."

"And are you?"

"I seem to have developed the standard symptoms – yes."

"Hmm."

"Mmm."

"Has she also pronounced who you are in love with?"

"No. Her ellipsis gets in the way of arithmetic, rather. But others have put two and two together."

"And come up with Bigby, I suppose?"

"That's what *they* suppose, certainly."

"I see. Whereas the truth is—?"

What to say? A direct answer seemed then quite ridiculous,

and not somewhat forlorn. She wished he *had* compromised her.
Adopting Astrid's device, she answered in the manner of a bad novel.

" 'The truth is, kind sir — I love another!' "

She had tried to give her answer lightly, as the rest of their
exchange, but couldn't find the right pitch in her voice to bring
it off. The thumping of her heart was in any case too loud in
her ears to judge these things finely, and that spongy feeling had
returned in her legs. She busied herself over the tea-caddy, where
the lid appeared stuck.

There was another silence, and then Kat heard the strangest thing.
It sounded a perfectly ordinary London accent, yet was coming from
this singular American – and quite convincingly delivered, too, as if
he had an ear for such. The words were those of the keeper – when
she had chosen the old spaniel at the Lost Dog's Home—

"That's very charitable of you, miss!"

The lid of the caddy came away then, and in her unsteady grip a
spray of black tea leaves scattered lightly across the draining-board.
Kat took a cloth with one hand, holding the tea-caddy out of the
way of further accidents with the other, and concentrated on wiping
the spillage.

She heard a further echo of the keeper, but in Boyd's natural
voice this time, low and close, and infinitely gentle.

"People don't usually like to give their hearts on such a short
return."

She stopped wiping, because he had taken the cloth away from
her, but she didn't dare to look up, though she knew he faced her.
She just managed to say:

"It would be worth it — for any return at all—"

She couldn't tell – between his reaching for her, and her legs
beginning to give way – which of the two happened first. All she
knew was that suddenly she felt her weight taken from her, and her
legs leave the ground, as Boyd snatched her up bodily, and cradled
her to him with a grip every bit as desperate and needful as her own.
To cling to him she had dropped the caddy, which hit the drainer
and sent a full quarter of tea in a black cascade to the floor, where
the dog approached warily in case any part of it was edible. Kat felt
the press of Boyd's beard, softer than she had imagined, against her
face and lips; felt the strength of his great arms as he clutched her

greedily to himself; felt a long shudder run the length of his frame. She wanted to look into his eyes but they were tightly closed, and she could see a tear squeezing into the corner of each. She strained to kiss his eyelids – *'with kisses four!'* – just as the kettle began to boil, whistling a note which, untended, rose steadily to a scream.

Chapter Ten

False Spring

The winter continued disagreeably, intermittently wet or foggy, and on occasions becoming both together. To Kat, while she was in love, and while the object of her love seemed to love her too, it seemed the very Spring of Life itself. She knew that there was only one first hour, and recognised this for hers. She knew, too, that like all first hours it couldn't last — and yet — it must!

Under cover of the world's believing her to be seeing Giles, she called upon Boyd as often as she dared, and found his door always open. Her only hindrance arose from the responsibility she felt to keep herself at least some of the time at a distance from him while he was writing, as she believed he must be now. But then – and this was strange – as with his drinking, so it was with his writing. Kat saw little evidence of it in his flat – no type-scripts strewn around, not even any hand-written notes, none of the paraphernalia of his art. And she never witnessed the process, never managed to arrive *while* he was writing. Usually she found him sitting by the fire; and she would apologise for disturbing him; and he would tell her that she had not. Never once did he make her feel she was distracting him, or taking up his time. He appeared, in fact, to have all the time in the world.

Nor, once, did he speak of his writing, even in passing. Its absence from his conversation was scrupulous, almost as if it was a superstition with him, and it seemed to Kat that it was not her place to break the taboo. That and one other subject aside, they roamed the wide world of ideas and imagination as they talked – sometimes discussing music and poetry, sometimes debating points in plays and books; or they would marvel at how a squirrel's nest

569

was constructed, or how a dog's back leg was curved. And sometimes they would say nothing of any consequence at all. It didn't matter to Kat what they talked of, for, in his company, the slightest thing was illuminated, and the most complex made accessible.

They continued to go to galleries, and at week-ends occasionally to matinées; they took further walks with 'Professor' in the park, and when the park was closed – as it was at dusk, occurring each evening a little later as the days lengthened – they walked instead around the ramshackle chain of mews which encircled his garden square. On cobbled ways once rung by horses' hooves and the wheels of stately black phaetons and commodious barouches – now the haunt of sleek sportscars in racing-green or white – they walked and talked, and laughed, and even kissed.

On just such a walk one evening, after a light rain had left the cobbles glistening and the carriage-lamps clouding over in newly-forming mist, Kat finally put the only question she had avoided asking hitherto. Taking a deep breath of the vapourish night air, and holding it in her lungs until she began to see flecks of light at the corners of her vision, she said at last, very quietly:

"Tell me about her."

"Tell you about who?" he asked, walking on, his heels still striking the cobbles at slow intervals.

"Your lost love."

He stopped, under the triumphal arch-way of one of the mews through which they were passing, like one struck then and there by revelation. It was as though he had heard her question from within himself, and not externally. Other than that, he made no sign, but led her back to the mansion block in utter silence, holding her hand tightly as a touchstone in his. If not for this last detail, Kat might have feared to have lost him forever, so total was his immersion in the sudden, dark, private recesses of his thoughts, into which her question had so plainly and instantly cast him.

In his apartment, he went straight to the dresser and, pulling open a drawer, wrenched out a sheaf of closely type-written pages – two or three inches thick and inexpertly bound in brown paper and string. Kat saw the wild glint dangerously livening his pale eyes, heard the note of earnest challenge in his voice as he thrust the parcel from him.

"Read it! – and tell me!"

Escorting her home, Boyd held her more tightly than ever, as though he were the one fearful of loss.

The mist continued to gather, and threaten more fog. As Michael came home for his supper from the House, *via* the smoking-room at the Remove, he found himself now tending to side with the Honourable Member who had challenged him that afternoon, suggesting from across the Floor that '*the notion of clean air in modern industrial society*' was as '*delusory as the phenomenon known as friar's lanthorn*'. Michael felt he might have been over-zealous in his reply, accusing the fellow (a Northern industrialist, though through no direct fault of his own) of mistrusting to breathe air which he could not actually see. Still, it was horrid stuff to swallow, this noxious cocktail of mechanisation. Two parts chimney, three of petrol, and a dash of carbonic oxide for good measure. Stir gently, and what did you have? Four thousand dead in one week! Michael paced on, hankering for the week-end, and the stainless vapours of Lippinghall.

Turning into South Square, he happened to glance across the road, and saw a pair of shadows standing together on the corner opposite his own. Though they were stationed beneath the only unlighted street-lamp there – no doubt deliberately – the shape their bodies made in the dimness was impossible to mistake. These were lovers – kissing good-night in the makeshift privacy of a chance patch of darkness. Michael let his gaze linger over the outline of that double shadow, stealthy yet somehow bold too, with the girl's head reaching up, and bent back submissively, her throat extended like a swan's – the man's face bent down over her, desirous, protective, jealous. An artist's brush could not have rendered their relationship more tellingly than the accidental *chiaroscuro* afforded by a broken light-bulb. They were there still, in much the same configuration, when Michael reached his doorstep and, from that vantage, turned to look at them again. Love! Another case of delusion — a true Will-o'-the-wisp, if ever there were one. Yet we all pursue it, he thought, we all follow those dancing lights, seeking substance — and grasping — shadow!

The girl, as Michael watched her, broke away from her lover's

571

arms, and for a second looked something like his daughter as her hair swung out in a dark flag behind her. Could it—? No. It couldn't be Kat, for a dozen reasons which sprang immediately to the parental mind – the least of which was that she always wore her hair up for work. Another was that the second shadow, even allowing for the angle of the nearest light, seemed rather tall to be cast by Giles Bigby. And now, as he continued to overlook the scene, Michael began to discern a third shape there, nearer the ground, as if one of the two had brought a piece of luggage. Then the girl stooped over the seeming valise, and it jumped up at her. A dog! —belonging to the man, he suspected, because it seemed as anxious to keep her in the darkness as he. The girl hesitated and, so aided, her lover drew her back to his arms, and the embrace began again. Feeling like a Peeping-Tom, despite being – as it were – in his own back-yard, Michael put his face to his front door and searched for his latch-key. He let himself inside and went straight up.

He looked in at the second-floor sitting-room they had installed for his mother; she was there, pulling a face at some misjudged stitch in her embroidery.

"Birds or bunnies?" Michael enquired, out of long familiarity with her expression.

"Bunnies! This one's lookin' cross and he should be happy – it's spring."

Em held up her work for scrutiny, and her son saw a rural scene – a convincing mead, scrolled around the edges in an abundance of mediaeval greenery and having passable swallows flitting overhead, but with the foreground quite dominated by a very disagreeable-looking white rabbit.

Michael kissed her cheek.

"Perhaps he's late," he suggested.

"That's a thought. He'll need a pocket-watch."

"And a waist-coat – for the pocket."

"Purple or blue?"

"Blue, against the green – and to match the swallows."

"I'll undo his mouth first. But it's the eyes that are wrong, I'm afraid."

"Only the left one, a little bit?"

Em squinted at her canvas.

"No. Both."

"Really?"

"Not bunny's – mine. I'm not seein' what I used to. Perhaps I ought to get vitamins again."

Michael considered his mother fondly, as she took her needle and began to tease out the white rabbit's pink upper lip. Far from not seeing, she grew more Sphinx-like each day.

"A and D they say, for the eyes. Or a good oculist."

"Or I could give him whiskers, and he could bless them. Who's dinin'?"

"Just 'us four', I think, unless Fleur's invited someone since breakfast."

"Kat ought to, sometime."

"I dare say she will – when she's ready."

With this Michael was hoping gently to remind her of the unwritten house-rule at South Square, which forbade the nudging of any member of the household by another on any matter of private affairs.

"I was ready after a month of your father. Lawrence had a way. He'd've got her confidin'."

On this point Michael agreed. Bart would have been Kat's natural *confidant* now – had been, in fact, when she was just a little thing and adored her grandfather. He saw his mother smile faintly: two tears, not quite together, started down her cheeks. He offered his handkerchief before they fell.

"Vitamins," she said sadly. "I was gettin' stout with your father — now I'm gettin' thin without him, Michael. I'll fatten bunny instead."

Fleur was in her bath – surrounded by a soft foam smelling of gardenias, her hair banded up, her eyes dreamily out of focus and directed vaguely towards her toes showing out of the water at the far end. How pretty she was! and to Michael she seemed still absurdly young — as if she had been ever too swift in all her movements, in all her thoughts, for Time to set its stamp upon her. She was unaware of him, suspended as he was in the half-open doorway, and Michael's guess – not uninformed on the subject, after all – was that he had caught her idling among recollections of lost love. He saw her lips open, as she smiled to herself at some passing fragment of memory, then watched them close again, as she frowned. Then it seemed she tossed away the thought altogether, with a sudden shake of her head above the bubbles. Feeling uncomfortably that he had progressed from being a Peeping-Tom outside his house, to being one inside, Michael pushed the door further inwards until it creaked, and his wife's face became its usual flawless mask as he went up to her.

Perching on the rolled edge of the bath, Michael pressed his lips onto her moist forehead. As he withdrew, Fleur put some of her bath onto the end of his nose.

"Thanks!" he said, and blew the bubbles away with an upward breath, making her smile. "Might I do your back?"

"You're too late – it's done," and the smile became a little yawn.

"Tired?"

"Bored."

And giving no indication that she intended to move, Fleur got up from her bath then, offering a soap-sudded vision to her husband for some seconds before she completed wrapping herself in an oversized towelling robe. She sat down on the cushions of an ottoman, and began to unwind the band from her hair.

"Just plain bored," she repeated with a sigh. "Tell me what's new, Michael. Something must be."

"Yes—" he replied mechanically, his best attention still distracted by that fleeting vista. "—Well," – he collected himself – "this is, certainly," and he reached into his jacket and brought out a fold of type-written papers, passing them to Fleur.

"What's this?"

"A short story by the heretic – the American – Vivian gave it me at the club. It's going out in the spring edition of *New Babylon* next month."

"Oh—?"

The mention of that celebrated literary quarterly – revered and reviled for carving out a ruggedly iconoclastic position for itself in the world of *belles-lettres* – aroused a tone of freshly piqued curiosity in her voice. Twisting a lock of hair between her fingers the while, she began to skim the pages, her clear hazel eyes scanning swiftly under their white lids. Within three minutes she had gleaned enough to say:

"It's 'real', as they say – and brave, up to a point. But there's no heart in it — just other organs and the viscera in between. Have you read it?"

Michael nodded. He had read the piece through at much greater length in the smoking-room of his club after Vivian left him there with it. He was of much the same opinion as his clear-sighted and quick-brained wife, but had taken several times as long to come to it.

"Pure 'Panjoy' stuff[1], I thought. Shades of *Canthar*. Vivian's betting there'll be a run-in with the Law over it."

"Naturally! If it causes a stir, then his American's well and truly launched. Did Vivian set this up?"

Michael nodded again. Really — her insight went through things like lightning!

"Apparently it's from the American's next novel, about a writer coming to terms with a tragedy in his life — all soul-searching, auto-biographical stuff. Vivian thought—"

But Fleur was already far ahead of him.

"—that he'd rather like me to break the ceremonial bottle over his maverick's bow here. Hmm. That might be fun."

Which was almost precisely the phrase Vivian had used when he suggested the whole thing at the Remove not above an hour before! For approaching the thousandth time, Michael wondered how this mercurial creature had put up with him, incurable slow-coach that he was, for these many, many years of marriage—As the prayer-book had it, it was an excellent mystery!

"A supper, I wonder?" he heard Fleur saying, now with a buzz of interest in her voice, as she took up a powder puff and began dusting herself with more gardenias. "The Nazings might come out of mothballs for him — Walter's such a Grand Old Man nowadays, he'd be bound to say something quotable — even actionable, who knows? And Amabel is still quite American. Perhaps I could rustle a cultural attaché from the Embassy, if I mentioned Francis Wilmot.

---

[1] *A condensed reference to Marjorie Ferrar's 'fast set'. known popularly as the Panjoys, who espoused freedom from moral convention in their tastes and recreational activities. The novel* Canthar, *by Perceval Calvin (pub. Editions Bruxelles, 1924) was one promoted by them, and gained much notoriety after being cited in Miss Ferrar's own notable libel suit (q.v.) of the following year.*

The Messengers, of course. What do you think, Michael?"

Michael recalled Vivian's description of the American author as the wolf at the door. According to that fable, as he remembered it, the wolf was kept out because of the havoc it wreaked when it was allowed inside the house. Even to alleviate her boredom – did she really want to risk having such a creature at her table?

Again, Fleur was already ahead.

"On second thoughts, drinks will do. We haven't had a cocktail-party for a while — it can be our first of the year."

Michael left her dressing – and planning – and went up a half-flight to his study, to sort papers for the next day. He sat down in the old campaign chair and, under the influence of all his caricatures, took a note-pad and began to sketch a wolf in writer's clothing snatching the tail-feathers from a brood of well-dressed chickens in Fleur's 'Grecian' parlour. Glancing up from his handiwork towards his open door, he saw Kat pass by on the landing, hurrying up to her own room, still in her coat and flushed from being out in the night air. He might have thought nothing of it, except for the way she had been clutching a brown-paper parcel to her heart. And, in the moment that she was framed by the doorway, Michael believed he had noticed two further details about his daughter. One was the distant, mystical smile on her face; the other was that her hair was down — and swinging out like a bright auburn flag behind her!

Chapter Eleven

Invitation

The typescript was untitled. By the time Kat had finished reading it – not until some hours into the dead of night, propped up against her pillows in bed – she understood that no title was possible, for none could have begun to encompass the nature of the work. The writing was plain, boldly unadorned, and relentlessly powerful; it swayed her by dangerous degrees, this way and that, as a tempest bends a sapling, mercilessly drenching her in its emotions. It left her exhausted, drained, yet indescribably replete, and not a little in awe of its writer – left her wondering, finally, how the soul of a man could endure such pain, and survive to tell of it with such honesty, such terrible persuasion.

She got up, gathered the pages and, sliding them back into their humble sheath of brown paper and string, put the unwieldy parcel in the drawer of her bureau. There she saw her own ledger, much neglected in recent weeks. Tired as she was, something nevertheless compelled her to take it out and find a pen. When at last she fell asleep, with several more of the pale blue pages covered in close record, a sharp-sighted bird in the square outside was already remarking an indiscernible dawn.

A week-end at Lippinghall intervening, it was a few days before Kat called again to the mansion block. She came upon Boyd unexpectedly in the ground-floor hallway, sifting through a communal pile of post, the old dog sitting at his heels. 'Professor' noticed her first, and gave a broken 'woo-ooo' at her arrival.

Boyd turned expressionlessly.

"Will you be there?" he asked her.

Kat was baffled to understand what plain of meaning his question was on, until he held up a square, cream-coloured envelope which he had just opened, and she recognised the swift, rounded slope of her mother's writing.

"The cocktail party! Yes – can you bear it?"

"No. But I dare say I'll go."

And, shooing the dog ahead of him, he took Kat's arm and led her upstairs.

They made toast – with the aid of a bent fork – in front of the gas fire, Boyd sitting in an easy chair, Kat at his feet on the stool. Boyd turned the bread, Kat buttered it when it was done. 'Professor' waited for the end of both processes, his tail scouring the carpet. After a while, all three of them were munching in a silence that seemed fully contented. Then Boyd said:

"Did you read it?"

Kat looked at him over her mug of tea.

"Yes."

"Do you understand now?"

"Yes. I think so. She — she was your first love."

He gave her a smile, though Kat thought there was a hint of something wretched behind it, in his eyes, until he said:

"And you're my last. Come here—"

She obeyed, and for some minutes there was no need for further exposition.

"I'm going away," he said, at the end of that interlude.

Sitting on his knee as she was, it was difficult for Kat to avoid his eyes. She managed it by turning her attention to one of his shirt buttons, which was undone, while the feeling of unbearable, all but childish disappointment began to well up in her.

"Oh," she said, after a moment. "Back to Paris?"

Paris would be bearable. She would be able to visit him in Paris – but he was shaking his head.

"No, not back to Paris," he said, smiling at her again.

"America?"

"Near enough — Mexico."

"Mexico!"

Of course! The classic destination for an American writer in self-imposed exile. The perfect hide-away for an intellectual *desperado* – a place where he could finally get away from the world, and live like

578

a prince on a dollar a day! Kat felt her eyes begin to swim, and knew her mouth was crumpling absurdly. She caught her lower lip between her teeth to stifle the expression, and again studied his shirt-button, fastening it with clumsy fingers. Boyd was looking at her intently — then he laughed in his throat, and suddenly Kat couldn't stand to hear the sound.

"Don't—!" she begged, but he only held her more closely, so that she felt like a little girl on his lap, as he continued to laugh, "—please don't!"

"Kat — Kat!" He caught her face in his hand so that she must look at him. When she did, he wiped away a tear from her cheek with his thumb, and said, "Come with me!"

The next afternoon, as Kat took the underground home from work, she was still thinking — as she had been all day, and all the previous night — about Boyd's suggestion. The last time she kissed him, she had felt something of what it would mean — to live alone with a man of such energy and passions and moods, to give herself up to him totally. She had felt a new urgency in his embrace, a feverishness in his kisses.

Buying the new edition of Astrid's magazine from a stand at the station, getting her ticket, jostling along the rat-runs of the tube with her fellow citizens — all her actions were achieved mechanically, through the automation of simple habit, while inwardly she turned that startling idea over and over.

She took a seat in the carriage, with the magazine opened at an article on who was going to be where in the seating arrangements at the Abbey for the Coronation — not three months away — which she had attempted to read at least five times while waiting on the platform at Embankment to change trains. But her good brain refused to make sense of even simple words, and so, as she waited for the train to leave the station, Kat turned to the gossip column, where the words were likely to be even simpler.

Over the signature 'Snooper', and under the eye-catching title *'Writer Finds His Mews'*, she read:

'Residents of a garden square in South Kensington have grown accustomed to the sight of a certain very tall American author walking his dog around their cobbled back-roads at all hours of the day and night – presumably in search of inspiration.

'The writer – so far known only for his 'continental' literary efforts – is one signed up at the end of last year by the Capital's noblest imprint. This association is thought to be particularly felicitous, since the middle-aged American is frequently accompanied on these walks by a young female member of his publisher's staff – at all hours of the day and night. . .'

As the meaning of that construction came to her – just as the train pulled away with a jolt – Kat felt a light tap on her knee.

"Snap!"

She looked up at an older, and presently more cheery, arrangement of her own colouring.

"Dinny!"

Her 'aunt' smiled sweetly, and held up another copy of the magazine. Lord! had she seen that piece?

"You were looking so worried, my dear – I thought you must have been reading about these new hemlines they want us to wear in the spring."

"Yes—!" Kat answered, thinking '*No—! She hasn't!*', and changing her expression quickly. "Their fashion-writer is a chum of mine – she says hems won't stop at the knee for long, either."

"Down again – or further up?"

Kat raised her finger in the direction of the hanging-straps overhead.

"Shocking!" Dinny laughed. "Well, I was too young to be a flapper first time around – I think I'm rather glad I shall be too old for the next circuit. I wondered whether they might have us back in farthingales, with all this talk about the New Elizabethans. Now, darling, tell me how you are – we haven't seen you for such a while."

This was true. Her mother had said something to her, to this effect but not as pleasantly put, only that morning. Kat knew she had hardly been seen anywhere outside of South Kensington since the new year – as someone at that magazine seemed to think, too.

"Oh – I've been jolly busy – at work."

"And afterwards?" Dinny's blue eyes were gentle but insistent. "First love can be jolly hard work, too."

She had no need for 'Snooper', Kat reflected – Dinny had her own line to the family oracle.

"The 'Lippinghall pronouncement' has reached you, I see."

Dinny nodded.

"Aunt Em *is* a bit uncanny on these things," she said. "I remember how she was with me—"

"When you met Uncle Eustace?" Kat asked hopefully. Dinny had been happily married for twenty years – and to an 'older man', too. It might be an omen.

"No," Dinny replied, and in her voice Kat heard the trace of something which sounded rather sad. "When I was going through *my* first love."

"Oh. I see."

The episode had evidently not been a successful one in Dinny's life, or there would have been another in Uncle Eustace's place. Kat's curiosity was suddenly curtailed – she didn't want to hear about it. She looked through the carriage window and saw that Westminster was approaching.

"Here's my stop—" Kat leaned across to Dinny and kissed her cheek. "Give my love to Uncle Eustace," she added, with more than a touch of fellow-feeling in the request.

"I will. Come and see us soon, won't you?"

Kat nodded, and rose. The train was stationary, but the doors weren't opening for some reason. Kat sighed – she was impatient to be away! She was aware of Dinny looking up at her, having caught the sound.

"Don't worry, darling – it is possible to survive it. Your mother and I both have!"

Before Kat could make sense of her aunt's last statement, the train doors slid open, and the flow of passengers carried her out.

At South Square, on the evening and at the hour appointed for the Monts' first cocktail-party of the year, guests began to arrive, and soon the air was sparkling and musical with all the *savoir* — as Michael put it — of those who had not to *faire*. The date had been fixed for the day of publication of the spring edition of *New*

Babylon, so that those who attended might have had a chance to see the short story – if they so wished – but not the critical firestorm that was predicted to follow.

A representative cull from all quarters of intelligent society spread through the ground floor of the house, where drawing-room and dining-room doors had been fastened open, making with the hall an accommodating H-shaped space for everyone to be intelligent and sociable in. Fleur had succeeded both with the American Embassy and with the Nazings, discovering that the latter were often invited to the former. She hadn't needed to mention Francis Wilmot. Amabel Nazing, at something close to sixty, still favoured backless dresses, and the attaché, it seemed, favoured older women. Walter had suggested to his hostess that they bring Gurdon Minho, 'the great novelist', along with them, who, being of severely advanced years and having published nothing for the last twenty of them, was tipped for a Nobel prize if he could survive until the nominations. When the future laureate appeared in the hallway, he was so old, and moved so slowly, with such minute movements – as though he were on weakly motorised castors – that Michael laid a private bet with himself that the old boy wouldn't last the evening. That the writer's dotage was either upon him, or nigh, was confirmed with his opening remark. He seemed agitated that he should be there at all.

"So kind of you, Lady Mont," he began as Fleur received him, "to think of inviting me – all you bright young things – but I'm sure I'll be quite a bore for everybody."

Michael, standing at Fleur's side, tried not to look as if he heartily agreed.

"We're none of us young any more, Mr Minho," said Fleur diplomatically, "and very few of us are still bright – you'll be our inspiration. Champagne, or a cocktail?"

"Oh!—a little champagne, I think, if I might. I was sorry to hear about the old Queen, you know.

"Yes – so was my aunt."

"Ah – is the lady a royalist?"

"Not particularly – but she's nearly ninety-five, so Queen Mary was always the *young* queen to her. Come and see my 'Grecian parlour'—"

Michael watched as the old boy – comforted and soothed – rolled away on Fleur's arm.

Pevensey Blythe – formerly editor of that much-mourned weekly, *The Outpost*,[1] and now editor of *New Babylon*, the demise of which was anticipated every quarter – appeared shortly after the Nazings. Michael saw him in.

"Hallo, Pev. Long time no. Have a glass."

"Michael – any scotch? – thanks. Is the Yankee here yet?"

"Coming with the Messengers. For a proponent, you don't sound keen."

"Bee-est fellow one ever met," said the Editor, scooping some salted almonds from a silver dish. "Dog which would bite one's hand for feeding it."

"Don't worry, then – Vivian's hand is somewhat further out than yours!"

"Bee right it is!" The Editor finished his first drink, as if in libation for the fact, and glanced around the room. "Who's that gorgeous girl in pink?"

"My daughter! Kat – come and meet Mr Blythe."

Kat had taken the decision to wear her 'damask rose' dress again, since Boyd had admired her in it. As yet untaken was the decision whether or not to throw her lot in with his and 'sail away for a year and a day'. How long remained to her, exactly, in which to decide, she didn't know, and was disinclined to ask. What she hoped for, privately, was some precipitating factor to aid her decision — and somehow, by an intuition which had prevailed with her all day, she felt that tonight would provide the setting for one to arise.

The Editor was still complimenting her on her dress when she saw Astrid and Giles arrive. They had been invited as useful 'make-weights', and so that the daughter of the house shouldn't be the only person under thirty in the room. Her putative attachment to Giles, Kat was sure, had also entered into the equation.

Extricating herself from Pevensey Blythe's mental clutches, Kat went up to her friends. She wanted to see Astrid before she got

---

[1] *Famous for championing Foggartism in the 'twenties. Mourned chiefly by those who missed anything so deserving of derision.*

caught up in the general babble – wanted particularly to look into her eyes—

"Katkin!"

"Astrid — Giles — here's the tray!"

Giles needed no further cue, and took two glasses as Timms scuttled by, passing one to his sister. Kat put out her face to be kissed on each cheek, and watched. No – there was nothing – no expression in Astrid's clear blue eyes which suggested she might know something about that item in the magazine. As for Giles – he looked blameless as ever. But — oh! dear — his kisses were always rather moist!

Astrid sipped her drink, and looked quickly around the room over the rim of her glass.

"Did you see my piece?" she asked.

A bold question, if she was dissembling!

"The one on hemlines?" Kat replied.

"Mmm." Astrid nodded and sipped some more, still looking around her. "Weren't the pictures absolutely marvellous! Is he here?"

Giles, being a head above his sister in height, answered.

"—don't see him. Or the 'old man', either."

"They're coming together," Kat said, and kept herself from looking towards the door. She wanted these two out of the hall before he arrived! "You haven't seen my mother's pre-Raphaelites, have you – I'm supposed to be like one of them."

This was enough for Giles – he peeled off to see *Psyche Bathing* – and Kat put Astrid in the way of meeting the Editor, who had been circling around for another try.

The H-shape was filling up. Everyone had arrived, save the publisher, his wife, and – most important of all – his new client. There would come a point – not many minutes away – when maximum anticipation had been reached. Kat saw her mother's eyes glancing every now and then towards the hall door, and began to feel quite anxious herself. Then she saw that Vivian was suddenly there, and her mother was flying across the room to greet him.

"Fleur, my angel — the Messenger brings bad news—"

Chapter Twelve

The Grey Beginning

When Kat saw her mother's face suddenly suspend its animation at Vivian's first words – which she was just close enough to hear – she knew that the decisive moment had come.

"Another bout of malaria—" she heard Vivian saying next, "only let me know just now. Sounded in a lousy way, but won't have the doctor. Really, it's too bad of the feller — Fleur, darling, I'm mortified—"

Kat did not wait to hear more, but slipped swiftly to her room. Two minutes later, she emerged again wearing her cape, with her little money purse tucked into an inner pocket.

Astrid was the first to see her coming back down the stairs. Kat caught the corner of her eye – unpleasantly sly and knowing, before Astrid could cover her reaction – and *knew*, in that second, that the gossip-column article had originated with her. In the same second, Kat felt all the old affection and loyalty of that bond drain from her. Her friendship with Astrid had been one of the considerations which had hampered her decision over these last few days – no more! She could bear to leave them all now, as Kit had done after the War – with impunity – with hardly a second glance.

One or two other guests had noticed her – the Editor, Vivian, the American attaché – but Kat was beyond feeling their stares. And, of course, Astrid had poked Giles, whose mouth was hanging open. She saw her father look up from the far side of the drawing-room – he was standing underneath the picture they said was like her – she saw his face take on a quizzical expression. Her mother was directly ahead, talking to the old novelist—

"Kat—?"

"I'm sorry, Mother," she said calmly, "but I must go. I'll be back later."

"Back? From where—?"

But Kat had already gone.

It had been alarming to witness, but the bout had passed – the worst of it, at least – and Kat refused to leave before making Boyd agree to let her bring a doctor with her when she returned the next morning. It was now Saturday evening, and rather more than twenty-four hours since she had fled into the night from South Square.

In that time she had nursed and fed, bathed and changed her lover, as readily and capably as if she were already his wife. He refused to let her fetch a doctor, saying only '*qu-quin-nine*' and '*o-o-oran-nge j-juice*' through chattering teeth when she asked him what would help his condition. These she found, in adequate supply, in the region of the kitchen where his whisky was kept.

"A sw-sweet an-gelic sl-slip of a th-thing," he stammered that morning, when he woke to find her bending over him. It was barely dawn, and Kat had tried with little success to sleep in the easy chair, as he had done on that first night. She was alert the moment he stirred, and went straight over to him.

She held his head up and helped him sip a little juice. After he had finished drinking he lay back on the pillow and stared up at the dim patch of the sky-light over his head. It was half an hour or so yet before dawn, and the light was still grey and dreary.

"Th-there's the gr-grey be-gin-ning—" he said, nodding upwards, and his eyes seemed trying to smile.

Kat was encouraged; two quotations from the same poem – it was progress! His brow felt cooler, too, with less fever under it, though his hands were cold to the marrow.

She waited until he fell asleep again, and went outside to walk the old dog. It was not until a postman, making his first deliveries of the day, gave her a strange look as he passed her, that she realised how she was dressed. She had quite forgotten the 'damask rose'!

Boyd seemed to improve over the course of the day, and by the evening she felt able to leave him. "M-must s-sleep," he had said to her finally. Now she was on her way back to South Square, having left her lover – as the whole world must by this time assume him to

586

be – sitting by the gas-fire, swaddled in blankets from the bed, weak as a kitten, but no longer shivering. The old dog, as always, was at his side.

Huddled into her cloak in the taxi's back seat, Kat tried to formulate how she would explain herself to her parents when she reached home. She had telephoned only once – last night, getting her father – to say where she was, and how long she expected to be, but had run out of pennies for the coin-box before he could ask many questions. As the taxi ticked along towards South Square, the formula seemed further and further away, and at last she gave up the exercise. She was too tired to worry about anything and, in any event, they would say what they would say.

She paid off the taxi at the corner of the square, feeling more comfortable than she had all day, to be under an evening sky once again in her tired evening clothes. She let herself in with her latch-key and, deliberately looking to neither side of the hallway, not wanting to know if either room was occupied, she went directly up to her bedroom, stripped down to her underthings, and drew a deep, hot bath.

A little revived from her soap-suds – still tired, but no longer bone-weary – wearing a long robe cinched at the middle, and a towel swathed around her washed hair, Kat decided to draw the sting. She left her own bedroom, with the intention of finding her mother's and having it out.

Passing her father's study on the way, she saw a light under the door. She knocked gently and, hearing his voice, entered.

"You're back!" he said, not crossly, but sounding if anything rather wistful.

His tone brought the tears swimming to her eyes.

"Oh, Kitten!" he said softly.

As that old nursery name undid her last resolve, Kat let her father put his arm around her, and guide her to his campaign chair as the hot tears rolled from her cheeks.

Michael perched on the edge of his desk – his back turned to the White Monkey, who seemed to find the whole affair highly ironical – and watched his daughter recover her calm in between gradually decreasing episodes of sniffles. Poor heart! he thought. It's a rotten thing, this business called love. Parliament ought to abolish it!

587

With that first brief outburst over, and her father's pocket handkerchief thoroughly 'christened' – as he used to say when she cried
as a little girl – it was easier for them both to proceed.

Michael decided it was his job, as the parent, to get the ball rolling.

"So tell me – are you very much in love?"

Kat looked up gratefully, and managed a little smile.

"Hopelessly. Sorry."

Michael gave a slow nod at her answer, and for a while couldn't
think of the next thing to say.

It was Kat who put the second question.

"What does Mother say?"

Michael shifted slightly on his perch.

"You know we both only want your happiness, Kat."

"That's not an answer, Dad."

"No. Do you want the proper one?"

"Yes."

"Well – right now she can't imagine how she ever gave birth
to such an idiotic daughter. I dare say she'll come round."

The attempt at humour brought a choked laugh from Kat,
which let out another little bout of tears after it.

"Oh, dear," she said into the damp ball of handkerchief. "I'm
sorry – but it's all just a bit overwhelming at the moment. I'll be
more coherent in the morning."

"Are you spending the night here?"

"Yes!"

She wished she had not seen the look of relief which came
over her father's face then.

"But after that — I must be with him, Dad — I must."

"I see."

"Do you?"

"Yes — really. But tell me — is that how he feels?"

"Yes."

"He says so?"

"Yes."

"I see," Michael repeated.

"No, I don't think you do, Dad. He's asked me to go away
with him."

"Abroad?"

She nodded.

"Mexico."

"Mexico—!"

Poor old Dad! Kat knew exactly what he was going through – in his face she could see the play of her own feelings when she had first heard that country mentioned.

"It may be," she added, "—or it needn't be. The truth is, I don't think it matters very much to him where he lives. He just wants me with him — wherever he goes."

"And you'd be happy with that?"

"I'd be happy with *him* – that's all that's important, isn't it?"

Kat waited till her father gave a brief, resigned nod in reply.

"I must get some sleep now," she said, getting up "—can we go through the rest of it in the morning? I'll make more sense then."

And she nuzzled her cheek against his for a moment or two, before leaving the room.

Kat slept dreamlessly. Or, rather, there was a dream somewhere around her, but she didn't seem able to get at it, and so it was as if she slept all the while in troubled limbo.

Then, with a terrible start, she awoke, utterly convinced that her heart had stopped beating. Panicked to her core, she was half out of bed before she came fully awake. As her feet touched the carpet, she knew something was wrong, very wrong – as wrong as it could be. She snapped on the light and dressed in moments, putting on skirt, blouse, and cardigan, taking no heed of colour, pulling anything from her cupboards that came to hand. Finally shuffling on her red coat with the hood, she found her purse, checked that there was still enough money for a taxi in it, and once again fled out of the house, and into the darkness.

The mansion block looked like a great gothic castle against the cloudy night sky. Kat told the driver to keep the whole of her last note – she had no time to wait for him to fumble around for change. The journey had already taken an age, her impatient heart wanting to course like an arrow over the house-tops to her destination, the chugging engine of the taxi seeming to weigh her down, and stop her flying on. She let herself in by means of the conveniently rigged door-bell, and raced up the spiralling stairs, not bothering to grope for the light-switch, not caring when she tripped over a frayed edge of stair-carpet and barked her shin – only minding that it delayed her desperate progress by precious seconds. In the darkness she was certain of only one thing — that she must get to him — or something too dreadful to be imagined would happen.

Reaching the top landing, opening the flat door, which she had left ajar, she felt a commotion around her legs. The dog had come to her, and was flurrying around her feet, keening faintly in odd bursts, as if knowing better than to make a noise, but not used to visitors arriving in the night.

"Good dog, Professor," she whispered, "good dog! Find master!"

The dog scampered ahead, and when Kat passed through the vestibule she saw Boyd sitting in the chair, almost exactly as she had left him. The gas fire was still burning and he seemed to have thrown off the blankets which were in a heap by the foot-stool. At the side of his chair, she saw by the firelight, was an empty scotch bottle, and no sign of a tumbler.

Oh, well, she thought — if it helps him sleep.

She stole up beside his chair, looking to see that he was sleeping. Yes!—eyes closed, face turned to the fire, supported by the chair back, looking peaceful as a baby. She reached over to smooth his hair, now dry again, and its usual flecked grey. His brow was nicely warm to her lips – but, for all that, she wondered whether he wasn't too close to the heat. One of his arms hung down, over the side of the chair. She took his great hand in hers – it was still stone cold, he must stay covered! – and rested it on the chair arm, while she turned to sort out a blanket from the tangled heap by the foot-stool.

As she turned her back, the dog set up a single, solid wail, long and pitiful — like a call for the dead!

At that mournful sound, Kat spun on her heel, and saw that Boyd's arm had slipped again from the side of the chair. She reached for his hand again, but the dog beat her to it, tucking his muzzle into his master's palm, nudging it repeatedly, as if desperate for a sign.

Something seized her heart then – an awful fear, too terrible to face, yet too frightening to run from. She took his hand a second time – watching the movement of her own hand with a strange dispassionateness, as if she had finally embarked upon the dream which she could not enter before – while the old dog shuffled his front paws to and fro, to and fro, in frantic agitation.

The writer's hand felt colder still — stone cold and lifeless. Like an insentient thing herself, Kat felt patiently, but in vain, for a pulse.

Somehow she had negotiated the obstacles of the telephone kiosk – dragging open its heavy red door with arms which suddenly had no strength in them. Then dialling – with stupid, useless fingers – speaking in a voice which seemed not her own – asking them – of all the senseless things – to hurry.

"Hold on, Miss," said an efficient voice in her ear, "we'll send a car."

The car seemed to materialise on the instant, its bell ringing first inside her head, and then outside on the street. In fact it had taken a little less than ten minutes – the station being only streets away – but, since Kat had fainted in the porch of the mansion block, she was unaware of the interval. A young man's face was bent close to hers, a strong arm was helping her to stand.

"Was it you who called us, Miss? – Miss? – Can you hear me?"

Kat nodded, tried to say 'Yes', but couldn't find a voice to form the word. There was just the ghost of the sound in her head.

"Have you got a key?"

'Press—' she said, in her ghost-voice, making no noise, and then she heard herself say raggedly, "—the bell. Flat Nine."

"Shock, Sarge," she heard the young man say to someone outside her line of vision.

The street door opened before Kat could explain how a dead man's door-bell would be answered. One of the other residents had heard the police car arrive. There was bustle for a few moments, a mêlée of different voices, people brushing past her, two officers going up and up, their footsteps neat and purposeful. The young man stayed with her, and was asking her questions from another world.

Gradually coming to the sense of her situation – as if there were any sense in it! – Kat answered the questions in toneless monosyllables.

591

"Yes ... (she knew the man) No ... (they were not related) Mont ... (her name) Boyd ... (his name) No ... (he had no family) Yes ... (they could contact her further) South Square ..."

An ambulance arrived – two more men swept past her up the stairs, carrying a stretcher between them. Suddenly she knew she must go up again. She stood shakily, and started up the stairs. The young officer made to stop her, but something in her expression, something which touched him mortally, made him reconsider, and holding her arm, he began to help her up the long coiling stair.

They must have tried to revive him, for when Kat stood once more inside that all-in-one parlour, where the fire was still hissing out warmth, she saw that the easy chair was empty, and that the screen was drawn discreetly around the bed. She could have spared them their effort, if she had known they would attempt resuscitation. She could have told them it was no use — they might as well have tried to revive her own stopped heart!

"No note anywhere," she heard the sergeant say to his colleague, but she didn't see the sense of the words. "Looks like he might've had a prescription for the powders, too. Probably just an accident, then."

Kat followed the line of the man's arm, as he pointed to the side of the easy chair, where she now noticed there were several opened folds of paper. '*A nifty cocktail*', her brain retrieved from nowhere, '*of scotch and sleeping powders*'. No! – please No! But now the sergeant's words made sense. No note – just an accident, then – a terrible, terrible accident.

Like a spirit from the other side, 'Professor' – now attached by a piece of string to one bed-post, she saw – let up another deadly wail.

"Can I take him?" Kat asked suddenly, to anyone who might hear her.

"Not for the moment, Miss," said the young officer, whom she had quite forgotten was still at her side. "We'll have to keep him in the pound – but if no one claims him," he looked momentarily embarrassed "—family, I mean – then he can come to you."

"How long will that take?"

"I don't really know – a month or so, I expect."

She looked at the dog, who was sitting on his haunches and

592

pawing the air at her, pleading to be helped. Suddenly she couldn't stand to be there any longer, in that little drab flat, with the presence of death under a sheet, and the old dog begging her again for his life.

"I must go," she said.

"Home, Miss?"

"Yes – home." Wherever that was—!

"Would you like us to drive you?"

She shook her head as she made for the door.

"No thank you – I'll walk."

Kat went out, into the dreary, pre-dawn light of the street, walking quickly, as if every step she took away from the place would put the same distance between her heart and its pain. She couldn't feel it yet – and guessed with that part of her brain which had been capable of dialling, capable of answering the young officer's questions, that she was in shock, and might well feel nothing for a while.

As the air got into her lungs – that reasonably fresh air of London on a Sunday – and as the walking pumped her blood, she felt, in fact, strangely lucid. So that was how these things happened! One read about the calamitous endings of great love affairs in novels – she had, at least, from her cradle – but never stopped to think that Life might really copy Art. It all seemed ridiculously final – that he was gone – that, however much she might conjure him now, he was gone from her for ever. The foreign prince she had imagined as a child, who had become her real-life American lover, had vanished, like the dream she had first constructed him from. It was perfect, in its way. Ashes to ashes, dreams to dreams . . .

She walked on, waiting for it to sink down into her feelings, and reach her heart. The pavements were empty, the roads almost without traffic. The city had that early-morning quiet about it, a sort of soft, deep, distant hum, like a giant about to wake.

She walked ever more quickly – not always by the straightest route to South Square, but taking each street in chance succession – variously along Brompton Road, Pont Street, Elizabeth Street and Buckingham Palace Road. However long she walked, she still seemed ahead of any traffic, and ahead of the dawn.

Then she heard an unexpected noise, coming from behind her.

The clipping of horses' hooves, and the crunch of carriage wheels turning. She looked over her shoulder as she walked, but could see nothing. But the sound persisted, drawing nearer. Kat stopped, and turned – and there it was – quite suddenly, coming towards her out of the eery dimness – the fairy carriage she had summoned as a child – bearing her foreign prince to whisk her away!

Kat stood like a dumb thing as the beautiful golden carriage, perfect in every detail – down to the high-stepping horses and liveried driver – moved slowly towards her. It was a dream — and she standing speechless in it!

A less than dream-like figure appeared alongside, out of the grey nothingness of the street—a policeman, looking like a fat seal under his cape.

"Stand back there, miss!" he called to her. "Royal coach coming through!"

Of course — the Coronation! They would be drilling everyone to get it right. Kat stood back on the pavement as ordered, unaware until then that she had strayed onto the road.

"That's right, miss. Don't want to get in the way of the practice-run, do you? Can't be late for the real thing, can we?"

And the coach passed her, and rumbled away.

Kat continued to stand where she had stopped, looking after it, watching as her fairy carriage disappeared along the road. Had that been her 'practice run', after all? Would she ever know 'the real thing' now?

She headed east, towards home. The light was starting to strengthen, the dimness gradually giving way to shape. Kat set her face towards the horizon, where the first dull rays of morning were showing. Yes—there it was! The grey beginning—!

THE END

FORSYTE FAMILY TREE

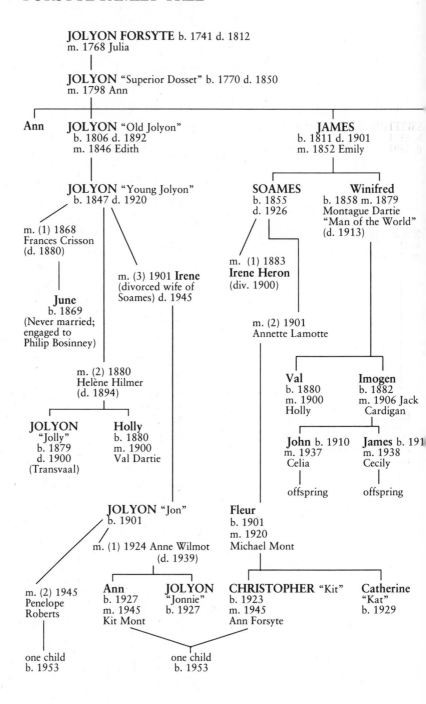

JOLYON FORSYTE b. 1741 d. 1812
m. 1768 Julia

JOLYON "Superior Dosset" b. 1770 d. 1850
m. 1798 Ann

Ann

JOLYON "Old Jolyon"
b. 1806 d. 1892
m. 1846 Edith

JAMES
b. 1811 d. 1901
m. 1852 Emily

JOLYON "Young Jolyon"
b. 1847 d. 1920

SOAMES
b. 1855
d. 1926

Winifred
b. 1858 m. 1879
Montague Dartie
"Man of the World"
(d. 1913)

m. (1) 1868
Frances Crisson
(d. 1880)

m. (3) 1901 **Irene**
(divorced wife of
Soames) d. 1945

m. (1) 1883
Irene Heron
(div. 1900)

June
b. 1869
(Never married;
engaged to
Philip Bosinney)

m. (2) 1901
Annette Lamotte

m. (2) 1880
Helène Hilmer
(d. 1894)

Val
b. 1880
m. 1900
Holly

Imogen
b. 1882
m. 1906 Jack
Cardigan

JOLYON
"Jolly"
b. 1879
d. 1900
(Transvaal)

Holly
b. 1880
m. 1900
Val Dartie

John b. 1910
m. 1937
Celia

James b. 191
m. 1938
Cecily

offspring

offspring

JOLYON "Jon"
b. 1901

Fleur
b. 1901
m. 1920
Michael Mont

m. (1) 1924 Anne Wilmot
(d. 1939)

m. (2) 1945
Penelope
Roberts

Ann
b. 1927
m. 1945
Kit Mont

JOLYON
"Jonnie"
b. 1927

CHRISTOPHER "Kit"
b. 1923
m. 1945
Ann Forsyte

Catherine
"Kat"
b. 1929

one child
b. 1953

one child
b. 1953